Masters
of the
Short Story

Edited
by Abraham H. Lass
and Leonard Kriegel

A MENTOR BOOK

NEW AMERICAN LIBRARY

NEW YORK AND SCARBOROUGH, ONTARIO

To
Betty, Janet, and Paul
and Mark and Bruce

There's an epidemic with 27 million victims. And no visible symptoms.

It's an epidemic of people who can't read.

Believe it or not, 27 million Americans are functionally illiterate, about one adult in five.

The solution to this problem is you... when you join the fight against illiteracy. So call the Coalition for Literacy at toll-free **1-800-228-8813** and volunteer.

Volunteer Against Illiteracy. The only degree you need is a degree of caring.

MENTOR Books of Plays (0451)

☐ **EIGHT GREAT TRAGEDIES edited by Sylvan Barnet, Morton Berman and William Burto.** The great dramatic literature of the ages. Eight memorable tragedies by Aeschylus, Euripides, Sophocles, Shakespeare, Ibsen, Strindberg, Yeats, and O'Neill. With essays on tragedy by Aristotle, Emerson and others. (625072—$4.50)*

☐ **EIGHT GREAT COMEDIES edited by Sylvan Barnet, Morton Berman and William Burto.** Complete texts of eight masterpieces of comic drama by Aristophanes, Machiavelli, Shakespeare, Molière, John Gay, Wilde, Chekhov, and Shaw. Includes essays on comedy by four distinguished critics and scholars. (623649—$4.95)

☐ **THE GENIUS OF THE EARLY ENGLISH THEATRE edited by Sylvan Barnet, Morton Berman and William Burto.** Complete plays including three anonymous plays—"Abraham and Isaac," "The Second Shepherd's Play," and "Everyman," and Marlowe's "Doctor Faustus," Shakespeare's "Macbeth," Jonson's "Volpone," and Milton's "Samson Agonistes," with critical essays. (624432—$4.95)*

☐ **THE MENTOR BOOK OF SHORT PLAYS edited by Richard Goldstone and Abraham H. Lass.** Introduction and "On Reading Plays" by the editors. Includes works of Granberry, Inge, Synge, Vidal, Chayefsky, Rose, Gregory, Wilde, Williams, Chekhov, Rostand, and Rattigan. (626311—$4.95)

☐ **SCENES AND MONOLOGUES FROM THE NEW AMERICAN THEATER Edited by Frank Pike and Thomas G. Dunn.** A collection of exciting, playable new scenes for two men, two women, or a man-woman team, plus 19 outstanding monologues. Fresh material from America's dynamic young playwrights. An essential book for every actor. (625471—$4.95)

☐ **PLAYS FROM THE CONTEMPORARY AMERICAN THEATER, edited and with an introduction by Brooks McNamara.** Modern American drama from the pens of eight noted playwrights: David Rabe, Arthur Kopit, A.R. Gurney, Christopher Durang, John Guare, Beth Henley, August Wilson, and Tina Howe. (625803—$6.95)

*Prices slightly higher in Canada

THE TOTAL SPECTRUM
OF HUMAN SENSIBILITY

It is one of the wonders of the short story form that it lends itself so well to such an extraordinary range of techniques, angles of vision, and emotions.

In this superbly edited anthology, we are led to experience the eerie terror of Pushkin and Poe . . . the elemental passions of Mérimée and Lawrence . . . the consummate artistry of Flaubert and Joyce . . . the delicious humor of Malamud and Singer . . . the rich romanticism of Kipling and Conrad . . . the sharp ironies of Babel . . . the compassionate humanity of Chekhov . . . the cerebral sophistication of Borges—to indicate but a few of the authors represented.

MASTERS OF THE SHORT STORY offers unforgettable insight into the greatness of literature—and into the beauty and innermost depths of life itself.

LEONARD KRIEGEL received his Ph.D. in American Studies from New York University in 1960. He has been awarded Guggenheim, Rockefeller, and Fulbright fellowships and is the author of numerous books and articles. Mr. Kriegel is also coeditor with Abraham Lass of the Mentor anthology STORIES OF THE AMERICAN EXPERIENCE.

ABRAHAM H. LASS, formerly principal of Brooklyn's Abraham Lincoln High School, is widely recognized as an anthologist. He has been a columnist on the *New York Post*, the *New York Herald Tribune*, and *The New York Times*. Other Mentor editions coedited by Mr. Lass are 21 GREAT STORIES, THE SECRET SHARER AND OTHER GREAT STORIES, STORIES OF THE AMERICAN EXPERIENCE, and THE MENTOR BOOK OF SHORT PLAYS.

SIGNET, SIGNET CLASSIC, MENTOR, ONYX, PLUME, MERIDIAN AND
NAL BOOKS are published *in the United States* by
NAL Penguin Inc.,
1633 Broadway, New York, New York 10019,
in Canada by The New American Library of Canada Limited,
81 Mack Avenue, Scarborough, Ontario M1L 1M8

First Printing, June, 1971

6 7 8 9 10 11 12 13 14

PRINTED IN CANADA

Table of Contents

INTRODUCTION

An anthology is, among other things, an argument between editor and reader. In presenting this personal selection of fiction by acknowledged masters of the short story, we expect the discriminating reader to counter with his own choice of masterpieces—that is to say, the stories more to his own taste.

Why have we chosen one story or writer rather than another? Sometimes the decision was made for us by the exigencies of space; in a few cases, as in the work of Ernest Hemingway, by the problems of rights and royalties. More often, in defining both masters and masterpieces of the short story, we followed a simple guideline: inclusion in this anthology was to be limited to writers of compelling and lasting literary sensibility. We would not prefer any particular tradition of the short story over another. We would consider every story in the light of whether it still had something to say to contemporary man and whether it promised to say something to him in the future. We, thus, excluded some writers who admittedly influenced the history and development of the short story. The reader will find Balzac represented in these pages; he will not find O. Henry. Balzac's "Passion in the Desert" has content and mood that still speak to us; the stories of O. Henry, despite their facility, have an artificial, sentimental tone which turns us off.

(The change in style is well illustrated in the work of Frank O'Connor, one of our finest short story writers. He did not wish to shape his stories into an artificial literary pattern; he did not approve of the sudden "twist" at the end that O. Henry loved, nor of a sudden change in character. If such a change occurred, said O'Connor, it must be like "the twisting of an iron bar"—a change growing directly out of the circumstances, which affects the personality of the character for life. O'Connor wished simply to present the life of the common people as it is lived. In his charming story in this collection, "My Oedipus Complex," O'Connor gives us a "modern" tale: loosely plotted, concerned with interior action, making use of myth and folklore, concerned with childhood as so many of our stories are concerned with adolescence. In this story, as in so many stories by Katherine Mansfield or Katherine Anne Porter, perhaps nothing "happens" in the Kiplingesque sense—yet everything is important.)

Fortunately there are no formulas for the creation of masterpieces, and the visions of the writers are as diverse as man himself. Stories as different from each other as "The Sire de Maletroit's Door" and "A Hunger Artist" derive from what is essential to the literary imagination: in the act of entertaining us, they reveal timeless insights into man.

"Every masterpiece was written this morning," said Thornton Wilder. We believe that every story in this collection qualifies as a masterpiece not only because it is still vital but also because it has the accent of artistry: that integration of theme, mood, and language which marks the greatest stories, modern or traditional. Each story in this book is the conveyor of an individual vision of character and action; it can be recognized as the work of one author rather than another. "The Magic Barrel" could have been written only by Malamud; "The Dead," only by Joyce. The style is the author; the subject comes to us as the author sees and creates it.

To define what we consider a "master" of the short story is even more difficult than to define a "masterpiece." Many writers have written one or two excellent short stories. But this, we felt, was not enough to warrant inclusion in this anthology. We have insisted that each writer here should be recognized for a body of work in the short story. Joyce has produced only a single volume of short stories, but it is a volume of incomparable brilliance and influence. Katherine Anne Porter and Frank O'Connor have achieved fame for several volumes of stories. The reader may quarrel with some of our nominations for the title of "master," but we hope that he will accept the achievement of each writer represented as the achievement of an artist.

Our chief aim in making this collection of short stories was to communicate our belief that the short story is among the most rewarding of literary forms for all readers. The demands it makes on the writer are considerable; the rewards it promises to the reader are even greater. Its economy and emotional concentration, its imaginative characterization of men and women in action or in situation comprehensible to all of us, its subtlety and ambiance—all of these depend on the writer's ability to translate a sometimes simple incident into an unforgettable experience for the reader. All of the stories in this collection have done that for the editors. It is our hope that they do it for our readers, too.

                                                    A.H.L.
1971   L.K.

Honoré de Balzac
(1799–1850)

Honoré de Balzac was born in Tours to an army father and a beautiful, wealthy mother. He studied law, but soon turned to writing. In 1829 he published Les Chouans, *the first of a remarkable number of novels. His two best-known novels,* Eugénie Grandet *(1833) and* Le Père Goriot *(1834) are part of his immense fictional undertaking,* La Comédie Humaine, *an analysis of French society, the most ambitious project undertaken by any nineteenth-century writer. Although it was never completed, the forty-seven volumes that Balzac wrote must be numbered among the most comprehensive and brilliant social portraits ever written. "I shall have carried an entire society in my head," he boasted.*

Balzac is generally recognized as the father of French realism. His stories exhibit the same qualities that mark the rest of his fiction: a broad, compassionate view of humanity; a faithful, undeviating confronting of the ills that plague man and society; a sharp, relentless psychological probing of a vast dramatis personae; *an unquenchable curiosity about the human condition; a sure dramatic feeling for the incident and denouement.*

"A Passion in the Desert" deals with the extraordinary relationship that develops between a French soldier lost in the Egyptian desert and a female panther. The strange friendship, trust, love, and finally betrayal that we witness in this story are curiously not unlike what happens in a purely human relationship. Under the influence of the love and companionship which the panther provides, the soldier comes to see the desert as a place of "sublime beauty" rather than of "frightful despair." The desert becomes for him, as it does for the protagonist in Albert Camus' "The Adulterous Woman," a place in which surrender to nature brings personal liberation. Some readers and critics see symbolic sexual overtones in the relationship between the soldier and the panther.

"A Passion in the Desert" is a powerful, exotic, fascinating story, brilliantly conceived and told with consummate skill.

A Passion in the Desert

"The whole show is dreadful," she cried, coming out of the menagerie of M. Martin. She had just been looking at that daring speculator "working with his hyena"—to speak in the style of the program.

"By what means," she continued, "can he have tamed these animals to such a point as to be certain of their affection for——"

"What seems to you a problem," said I, interrupting, "is really quite natural."

"Oh!" she cried, letting an incredulous smile wander over her lips.

"You think that beasts are wholly without passions?" I asked her. "Quite the reverse; we can communicate to them all the vices arising in our own state of civilization."

She looked at me with an air of astonishment.

"Nevertheless," I continued, "the first time I saw M. Martin, I admit, like you, I did give vent to an exclamation of surprise. I found myself next to an old soldier with the right leg amputated, who had come in with me. His face had struck me. He had one of those intrepid heads, stamped with the seal of warfare, and on which the battles of Napoleon are written. Besides, he had that frank good-humored expression which always impresses me favorably. He was without doubt one of those troopers who are surprised at nothing, who find matter for laughter in the contortions of a dying comrade, who bury or plunder him quite light-heartedly, who stand intrepidly in the way of bullets; in fact, one of those men who waste no time in deliberation, and would not hesitate to make friends with the devil himself. After looking very attentively at the proprietor of the menagerie getting out of his box, my companion pursed up his lips with an air of mockery and contempt, with that peculiar and expressive twist which superior people assume to show they are not taken in. Then when I was expatiating on the courage of M. Martin, he smiled, shook his head knowingly, and said, 'Well known.'

"How 'well known'?" I said. "If you would only explain to me the mystery I should be vastly obliged."

"After a few minutes, during which we made acquaintance, we went to dine at the first *restaurateur's* whose shop caught our eye. At dessert a bottle of champagne completely refreshed and brightened up the memories of this odd old soldier. He told me his story, and I said he had every reason to exclaim, 'Well known.' "

When she got home, she teased me to that extent and made so many promises, that I consented to communicate to her the old soldier's confidences. Next day she received the following episode of an epic which one might call "The Frenchman in Egypt."

During the expedition in Upper Egypt under General Desaix, a Provençal soldier fell into the hands of the Mangrabins, and was taken by these Arabs into the deserts beyond the falls of the Nile.

In order to place a sufficient distance between themselves and the French army, the Mangrabins made forced marches, and only rested during the night. They camped round a well overshadowed by palm trees under which they had previously concealed a store of provisions. Not surmising that the notion of flight would occur to their prisoner, they contented themselves with binding his hands, and after eating a few dates and giving provender to their horses, went to sleep.

When the brave Provençal saw that his enemies were no longer watching him, he made use of his teeth to steal a scimitar, fixed the blade between his knees, and cut the cords which prevented using his hands; in a moment he was free. He at once seized a rifle and dagger, then taking the precaution to provide himself with a sack of dried dates, oats, and powder and shot, and to fasten a scimitar to his waist he leaped onto a horse, and spurred on vigorously in the direction where he thought to find the French army. So impatient was he to see a bivouac again that he pressed on the already tired courser at such speed that its flanks were lacerated with his spurs, and at last the poor animal died, leaving the Frenchman alone in the desert. After walking some time in the sand with all the courage of an escaped convict, the soldier was obliged to stop, as the day had already ended. In spite of the beauty of an oriental sky at night, he felt he had not strength enough to go on. Fortunately he had been able to find a small hill, on the summit of which a few palm trees shot up into the air; it was their verdure seen from afar which had brought hope and consolation to his heart. His fatigue was so great that he lay down upon a rock of granite, capriciously cut out like a camp-bed; there he fell asleep without taking any precaution to defend himself while he slept. He had made the sacrifice of his life. His last thought was one of regret. He repented having left the Mangrabins, whose nomad life seemed to smile on him now that he was afar from them and without help. He was awakened by the sun, whose pitiless rays fell with all their force on the granite and produced an intolerable heat—for he had had the stupidity to place himself inversely to the shadow thrown by the verdant majestic heads of the palm trees. He looked at the solitary trees and shuddered—they reminded him of the graceful shafts crowned with foliage which characterize the Saracen columns in the cathedral of Ares.

But when, after counting the palm trees, he cast his eye around him, the most horrible despair was infused into his soul. Before him stretched an ocean without limit. The dark sand of the desert spread farther than sight could reach in every direction, and glittered like steel struck with a bright light. It might have been a sea of looking-glass, or lakes melted together in a mirror. A fiery vapor carried up in streaks made a perpetual whirlwind over the quivering land. The sky was lit with an oriental splendor of insupportable purity, leaving naught for the imagination to desire. Heaven and earth were on fire.

The silence was awful in its wild and terrible majesty. Infinity, immensity, closed in upon the soul from every side. Not a cloud in the sky, not a breath in the air, not a flaw on the bosom of the sand, ever moving in diminutive waves; the horizon ended as at sea on a clear day, with one line of light, definite as the cut of a sword.

The Provençal threw his arms around the trunk of one of the palm trees, as though it were the body of a friend, and then in the shelter of the thin straight shadow that the palm cast upon the granite, he wept. Then sitting down he remained as he was, contemplating with profound sadness the implacable scene, which was all he had to look upon. He cried aloud, to measure the solitude. His voice, lost in the hollows of the hill, sounded faintly, and aroused no echo—the echo was in his own heart. The Provençal was twenty-two years old;—he loaded his carbine.

"There'll be time enough," he said to himself, laying on the ground the weapon which alone could bring him deliverance.

Looking by turns at the black expanse and the blue expanse, the soldier dreamed of France—he smelt with delight the gutters of Paris—he remembered the towns through which he had passed, the faces of his fellow-soldiers, the most minute details of his life. His southern fancy soon showed him the stones of his beloved Provence, in the play of the heat which waved over the spread sheet of the desert. Fearing the danger of this cruel mirage, he went down the opposite side of the hill to that by which he had come up the day before. The remains of a rug showed that this place of refuge had at one time been inhabited; at a short distance he saw some palm trees full of dates. Then the instinct which binds us to life awoke again in his heart. He hoped to live long enough to await the passing of some Arabs, or perhaps he might hear the sound of cannon; for at this time Bonaparte was traversing Egypt.

This thought gave him new life. The palm tree seemed to bend with the weight of the ripe fruit. He shook some of it down. When he tasted this unhoped-for manna, he felt sure that the palms had been cultivated by a former inhabitant—the savory, fresh meat of the dates was proof of the care of his predecessor. He passed suddenly from dark despair to an almost insane joy. He went up again to the top of the hill, and spent the rest of the day in cutting down one of the sterile palm trees, which the night before had served him for shelter. A vague memory made him think of the animals of the desert; and in case they might come to drink at the spring, visible from the base of the rocks but lost farther down, he resolved to guard himself from their visits by placing a barrier at the entrance of his hermitage.

In spite of his diligence, and the strength which the fear of being devoured asleep gave him, he was unable to cut the palm in pieces, though he succeeded in cutting it down. At eventide the king of the desert fell; the sound of its fall resounded far and wide, like a sign in the solitude; the soldier shuddered as though he had heard some voice predicting woe.

But like an heir who does not long bewail a deceased parent, he tore off from this beautiful tree the tall broad green leaves which are its poetic adornment, and used them to mend the mat on which he was to sleep.

Fatigued by the heat and his work, he fell asleep under the red curtains of his wet cave.

In the middle of the night his sleep was troubled by an extraordinary noise; he sat up, and the deep silence around him allowed him to distinguish the alternative accents of a respiration whose savage energy could not belong to a human creature.

A profound terror, increased still further by the darkness, the silence, and his waking images, froze his heart within him. He almost felt his hair stand on end, when by straining his eyes to their utmost he perceived through the shadows two faint yellow lights. At first he attributed these lights to the reflection of his own pupils, but soon the vivid brilliance of the night aided him gradually to distinguish the objects around him in the cave, and he beheld a huge animal lying but two steps from him. Was it a lion, a tiger, or a crocodile?

The Provençal was not educated enough to know under what species his enemy ought to be classed; but his fright was all the greater, as his ignorance led him to imagine all terrors at once; he endured a cruel torture, noting every variation of the breathing close to him without daring to make the slightest movement. An odor, pungent like that of a fox, but more penetrating, profounder—so to speak— filled the cave, and when the Provençal became sensible of this, his terror reached its height, for he could not longer doubt the proximity of a terrible companion, whose royal dwelling served him for shelter.

Presently the reflection of the moon, descending on the horizon, lit up the den, rendering gradually visible and resplendent the spotted skin of a panther.

The lion of Egypt slept, curled up like a big dog, the peaceful possessor of a sumptuous niche at the gate of an hotel; its eyes opened for a moment and closed again; its face was turned toward the man. A thousand confused thoughts passed through the Frenchman's mind; first he thought of killing it with a bullet from his gun, but he saw there was not enough distance between them for him to take proper aim—the shot would miss the mark. And if it were to wake!—the thought made his limbs rigid. He listened to his own heart beating in the midst of the silence, and cursed the too violent pulsations which the flow of blood brought on, fearing to disturb that sleep which allowed him time to think of some means of escape.

Twice he placed his hand on his scimitar, intending to cut off the head of his enemy; but the difficulty of cutting the stiff, short hair compelled him to abandon this daring project. To miss would be to die for *certain*, he thought; he preferred the chances of fair fight, and made up his mind to wait till morning; the morning did not leave him long to wait.

He could now examine the panther at ease; its muzzle was smeared with blood.

"She's had a good dinner," he thought, without troubling himself as to whether her feast might have been on human flesh. "She won't be hungry when she gets up."

It was a female. The fur on her belly and flanks was glistening white; many small marks like velvet formed beautiful bracelets round her feet; her sinuous tail was also white, ending with black rings; the overpart of her dress, yellow like unburnished gold, very lissom and soft, had the characteristic blotches in the form of rosettes, which distinguish the panther from every other feline species.

This tranquil and formidable hostess snored in an attitude as graceful as that of a cat lying on a cushion. Her blood-stained paws, nervous and well-armed, were stretched out before her face, which rested upon them, and from which radiated her straight, slender whiskers, like threads of silver.

If she had been like that in a cage, the Provençal would doubtless have admired the grace of the animal, and the vigorous contrasts of vivid color which gave her robe an imperial splendor; but just then his sight was troubled by her sinister appearance.

The presence of the panther, even asleep, could not fail to produce the effect which the magnetic eyes of the serpent are said to have on the nightingale.

For a moment the courage of the soldier began to fail before this danger, though no doubt it would have risen at the mouth of a cannon charged with shell. Nevertheless, a bold thought brought daylight to his soul and sealed up the source of the cold sweat which sprang forth on his brow. Like men driven to bay who defy death and offer their body to the smiter, so he, seeing in this merely a tragic episode, resolved to play his part with honor to the last.

"The day before yesterday the Arabs would have killed me perhaps," he said; so considering himself as good as dead already, he waited bravely, with excited curiosity, his enemy's awakening.

When the sun appeared, the panther suddenly opened her eyes; then she put out her paws with energy, as if to stretch them and get rid of cramp. At last she yawned, showing the formidable apparatus of her teeth and pointed tongue, rough as a file.

"A regular *petite maîtresse*," thought the Frenchman, seeing her roll herself about so softly and coquettishly. She licked off the blood which stained her paws and muzzle, and scratched her head with reiterated gestures full of prettiness. "All right, make a little toilet," the Frenchman said to himself, beginning to recover his gaiety with his courage; "we'll say good morning to each other presently," and he seized the small, short dagger which he had taken from the Mangrabins. At this moment the panther turned her head toward the man and looked at him fixedly without moving.

The rigidity of her metallic eyes and their insupportable luster made him shudder, especially when the animal walked toward him. But he looked at her caressingly, staring into her eyes in order to magnetize her, and let her come quite close to him; then with a movement both gentle and amorous, as though he were caressing the most beautiful of women, he passed his hand over her whole body, from the head to the tail, scratching the flexible vertebrae which divided the panther's yellow back. The animal waved her tail voluptuously, and her eyes grew gentle; and when for the third time the Frenchman accomplished this interesting flattery, she gave forth one of those purrings by which our cats express their pleasure; but this murmur issued from a throat so powerful and so deep, that it resounded through the cave like the last vibrations of an organ in a church. The man, understanding the importance of his caresses, redoubled them in such a way as to surprise and stupefy his imperious courtesan. When he felt sure of having extinguished the ferocity of his capricious companion, whose hunger had so fortunately been satisfied the day before, he got up to go out of the cave; the panther let him go out, but when he had reached the summit of the hill she sprang with the lightness of a sparrow hopping from twig to twig, and rubbed herself against his legs, putting up her back after the manner of all the race of cats. Then regarding her guest with eyes whose glare had softened a little, she gave vent to that wild cry which naturalists compare to the grating of a saw.

"She is exacting," said the Frenchman, smilingly.

He was bold enough to play with her ears; he caressed her belly and scratched her head as hard as he could.

When he saw that he was successful, he tickled her skull with the point of his dagger, watching for the right moment to kill her, but the hardness of her bones made him tremble for his success.

The sultana of the desert showed herself gracious to her slave; she lifted her head, stretched out her neck, and manifested her delight by the tranquillity of her attitude. It suddenly occurred to the soldier that to kill this savage princess with one blow he must poignard her in the throat.

He raised the blade, when the panther, satisfied no doubt, laid herself gracefully at his feet, and cast up at him glances in which, in spite of their natural fierceness, was mingled confusedly a kind of good-will. The poor Provençal ate his dates, leaning against one of the palm trees, and casting his eyes alternately on the desert in quest of some liberator and on his terrible companion to watch her uncertain clemency.

The panther looked at the place where the date stones fell, and every time that he threw one down, her eyes expressed an incredible mistrust.

She examined the man with an almost commercial prudence. However, this examination was favorable to him, for when he had finished his meager meal she licked his boots with her powerful rough tongue, brushing off with marvellous skill the dust gathered in the creases.

"Ah, but when she's really hungry!" thought the Frenchman. In spite of the shudder this thought caused him, the soldier began to measure curiously the proportions of the panther, certainly one of the most splendid specimens of its race. She was three feet high and four feet long without counting her tail; this powerful weapon, rounded like a cudgel, was nearly three feet long. The head, large as that of a lioness, was distinguished by a rare expression of refinement. The cold cruelty of a tiger was dominant, it was true, but there was also a vague resemblance to the face of a sensual woman. Indeed, the face of this solitary queen had something of the gaiety of a drunken Nero: she had satiated herself with blood, and she wanted to play.

The soldier tried if he might walk up and down, and the panther left him free, contenting herself with following him with her eyes, less like a faithful dog than a big Angora cat, observing everything, and every movement of her master.

When he looked around, he saw, by the spring, the remains of his horse; the panther had dragged the carcass all that way; about two-thirds of it had been devoured already. The sight reassured him.

It was easy to explain the panther's absence, and the respect she had had for him while he slept. The first piece of good luck emboldened him to tempt the future, and he conceived the wild hope of continuing on good terms with the panther during the entire day, neglecting no means of taming her, and remaining in her good graces.

He returned to her, and had the unspeakable joy of seeing her wag her tail with an almost imperceptible movement at his approach. He sat down then, without fear, by her side, and they began to play together; he took her paws and muzzle, pulled her ears, rolled her over on her back, stroked her warm, delicate flanks. She let him do whatever he liked, and when he began to stroke the hair on her feet she drew her claws in carefully.

The man, keeping the dagger in one hand, thought to plunge it into the belly of the too-confiding panther, but he was afraid that he would be immediately strangled in her last convulsive struggle; besides, he felt in his heart a sort of remorse which bid him respect a creature that had done him no harm. He seemed to have found a friend, in a boundless desert; half unconsciously he thought of his first sweetheart, whom he had nicknamed "Mignonne" by way of contrast, because she was so atrociously jealous that all the time of their love he was in fear of the knife with which she had always threatened him.

This memory of his early days suggested to him the idea of making the young panther answer to this name, now that he began to admire with less terror her swiftness, suppleness, and softness. Toward the end of the day he had familiarized himself with his perilous position; he now almost liked the painfulness of it. At last his companion had got into the habit of looking up at him whenever he cried in a falsetto voice, "Mignonne."

At the setting of the sun Mignonne gave, several times running, a profound melancholy cry. "She's been well brought up," said the light-hearted soldier; "she says her prayers." But this mental joke only occurred to him when he noticed what a pacific attitude his companion remained in. "Come, *ma petite blonde,* I'll let you go to bed first," he said to her, counting on the activity of his own legs to run away as quickly as possible, directly she was asleep, and seek another shelter for the night.

The soldier waited with impatience the hour of his flight, and when it had arrived he walked vigorously in the direction of the Nile; but hardly had he made a quarter of a league in the sand when he heard the panther bounding after him, crying with that saw-like cry more dreadful even than the sound of her leaping.

"Ah!" he said, "then she's taken a fancy to me; she has never met any one before, and it is really quite flattering to have her first love." That instant the man fell into one of those movable quicksands so terrible to travellers and from which it is impossible to save oneself. Feeling himself caught, he gave a shriek of alarm; the panther seized him

with her teeth by the collar, and, springing vigorously
backward, drew him as if by magic out of the whirling sand.

"Ah, Mignonne!" cried the soldier, caressing her en-
thusiastically; "we're bound together for life and death—
but no jokes, mind!" and he retraced his steps.

From that time the desert seemed inhabited. It contained
a being to whom the man could talk, and whose ferocity
was rendered gentle by him, though he could not explain
to himself the reason for their strange friendship. Great as
was the soldier's desire to stay upon guard, he slept.

On awakening he could not find Mignonne; he mounted
the hill, and in the distance saw her springing toward him
after the habit of these animals, who cannot run on account
of the extreme flexibility of the vertebral column. Mignonne arrived, her jaws covered with blood; she received
the wonted caress of her companion, showing with much
purring how happy it made her. Her eyes, full of languor,
turned still more gently than the day before toward the
Provençal who talked to her as one would to a tame animal.

"Ah! Mademoiselle, you are a nice girl, aren't you? Just
look at that! so we like to be made much of, don't we?
Aren't you ashamed of yourself? So you have been eating
some Arab or other, have you? that doesn't matter. They're
animals just the same as you are; but don't you take to eating Frenchmen, or I shan't like you any longer."

She played like a dog with its master, letting herself be
rolled over, knocked about, and stroked, alternately; sometimes she herself would provoke the soldier, putting up her
paw with a soliciting gesture.

Some days passed in this manner. This companionship
permitted the Provençal to appreciate the sublime beauty of
the desert; now that he had a living thing to think about,
alternations of fear and quiet, and plenty to eat, his mind
became filled with contrast and his life began to be diversi-
fied.

Solitude revealed to him all her secrets, and enveloped
him in her delights. He discovered in the rising and setting
of the sun sights unknown to the world. He knew what it
was to tremble when he heard over his head the hiss of a
bird's wing, so rarely did they pass, or when he saw the
clouds, changing and many-colored travellers, melt one
into another. He studied in the night time the effect of the
moon upon the ocean of sand, where the simoom made
waves swift of movement and rapid in their change. He
lived the life of the Eastern day, marvelling at its wonderful pomp; then, after having revelled in the sight of a

hurricane over the plain where the whirling sands made red,
dry mists and death-bearing clouds, he would welcome the
night with joy, for then fell the healthful freshness of the
stars, and he listened to imaginary music in the skies. Then
solitude taught him to unroll the treasures of dreams. He
passed whole hours in remembering mere nothings, and
comparing his present life with his past.

At last he grew passionately fond of the panther; for
some sort of affection was a necessity.

Whether it was that his will powerfully projected had
modified the character of his companion, or whether, because she found abundant food in her predatory excursions
in the desert, she respected the man's life, he began to fear
for it no longer, seeing her so well tamed.

He devoted the greater part of his time to sleep, but he
was obliged to watch like a spider in its web that the
moment of his deliverance might not escape him, if any
one should pass the line marked by the horizon. He had
sacrificed his shirt to make a flag with, which he hung at
the top of a palm tree, whose foliage he had torn off. Taught
by necessity, he found the means of keeping it spread out,
by fastening it with little sticks; for the wind might not be
blowing at the moment when the passing traveller was looking through the desert.

It was during the long hours, when he had abandoned
hope, that he amused himself with the panther. He had
come to learn the different inflections of her voice, the
expressions of her eyes; he had studied the capricious patterns of all the rosettes which marked the gold of her robe.
Mignonne was not even angry when he took hold of the
tuft at the end of her tail to count her rings, those graceful
ornaments which glittered in the sun like jewelry. It gave
him pleasure to contemplate the supple, fine outlines of her
form, the whiteness of her belly, the graceful pose of her
head. But it was especially when she was playing that he
felt most pleasure in looking at her; the agility and youthful lightness of her movements were a continual surprise to
him; he wondered at the supple way in which she jumped
and climbed, washed herself and arranged her fur, crouched
down and prepared to spring. However rapid her spring
might be, however slippery the stone she was on, she would
always stop short at the word "Mignonne."

One day, in a bright mid-day sun, an enormous bird
coursed through the air. The man left his panther to look
at this new guest; but after waiting a moment the deserted
sultana growled deeply.

"My goodness! I do believe she's jealous," he cried, seeing her eyes become hard again; "the soul of Virginie has passed into her body; that's certain."

The eagle disappeared into the air, while the soldier admired the curved contour of the panther.

But there was such youth and grace in her form! she was beautiful as a woman! the blond fur of her robe mingled well with the delicate tints of faint white which marked her flanks.

The profuse light cast down by the sun made this living gold, these russet markings, to burn in a way to give them an indefinable attraction.

The man and the panther looked at one another with a look full of meaning; the coquette quivered when she felt her friend stroke her head; her eyes flashed like lightning —then she shut them tightly.

"She has a soul," he said, looking at the stillness of this queen of the sands, golden like them, white like them, solitary and burning like them.

"Well," she said, "I have read your plea in favor of beasts; but how did two so well adapted to understand each other end?"

"Ah, well! you see, they ended as all great passions do end—by a misunderstanding. For some reason *one* suspects the other of treason; they don't come to an explanation through pride, and quarrel and part from sheer obstinacy."

"Yet sometimes at the best moments a single word or a look is enough—but anyhow go on with your story."

"It's horribly difficult, but you will understand, after what the old villain told me over his champagne.

"He said—'I don't know if I hurt her, but she turned round, as if enraged, and with her sharp teeth caught hold of my leg—gently, I daresay; but I, thinking she would devour me, plunged my dagger into her throat. She rolled over, giving a cry that froze my heart; and I saw her dying, still looking at me without anger. I would have given all the world—my cross even, which I had not got then—to have brought her to life again. It was as though I had murdered a real person; and the soldiers who had seen my flag, and were come to my assistance, found me in tears.'

" 'Well sir,' he said, after a moment of silence, 'since then I have been in war in Germany, in Spain, in Russia, in France; I've certainly carried my carcass about a good deal, but never have I seen anything like the desert. Ah! yes, it is very beautiful!'

" 'What did you feel there?' I asked him.

" 'Oh! that can't be described, young man. Besides, I am not always regretting my palm trees and my panther; I should have to be very melancholy for that. In the desert, you see, there is everything, and nothing.'

" 'Yes, but explain——'

" 'Well,' he said, with an impatient gesture, 'it is God without mankind.' "

Alexander Pushkin

(1799–1837)

Like Chekhov, Alexander Pushkin died young; like Chekhov, too, his influence upon Russian literature is almost too pervasive to measure. But in virtually every other respect, Pushkin is the antithesis of Chekhov. Chekhov was the son of a small shopkeeper and the grandson of a serf. Pushkin was descended from an old aristocratic family with more than its touch of the exotic, including his maternal great-grandfather, an Abyssinian prince. Chekhov had to write in order to meet his indebted family's financial obligations; Pushkin, like Byron, after whom he consciously modeled himself, effectively combined writing and dissipation. The greatest difference between them, however, lies in their literary and philosophical outlook. Chekhov is the greatest of Russian realists; Pushkin the greatest of Russian romantics.

Pushkin has been aptly called the "Byron of Russia." His life and career parallel those of the English poet. Pushkin is primarily a poet, despite his short stories and a historical novel about his great-grandfather that he wrote while very young. His poems brought him recognition as a fiery liberal, since they lauded freedom and condemned oppression—an attitude shared by most romantics but especially dangerous in Russia which was far more despotic and autocratic than any other European country. Pushkin joined the Russian diplomatic corps, but his reputation as a political liberal shortly resulted in his banishment to the south and finally his dismissal. He married a beautiful, dazzling Russian, but the marriage was tempestuous and ended, along with Pushkin's life, six years later when he was killed in a duel brought on by his wife's extramarital affairs.

Pushkin's work inspired many composers. Tschaikovsky created operas out of Eugen Onegin *(1833), Pushkin's romantic verse satire, and the story "The Queen of Spades." Moussorgsky fashioned a brilliant opera out of* Boris Godunov *(1825), Pushkin's blank verse historical tragedy about a Russian Tzar modeled upon Shakespeare's chronicle plays. Rimsky-Korsakov was inspired*

27

by Pushkin's Le Coq d'or. *Glinka adapted his* Russlan
and Ludmilla.

Pushkin's Tales of Belkin *(1830), in which "The Queen
of Spades" was first published, constitute his major contribution to the Russian short story. There is an air of
rich romanticism about this fascinating, skillfully contrived tale of the aristocratic world of the gaming table
and the salon as Pushkin knew it. Yet the major characters
are brilliantly conceived and realized. Pushkin never sacrifices his characters to achieve the potent impact of this
story.*

The Queen of Spades

*The Queen of Spades
stands for secret enmity.*
LATEST BOOK OF DREAMS

> *On a cold winter day
> They would gather and play,
> Smoking,*
>
> *And many a stake
> Those youngsters would make,
> Joking.*
>
> *Of the stakes that they won
> They chalked up every one,
> Paying,*
>
> *And so, many a day
> They would squander away,
> Playing.*

One

Card playing was going on in the quarters of Narumov,
an officer in the Horse Guards. The long winter night
passed imperceptibly; it was five in the morning when they
sat down to supper. Those who had won plied their forks
eagerly; the rest sat in front of their empty plates with an

air of abstraction. But champagne was set on the table, the talk became lively, and all took part in it.

"How did you get on, Surin?" asked the host.

"Lost as usual. It must be admitted that I am unlucky. I play for low stakes, I never get excited, always keep my head, and yet I lose all the time."

"And are you never tempted? Don't you ever long to raise the stakes on a card? Your firmness amazes me."

"Look at Hermann!" said one of the guests, pointing to a young officer from an engineer regiment. "Never picked up a card his whole life, never doubled a stake, and sits beside us till five o'clock, watching our play!"

"I take a great interest in cards," said Hermann, "but I am not in a position to sacrifice what is necessary in the hope of gaining what is superfluous."

"Hermann's a Teuton, and therefore cautious—that's all!" remarked Tomsky. "Now, my grandmother, Countess Anna Fedotovna—she's an enigma, if there ever was one."

"What? What's that?" cried the guests.

"I can't understand," continued Tomsky, "how it is that my grandmother never gambles."

"What is there remarkable about an eighty-year-old woman not wanting to gamble?" said Narumov.

"D'you mean to say you don't know anything about her?"

"Nothing whatsoever. Upon my word!"

"Then let me tell you.

"You must know that my grandmother, sixty years ago, visited Paris, and was all the fashion there. People followed her about to have a look at *la Vénus Moscovite;* Richelieu paid her court, and my grandmother vows that her cruelty almost drove him to suicide.

"In those days ladies used to play faro. One day, while playing cards at court, she incurred a debt of honor for a great sum of money to the Duc d'Orléans. When she got home, my grandmother, while removing the patches off her face and slipping out of her hooped skirt, recounted her losses to my grandfather and ordered him to pay up.

"My late grandfather, as far as I can remember, was a kind of steward to my grandmother. He feared her like the plague; but when he heard of such appalling losses he flew into a rage, took up the abacus, and proved to her that they had spent half a million during the last six months, that they had no Moscow or Saratov estates in the neighborhood of Paris, and flatly refused to pay. My grandmother gave him a box on the ears and banished him from her bedroom, as a token of her disfavor.

"The next day she sent for her husband, hoping that the domestic chastisement would have had its effect on him, but she found him adamant. For the first time in their married life she condescended to argument and explanations. She tried to shame him by pointing out condescendingly that there were debts and debts, and that there was a difference between a prince and a coachmaker. Useless! My grandfather rebelled. He said no, and his 'no' must be final. My grandmother was at her wits' end.

"Among her intimates was a very remarkable individual. You have heard of Comte St. Germain, of whom such extraordinary tales are told. You know he gave himself out to be the Eternal Jew, the discoverer of the elixir of life and the philosopher's stone, and so on. People laughed at him as a charlatan, and Casanova wrote in his *Memoirs* that he was a spy; despite his mysterious reputation, however, St. Germain had a most respectable appearance and knew how to make himself agreeable in society. My grandmother loves him to distraction to this day, and will not allow him to be spoken of disrespectfully. She knew St. Germain had a great amount of money at his disposal, and, deciding to have recourse to his aid, sent him a note asking him to come to her at once.

"The old eccentric responded to her summons immediately and found my grandmother overcome with grief. She painted in the darkest colors her husband's cruelty and ended by declaring that her only hope was in St. Germain's friendship and chivalry.

"St. Germain pondered. 'I could let you have this sum,' he said, 'but I know you would never have any peace until you had paid me back, and I should not like to cause you fresh cares. There is another means—you can win it back.'

"'But my dear Count,' replied my grandmother, 'I tell you we have no money at all.' 'You will not need money,' said the count. 'Be so kind as to hear me out.' And he told her a secret which any one of us would pay dear to know. . . ."

The youthful gamblers redoubled their attention. Tomsky lit his pipe, inhaled the smoke, and continued:

"That same night my grandmother appeared at Versailles, *au jeu de la Reine*. The Doc d'Orléans dealt. My grandmother gave some slight apology for not having brought the money for her debt, inventing a little story in her justification, and began playing against him. She

selected three cards, which she played one after another—
all three proved to be winning cards, and my grandmother
won back the whole of her debt."

"A mere fluke!" said one of the guests.

"A fairy tale," said Hermann.

"Perhaps the cards were marked," put in another.

"Hardly," replied Tomsky with dignity.

"What!" said Narumov. "You have a grandmother who
can play three winning cards running, and you have not yet
been able to discover the secret of these cabalistics!"

"It's not so simple, devil take it!" replied Tomsky. "She
had four sons, of whom one was my father. All four were
desperate gamblers, and she did not disclose her secret to
any of them, although this would have been no bad thing
for them—nor for me either, for that matter. But this is
what my uncle, Count Ivan Ilyich, told me, on his word
of honor. The late Chaplitsky, that same Chaplitsky who
died in poverty, having squandered millions, once lost
about three hundred thousand rubles in his youth—to
Zorich, I think. He was in despair. My grandmother, who
was always very hard on vagaries of young men, for some
reason took pity on Chaplitsky. She named three cards to
him, which he was to play in succession, but extorted from
him the promise, on his word of honor, never to gamble
any more. Chaplitsky went to the rooms of his fortunate
opponent, and they sat down at the card table. Chaplitsky
staked fifty thousand on the first card and won; then he
doubled and redoubled the stake, and won back his losses,
with a generous margin. . . .

"But it's time to go to bed—it's a quarter to six." Indeed
it was getting light already—the young men finished what
was in their glasses and dispersed.

—*Il paraît que monsieur est
décidément pour les suivantes.*
—*Que voulez-vous, madame?
Elles sont plus fraîches.*
SOCIETY TALK

Two

The old countess ———— was sitting in her dressing room
in front of her mirror. Three serving maids hovered around

her. One held a pot of rouge, another a box of hairpins, and the third a high cap with flame-colored ribbons. The countess, who had not the slightest pretensions to beauty, which had long faded, neverthless preserved all the habits of her youth, adhering strictly to the fashions of the 1770's, and spending as much time and energy over her toilet as she had done sixty years before. Seated before a tambour at the window was a young lady, the countess's companion.

"Good morning, *Grand'maman!*" said a young officer who had just come into the room. *"Bonjour, Mademoiselle Lise.* I have come to ask a favor of you, *Grand'maman.*"

"What is it, Paul?"

"Permit me to introduce a friend of mine to you, and to bring him to your ball on Friday."

"Bring him straight to the ball, you can introduce him to me there. Were you at the ————'s yesterday?"

"Oh, yes! It was very gay. We danced till five. Eletskaya was exquisite."

"Eh, my dear! What can you see in her? You should have seen her grandmother, the Princess Darya Petrovna! She must be very old now, I suppose—the Princess Darya Petrovna."

"Old?" replied Tomsky absently. "She's been dead these seven years."

The young lady at the window raised her head and made a sign to the young man. He remembered that the death of her contemporaries was always kept from the old countess, and bit his lip. But the countess received this information, which was news to her, with the utmost indifference.

"Dead!" she repeated. "And I did not know! We became maids of honor at the same time, and when we were presented, the Empress. . . ."

And the countess told her story to her grandson for the hundredth time.

"Well, Paul," she said, after a pause. "Now help me to get up. Lise, where's my snuff box?"

And the countess retired behind a screen, accompanied by her maids, to finish her toilet. Tomsky remained with the young lady.

"Whom do you wish to introduce to her?" asked Lisaveta Ivanovna in low tones.

"Narumov. Do you know him?"

"No. Is he a military or a civilian?"

"Military."

"An engineer?"

"No. A cavalryman. What made you think he was an engineer?"

The girl gave a short laugh, but answered not a word.

"Paul!" cried the countess from behind the screen. "Send me a new novel, but not a modern one, if you please."

"What do you mean, *Grand'maman?*"

"I mean a novel in which the hero strangles neither his father nor his mother, and in which there are no drowned bodies. I have a perfect horror of drowned bodies!"

"There are no such novels, nowadays. Unless, of course, you would like a Russian novel."

"Are there any Russian novels? Send me one, sir, by all means, send me one!"

"I must say good-bye to you *Grand'maman*. I am pressed for time. Good-bye, Lisaveta Ivanovna. What made you think Narumov was an engineer?"

And Tomsky went out of the dressing room.

Lisaveta Ivanovna remained alone—she turned from her embroidery and began looking out of the window. Very soon a young looking officer made his appearance around the corner on the other side of the street. A blush covered her cheeks; she took up her work again, bending her head low over the canvas. Just then the countess reappeared, fully dressed.

"Order the carriage, Lisanka," she said. "We'll go for a drive."

Lise rose from the embroidery frame and began putting away her work.

"Are you deaf, child?" cried the countess. "Order the carriage instantly!"

"Yes, *Grand'maman,*" said the girl softly, and went quickly into the entrance hall.

A servant entered with some books for the countess from Prince Pavel Alexandrovich.

"Very good. Give him my thanks," said the countess. "Lise! Lise! Where are you going?"

"To dress."

"There's plenty of time, child! Stay where you are! Open the first volume. Read to me. . . ."

The girl picked up the book and read a few lines.

"Louder!" said the countess. "What's the matter with you, my dear? Have you lost your voice? Wait a minute—give me a footstool. Nearer, can't you?"

Lisaveta Ivanovna read two more pages. The countess yawned.

"Put the book down," she said. "A lot of nonsense! Send

it back to Prince Pavel with my thanks. Well, where's the carriage?"

"The carriage is ready," said Lisaveta Ivanovna, glancing out of the window.

"And why aren't you dressed?" said the countess. "You always keep me waiting. It's intolerable, my dear!"

Lise ran to her room. Before two minutes had passed the countess began ringing her bell with all her might. The three maids came running in at one door, and the footman at the other.

"Can't you come when you're called?" exclaimed the countess. "Tell Lisaveta Ivanovna I'm waiting for her."

Lisaveta Ivanovna came in, in her cloak and hat.

"At last!" said the countess. "How you're dressed up! What for, I wonder? Whom do you want to conquer? What's the weather like? It seems to be windy."

"Not at all, Your Highness. It's very still weather," replied the footman.

"You always say the first thing that comes into your head. Open the *fortochka.** There, I knew there was a wind, and a very cold one, too! Send away the carriage. We're not going, Lise. You needn't have dressed yourself up."

"And this is my life!" thought Lisaveta Ivanovna.

In truth, Lisaveta Ivanovna was a most unhappy creature. The bread of charity is bitter, said Dante, and the steps to a stranger's house are steep, and who knows that bitterness so well as a poor girl dependent on an aristocratic old dame? The Countess ———— did not really have a bad disposition, but she was capricious, like all women who have once been the spoiled darlings of society, and she was stingy, completely absorbed in her cold selfishness, like all old people who, having expended their tenderer emotions during a long lifetime, feel that they do not belong to the present. She participated in all the vanities of high society, dragging herself to balls, where, seated in a corner, rouged and dressed according to the fashion of ancient days, she was the hideous and essential ornament of the ballroom; newly arrived guests went up to her and bowed low, as though in obedience to an established ritual, after which nobody took any notice of her. In her own home she received the whole town, observing the strictest etiquette, though she did not recognize any of her guests. Her innumerable household, growing fat and gray in her hall and

_____
* Small ventilation pane in window.

in the servants' quarters, did whatever they liked and vied with one another in plundering the dying old woman. Lisaveta Ivanovna was a domestic martyr. She poured out tea and was scolded for the waste of sugar; she read novels aloud and was held guilty for all the author's shortcomings; she accompanied the old lady on her drives, and had to answer for the weather and the state of the road. She was allotted a salary which she never received in full; and was expected to be dressed like everyone else, which is to say like very few. In society she played the most pitiable role. Everyone knew her and no one took any notice of her; at balls, she only danced when a *vis-à-vis* was needed, and the ladies took her arm whenever they had to retire in order to set to rights some detail of their toilet. Sensitive and therefore fully alive to her position, she was always on the lookout for the deliverer she awaited so impatiently. But the young men, vain and calculating, did not honor her with their attention, although Lisaveta Ivanovna was infinitely more attractive than the cold, arrogant maidens upon whom they danced attendance. How many times, noiselessly departing from the dull, luxurious drawing room, did she retire to weep in her humble chamber, with its wallpapered screen, its chest of drawers, its little mirror and painted bedstead, in which a tallow candle in a brass candlestick burned dimly!

Once—a day or two after the evening described in the beginning of this tale, and two weeks before the scene just enacted—Lisaveta Ivanovna, seated before her tambour at the window, happened to glance into the street, and caught sight of a young man in the uniform of an engineer regiment standing motionless, his eyes fixed on her window. She lowered her head and resumed her work; five minutes later she looked out again—the young officer was still there. Not being in the habit of flirting with passing officers, she stopped looking out of the window and went on stitching for another two hours or so without raising her head. Dinner was served. Rising, she began to put away her tambour and, glancing out of the window, observed that the officer was still there. This struck her as somewhat strange. After dinner she went to the window with uneasy feelings, but the officer was no longer there—and she forgot about him. . . .

Two days later, while going out with the countess to get into the carriage, she saw him again. He was standing right at the porch, his beaver collar turned up to hide his face— a pair of black eyes gleaming from beneath his cap. Lisaveta

Ivanovna was alarmed, she knew not why, and seated herself in the carriage with inexplicable trepidation.

As soon as she returned home she ran to the window—the officer was standing in his former place, his eyes fixed on her; she moved away, tortured by curiosity and an agitation which was quite new to her.

From that time, not a day passed without the young man appearing beneath the windows of their house at a certain hour. A curious relationship sprang up between them. While seated at her work she would feel his approach and raise her head, her glance resting on him for a longer space of time every day. The young man seemed to be beholden to her for this; with the keen sight of youth, she saw the instant blush which covered his pale cheeks whenever their eyes met.

A week later, and she was greeting him with a smile. . . .

When Tomsky asked permission to introduce his friend to the countess, the poor girl's heart began to beat. But when she learned that Narumov was not an engineer but a horse guardsman, she regretted that, by her indiscreet question, she had given away her secret to the volatile Tomsky.

Hermann was the son of a Russianized German who had left him a very small fortune. Firmly convinced of the necessity of consolidating his independence, Hermann did not even touch the interest from it and lived exclusively on his pay, never allowing himself the slightest indulgences. He was, however, reserved and ambitious, and his comrades seldom had occasion to laugh at his excessive thriftiness. He was a man of strong passions and a fiery imagination, but his firmness of character saved him from the usual errors of youth. Thus, while by nature a gambler, he never played cards, calculating that his fortune was not such as to allow him (to use his own words) *to sacrifice the necessary in the hope of gaining the superfluous,* and yet he would sit beside the card tables all night long, following with feverish excitement the vicissitudes of the game.

The story of the three cards affected his imagination powerfully, and he could not get it out of his head all night. "Supposing," he said to himself, roaming the streets of Petersburg the next night, "supposing the old countess were to reveal her secret to me? Supposing she was to tell me the names of those three infallible cards? Why should I not try my luck? Present myself to her, get into her favor —perhaps become her lover . . . but all this would take time, and she is eighty-seven; she might die next week, the day after tomorrow! And the story itself—is it to be believed? No! Caution, moderation, and diligence—these are my three faithful cards; with these I will treble my fortune, increase it sevenfold, achieve tranquillity and independence."

Thus meditating, he found himself in one of the principal streets of Petersburg, before a house of ancient architecture. The street was thronged with carriages, which were still rolling up one after another to the brilliantly lighted porch. The slender foot of some young belle, a jackboot with jingling spurs, the striped stocking and the slipper of an ambassador, were thrust in rapid succession from the carriage doors. Furred mantles and cloaks flashed past the majestic footman. Hermann came to a standstill.

"Whose house is this?" Hermann asked the gendarme at the corner.

"The Countess ———'s," replied the latter.

Hermann was thrown into trepidation. The marvelous story again rose before the eye of his fancy. He began walking up and down in front of the house, thinking of its mistress and her miraculous power. It was late when he returned to his humble dwelling; he lay awake a long time, and when sleep overcame him he dreamed of cards, the baize-covered table, heaps of notes, piles of golden coins. He staked one card after another, firmly doubled the stakes, won repeatedly, scraped the gold toward him, pocketed the notes. He awoke late, sighing for the loss of his fantastic riches, and once more went to roam the city, once more found himself in front of the countess's mansion. It was as if some mysterious force had drawn him to it. He stood still and looked up at the windows. Behind one of them he saw a dark head bent either over a book or work. The head was lifted. Hermann saw a youthful face and black eyes. This moment decided his fate.

> *Vous m'écrivez, mon ange, des*
> *lettres de quatre pages plus vite*
> *que je ne puis les lire.*
> CORRESPONDENCE

Three

Hardly had Lisaveta Ivanovna taken off her cloak and hat, when the countess sent for her and ordered the car-

riage to be brought around again. And so they went out of
the house to get into it. Just at the moment when two
footmen were half-lifting, half-pushing the old dame
through the carriage door, Lisaveta Ivanovna saw her
engineer standing close to the wheels. He seized her hand;
she was almost stupefied with terror; the young man
vanished—a letter remained in her hand. She hid it inside
her glove and neither saw nor heard anything during the
whole drive. It was the countess's habit to fire off question
after question when in the carriage—Who's that, just gone
by? What bridge is that? What's written on that sign? This
time Lisaveta Ivanovna answered at random, and her
meaningless remarks angered the countess.

"What's come over you, my dear? Have you had a stroke
all of a sudden? Don't you hear me, or is it that you don't
understand what I say? . . . I don't lisp, thank the Lord,
and I am still in possession of my wits!"

Lisaveta Ivanovna in truth was not listening. As soon
as she got back she hastened to her room and drew the
missive out of her glove—it was unsealed. Lisaveta Ivanovna ran her eye over it. The letter contained professions
of love: it was tender and respectful, copied word-for-
word from a German novel. But Lisaveta Ivanovna, who
did not know German, was enchanted with the letter.

The letter she had received nevertheless caused her excessive agitation. It was the first time she had entered upon
secret, intimate relations with a young man. His audacity
appalled her. She reproached herself with indiscreet behavior, and could not make up her mind what to do. Should
she stop sitting at the window and cool the officer's desire
for further pursuit by displaying indifference? Ought she
to send him back his letter, or, perhaps, answer it coldly
and decisively? There was no one for her to consult—
she had neither friends nor counselors. Lisaveta Ivanovna
made up her mind to reply.

She sat down at her little writing table, got out pen and
paper, and fell to musing. She began her letter several
times, tearing it up each time—her words seemed to her
either too indulgent, or too severe. At last she succeeded
in writing a few lines with which she could be satisfied:
"I am confident," she wrote, "that your intentions are
honorable and that you would not wish to insult me by a
thoughtless act; but our acquaintance must not begin in
this wise. I return you your letter and trust that in future
I shall have no cause to complain of unmerited disrespect."

The next day, as soon as she saw Hermann approaching,

Lisaveta Ivanovna rose from her tambour, went into the adjoining room, opened the *fortochka,* and tossed her letter out of the window, relying on the young officer's dexterity. Hermann ran to the spot where the letter had fallen, picked it up, and entered the shop of a pastry cook. Breaking the seal, he found his own letter and the reply of Lisaveta Ivanovna. It was what he had expected and he went home, deeply absorbed in his intrigue.

Three days after this, a sharp-eyed girl from a milliner's shop brought Lisaveta Ivanovna a note.

Lisaveta Ivanovna opened it anxiously, fearing it might be a dun, when she suddenly recognized Hermann's handwriting.

"You've made a mistake, child," she said. "This note is not for me."

"It is, it is! It's for you," answered the bold girl, not troubling to conceal a sly smile. "Be so good as to read it."

Lisaveta Ivanovna ran her eye hastily over the note. Hermann demanded an interview.

"You must be mistaken, my girl," said Lisaveta Ivanovna, alarmed both by the precipitancy of the demand and the means employed by Hermann. "This letter is probably not intended for me." And she tore it into fragments.

"If it's not for you, then why did you tear it up?" said the shopgirl. "I could have given it back to the person who sent it."

"I would ask you not to bring me any more notes, for the future, child," said Lisaveta Ivanovna, flushing at the girl's remark. "And tell the person who sent you that he ought to be ashamed of himself. . . ."

But Hermann did not desist from his efforts. Lisaveta Ivanovna received letters from him daily, through various channels. They were no longer translated from German. Hermann wrote them under the inspiration of passion, and used language which was natural to him—his letters expressed both his unwavering desire and the chaos of his unbridled imagination. Lisaveta Ivanovna no longer attempted to return them to him. She reveled in them; she began answering them, and her notes became longer and more tender with every day. At last she threw the following letter out of the window to him:

"There is a ball at the ———— Embassy tonight. The countess will be there. We shall be there till two o'clock. This would be your chance to see me alone. As soon as the countess leaves, her servants are sure to go away; there will be only the doorman in the porch, and he usually goes into his own little room. Come at half-past eleven. Go straight upstairs. If you find anyone in the hall, ask for the countess. They'll tell you she isn't at home, and there will be nothing for you to do but go. But you will probably meet no one. The maids stay in their own room, all together. From the hall, turn to the left and go straight on till you get to the countess's bedroom. There you will see a screen in front of two little doors. The one on the right leads to the study, where the countess never goes. The one on the left leads to a passage, from which there is a narrow spiral staircase to my room."

Hermann awaited the appointed time, like a tiger ready to pounce. By ten o'clock he had already taken up his position in front of the countess's house. The weather was atrocious, the wind howled and snow fell in moist flakes. The lamps burned dimly, the streets were deserted. Every now and then a cabby drove his lean hack by, in the hope of picking up a belated wayfarer. Hermann had nothing on over his frockcoat, but was conscious neither of wind nor snow. At last the countess's carriage was brought around. Hermann saw the footmen come out, supporting on either side the bowed form of the old woman in her sable cloak, and her youthful companion slip by after her, in her thin wrap, with flowers in her hair. The carriage door slammed. The carriage rolled heavily over the loose snow. The doorman closed the front door. The windows went dark. Hermann began walking up and down in front of the deserted mansion. When he got to a street light he glanced at his watch—it was twenty minutes past eleven. He stood in the light of the lamp, his eyes fixed on the hands of his watch, waiting for the remaining minutes to pass. Precisely at half-past eleven he stepped onto the countess's porch and into the brightly lit entrance. The doorman was not there. Hermann ran up the stairs, opened the door into the hall, and saw a serving man asleep beneath a lamp, in an ancient, greasy armchair. Hermann passed him with a light, firm tread. The ballroom and drawing room were dark. The lamp in the hall shed a dim light on them. Hermann entered the bedroom. A gilded lamp swung in front of an iconostasis filled with ancient icons. Armchairs upholstered in faded damask, and down-stuffed sofas with the gilt wearing off in patches, stood in mournful symmetry along the walls, which were hung with Chinese wallpaper. There were two portraits painted in Paris by Madame Lebrun on the walls. One was the likeness of a man of some forty years, rosy-cheeked and stout, in a bright-green uniform with a star on the breast; the other showed a young belle with an aquiline nose, in whose powdered locks, brushed up from the temples, was a rose. In every corner could be seen porcelain shepherdesses, clocks from the skilled hand of Leroy, ornamental boxes, tops, fans, and various toys invented for the amusement of ladies in the end of the previous century, along with Montgolfier's balloon and Mesmer's magnetism. Hermann went behind the screen. There stood a small iron bedstead; on the right was the door of the study, on the left the door into the passage. Hermann opened it and saw the narrow spiral staircase leading to the poor young lady's room. But he turned back and entered the dark study.

The hours passed slowly. All was quiet. The clock in the drawing room struck midnight. Clocks in all the other rooms chimed in one after the other. And all was quiet again. Hermann stood leaning against the cold stove. He was quite calm; his heart pulsed regularly, like that of one who has resolved upon what is dangerous, but inevitable. The clocks struck one, and then two—and he heard the distant sound of carriage wheels. He was thrown into a state of agitation. The carriage drove up and came to a stop. He could hear the clatter of the steps being let down. There were sounds of bustle in the house. People came running, voices were heard, and the house lit up. Three elderly lady's maids hastened into the bedroom, and the countess, more dead than alive, entered and sank into the high-backed armchair. Hermann peeped through a crack in the door. Lisaveta Ivanovna passed close to him. He could hear her hurried footsteps ascending her staircase. He felt something like a pang of remorse, but it died down at once. He stood as if turned to stone.

The countess began undressing in front of the mirror. Her maids unpinned her rose-trimmed cap, removed the powdered wig from her gray, closely cropped head. Pins fell from her in showers. The yellow dress embroidered in silver dropped to her swollen feet. Hermann was a witness of the horrid secrets of her toilet. At last the countess was clad in nothing but a nightgown and nightcap—in this attire, more appropriate to her age, she was not so sinister and hideous.

Like all old people, the countess suffered from insomnia. When her maids had undressed her she sat down near the window in the high-backed armchair and dismissed them. The candles were carried out, and once more the only light in the room came from the icon lamp. Her face a bilious

yellow, her drooping lips twitching, the countess swayed
from left to right in her chair. Utter absence of thought
could be seen in her dim eyes. Looking at her, one might
have supposed that the terrible old woman swayed from
side to side, not of her own accord, but under the influence of some concealed galvanic force.

Suddenly an indescribable change came over her death-
like countenance. Her lips ceased their twitching, and a
light came into her eyes. A strange man stood before the
countess.

"Do not be afraid, for God's sake, do not be afraid!" he
was saying in low, clear tones. "I have no intention of
harming you—I have come to beg a single favor of you."

The old woman gazed at him in silence, but seemed not
to have heard him. Hermann, supposing her to be deaf,
bent right over her ear and repeated his words. The old
woman was as silent as ever.

"You can make me happy for life," continued Hermann, "and it will cost you nothing. I know that you are
able to guess three cards to be played in succession. . . ."

Hermann broke off. Evidently the countess understood
what was wanted of her, and was searching for words to
answer him with.

"It was only a jest," she said at last. "I swear to you!
It was a jest!"

"This is no jesting matter," replied Hermann sternly.
"Remember Chaplitsky whom you helped to win back his
losses."

The countess was visibly embarrassed. Some powerful
emotion showed itself in her face, but very soon she sank
back into her former apathy.

"Can you name me these three infallible cards?" continued Hermann.

The countess remained silent. Hermann continued:

"For whom are you treasuring your secret? For your
grandchildren? They are rich, as it is; they do not understand the value of money. Your three cards will not help a
spendthrift. He who allows a father's legacy to slip through
his fingers will die in poverty, despite any diabolical
efforts. I am no spendthrift. I know the value of money.
Your three cards will not be wasted on me. Come now! . . ."

He ceased speaking, and waited anxiously for her reply.
The countess remained silent. Hermann fell on his knees.

"If your heart ever knew the feeling of love," he said, "if
you remember its ecstasies, if you have only once smiled
to hear the crying of a newborn son, if anything human

ever beat in your bosom, I appeal to you as wife, mistress, mother, by all that is sacred in life, do not refuse my request! Reveal your secret to me! Perchance it may be linked with some terrible sin, with the forfeiture of eternal bliss, a pact with the devil. Bethink yourself that you are old, you have not long to live. I am ready to take your sins on myself. Only reveal to me your secret. Bethink yourself that the happiness of a human being is in your hands. That not only I, but my children, grandchildren and great-grand-children will bless your memory, and hold it sacred. . . ."

The old woman answered not a word.

Hermann rose.

"Old witch!" he said, clenching his teeth. "Then I will compel you to answer me!"

With these words he drew a pistol from his pocket.

At the sight of the pistol the countess again showed signs of powerful emotion. She jerked back her head and raised her hand, as if to ward off a shot. . . . Then she fell against the back of her chair . . . and remained motionless.

"Come, you are not a child!" said Hermann, taking her hand. "I ask you for the last time—do you intend to tell me what these three cards are? Yes or no?"

The countess made no answer. Hermann saw that she was dead.

7 Mai 18 . .
Homme sans mœurs et sans religion.
CORRESPONDENCE

Four

Lisaveta Ivanovna was seated in her room, still in her ball dress, absorbed in profound meditation. As soon as she got home she hastily dismissed her drowsy maid, who offered her services reluctantly, and said she would undress herself. Then she went up to her own room with a fluttering heart, hoping to find Hermann there, and desiring not to find him. She saw at a glance that he was not there, and thanked her stars for the obstacle in the way of their interview. She sat down without taking off her clothes and began to go over in her mind all the circumstances which had carried her so far in such a short space of time. Four weeks had not yet

elapsed since the day she had first seen the young man beneath her window—and she was already corresponding with
him, while he had wrung from her the promise of a nocturnal interview. If she knew his name, it was only because
some of his letters had been signed. She had never spoken
to him, never heard his voice, never heard anything about
him—till this very evening. And strange to say, at the ball,
Tomsky, vexed with the youthful Princess Pauline —— for
flirting with someone else for a change, wished to revenge
himself and show his indifference. He invited Lisaveta Ivanovna to dance with him, and went through the endless
mazes of the mazurka with her. He had jested the whole
time about her partiality for engineers, assuring her that he
knew a great deal more than she could possibly imagine,
and some of his jests so nearly hit the mark that Lisaveta
Ivanovna could not help thinking, more than once, that he
knew her secret.

"Who told you all this?" she asked him, laughing.

"A friend of a certain person whom you know," replied
Tomsky. "A most remarkable man."

"And who is the remarkable person?"

"His name is Hermann."

Lisaveta Ivanovna made no reply, but her hands and feet
turned cold as ice.

"This Hermann," continued Tomsky, "is a most romantic
individual. He has the profile of a Napoleon, and the soul
of a Mephistopheles. I believe he has at least three crimes
on his conscience. How pale you are! . . ."

"My head aches. . . . What did that, what's his name—
Hermann—tell you?"

"Hermann is greatly displeased with his friend. He says
he would have acted quite differently, himself. . . . I'm inclined to think that Hermann has an eye on you himself,
for he listens with great interest to the enamored exclama-
tions of his friend."

"But where can he have seen me?"

"At church, perhaps, or out driving. . . . God knows—
perhaps in your room, while you were asleep. Anything
may be expected of him."

Three ladies came up to them with the question, *"Oubli
ou regret?"* and the conversation, of such agonizing interest for Lisaveta Ivanovna, had to be interrupted.

The lady whom Tomsky chose was the Princess ——
herself. During one round of the ballroom and a turn in
front of her chair they had come to an understanding, and
by the time Tomsky got back to his place he was no longer

interested either in Hermann or in Lisaveta Ivanovna. She was longing to revive the interrupted conversation; but the mazurka came to an end, and soon after the old countess took her departure.

Tomsky's words had been nothing but ballroom small talk, but they had sunk deep into the soul of the romantic girl. The portrait sketched by Tomsky coincided with the image she had herself formed, and this type, which the latest novels have made a commonplace, at once alarmed and captivated her imagination. She sat with her bare arms folded, her head, with the flowers still in her hair, drooping over her half-exposed breast. . . . Suddenly the door opened and Hermann entered. She felt a profound thrill. . . .

"Where have you been?" she asked in a frightened whisper.

"In the old countess's bedroom," replied Hermann. "I've just come from her. The countess is dead."

"Dear God! What d'you mean?"

"And it seems," continued Hermann, "that it was I who caused her death."

Lisaveta Ivanovna glanced at him, and Tomsky's words echoed in her heart: *That man has at least three crimes on his conscience.* Hermann seated himself on the window sill next to her and told her all.

Lisaveta Ivanovna heard him with horror. And so it was not love that had inspired all those passionate letters, those ardent requests, that audacious, stubborn pursuit! Money —that was what his soul thirsted after. It was not she who could quench his desires and make him happy. The poor companion had been nothing but the blind accomplice of a criminal, the murderer of her old benefactress. She wept bitterly, in her belated, anguished repentance. Hermann looked at her in silence—he, too, felt a pang, but it was not the poor girl's tears, nor the exquisite beauty of her grief which stirred his hard heart. He felt no remorse at the thought of the old woman who was dead. Only one thing appalled him—the irretrievable loss of the secret which he had hoped would enrich him.

"You are a monster," said Lisaveta Ivanovna at last.

"I did not desire her death," replied Hermann. "My pistol was not loaded."

They were both silent.

Day began to break. Lisaveta Ivanovna extinguished the dying candle—a pale light crept into the room. She dried her eyes, which were red with weeping, and raised them to

Hermann's face: he was sitting on the window sill with his arms crossed, frowning ominously. In this pose he strikingly resembled a portrait of Napoleon. Even Lisaveta Ivanovna was impressed by the likeness.

"How are you to get out of the house?" she said, after a pause. "I had intended to take you by a concealed stairway, but we should have to go past her bedroom, and I am afraid."

"Tell me how I can find this concealed stairway. I will go."

Lisaveta Ivanovna rose, went to her chest of drawers, and took out a key which she handed to Hermann, giving him full instructions. Hermann pressed her cold, passive hand, kissed the top of her bent head, and went away.

He descended the spiral staircase and once more entered the bedroom of the old countess. The dead old woman sat there as if turned to stone; there was an expression of profound calm on her features. Hermann stood before her, gazed long at her, as if desirous of confirming to himself the appalling truth. At last he went into the study, felt for the papered door in the wall, and began descending a dark staircase, a prey to the strangest sensations. By this very staircase, he told himself, sixty years ago into this very bedroom, at this very hour, in a long embroidered coat, his hair brushed *à l'oiseau royal,* his three-cornered hat pressed to his heart, may have stolen a young fortunate, now long moldering in the grave, while the heart of his aged mistress had this day ceased to beat. . . .

At the foot of the staircase Hermann found a door, which he unlocked with the same key, and emerged in a passage leading right through the house to the street.

> *The late Baroness von V—— appeared*
> *to me in a dream tonight.*
> *She was attired in white and said to me:*
> *"Greetings, Mr. Privy Councilor."*
> SWEDENBORG

Five

Three days after the fatal night, Hermann went to the —— monastery, where a service was to be held over the

remains of the defunct countess. While he felt no remorse
he could not, however, quite silence the voice of conscience, which told him: it is you who murdered the old
woman. He had little true faith, but many superstitious
beliefs. He believed that the dead countess might have an
injurious influence on his life—and resolved to attend her
funeral in order to beg her forgiveness.

The church was full. Hermann could hardly push his
way through the crowd of mourners. The coffin stood on a
rich bier beneath a velvet pall. The dead woman lay with
hands folded on her breast, clad in a lace cap and white
satin dress. Around the coffin stood her household—the
servants in black liveries, with crested ribbons on their
shoulders, holding candles, the relatives—her children,
grandchildren, and great-grandchildren—in deep mourning.
No one wept; tears would have been *une affectation*. The
countess had been so old that her death caused no surprise
to anyone, and her relatives had long regarded her as one
who had outlived her time. A youthful priest preached the
funeral sermon. He described in simple and touching
phrases the peaceful end of the pious lady, for whom the
long years had been a calm affecting preparation for a
Christian death. "The angel of death," said the preacher,
"found her awake, in the midst of holy meditations, awaiting the midnight bridegroom." The service was accomplished with mournful propriety. The relatives went first
to bid farewell to the body. After them, the innumerable
guests, who had come to pay obeisance to her who had
so long been a participator in their vain festivities, moved
towards the coffin. Then came the members of the household. And finally there approached an ancient serving
maid, who was the same age as her mistress. Two youthful
serving maids held her up beneath her arms. She had not
the strength to bow down to the ground, and, alone of
them all, shed a few tears as she kissed the cold hand of
her late mistress. After her, Hermann ventured to approach
the coffin. He bowed to the ground, prostrating himself
for a few moments on the cold paving stones, strewn with
branches of fir. Then he rose, as white as the corpse itself,
ascended the steps of the bier, and bent down. . . . It
seemed to him that the dead woman looked at him
quizzically, and winked. Retreating hastily, he missed the
step, and fell flat on the ground. He was picked up. At
that very moment Lisaveta Ivanovna was carried out to
the porch of the church in a swoon. This incident disturbed
for a few moments the solemnity of the gloomy ritual. A

hollow murmur arose from the crowd, and a lean courtier, a near relation to the deceased, whispered in the ear of an Englishman standing beside him that the young officer was her natural son, to which the Englishman replied with a dry: "Oh?"

Hermann was in a state of excessive agitation the whole day. He dined in a lonely tavern and, contrary to his custom, drank a great deal, in the hope of drowning his anxiety. But the wine only inflamed his imagination still more. As soon as he got home, he threw himself down on his bed in his clothes and fell sound asleep.

When he woke up it was night; the moon lit up his room. He glanced at his watch—it was a quarter to three. He no longer wanted to sleep, and sat up in bed, thinking about the old countess's funeral.

Just then someone in the street looked at him through the window, and immediately stepped back. Hermann paid no attention to this. A minute later he heard the front door being opened. He thought it was his orderly, drunk as usual, returning from his nocturnal revelries. But he heard unfamiliar footsteps: someone approached with softly shuffling slippers. The door of his room opened and a woman in a white dress entered. Hermann took her for his own nurse and wondered what could have brought her there at such a time. But the white woman glided forward, and was suddenly quite close to him—and Hermann recognized the countess.

"I have come to you against my will," she said in firm tones. "I have been bidden to fulfill your request. A three, a seven, and an ace in succession are your winning cards, but only on condition that you do not stake more than one card a day, and after that never again play your whole life long. I forgive you my death, on condition that you marry my protégée Lisaveta Ivanovna. . . ."

With these words she turned softly toward the door and shuffled out. Hermann heard the door in the porch bang, and saw someone peer through the window into his room again.

It was a long time before he could recover his senses. He went into the next room. The orderly was asleep on the floor. Hermann roused him with great difficulty. He was drunk as usual, and Hermann could get nothing out of him. The door to the porch was bolted. Hermann went back to his room, lit a candle, and wrote an account of the vision he had seen.

"Attendez!"
"How dare you tell me *attendez?*"
"I said *'attendez-vous,'* Your Excellency."

Six

Two fixed ideas cannot exist simultaneously in our moral nature, any more than two bodies can occupy one and the same place in the physical world. The three, the seven, the ace soon blurred the image of the dead old woman in Hermann's imagination. The three, the seven, the ace were continually in his mind, and hovered on his lips. When he caught sight of a young girl he said: "How graceful she was—a regular three of hearts!" When asked what the time was, he answered five minutes to the seven. Every paunchy man he came across reminded him of the ace. The three, the seven, the ace haunted his dreams, assuming all sorts of forms. The three blossomed out before his eyes in the image of an enormous flower, the seven was represented by Gothic portals, the ace by a huge spider. All his thoughts were merged in a single one—to profit by the secret which had cost him so dear. He began thinking of retiring and traveling. He longed to wrench the treasure from enchanted Fortune in the public gambling salons of Paris. Chance relieved him of these cares.

At that time there was a society of wealthy gamblers in Moscow presided over by the renowned Chekalinsky, whose whole life had been spent playing cards, and who had accumulated millions, winning promissory notes and losing ready cash. His experience and wisdom had earned him the confidence of his comrades, and his hospitality, famous chef, kindliness, and cheerfulness had gained him the esteem of the public. He came to Petersburg. The young men flocked to him, neglecting balls for card playing and preferring the seductions of faro to the sweets of courting. Narumov brought Hermann to his house.

They passed through a suite of resplendent rooms lined with respectful menservants. A few generals and privy councilors were playing whist. Young men sprawled on the damask sofas, eating ices and smoking pipes. The host was keeping the bank at a long table in the drawing room, around which crowded some twenty gamblers. He was a man of about sixty of the most genteel appearance. His hair was a silvery gray; his plump, fresh-colored countenance expressed good humor; his eyes shone, lit up by a continual smile. Narumov introduced Hermann to him. Chekalinsky pressed his hand cordially, asked him not to stand upon ceremony, and went on playing.

The game was a long one. There were over thirty cards on the table. Chekalinsky paused after every deal in order to give the players time to look over their hands, jotted down losses, lent a courteous ear to all demands, and still more courteously smoothed back the corner of a card bent over by a careless hand. At last the game came to an end. Chekalinsky shuffled the cards and prepared to begin another.

"I would like to stake a card, if you please," said Hermann, stretching out his hand from behind a fat gentleman at the card table. Chekalinsky smiled and bowed silently, in token of submissive consent. Narumov laughingly congratulated Hermann on the breaking of his long fast, and wished him good luck.

"I am ready!" said Hermann, writing the sum in chalk above his card.

"What's that?" asked the holder of the bank, screwing up his eyes. "I am not sure that I read your sum right."

"Forty-seven thousand," replied Hermann.

At the sound of these words all heads were turned immediately, and all eyes were fixed on Hermann.

"He's gone mad," thought Narumov.

"Allow me to remark," said Chekalinsky, with his habitual smile, "that your stake is high. No one has ever staked more than two hundred and seventy-five *simple* here."

"Well?" replied Hermann. "Will you play?"

Chekalinsky bowed with his usual air of submission.

"I only wished to inform you," he said, "that, since I am honored with the confidence of my friends, I am obliged to play for cash only. For my part, I am, of course, willing to rely on your word, but for form's sake and to avoid misunderstanding I would ask you to place your money on the table."

Hermann took a bank note from his pocket and handed it to Chekalinsky, who, glancing rapidly at it, placed it on Hermann's card.

He began dealing. On the right lay a nine, on the left a three.

"Mine!" said Hermann, showing his card.

A murmur rose from the players. Chekalinsky frowned, but the smile returned immediately to his face.

"Shall I give it you now?" he asked Hermann.

"If it's no trouble."

Chekalinsky drew a bundle of bank notes from his pocket and counted out the required sum. Hermann took his winnings and retired from the table. Narumov was almost beside himself. Hermann drank a glass of lemonade and went home.

On the evening of the next day he repaired to Chekalinsky's again. The host was dealing. Hermann went up to the table; the other players immediately made room for him. Chekalinsky bowed to him urbanely.

Hermann waited for a fresh deal, and laid down a card, on which he placed his forty-seven thousand and his winnings of the previous night.

Chekalinsky began dealing. A knave was on the right, a seven on the left.

Hermann turned up a seven.

Everyone gasped. Chekalinsky was visibly disconcerted. He counted out ninety-four thousand in notes and handed them to Hermann. Hermann received them with the utmost *sang-froid* and immediately withdrew.

On the following evening Hermann was again at the table. Everyone was expecting him. The generals and privy councilors abandoned their rubber of whist to watch the unusual play. The young officers sprang up from the sofas. All the menservants were gathered in the drawing room. Everyone pressed around Hermann. The other players did not put down their stakes, but waited eagerly to see how the game would go. Hermann stood at the table, ready to play against the pale, but ever-smiling Chekalinsky. Each unsealed a new pack of cards. Chekalinsky shuffled. Hermann cut and laid down his card, covering it with a heap of bank notes. It was like a duel. Profound silence reigned in the room.

Chekalinsky began to deal with an unsteady hand. On the right, he turned up a queen, on the left, an ace.

"The ace wins," said Hermann, and showed his card.

"Your queen is covered," said Chekalinsky urbanely.

Hermann started: it was true—instead of an ace there lay the queen of spades. He could hardly believe his eyes, and wondered how he could have made such a blunder.

And all of a sudden it seemed to him that the queen of spades was narrowing her eyes and laughing at him. He was struck by an extraordinary likeness.

"The old woman!" he cried in horror.

Chekalinsky drew his winnings toward him. Hermann stood motionless. When he went away from the table everyone started talking loudly. "What a game!" exclaimed the players. Chekalinsky again shuffled the cards: the game went on as usual.

Conclusion

Hermann has gone mad. He is in Ward Number 17 of the Obukhov Hospital, and never answers when he is spoken to, only muttering over and over again with extraordinary rapidity: "Three, seven, ace . . . three, seven, queen! . . ."

Lisaveta Ivanovna married a very well-bred young man; he works in a government office and is the possessor of a considerable fortune. He is the son of the old countess's former steward. Lisaveta Ivanovna is bringing up an impoverished female relative.

Tomsky has been promoted to a captaincy and is going to marry the Princess Pauline.

Prosper Mérimée

(1803–1870)

Although Prosper Mérimée began to publish in 1829 at the age of twenty-six and continued writing for forty years, his reputation remains linked to his simple but powerful stories. Mérimée's novels and essays have not survived the passage of time.

In short fiction, he seems one of the precursors of Hemingway, Camus, and the other moderns who strip their characters and prose down to the fundamental simplicities. Mérimée's style is tightly wrought; his settings are carefully, sparsely, but accurately delineated; and his dialogue, like the dialogue of Hemingway, is taut and highly suggestive. His stories carry an almost visceral impact.

Mérimée was among the first of his contemporaries to break with the baroque ornateness of current prose. He preferred simplicity and directness of statement, foreshadowing, and tone. The characters in many of his stories, such as "Mateo Falcone," possess an archaic, almost Homeric dignity. Their lives are rooted in essentials, in enduring loyalties and habits. The appeal that Mérimée makes is to our deepest emotions. Mateo acts according to an ancient, unchanging code of honor which defines not only his point of view about life but his very capacity to continue to live. His son's betrayal of the code is, in his eyes, an indication of his inability to meet his primary responsibility as a human being. He has violated the moral law, the inviolable tribal code. His punishment is swift, terrible, inexorable.

Mateo Falcone

Coming out of Porto-Vecchio, and turning northwest toward the interior of the island, the ground rises somewhat rapidly, and, after a three hours' walk along winding paths, blocked by huge rocky boulders, and sometimes cut by ravines, you come to the edge of a wide *mâquis*. The *mâquis*, or high plateau, is the home of the Corsican shepherds and of all those who wish to escape the police. I would have you understand that the Corsican peasant sets fire to a stretch of woodland to save himself the trouble of manuring his fields. If the flames spread further than they should, so much the worse. In any case, he is sure of a good crop if he sows on this ground, which has been fertilized by the ashes of the trees which grew on it. When the corn has been harvested, they leave the straw, because it takes too much time to gather it up. The roots of the burned trees, which have been left in the ground undamaged, put forth very thick shoots in the following spring, and these shoots, before many years, attain a height of seven or eight feet. It is this sort of undergrowth which is called a *mâquis*. It is composed of all sorts of trees and shrubs mingled and tangled every which way. A man has to hew his way through with an axe, and there are *mâquis* so thick and tangled that even wild rams cannot penetrate them.

If you have killed a man, go into the *mâquis* of Porto-Vecchio with a good gun and powder and shot. You will live there quite safely, but don't forget to bring along a brown cloak and hood for your blanket and mattress. The shepherds will give you milk, cheese, and chestnuts, and you need not trouble your head about the law or the dead man's relatives, except when you are compelled to go down into the town to renew your ammunition.

When I was in Corsica in 18—, Mateo Falcone's house stood half a league away from the *mâquis*. He was a fairly rich man for that country. He lived like a lord, that is to say, without toil, on the produce of his flocks, which the nomadic shepherds pastured here and there on the mountains. When I saw him, two years later than the incident which I am about to relate, he did not seem to be more than fifty years of age.

Picture a small, sturdy man, with jet-black curly hair, a Roman nose, thin lips, large piercing eyes, and a weatherbeaten complexion. His skill as a marksman was extraordinary, even in this country, where everyone is a good shot. For instance, Mateo would never fire on a wild ram with small shot, but at a hundred and twenty paces he would bring it down with a bullet in its head or its shoulder, just as he fancied. He used his rifle at night as easily as in the daytime, and I was given the following illustration of his skill, which may seem incredible, perhaps, to those who have never travelled in Corsica. He placed a lighted candle behind a piece of transparent paper as big as a plate, and aimed at it from eighty paces away. He extinguished the candle; and a moment later, in utter darkness, fired and pierced the paper three times out of four.

With this extraordinary skill Mateo Falcone had gained a great reputation. He was said to be a good friend and a dangerous enemy. Obliging and charitable, he lived at peace with all his neighbors around Porto-Vecchio. But they said of him that once, at Corte, whence he had brought home his wife, he had quickly freed himself of a rival reputed to be as fearful in war as in love. At any rate, people gave Mateo the credit for a certain shot which had surprised his rival shaving in front of a small mirror hung up in his window. The matter was hushed up and Mateo married the girl. His wife Giuseppa presented him at first, to his fury, with three daughters, but at last came a son whom he christened Fortunato, the hope of the family and the heir to its name. The girls were married off satisfactorily. At a pinch their father could count on the daggers and rifles of his sons-in-law. The son was only ten years old, but already gave promise for the future.

One autumn day, Mateo and his wife set forth to visit one of his flocks in a clearing on the *mâquis*. Little Fortunato wanted to come along, but the clearing was too far off, and moreover, someone had to stay to look after the house. His father refused to take him. We shall see that he was sorry for this afterwards.

He had been gone several hours, and little Fortunato lay stretched out quietly in the sunshine, gazing at the blue mountains, and thinking that next Sunday he would be going to town to have dinner with his uncle, the magistrate, when he was suddenly startled by a rifle shot. He rose and turned toward the side of the plain whence the sound had come. Other shots followed, fired at irregular intervals, and they sounded nearer and nearer, till, finally, he saw a man on the path which led from the plain up to Mateo's house. He wore a mountaineer's peaked cap, had a beard, and was clad in rags. He dragged himself along with difficulty, leaning on his gun. He had just been shot in the thigh. The man was an outlaw from justice, who, having set out at nightfall to buy ammunition in the town, had fallen on the way into an ambuscade of Corsican gendarmes. After a vigorous defense, he had succeeded in making his escape, but the gendarmes had pursued him closely and fired at him from rock to rock. He had been just ahead of the soldiers, and his wound made it impossible for him to reach the *mâquis* without being captured.

He came up to Fortunato and asked:

"Are you Mateo Falcone's son?"

"Yes, I am."

"I'm Gianetto Sanpiero. The yellow necks are after me. Hide me, for I can go no farther."

"But what will my father say, if I hide you without his permission?"

"He will say that you did the right thing."

"How can I be sure of that?"

"Quick! Hide me! Here they come!"

"Wait till my father comes back."

"How the devil can I wait? They'll be here in five minutes. Come now, hide me, or I shall kill you."

Fortunato replied as cool as a cucumber:

"Your rifle is not loaded, and there are no cartridges in your pouch."

"I have my stiletto."

"But can you run as fast as I can?"

He bounded out of the man's reach.

"You are no son of Mateo Falcone. Will you let me be captured in front of his house?"

The child seemed touched.

"What will you give me if I hide you?" he said, coming nearer to him.

The fugitive felt in a leather wallet that hung from his belt, and took out a five-franc piece which he had been saving, no doubt, to buy powder. Fortunato smiled when he saw the piece of silver. He snatched it and said to Gianetto:

"Have no fear."

He made a large hole at once in a haystack beside the house. Gianetto huddled down in it, and the boy covered him up so as to leave a little breathing space, and yet so that no one could possibly suspect that a man was hidden there. He showed his ingenious wild cunning by another trick. He fetched a cat and her kittens and put them on top of the haystack, so that anyone who passed would think that it had not been disturbed for a long time. Then he noticed some bloodstains on the path in front of the house and covered them over carefully with dust. When he had finished, he lay down again in the sun looking as calm as ever.

A few minutes later, six men in brown uniforms with yellow collars, led by an adjutant, stopped in front of Mateo's door. The adjutant was a distant cousin of Falcone. (You know that degrees of kindred are traced farther in Corsica than anywhere else.) His name was Tiodoro Gamba. He was an energetic man, much feared by the outlaws, many of whom he had already hunted down.

"Good morning, little cousin," he said, accosting Fortunato. "How you have grown! Did you see a man go by just now?"

"Oh, I'm not as tall as you are yet, cousin," replied the child with an innocent smile.

"It won't take long. But, tell me, didn't you see a man go by?"

"Did I see a man go by?"

"Yes, a man with a black velvet peaked cap and a waistcoat embroidered in red and yellow?"

"A man with a black velvet peaked cap, and a waistcoat embroidered in red and yellow?"

"Yes. Hurry up and answer me, and don't keep repeating my questions."

"Monsieur the Curé went by this morning on his horse Pierrot. He enquired after papa's health, and I said to him that——"

"You are making a fool of me, you limb of the devil! Tell me at once which way Gianetto went. He's the man we're looking for, and I'm sure he went this way."

"How do you know?"

"How do I know? I know you've seen him."

"Can I see people pass by in my sleep?"

"You weren't asleep, you rascal. Our shots would wake you."

"So you think, cousin, that your rifles make all that hullabaloo? My father's rifle makes much more noise."

"The devil take you, you little scamp. I am positive that you have seen Gianetto. Maybe you've hidden him, in fact. Here, boys, search the house and see if our man isn't there. He could only walk on one foot, and he has too much sense, the rascal, to try and reach the *mâquis* limping. Besides, the trail of blood stops here."

"What will papa say?" asked Fortunato. "What will he say when he discovers that his house has been searched during his absence?"

"Do you realize that I can make you change your tune, you rogue?" cried the adjutant, as he pulled his ear. "Per-

haps you will have something more to say when I have
thrashed you with the flat of my sword."

Fortunato laughed in derision.

"My father is Mateo Falcone," he said meaningly.

"Do you realize, you rascal, that I can haul you off to
Corte or to Bastia? I shall put you in a dungeon on straw,
with your feet in irons, and I'll have your head chopped
off unless you tell me where to find Gianetto Sanpiero."

The child laughed again derisively at this silly threat. He
repeated:

"My father is Mateo Falcone."

"Adjutant, don't get us into trouble with Mateo," muttered one of the gendarmes.

You could see that Gamba was embarrassed. He whispered to his men, who had already searched the house
thoroughly. This was not a lengthy matter, for a Corsican
hut consists of one square room. There is no furniture
other than a table, benches, chests, cooking utensils, and
weapons. Meanwhile, little Fortunato was stroking the cat,
and seemed to take a malicious satisfaction in the dis-
comfiture of his cousin and the gendarmes.

One gendarme approached the haystack. He looked at
the cat and carelessly stuck a bayonet into the hay, shrugging his shoulders as if he thought the precaution absurd.
Nothing stirred, and the child's face remained perfectly
calm.

The adjutant and his men were desperate. They looked
seriously out across the plain, as if they were inclined to
go back home, when their leader, satisfied that threats
would make no impression on Falcone's son, decided to
make a final attempt, and see what coaxing and gifts might
do.

"Little cousin," said he, "I can see that your eyes are
open. You'll get on in life. But you are playing a risky
game with me, and, if it weren't for the trouble it would
give my cousin Mateo, God help me if I wouldn't carry
you off with me."

"Nonsense!"

"But, when my cousin returns, I am going to tell him
all about it, and he'll horsewhip you till the blood comes
because you've been telling me lies."

"How do you know?"

"You'll see! . . . But see here! Be a good boy, and I'll
give you a present."

"I advise you to go and look for Gianetto in the *mâquis*,
cousin. If you hang about here much longer, it will take

a cleverer man than you to catch him." The adjutant took a silver watch worth ten dollars out of his pocket. He noticed that little Fortunato's eyes sparkled as he looked at it, and he dangled the watch out to him at the end of its steel chain as he said:

"You scamp, wouldn't you like to have a watch like this hanging round your neck, and to strut up and down the streets of Porto-Vecchio as proud as a peacock? Folk would ask you what time it was and you would say, 'Look at my watch!'"

"When I'm a big boy, my uncle, the magistrate, will give me a watch."

"Yes, but your uncle's son has one already—not as fine as this, to be sure—but he is younger than you are."

The boy sighed.

"Well, would you like this watch, little cousin?"

Fortunato kept eyeing the watch out of the corner of his eye, like a cat that has been given a whole chicken to play with. It does not dare to pounce upon it, because it is afraid folk are laughing at it, but it turns its eyes away now and then so as to avoid temptation, and keeps licking its lips, as much as to say to its master: "What a cruel trick to play on a cat!" And yet Gamba seemed to be really offering him the watch. Fortunato did not hold out his hand, but said with a bitter smile:

"Why are you mocking me?"

"I swear that I am not mocking you. Only tell me where Gianetto is, and the watch is yours."

Fortunato smiled incredulously and fixed his dark eyes on those of the adjutant, trying to read them to see if the man could be trusted.

"May I lose my epaulettes," cried the adjutant, "if I do not give you the watch on this one condition! My men are witnesses, and I cannot back out of it."

As he spoke, he held the watch nearer and nearer till it almost touched the pale cheek of the boy, whose face clearly showed the struggle going on in his heart between greed and the claims of hospitality. His bare breast heaved till he was almost suffocated. Meanwhile the watch dangled and twisted and even touched the tip of his nose. Little by little, his right hand rose toward it, the tips of his fingers touched it, and the whole weight of it rested on his hand, although the adjutant still had it by the chain. . . . The face of the watch was blue. . . . The case was newly burnished. . . . It flamed like fire in the sun. . . . The temptation was too great.

Fortunato raised his left hand and pointed with his thumb over his shoulder to the haystack on which he was leaning. The adjutant understood him at once and let go the end of the chain. Fortunato felt that he was now sole possessor of the watch. He leaped away like a deer, and paused ten paces from the haystack which the gendarmes began to tumble over at once.

It was not long before they saw the hay begin to stir and a bleeding man came out with a stiletto in his hand. But when he tried to rise to his feet, his congealed wound prevented him from standing. He fell down. The adjutant flung himself upon his prey and wrested the stiletto from his grasp. He was speedily trussed up, in spite of his resistance, bound securely, and flung on the ground like a bundle of sticks. He turned his head toward Fortunato who had drawn near again.

"Son of . . . !" he exclaimed, more in contempt than in anger.

The child threw him the piece of silver, realizing that he no longer deserved it, but the fugitive paid no attention to it. He merely said quietly to the adjutant:

"My dear Gamba, I cannot walk. You must carry me to town."

"You were running as fast as a kid just now," retorted his captor, roughly. "But don't worry! I'm so glad to have caught you that I could carry you a league on my own back without feeling it. Anyhow, my friend, we'll make a litter for you out of branches and your cloak. We'll find horses at the farm at Crespoli."

"Very well," said the prisoner. "I suppose you will put a little straw on the litter to make it easier for me."

While the gendarmes were busy, some making a crude litter of chestnut boughs, and others dressing Gianetto's wound, Mateo Falcone and his wife suddenly appeared at a turn of the path which led from the *mâquis*. His wife came first, bowed low beneath the weight of a huge sack of chestnuts, while her husband strolled along, carrying a gun in one hand, and another slung over his shoulder. It is beneath a man's dignity to carry any other burden than his weapons.

As soon as he saw the soldiers, Mateo's first thought was that they must have come to arrest him. But there was no reason for it. He had no quarrel with the forces of law and order. He had an excellent reputation. He was "well thought of," as they say, but he was a Corsican, and a mountaineer, and there are very few Corsican mountain-

eers who, if they search their past sufficiently, cannot find
some peccadillo, a rifle shot or a thrust with a stiletto or
some other trifle. Mateo had a clearer conscience than
most of his friends, for it was at least ten years since he
had pointed a rifle at a man; but all the same it behooved
him to be cautious, and he prepared to put up a good
defense, if necessary.

"Wife," he said, "put down your sack and be on your
guard."

She obeyed at once. He gave her the gun from his
shoulder belt, as it seemed likely that it might be in his
way. He cocked the other rifle, and advanced in a leisurely
manner toward the house, skirting the trees beside the path,
and ready, at the least sign of hostility, to throw himself
behind the largest trunk and fire from cover. His wife
followed close behind him, holding her loaded rifle and his
cartridges. It was a good wife's duty, in case of trouble,
to reload her husband's arms.

The adjutant, on his side, was much troubled at seeing
Mateo advance upon him so with measured steps, pointing
his rifle, and keeping his finger on the trigger.

"If it should happen," thought he, "that Gianetto turns
out to be Mateo's relative or friend, and he wishes to
defend him, two of his bullets will reach us as sure as a
letter goes by post, and if he aims at me, in spite of our
kinship . . . !"

In his perplexity, he put the best face he could on the
matter, and went forward by himself to meet Mateo and
tell him all that had happened, greeting him like an old
friend. But the short distance between him and Mateo
seemed fearfully long.

"Hello, there, old comrade!" he cried out. "How are
you? I'm your cousin Gamba."

Mateo stood still and said not a word. As the other man
spoke, he slowly raised the barrel of his rifle so that, by
the time the adjutant came up to him, it was pointing to
the sky.

"Good-day, brother," said the adjutant, holding out his
hand. "It's an age since I've seen you."

"Good-day, brother."

"I just stopped by to pass the time of day with you and
cousin Pepa. We've had a long march to-day, but we can't
complain, for we've made a famous haul. We've just
caught Gianetto Sanpiero."

"Heaven be praised!" exclaimed Giuseppa. "He stole
one of our milch goats a week ago."

Gamba was delighted at her words.

"Poor devil!" said Mateo, "he was hungry."

"The chap fought like a lion," pursued the adjutant, somewhat annoyed. "He killed one of my men, and as if that were not enough, broke Corporal Chardon's arm; not that it matters, he's only a Frenchman. . . . Then he hid himself so cleverly that the devil himself couldn't find him. If it hadn't been for my little cousin Fortunato, I should never have found him."

"Fortunato?" cried Mateo.

"Fortunato?" echoed Giuseppa.

"Yes! Gianetto was hidden in your haystack over there, but my little cousin soon showed up his tricks. I shall tell his uncle, the magistrate, and he'll send him a fine present as a reward. And both his name and yours shall be in the report that I'm sending to the Public Prosecutor."

"Damn you!" muttered Mateo under his breath.

They had now rejoined the gendarmes. Gianetto was already laid on his litter, and they were all ready to start. When he saw Mateo in Gamba's company, he smiled oddly; then, turning toward the door of the house, he spat at the threshold.

"The house of a traitor!"

It was asking for death to call Falcone a traitor. A quick stiletto thrust, and no need of a second, would have instantly wiped out the insult. But Mateo's only movement was to put his hand to his head as if he were stunned.

Fortunato had gone into the house when he saw his father coming. Presently he reappeared with a bowl of milk, which he offered with downcast eyes to Gianetto.

"Keep away from me!" thundered the outlaw.

Then, turning to one of the gendarmes, he said:

"Comrade, will you give me a drink?"

The gendarme put the flask in his hand, and the outlaw drank the water given him by the man with whom he had just been exchanging rifle shots. Then he requested that his hands might be tied crossed on his breast instead of behind his back.

"I would rather," he said, "lie comfortably."

They gratified his request. Then, at a sign from the adjutant, saying good-bye to Mateo, who vouchsafed no answer, they set off quickly toward the plain.

Ten minutes passed before Mateo opened his mouth. The child looked uneasily, first at his mother, then at his father, who was leaning on his gun and gazing at him with an expression of concentrated fury.

"You begin well," said Mateo at last, in a calm voice, terrifying enough to those who knew the man.

"Father!" cried the boy, with tears in his eyes, coming nearer as if to throw himself at his father's knee.

"Out of my sight!" Mateo shouted.

The child stopped short a few paces away from his father, and sobbed.

Giuseppa approached him. She had just noticed the watch-chain hanging out of his shirt.

"Who gave you that watch?" she asked sternly.

"My cousin, the adjutant."

Falcone snatched the watch and flung it against a stone with such violence that it was shattered into a thousand fragments.

"Woman," he said, "is this a child of mine?"

Giuseppa's brown cheeks flushed brick red.

"What are you saying, Mateo? Do you realize to whom you are speaking?"

"Yes, perfectly well. This child is the first traitor in my family."

Fortunato redoubled his sobs and choking, and Falcone kept watching him like a hawk. At last he struck the ground with the butt of his rifle, then flung it across his shoulder, returned to the path which led toward the *mâquis,* and commanded Fortunato to follow him. The child obeyed.

Giuseppa ran after Mateo and clutched his arm.

"He is your son," she said in a trembling voice, fixing her dark eyes on those of her husband, as if to read all that was passing in his soul.

"Leave me," replied Mateo. "I am his father."

Giuseppa kissed her son and went back weeping into the house. She flung herself on her knees before an image of the Blessed Virgin and prayed fervently. Falcone walked about two hundred paces along the path, and went down a little ravine where he stopped. He tested the ground with the butt of his rifle, and found it soft and easy to dig. The spot seemed suitable for his purpose.

"Fortunato, go over to that big rock."

The boy did as he was told. He knelt down.

"Father, Father, do not kill me!"

"Say your prayers!" shouted Mateo in a terrible voice.

The boy, stammering and sobbing, recited the Our Father and the Apostles' Creed. The father said "Amen!" in a firm voice at the end of each prayer.

"Are those all the prayers you know?"

"I know the Hail Mary, too, and the Litany my aunt taught me, Father."

"It is long, but never mind."

The boy finished the Litany in a stifled voice.

"Have you finished?"

"Oh, Father, forgive me! Forgive me! I'll never do it again. I'll beg my cousin, the magistrate, ever so hard to pardon Gianetto!"

He kept beseeching his father. Mateo loaded his gun and took aim.

"God forgive you!" he said.

The boy made a desperate effort to rise and clasp his father's knees, but he had no time. Mateo fired and Fortunato fell stone-dead.

Without glancing at the body, Mateo returned to the house to fetch a spade with which to dig his son's grave. He had only gone a few steps along the path when he met Giuseppa, running, for she had been alarmed by the rifle shot.

"What have you done?" she cried.

"Justice!"

"Where is he?"

"In the ravine. I am going to bury him. He died a Christian. I shall have a Mass said for him. Send word to my son-in-law, Tiodoro Bianchi, that he is to come and live with us."

Nathaniel Hawthorne

(1804–1864)

*Born into an old New England family, which numbered
among its luminaries one of the judges in the Salem
witchcraft trials of 1692–1693, Hawthorne's preoccupation with the Puritan past came to him naturally. His
father was a sea captain who died in Surinam when
Hawthorne was four years old. The task of raising him
fell to his mother and her family. His uncles sent him
to Bowdoin College where his two closest friends were
the future poet, Henry Wadsworth Longfellow, and the
future president, Franklin Pierce, who was later to reward Hawthorne for his campaign efforts on his behalf
by appointing him as American consul in Liverpool.*

*The young Hawthorne wanted only to perfect himself
as a writer. After graduating from Bowdoin, he spent
the next twelve years sequestered in his family home
methodically learning his craft. Though they went
virtually unnoticed, the stories he published in his first
book,* Twice-Told Tales *(1837), are in no sense the work
of a young writer. Hawthorne's style is polished and
mature, and he has already seized upon what was to remain his chief preoccupation as a writer—sin and its
consequences.*

*Hawthorne spent a year as a clerk in the Boston
Custom House and another year as a member of the
experimental socialist community, Brook Farm, an experience which formed the basis for* The Blithedale
Romance *(1852). In 1842 he married Sophia Peabody
and spent what was probably the happiest period of his
life at the Old Manse in Concord* (Mosses From an Old
Manse, *1846). Here he became friendly with Emerson
and Thoreau. He returned to his boyhood home, Salem,
in order to accept an appointment as surveyor in the
Custom House, a job which a change in political admin-
istrations forced him to relinquish in 1849. In 1850 he
produced* The Scarlet Letter, *his best-known romance
and one of the finest nineteenth-century American novels.
Along with* The Blithedale Romance, The House of Seven
Gables *(1851), and Hawthorne's European novel,* The
Marble Faun *(1860),* The Scarlet Letter *subordinated*

65

Gothic terror to the more fundamental probing of the dark recesses of man's soul.

Hawthorne's interest in Puritanism arose out of his conviction that it had created in New England men and women whose passions and emotions were stifled. And yet, Hawthorne was more ambiguous about the Puritan ethic than he seemed. A closer examination of his writings reveals him to be as much the captive of Puritanism as he was its critic. He was not able to probe the split between man's rational and emotional needs as effectively as his friend Herman Melville did in Moby Dick.

All of Hawthorne's four important novels, what he called "romances," were written in the single decade 1850–1860; his major short stories were written earlier. In the past, he has been criticized for the excessively allegorical nature of his tales. He has been charged with being unable to create character. More recently, however, we have come to recognize that Hawthorne managed to combine narrative and symbol in a way wholly new to American fiction. His stories now seem at the very center of his literary fame. A story such as "Wakefield" indicates that he understood what was happening to modern man long before such contemporary concepts as "alienation" became the mode. As a character, Wakefield is almost existential in his distrustful and alienated reaction to society. In his intricate modernity, he is a memorable creation.

Wakefield

In some old magazine or newspaper I recollect a story, told as truth, of a man—let us call him Wakefield—who absented himself for a long time from his wife. The fact, thus abstractedly stated, is not very uncommon, nor—without a proper distinction of circumstances—to be condemned either as naughty or nonsensical. Howbeit, this, though far from the most aggravated, is perhaps the strangest, instance on record, of marital delinquency; and, moreover, as remarkable a freak as may be found in the whole list of human oddities. The wedded couple lived in London. The man, under pretence of going on a journey, took lodgings in the next street to his own house, and there, unheard of by his wife or friends, and without the shadow of a reason for such self-banishment, dwelt upwards of twenty years. During that period, he beheld his home every day, and frequently the forlorn Mrs. Wakefield. And after so great a gap in his matrimonial felicity—when his death was reckoned certain, his estate settled, his name dismissed from memory, and his wife, long, long ago, resigned to her autumnal widowhood—he entered the door one evening, quietly, as from a day's absence, and became a loving spouse till death.

This outline is all that I remember. But the incident, though of the purest originality, unexampled, and probably never to be repeated, is one, I think, which appeals to the generous sympathies of mankind. We know, each for himself, that none of us would perpetrate such a folly, yet feel as if some other might. To my own contemplations, at least, it has often recurred, always exciting wonder, but with a sense that the story must be true, and a conception of its hero's character. Whenever any subject so forcibly affects the mind, time is well spent in thinking of it. If the reader choose, let him do his own meditation; or if he prefer to ramble with me through the twenty years of Wakefield's vagary, I bid him welcome; trusting that there will be a pervading spirit and a moral, even should we fail to find them, done up neatly, and condensed into the final sentence. Thought has always its efficacy, and every striking incident its moral.

What sort of a man was Wakefield? We are free to shape out our own idea, and call it by his name. He was now in the meridian of life; his matrimonial affections, never violent, were sobered into a calm, habitual sentiment; of all husbands, he was likely to be the most constant, because a certain sluggishness would keep his heart at rest, wherever it might be placed. He was intellectual, but not actively so; his mind occupied itself in long and lazy musings, that ended to no purpose, or had not vigor to attain it; his thoughts were seldom so energetic as to seize hold of words. Imagination, in the proper meaning of the term, made no part of Wakefield's gifts. With a cold but not depraved nor wandering heart, and a mind never feverish with riotous thoughts, nor perplexed with originality, who could have anticipated that our friend would entitle himself to a foremost place among the doers of eccentric deeds? Had his acquaintances been asked, who was the man in London the surest to perform nothing to-day which should be remembered on the morrow, they would have thought of Wakefield. Only the wife of his

bosom might have hesitated. She, without having analyzed
his character, was partly aware of a quiet selfishness, that
had rusted into his inactive mind; of a peculiar sort of
vanity, the most uneasy attribute about him; of a disposition to craft, which had seldom produced more positive
effects than the keeping of petty secrets, hardly worth
revealing; and, lastly, of what she called a little strangeness,
sometimes, in the good man. This latter quality is indefinable, and perhaps non-existent.

Let us now imagine Wakefield bidding adieu to his wife.
It is the dusk of an October evening. His equipment is a
drab greatcoat, a hat covered with an oilcloth, top-boots,
an umbrella in one hand and a small portmanteau in the
other. He has informed Mrs. Wakefield that he is to take
the night coach into the country. She would fain inquire
the length of his journey, its object, and the probable time
of his return; but, indulgent to his harmless love of
mystery, interrogates him only by a look. He tells her not
to expect him positively by the return coach, nor to be
alarmed should he tarry three or four days; but, at all
events, to look for him at supper on Friday evening. Wakefield himself, be it considered, has no suspicion of what is
before him. He holds out his hand, she gives her own, and
meets his parting kiss in the matter-of-course way of a ten
years' matrimony; and forth goes the middle-aged Mr.
Wakefield, almost resolved to perplex his good lady by a
whole week's absence. After the door has closed behind
him, she perceives it thrust partly open, and a vision of her
husband's face, through the aperture, smiling on her, and
gone in a moment. For the time, this little incident is dismissed without a thought. But, long afterwards, when she
has been more years a widow than a wife, that smile
recurs, and flickers across all her reminiscences of Wakefield's visage. In her many musings, she surrounds the
original smile with a multitude of fantasies, which make it
strange and awful: as, for instance, if she imagines him in
a coffin, that parting look is frozen on his pale features;
or, if she dreams of him in heaven, still his blessed spirit
wears a quiet and crafty smile. Yet, for its sake, when all
others have given him up for dead, she sometimes doubts
whether she is a widow.

But our business is with the husband. We must hurry
after him along the street, ere he lose his individuality,
and melt into the great mass of London life. It would be
vain searching for him there. Let us follow close at his
heels, therefore, until, after several superfluous turns and

doublings, we find him comfortably established by the fire-
side of a small apartment, previously bespoken. He is in
the next street to his own, and at his journey's end. He
can scarcely trust his good fortune, in having got thither
unperceived—recollecting that, at one time, he was delayed
by the throng, in the very focus of a lighted lantern; and,
again, there were footsteps that seemed to tread behind
his own, distinct from the multitudinous tramp around
him; and, anon, he heard a voice shouting afar, and fancied
that it called his name. Doubtless, a dozen busybodies had
been watching him, and told his wife the whole affair. Poor
Wakefield! Little knowest thou thine own insignificance in
this great world! No mortal eye but mine has traced thee.
Go quietly to thy bed, foolish man; and, on the morrow,
if thou wilt be wise, get thee home to good Mrs. Wakefield,
and tell her the truth. Remove not thyself, even for a little
week, from thy place in her chaste bosom. Were she, for
a single moment, to deem thee dead, or lost, or lastingly
divided from her, thou wouldst be wofully conscious of
a change in thy true wife forever after. It is perilous to
make a chasm in human affections; not that they gape so
long and wide—but so quickly close again!

Almost repenting of his frolic, or whatever it may be
termed, Wakefield lies down betimes, and starting from
his first nap, spreads forth his arms into the wide and
solitary waste of the unaccustomed bed. "No,"—thinks he,
gathering the bedclothes about him,—"I will not sleep
alone another night."

In the morning he rises earlier than usual, and sets himself to consider what he really means to do. Such are his
loose and rambling modes of thought that he has taken
this very singular step with the consciousness of a purpose,
indeed, but without being able to define it sufficiently for
his own contemplation. The vagueness of the project, and
the convulsive effort with which he plunges into the execution of it, are equally characteristic of a feeble-minded
man. Wakefield sifts his ideas, however, as minutely as
he may, and finds himself curious to know the progress
of matters at home—how his exemplary wife will endure
her widowhood of a week; and, briefly, how the little
sphere of creatures and circumstances, in which he was a
central object, will be affected by his removal. A morbid
vanity, therefore, lies nearest the bottom of the affair. But,
how is he to attain his ends? Not, certainly, by keeping
close in this comfortable lodging, where, though he slept
and awoke in the next street to his home, he is as effectu-

ally abroad as if the stage-coach had been whirling him away all night. Yet, should he reappear, the whole project is knocked in the head. His poor brains being hopelessly puzzled with this dilemma, he at length ventures out, partly resolving to cross the head of the street, and send one hasty glance towards his forsaken domicile. Habit—for he is a man of habits—takes him by the hand, and guides him, wholly unaware, to his own door, where, just at the critical moment, he is aroused by the scraping of his foot upon the step. Wakefield! whither are you going?

At that instant his fate was turning on the pivot. Little dreaming of the doom to which his first backward step devotes him, he hurries away, breathless with agitation hitherto unfelt, and hardly dares turn his head at the distant corner. Can it be that nobody caught sight of him? Will not the whole household—the decent Mrs. Wakefield, the smart maid servant, and the dirty little footboy—raise a hue and cry, through London streets, in pursuit of their fugitive lord and master? Wonderful escape! He gathers courage to pause and look homeward, but is perplexed with a sense of change about the familiar edifice, such as affects us all, when, after a separation of months or years, we again see some hill or lake, or work of art, with which we were friends of old. In ordinary cases, this indescribable impression is caused by the comparison and contrast between our imperfect reminiscences and the reality. In Wakefield, the magic of a single night has wrought a similar transformation, because, in that brief period, a great moral change has been effected. But this is a secret from himself. Before leaving the spot, he catches a far and momentary glimpse of his wife, passing athwart the front window, with her face turned towards the head of the street. The crafty nincompoop takes to his heels, scared with the idea that, among a thousand such atoms of mortality, her eye must have detected him. Right glad is his heart, though his brain be somewhat dizzy, when he finds himself by the coal fire of his lodgings.

So much for the commencement of this long whim-wham. After the initial conception, and the stirring up of the man's sluggish temperament to put it in practice, the whole matter evolves itself in a natural train. We may suppose him, as the result of deep deliberation, buying a new wig, of reddish hair, and selecting sundry garments, in a fashion unlike his customary suit of brown, from a Jew's old-clothes bag. It is accomplished. Wakefield is another man. The new system being now established, a retrograde movement to the old would be almost as difficult as the step that placed him in his unparalleled position. Furthermore, he is rendered obstinate by a sulkiness occasionally incident to his temper, and brought on at present by the inadequate sensation which he conceives to have been produced in the bosom of Mrs. Wakefield. He will not go back until she be frightened half to death. Well; twice or thrice has she passed before his sight, each time with a heavier step, a paler cheek, and more anxious brow; and in the third week of his non-appearance he detects a portent of evil entering the house, in the guise of an apothecary. Next day the knocker is muffled. Towards nightfall comes the chariot of a physician, and deposits its big-wigged and solemn burden at Wakefield's door, whence, after a quarter of an hour's visit, he emerges, perchance the herald of a funeral. Dear woman! Will she die? By this time, Wakefield is excited to something like energy of feeling, but still lingers away from his wife's bedside, pleading with his conscience that she must not be disturbed at such a juncture. If aught else restrains him, he does not know it. In the course of a few weeks she gradually recovers; the crisis is over; her heart is sad, perhaps, but quiet; and, let him return soon or late, it will never be feverish for him again. Such ideas glimmer through the mist of Wakefield's mind, and render him indistinctly conscious that an almost impassable gulf divides his hired apartment from his former home. "It is but in the next street!" he sometimes says. Fool! it is in another world. Hitherto, he has put off his return from one particular day to another; henceforward, he leaves the precise time undetermined. Not to-morrow—probably next week—pretty soon. Poor man! The dead have nearly as much chance of revisiting their earthly homes as the self-banished Wakefield.

Would that I had a folio to write, instead of an article of a dozen pages! Then might I exemplify how an influence beyond our control lays its strong hand on every deed which we do, and weaves its consequences into an iron tissue of necessity. Wakefield is spell-bound. We must leave him, for ten years or so, to haunt around his house, without once crossing the threshold, and to be faithful to his wife, with all the affection of which his heart is capable, while he is slowly fading out of hers. Long since, it must be remarked, he had lost the perception of singularity in his conduct.

Now for a scene! Amid the throng of a London street

we distinguish a man, now waxing elderly, with few characteristics to attract careless observers, yet bearing, in his whole aspect, the handwriting of no common fate, for such as have the skill to read it. He is meagre; his low and narrow forehead is deeply wrinkled; his eyes, small and lustreless, sometimes wander apprehensively about him, but oftener seem to look inward. He bends his head, and moves with an indescribable obliquity of gait, as if unwilling to display his full front to the world. Watch him long enough to see what we have described, and you will allow that circumstances—which often produce remarkable men from nature's ordinary handiwork—have produced one such here. Next, leaving him to sidle along the footwalk, cast your eyes in the opposite direction, where a portly female, considerably in the wane of life, with a prayer-book in her hand, is proceeding to yonder church. She has the placid mien of settled widowhood. Her regrets have either died away, or have become so essential to her heart, that they would be poorly exchanged for joy. Just as the lean man and well-conditioned woman are passing, a slight obstruction occurs, and brings these two figures directly into contact. Their hands touch; the pressure of the crowd forces her bosom against his shoulder; they stand, face to face, staring into each other's eyes. After a ten years' separation, thus Wakefield meets his wife!

The throng eddies away, and carries them asunder. The sober widow, resuming her former pace, proceeds to church, but pauses in the portal, and throws a perplexed glance along the street. She passes in, however, opening her prayer-book as she goes. And the man! with so wild a face that busy and selfish London stands to gaze after him, he hurries to his lodgings, bolts the door, and throws himself upon the bed. The latent feelings of years break out; his feeble mind acquires a brief energy from their strength; all the miserable strangeness of his life is revealed to him at a glance: and he cries out, passionately, "Wakefield! Wakefield! You are mad!"

Perhaps he was so. The singularity of his situation must have so moulded him to himself, that, considered in regard to his fellow-creatures and the business of life, he could not be said to possess his right mind. He had contrived, or rather he had happened, to dissever himself from the world—to vanish—to give up his place and privileges with living men, without being admitted among the dead. The life of a hermit is nowise parallel to his. He was in the bustle of the city, as of old; but the crowd swept by and saw him not; he was, we may figuratively say, always beside his wife and at his hearth, yet must never feel the warmth of the one nor the affection of the other. It was Wakefield's unprecedented fate to retain his original share of human sympathies, and to be still involved in human interests, while he had lost his reciprocal influence on them. It would be a most curious speculation to trace out the effect of such circumstances on his heart and intellect, separately, and in unison. Yet, changed as he was, he would seldom be conscious of it, but deem himself the same man as ever; glimpses of the truth, indeed, would come, but only for the moment; and still he would keep saying, "I shall soon go back!"—nor reflect that he had been saying so for twenty years.

I conceive, also, that these twenty years would appear, in the retrospect, scarcely longer than the week to which Wakefield had at first limited his absence. He would look on the affair as no more than an interlude in the main business of his life. When, after a little while more, he should deem it time to reënter his parlor, his wife would clap her hands for joy, on beholding the middle-aged Mr. Wakefield. Alas, what a mistake! Would Time but await the close of our favorite follies, we should be young men, all of us, and till Doomsday.

One evening, in the twentieth year since he vanished, Wakefield is taking his customary walk towards the dwelling which he still calls his own. It is a gusty night of autumn, with frequent showers that patter down upon the pavement, and are gone before a man can put up his umbrella. Pausing near the house, Wakefield discerns, through the parlor windows of the second floor, the red glow and the glimmer and fitful flash of a comfortable fire. On the ceiling appears a grotesque shadow of good Mrs. Wakefield. The cap, the nose and chin, and the broad waist, form an admirable caricature, which dances, more-over, with the up-flickering and down-sinking blaze, almost too merrily for the shade of an elderly widow. At this instant a shower chances to fall, and is driven, by the un-mannerly gust, full into Wakefield's face and bosom. He is quite penetrated with its autumnal chill. Shall he stand, wet and shivering here, when his own hearth has a good fire to warm him, and his own wife will run to fetch the gray coat and small-clothes, which, doubtless, she has kept carefully in the closet of their bed chamber? No! Wake-field is no such fool. He ascends the steps—heavily!—for twenty years have stiffened his legs since he came down—

but he knows it not. Stay, Wakefield! Would you go to
the sole home that is left you? Then step into your grave!
The door opens. As he passes in, we have a parting glimpse
of his visage, and recognize the crafty smile, which was
the precursor of the little joke that he has ever since been
playing off at his wife's expense. How unmercifully has
he quizzed the poor woman! Well, a good night's rest to
Wakefield!

This happy event—supposing it to be such—could only
have occurred at an unpremeditated moment. We will not
follow our friend across the threshold. He has left us
much food for thought, a portion of which shall lend its
wisdom to a moral, and be shaped into a figure. Amid the
seeming confusion of our mysterious world, individuals
are so nicely adjusted to a system, and systems to one
another and to a whole, that, by stepping aside for a
moment, a man exposes himself to a fearful risk of losing
his place forever. Like Wakefield, he may become, as it
were, the Outcast of the Universe.

Edgar Allan Poe

(1809–1849)

*The son of a professional actor who deserted his wife
soon after Poe's birth and a professional actress who
died when he was only two, Poe seems to have struggled
with a lifelong identity crisis. He was raised by a wealthy
Virginia merchant, John Allan, and his wife, who sent
him to excellent schools in Richmond and in England,
but did not legally adopt him. Poe attended the University
of Virginia for one year and left because of his drinking and gambling, which were to plague him throughout
his life. His first collection of poems was published in
1827, when his foster father secured him an appointment to West Point. His dismissal from West Point produced a final break with Allan. Poe was left to make his
living as an itinerant journalist and writer.*

*Poe's first literary success was the short story "Ms
Found in a Bottle" (1831), which eventually led to his
becoming editor of the* Southern Literary Messenger. *In
1836 he left the* Messenger *for New York, married his
fourteen-year-old cousin, and spent the next twelve
years shuttling between New York and Philadelphia,
working as a journalist, short story writer, critic, and
literary hack. His wife died in 1847, after an illness
caused in large part by the poverty in which she had
lived. Two years later Poe was found in Baltimore in a
stupor. He died without regaining consciousness, exhausted from his struggle with poverty, drink, and his
severe psychological problems.*

*Poe is one of the seminal forces in modern literature.
His symbolic and impressionistic modes influenced Baudelaire, Verlaine, and Mallarmé. His science-fiction tales
(a genre which he can virtually be credited with inventing) deeply affected Jules Verne and H. G. Wells. His
"tales of ratiocination" evolved into the modern detective story.*

*Utilizing the conventions of the Gothic tale, Poe gave
new dimensions to the traditional horror story. His
stories are filled with the familiar Gothic images and
stage effects—old castles, dungeons, secret passages—
but these are kept subordinate to the particular effect
Poe wishes to produce—to internalize the horror. This*

*is what Poe meant when he spoke of terror being "not
of Germany, but of the soul."*

    *Unlike other practitioners of the horrible, Poe was
interested in the psychology of his victims. His famous
story, "The Pit and the Pendulum," is an almost unbearable tale of a man's expectation of tortures. Man's
irrationality had always intrigued him, and it was this,
rather than any supernatural occurrences, which absorbed
his attention. He was not so much interested in the murder as he was in the mind of the murderer. "The Black
Cat," in which Poe once again sets himself the task of
explicating "the spirit of* PERVERSENESS," *is narrated by
a man awaiting execution for the murder of his wife. The
style is highly compressed and dramatic—considerably
different from the ornateness which so often characterizes Poe's literary technique.*

The Black Cat

For the most wild, yet most homely narrative which I am
about to pen, I neither expect nor solicit belief. Mad indeed
would I be to expect it, in a case where my very senses
reject their own evidence. Yet, mad am I not—and very
surely do I not dream. But to-morrow I die, and to-day I
would unburthen my soul. My immediate purpose is to
place before the world, plainly, succinctly, and without
comment, a series of mere household events. In their consequences, these events have terrified—have tortured—
have destroyed me. Yet I will not attempt to expound
them. To me, they have presented little but Horror—to
many they will seem less terrible than *baroques*. Hereafter,
perhaps, some intellect may be found which will reduce
my phantasm to the common-place—some intellect more
calm, more logical, and far less excitable than my own,
which will perceive, in the circumstances I detail with awe,
nothing more than an ordinary succession of very natural
causes and effects.

    From my infancy I was noted for the docility and
humanity of my disposition. My tenderness of heart was
even so conspicuous as to make me the jest of my companions. I was especially fond of animals, and was indulged by my parents with a great variety of pets. With

these I spent most of my time, and never was so happy as when feeding and caressing them. This peculiarity of character grew with my growth, and, in my manhood, I derived from it one of my principal sources of pleasure. To those who have cherished an affection for a faithful and sagacious dog, I need hardly be at the trouble of explaining the nature or the intensity of the gratification thus derivable. There is something in the unselfish and self-sacrificing love of a brute, which goes directly to the heart of him who has had frequent occasion to test the paltry friendship and gossamer fidelity of mere *Man*.

I married early, and was happy to find in my wife a disposition not uncongenial with my own. Observing my partiality for domestic pets, she lost no opportunity of procuring those of the most agreeable kind. We had birds, goldfish, a fine dog, rabbits, a small monkey, and *a cat*.

This latter was a remarkably large and beautiful animal, entirely black, and sagacious to an astonishing degree. In speaking of his intelligence, my wife, who at heart was not a little tinctured with superstition, made frequent allusion to the ancient popular notion, which regarded all black cats as witches in disguise. Not that she was ever *serious* upon this point—and I mention the matter at all for no better reason than that it happens, just now, to be remembered.

Pluto—this was the cat's name—was my favorite pet and playmate. I alone fed him, and he attended me wherever I went about the house. It was even with difficulty that I could prevent him from following me through the streets.

Our friendship lasted, in this manner, for several years, during which my general temperament and character—through the instrumentality of the Fiend Intemperance—had (I blush to confess it) experienced a radical alteration for the worse. I grew, day by day, more moody, more irritable, more regardless of the feelings of others. I suffered myself to use intemperate language to my wife. At length, I even offered her personal violence. My pets, of course, were made to feel the change in my disposition. I not only neglected, but ill-used them. For Pluto, however, I still retained sufficient regard to restrain me from maltreating him, as I made no scruple of maltreating the rabbits, the monkey, or even the dog, when by accident, or through affection, they came in my way. But my disease grew upon me—for what disease is like Alcohol!—and at length even Pluto, who was now becoming old, and consequently somewhat peevish—even Pluto began to experience the effects of my ill temper.

One night, returning home, much intoxicated, from one of my haunts about town, I fancied that the cat avoided my presence. I seized him; when, in his fright at my violence, he inflicted a slight wound upon my hand with his teeth. The fury of a demon instantly possessed me. I knew myself no longer. My original soul seemed, at once, to take its flight from my body; and a more than fiendish malevolence, gin-nurtured, thrilled every fibre of my frame. I took from my waistcoat-pocket a penknife, opened it, grasped the poor beast by the throat, and deliberately cut one of its eyes from the socket! I blush, I burn, I shudder, while I pen the damnable atrocity.

When reason returned with the morning—when I had slept off the fumes of the night's debauch—I experienced a sentiment half of horror, half of remorse, for the crime of which I had been guilty; but it was, at least, a feeble and equivocal feeling, and the soul remained untouched. I again plunged into excess, and soon drowned in wine all memory of the deed.

In the meantime the cat slowly recovered. The socket of the lost eye presented, it is true, a frightful appearance, but he no longer appeared to suffer any pain. He went about the house as usual, but, as might be expected, fled in extreme terror at my approach. I had so much of my old heart left, as to be at first grieved by this evident dislike on the part of a creature which had once so loved me. But this feeling soon gave place to irritation. And then came, as if to my final and irrevocable overthrow, the spirit of PERVERSENESS. Of this spirit philosophy takes no account. Yet I am not more sure that my soul lives, than I am that perverseness is one of the primitive impulses of the human heart—one of the indivisible primary faculties, or sentiments, which give direction to the character of Man. Who has not, a hundred times, found himself committing a vile or a silly action, for no other reason than because he knows he should *not?* Have we not a perpetual inclination, in the teeth of our best judgment, to violate that which is *Law,* merely because we understand it to be such? This spirit of perverseness, I say, came to my final overthrow. It was this unfathomable longing of the soul *to vex itself*—to offer violence to its own nature—to do wrong for the wrong's sake only—that urged me to continue and finally to consummate the injury I had inflicted upon the unoffending brute. One morning, in cool blood,

I slipped a noose about its neck and hung it to the limb of a tree;—hung it with the tears streaming from my eyes, and with the bitterest remorse at my heart;—hung it *because* I knew that it had loved me, and *because* I felt it had given me no reason of offence;—hung it *because* I knew that in so doing I was committing a sin—a deadly sin that would so jeopardize my immortal soul as to place it—if such a thing were possible—even beyond the reach of the infinite mercy of the Most Merciful and Most Terrible God.

On the night of the day on which this cruel deed was done, I was aroused from sleep by the cry of fire. The curtains of my bed were in flames. The whole house was blazing. It was with great difficulty that my wife, a servant, and myself, made our escape from the conflagration. The destruction was complete. My entire worldly wealth was swallowed up, and I resigned myself thenceforward to despair.

I am above the weakness of seeking to establish a sequence of cause and effect, between the disaster and the atrocity. But I am detailing a chain of facts—and wish not to leave even a possible link imperfect. On the day succeeding the fire, I visited the ruins. The walls, with one exception, had fallen in. This exception was found in a compartment wall, not very thick, which stood about the middle of the house, and against which had rested the head of my bed. The plastering had here, in great measure, resisted the action of the fire—a fact which I attributed to its having been recently spread. About this wall a dense crowd were collected, and many persons seemed to be examining a particular portion of it with very minute and eager attention. The words "strange!" "singular!" and other similar expressions, excited my curiosity. I approached and saw, as if graven in *bas relief* upon the white surface, the figure of a gigantic *cat*. The impression was given with an accuracy truly marvellous. There was a rope about the animal's neck.

When I first beheld this apparition—for I could scarcely regard it as less—my wonder and my terror were extreme. But at length reflection came to my aid. The cat, I remembered, had been hung in a garden adjacent to the house. Upon the alarm of fire, this garden had been immediately filled by the crowd—by some one of whom the animal must have been cut from the tree and thrown, through an open window, into my chamber. This had probably been done with the view of arousing me from sleep. The falling

of other walls had compressed the victim of my cruelty
into the substance of the freshly-spread plaster; the lime
of which, with the flames, and the *ammonia* from the carcass, had then accomplished the portraiture as I saw it.

Although I thus readily accounted to my reason, if not
altogether to my conscience, for the startling fact just
detailed, it did not the less fail to make a deep impression
upon my fancy. For months I could not rid myself of the
phantasm of the cat; and, during this period, there came
back into my spirit a half-sentiment that seemed, but was
not, remorse. I went so far as to regret the loss of the
animal, and to look about me, among the vile haunts which
I now habitually frequented, for another pet of the same
species, and of somewhat similar appearance, with which
to supply its place.

One night as I sat, half stupefied, in a den of more
than infamy, my attention was suddenly drawn to some
black object, reposing upon the head of one of the immense hogsheads of Gin, or of Rum, which constituted the
chief furniture of the apartment. I had been looking
steadily at the top of this hogshead for some minutes, and
what now caused me surprise was the fact that I had not
sooner perceived the object thereupon. I approached it,
and touched it with my hand. It was a black cat—a very
large one—fully as large as Pluto, and closely resembling
him in every respect but one. Pluto had not a white hair
upon any portion of his body; but this cat had a large,
although indefinite, splotch of white, covering nearly the
whole region of the breast.

Upon my touching him, he immediately arose, purred
loudly, rubbed against my hand, and appeared delighted
with my notice. This, then, was the very creature of which
I was in search. I at once offered to purchase it of the
landlord; but this person made no claim to it—knew
nothing of it—had never seen it before.

I continued my caresses, and, when I prepared to go
home, the animal evinced a disposition to accompany me.
I permitted it to do so; occasionally stooping and patting
it as I proceeded. When it reached the house it domesti-
cated itself at once, and became immediately a great
favorite with my wife.

For my own part, I soon found a dislike to it arising
within me. This was just the reverse of what I had anticipated; but I know not how or why it was—its evident
fondness for myself rather disgusted and annoyed. By slow
degrees, these feelings of disgust and annoyance rose into

the bitterness of hatred. I avoided the creature; a certain
sense of shame, and the remembrance of my former deed
of cruelty, preventing me from physically abusing it. I did
not, for some weeks, strike, or otherwise violently ill use
it; but gradually—very gradually—I came to look upon it
with unutterable loathing, and to flee silently from its
odious presence, as from the breath of a pestilence.

What added, no doubt, to my hatred of the beast, was
the discovery, on the morning after I brought it home, that,
like Pluto, it also had been deprived of one of its eyes.
This circumstance, however, only endeared it to my wife,
who, as I have already said, possessed, in a high degree,
that humanity of feeling which had once been my dis-
tinguishing trait, and the source of many of my simplest
and purest pleasures.

With my aversion to this cat, however, its partiality for
myself seemed to increase. It followed my footsteps with
a pertinacity which it would be difficult to make the reader
comprehend. Whenever I sat, it would crouch beneath my
chair, or spring upon my knees, covering me with its
loathsome caresses. If I arose to walk it would get between
my feet and thus nearly throw me down, or, fastening its
long and sharp claws in my dress, clamber, in this manner,
to my breast. At such times, although I longed to destroy
it with a blow, I was yet withheld from so doing, partly
by a memory of my former crime, but chiefly—let me
confess it at once—by absolute *dread* of the beast.

This dread was not exactly a dread of physical evil—
and yet I should be at a loss how otherwise to define it.
I am almost ashamed to own—yes, even in this felon's
cell, I am almost ashamed to own—that the terror and
horror with which the animal inspired me, had been
heightened by one of the merest chimæras it would be
possible to conceive. My wife had called my attention,
more than once, to the character of the mark of white
hair, of which I have spoken, and which constituted the
sole visible difference between the strange beast and the
one I had destroyed. The reader will remember that this
mark, although large, had been originally very indefinite;
but, by slow degrees—degrees nearly imperceptible, and
which for a long time my Reason struggled to reject as
fanciful—it had, at length, assumed a rigorous distinctness
of outline. It was now the representation of an object that
I shudder to name—and for this, above all, I loathed, and
dreaded, and would have rid myself of the monster *had I
dared*—it was now, I say, the image of a hideous—of a

ghastly thing—of the GALLOWS—oh, mournful and terrible
engine of Horror and of Crime—of Agony and of Death!

And now was I indeed wretched beyond the wretchedness of mere Humanity. And a *brute beast*—whose fellow
I had contemptuously destroyed—*a brute beast* to work
out for *me*—for me a man, fashioned in the image of the
High God—so much of insufferable woe! Alas! neither
by day nor by night knew I the blessing of Rest any more!
During the former the creature left me no moment alone;
and, in the latter, I started, hourly, from dreams of unutterable fear, to find the hot breath of *the thing* upon my
face, and its vast weight—an incarnate Night-Mare that
I had no power to shake off—incumbent eternally upon my
heart!

Beneath the pressure of torments such as these, the feeble remnant of the good within me succumbed. Evil
thoughts became my sole intimates—the darkest and most
evil of thoughts. The moodiness of my usual temper increased to hatred of all things and of all mankind; while,
from the sudden, frequent, and ungovernable outbursts of
a fury to which I now blindly abandoned myself, my un-
complaining wife, alas! was the most usual and the most
patient of sufferers.

One day she accompanied me, upon some household
errand, into the cellar of the old building which our poverty
compelled us to inhabit. The cat followed me down the
steep stairs, and, nearly throwing me headlong, exasperated me to madness. Uplifting an axe, and forgetting, in
my wrath, the childish dread which had hitherto stayed
my hand, I aimed a blow at the animal which, of course,
would have proved instantly fatal had it descended as I
wished. But this blow was arrested by the hand of my
wife. Goaded, by the interference, into a rage more than
demoniacal, I withdrew my arm from her grasp and buried
the axe in her brain. She fell dead upon the spot, without a
groan.

This hideous murder accomplished, I set myself forth-
with, and with entire deliberation, to the task of concealing
the body. I knew that I could not remove it from the
house, either by day or by night, without the risk of being
observed by the neighbors. Many projects entered my
mind. At one period I thought of cutting the corpse into
minute fragments, and destroying them by fire. At another,
I resolved to dig a grave for it in the floor of the cellar.
Again, I deliberated about casting it in the well in the
yard—about packing it in a box, as if merchandize, with the

usual arrangements, and so getting a porter to take it from the house. Finally I hit upon what I considered a far better expedient than either of these. I determined to wall it up in the cellar—as the monks of the middle ages are recorded to have walled up their victims.

For a purpose such as this the cellar was well adapted. Its walls were loosely constructed, and had lately been plastered throughout with a rough plaster, which the dampness of the atmosphere had prevented from hardening. Moreover, in one of the walls was a projection, caused by a false chimney, or fireplace, that had been filled up, and made to resemble the rest of the cellar. I made no doubt that I could readily displace the bricks at this point, insert the corpse, and wall the whole up as before, so that no eye could detect anything suspicious.

And in this calculation I was not deceived. By means of a crow-bar I easily dislodged the bricks, and, having carefully deposited the body against the inner wall, I propped it in that position, while, with little trouble, I re-laid the whole structure as it originally stood. Having procured mortar, sand, and hair, with every possible precaution, I prepared a plaster which could not be distinguished from the old, and with this I very carefully went over the new brick-work. When I had finished, I felt satisfied that all was right. The wall did not present the slightest appearance of having been disturbed. The rubbish on the floor was picked up with the minutest care. I looked around triumphantly, and said to myself—"Here at least, then, my labor has not been in vain."

My next step was to look for the beast which had been the cause of so much wretchedness; for I had, at length, firmly resolved to put it to death. Had I been able to meet with it, at the moment, there could have been no doubt of its fate, but it appeared that the crafty animal had been alarmed at the violence of my previous anger, and forebore to present itself in my present mood. It is impossible to describe, or to imagine, the deep, the blissful sense of relief which the absence of the detested creature occasioned in my bosom. It did not make its appearance during the night—and thus for one night at least, since its introduction into the house, I soundly and tranquilly slept; aye, *slept* even with the burden of murder upon my soul!

The second and the third day passed, and still my tormentor came not. Once again I breathed as a free man. The monster, in terror, had fled the premises forever! I should behold it no more! My happiness was su-

preme! The guilt of my dark deed disturbed me but little.
Some few inquiries had been made, but these had been
readily answered. Even a search had been instituted—but
of course nothing was to be discovered. I looked upon my
future felicity as secured.

Upon the fourth day of the assassination, a party of
the police came, very unexpectedly, into the house, and
proceeded again to make rigorous investigation of the
premises. Secure, however, in the inscrutability of my
place of concealment, I felt no embarrassment whatever.
The officers bade me accompany them in their search.
They left no nook or corner unexplored. At length, for the
third or fourth time, they descended into the cellar. I
quivered not a muscle. My heart beat calmly as that of one
who slumbers in innocence. I walked the cellar from end
to end. I folded my arms upon my bosom, and roamed
easily to and fro. The police were thoroughly satisfied and
prepared to depart. The glee at my heart was too strong
to be restrained. I burned to say if but one word, by way
of triumph, and to render doubly sure their assurance of
my guiltlessness.

"Gentlemen," I said at last, as the party ascended the
steps, "I delight to have allayed your suspicions. I wish you
all health, and a little more courtesy. By the bye, gentlemen, this—this is a very well constructed house." [In the
rabid desire to say something easily, I scarcely knew what
I uttered at all.]—"I may say an *excellently* well constructed house. These walls—are you going, gentlemen?—
these walls are solidly put together;" and here, through the
mere phrenzy of bravado, I rapped heavily, with a cane
which I held in my hand, upon that very portion of the
brick-work behind which stood the corpse of the wife of
my bosom.

But may God shield and deliver me from the fangs of
the Arch-Fiend! No sooner had the reverberation of my
blows sunk into silence, than I was answered by a voice
from within the tomb!—by a cry, at first muffled and
broken, like the sobbing of a child, and then quickly
swelling into one long, loud, and continuous scream, utterly anomalous and inhuman—a howl—a wailing shriek, half
of horror and half of triumph, such as might have arisen
only out of hell, conjointly from the throats of the damned
in their agony and of the demons that exult in the damnation.

Of my own thoughts it is folly to speak. Swooning, I
staggered to the opposite wall. For one instant the party

upon the stairs remained motionless, through extremity of terror and of awe. In the next, a dozen stout arms were toiling at the wall. It fell bodily. The corpse, already greatly decayed and clotted with gore, stood erect before the eyes of the spectators. Upon its head, with red extended mouth and solitary eye of fire, sat the hideous beast whose craft had seduced me into murder, and whose informing voice had consigned me to the hangman. I had walled the monster up within the tomb!

Nikolai Vasilyevich Gogol
(1809–1852)

As a young man, Gogol attempted to achieve fame as both an actor and a poet. An intense and fearful individual, he published his first poem under a pseudonym in 1829. Because it was reviewed unfavorably, the sensitive Gogol bought and burned all the copies he could find and then fled Russia. His first literary success, Evenings On A Farm Near Dikanka *(1831)* brought him recognition as a writer, but he did not pursue his literary career in earnest until he had failed as an assistant professor of medieval history at the University of St. Petersburg. He then published two short story collections, Arabesques *(1835)* and Mirogorod *(1836)* and his famous story, "The Nose," a part of the anatomy which Gogol viewed with almost fetishistic delight. He has been credited, by no less an authority than Vladimir Nabokov, with being the writer whose "long sensitive nose . . . discovered new smells in literature. . . ."

Gogol's farce The Inspector General *(1836)*, a satire on rapacious and bungling bureaucrats, met with great success and won the approval of the Czar himself, although it enraged the officials who were the object of Gogol's ridicule. For the next twelve years, Gogol frequently lived abroad in Western Europe. Dead Souls *(1842)*, the novel which is generally considered Gogol's masterpiece, had placed him in what he considered an untenable situation. Gogol did not actually mean to disturb the Russian system of government, but his novel which attacked the institution of serfdom was naturally viewed as an attack. Gogol's purpose was not so much to reform Russia as it was to initiate a spiritual regeneration in his country. The second part of Dead Souls, which Gogol was to burn under the influence of a spiritual fanatic, the ascetic Father Matthew Konstantinovsky, was intended to portray all of Russia. But the ascetic priest played upon Gogol's belief that he was already eternally damned, a belief that had sent him on a pilgrimage to Palestine in 1848. He urged Gogol to renounce literature and to enter a monastery. Gogol so lacerated himself spiritually that he died of starvation induced by excessive self-mortification and fasting. Shortly before he died, he burned all of his remaining *manuscripts. All that we have left of the second part of* Dead Souls *are a few scattered pages.*

Gogol is generally recognized as the father of the Russian realistic novel. It is from his work that the great trio of Russian realists—Turgenev, Tolstoy, Dostoyevsky —drew much of their inspiration. What characterizes Gogol's fiction, and what gives it its breadth and humanity, can be seen in the relationship between the two men in "The Overcoat." There is a warmth to Gogol's writing, even when he is being satirical, that is not ordinarily to be found in the work of Dostoyevsky or Turgenev. As any reader of "The Overcoat" will discover, Gogol is perhaps the most Russian (with the possible exception of Dostoyevsky) of the great Russian realists.

The Overcoat

Once, in a department . . . but better not mention which department. There is nothing touchier than departments, regiments, bureaus, in fact, any caste of officials. Things have reached the point where every individual takes an insult to himself as a slur on society as a whole. It seems that not long ago a complaint was lodged by the police inspector of I forget which town, in which he stated clearly that government institutions had been imperiled and his own sacred name taken in vain. In evidence he produced a huge volume, practically a novel, in which, every ten pages, a police inspector appears, and what's more, at times completely drunk. So, to stay out of trouble, let us refer to it just as *a department*.

And so, once, in *a department*, there worked a clerk. This clerk was nothing much to speak of: he was small, somewhat pockmarked, his hair was somewhat reddish and he even looked somewhat blind. Moreover, he was getting thin on top, had wrinkled cheeks and a complexion that might be aptly described as hemorrhoidal. But that's the Petersburg climate for you.

As to his civil-service category (for first a man's standing should be established), he was what is called an eternal pen-pusher, a lowly ninth-class clerk, the usual butt of the jeers and jokes of those writers who have the congenial habit of biting those who cannot bite back.

The clerk's name was Shoenik. There is no doubt that

this name derives from shoe but we know nothing of how, why, or when. His father, his grandfather, and even his brother-in-law wore boots, having new soles put on them not more than three times a year.

His first name was Akaky, like his father's, which made him Akaky Akakievich. This may sound somewhat strange and contrived but it is not contrived at all, and, in view of the circumstances, any other name was unthinkable. If I am not mistaken, Akaky Akakievich was born on the night between the 22nd and the 23rd of March. His late mother, an excellent woman and the wife of a clerk, had made all the arrangements for the child's christening, and, while she was still confined to her bed, the godparents arrived: the worthy Ivan Yeroshkin, head clerk in the Senate, and Arina Whitetumkin, the wife of a police captain, a woman of rare virtue.

The new mother was given her pick of the following three names for her son: Mochius, Sossius, and that of the martyr, Hotzazat. "That won't do," Akaky's late mother thought. "Those names are . . . how shall I put it . . ." To please her, the godparents opened the calendar at another page and again three names came out: Strifilius, Dulius, and Varachasius.

"We're in a mess," the old woman said. "Who ever heard of such names? If it was something like Varadat or Varuch, I wouldn't object . . . but Strifilius and Varachasius . . ."

So they turned to yet another page and out came Pavsicachius and Vachtisius.

"Well, that's that," the mother said. "That settles it. He'll just have to be Akaky like his father."

So that's how Akaky Akakievich originated.

And when they christened the child it cried and twisted its features into a sour expression as though it had a foreboding that it would become a ninth-class clerk.

Well, that's how it all happened and it has been reported here just to show that the child couldn't have been called anything but Akaky.

No one remembers who helped him get his appointment to the department or when he started working there. Directors and all sorts of chiefs came and went but he was always to be found at the same place, in the same position, and in the same capacity, that of copying clerk. Until, after a while, people began to believe that he must have been born just as he was, shabby frock coat, bald patch, and all.

In the office, not the slightest respect was shown him. The porters didn't get up when he passed. In fact, they didn't even raise their eyes, as if nothing but an ordinary fly had passed through the reception room. His chiefs were cold and despotic with him. Some head clerks would just thrust a paper under his nose without even saying, "Copy this," or "Here's a nice interesting little job for you," or some such pleasant remark as is current in well-bred offices. And Akaky Akakievich would take the paper without glancing up to see who had put it under his nose or whether the person was entitled to do so. And right away he would set about copying it.

The young clerks laughed at him and played tricks on him to the limit of their clerkish wit. They made up stories about him and told them in front of him. They said that his seventy-year-old landlady beat him and asked him when the wedding would be. They scattered scraps of paper which they said was snow over his head. But with all this going on, Akaky Akakievich never said a word and even acted as though no one were there. It didn't even affect his work and in spite of their loud badgering he made no mistakes in his copying. Only when they tormented him unbearably, when they jogged his elbow and prevented him from getting on with his work, would he say:

"Let me be. Why do you do this to me? . . ."

And his words and the way he said them sounded strange. There was something touching about them. Once a young man who was new to the office started to tease him, following the crowd. Suddenly he stopped as if awakened from a trance and, after that, he couldn't stand the others, whom at first he had deemed decent people. And for a long time to come, during his gayest moments, he would suddenly see in his mind's eye the little, balding clerk and he would hear the words, "Let me be. Why do you do this to me?" and within those words rang the phrase, "I am your brother." And the young man would cover his face with his hands. Later in life, he often shuddered, musing about the wickedness of man toward man and all the cruelty and vulgarity which are concealed under refined manners. And this, he decided, was also true of men who were considered upright and honorable.

It would be hard to find a man who so lived for his job. It would not be enough to say that he worked conscientiously—he worked with love. There, in his copying, he found an interesting, pleasant world for himself and his

delight was reflected in his face. He had his favorites
among the letters of the alphabet and, when he came to
them, he would chuckle, wink and help them along with
his lips so that they could almost be read on his face as
they were formed by his pen.

Had he been rewarded in proportion with his zeal, he
would, perhaps to his own surprise, have been promoted
to fifth-class clerk. But all he got out of it was, as his
witty colleagues put it, a pin for his buttonhole and hemor-
rhoids to sit on.

Still, it would be unfair to say that no attention had ever
been paid him. One of the successive directors, a kindly
man, who thought Akaky Akakievich should be rewarded
for his long service, suggested that he be given something
more interesting than ordinary copying. So he was asked
to prepare an already drawn-up document for referral to
another department. Actually, all he had to do was to give
it a new heading and change some of the verbs from the
first to the third person. But Akaky Akakievich found this
work so complicated that he broke into a sweat and finally,
mopping his brow, he said:

"Oh no, I would rather have something to copy instead."

After that they left him to his copying forever. And aside
from it, it seemed, nothing existed for him.

He never gave a thought to his clothes. His frock coat,
which was supposed to be green, had turned a sort of
mealy reddish. Its collar was very low and very narrow
so that his neck, which was really quite ordinary, looked
incredibly long—like the spring necks of the head-shaking
plaster kittens which foreign peddlers carry around on their
heads on trays. And, somehow, there was always something stuck to Akaky Akakievich's frock coat, a wisp of
hay, a little thread. Then too, he had a knack of passing
under windows just when refuse happened to be thrown
out and as a result was forever carrying around on his hat
melon rinds and other such rubbish.

Never did he pay any attention to what was going on
around him in the street. In this he was very different from
the other members of the pen-pushing brotherhood, who
are so keen-eyed and observant that they'll notice an undone strap on the bottom of someone's trousers, an observation that unfailingly molds their features into a sly
sneer. But even when Akaky Akakievich's eyes were resting on something, he saw superimposed on it his own well-
formed, neat handwriting. Perhaps it was only when, out
of nowhere, a horse rested its head on his shoulder and

sent a blast of wind down his cheek that he'd realize he
was not in the middle of a line but in the middle of a
street.

When he got home he would sit straight down to the
table and quickly gulp his cabbage soup, followed by beef
and onions. He never noticed the taste and ate it with
flies and whatever else God happened to send along. When
his stomach began to feel bloated, he would get up from
the table, take out his inkwell, and copy papers he had
brought with him from the office. And if there weren't any
papers to copy for the office, he would make a copy for
his own pleasure, especially if the document were unusual.
Unusual, not for the beauty of its style, but because it was
addressed to some new or important personage.

Even during those hours when light has completely disappeared from the gray Petersburg sky and the pen-pushing brotherhood have filled themselves with dinner of one
sort of another, each as best he can according to his income and his preference; when everyone has rested from
the scraping of pens in the office, from running around on
their own and others' errands; when the restless human
being has relaxed after the tasks, sometimes unnecessary,
he sets himself; and the clerks hasten to give over the remaining hours to pleasure—the more enterprising among
them rushes to the theater, another walks in the streets,
allotting his time to the inspection of ladies' hats; another
spends his evening paying compliments to some prettyish
damsel, the queen of a small circle of clerks; another, the
most frequent case, goes to visit a brother clerk, who lives
somewhere on the third or fourth floor, in two small
rooms with a hall of a kitchen and some little pretensions
to fashion, a lamp or some other article bought at great
sacrifice, such as going without dinner or outside pleasures
—in brief, at the time when all clerks have dispersed
among the lodgings of their friends to play a little game
of whist, sipping tea from glasses and nibbling biscuits,
inhaling the smoke from their long pipes, relaying, while
the cards are dealt, some bit of gossip that has trickled
down from high society, a thing which a Russian cannot do
without whatever his circumstances, and even, when there's
nothing else to talk about, telling once again the ancient
joke about the commandant to whom it was reported that
someone had hacked the tail off the horse of the monument to Peter the First—in a word, when everyone else

was trying to have a good time, Akaky Akakievich was not even thinking of diverting himself.

No one had ever seen him at a party in the evening. Having written to his heart's content, he would go to bed, smiling in anticipation of the morrow, of what God would send him to copy.

Thus flowed the life of a man who, on a yearly salary of four hundred rubles, was content with his lot. And perhaps it would have flowed on to old age if it hadn't been for the various disasters which are scattered along life's paths, not only for ninth-class clerks, but even for eighth-, seventh-, sixth-class clerks and all the way up to State Councilors, Privy Councilors, and even to those who counsel no one, not even themselves.

In Petersburg, there's a formidable enemy for all those who receive a salary in the neighborhood of four hundred rubles a year. The enemy is none other than our northern cold, although they say it's very healthy.

Between eight and nine in the morning, at just the time when the streets are filled with people walking to their offices, the cold starts to mete out indiscriminately such hard, stinging flicks on noses that the wretched clerks don't know where to put them. And when the cold pinches the brows and brings tears to the eyes of those in high positions, ninth-class clerks are completely defenseless. They can only wrap themselves in their threadbare overcoats and run as fast as they can the five or six blocks to the office. Once arrived, they have to stamp their feet in the vestibule until their abilities and talents, which have been frozen on the way, thaw out once again.

Akaky Akakievich had noticed that for some time the cold had been attacking his back and shoulders quite viciously, try as he might to sprint the prescribed distance. He finally began to wonder whether the fault did not lie with his overcoat. When he gave it a good looking-over in his room, he discovered that in two or three places—the shoulders and back—it had become very much like gauze. The cloth was worn so thin that it let the draft in, and, to make things worse, the lining had disintegrated.

It must be noted that Akaky Akakievich's overcoat had also been a butt of the clerk's jokes. They had even deprived it of its respectable name, referring to it as the old dressing gown. And, as far as that goes, it did have a strange shape. Its collar shrank with every year, since it was used to patch other areas. And the patching, which did not flatter the tailor, made the overcoat baggy and ugly.

Having located the trouble, Akaky Akakievich decided to take the cloak to Petrovich, a tailor who lived somewhere on the fourth floor, up a back stairs, and who, one-eyed and pockmarked as he was, was still quite good at repairing clerks' and other such people's trousers and frock coats, provided he happened to be sober and hadn't other things on his mind.

We shouldn't, of course, waste too many words on the tailor, but since it has become the fashion to give a thorough description of every character figuring in a story, there's nothing to be done but to give you Petrovich.

At first he was called just Grigory and was the serf of some gentleman or other. He began to call himself Petrovich when he received his freedom and took to drinking rather heavily on all holidays, on the big ones at first and then, without distinction, on all church holidays—on any day marked by a little cross on the calendar. In this he was true to the traditions of his forefathers, and, when his wife nagged him about it, he called her impious and a German. Now that we've mentioned his wife, we'd better say a word or two about her, too. But unfortunately very little is known about her, except that Petrovich had a wife who wore a bonnet instead of a kerchief, but was apparently no beauty, since, on meeting her, it occurred to no one but an occasional soldier to peek under that bonnet of hers, twitching his mustache and making gurgling sounds.

Going up the stairs leading to Petrovich's place, which, to be honest about it, were saturated with water and slops and exuded that ammonia smell which burns your eyes and which you'll always find on the back stairs of all Petersburg houses—going up those stairs, Akaky Akakievich was already conjecturing how much Petrovich would ask and making up his mind not to pay more than two rubles.

The door stood open because Petrovich's wife was cooking some fish or other and had made so much smoke in the kitchen that you couldn't even see the cockroaches. Akaky Akakievich went through the kitchen without even seeing Mrs. Petrovich and finally reached the other room, where he saw Petrovich sitting on a wide, unpainted wooden table, with his legs crossed under him like a Turkish pasha.

He was barefoot, as tailors at work usually are, and the first thing Akaky Akakievich saw was Petrovich's big toe, with its twisted nail, thick and hard like a tortoise shell.

A skein of silk and cotton thread hung around Petrovich's neck. On his knees there was some old garment. For the past three minutes he had been trying to thread his needle, very irritated at the darkness of the room and even with the thread itself, muttering under his breath: "It won't go through, the pig, it's killing me, the bitch!" Akaky Akakievich was unhappy to find Petrovich so irritated. He preferred to negotiate when the tailor was a little under the weather, or, as his wife put it, "when the one-eyed buzzard had a load on." When caught in such a state, Petrovich usually gave way very readily on the price and would even thank Akaky Akakievich with respectful bows and all that. True, afterwards, his wife would come whining that her husband had charged too little because he was drunk; but all you had to do was to add ten kopeks and it was a deal.

This time, however, Petrovich seemed to be sober and therefore curt, intractable, and likely to charge an outrageous price. Akaky Akakievich realized this and would have liked to beat a hasty retreat, but the die was cast. Petrovich had fixed his one eye on him and Akaky Akakievich involuntarily came out with:

"Hello, Petrovich."

"Wish you good day, sir," said Petrovich and bent his eye toward Akaky Akakievich's hands to see what kind of spoil he had brought him.

"Well, Petrovich, I've come . . . see . . . the thing is . . . to . . ."

It should be realized that Akaky Akakievich used all sorts of prepositions, adverbs and all those meaningless little parts of speech when he spoke. Moreover, if the matter were very involved, he generally didn't finish his sentences and opened them with the words: "This, really, is absolutely, I mean to say . . ." and then nothing more— he had forgotten that he hadn't said what he wanted to.

"What is it then?" Petrovich asked, looking over Akaky Akakievich's frock coat with his one eye, the collar, the sleeves, the back, the tails, the buttonholes, all of which he was already acquainted with, since, repairs and all, it was his own work. That's just what tailors do as soon as they see you.

"Well, it's like this, Petrovich . . . my cloak, well, the material . . . look, you can see, everywhere else it's very strong, well, it's a bit dusty and it looks rather shabby, but it's not really . . . look, it's just in one place it's a little . . . on the back here, and here too . . . it's a little worn . . . and here on this shoulder too, a little—and that's all. There's not much work . . ."

Petrovich took Akaky Akakievich's old dressing gown, as his colleagues called it, spread it out on the table and looked it over at length. Then he shook his head and, stretching out his hand, took from the window sill a snuff-box embellished with the portrait of a general, though just what general it was impossible to tell since right where his face used to be there was now a dent glued over with a piece of paper. Taking some snuff, Petrovich spread the overcoat out on his hands, held it up against the light and again shook his head. Then he turned the overcoat inside out, with the lining up, and shook his head again. Then, once more, he removed the snuffbox lid with its general under the piece of paper, and, stuffing snuff into his nose, closed the box, put it away, and finally said:

"No. It can't be mended. It's no use."

At these words, Akaky Akakievich's heart turned over.

"But why can't it be, Petrovich?" he said in the imploring voice of a child. "Look, the only trouble is that it's worn around the shoulders. I'm sure you have some scraps of cloth . . ."

"As for scraps, I suppose I could find them," Petrovich said, "but I couldn't sew them on. The whole thing is rotten. It'd go to pieces the moment you touched it with a needle."

"Well, if it starts to go, you'll catch it with a patch . . ."

"But there's nothing for patches to hold to. It's too far gone. It's only cloth in name—a puff of wind and it'll disintegrate."

"Still, I'm sure you can make them hold just the same. Otherwise, really, Petrovich, see what I mean . . ."

"No," Petrovich said with finality, "nothing can be done with it. It's just no good. You'd better make yourself some bands out of it to wrap round your legs when it's cold and socks aren't enough to keep you warm. The Germans thought up those things to make money for themselves." —Petrovich liked to take a dig at the Germans whenever there was a chance.—"As to the overcoat, it looks as if you'll have to have a new one made."

At the word "new" Akaky Akakievich's vision became foggy and the whole room began to sway. The only thing he saw clearly was the general with the paper-covered face on the lid of Petrovich's snuffbox.

"What do you mean a *new* one?" he said, talking as if in a dream. "I haven't even got the money . . ."

"A new one," Petrovich repeated with savage calm.

"Well, but if I really had to have a new one, how would it be that . . ."

"That is, what will it cost?"

"Yes."

"Well, it will be over one hundred and fifty rubles," Petrovich said, pursing his lips meaningfully. He liked strong effects, he liked to perplex someone suddenly and then observe the grimace that his words produced.

"A hundred and fifty rubles for an overcoat!" shrieked the poor Akaky Akakievich, shrieked perhaps for the first time in his life, since he was always noted for his quietness.

"Yes, sir," said Petrovich, "but what an overcoat! And if it is to have marten on the collar and a silk-lined hood, that'll bring it up to two hundred."

"Please, Petrovich, please," Akaky Akakievich said beseechingly, not taking in Petrovich's words or noticing his dramatic effects, "mend it somehow, just enough to make it last a little longer."

"No sir, it won't work. It would be a waste of labor and money."

Akaky Akakievich left completely crushed. And when he left, Petrovich, instead of going back to his work, remained for a long time immobile, his lips pursed meaningfully. He was pleased with himself for having upheld his own honor as well as that of the entire tailoring profession.

Akaky Akakievich emerged into the street feeling as if he were in a dream. "So that's it," he repeated to himself. "I never suspected it would turn out this way . . ." and then, after a brief pause, he went on: "So that's it! Here's how it turns out in the end, and I, really, simply couldn't have foreseen it." After another, longer pause, he added: "And so here we are! Here's how things stand. I in no way expected . . . but this is impossible . . . what a business!" Muttering thus, instead of going home, he went in the opposite direction, without having the slightest idea of what was going on.

As he was walking, a chimney sweep brushed his dirty side against him and blackened his whole shoulder; a whole bucketful of lime was showered over him from the top of a house under construction. But he noticed nothing and only when he bumped into a watchman who, resting his halberd near him, was shaking some snuff out of a horn into his calloused palm, did he come to a little and that only because the watchman said:

"Ya hafta knock my head off? Ya got the whole side-walk, ain'tcha?"

This caused him to look about him and turn back toward home. Only then did he start to collect his thoughts and to see his real position clearly. He began to talk to himself, not in bits of phrases now but sensibly, as to a wise friend in whom he could confide.

"Oh no," he said, "this wasn't the moment to speak to Petrovich. Right now he's sort of . . . his wife obviously has given him a beating . . . that sort of thing. It'd be better if I went and saw him Sunday morning. After Saturday night, his one eye will be wandering and he'll be tired and in need of another drink, and his wife won't give him the money. So I'll slip him a quarter and that will make him more reasonable and so, for the overcoat . . ." Thus Akaky Akakievich tried to reassure himself, and persuaded himself to wait for Sunday.

When that day came, he waited at a distance until he saw Petrovich's wife leave the house and then went up. After his Saturday night libations, Petrovich's eye certainly was wandering. He hung his head and looked terribly sleepy. But, despite all that, as soon as he learned what Akaky Akakievich had come about, it was as if the devil had poked him.

"It can't be done," he said. "You must order a new one."

Here Akaky Akakievich pressed the quarter on him.

"Thank you," Petrovich said. "I'll drink a short one to you, sir. And as to the overcoat, you can stop worrying. It's worthless. But I'll make you a first-rate new one. That I'll see to."

Akaky Akakievich tried once more to bring the conver-sation around to mending, but Petrovich, instead of lis-tening, said:

"I'll make you a new one, sir, and you can count on me to do my best. I may even make the collar fastened with silver-plated clasps for you."

At this point Akaky Akakievich saw that he'd have to have a new overcoat and he became utterly depressed. Where was he going to get the money? There was of course the next holiday bonus. But the sum involved had long ago been allotted to other needs. He had to order new trousers, to pay the cobbler for replacing the tops on his boots. He owed the seamstress for three shirts and simply had to have two items of underwear which one cannot refer to in print. In fact, all the money, to the last kopek, was owed, and even if the director made an unexpectedly generous gesture and allotted him, instead of forty rubles, a whole forty-five or even fifty, the difference would be a drop in the ocean in the overcoat outlay.

It is true Akaky Akakievich knew that, on occasions, Petrovich slapped on heaven knows what exorbitant price, so that even his wife couldn't refrain from exclaiming:

"Have you gone mad, you fool! One day he accepts work for nothing, and the next, something gets into him and makes him ask for more than he's worth himself."

But he also knew that Petrovich would agree to make him a new overcoat for eighty rubles. Even so, where was he to find the eighty? He could perhaps scrape together half that sum. Even a little more. But where would he get the other half? . . . Let us, however, start with the first half and see where it was to come from.

Akaky Akakievich had a rule: whenever he spent one ruble, he slipped a copper into a little box with a slot in its side. Every six months, he counted the coppers and changed them for silver. He'd been doing this for a long time and, after all these years, had accumulated more than forty rubles. So this came to one half. But what about the remaining forty rubles?

Akaky Akakievich thought and thought and decided that he would have to reduce his regular expenses for an entire year at least. It would mean going without his evening tea; not burning candles at night, and, if he absolutely had to have light, going to his landlady's room and working by her candle. It would mean, when walking in the street, stepping as carefully as possible over the cobbles and paving stones, almost tiptoeing, so as not to wear out the soles of his boots too rapidly, and giving out his laundry as seldom as possible, and, so that it shouldn't get too soiled, undressing as soon as he got home and staying in just his thin cotton dressing gown, which, if time hadn't taken pity on it, would itself have collapsed long ago.

It must be admitted that, at first, he suffered somewhat from these restrictions. But then he became accustomed to them somehow and things went smoothly again. He even got used to going hungry in the evenings, but then he was able to feed himself spiritually, carrying within him the eternal idea of his overcoat-to-be. It was as if his existence had become somehow fuller, as if he had married and another human being were there with him, as if he were no longer alone on life's road but walking by the side of a delightful companion. And that companion was none other than the overcoat itself, with its thick padding and strong lining that would last forever. In some way, he became more alive, even stronger-minded, like a man who has determined his ultimate goal in life.

From his face and actions all the marks of vacillation and indecision vanished.

At times, there was even a fire in his eyes and the boldest, wildest notions flashed through his head—perhaps he should really consider having marten put on the collar? The intensity of these thoughts almost distracted his attention from his work. Once he almost made a mistake, which caused him to exclaim—true, very softly—"Oof!" and to cross himself.

At least once each month he looked in on Petrovich to discuss the overcoat—the best place to buy the material, its color, its price . . . Then, on the way home, a little worried but always pleased, he mused about how, finally, all this buying would be over and the coat would be made.

Things went ahead faster than he had expected. Beyond all expectations, the director granted Akaky Akakievich not forty, nor forty-five, but a whole sixty rubles. Could he have had a premonition that Akaky Akakievich needed a new overcoat, or had it just happened by itself? Whatever it was, Akaky Akakievich wound up with an extra twenty rubles. This circumstance speeded matters up. Another two or three months of moderate hunger and he had almost all of the eighty rubles he needed. His heartbeat, generally very quiet, grew faster.

As soon as he could, he set out for the store with Petrovich. They bought excellent material, which is not surprising since they had been planning the move for all of six months, and a month had seldom gone by without Akaky Akakievich dropping into the shop to work out prices. Petrovich himself said that there was no better material to be had.

For the lining they chose calico, but so good and thick that, Petrovich said, it even looked better and glossier than silk. They did not buy marten because it was too expensive. Instead they got cat, the best available—cat which at a distance could always be taken for marten. Petrovich spent two full weeks on the overcoat because of all the quilting he had to do. He charged twelve rubles for his work—it was impossible to take less; it had been sewn with silk, with fine double seams, and Petrovich had gone over each seam again afterwards with his own teeth, squeezing out different patterns with them.

It was—well, it's hard to say exactly which day it was, but it was probably the most solemn day in Akaky Akakievich's life, the day Petrovich finally brought him the overcoat. He brought it in the morning, just before it was time to go to the office. There couldn't have been a better moment for the coat to arrive, because cold spells had been creeping in and threatened to become even more severe. Petrovich appeared with the coat, as befits a good tailor. He had an expression of importance on his face that Akaky Akakievich had never seen before. He looked very much aware of having performed an important act, an act that carries tailors over the chasm which separates those who merely put in linings and do repairs from those who create.

He took the overcoat out of the gigantic handkerchief—just fresh from the wash—in which he had wrapped it to deliver it. The handkerchief he folded neatly and put in his pocket, ready for use. Then he took the coat, looked at it with great pride and, holding it in both hands, threw it quite deftly around Akaky Akakievich's shoulders. He pulled and smoothed it down at the back, wrapped it around Akaky Akakievich, leaving it a little open at the front. Akaky Akakievich, a down-to-earth sort of man, wanted to try out the sleeves. Petrovich helped him to pull his arms through and it turned out that with the sleeves too it was good. In a word, it was clear that the coat fitted perfectly.

Petrovich didn't fail to take advantage of the occasion to remark that it was only because he did without a signboard, lived in a small side street, and had known Akaky Akakievich for a long time that he had charged him so little. On Nevsky Avenue, nowadays, he said, they'd have taken seventy-five rubles for the work alone. Akaky Akakievich had no desire to debate the point with Petrovich—he was always rather awed by the big sums which Petrovich liked to mention to impress people. He paid up, thanked Petrovich, and left for the office wearing his new overcoat.

Petrovich followed him and stood for a long time in the street, gazing at the overcoat from a distance. Then he plunged into a curving side street, took a short cut, and re-emerged on the street ahead of Akaky Akakievich, so that he could have another look at the coat from another angle.

Meanwhile, Akaky Akakievich walked on, bubbling with good spirits. Every second of every minute he felt the new overcoat on his shoulders and several times he even let out a little chuckle of inward pleasure. Indeed, the over-

coat presented him with a double advantage: it was warm
and it was good. He didn't notice his trip at all and suddenly found himself before the office building. In the porter's lodge, he slipped off the overcoat, inspected it, and en-
trusted it to the porter's special care.

No one knows how, but it suddenly became general
knowledge in the office that Akaky Akakievich had a new
overcoat and that the old dressing gown no longer existed.
Elbowing one another, they all rushed to the cloakroom to
see the new coat. Then they proceeded to congratulate him.
He smiled at first, but then the congratulations became too
exuberant, and he felt embarrassed. And when they surrounded him and started trying to persuade him that the
very least he could do was to invite them over one evening
to drink to the coat, Akaky Akakievich felt completely at
a loss, didn't know what to do with himself, what to say
or how to talk himself out of it. And a few minutes later,
all red in the face, he was trying rather naively to convince
them that it wasn't a new overcoat at all, that it wasn't
much, that it was an old one.

In the end, a clerk, no lesser person than an assistant to
the head clerk, probably wanting to show that he wasn't
too proud to mingle with those beneath him, said:

"All right then, I'll do it instead of Akaky Akakievich.
I invite you all over for a party. Come over to my place to-
night. Incidentally, it happens to be my birthday today."

Naturally the clerks now congratulated the head clerk's
assistant and happily accepted his invitation. Akaky Akakievich started to excuse himself, but he was told that it
would be rude on his part, a disgrace, so he had to give
way in the end. And later he was even rather pleased that
he had accepted, since it would give him an opportunity
to wear the new coat in the evening too.

Akaky Akakievich felt as if it were a holiday. He arrived home in the happiest frame of mind, took off the
overcoat, hung it up very carefully on the wall, gave the
material and the lining one more admiring inspection. Then
he took out that ragged item known as the old dressing
gown and put it next to the new overcoat, looked at it and
began to laugh, so great was the difference between the
two. And long after that, while eating his dinner, he snorted
every time he thought of the dressing gown. He felt very
gay during his dinner, and afterwards he did no copying
whatsoever. Instead he wallowed in luxury for a while,

lying on his bed until dark. Then, without further dallying, he dressed, pulled on his new overcoat and went out.

It is, alas, impossible to say just where the party-giving clerk lived. My memory is beginning to fail me badly and everything in Petersburg, streets and houses, has become so mixed up in my head that it's very difficult to extract anything from it and to present it in an orderly fashion. Be that as it may, it is a fact that the clerk in question lived in a better district of the city, which means not too close to Akaky Akakievich.

To start with, Akaky Akakievich had to pass through a maze of deserted, dimly lit streets, but, toward the clerk's house, the streets became lighter and livelier. More pedestrians began flashing by more often; there were some well-dressed ladies and men with beaver collars. And, instead of the drivers with their wooden, fretworked sledges studded with gilt nails, he came across smart coachmen in crimson velvet caps, in lacquered sledges, with bearskin lap rugs. He even saw some carriages darting past with decorated boxes, their wheels squeaking on the snow.

Akaky Akakievich gazed around him. For several years now he hadn't been out in the evening. He stopped before the small, lighted window of a shop, staring curiously at a picture of a pretty woman kicking off her shoe and thereby showing her whole leg, which was not bad at all; in the background, some man or other with side whiskers and a handsome Spanish goatee was sticking his head through a door leading to another room. Akaky Akakievich shook his head, snorted, smiled and walked on. Why did he snort? Was it because he had come across something that, although completely strange to him, still aroused in him, as it would in anyone, a certain instinct—or did he think, as many clerks do, along the following lines: "Well, really, the French! If they are after something . . . that sort of thing . . . then, really! . . ." Maybe he didn't even think that. After all, one can't just creep into a man's soul and find out everything he's thinking.

At last he reached the house in which the head clerk's assistant lived. And he lived in style, on the second floor, with the staircase lighted by a lantern. In the hall, Akaky Akakievich found several rows of galoshes. Amidst the galoshes, a samovar was hissing and puffing steam. All around the walls hung overcoats and cloaks, some with beaver collars and others with velvet lapels. The noise and talk that could be heard through the partition became suddenly clear and resounding when the door opened and a servant came out with a tray of empty glasses, a cream jug, and a basket of cookies. It was clear that the clerks had arrived long before and had already drunk their first round of tea.

Akaky Akakievich hung his coat up and went in. In a flash, he took in the candles, the clerks, the pipes, the card tables, while his ears were filled with the hubbub of voices rising all around him and the banging of chairs being moved. Awkwardly, he paused in the middle of the room, trying to think what to do. But he had been noticed and his arrival was greeted with a huge yell. Immediately everybody rushed out into the hall to have another look at his new overcoat. Akaky Akakievich felt a bit confused, but, being an uncomplicated man, he was rather pleased when everyone agreed that it was a good overcoat.

Soon, however, they abandoned him and his overcoat and turned their attention, as was to be expected, to the card tables.

The din, the voices, the presence of so many people —all this was unreal to Akaky Akakievich. He had no idea how to behave, where to put his hands, his feet, or, for that matter, his whole body. He sat down near a card table, stared at the cards and peeked in turn into the faces of the players. In a little while he got bored and began to yawn, feeling rather sleepy—it was long past his usual bedtime. He wanted to take leave of the host, but they wouldn't let him go. He really had to toast his new over-coat with champagne, they insisted. They made Akaky Akakievich drink two glasses of champagne, after which he felt that the party was becoming gayer, but nevertheless he was quite unable to forget that it was now midnight and that he should have gone home long ago.

In spite of everything his host could think up to keep him, he went quietly out into the hall, found his overcoat, which to his annoyance was lying on the floor, shook it, carefully removed every speck he could find on it, put it on and walked down the stairs and out into the street.

The street was still lighted. Some little stores, those meeting places for servants and people of every sort, were open, while others, although closed, still showed a long streak of light under their doors, which indicated that the company had not yet dispersed and that the menservants and maids were finishing up their gossip and their conver-sations, leaving their masters perplexed as to their where-abouts.

Akaky Akakievich walked along in such a gay mood that, who knows why, he almost darted after a lady who flashed by him like a streak of lightning, every part of her body astir with independent, fascinating motion. Still, he restrained himself immediately, went back to walking slowly and even wondered where that compulsion to gallop had come from.

Soon there stretched out before him those deserted streets which, even in the daytime, are not so gay, and, now that it was night, looked even more desolate. Fewer street lamps were lit—obviously a smaller oil allowance was given out in this district. Then came wooden houses and fences; not a soul around, nothing but glistening snow and the black silhouettes of the low, sleeping hovels with their shuttered windows. He came to the spot where the street cut through a square so immense that the houses opposite were hardly visible beyond its sinister emptiness.

God knows where, far away on the edge of the world, he could see the glow of a brazier by a watchman's hut.

Akaky Akakievich's gay mood definitely waned. He could not suppress a shiver as he stepped out into the square, a foreboding of evil in his heart. He glanced behind him and to either side—it was like being in the middle of the sea. "No, it's better not to look," he thought, and walked on with his eyes shut. And when he opened them again to see if the other side of the square was close, he saw instead, standing there, almost in front of his nose, people with mustaches, although he couldn't make out exactly who or what. Then his vision became foggy and there was a beating in his chest.

"Why, here's my overcoat," one of the people thundered, grabbing him by the collar.

Akaky Akakievich was just going to shout out "Help!" when another brought a fist about the size of a clerk's head up to his very mouth, and said:

"You just try and yell . . ."

Akaky Akakievich felt them pull off his coat, then he received a knee in the groin. He went down on his back and after that he lay in the snow and felt nothing more.

When he came to a few minutes later and scrambled to his feet, there was no one around. He felt cold and, when he realized that the overcoat was gone, desperate. He let out a yell. But his voice didn't come close to reaching the other side of the square.

Frantic, he hollered all the way across the square as he scrambled straight toward the watchman's hut. The watchman was standing beside it, leaning on his halberd, and gazing out across the square, wondering who it could be running toward him and shouting. At last Akaky Akakievich reached him. Gasping for breath, he began shouting at him—what sort of a watchman did he think he was, hadn't he seen anything, and why the devil had he allowed them to rob a man? The watchman said he had seen no one except the two men who had stopped Akaky Akakievich in the middle of the square, who he had thought were friends of his, and that instead of hollering at the watchman, he'd better go and see the police inspector tomorrow and the inspector would find out who had taken the overcoat.

Akaky Akakievich hurried home; he was in a terrible state. The little hair he had left, on his temples and on the back of his head, was completely disheveled, there was snow all down one side of him and on his chest and all over his trousers. His old landlady, hearing his impatient banging on the door, jumped out of bed and, with only one shoe on, ran to open up, clutching her nightgown at the neck, probably out of modesty. When she saw the state Akaky Akakievich was in, she stepped back.

When he told her what had happened, she threw up her hands and said that he should go straight to the borough police Commissioner, that the local police inspector could not be trusted, that he'd just make promises and give him the runaround. So it was best, she said, to go straight to the borough Commissioner. In fact, she even knew him because Anna, her former Finnish cook, had now got a job as a nanny at his house. And the landlady herself often saw him driving past their house. Moreover, she knew he went to church every Sunday and prayed and at the same time looked cheerful and was obviously a good man. Having heard her advice, Akaky Akakievich trudged off sadly to his room and somehow got through the night, though exactly how must be imagined by those who know how to put themselves in another man's place.

Early the next morning, he went to the borough Commissioner's. But it turned out that he was still asleep. He returned at ten and again was told he was asleep. He went back at eleven and was told that the Commissioner was not home. He tried again during the dinner hour but the secretaries in the reception room would not let him in and wanted to know what business had brought him. For once in his life Akaky Akakievich decided to show some character and told them curtly that he must see the Commissioner personally, that they'd better let him in since he was on official government business, that he would lodge a complaint against them and that then they would see.

The secretaries didn't dare say anything to that and one of them went to call the Commissioner. The Commissioner reacted very strangely to Akaky Akakievich's story of the robbery. Instead of concentrating on the main point, he asked Akaky Akakievich what he had been doing out so late, whether he had stopped off somewhere on his way, hadn't he been to a house of ill repute. Akaky Akakievich became very confused and when he left he wasn't sure whether something would be done about his overcoat or not.

That day he did not go to his office for the first time in his life. The next day he appeared, looking very pale and wearing his old dressing gown, which now seemed shabbier than ever. His account of the theft of his overcoat touched many of the clerks, although, even now, there were some who poked fun at him. They decided on the spot to take up a collection for him but they collected next to nothing because the department employees had already had to donate money for a portrait of the Director and to subscribe to some book or other, on the suggestion of the section chief, who was a friend of the author's. So the sum turned out to be the merest trifle.

Someone, moved by compassion, decided to help Akaky Akakievich by giving him good advice. He told him that he had better not go to his local inspector because, even supposing the inspector wanted to impress his superiors and managed to recover the coat, Akaky Akakievich would still find it difficult to obtain it at the police station unless he could present irrefutable proof of ownership. The best thing was to go through a certain important personage who, by writing and contacting the right people, would set things moving faster. So Akaky Akakievich decided to seek an audience with the important personage.

Even to this day, it is not known exactly what position the important personage held or what his duties consisted of. All we need to know is that this important personage had become important quite recently and that formerly he had been an unimportant person. And even his present position was unimportant compared with other, more important ones. But there is always a category of people for whom somebody who is unimportant to others is an important personage. And the personage in question used various devices to play up his importance: for instance, he made

the civil servants of lower categories come out to meet
him on the stairs before he'd even reached his office; and
a subordinate could not approach him directly but had to
go through proper channels. That's the way things are in
Holy Russia—everyone tries to ape his superior.

They say that one ninth-class clerk, when he was named
section chief in a small office, immediately had a partition
put up to make a separate room, which he called the conference room. He stationed an usher at the door who had
to open it for all those who came in, although the conference room had hardly enough space for a writing table,
even without visitors. The audiences and the manner of
our important personage were impressive and stately, but
quite uncomplicated. The key to his system was severity.
He liked to say: "Severity, severity, severity," and as he
uttered the word for the third time, he usually looked very
meaningfully into the face of the person he was talking to.
True, it was not too clear what need there was for all this
severity since the ten-odd employees who made up the
whole administrative apparatus of his office were quite
frightened enough as it was. Seeing him coming, they
would leave their work and stand to attention until he had
crossed the room. His usual communication with his inferiors was full of severity and consisted almost entirely
of three phrases: "How dare you!" "Who do you think
you're talking to?" and "Do you appreciate who I am?"
Actually, he was a kindly man, a good friend and obliging,
but promotion to a high rank had gone to his head,
knocked him completely off balance, and he just didn't
know how to act. When he happened to be with equals, he
was still a decent fellow, and, in a way, by no means stupid.
But whenever he found himself among those who were
below him—even a single rank—he became impossible.
He fell silent and was quite pitiable, because even he himself realized that he could have been having a much better
time. Sometimes he was obviously longing to join some
group in a lively conversation, but he would be stopped
by the thought that he would be going too far, putting
himself on familiar terms and thereby losing face. And so
he remained eternally in silent, aloof isolation, only occasionally uttering some monosyllabic sounds, and, as a
result, he acquired a reputation as a deadly bore.

It was to this important personage that Akaky Akakievich presented himself, and at a most unpropitious moment
to boot. That is, very unpropitious for him, although quite
suitable for the important personage. The latter was in his

office talking gaily to a childhood friend who had recently come to Petersburg and whom he hadn't seen for many years. This was the moment when they announced that there was a man named Shoenik to see him.

"Who's he?" the personage wanted to know.

"Some clerk," they told him.

"I see. Let him wait. I am not available now."

Here it should be noted that the important personage was greatly exaggerating. He was available. He and his friend had talked over everything imaginable. For some time now the conversation had been interlaced with lengthy silences, and they weren't doing much more than slapping each other on the thigh and saying:

"So that's how it is, Ivan Abramovich."

"Yes, indeed, Stepan Varlamovich!"

Still Akaky Akakievich had to wait, so that his friend, who had left the government service long ago and now lived in the country, could see what a long time employees had to wait in his reception room.

At last, when they had talked and had sat silent facing each other for as long as they could stand it, when they had smoked a cigar reclining in comfortable armchairs with sloping backs, the important personage, as if he had just recalled it, said to his secretary who was standing at the door with papers for a report:

"Wait a minute. Wasn't there a clerk waiting? Tell him to come in."

Seeing Akaky Akakievich's humble appearance and his wretched old frock coat, he turned abruptly to face him and said: "What do you want?"

He spoke in the hard, sharp voice which he had deliberately developed by practicing at home before a mirror an entire week before he had taken over his present exalted position.

Akaky Akakievich, who had felt properly subdued even before this, felt decidedly embarrassed. He did his best, as far as he could control his tongue, to explain what had happened. Of course, he added even more than his usual share of phrases like "that is to say" and "so to speak." The overcoat, he explained, was completely new and had been cruelly taken away from him and he had turned to the important personage, that is to say, come to him, in the hope that he would, so to speak, intercede for him somehow, that is to say, write to the Superintendent of Police or, so to speak, to someone, and find the overcoat.

For some unimaginable reason the important personage found his manner too familiar.

"My dear sir," he answered sharply, "don't you know the proper channels? Do you realize whom you're addressing and what the proper procedure should be? You should first have handed in a petition to the office. It would have gone to the head clerk. From him it would have reached the section head, who would have approached my secretary and only then would the secretary have presented it to me. . . ."

"But, Your Excellency," said Akaky Akakievich, trying to gather what little composure he had and feeling at the same time that he was sweating terribly, "I, Your Excellency, ventured to trouble you because secretaries, that is to say . . . are, so to speak, an unreliable lot. . . ."

"What, what, what?" demanded the important personage. "Where did you pick up such an attitude? Where did you get such ideas? What is this insubordination that is spreading among young people against their chiefs and superiors?"

The important personage, apparently, had not noticed that Akaky Akakievich was well over fifty. Thus, surely, if he could be called young at all it would only be relatively, that is, to someone of seventy.

"Do you realize to whom you are talking? Do you appreciate who I am? Do you really realize, do you, I'm asking you?"

Here he stamped his foot and raised his voice to such a pitch that there was no need to be an Akaky Akakievich to be frightened.

And Akaky Akakievich froze completely. He staggered, his whole body shook, and he was quite unable to keep his feet. If a messenger hadn't rushed over and supported him, he would have collapsed onto the floor. They carried him out almost unconscious.

And the important personage, pleased to see that his dramatic effect had exceeded his expectations, and completely delighted with the idea that a word from him could knock a man unconscious, glanced at his friend to see what he thought of it all and was pleased to see that the friend looked somewhat at a loss and that fear had extended to him too.

Akaky Akakievich remembered nothing about getting downstairs and out into the street. He could feel neither hand nor foot. In all his life he had never been so severely reprimanded by a high official, and not a direct chief of his at that. He walked open-mouthed through a blizzard, again and again stumbling off the sidewalk. The wind, according to Petersburg custom, blew at him from all four sides at once, out of every side street. In no time it had blown him a sore throat and he got himself home at last quite unable to say a word. His throat was swollen and he went straight to bed. That's how severe the effects of an adequate reprimand can be.

The next day he was found to have a high fever. Thanks to the generous assistance of the Petersburg climate, the illness progressed beyond all expectations. A doctor came, felt his pulse, found there was nothing he could do and prescribed a poultice. That was done so that the patient would not be deprived of the beneficial aid of medicine. The doctor added, however, that, by the way, the patient had another day and a half to go, after which he would be what is called kaput. Then, turning to the landlady, the doctor said:

"And you, my good woman, I'd not waste my time if I were you. I'd order him the coffin right away. A pine one. The oak ones, I imagine, would be too expensive for him."

Whether Akaky Akakievich heard what for him were fateful words, and, if he heard, whether they had a shattering effect on him and whether he was sorry to lose his wretched life, are matters of conjecture. He was feverish and delirious the whole time. Apparitions, each stranger than the last, kept crowding before him. He saw Petrovich and ordered an overcoat containing some sort of concealed traps to catch the thieves who were hiding under his bed, so that every minute he kept calling his landlady to come and pull out the one who had even slipped under his blanket. Next, he would ask why his old dressing gown was hanging there in front of him when he had a new overcoat. Then he would find himself standing before the important personage, listening to the reprimand and repeating over and over: "I am sorry, Your Excellency, I am sorry."

Then he began to swear, using the most frightful words, which caused his old landlady to cross herself in horror; never in her life had she heard anything like it from him, and what made it even worse was that they came pouring out on the heels of the phrase, "Your Excellency." After that he talked complete nonsense and it was impossible to make out anything he was saying, except that his disconnected words kept groping for that lost overcoat of his. Then, at last, poor Akaky Akakievich gave up the ghost.

They did not bother to seal his room or his belongings because there were no heirs and, moreover, very little to inherit—namely, a bundle of goose quills, a quire of white government paper, three pairs of socks, a few buttons that had come off his trousers, and the old dressing-gown coat already mentioned. God knows whom they went to; even the reporter of this story did not care enough to find out.

They took Akaky Akakievich away and buried him. And Petersburg went on without him exactly as if he had never existed. A creature had vanished, disappeared. He had had no one to protect him. No one had ever paid him the slightest attention. Not even that which a naturalist pays to a common fly which he mounts on a pin and looks at through his microscope. True, this creature, who had meekly borne the office jokes and gone quietly to his grave, had had, toward the end of his life, a cherished visitor—the overcoat, which for a brief moment had brightened his wretched existence. Then a crushing blow had finished everything, a blow such as befalls the powerful of the earth. . . .

A few days after his death, a messenger from his office was sent to his lodgings with an order summoning him to report immediately; the chief was asking for him. But the messenger had to return alone and to report that Akaky Akakievich could not come.

"Why not?" he was asked.

"Because," the messenger said, "he died. They buried him four days ago."

That is how the department found out about Akaky Akakievich's death, and the next day a new clerk sat in his place: he was much taller and his handwriting was not as straight. In fact, his letters slanted considerably.

But who would have imagined that that was not the end of Akaky Akakievich, that he was fated to live on and make his presence felt for a few days after his death as if in compensation for having spent his life unnoticed by anyone? But that's the way it happened and our little story gains an unexpectedly fantastic ending. Rumors suddenly started to fly around Petersburg that a ghost was haunting the streets at night in the vicinity of the Kalinkin Bridge. The ghost, which looked like a little clerk, was purportedly searching for a stolen overcoat and used this pretext to pull the coats off the shoulders of everyone he met without regard for rank or title. And it made no difference what kind of coat it was—cat, beaver, fox, bearskin, in fact any of the furs and skins people have thought up to cover their own skins with.

One of the department employees saw the ghost with his own eyes and instantly recognized Akaky Akakievich. However, he was so terrified that he dashed off as fast as his legs would carry him and so didn't get a good look; he only saw from a distance that the ghost was shaking his finger at him. Complaints kept pouring in, and not only from petty employees, which would have been understandable. One and all, even Privy Councilors, were catching chills in their backs and shoulders from having their overcoats peeled off. The police were ordered to catch the ghost at any cost, dead or alive, and to punish him with due severity as a warning to others. And what's more, they nearly succeeded.

To be precise, a watchman caught the ghost red-handed, grabbed it by the collar, in Kiryushkin Alley, as it was trying to pull the coat off a retired musician who, in his day, used to tootle on the flute. Grabbing it, he called for help from two colleagues of his and asked them to hold on to it for just a minute. He had, he said, to get his snuff-box out of his boot so that he could bring some feeling back to his nose, which had been frostbitten six times in his life. But it was evidently snuff that even a ghost couldn't stand. The man, closing his right nostril with his finger, had hardly sniffed up half a fistful into the left when the ghost sneezed so violently that the three watchmen were blinded by the resulting shower. They all raised their fists to wipe their eyes and, when they could see again, the ghost had vanished. They even wondered whether they had really held him at all. After that, watchmen were so afraid of the ghost that they felt reluctant to interfere with live robbers and contented themselves with shouting from a distance: "Hey you! On your way!"

And the clerk's ghost began to haunt the streets well beyond the Kalinkin Bridge, spreading terror among the meek.

However, we have completely neglected the important personage, who really, in a sense, was the cause of the fantastic direction that this story—which, by the way, is completely true—has taken. First of all, it is only fair to say that, shortly after poor Akaky Akakievich, reduced to a pulp, had left his office, the important personage felt a twinge of regret. Compassion was not foreign to him— many good impulses stirred his heart, although his position usually prevented them from coming to the surface. As soon as his visiting friend had left the office, his thoughts returned to Akaky Akakievich. And after that, almost every day, he saw in his mind's eye the bloodless face of the little clerk who had been unable to take a proper reprimand. This thought was so disturbing that a week later he went so far as to send a clerk from his office to see how Akaky Akakievich was doing and to find out whether, in fact, there was any way to help him. And when he heard the news that Akaky Akakievich had died suddenly of a fever, it was almost a blow to him, even made him feel guilty and spoiled his mood for the whole day.

Trying to rid himself of these thoughts, to forget the whole unpleasant business, he went to a party at a friend's house. There he found himself in respectable company and, what's more, among people nearly all of whom were of the same standing so that there was absolutely nothing to oppress him. A great change came over him. He let himself go, chatted pleasantly, was amiable, in a word, spent a very pleasant evening. At supper, he drank a couple of glasses of champagne, a well-recommended prescription for inducing good spirits. The champagne gave him an inclination for something special and so he decided not to go home but instead to pay a little visit to a certain well-known lady named Karolina Ivanovna, a lady, it seems, of German extraction, toward whom he felt very friendly. It should be said that the important personage was no longer a young man, that he was a good husband, the respected father of a family. His two sons, one of whom already had a civil-service post, and his sweet-faced sixteen-year-old daughter, who had a slightly hooked but nevertheless pretty little nose, greeted him every day with a "Bon jour, Papa." His wife, a youngish woman and not unattractive at that, gave him her hand to kiss and then kissed his. But although the important personage was quite content with these displays of family affection, he considered it the proper thing to do to have, for friendship's sake, a lady friend in another part of the city. This lady friend was not a bit prettier or younger than his wife, but the world is full of such puzzling things and it is not our business to judge them.

So the important personage came down the steps, stepped inside his sledge, and said to the coachman:

"To Karolina Ivanovna's."

Wrapping his warm luxurious fur coat around him, he sat back in his seat. He was in that state so cherished by Russians, in which, without your having to make any effort, thoughts, each one pleasanter than the last, slip into your head by themselves.

Perfectly content, he went over all the most pleasant moments at the party, over the clever retorts that had caused that select gathering to laugh. He even repeated many of them under his breath and, still finding them funny, laughed heartily at them all over again, which was natural enough. However, he kept being bothered by gusts of wind which would suddenly blow, God knows from where or for what reason, cutting his face, throwing lumps of snow into it, filling the cape of his coat like a sail and throwing it over his head, so that he had to extricate himself from it again and again.

Suddenly the important personage felt someone grab him violently from behind. He turned around and saw a small man in a worn-out frock coat. Terrified, he recognized Akaky Akakievich, his face as white as the snow and looking altogether very ghostly indeed. Fear took over completely when the important personage saw the ghost's mouth twist and, sending a whiff of the grave into his face, utter the following words:

"I've caught you at last. I've got you by the collar now! It's the coat I need. You did nothing about mine and hollered at me to boot. Now I'll take yours!"

The poor important personage almost died. He may have displayed force of character in the office and, in general, toward his inferiors, so that after one glance at his strong face and manly figure, people would say: "Quite a man," but now, like many other mighty-looking people, he was so frightened that he began to think, and not without reason, that he was about to have an attack of something or other. He was even very helpful in peeling off his coat, after which he shouted to the coachman in a ferocious tone:

"Home! As fast as you can!"

The coachman, hearing the ferocious tone which the important personage used in critical moments and which was sometimes accompanied with something even more drastic, instinctively ducked his head and cracked his whip, so that they tore away like a streak. In a little over six minutes the important personage was in front of his house. Instead of being at Karolina Ivanovna's, he was somehow staggering to his room, pale, terrified, and coatless. There he spent such a restless night that the next morning, at breakfast, his daughter said:

"You look terribly pale this morning, Papa."

But Papa was silent, and he didn't say a word to anyone about what had happened to him, or where he had been or where he had intended to go. This incident made a deep impression upon him. From then on his subordinates heard far less often: "How dare you!" and "Do you know whom you're talking to?" And even when he did use these expressions it was after listening to what others had to say.

But even more remarkable—after that night, Akaky Akakievich's ghost was never seen again. The important personage's overcoat must have fitted him snugly. At any rate, one no longer heard of coats being torn from people's shoulders. However, many busybodies wouldn't let the matter rest there and maintained that the ghost was still haunting certain distant parts of the city. And, sure enough, a watchman in the Kolomna district caught a glimpse of the ghost behind a house. But he was rather a frail watchman. (Once an ordinary, but mature, piglet, rushing out of a private house, knocked him off his feet to the huge delight of a bunch of cabbies, whom he fined two kopeks each for their lack of respect—then he spent the proceeds on tobacco.) So, being rather frail, the watchman didn't dare to arrest the ghost. Instead he followed it in the darkness until at last it stopped suddenly, turned to face him, and asked:

"You looking for trouble?"

And it shook a huge fist at him, much larger than any you'll find among the living.

"No," the watchman said, turning away.

This ghost, however, was a much taller one and wore an enormous mustache. It walked off, it seems, in the direction of the Obukhov Bridge and soon dissolved into the gloom of night.

Gustave Flaubert

(1821–1880)

Gustave Flaubert's father was a surgeon and director of the public hospital in Rouen, France. The young Flaubert was raised in clinical-hospital surroundings. The effect of this environment on Flaubert was considerable. It is undoubtedly among the chief sources of his incredible quest for precision, the search for le mot juste, *with which he created a quiet revolution in the art of narrative. "I have never seen a child without thinking that he would become an old man, nor a cradle without thinking of a grave. The contemplation of a woman makes me wonder about her skeleton."*

Flaubert was ideally endowed with those virtues of the classical temperament which so uniquely characterize his contribution to the art of the novel: distance, restraint, skepticism, an insistence on the concrete and the objective, a refusal to sacrifice the narrative line of a story to the ego of the author. His extraordinary, selfless devotion (the cornerstone of both the classical temperament and the narrative art which he practices) is dramatically apparent in the way in which, after having studied law in Paris only to discover that he liked neither the city nor the profession, he immersed himself in the task of writing, returning to his family in order to become "a galley-slave of letters."

Flaubert's output is rather meager, but each of his books can be said to have left a permanent imprint upon the development of French literature. He worked on Madame Bovary (1857) *for more than five years. After its publication, he was indicted for having written a book that was an "outrage to public morals and religion." He was acquitted and found himself the most celebrated naturalist in France.* Madame Bovary *is an indictment of the French provincial bourgeoisie. With absolute objectivity Flaubert traces Emma Bovary's development into the quintessence of the nineteenth-century woman, a victim of forces beyond her control. Flaubert continued his quest for literary objectivity in* Salammbô (1862), *a historical novel for the writing of which he traveled to the site of ancient Carthage. This was followed by* L'Education Sentimentale (1869), *a novel which re-creates the experience of the revolutionary*

116

epoch of 1848 through a kind of male Emma Bovary.
Flaubert's most romantic novel La Tentation de Saint-
Antoine *(1874) is an expression of his intense interest*
in religious creeds.

Trois Contes (1877) contains three long short stories,
of which the one published here, "A Simple Heart," is
most famous. Along with the story, it offers the reader
a virtual handbook of Flaubert's literary technique. The
tone is impartial and objective. The events of Félicité's
life seem to unfold according to a natural order. Each
detail described is endowed with an importance all its
own. The selection of detail is matched by the meticulous,
intensive, succinct exploration of character. So powerful
is Flaubert's seemingly quiet technique that the reader is
swept up into the lives of these people with a totality
he has rarely experienced in fiction.

A Simple Heart

1

For half a century the womenfolk of Pont-l'Évêque be-
grudged Mme. Aubain her servant, Félicité.

For one hundred francs a year she cooked and did the
housework, sewed, washed, ironed, and knew how to bridle
a horse, how to "fatten" the chickens, how to make butter,
and she remained loyal to her mistress who, it must be
noted, was not a very easy person to get along with.

Mme. Aubain had married a handsome fellow, without
means, who had died at the beginning of the year 1809,
leaving her with two very young children and many debts.
At that time she sold what landed property she possessed,
except two farms, one at Toucques and another at Geffosses, the income of which brought her, at most, five
thousand francs a year; and she gave up her house at Saint-
Melaine to move into another less costly to maintain—a
house that had belonged to her ancestors and that was
situated behind the market square.

This house, with its slate roof, stood between an alley
and a little street that led to the river. Inside it had different
levels which caused one to stumble. A narrow vestibule

separated the kitchen from the parlor where Mme. Aubain, seated near the casement window in her wicker chair, spent the entire day. Against the wainscoting, painted white, were aligned eight mahogany chairs. A pyramid of wooden boxes and pasteboard cartons were piled up on an old piano, underneath a barometer. Two small stuffed armchairs flanked the yellow marble fireplace, in the style of Louis XV. The clock in the center depicted a temple of Vesta—the whole room smelled slightly musty, because the floor was on a level lower than the garden.

On the first floor, there was first Madame's bedroom, very large, papered in a pale flower design, with a portrait of "Monsieur" in a foppish costume on the wall. A smaller room in which were to be seen two children's beds, without mattresses, adjoined hers. Next came the salon, always kept locked, and cluttered with furniture covered over with sheets. Then a corridor led to the study; books and miscellaneous papers filled the shelves of a bookcase, the three sections of which surrounded a large desk made of black wood. The two panels in the corner were almost completely covered with pen sketches, water colors, and engravings by Audran—souvenirs of better times and vanished luxury. A dormer window on the second floor lighted Félicité's room, which overlooked the fields.

Félicité rose at daybreak so as not to miss mass, and she worked till evening without interruption; then, when dinner was over, the dishes done, the door bolted, she would smother the burning log in the ashes and fall asleep before the hearth, her rosary beads still in her hand. No one was better at stubborn bargaining in the marketplace than she. As for cleanliness, the shine on her pots and pans was the despair of the other servants. Very thrifty, she ate slowly and gathered together with her finger the bread crumbs on the table—her bread, which weighed twelve pounds, was especially baked for her, and lasted twenty days.

During all seasons she wore a calico neckerchief over her shoulders, pinned at the back, a bonnet hiding her hair, gray stockings, a red petticoat, and over her bodice an apron like those worn by hospital nurses.

Her face was thin and her voice sharp. At twenty-five, people took her to be forty. After she reached fifty, she showed no age at all; and always taciturn, with her erect posture and measured movements, she seemed like a woman made of wood, performing like an automaton.

2

Like any other, Félicité had had her love story.

Her father, a stonemason, had been killed by a fall from a scaffold. Then her mother died, her sisters wandered away, a farmer took her in and employed her, while still very young, to watch over his cows in the pasture. She shivered in her thin rags; drank water, lying on her stomach, from ponds; for no reason received whippings, and finally was sent away because of a theft of thirty sous—a crime she had not committed. She went to another farm, tended the poultry yard, and because she pleased her employers the other servants became jealous of her.

One evening in August (she was then eighteen) she was taken to a party at Colleville. Immediately she was bewildered, dazzled by the noise of the fiddlers, the lights hanging from the trees, the medley of costumes, the laces, the gold crosses, the immense crowd of people all bustling about. She was standing modestly aside, when a young, well-dressed man, smoking a pipe while resting his elbows on the shaft of a cart, came over and asked her to dance. He bought her cider, coffee and cakes, and a silk scarf, and, imagining that she guessed what he was thinking about, offered to take her home. On their way past a field of oats, he threw her backward very roughly. She was frightened and began to scream. He ran off.

Another evening, on the road to Beaumont, she wanted to pass a large wagon of hay that was going along slowly, and brushing against the wheels, she recognized Théodore.

He addressed her calmly, saying that she must forgive him everything, since it was "the fault of the drink."

She did not know what to say; and she wanted to run away.

Immediately he began to speak about the harvesting and the important people of the commune, for his father had left Colleville and had taken over the farm at Écots, so that now they were neighbors. "Oh!" she said. He went on to say that they wanted him to settle down. However, he was in no hurry, and was going to wait till he found a wife to his taste. She lowered her head. Then he asked her had she thought of marriage. She replied, smiling, that it wasn't nice to make fun of her.

"But I'm not making fun of you, I swear!" said he, putting his left arm around her waist. She walked along leaning on him. They slowed their pace. The wind was gentle, stars were shining; in front of them the huge hay wagon swayed from side to side; the four horses, dragging their hoofs, were stirring up dust. Then suddenly the horses veered to the right. He kissed her once more. She disappeared into the darkness.

The following week, Théodore had several meetings with her.

They met in remote farmyards, behind walls, or under some isolated tree. She was not innocent like well-bred young ladies—she had learned from being around animals; but reason and her self-esteem kept her from giving in. Her resistance exasperated Théodore's passion, so much so that to satisfy it (or perhaps naïvely) he proposed marriage to her. At first she doubted his sincerity, but he made strong vows of love.

Soon afterward, he confessed to her a troublesome bit of news: his parents, the year before, had bought him a substitute for the army, but any day now he could be drafted again; the idea of military service frightened him. Félicité interpreted this cowardice as proof of his affection, and it redoubled hers. She stole away at night to meet him, and while they were together Théodore tortured her with his problems and entreaties.

At last, he declared that he would go himself to the prefecture for information, and that he would inform her of what he found out on the following Sunday, between eleven o'clock and midnight.

When the moment arrived she hastened to her lover.

In his stead, she found one of his friends.

He told her that she was never to see Théodore again. To prevent himself from being drafted, Théodore had married a very rich *old* lady, Mme. Lehoussais of Toucques.

Félicité, beside herself with grief, threw herself to the ground, uttering cries and calling upon the merciful God above. All alone she stayed there in the fields, and wept till morning. Then she went back to the farm and announced that she was leaving; and, at the end of the month, when she had received her wages, she bundled up her few little belongings in a handkerchief and went to Pont-l'-Évêque.

In front of the inn, she made some inquiries of a woman

wearing a widow's cap, and who, it just so happened, was looking for a cook. This young girl did not know much, but she seemed so willing and was asking for so little that Mme. Aubain ended by saying: "All right, I'll take you!"

Fifteen minutes later, Félicité was settled in her new house.

At first, she lived there in a sort of fear and trembling caused by "the tone of the house" and by the vivid memory of "Monsieur" which hovered over everything! Madame's children, Paul and Virginie, one seven and the other four, respectively, seemed to her to be made of some rare substance; she liked to carry them piggyback. But Mme. Aubain forbade her to kiss them too often, which mortified Félicité. However, she was happy. The gentleness of her surroundings had softened her grief.

Every Thursday, the close friends of Mme. Aubain used to come for a game of "Boston." Félicité had to get the cards and foot warmers ready in advance. They always arrived precisely at eight and left before the clock struck eleven.

Every Monday morning, the junk dealer who lived on the same street used to spread out his wares on the ground. Then the whole town was filled with the hum of many voices—together with the neighing of horses, the bleating of sheep, the grunting of pigs, and the rattle of carts down the street. About noon, when market time reached its peak, a tall, old peasant with a hooked nose, wearing his cap on the back of his head, would appear and stand in the doorway—this was Robelin, a farmer of Geffosses. A little while later, Liébard, a farmer from Toucques, short, ruddy, corpulent, wearing a gray coat and spurs, appeared in the same place.

Both brought chickens and cheeses to their landlady, Mme. Aubain. Invariably Félicité would cunningly outwit them, and they would go away with more respect for her shrewdness.

At various times, the Marquis of Gremanville, one of Mme. Aubain's uncles, used to visit her. He had ruined himself by debauchery and was now living in Falaise on his last bit of farmland. He invariably came at lunch time, accompanied by a dreadful poodle that always dirtied the furniture with its paws. Despite his efforts to play the role of the gentleman (he would raise his hat every time he said, "my late father"), force of habit compelled him to drink one glass after another and to blurt out risqué stories. Félicité would politely usher him out the door, saying,

"You have had enough, Monsieur de Gremanville! Some other time!" And she would shut the door on him.

To M. Bourais, a retired lawyer, the door was invitingly opened. His white cravat, his bald head, his frilled shirt, his full-fitting brown frock coat, his way of flourishing his arm when he took snuff—his whole person produced in her a certain excitement such as we all experience at the sight of extraordinary men.

As he was the manager of Madame's properties, he spent hours with her in "Monsieur's" study, all the time fearful of compromising his position. He had great respect for the bench. Moreover, he had some pretensions to being a Latin scholar.

To make learning pleasant for the children, he gave them a geography book consisting of prints. There were representative scenes from all over the world: cannibals with feathered headdresses; a monkey carrying away a damsel; Bedouins in the desert; a whale being harpooned, and so on.

Paul explained these pictures to Félicité. And this was the extent of her literary education.

The children's education was in the hands of Guyot, a wretched individual working at the Town Hall, who was famous for his beautiful handwriting and for the way he sharpened his penknife on his boot.

When the weather was clear, they all used to start early for the Geffosses farm.

The farmyard is on the side of a slope, with the house in the middle; and the sea, from a distance, looks like a gray blot.

Félicité would take out slices of cold meat from her basket, and they all would eat in a room that adjoined the milk house. It was all that remained of a once elegant country house. Now the wallpaper hung like tattered ribbons, and rustled with the drafts from the window. Mme. Aubain would bow her head, weighed down by memories of the past; the children would no longer dare to speak. "Go out and play!" she would say to them; and off they would go.

Paul climbed up in the barn, caught birds, played ducks and drakes, or tapped with a stick the huge barrels that rumbled like drums.

Virginie fed the rabbits and scampered away to pick cornflowers, her legs moving so quickly that you could see her little lace-trimmed drawers.

One autumn evening they were returning through the fields.

The moon in its first quarter lit a segment of the sky, and a haze floated like a scarf over the winding Toucques River. Cattle, lying in the middle of the meadow, gazed contentedly at these four people. In the third pasture, some of the cows got up and circled them. "Don't be afraid!" said Félicité, and stroking the back of the one nearest to her, she murmured a sort of lament. It turned around and the others did the same. But, when they crossed the next field, they heard a loud bellow. It was a bull, hidden in the haze. He came toward the two women. Mme. Aubain was about to run. "No, no, not so fast!" Nevertheless, though they quickened their steps, they heard back of them the sound of snorting, coming closer and closer. His hoofs beat like hammer blows on the meadow grass. Now he was galloping toward them! Félicité turned around and, with both hands, snatched up clods of turf to throw into the bull's eyes. He lowered his head, shook his horns, and, trembling with fury, bellowed terribly. Mme. Aubain, at the end of the pasture with the two little ones, looked frantically for a way to get over the high bank. Félicité backed steadily away from the bull, throwing grass and dirt at him all the time, to blind him, while at the same time she shouted, "Hurry! Hurry!"

Mme. Aubain jumped into the ditch, pushing Virginie, then Paul, in front of her. She stumbled several times, struggling to climb the bank, and by sheer courage finally succeeded.

The bull had backed Félicité against a fence; his slaver spattered her face; a second more and he would have gored her. She just had time to crawl between two fence rails. The huge animal stopped, amazed.

At Pont-l'Évêque, they talked of this adventure for many years. However, Félicité was not proud of it, nor did she think that she had done anything heroic.

Virginie took up all her time—for, as a result of her fright, she had developed a nervous disorder, and M. Poupart, the physician, advised sea-baths for her at Trouville.

At that time not many people frequented Trouville. Mme. Aubain sought information about the place, consulted with Bourais, and made preparations as if embarking on a long voyage.

They sent off her baggage the day before, in Liébard's cart. The next day, he brought to the house two horses, one of which had a lady's saddle, with a velvet back; the other had a cloak rolled up like a seat on the crupper.

Mme. Aubain mounted her horse, behind Liébard. Félicité took charge of Virginie, and Paul rode M. Lechaptois' donkey, lent to him on condition that he take good care of it.

The road was so bad that it took two hours to go five miles. The horses sank into mud up to their pasterns, and had to make strenuous movements with their haunches to extricate themselves; they would sometimes stumble in ruts; other times they had to leap over them. In some places Liébard's mare would stop all of a sudden. Patiently he would wait for her to go on again; meantime he talked about the people whose property bordered the road, interpolating moral reflections on the story told. Thus, while they were in the middle of Touncques, as they were passing under a window full of nasturtiums, he remarked, shrugging his shoulders: "There's that Mme. Lehoussais, who instead of taking in a young man . . ." Félicité did not hear the rest; the horses were trotting; the donkey was galloping. They all filed down the path, a gate swung open, two boys appeared, and they dismounted in front of a dung heap on the very threshold.

When Mme. Liébard spotted her mistress, she was profuse in her expressions of delight. She served her a luncheon of sirloin of beef, tripe, black pudding, a fricassee of chicken, frothy cider, a fruit tart, and plums in brandy—all the time paying the Madame polite compliments, saying how wonderful she looked, how Mademoiselle was becoming "magnificent," and how Paul was growing so strong. Nor did she forget their deceased grandparents, whom the Liébards had known, as they had been in the service of the family for generations. The farm, like them, had the quality of oldness. The ceiling beams were worm-eaten, the walls black with smoke, the window panes gray with dust. On an oak sideboard were set all sorts of utensils, jugs, dishes, pewter bowls, wolf-traps, and sheep shears; and a big syringe made the children laugh. There was not a tree in the three courtyards that did not have mushrooms growing at its base or a tuft of mistletoe on its branches. The wind had blown some of the trees down. They had begun to grow again in the middle; and all of them were bent under the weight of the apples. The thatched roofs, like brown velvet and varying in thickness, had withstood the most violent gales. However, the wagon shed was fall-

ing into ruin. Mme. Aubain said she would tend to it later,
and ordered the animals to be resaddled.

It was another half hour before they arrived in Trouville.
The little caravan dismounted to pass Écores—a cliff jut-
ting out over some boats—and three minutes later, at the
end of the quay, they entered the courtyard of the "Golden
Lamb" kept by Mme. David.

Virginie, from the very first days there, began to feel
less weak—the result of the change of air and the effect
of the baths, which she took in her chemise, for want of a
bathing costume. Her nurse dressed her in a custom-house
shed, which was used by the bathers.

In the afternoon, with the donkey, they rode off beyond
the Roches-Noires, in the direction of Hennequeville. The
path rose, at first, over hilly terrain like the lawn of a
park; then it reached a plateau where meadows alternated
with plowed fields. By the edge of the road, in briar
thickets, stood holly bushes; here and there, a great lifeless
tree made zigzags in the blue sky with its naked branches.

Nearly always they would rest awhile in a meadow, with
Deauville to their left, Le Havre to the right, and before
them the open sea. It sparkled in the sun, smooth like a
mirror, so calm that you could hardly hear its murmuring.
Unseen sparrows chirped, and the immense vault of heaven
hung over everything. Mme. Aubain sat on the ground,
doing her sewing; Virginie, next to her, plaited rushes;
Félicité was weeding some lavender flowers; Paul was
bored and wanted to go back.

On other occasions, they would go by boat across the
Toucques, looking for shells. At low tide, they found sea
urchins, starfish, and jellyfish; and the children would chase
the flakes of foam carried by the wind. The waves, breaking on the sand, unrolled sleepily along the beach. The
latter stretched as far as you could see, but on the landward
side, it ended in the dunes that separated it from the
Marais, a wide meadow shaped like an arena. When they
returned that way, Trouville, on the hill slope in the background, loomed larger with every step, and its houses, with
their uneven rooftops, seemed to be spread in colorful
disorder.

On days when it was too hot, they did not leave their
room. The dazzling brightness from outside made golden
streaks through the venetian blinds. The village was silent.
No one was to be seen on the sidewalks below. The all-
pervading silence intensified the peacefulness. In the dis-

tance the hammers of the caulkers tapped on the hulls of the boats and a warm breeze wafted up the odor of tar.

The chief amusement was watching the ships return. As soon as they had passed the buoys, they began to maneuver. They lowered the sails on two of the three masts, and, with the foresail swelling like a balloon, they moved in gliding fashion over the chopping waves, until they reached the middle of the harbor where they suddenly dropped anchor. Then the boat docked against the pier. The sailors threw squirming fish over the side; a line of carts was awaiting them, and women in cotton bonnets rushed forward to take the baskets and to kiss their men.

One day one of them came up to Félicité, who, a little later, went to her room overjoyed. She had found a sister, Nastasie Barette, whose married name was Leroux, nursing an infant; and on her right-hand side was another child, and at her left was a little cabin boy with his hands on his hips and a beret cocked over his ear.

After fifteen minutes, Mme. Aubain sent them away.

But they were always to be seen outside her kitchen or on their walks. The husband never appeared.

Félicité took a liking to them. She bought them a blanket, some shirts, and a stove; it was obvious they were taking advantage of her. And this weakness of hers annoyed Mme. Aubain, who, moreover, did not like the familiar ways of Félicité's nephew with her son. And, as Virginie was coughing and the weather was no longer good, she decided to go back to Pont-l'Évêque.

M. Bourais advised her on the choice of a school for Paul. The one at Caen was considered to be the best, so he was sent there. He said his goodbyes bravely and was content to be going to live in a house where he would have companions his age.

Mme. Aubain resigned herself to her son's departure, because it was necessary. Virginie thought about it less and less. Félicité missed his noise. But a new interest diverted her: from Christmas time onward, she took the little girl to her catechism lesson every day.

3

When she had made her genuflection at the door of the church, Félicité walked under the lofty nave between the double row of chairs, opened Mme. Aubain's pew, sat down, and gazed around.

The choir stalls were filled with boys on the right and girls on the left; the curé was standing next to the lectern. One stained-glass window in the apse depicted the Holy Ghost hovering over the Virgin; another showed her on her knees before the Christ Child, and behind the tabernacle a group carved in wood depicted St. Michael overcoming the dragon.

The priest began with an outline of Sacred History. Félicité formed vivid pictures in her mind of Paradise, the Flood, the Tower of Babel, cities in flames, people dying, idols being overturned. She learned from these bewildering scenes a reverence for the Most High and a fear of His wrath. Then, she wept when the Passion was narrated. Why had they crucified Him—He who loved the little children, He who fed the multitudes, He who cured the blind, and He who had consented, out of meekness, to be born among the poor in a stable? The sowings, the harvests, the wine presses, all these familiar things the Gospel speaks of, were a part of her life; they had been sanctified by God's sojourn on earth. She loved lambs more tenderly out of love for the Lamb, and doves because of the Holy Ghost.

She found it difficult to imagine His person, for He was not only a bird, but a flame as well, and at still other times, a breath. She thought perhaps it is His light that hovers at night on the edge of the marshes, His breath that moves the clouds, His voice that gives the bells their harmony! Thus she sat in adoration, delighting in the cool walls and the peacefulness of the church.

As for Church dogmas, she did not understand or even try to understand them. The priest gave his sermon, the children recited, and she finally fell asleep. She woke up again with a start, when the people, leaving the church, clattered with their wooden shoes on the flagstones.

This is how Félicité, whose religious education had been neglected in her youth, learned her catechism—by hearing it repeated; and from that time on she imitated all of Virginie's practices, fasting when she did and going to confession with her. On Corpus Christi they made a small altar together.

She had looked forward with consternation to Virginie's first communion. Félicité made much ado about the little girl's rosary beads, her shoes, her prayerbook, her gloves. How she trembled as she helped Virginie's mother dress the child!

All through the mass, Félicité felt a terrible anxiety. She could not see one side of the choir—M. Bourais was in the way; but just in front of her, the band of young virgins, wearing white crowns over their lowered veils, looked to her like a field of snow. From afar she could recognize her precious little Virginie by her slender neck and by her enraptured bearing.

The altar bell tinkled. Heads bowed. There was silence. When the organ began to play again, the choir members and the whole congregation chanted the *Agnus Dei*. Then the boys began to move from their pews. After them the girls rose. Reverently, with their hands joined, they made their way to the brilliantly lit altar, and knelt on the first step, to receive the Divine Host in turn. Afterward they came back to their *prie-dieus* in the same order.

When it was Virginie's turn, Félicité leaned forward to see her; and in imagination, stimulated by genuine affection, she felt that she herself was this child. Virginie's face became her own; Virginie's dress clothed her; Virginie's heart throbbed in her own breast; when Virginie opened her mouth and closed her eyes, Félicité almost fainted.

Early the next morning, she went to the sacristy and asked M. le Curé to give her communion. She received it with devotion, but she did not feel the same ecstatic rapture.

Mme. Aubain wanted to make an accomplished person of her daughter; and, as Guyot could not teach her either English or music, she decided to board Virginie in the Ursuline Convent at Honfleur.

Virginie did not object. Félicité sighed and thought Madame was unfeeling. Then she decided that her mistress was, perhaps, right. These things were too much for Félicité to grasp.

So, one day, an old coach stopped in front of the door, and out stepped a nun who had come to fetch Virginie. Félicité lifted Virginie's baggage to the top of the vehicle, gave some instructions to the driver, and put on the seat six jars of jam, a dozen pears, and a bouquet of violets.

Virginie, at the last moment, began to sob; she hugged her mother who kissed her on the forehead and kept saying, "Come on, now! Be brave. Don't cry!" The side step was raised and the coach drove off.

Then Mme. Aubain broke down. That evening all her friends—the Lormeau family, Mme. Lechaptois, the Rochefeville ladies, M. de Houppeville, and Bourais—came to comfort her.

At first, her daughter's absence caused Mme. Aubain much grief. But three times a week she received a letter from Virginie. She wrote to her daughter on the other days, took strolls in the garden, or read a little, and in this way managed to fill the lonely hours.

Every morning, regularly, Félicité would go into Virginie's room and look around. It distressed her not to have to comb the girl's hair any more, not to lace her shoes, not to tuck her into bed—not to see her perpetually radiant face, not to hold her hand anymore when they went out together. For want of something to do, Félicité tried making lace, but her clumsy fingers broke the threads; she could not do anything, she could not sleep, and was, to use her own expression, "done in." To "distract herself," she asked permission to have her nephew Victor visit her.

He came on Sundays after mass—rosy-cheeked, barechested, and smelling of the fields he had crossed. Immediately Félicité set the table and they sat down to lunch facing each other. Félicité, eating as little as possible to save expense, stuffed him so much that finally he fell asleep. When vespers sounded, she woke him, brushed his trousers, knotted his tie, and went to the church with him, leaning on his arm with a kind of maternal pride.

His parents always instructed him to get something out of her—either a box of brown sugar, some soap, some brandy, or sometimes even money. He always brought his old clothes to Félicité to be mended. She was happy to do this task because it meant he had to come back.

In August his father took him off on a cruise along the coast.

It was vacation time, and the arrival of the children consoled her in the absence of her nephew. But Paul was getting contrary and Virginie was now too old to be addressed familiarly. Now there was a barrier—a feeling of uneasiness—between Virginie and Félicité.

Victor went to Morlaix, Dunkirk, and then to Brighton; and on his return from each trip he brought Félicité a present. The first time it was a box made of sea shells; then it was a coffee cup; from his third trip it was a large gingerbread man. Victor was becoming good-looking: he was well-built, he wore a small mustache, his eyes were attractively frank, and he cocked his small leather cap back like a pilot's. He amused her by telling stories mixed with sailors' lingo.

One Monday, July 14, 1819 (she never forgot the date), Victor told her that he had signed up for a long voyage, and that during the night of the following day, he would take the Honfleur boat to join his schooner which was to weigh anchor from Le Havre soon afterward. He would, perhaps, be gone for two years.

The thought of such a long absence dismayed Félicité, and, to say goodbye to him again, on Wednesday evening, after Madame's dinner, she put on her clogs and traveled the long twelve miles between Pont-l'Évêque and Honfleur.

When she arrived at the Calvary instead of turning left, she went right, got lost in the shipyards, and had to retrace her steps. Some people whom she approached advised her to hurry along. She went all around the ship-filled harbor, stumbling over the moorings. Where the ground sloped, lights criss-crossed. Félicité thought she was losing her mind, for she saw horses in the heavens.

On the wharf's edge, horses, frightened by the sea, were neighing. A crane was lifting them and lowering them into a boat where passengers were jostling one another amid cider casks, baskets of cheese, and grain sacks. Over the cackling of the chickens, one could hear the captain cursing. A cabin boy, undisturbed by all the confusion, leaned over the bow.

Félicité, who had not recognized him, suddenly called, "Victor!" He raised his head; she darted toward him, but at that moment the gangplank was raised.

The boat, towed by singing women, eased away from the wharf. Her hull creaked, and heavy water lashed against the prow. The sail had been turned around, hence no one could be seen any longer on her decks. On the silvery, moonlit sea, she became a black spot that gradually faded out of sight, then sank below the horizon.

As Félicité passed Calvary she wanted to commend to God this boy whom she loved most. She stood there a long time praying, her face bathed in tears, her eyes raised to heaven.

The town slept; only custom officials walked about. There was the sound of water, like that of a torrent, pouring through the holes of a sluice. The town clock struck two.

The convent reception room would not be open before morning. If she was late, Madame would surely be annoyed; so, in spite of a great desire to see Virginie, she returned home. The serving girls of the inn were just getting up when she reached Pont-l'Évêque.

"For months and months that poor boy is going to be tossing about on the waves!" thought Félicité. She had not been frightened by his previous voyages. One always returned safely from England or Brittany; but America, the colonies, the islands—all these were lost in a hazy region at the other end of the world.

From this moment on, Félicité thought of nothing but her nephew. On sunny days, she imagined he was thirsty; when it was stormy, she feared for him the lightning. As she listened to the wind howling down the chimney or heard it carrying off the slates, she saw him battered by this same storm, as he clung to the top of a broken masthead, his body bent back under the wash of the waves. At other times—remembering the geography prints—she imagined him being eaten by cannibals, captured by apes in the jungle, or lying dead on some deserted beach. But never did she speak of these secret apprehensions.

Mme. Aubain had her own apprehensions about her daughter.

The good nuns thought Virginie an affectionate but delicate child. The least bit of excitement upset her. She had to give up her piano lessons.

Her mother demanded from the convent authorities a regular flow of letters. One morning when there was no mail, she became very impatient; she walked up and down her room from the chair to the window. It was very strange indeed! No mail in four days!

To console her, Félicité said, "Look at me, Madame, it has been six months since I received any . . . !"

"From whom? . . ."

"Why . . . from my nephew!" meekly replied the servant.

"Oh! your nephew!" Mme. Aubain began to pace again, shrugging her shoulders as if to say: "I wasn't thinking of him! . . . Besides, he is nothing to me! A cabin boy, a little scamp! . . . While my daughter . . . just think!"

Félicité, though accustomed to rudeness, felt indignant at Madame, but overlooked it as usual.

It seemed very natural to her that one could lose one's head over a little girl.

The two children, Virginie and her nephew, were equally dear to her—they both shared her heart! And their destinies were to be the same.

The druggist told her that Victor's boat had docked in Havana. He had read this bit of news in a newspaper.

On account of cigars, she imagined Havana to be a country where everyone did nothing but smoke. She could visualize Victor moving among the Negroes in a cloud of tobacco fumes. Could one "in case of necessity" return from Havana by land, she wondered. How far was it from Pont-l'Évêque? For answers to these questions, she turned to M. Bourais.

He took out his atlas and began explaining longitudes; and smiled in a pedantic manner at Félicité's amazement. Then with his pencil he pointed to an almost imperceptible black dot on an oval spot, and said, "Here it is." She leaned over the map. This network of colored lines blurred her vision and meant nothing to her; and when Bourais asked her to say what was puzzling her, she begged him to point to the house where Victor was staying. Bourais threw up his arms, sneezed, and roared with laughter; such simplicity was sheer joy to him. But Félicité did not understand why he was so amused—how could she when she perhaps expected to see her nephew's portrait on the map—so limited was her understanding!

It was two weeks afterward that Liébard came into the kitchen at market time as usual, and handed her a letter from her brother-in-law. Since neither of them could read, she took it to her mistress.

Mme. Aubain, who was counting stitches in her knitting, put her work aside, opened the letter, trembled, and with a look full of meaning, said in a low voice, "It is bad news . . . that they have to tell you. Your nephew . . ."

He was dead. The letter said no more.

Félicité slumped into a chair, and leaned her head back. She closed her eyelids which had suddenly become pink. Then, with her head down, her hands hanging idly, her eyes fixed, she kept saying over and over, "Poor boy! Poor little boy!"

Liébard, murmuring sighs of consolation, watched her. Mme. Aubain was still shaking a little. She suggested to Félicité that she go visit with her sister at Trouville.

Félicité made a gesture to indicate there was no need to do so.

There was silence. Liébard thought it wise that they leave Félicité alone.

Then Félicité said, "They don't care! It means nothing to them!"

She dropped her head again, but, from time to time, she mechanically picked up the long knitting needles from the worktable.

Women passed in the courtyard with their barrows of dripping linen.

Seeing them through the window, Félicité remembered

her own washing. Having soaked it the day before, she
had to rinse it today; and she left the room.

Her plank and wooden bucket were down by the
Toucques. She threw a pile of underclothing on the river
bank, rolled up her sleeves, and took the paddle in her
hand. The heavy beating she gave her laundry could be
heard in the nearby gardens. The meadows were empty, the
wind made ripples on the surface of the water; while deep
down, tall weeds swayed, like the hair of corpses floating in
the water. Félicité suppressed her grief and was very brave
till evening; but in her room, she broke down completely
and lay on her bed with her face buried in the pillow and
her hands clenched against her temples.

Much later, she heard from the captain himself the
circumstances of Victor's death. He had had yellow fever.
Four doctors had held him while they bled him—too
much—at the hospital. He died immediately and the head
doctor said: "There! Another one!"

Victor's parents had always been brutal to him. Félicité
preferred not to see them again; and they in turn made no
attempt to see her, either because they had forgotten about
her, or because of the callousness of the poor.

Meanwhile, at the convent, Virginie became weaker.
Congestion in her lungs, coughing, a continuous fever,
and splotches on her cheekbones indicated some deep-
seated illness. M. Poupart prescribed a few days in Provence. Mme. Aubain agreed to that, and would have
brought her daughter home at once were it not for the
climate of Pont-l'Évêque.

She chartered a carriage and was driven to the convent
every Tuesday. There is a terrace in the garden from
which you can see the Seine. Virginie would walk there
on her mother's arm, over the fallen vine leaves. Sometimes the sun piercing through the clouds made her blink,
as she gazed at the distant sails and the whole horizon—
from the Château of Tancarville to the lighthouse of
Le Havre. Then they would rest under an arbor. Her
mother had with her a little flask of excellent Malaga
wine, and, laughing at the idea of getting a little tipsy,
Virginie would drink just a little, no more.

She regained strength. Autumn passed pleasantly. Félicité reassured Mme. Aubain. But, one evening when she
had been running errands in the neighborhood, she saw
on her return M. Poupart's carriage in front of the door.
He was in the vestibule. Mme. Aubain was tying on her
hat.

"Give me my foot warmer, my handbag, and gloves! Hurry!"

Virginie had pneumonia. Perhaps her case was already hopeless.

"Not yet!" said the doctor and both got into his carriage, under whirling flakes of snow. Night was falling. It was very cold.

Félicité rushed into church to light a candle. Then she ran after the carriage which she overtook an hour later. She had jumped nimbly on behind, and was holding on to the straps, when she suddenly thought: "The courtyard isn't locked! Suppose thieves break in!" And she jumped off.

At dawn of the following day, she went to the doctor's house. He had returned, but had left again for the country. Then she stayed at the inn, thinking some stranger would bring a letter. Finally, at dusk, she took the Lisieux stagecoach.

The convent was at the bottom of a steep lane. About halfway down, Félicité heard strange sounds—a death knell. "It's for someone else," she thought. But she knocked violently on the door.

After several minutes, she heard the shuffling of slippers; the door was opened a crack and a nun appeared.

The good sister, with a compassionate air, said that Virginie "had just passed away." At that moment, the tolling at Saint-Léonard's became louder.

Félicité went up to the second floor of the convent.

From the doorway she could see Virginie lying on her back, her hands folded, her mouth open, and her head tilted back under an overhanging black cross between two motionless curtains, less pale than her face. Mme. Aubain, clutching the foot of the bed, was sobbing uncontrollably. The Mother Superior was standing on the right. Three candles on the dresser made shafts of red light, and mist whitened the windowpanes. Some nuns led Mme. Aubain away.

For two nights Félicité did not leave her death watch. She repeated the same prayers, sprinkled the sheets with holy water, sat down again, and gazed at the dead girl. At the end of the first night, she noticed that the face had yellowed, the lips had turned blue, the nose was sharper and the eyes were deeper. She kissed them several times, and would not have been surprised if they had opened again; for to minds like hers the supernatural is quite simple. She dressed her, wrapped her in a shroud, laid her body in the coffin, arranged her hair, and placed a wreath upon her head. The hair was blond and extraordinarily long for her age. Félicité cut a thick lock of it and slipped half of it into Virginie's bosom. She resolved never to part with hers.

The corpse was brought back to Pont-l'Évêque, according to the wishes of Mme. Aubain, who followed the hearse in a closed carriage.

After the mass, it took another three-quarters of an hour to reach the cemetery. Paul, sobbing, walked ahead of the cortege. M. Bourais walked behind, followed by the principal residents of the village, the women wearing black mantles, and Félicité. She was thinking of her nephew, and because she had not been able to pay these respects to him, her sadness was intensified, as if he were being interred with Virginie.

Mme. Aubain's despair knew no limits.

At first she cried out against God, thinking it unjust for Him to have taken her daughter—Virginie who had never hurt anyone, and whose soul was so pure! But no! She should have taken her to the south. Other doctors could have saved her! She railed at herself, she wanted to join Virginie in death, she cried out distressfully in her dreams. One dream especially haunted her. Her husband, dressed like a sailor, came back from a long voyage and told her tearfully that he had received orders to take Virginie away. Then, they both tried to find a hiding place somewhere.

Once Mme. Aubain came in from the garden terribly upset. A little while before (she could point out the spot) the father and daughter, standing side by side, had appeared to her; they did nothing; they just looked at her.

For several months she kept to her room—apathetic. Félicité reproached her gently, saying her mistress must take care of herself for the sake of her son, and in remembrance of "her."

"Her?" replied Mme. Aubain as though she were emerging from sleep. "Ah yes! . . . Yes! You do not forget her!" This was an allusion to the cemetery which Mme. Aubain was strictly forbidden to visit.

Félicité went there every day.

At exactly four o'clock, she would go by the houses, climb the hill, open the gate, and come to Virginie's grave. There was a little column of pink marble with a plaque at its base, to which was fastened a chain that enclosed a miniature garden. The borders disappeared under beds of

flowers. Félicité watered the plants, upturned the gravel,
and knelt down better to dress the ground. Mme. Aubain,
when at last she could visit the grave, felt a relief and a
kind of consolation.

The years slipped by uneventfully and without any incidents other than the return of the great feast days: Easter,
Assumption, All Saints' Day. Only household events were
spoken of as important in the years that followed: for
example, in 1825, two workmen whitewashed the vestibule;
in 1827, part of the roof, falling into the courtyard, almost
killed a man; in the summer of 1827, it became Madame's
turn to offer the consecrated bread; Bourais, about this
time, was mysteriously not around; and the old acquaintances one by one went away: Guyot, Liébard, Mme.
Lechaptois, Robelin, Uncle Gremanville, who had been
paralyzed for a long time now.

One night the driver of the mail coach announced in
Pont-l'Évêque the July Revolution. A new subprefect was
appointed a few days later: Baron de Larsonnière, an ex-
consular official in America, and a man who had brought
with him, in addition to his wife, his sister-in-law and
her three daughters, almost grown up. They could be seen
on their lawn, dressed in loose-fitting blouses; they had
a Negro servant and a parrot. They paid a visit to Mme.
Aubain, who returned their call promptly. Whenever
Félicité saw them coming, she always ran to her mistress
to forewarn her. But the only thing really capable of arousing Madame was letters from her son.

He could not follow any profession, since he spent most
of his time in taverns. She paid his debts, but he contracted
others; and the sighs that Mme. Aubain uttered, as she
sat knitting by the window, reached Félicité as she turned
her spinning wheel in the kitchen.

They took walks together along the espalier, and talked
always about Virginie, wondering whether such and such
would have pleased her, or what she would probably have
said on this or that occasion.

All her little belongings were in a cupboard in the room
with two beds. Mme. Aubain inspected them as seldom as
possible. One summer day she resigned herself to doing
so, and moths flew out of the cupboard.

Her dresses were arranged under a shelf on which sat
three dolls, some hoops, a doll's house, and the basin that
she used daily. They took out her petticoats, stockings,
and handkerchiefs and spread them on the two beds, before
folding them again. The sun, shining on these pitiful ob-

jects, brought out the spots and the creases made by the
movements of Virginie's body. Outside, the sky was blue,
the air was warm, a blackbird warbled. Everything seemed
vibrant with a heartfelt sweetness. They found a little hat
of deeply piled plush, chestnut-colored; but it was all moth-
eaten. Félicité wanted it for herself. They looked at each
other and their eyes filled with tears; at last the mistress
opened her arms and the servant threw herself into them.
They held each other close, assuaging their grief in a kiss
that made them equal.

This was the first time in their lives, for Mme. Aubain
was not demonstrative by nature. Félicité was as grateful
as if she had been presented with a gift; and from then on
she cherished Mme. Aubain with a devotion that was
almost animal and with an almost religious veneration.

The kindness of her heart grew.

When she heard in the street the drums of a marching
regiment, she stood at the front door with a pitcher of cider
and asked the soldiers to drink. She took care of cholera
patients. She protected the Poles, and there was even one
who wanted to marry her. But they quarreled, for one
morning, returning from the Angelus, she found that he had
entered her kitchen, prepared a salad, and was nonchalant-
ly eating it.

After the Poles came Papa Colmiche, an old man who
was supposed to have been guilty of some atrocities in '93.
He lived along the riverbank, in a tumble-down pigsty.
The little boys used to spy on him through cracks in the
wall and throw stones at him that always landed on the
squalid bed where he lay, continually racked by a cough.
His hair was long, his eyes inflamed, and on his arm grew
a tumor bigger than his head. Félicité supplied him with
linen and tried to keep his miserable hut clean. It was her
wish to have him installed in the bakehouse without his
annoying Madame. When the tumor opened, she dressed
it every day. Sometimes she brought him some cake. She
used to lay him in the sun on a bed of straw. The poor
old fellow, slobbering and shaking, would thank her in his
weak voice. He was afraid of losing her, and would stretch
out his hand when he saw her going away. He died. She
had a mass said for the repose of his soul.

On that day, fortune smiled on her: at the dinner hour,
the Negro servant of Mme. de Larsonnière came carrying
the parrot in a cage, with perch, chain, and padlock. A
note from the baroness informed Mme. Aubain that, because her husband was promoted to a prefecture, they

were leaving that evening; and she begged her to accept the
bird as a remembrance and a mark of her esteem.

For a long time this bird had occupied Félicité's
thoughts, because he came from America and America
reminded her of Victor—so much so that she questioned
the Negro about that country. Once she had even remarked: "How happy Madame would be to have him!"

The Negro had told this to his mistress, and since she
could not take the bird with her, she disposed of him in this
fashion.

4

The parrot was called Loulou. His body was green, the
tip of his wings pink, his forehead blue, and his throat
golden.

But he had the tiresome habit of biting his perch, plucking his feathers, scattering his mess about, and spattering
the water of his bath. Mme. Aubain thought the bird was
a nuisance and gave him to Félicité to keep.

She set out to train the parrot; soon he could repeat:
"Nice boy," "Your servant, sir," "Hello, Mary!" He was
placed next to the door, and people were surprised that he
would not answer to Jacquot, for weren't all parrots called
Jacquot? They likened him to a turkey, to a log of wood;
and each time they did so Félicité was hurt to the quick!
But Loulou was curiously stubborn! He stopped talking
when one looked at him!

Yet he liked company, for on Sunday, while those
Rochefeuille ladies, M. de Houppeville, and some new
habitués—Onfray the apothecary, M. Varin, and Captain
Mathieu—were playing cards, he would beat the windowpanes with his wings, and would fling himself about so
violently that it was impossible to hear oneself speak.

Bourais' face, undoubtedly, struck him as being very
funny. As soon as he spotted Bourais, he would begin to
laugh—to laugh with all his might. His noises reverber-
ated through the courtyard, echoes repeated them, the
neighbors stood at their windows and laughed too. Therefore, so as not to be seen by the parrot, M. Bourais would
slither along the wall, hiding his face under his hat, and,
getting down to the river, would enter the house by the

garden door. The looks he then shot at the bird were far from tender.

Loulou had been slapped by the butcher boy for taking the liberty of putting his head into the meat basket. Since then, the bird always tried to pinch him through his shirt. Fabu threatened to wring Loulou's neck, although he was not cruel, in spite of his tattooed arms and long sideburns. On the contrary! He was rather fond of the parrot and, in a jovial mood, he even wanted to teach him some curse words. Félicité, alarmed by all these tricks, removed the parrot to the kitchen.

Later, his little chain was removed and he roamed about the house. He would come downstairs by hooking his curved beak on the steps, lifting first his right leg, then his left. Félicité was afraid that all these gymnastics would make the bird dizzy. Sure enough, he did become ill and could neither talk nor eat. There was a thickness under his tongue such as chickens sometimes develop. She cured him by scratching out this thickness with her fingernail.

M. Paul, one day, had the effrontery to blow cigar smoke into the parrot's nostrils. Another time, when Mme. Lormeau was teasing him with the end of her parasol, Loulou snapped at the metal ring. Finally, the bird got lost.

Félicité had put him on the grass to give him some fresh air and had gone away for a minute. When she returned, the parrot was gone! First, she searched in the bushes, then by the riverbank, and on the roofs, paying no attention to her mistress who was screaming, "Be careful! You must be out of your mind!"

Then Félicité looked in all the gardens of Pont-l'Évêque, and she stopped everyone passing by—"You haven't seen my parrot, by chance, have you?" To those who did not know the bird, she gave a description. Suddenly, she thought she spotted something green fluttering behind the mill at the bottom of the hill. But when she approached— nothing! A peddler told her he had seen a parrot a little while ago at Saint-Melaine, in Mère Simon's shop. She ran all the way. They didn't know what she was talking about. Finally, she came home, exhausted, her slippers in shreds, her heart broken by disappointment. As she was sitting on a bench close to Mme. Aubain and was telling her everywhere she had been, a light weight fell on her shoulder. It was Loulou! What the devil had he been doing? Probably taking a stroll in the neighborhood!

Félicité had trouble getting over this—or rather, she never did recover from it.

As a result of a cold, Félicité had an attack of quinsy, and a little later an ear infection. Three years later she was deaf; and she spoke very loud, even in church. Though her sins might have been bruited abroad to all corners of the diocese without shame to her or scandal to anyone, the parish priest thought it best henceforth to hear her confession only in the sacristy.

Imaginary buzzings in the head added to her afflictions. Often her mistress would say to her: "My word, how stupid you are!" She would simply answer, "Yes, Madame," and go look for something to do near her.

The small scope of her ideas became smaller still, and the pealing of the church bells and the lowing of the cattle ceased to exist for her. All living creatures moved about silently as ghosts. The only sound that she could hear now was the voice of the parrot.

As if to distract her, Loulou would mimic the tic-tac of the turnspit, the shrill cry of the the fish vendor, the noise of the carpenter's saw across the road, and when the bell rang, he would imitate Mme. Aubain—"Félicité! The door, the door!"

They had conversations, Loulou incessantly repeating the three short phrases in his repertory, to which Félicité would reply with phrases just as disconnected, but in which there was deep sincerity. Loulou was almost a son and lover to her in her isolated world. He would climb on her fingers, nibble at her lips, and cling to her kerchief; and, when she leaned forward, shaking her head as nurses do, the long wings of her bonnet and those of the bird moved together.

When the clouds were banked on top of one another and the thunder began to roll, Loulou would utter cries, remembering, perhaps, the downpours in his native forests. Teeming rain made him absolutely mad with joy; he fluttered about wildly, he climbed the ceiling, knocked everything over, and went out through the window to splash in the garden; but he would come back quickly and alight on one of the andirons, and hopping about to dry his feathers, he would show first his tail, then his beak.

One morning in the terrible winter of 1837, when Félicité had put Loulou in front of the fireplace because of the cold, she found him dead, in the center of his cage, his head down, and his claws clutching the wire bars. Undoubtedly, he had died of a congestion. But Félicité thought he had been poisoned with parsley, and despite all lack of evidence, she suspected Fabu.

She wept so bitterly that her mistress said to her: "Well then, have the bird stuffed."

She asked the pharmacist's advice, since he had always been kind to the parrot.

He wrote to Le Havre. A certain man named Fellacher undertook the job. But as parcels sometimes got lost when sent by the stagecoach, she decided to take it herself as far as Honfleur.

Leafless apple trees lined both sides of the road. Ice covered the ditches. Dogs barked on the farms. Félicité, with her hands under her cloak, carrying her basket, and wearing her little black sabots, walked briskly along in the middle of the road.

She went through the forest, passed Haut-Chêne, and reached Saint-Gatien.

Behind her, in a cloud of dust, gathering speed down a steep hill, came a mail coach, with horses at full gallop, like the wind. Seeing this woman who was not paying any attention, the driver stood up, and the postilion shouted, too. All the while the four horses which the driver could not hold back gained speed. The first two horses grazed Félicité. With a pull on the reins, he veered to the side, but, furious, he raised his arm, and in full flight, with his heavy whip he gave her such a lash from her stomach to her neck that she fell on her back.

Her first action, when she regained consciousness, was to open the basket. Fortunately, Loulou was all right. She felt a burning on her right cheek, and when she touched it, her hands were red. The blood was streaming.

She sat down on a pile of stones and dabbed her face with a handkerchief; then she ate a crust of bread which she had put in her basket just in case, and took consolation for her own wound in gazing at the bird.

When she arrived at Ecquemauville, she could see below the lights of Honfleur, which twinkled in the night like a cluster of stars; the sea, beyond, spread out indistinctly. Then weakness forced her to stop; and her wretched childhood, the disillusion of her first love, the departure of her nephew, Virginie's death, all came back to her like the waves of a tide, rising to her throat and choking her.

Later she spoke to the captain of the boat; and without telling him what she was sending, she gave him instructions.

Fellacher kept the parrot a long time. He was always promising it for the following week. At the end of six months he announced it had been dispatched in a box; and then nothing more was heard about it. It seemed that

Loulou was never coming back. "They have stolen him from me!" she thought.

Finally he did arrive—and how wonderful he looked, sitting upright on a branch that was screwed to a mahogany base. One foot was held in the air. His head was tilted sidewise, and he was biting on a nut that the taxidermist, carried away by a flair for the grandiose, had painted gold!

Félicité put Loulou in her room.

This place, to which she admitted few, had so many religious objects and so many unusual things that it looked like a chapel and a bazaar combined.

A large wardrobe made it difficult to open the door. Opposite the window overlooking the garden, a small circular window looked down upon the courtyard. On a table near the folding bed stood a water pitcher, two combs, and a bar of blue soap on a chipped plate. On the walls hung rosary beads, medallions, several statues of the Virgin, and a holy water font made of a coconut; on the commode, covered with a cloth like that on altars, stood the box made of shells which Victor had given to her, a watering can, a balloon, some writing books, the geography picture book, and a pair of boots. Fastened by its ribbons to a nail on the mirror hung the small plush hat! Félicité carried this kind of respect to such extremes that she even kept one of Monsieur's frock coats. All the old things Mme. Aubain no longer wanted Félicité took to her room. For this reason there were artificial flowers on the edge of the commode, and a portrait of the Comte d'Artois in the recess of the dormer window.

By means of a small shelf, Loulou was set prominently on the chimney piece that projected into the room. Every morning, when Félicité woke up, she could see him in the dawn's light, and she would recall painlessly and peacefully the old days with their insignificant events down to their last detail.

Communicating with no one, she lived in a kind of sleep-walking trance. The Corpus Christi processions rejuvenated her. She would go to her neighbors begging tapers and mats with which to decorate the altar being erected in the street.

In church she always sat gazing at the stained-glass window that portrayed the Holy Ghost, and noticed there was something of the parrot about it. The resemblance seemed to her more pronounced in a picture that depicted the Baptism of Our Lord. With its purple wings and its emerald body, it was really Loulou's portrait.

She bought this picture and hung it in the place formerly occupied by the Comte d'Artois—so that, with one glance, she could see them together. They became associated in her mind, the parrot becoming sanctified by this association with the Holy Ghost, which became more real in her eyes and easier to comprehend. God the Father, to reveal Himself, could not have chosen a dove, since those birds have no voices, but rather one of Loulou's ancestors. And Félicité, although she looked at the picture as she said her prayers, would turn from time to time toward the parrot.

She wanted to join the Ladies of the Blessed Virgin, but Mme. Aubain dissuaded her.

Then a great event occurred: Paul's marriage.

After having been in succession a clerk in a notary's office, in business, in the customs office, in the revenue service, and having even made efforts to get into the bureau of waters and forests—suddenly, at thirty-six, by an inspiration from heaven, he had discovered his career: that of registrar! He showed such aptitude for this kind of work that an inspector had offered him his daughter in marriage, promising to use his influence on Paul's behalf.

Paul, serious-minded now, brought the girl to see his mother.

She sniffed at the ways of Pont-l'Évêque, gave herself the airs of a princess, and hurt Félicité's feelings. Mme. Aubain felt relieved when the visitor left.

The following week news was brought of Bourais' death in an inn in lower Brittany. Rumors of suicide were later confirmed and doubts of his integrity were raised. Mme. Aubain pored over his accounts, and it didn't take her long to discover a long list of his misdeeds: embezzlements, fictitious sales of wood, forged receipts, etc. Besides that, he had an illegitimate child, and "relations with a certain person from Dozulé."

These scandalous acts distressed Madame very much. In March 1853, she was seized with a pain in her chest; her tongue was coated, and leeches did not give her any relief. On the ninth evening she died, having just reached her seventy-second birthday.

Everyone thought she was younger than she really was, because of her brown hair, braids of which framed her pallid, pockmarked face. Few friends regretted her passing, for with her haughty manner she kept people at a distance.

But Félicité mourned her as masters are seldom

mourned. That Madame should have died before her disturbed her thoughts, seemed to her contrary to the nature of things, something inadmissible and monstrous.

Ten days later (the time it took to travel from Besançon) the heirs arrived. The daughter-in-law rummaged through drawers, selected certain pieces of furniture, sold the rest. Then they left, and Paul returned to his registering.

Madame's armchair, her small round table, her foot warmer, the eight chairs were gone! On the walls were yellow squares that marked where pictures used to hang. They had carried off the two beds, with the mattresses, and Virginie's belongings were no longer to be seen in the cupboard! Félicité, numb with sadness, wandered from floor to floor.

Next day there was a notice on the door. The apothecary shouted in her ear that the house was for sale.

She staggered and had to sit down. What distressed her most of all was that she might have to give up her room—so comfortable for poor little Loulou. Gazing at the bird with a look of anguish, she prayed to the Holy Ghost. She had formed the idolatrous habit of saying her prayers on her knees in front of the parrot. Sometimes the sun breaking through the window caught his glass eye, and a long luminous ray would dart from it, throwing Félicité into ecstasy.

She had an income of three hundred and eighty francs a year, willed to her by Mme. Aubain. The garden provided her with vegetables. As for clothes, she had enough to last till the end of her days, and she saved on lighting by going to bed at dusk.

She rarely went out, in order to avoid the secondhand shop where some pieces of the old furniture were displayed for sale. Ever since her shock, she dragged one leg; and as her strength was failing, Mère Simon, whose grocery business had fallen into ruin, used to come every morning to chop her wood and pump her water.

Félicité's eyesight became weak.

The shutters of the house would no longer open. Many years passed, but the place was not rented or sold.

For fear of being turned out, Félicité never asked for repairs. The laths of the roof began to rot, so that for a whole year the bolster of her bed was damp. After Easter she began to spit blood.

This time Mère Simon called a doctor. Félicité wanted to know what was the matter with her. But, too deaf to hear, she caught only one word: "Pneumonia." It was familiar enough to her and she answered, softly, "Ah! like Madame," thinking it natural that she should thus follow her mistress.

The time for preparing the altars was nearing. The first of them was always erected at the bottom of the hill, the second in front of the post office, and the third about halfway down the street. There was some difference of opinion concerning this last-mentioned, and the parishioners at last decided to put it in Mme. Aubain's courtyard.

The pain in Félicité's chest and her fever continued to increase. Félicité was annoyed because she could do nothing for the altar. If only she could have at least put something on it. Then she thought of the parrot. But the neighbors objected: it wasn't proper. However, the curé granted permission and this made her so happy that she begged him to accept Loulou, her sole valuable possession, when she died.

From Tuesday to Saturday, the eve of Corpus Christi, she coughed more and more. By the evening, her face was pinched, her lips clung to her gums, and she began to vomit, and next day at early dawn, feeling very weak, she sent for a priest.

Three kindly old women stood around while she received extreme unction. Then she said she wanted to speak to Fabu.

He came in his Sunday clothes, ill at ease in this sad atmosphere.

"Forgive me," she said, with an effort to extend her arm, "I thought it was you who had killed him!"

What did she mean by this nonsense? Suspecting a man like him of being a murderer! He was indignant, and was about to make a scene.

"As you can see, she makes no sense at all."

Every once in a while Félicité would talk to shadows. The three ladies went away and Mère Simon went to breakfast.

A little later Mère Simon took Loulou and, holding him near Félicité, said: "Come, now, say goodbye to him!"

Though he was not a corpse, the worms had begun to devour the dead bird; one of his wings was broken, and the stuffing was coming out of his body. But Félicité, now blind, kissed Loulou's forehead, and pressed him against her cheek. Mère Simon took him away and placed him on the altar.

5

A scent of summer drifted from the meadow; flies buzzed;
the sun made the surface of the river glisten and heated
the slate roofs. Mère Simon had come back into the room,
and was dozing peacefully.

The tolling of the church bell awakened her; the people
were coming from vespers. Félicité's delirium ceased. She
thought of the procession, and saw it as if she had been
there.

All the children from the schools, the choir singers,
together with the firemen, walked along on the pavement,
while in the middle of the road marched first the verger
armed with his halberd, the beadle carrying his large
cross, the schoolmaster watching his small charges, and
the sister anxious for her little girls; three of the cutest of
these, with curls like angels, were throwing rose petals in
the air; the deacon, with his arms outstretched, was leading
the music; and two incense bearers bowed at every step in
front of the Blessed Sacrament, carried by M. le Curé
wearing a beautiful chasuble, beneath a flaming red canopy,
held by four churchwardens. Waves of people surged behind, between the white cloths covering the walls of
the houses. They arrived at the foot of the hill.

Beads of cold sweat dampened Félicité's temples. Mère
Simon sponged them with a piece of cloth, saying to herself that one day she would have to go too.

The murmur of the crowd mounted; for a moment, it
was very loud, then it faded.

A fusillade rattled the windowpanes. It was the postilions
saluting the monstrance. Félicité rolled her eyes and said as
softly as she could:

"Is he all right?" She was anxiously thinking of her
parrot.

Her death agony began. A rattle, more and more violent,
shook her sides. Froth appeared at the corners of her mouth
and her whole body was trembling.

Soon, above the blaring of the wind instruments, the
clear voices of the children and the deep voices of men
could be distinguished. At intervals, all was silent, except
for the tread of feet shuffling over the strewn flowers,
sounding like sheep on the grass.

The priests appeared in the courtyard. Mère Simon climbed on one of the chairs to look through the round window. In this way she could look down upon the altar.

Green wreaths hung from the altar, which was decorated with a flounce of English lace. In the middle there was a small receptacle containing relics; two orange trees stood at the corners, and all along were silver candlesticks and porcelain vases, filled with sunflowers, lilies, peonies, foxgloves, and tufts of hydrangea. This mass of brilliant colors banked from the level of the altar to the rug spread over the pavement. Strange objects caught the eye: a vermilion sugar bowl held a wreath of violets; pendants of Alençon stone glittered on the moss; two Chinese screens depicted landscapes. Loulou, concealed by the roses, showed nothing but his blue forehead, like a piece of lapis lazuli.

The churchwardens, choristers, and children stood in rows on three sides of the courtyard. The priest ascended the steps slowly, and put down his great, shining, golden monstrance on the lacework cloth. All knelt. There was a deep silence; and the censers, swinging to and fro, glided on their little chains.

A blue cloud of smoke rose to Félicité's room. She distended her nostrils, breathing it in with a mystical sensuousness; then she closed her eyes. Her lips were smiling. The beating of her heart became fainter and fainter, softer like an exhausted fountain, like a fading echo; and when she breathed her last breath, she thought she saw in the opening heavens a gigantic parrot, hovering above her head.

Robert Louis Stevenson

(1850–1894)

*Were he alive today, Robert Louis Stevenson would not
be displeased to find that his best-known and best-loved
works are affectionately called "adventure classics." For,
in a sense, Stevenson's life was a robust, colorful adventure, much different from the staid, correct, musty
Victorianism of his time. Born in Scotland, Stevenson
early achieved prominence as an essayist, an adventure
novelist, a poet, and an accomplished travel writer.
But his substantial achievements in these areas are
overshadowed by his preeminence as a writer of short
stories. It was Stevenson who, more than any other
English writer, opened the past to short story writers.
Just as he brought to the novel a zest for action and
romance, so in the short story he rekindled a feeling
for the romantic past. Stories such as "A Lodging for
the Night," "The Sire de Malétroit's Door," "Will of
the Mill" speak to the incurable, ineradicable romantic
in all of us. They are also memorable portraits of a
past that by virtue of its very distance from us makes its
wholly different set of values seem even more acceptable
than our own.*

*The Irish critic and short story writer, Sean O'Faolain,
has described the paraphernalia of Stevenson's stories as
"the hieroglyphics of imaginative art, like Henry Moore's
pinheaded statues or Picasso's women with one, two, or
three eyes, or Titian's naked goddesses." The point is
well taken, for Stevenson is a writer of wide romantic
and imaginative range. Like Hemingway and Camus,
he espouses a code of behavior which moves men to act
nobly and unselfishly and with dignity. Though Stevenson's morality seems somewhat less relevant to us,
placed as it is in the romantic settings and trappings of
his stories—hidden doors, lovely young girls, immediate,
irreversible choices between love or death—it does not
diminish our great pleasure in the stories.*

*"The Sire de Malétroit's Door" is a superb story with
its glowing evocation of the feel, color, and movement
of a bygone age, skillfully wrought plot, swift and deft
characterization, rich, flawless style. It is Stevenson's
"passion for the craft of letters" as we see it expressed in*

*this story that called forth Henry James' comment, "It
is a luxury, in this immoral age, to encounter someone
who does write—who is really acquainted with that
lovely art."*

The Sire de Malétroit's Door

Denis de Beaulieu was not yet two-and-twenty, but he
counted himself a grown man, and a very accomplished
cavalier into the bargain. Lads were early formed in that
rough, warfaring epoch; and when one has been in a
pitched battle and a dozen raids, has killed one's man in
an honourable fashion, and knows a thing or two of
strategy and mankind, a certain swagger in the gait is
surely to be pardoned. He had put up his horse with due
care, and supped with due deliberation; and then, in a
very agreeable frame of mind, went out to pay a visit in
the grey of the evening. It was not a very wise proceeding
on the young man's part. He would have done better to
remain beside the fire or go decently to bed. For the town
was full of the troops of Burgundy and England under a
mixed command; and though Denis was there on safe-conduct, his safe-conduct was like to serve him little on a
chance encounter.

It was September, 1429; the weather had fallen sharp; a
flighty, piping wind, laden with showers, beat about the
township; and the dead leaves ran riot along the streets.
Here and there a window was already lighted up; and the
noise of men-at-arms making merry over supper within,
came forth in fits and was swallowed up and carried away
by the wind. The night fell swiftly; the flag of England,
fluttering on the spire-top, grew ever fainter and fainter
against the flying clouds—a black speck like a swallow in
the tumultuous, leaden chaos of the sky. As the night fell
the wind rose, and began to hoot under archways and roar
amid the tree-tops in the valley below the town.

Denis de Beaulieu walked fast and was soon knocking
at his friend's door; but though he promised himself to
stay only a little while and make an early return, his
welcome was so pleasant, and he found so much to delay
him, that it was already long past midnight before he said
good-bye upon the threshold. The wind had fallen again

in the meanwhile; the night was as black as the grave; not
a star nor a glimmer of moonshine slipped through the
canopy of cloud. Denis was ill-acquainted with the intricate
lanes of Château Landon; even by daylight he had found
some trouble in picking his way; and in this absolute darkness he soon lost it altogether. He was certain of one thing
only—to keep mounting the hill; for his friend's house lay
at the lower end, or tail, of Château Landon, while the
inn was up at the head, under the great church spire. With
this clue to go upon he stumbled and groped forward, now
breathing more freely in open places where there was a
good slice of sky overhead, now feeling along the wall in
stifling closeness. It is an eerie and mysterious position to
be thus submerged in opaque blackness in an almost unknown town. The silence is terrifying in its possibilities. The
touch of cold window bars to the exploring hand startles
the man like the touch of a toad; the inequalities of the
pavement shake his heart into his mouth; a piece of denser
darkness threatens an ambuscade or a chasm in the pathway; and where the air is brighter, the houses put cn strange
and bewildering appearances, as if to lead him farther from
his way. For Denis, who had to regain his inn without at-
tracting notice, there was real danger as well as mere discomfort in the walk; and he went warily and boldly at
once, and at every corner paused to make an observation.

He had been for some time threading a lane so narrow
that he could touch a wall with either hand; when it began
to open out and go sharply downward. Plainly this lay no
longer in the direction of his inn; but the hope of a little
more light tempted him forward to reconnoitre. The lane
ended in a terrace with a bartizan wall, which gave an
outlook between high houses, as out of an embrasure, into
the valley lying dark and formless several hundred feet below. Denis looked down, and could discern a few tree-tops
waving and a single speck of brightness where the river ran
across a weir. The weather was clearing up, and the sky
had lightened, so as to show the outline of the heavier
clouds and the dark margin of the hills. By the uncertain glimmer, the house on his left hand should be a place
of some pretensions; it was surmounted by several pin-
nacles and turret-tops; the round stern of a chapel, with a
fringe of flying buttresses, projected boldly from the main
block; and the door was sheltered under a deep porch
carved with figures and overhung by two long gargoyles.
The windows of the chapel gleamed through their intricate
tracery with a light as of many tapers, and threw out the

buttresses and the peaked roof in a more intense blackness against the sky. It was plainly the hotel of some great family of the neighbourhood; and as it reminded Denis of a town house of his own at Bourges, he stood for some time gazing up at it and mentally gauging the skill of the architects and the consideration of the two families.

There seemed to be no issue to the terrace but the lane by which he had reached it; he could only retrace his steps, but he had gained some notion of his whereabouts, and hoped by this means to hit the main thoroughfare and speedily regain the inn. He was reckoning without that chapter of accidents which was to make this night memorable above all others in his career; for he had not gone back above a hundred yards before he saw a light coming to meet him, and heard loud voices speaking together in the echoing narrows of the lane. It was a party of men-at-arms going the night round with torches. Denis assured himself that they had all been making free with the wine-bowl, and were in no mood to be particular about safe-conducts or the niceties of chivalrous war. It was as like as not that they would kill him like a dog and leave him where he fell. The situation was inspiriting but nervous. Their own torches would conceal him from sight, he reflected; and he hoped that they would drown the noise of his footsteps with their own empty voices. If he were but fleet and silent, he might evade their notice altogether.

Unfortunately, as he turned to beat a retreat, his foot rolled upon a pebble; he fell against the wall with an ejaculation, and his sword rang loudly on the stones. Two or three voices demanded who went there—some in French, some in English; but Denis made no reply, and ran the faster down the lane. Once upon the terrace, he paused to look back. They still kept calling after him, and just then began to double the pace in pursuit, with a considerable clank of armour, and great tossing of the torchlight to and fro in the narrow jaws of the passage.

Denis cast a look around and darted into the porch. There he might escape observation, or—if that were too much to expect—was in a capital posture whether for parley or defence. So thinking, he drew his sword and tried to set his back against the door. To his surprise, it yielded behind his weight; and though he turned in a moment, continued to swing back on oiled and noiseless hinges, until it stood wide open on a black interior. When things fall out opportunely for the person concerned, he is not apt to be critical about the how or why, his own im-

mediate personal convenience seeming a sufficient reason
for the strangest oddities and revolutions in our sublunary
things; and so Denis, without a moment's hesitation, stepped
within and partly closed the door behind him to conceal
his place of refuge. Nothing was further from his thoughts
than to close it altogether; but for some inexplicable reason
—perhaps by a spring or a weight—the ponderous mass of
oak whipped itself out of his fingers and clanked to, with a
formidable rumble and a noise like the falling of an auto-
matic bar.

The round, at that very moment, debouched upon the
terrace and proceeded to summon him with shouts and
curses. He heard them ferreting in the dark corners; the
stock of a lance even rattled along the outer surface of the
door behind which he stood; but these gentlemen were in
too high a humour to be long delayed, and soon made
off down a corkscrew pathway which had escaped Denis'
observation, and passed out of sight and hearing along the
battlements of the town.

Denis breathed again. He gave them a few minutes' grace
for fear of accidents, and then groped about for some means
of opening the door and slipping forth again. The inner surface was quite smooth, not a handle, not a moulding, not
a projection of any sort. He got his finger-nails round the
edges and pulled, but the mass was immovable. He shook it,
it was as firm as a rock. Denis de Beaulieu frowned and
gave vent to a little noiseless whistle. What ailed the door?
he wondered. Why was it open? How came it to shut so
easily and so effectually after him? There was something
obscure and underhand about all this, that was little to the
young man's fancy. It looked like a snare; and yet who
could suppose a snare in such a quiet by-street and in a
house of so prosperous and even noble an exterior? And yet
—snare or no snare, intentionally or unintentionally—here
he was, prettily trapped; and for the life of him he could
see no way out of it again. The darkness began to weigh
upon him. He gave ear; all was silent without, but within
and close by he seemed to catch a faint sighing, a faint
sobbing rustle, a little stealthy creak—as though many persons were at his side, holding themselves quite still, and
governing even their respiration with the extreme of sly-
ness. The idea went to his vitals with a shock, and he
faced about suddenly as if to defend his life. Then, for the
first time, he became aware of a light about the level of
his eyes and at some distance in the interior of the house—
a vertical thread of light, widening towards the bottom,

such as might escape between two wings of arras over a
doorway. To see anything was a relief to Denis; it was like
a piece of solid ground to a man labouring in a morass;
his mind seized upon it with avidity; and he stood staring at
it and trying to piece together some logical conception of
his surroundings. Plainly there was a flight of steps ascending from his own level to that of the illuminated doorway;
and indeed he thought he could make out another thread
of light, as fine as a needle and as faint as phosphorescence,
which might very well be reflected along the polished wood
of a handrail. Since he had begun to suspect that he was
not alone, his heart had continued to beat with smothering
violence, and an intolerable desire for action of any sort
had possessed itself of his spirit. He was in deadly peril, he
believed. What could be more natural than to mount the
staircase, lift the curtain, and confront his difficulty at once?
At least he would be dealing with something tangible; at
least he would be no longer in the dark. He stepped slowly
forward with outstretched hands, until his foot struck the
bottom step; then he rapidly scaled the stairs, stood for
a moment to compose his expression, lifted the arras, and
went in.

He found himself in a large apartment of polished stone.
There were three doors; one on each of three sides; all
similarly curtained with tapestry. The fourth side was occupied by two large windows and a great stone chimney-
piece, carved with the arms of the Malétroits. Denis recognized the bearings, and was gratified to find himself in
such good hands. The room was strongly illuminated; but it
contained little furniture except a heavy table and a chair
or two, the hearth was innocent of fire, and the pavement
was but sparsely strewn with rushes clearly many days old.

On a high chair beside the chimney, and directly facing
Denis as he entered, sat a little old gentleman in a fur tippet.
He sat with his legs crossed and his hands folded, and a
cup of spiced wine stood by his elbow on a bracket on the
wall. His countenance had a strongly masculine cast; not
properly human, but such as we see in the bull, the goat,
or the domestic boar, something equivocal and wheedling,
something greedy, brutal, and dangerous. The upper lip
was inordinately full, as though swollen by a blow or a
toothache; and the smile, the peaked eyebrows, and the
small, strong eyes were quaintly and almost comically evil
in expression. Beautiful white hair hung straight all round
his head, like a saint's, and fell in a single curl upon the
tippet. His beard and moustache were the pink of vener-

able sweetness. Age, probably in consequence of inordinate precautions, had left no mark upon his hands; and the Malétroit hand was famous. It would be difficult to imagine anything at once so fleshy and so delicate in design; the tapered sensual fingers were like those of one of Leonardo's women; the fork of the thumb made a dimpled protuberance when closed; the nails were perfectly shaped, and of a dead, surprising whiteness. It rendered his aspect tenfold more redoubtable, that a man with hands like these should keep them devoutly folded in his lap like a virgin martyr—that a man with so intense and startling an expression of face should sit patiently on his seat and contemplate people with an unwinking stare, like a god, or a god's statue. His quiescence seemed ironical and treacherous, it fitted so poorly with his looks.

Such was Alain, Sire de Malétroit.

Denis and he looked silently at each other for a second or two.

"Pray step in," said the Sire de Malétroit. "I have been expecting you all the evening."

He had not risen, but he accompanied his words with a smile and a slight but courteous inclination of the head. Partly from the smile, partly from the strange musical murmur with which the Sire prefaced his observation, Denis felt a strong shudder of disgust go through his marrow. And what with disgust and honest confusion of mind, he could scarcely get words together in reply.

"I fear," he said, "that this is a double accident. I am not the person you suppose me. It seems you were looking for a visit; but for my part, nothing was further from my thoughts—nothing could be more contrary to my wishes—than this intrusion."

"Well, well," replied the old gentleman indulgently, "here you are, which is the main point. Seat yourself, my friend, and put yourself entirely at your ease. We shall arrange our little affairs presently."

Denis perceived that the matter was still complicated with some misconception, and he hastened to continue his explanation.

"Your door . . ." he began.

"About my door?" asked the other, raising his peaked eyebrows. "A little piece of ingenuity." And he shrugged his shoulders. "A hospitable fancy! By your own account, you were not desirous of making my acquaintance. We old people look for such reluctance now and then; and when it touches our honours, we cast about until we find some way of overcoming it. You arrive uninvited, but believe me, very welcome."

"You persist in error, sir," said Denis. "There can be no question between you and me. I am a stranger in this countryside. My name is Denis, Damoiseau de Beaulieu. If you see me in your house, it is only—"

"My found friend," interrupted the other, "you will permit me to have my own ideas on that subject. They probably differ from yours at the present moment," he added with a leer, "but time will show which of us is in the right."

Denis was convinced he had to do with a lunatic. He seated himself with a shrug, content to wait the upshot; and a pause ensued, during which he thought he could distinguish a hurried gabbling as of prayer from behind the arras immediately opposite him. Sometimes there seemed to be but one person engaged, sometimes two; and the vehemence of the voice, low as it was, seemed to indicate either great haste or an agony of spirit. It occurred to him that this piece of tapestry covered the entrance to the chapel he had noticed from without.

The old gentleman meanwhile surveyed Denis from head to foot with a smile, and from time to time emitted little noises like a bird or a mouse, which seemed to indicate a high degree of satisfaction. This state of matters became rapidly insupportable; and Denis, to put an end to it, remarked politely that the wind had gone down.

The old gentleman fell into a fit of silent laughter, so prolonged and violent that he became quite red in the face. Denis got upon his feet at once, and put on his hat with a flourish.

"Sir," he said, "if you are in your wits, you have affronted me grossly. If you are out of them, I flatter myself I can find better employment for my brains than to talk with lunatics. My conscience is clear; you have made a fool of me from the first moment; you have refused to hear my explanations; and now there is no power under God will make me stay here any longer; and if I cannot make my way out in a more decent fashion, I will hack your door in pieces with my sword."

The Sire de Malétroit raised his right hand and wagged it at Denis with the fore and little fingers extended.

"My dear nephew," he said, "sit down."

"Nephew!" retorted Denis, "you lie in your throat"; and he snapped his fingers in his face.

"Sit down, you rogue!" cried the old gentleman, in a

sudden, harsh voice, like the barking of a dog. "Do you fancy," he went on, "that when I had made my little contrivance for the door I had stopped short with that? If you prefer to be bound hand and foot till your bones ache, rise and try to go away. If you choose to remain a free young buck, agreeably conversing with an old gentleman —why, sit where you are in peace, and God be with you."

"Do you mean I am a prisoner?" demanded Denis.

"I state the facts," replied the other. "I would rather leave the conclusion to yourself."

Denis sat down again. Externally he managed to keep pretty calm; but within, he was now boiling with anger, now chilled with apprehension. He no longer felt convinced that he was dealing with a madman. And if the old gentleman was sane, what, in God's name, had he to look for? What absurd or tragical adventure had befallen him? What countenance was he to assume?

While he was thus unpleasantly reflecting, the arras that overhung the chapel door was raised, and a tall priest in his robes came forth and, giving a long, keen stare at Denis, said something in an undertone to Sire de Malétroit.

"She is in a better frame of spirit?" asked the latter.

"She is more resigned, messire," replied the priest.

"Now the Lord help her, she is hard to please!" sneered the old gentleman. "A likely stripling—not ill-born—and of her own choosing, too? Why, what more would the jade have?"

"The situation is not usual for a young damsel," said the other, "and somewhat trying to her blushes."

"She should have thought of that before she began the dance. It was none of my choosing, God knows that: but since she is in it, by our Lady, she shall carry it to the end." And then addressing Denis, "Monsieur de Beaulieu," he asked, "may I present you to my niece? She has been waiting your arrival, I may say, with even greater impatience than myself."

Denis had resigned himself with a good grace—all he desired was to know the worst of it as speedily as possible; so he rose at once, and bowed in acquiescence. The Sire de Malétroit followed his example and limped, with the assistance of the chaplain's arm, towards the chapel door. The priest pulled aside the arras, and all three entered. The building had considerable architectural pretensions. A light groining sprang from six stout columns, and hung down in two rich pendants from the centre of the vault. The place terminated behind the altar in a round end,

embossed and honeycombed with a superfluity of ornament in relief, and pierced by many little windows shaped
like stars, trefoils, or wheels. These windows were im-
perfectly glazed, so that the night air circulated freely in
the chapel. The tapers, of which there must have been
half a hundred burning on the altar, were unmercifully
blown about; and the light went through many different
phases of brilliancy and semi-eclipse. On the steps in
front of the altar knelt a young girl richly attired as a
bride. A chill settled over Denis as he observed her costume; he fought with desperate energy against the conclusion that was being thrust upon his mind; it could not—it
should not—be as he feared.

"Blanche," said the Sire, in his most flute-like tones, "I
have brought a friend to see you, my little girl; turn
around and give him your pretty hand. It is good to be
devout; but it is necessary to be polite, my niece."

The girl rose to her feet and turned towards the new
comer. She moved all of a piece; and shame and exhaustion were expressed in every line of her fresh young body;
and she held her head down and kept her eyes upon the
pavement, as she came slowly forward. In the course of
her advance, her eyes fell upon Denis de Beaulieu's feet—
feet of which he was justly vain, be it remarked, and wore
in the most elegant accoutrement even while traveling.
She paused—started, as if his yellow boots had conveyed
some shocking meaning—and glanced suddenly up into
the wearer's countenance. Their eyes met; shame gave
place to horror and terror in her looks; the blood left
her lips; with a piercing scream she covered her face with
her hands and sank upon the chapel floor.

"That is not the man!" she cried. "My uncle, that is not
the man!"

The Sire de Malétroit chirped agreeably. "Of course
not," he said; "I expected as much. It was so unfortunate
you could not remember his name."

"Indeed," she cried, "indeed, I have never seen this
person till this moment—I have never so much as set
eyes upon him—I never wish to see him again. Sir," she
said, turning to Denis, "if you are a gentleman, you will
bear me out. Have I ever seen you—have you ever seen
me—before this accursed hour?"

"To speak for myself, I have never had that pleasure,"
answered the young man. "This is the first time, messire,
that I have met with your engaging niece."

The old gentleman shrugged his shoulders.

"I am distressed to hear it," he said. "But it is never too late to begin. I had little more acquaintance with my own late lady ere I married her; which proves," he added with a grimace, "that these impromptu marriages may often produce an excellent understanding in the long-run. As the bridegroom is to have a voice in the matter, I will give him two hours to make up for lost time before we proceed with the ceremony." And he turned towards the door, followed by the clergyman.

The girl was on her feet in a moment. "My uncle, you cannot be in earnest," she said. "I declare before God I will stab myself rather than be forced on that young man. The heart rises at it; God forbids such marriages; you dishonour your white hair. Oh, my uncle, pity me! There is not a woman in all the world but would prefer death to such a nuptial. Is it possible," she added, faltering—"is it possible that you do not believe me—that you still think this"—and she pointed at Denis with a tremor of anger and contempt—"that you still think *this* to be the man?"

"Frankly," said the old gentleman, pausing on the threshold, "I do. But let me explain to you once for all, Blanche de Malétroit, my way of thinking about this affair. When you took it into your head to dishonour my family and the name that I have borne, in peace and war, for more than three-score years, you forfeited, not only the right to question my designs, but that of looking me in the face. If your father had been alive, he would have spat on you and turned you out of doors. His was the hand of iron. You may bless your God you have only to deal with the hand of velvet, mademoiselle. It was my duty to get you married without delay. Out of pure good-will, I have tried to find your own gallant for you. And I believe I have succeeded. But before God and all the holy angels, Blanche de Malétroit, if I have not, I care not one jack-straw. So let me recommend you to be polite to our young friend; for upon my word, your next groom may be less appetising."

And with that he went out, with the chaplain at his heels; and the arras fell behind the pair.

The girl turned upon Denis with flashing eyes.

"And what, sir," she demanded, "may be the meaning of all this?"

"God knows," returned Denis gloomily. "I am a prisoner in this house, which seems full of mad people. More I know not; and nothing do I understand."

"And pray how came you here?" she asked.

He told her as briefly as he could. "For the rest," he added, "perhaps you will follow my example, and tell me the answer to all these riddles, and what, in God's name, is like to be the end of it."

She stood silent for a little, and he could see her lips tremble and her tearless eyes burn with a feverish lustre. Then she pressed her forehead in both hands.

"Alas, how my head aches!" she said wearily—"to say nothing of my poor heart! But it is due to you to know my story, unmaidenly as it must seem. I am called Blanche de Malétroit; I have been without father or mother—oh! for as long as I can recollect, and indeed I have been most unhappy all my life. Three months ago a young captain began to stand near me every day in church. I could see that I pleased him; I am much to blame, but I was so glad that any one should love me; and when he passed me a letter, I took it home with me and read it with great pleasure. Since that time he has written many. He was so anxious to speak with me, poor fellow! and kept asking me to leave the door open some evening that we might have two words upon the stair. For he knew how much my uncle trusted me." She gave something like a sob at that, and it was a moment before she could go on. "My uncle is a hard man, but he is very shrewd," she said at last. "He has performed many feats in war, and was a great person at court, and much trusted by Queen Isabeau in old days. How he came to suspect me I cannot tell; but it is hard to keep anything from his knowledge; and this morning, as we came from mass, he took my hand in his, forced it open, and read my little billet, walking by my side all the while. When he had finished, he gave it back to me with great politeness. It contained another request to have the door left open; and this has been the ruin of us all. My uncle kept me strictly in my room until evening, and then ordered me to dress myself as you see me— a hard mockery for a young girl, do you not think so? I suppose, when he could not prevail with me to tell him the young captain's name, he must have laid a trap for him: into which, alas! you have fallen in the anger of God. I looked for much confusion; for how could I tell whether he was willing to take me for his wife on these sharp terms? He might have been trifling with me from the first; or I might have made myself too cheap in his eyes. But truly I had not looked for such a shameful punishment as this? I could not think that God would let a girl be so disgraced before a young man. And now I have told you all; and I can scarcely hope that you will not despise me."

Denis made her a respectful inclination.

"Madam," he said, "you have honoured me by your confidence. It remains for me to prove that I am not unworthy of the honour. Is Messire de Malétroit at hand?"

"I believe he is writing in the salle without," she answered.

"May I lead you thither, madam?" asked Denis, offering his hand with his most courtly bearing.

She accepted it; and the pair passed out of the chapel, Blanche in a very drooping and shamefaced condition, but Denis strutting and ruffling in the consciousness of a mission, and the boyish certainty of accomplishing it with honour.

The Sire de Malétroit rose to meet them with an ironical obeisance.

"Sir," said Denis, with the grandest possible air, "I believe I am to have some say in the matter of this marriage; and let me tell you at once, I will be no party to forcing the inclination of this young lady. Had it been freely offered to me, I should have been proud to accept her hand, for I perceive she is as good as she is beautiful; but as things are, I have now the honour, messire, of refusing."

Blanche looked at him with gratitude in her eyes; but the old gentleman only smiled and smiled; until his smile grew positively sickening to Denis.

"I am afraid," he said, "Monsieur de Beaulieu, that you do not perfectly understand the choice I have to offer you. Follow me, I beseech you, to this window." And he led the way to one of the large windows which stood open on the night. "You observe," he went on, "there is an iron ring in the upper masonry, and reeved through that, a very efficacious rope. Now, mark my words: if you should find your disinclination to my niece's person insurmountable, I shall have you hanged out of this window before sunrise. I shall only proceed to such an extremity with the greatest regret, you may believe me. For it is not at all your death that I desire, but my niece's establishment in life. At the same time, it must come to that if you prove obstinate. Your family, Monsieur de Beaulieu, is very well in its way; but if you sprang from Charlemagne, you should not refuse the hand of a Malétroit with impunity—not if she had been as common as the Paris road—not if she were as hideous as the gargoyle over my door. Neither my niece nor you, nor my own

private feelings, move me at all in this matter. The honour
of my house has been compromised; I believe you to be
the guilty person; at least you are now in the secret; and
you can hardly wonder if I request you to wipe out the
stain. If you will not, your blood be on your own head! It
will be no great satisfaction to me to have your interesting
relics kicking their heels in the breeze below my windows;
but half a loaf is better than no bread, and if I cannot cure
the dishonour, I shall at least stop the scandal."

There was a pause.

"I believe there are other ways of settling such im-
broglios among gentlemen," said Denis. "You wear a
sword, and I hear you have used it with distinction."

The Sire de Malétroit made a signal to the chaplain,
who crossed the room with long silent strides and raised
the arras over the third of the three doors. It was only
a moment before he let it fall again; but Denis had time
to see a dusky passage full of armed men.

"When I was a little younger, I should have been delighted to honour you, Monsieur de Beaulieu," said Sire
Alain; "but I am now too old. Faithful retainers are the
sinews of age, and I must employ the strength I have.
This is one of the hardest things to swallow as a man
grows up in years; but with a little patience, even this becomes habitual. You and the lady seem to prefer the salle
for what remains of your two hours; and as I have no
desire to cross your preference, I shall resign it to your
use with all the pleasure in the world. No haste!" he
added, holding up his hand, as he saw a dangerous look
come into Denis de Beaulieu's face. "If your mind revolts
against hanging, it will be time enough two hours hence
to throw yourself out of the window or upon the pikes of
my retainers. Two hours of life are always two hours. A
great many things may turn up in even as little a while as
that. And besides, if I understand her appearance, my
niece has still something to say to you. You will not dis-
figure your last hours by a want of politeness to a lady?"

Denis looked at Blanche, and she made him an imploring gesture.

It is likely that the old gentleman was hugely pleased
at this symptom of an understanding; for he smiled on
both, and added sweetly: "If you will give me your word
of honour, Monsieur de Beaulieu, to await my return
at the end of the two hours before attempting anything
desperate, I shall withdraw my retainers, and let you
speak in greater privacy with mademoiselle."

Denis again glanced at the girl, who seemed to beseech him to agree.

"I give you my word of honour," he said.

Messire de Malétroit bowed, and proceeded to limp about the apartment, clearing his throat the while with that odd musical chirp which had already grown so irritating in the ears of Denis de Beaulieu. He first possessed himself of some papers which lay upon the table; then he went to the mouth of the passage and appeared to give an order to the men behind the arras; and lastly he hobbled out through the door by which Denis had come in, turning upon the threshold to address a last smiling bow to the young couple, and followed by the chaplain with a hand-lamp.

No sooner were they alone than Blanche advanced towards Denis with her hands extended. Her face was flushed and excited, and her eyes shone with tears.

"You shall not die!" she cried, "you shall marry me after all."

"You seem to think, madam," replied Denis, "that I stand much in fear of death."

"Oh, no, no," she said, "I see you are no poltroon. It is for my own sake—I could not bear to have you slain for such a scruple."

"I am afraid," returned Denis, "that you underrate the difficulty, madam. What you may be too generous to refuse, I may be too proud to accept. In a moment of noble feeling towards me, you forget what you perhaps owe to others."

He had the decency to keep his eyes upon the floor as he said this, and after he had finished, so as not to spy upon her confusion. She stood silent for a moment, then walked suddenly away, and falling on her uncle's chair, fairly burst out sobbing. Denis was in the acme of embarrassment. He looked round, as if to seek for inspiration, and seeing a stool, plumped down upon it for something to do. There he sat, playing with the guard of his rapier, and wishing himself dead a thousand times over, and buried in the nastiest kitchen-heap in France. His eyes wandered round the apartment but found nothing to arrest them. There were such wide spaces between the furniture, the light fell so badly and cheerlessly over all, the dark outside air looked in so coldly through the windows, that he thought he had never seen a church so vast, nor a tomb so melancholy. The regular sobs of Blanche de Malétroit measured out the time like the ticking of a

clock. He read the device upon the shield over and over
again, until his eyes became obscured; he stared into
shadowy corners until he imagined they were swarming
with horrible animals; and every now and again he awoke
with a start, to remember that his last two hours were
running and death was on the march.

Oftener and oftener, as the time went on, did his glance
settle on the girl herself. Her face was bowed forward
and covered with her hands, and she was shaken at intervals by the convulsive hiccup of grief. Even thus she was
not an unpleasant object to dwell upon, so plump and
yet so fine, with a warm brown skin, and the most beautiful hair, Denis thought, in the whole world of woman-
kind. Her hands were like her uncle's; but they were more
in place at the end of her young arms, and looked infinitely soft and caressing. He remembered how her blue
eyes had shone upon him, full of anger, pity, and innocence. And the more he dwelt on her perfections, the
uglier death looked, and the more deeply was he smitten
with penitence at her continued tears. Now he felt that
no man could have the courage to leave a world which
contained so beautiful a creature; and now he would have
given forty minutes of his last hour to have unsaid his
cruel speech.

Suddenly a hoarse and ragged peal of cockcrow rose
to their ears from the dark valley below the windows. And
this shattering noise in the silence all around was like a
light in a dark place, and shook them both out of their
reflections.

"Alas, can I do nothing to help you?" she said, looking
up.

"Madam," replied Denis, with a fine irrelevancy, "if I
have said anything to wound you, believe me, it was for
your own sake and not for mine."

She thanked him with a tearful look.

"I feel your position cruelly," he went on. "The world
has been bitter hard on you. Your uncle is a disgrace to
mankind. Believe me, madam, there is no young gentleman in all France but would be glad of my opportunity,
to die in doing you a momentary service."

"I know already that you can be very brave and generous," she answered. "What I *want* to know is whether
I can serve you—now or afterwards," she added, with a
quaver.

"Most certainly," he answered with a smile. "Let me
sit beside you as if I were a friend, instead of a foolish

intruder; try to forget how awkwardly we are placed to
one another; make my last moments go pleasantly; and
you will do me the chief service possible."

"You are very gallant," she added, with a yet deeper sadness . . . "very gallant . . . and it somehow pains me. But
draw nearer, if you please, and if you find anything to say
to me, you will at least make certain of a very friendly
listener. Ah! Monsieur de Beaulieu, how can I look you in
the face?" And she fell to weeping again with a renewed
effusion.

"Madam," said Denis, taking her hand in both of his,
"reflect on the little time I have before me, and the great
bitterness into which I am cast by the sight of your distress.
Spare me, in my last moments, the spectacle of what I
cannot cure even with the sacrifice of my life."

"I am very selfish," answered Blanche. "I will be braver,
Monsieur de Beaulieu, for your sake. But think if I can do
you no kindness in the future—if you have no friends to
whom I could carry your adieux. Charge me as heavily as
you can; every burden will lighten, by so little, the invaluable gratitude I owe you. Put it in my power to do
something more for you than weep."

"My mother is married again, and has a young family to
care for. My brother Guichard will inherit my fiefs; and if
I am not in error, that will content him amply for my
death. Life is a little vapour that passeth away, as we are
told by those in holy orders. When a man is in a fair
way and sees all life open in front of him, he seems to
himself to make a very important figure in the world. His
horse whinnies to him; the trumpets blow and the girls look
out of window as he rides into town before his company;
he receives many assurances of trust and regard—sometimes by express in a letter—sometimes face to face, with
persons of great consequence falling on his neck. It is not
wonderful if his head is turned for a time. But once he is
dead, were he as brave as Hercules or as wise as Solomon,
he is soon forgotten. It is not ten years since my father
fell, with many other knights around him, in a very fierce
encounter, and I do not think that any one of them, nor
so much as the name of the fight, is now remembered. No,
no, madam, the nearer you come to it, you see that death
is a dark and dusty corner, where a man gets into his
tomb and has the door shut after him till the judgment
day. I have few friends just now, and once I am dead I
shall have none."

"Ah, Monsieur de Beaulieu!" she exclaimed, "you forget Blanche de Malétroit."

"You have a sweet nature, madam, and you are pleased to estimate a little service far beyond its worth."

"It is not that," she answered. "You mistake me if you think I am so easily touched by my own concerns. I say so, because you are the noblest man I have ever met; because I recognise in you a spirit that would have made even a common person famous in the land."

"And yet here I die in a mouse-trap—with no more noise about it than my own speaking," answered he.

A look of pain crossed her face, and she was silent for a little while. Then a light came into her eyes, and with a smile she spoke again.

"I cannot have my champion think meanly of himself. Anyone who gives his life for another will be met in Paradise by all the heralds and angels of the Lord God. And you have no such cause to hang your head. For . . . Pray, do you think me beautiful?" she asked, with a deep flush.

"Indeed, madam, I do," he said.

"I am glad of that," she answered, heartily. "Do you think there are many men in France who have been asked in marriage by a beautiful maiden—with her own lips—and who have refused her to her face? I know you men would half despise such a triumph; but believe me, we women know more of what is precious in love. There is nothing that should set a person higher in his own esteem; and we women would prize nothing more dearly."

"You are very good," he said; "but you cannot make me forget that I was asked in pity and not for love."

"I am not so sure of that," she replied, holding down her head. "Hear me to an end, Monsieur de Beaulieu. I know how you must despise me; I feel you are right to do so; I am too poor a creature to occupy one thought of your mind, although, alas! you must die for me this morning. But when I asked you to marry me, indeed, and indeed, it was because I respected and admired you, and loved you with my whole soul, from the very moment that you took my part against my uncle. If you had seen yourself, and how noble you looked, you would pity rather than despise me. And now," she went on, hurriedly checking him with her hand, "although I have laid aside all reserve and told you so much, remember that I know your sentiments towards me already. I would not, believe me, being nobly born, weary you with importunities into consent. I too have a pride of my own: and I declare before the holy mothers of God, if you should now go back from your word already given, I would no more marry you than I would marry my uncle's groom."

Denis smiled a little bitterly.

"It is a small love," he said, "that shies at a little pride."

She made no answer, although she probably had her own thought.

"Come hither to the window," he said, with a sigh. "Here is the dawn."

And indeed the dawn was already beginning. The hollow of the sky was full of essential daylight, colourless and clean; and the valley underneath was flooded with a grey reflection. A few thin vapors clung in the coves of the forest or lay along the winding course of the river. The scene disengaged a surprising effect of stillness, which was hardly interrupted when the cocks began once more to crow among the steadings. Perhaps the same fellow who had made so horrid a clangour in the darkness not half an hour before, now sent up the merriest cheer to greet the coming day. A little wind went bustling and eddying among the tree-tops underneath the windows. And still the daylight kept flooding insensibly out of the east, which was soon to grow incandescent and cast up that red-hot cannon-ball, the rising sun.

Denis looked out over all this with a bit of a shiver. He had taken her hand and retained it in his almost unconsciously.

"Has the day begun already?" she said; and then, illogically enough: "the night has been so long! Alas! what shall we say to my uncle when he returns?"

"What you will," said Denis, and he pressed her fingers in his.

She was silent.

"Blanche," he said, with a swift, uncertain, passionate utterance, "you have seen whether I fear death. You must know well enough that I would as gladly leap out of the window into the empty air as to lay a finger on you without your free and full consent. But if you care for me at all do not let me lose my life in a misapprehension; for I love you better than the whole world; and though I will die for you blithely, it would be like all the joys of Paradise to live on and spend my life in your service."

As he stopped speaking, a bell began to ring loudly in the interior of the house, and a clatter of armour in the corridor showed that the retainers were returning to their post, and the two hours were at an end.

"After all that you have heard?" she whispered, leaning towards him with her lips and eyes.

"I have heard nothing," he replied.

"The captain's name was Florimond de Champdivers," she said in his ear.

"I did not hear it," he answered, taking her supple body in his arms and covering her wet face with kisses.

A melodious chirping was audible behind, followed by a beautiful chuckle, and the voice of Messire de Malétroit wished his new nephew a good morning.

Guy de Maupassant

(1850–1893)

A disciple of Gustave Flaubert, who was a friend of his family and who, like him, was a Norman, Guy de Maupassant finished his army service and entered upon a career as a government clerk before he began seriously to consider a literary career. Flaubert introduced him to his friends Turgenev, Daudet, Zola. De Maupassant soon became a distinguished devotee of the objective realism of Flaubert and his school. But de Maupassant's stories are distinctively his own, not mere Flaubertian imitations. Like Flaubert's, his narrative tone tends to be impersonal, but he is both more satirical and more bitter about human imperfections than was Flaubert. Unlike his master, de Maupassant is totally devoid of religious feeling or interest. He is, in fact, one of the most jaundiced and skeptical short story writers of the nineteenth century. He ridicules middle-class values and conventions, analyzes romantic love with scientific precision and detachment, and treats the bourgeoisie, the peasantry, and the declining aristocracy with the same skepticism and contempt. His stories reflect his deep feeling for the sensual.

De Maupassant experienced a physical and mental breakdown as a result of his intensive work during his most productive decade (1880–1890) when he wrote over three hundred short stories, five novels, some plays, and some poetry. His relentless debauchery during this period hastened his disintegration. He ended his days insane and institutionalized.

De Maupassant's claim to fame rests on his uniquely masterful command of the short story. His short stories are told with a crystalline precision, filled with sharply etched details and a vivid sense of scene. A scrupulous economy of phrase and narrative pace give de Maupassant's tales a fresh and immediately recognizable quality.

"Father and Son" is de Maupassant at his best. Its power springs from its economy, its accurate and sympathetic etching of its characters. The Norman background, with which de Maupassant was so familiar, serves him here as a backdrop against which these simple but enduring people play their inevitable, subdued roles.

Father and Son

Hautot Senior and Junior

The dogs fastened to the apple trees in the grounds in front of the house were giving tongue at the sight of the game bags carried by the gamekeepers and small boys. It was half farm and half manor house, one of those quasi-seignorial country residences, now occupied by large farmers. In the spacious dining-room-kitchen, Hautot Senior and Hautot Junior, M. Bermont, the tax collector, and M. Mondaru, the notary, were eating a mouthful and drinking a glass before going out shooting, for it was the first day of the season.

Hautot Senior, proud of all his possessions, talked boastfully of the game which his guests were going to find on his lands. He was a big Norman, one of those powerful, ruddy men, with large bones, who lift wagon loads of apples on their shoulders. Half peasant, half gentleman, rich, respected, influential, autocratic, he obliged his son César to go through the third form at college so that he might be an educated man, and there he had brought his studies to an end, for fear of his becoming a fine gentleman and paying no attention to the land.

César Hautot, almost as tall as his father, but thinner, was a good son, docile, content with everything, full of admiration, respect, and deference for the wishes and opinions of Hautot Senior.

M. Bermont, the tax collector, a stout little man, who showed on his red cheeks a thin network of violet veins resembling the tributaries and the winding courses of rivers on maps, asked:

"And hares—are there any hares?"

Hautot Senior answered:

"As many as you wish, especially in the Puysatier land."

"How shall we set out?" asked the notary, an epicure of a notary, pale and corpulent, with a brand-new hunting costume, belted in, that he had bought at Rouen.

"Well, that way, through the bottoms. We will drive the partridges into the plain, and we can get them there."

And Hautot Senior rose up. They all followed his example, took their guns out of the corners, examined the locks, stamped their feet in order to adjust their boots, which were rather hard, not having become flexible from wear. Then they went out; and the dogs, standing on their hind legs at the ends of their leashes, gave tongue while beating the air with their paws.

They set out toward the bottoms referred to. These consisted of a little valley, or, rather, a long, undulating stretch of poor land, which had on that account remained uncultivated, furrowed with ditches and covered with ferns, an excellent preserve for game.

The sportsmen took up their positions at some distance from each other, Hautot Senior at the right, Hautot Junior at the left, and the two guests in the middle. The game-keeper, and the men carrying the game bags, followed. It was the solemn moment when the first shot is awaited, when the heart beats a little, while the nervous finger keeps feeling the trigger.

Suddenly a shot went off. Hautot Senior had fired. They all stopped, and saw a partridge separate from a covey which had risen, and fall down into a deep ditch under a thick growth of brush. The sportsman, becoming excited, rushed forward with rapid strides, thrusting aside the briars which stood in his path, and disappeared in his turn into the thicket, in quest of his game.

Almost at the same instant, a second shot was heard.

"Ha! ha! the rascal!" exclaimed M. Bermont, "he must have started a hare down there."

They all waited, with their eyes riveted on the mass of brush which their gaze failed to penetrate.

The notary, making a speaking trumpet of his hands, shouted:

"Have you got them?"

Hautot Senior made no response.

Then César, turning toward the gamekeeper, said:

"Just go and assist him, Joseph. We must keep walking in line. We'll wait."

And Joseph, an old stump of a man, lean and knotty, all of whose joints formed protuberances, set off at an easy pace down into the ditch, searching every opening through which a passage could be effected with the cautiousness of a fox. Then, suddenly, he cried:

"Oh! come! come! an accident has occurred."

They all hurried forward, plunging through the briars.

The elder Hautot had fallen on his side, in a faint, with

both hands pressed to his abdomen, from which blood trickled through his shooting jacket, torn by a bullet. Letting go of his gun, in order to pick up the dead partridge, he had let the firearm fall, and the second discharge, going off with the shock, had torn open his entrails. They drew him out of the trench, removed his clothes, and saw a frightful wound, through which the intestines protruded. Then, after having ligatured him the best way they could, they brought him back to his own house, and awaited the doctor, who had been sent for, as well as the priest.

When the doctor arrived he gravely shook his head, and, turning toward young Hautot, who was sobbing on a chair, he said:

"My poor boy, this does not look favorable."

But, when the wound was dressed, the wounded man moved his fingers, opened his mouth, then his eyes, cast around him troubled, haggard glances, then appeared to be trying to recall, to understand, and he murmured:

"Ah! good God! this has finished me!"

The doctor held his hand.

"Why, no; why, no; some days of rest merely—it will be nothing."

Hautot returned:

"It has finished me! My abdomen is gashed! I know it well."

Then, all of a sudden:

"I want to talk to my son, if I have time."

Hautot Junior, in spite of himself, shed tears, and kept repeating like a little boy:

"Papa, papa, poor papa!"

But the father, in a firm tone, said:

"Come! stop crying—this is no time for it. I have something to say to you. Sit down there, quite close to me. It will not take long, and I shall be more calm. As for the rest of you, kindly leave us alone for a minute."

They all went out, leaving the father and son together.

As soon as they were alone:

"Listen, son!" he said, "you are twenty-four; one can talk to you. And then there is not such mystery about these matters as we attach to them. You know, do you not, that your mother has been dead seven years, and that I am not more than forty-five years myself, seeing that I was married at nineteen. Is not that true?"

The son faltered:

"Yes, it is true."

"So then your mother is dead seven years, and I have

remained a widower. Well! a man like me cannot remain without a wife at thirty-seven, isn't that true?"

The son replied:

"Yes, it is true."

The father, out of breath, very pale, and his face contracted with suffering, went on:

"God! how I suffer! Well, you understand. Man is not made to live alone, but I did not want to take a successor to your mother, since I promised her not to do so. Therefore—you understand?"

"Yes, father."

"Well, I kept a young girl at Rouen, number eighteen, Rue de l'Éperlan, on the third floor, the second door—I am telling you all this, don't forget—a young girl, who has been very nice to me, loving, devoted, a true woman, eh? You understand, my lad?"

"Yes, father."

"So then, if I am carried off, I owe something to her, something substantial, that will place her beyond the reach of want. You understand?"

"Yes, father."

"I tell you that she is a good girl, and, but for you, and the remembrance of your mother, and also because we three lived together in this house, I would have brought her here, and then married her. Listen—listen, my boy—I might have made a will—I haven't done so. I did not wish to do so—for it is not necessary to write down things —things of this sort—it is too damaging to the legitmate children—and then it makes confusion—it ruins every one! Look you, lawyers, there's no need of them—never consult one. If I am rich, it is because I never employed one in all my life. You understand, my son?"

"Yes, father."

"Listen again—listen attentively! So then, I have made no will—I did not desire to do so—and then I knew you; you have a good heart, you are not covetous, not stingy, and I said to myself that when my end approached I would tell you all about it, and that I would beg of you not to forget the girl. And then, listen again! When I am gone, go and see her at once—and make such arrangements that she may not blame my memory. You have plenty of means. You can spare it—I leave you enough. Listen! You won't find her at home every day in the week. She works at Madame Moreau's in the Rue Beauvoisine. Go there on a Thursday. That is the day she expects me. It has been my day for the past six years. Poor little girl! she will weep!

I say all this to you, because I know you so well, my son.
One does not tell these things in public, either to the notary
or to the priest. They happen—every one knows that—but
they are not talked about, save in case of necessity. Then
there must be no outsider in the secret, nobody except the
family, because the family consists of one person alone.
You understand?"

"Yes, father."

"Do you promise?"

"Yes, father."

"Do you swear it?"

"Yes, father."

"I beg of you, I implore of you, son, do not forget. I
insist on this."

"No, father."

"You will go yourself. I want you to make sure of
everything."

"Yes, father."

"And then, you will see—you will see what she will
explain to you. As for me, I can say no more to you. You
have sworn to do it."

"Yes, father."

"That's good, my son. Embrace me. Farewell. I am
going to die, I'm sure. Tell them they may come in."

Young Hautot embraced his father, groaning as he did
so; then, always docile, he opened the door, and the priest
appeared in a white surplice, carrying the holy oils.

But the dying man had closed his eyes and refused to
open them again; he refused to answer, and even to show
by a sign that he understood.

He had talked enough, this man; he could speak no
longer. Besides, he now felt his heart at ease and wanted
to die in peace. What need had he to make a confession
to the deputy of God, since he had just confessed to his
son, who constituted his family?

He received the last rites, was purified, and received
absolution, surrounded by his friends and his servants on
their bended knees, without any movement of his face
indicating that he still lived.

He expired about midnight, after four hours of spasms,
which showed that he must have suffered dreadfully.

Part II

He was buried on Tuesday, the shooting season having
opened on Sunday. On returning home after the funeral
César Hautot spent the rest of the day weeping. He
scarcely slept that night, and felt so sad on awaking that
he asked himself how he could go on living.

However, he kept thinking that, in order to obey his
father's dying wish, he must go to Rouen the following
day, and see this girl Caroline Donet, who lived at eighteen
Rue d'Éperlan, the third story, second door. He had muttered to himself this name and address a countless number
of times, just as a child repeats a prayer, so that he might
not forget them, and he ended by repeating them continually, without thinking, so impressed were they on his mind.

Accordingly, on the following day, about eight o'clock,
he ordered Graindorge to be harnessed to the tilbury, and
set forth, at the long, swinging pace of the heavy Norman
horse, along the high road from Ainville to Rouen. He
wore his black frock coat, his tall silk hat, and his trousers
strapped under his shoes, and, being in mourning, did not
put on his blue dust coat.

He entered Rouen just as it was striking ten o'clock,
put up, as he had always done, at the Hotel des Bons-
Enfants, in the Rue des Trois-Mares, and submitted to
the embraces of the landlord and his wife and their five
children, for they had heard the melancholy news; after
that, he had to tell them all the particulars of the accident,
which caused him to shed tears; to repel all the proffered
attentions which they sought to thrust upon him merely
because he was wealthy; and to decline even the luncheon
they wanted him to partake of, thus wounding their sensi-
bilities.

Then, having wiped the dust off his hat, brushed his
coat, and removed the mud stains from his boots, he set
forth in search of the Rue de l'Éperlan, without venturing
to make inquiries from any one, for fear of being recognized and of arousing suspicion.

At length, unable to find the place, he saw a priest
passing by, and, trusting to the professional discretion of
the clergy, he questioned the ecclesiastic.

He had only a hundred steps farther to go; it was the second street to the right.

Then he hesitated. Up to that moment he had obeyed, like a mere animal, the expressed wish of the deceased. Now he felt quite agitated, confused, humiliated, at the idea of finding himself—the son—in the presence of this woman who had been his father's sweetheart. All the morality we possess, which lies buried at the bottom of our emotions through centuries of hereditary instruction, all that he had been taught since he had learned his catechism about creatures of evil life, the instinctive contempt which every man entertains toward them, even though he may marry one of them, all the narrow honesty of the peasant in his character, was stirred up within him, and held him back, making him grow red with shame.

But he said to himself:

"I promised father. I must not break my promise."

So he pushed open the partly opened door of number eighteen, saw a gloomy-looking staircase, ascended three flights, perceived a door, then a second door, saw a bell rope, and pulled it. The ringing, which resounded in the apartment, sent a shiver through his frame. The door was opened, and he found himself face to face with a well-dressed young lady, a brunette with rosy cheeks, who gazed at him with eyes of astonishment.

He did not know what to say to her, and she, who suspected nothing, and who was waiting for the father, did not invite him to come in. They stood looking thus at one another for nearly half a minute, at the end of which she said in a questioning tone:

"Do you want anything, monsieur?"

He falteringly replied:

"I am M. Hautot's son."

She gave a start, turned pale, and stammered out as if she had known him for a long time:

"Monsieur César?"

"Yes."

"And what then?"

"I have come with a message to you from my father."

She exclaimed:

"Oh, my God!" and then drew back so that he might enter. He shut the door and followed her into the apartment. Then he perceived a little boy of four or five years playing with a cat, seated on the floor in front of a stove, from which rose an odor of food being kept hot.

"Take a seat," she said.

He sat down.

"Well?" she questioned.

He no longer ventured to speak, keeping his eyes fixed on the table which stood in the centre of the room, with three covers laid on it, one of which was for a child, and a bottle of claret that had been opened, and one of white wine that had not been uncorked. He glanced at the chair with its back turned to the fire. That was his father's chair! They were expecting him. That was his bread which he saw at his place, for the crust had been removed on account of Hautot's bad teeth. Then, raising his eyes, he noticed on the wall his father's portrait, the large photograph taken at Paris the year of the exhibition, the same as that which hung above the bed in the sleeping apartment at Ainville.

The young woman again asked:

"Well, Monsieur César?"

He kept staring at her. Her face was livid with anxiety, and she waited, her hands trembling with fear.

Then he took courage.

"Well, mam'zelle, papa died on Sunday last just after he had opened the shooting season."

She was so overwhelmed that she did not move. After a silence of a few seconds, she faltered in an almost inaudible tone:

"Oh, it is not possible!"

Then, on a sudden, tears came into her eyes, and, covering her face with her hands, she burst out sobbing.

At that point the little boy turned round, and, seeing his mother weeping, began to roar. Then, realizing that this sudden trouble was brought about by the stranger, he rushed at César, caught hold of his trousers with one hand and with the other hit him with all his strength on the thigh. And César remained bewildered, deeply affected; with this woman mourning for his father on the one hand, and the little boy defending his mother on the other. He felt their emotion taking possession of him, and his eyes were beginning to fill with tears; so, to recover his self-command, he began to talk:

"Yes," he said, "the accident occurred on Sunday, at eight o'clock——"

And he told all the facts as if she were listening to him, without forgetting a single detail, mentioning the most trivial matters with the minuteness of a countryman. And the child still kept attacking him, kicking his ankles.

When he came to what his father had said about her, she took her hands from her face and said:

"Pardon me! I was not following you; I would like to know—— Would you mind beginning over again?"

He repeated everything in the same words, with pauses and reflections of his own from time to time. She listened eagerly now, perceiving, with a woman's keen sensibility, all the sudden changes of fortune which his narrative implied, and trembling with horror, every now and then exclaiming:

"Oh, my God!"

The little fellow, believing that she had calmed down, ceased beating César, in order to take his mother's hand, and he listened, too, as if he understood.

When the narrative was finished, young Hautot continued:

"Now, we will settle matters together, in accordance with his wishes. I am well off, he has left me plenty of means. I don't want you to have anything to complain about——"

But she quickly interrupted him.

"Oh! Monsieur César, Monsieur César, not to-day. I am cut to the heart—another time—another day. No, not to-day. If I accept, listen—it is not for myself—no, no, no, I swear to you, it is for the child. Besides, this sum will be placed to his account."

Thereupon, César, horrified, guessed the truth, and stammered:

"So then—it is his—the child?"

"Why, yes," she said.

And Hautot Junior gazed at his brother with a confused emotion, intense and painful.

After a long silence, for she had begun to weep afresh, César, quite embarrassed, went on:

"Well, then, Mam'zelle Donet, I am going. When would you wish to talk this over with me?"

She exclaimed:

"Oh! no, don't go! don't go! Don't leave me all alone with Émile. I would die of grief. I have no longer any one, any one but my child. Oh! what wretchedness, what wretchedness. Monsieur César! Come, sit down again. Tell me something more. Tell me what he did at home all the week."

And César resumed his seat, accustomed to obey.

She drew over another chair for herself in front of the stove, where the dishes had all this time been heating, took

Émile upon her knees, and asked César a thousand questions about his father—questions of an intimate nature, which made him feel, without reasoning on the subject, that she had loved Hautot with all the strength of her weak woman's heart.

And, by the natural sequence of his ideas—which were rather limited in number—he recurred once more to the accident, and set about telling the story over again with all the same details.

When he said:

"He had a hole in his stomach that you could put your two fists into," she gave a sort of shriek, and her eyes again filled with tears.

Then, seized by the contagion of her grief, César began to weep, too, and as tears always soften the fibres of the heart, he bent over Émile, whose forehead was close to his own mouth, and kissed him.

The mother, recovering her breath, murmured:

"Poor child, he is an orphan now!"

"And so am I," said César.

And they were silent.

But suddenly the practical instinct of the housewife, accustomed to think of everything, revived in the young woman's breast.

"You have perhaps had nothing to eat all the morning, Monsieur César."

"No, mam'zelle."

"Oh! you must be hungry. You will eat a morsel."

"Thank you," he said, "I am not hungry; I have had too much sorrow."

She replied:

"In spite of sorrow, we must live. You will not refuse to let me get something for you! And then you will remain a little longer. When you are gone, I don't know what will become of me."

He yielded after some further resistance, and, sitting down with his back to the fire, facing her, he ate a plateful of tripe, which had been drying up in the gravy, and drank a glass of red wine. But he would not allow her to uncork the bottle of white wine. He several times wiped the mouth of the little boy who had smeared all his chin with gravy.

As he rose to take his leave, he asked:

"When would you like me to come back to talk about this matter, Mam'zelle Donet?"

"If it is all the same to you, say next Thursday, Monsieur César. In that way I shall not waste my time, as I always have my Thursdays free."

"That will suit me—next Thursday."

"You will come to luncheon, won't you?"

"Oh! As to that I can't promise."

"The reason I suggested it is, that people can chat better when they are eating. One has more time, too."

"Well, be it so. About twelve o'clock, then."

And he took his departure, after he had again kissed little Émile, and pressed Mademoiselle Donet's hand.

Part III

The week appeared long to César Hautot. He had never before lived alone, and the isolation seemed to him unendurable. Till now, he had lived at his father's side, just like his shadow, followed him into the fields, superintended the execution of his orders, and if they were separated for a short time they again met at dinner. They spent the evenings smoking their pipes together, sitting opposite each other, chatting about horses, cows, or sheep; and the grip of their hands when they rose in the morning was a manifestation of deep family affection.

Now César was alone. He went mechanically about his autumn duties on the farm, expecting any moment to see his father's tall, energetic outline rising up at the end of a level field. To kill time, he visited his neighbors, told about the accident to all who had not heard of it, and sometimes repeated it to the others. Then, having exhausted his occupations and his reflections, he would sit down at the side of the road, asking himself whether this kind of life was going to last forever.

He frequently thought of Mademoiselle Donet. He liked her. He considered her thoroughly respectable, a gentle, good young woman, as his father had said. Yes, undoubtedly she was a good girl. He resolved to act handsomely toward her, and to give her two thousand francs a year, settling the capital on the child. He even experienced a certain pleasure in thinking that he was going to see her on the following Thursday and arrange this matter with her. And then the thought of this brother, this little chap of five, who was his father's son, worried him, annoyed him a little, and, at the same time, pleased him. He had, as it were, a family in this youngster, sprung from a clandestine alliance, who would never bear the name of Hautot—a family which he might take or leave, just as he pleased, but which reminded him of his father.

And so, when he saw himself on the road to Rouen on Thursday morning, borne along by Graindorge with his measured trot, he felt his heart lighter, more at peace than it had been since his bereavement.

On entering Mademoiselle Donet's apartment, he saw the table laid as on the previous Thursday, with the sole difference that the crust had not been removed from the bread. He pressed the young woman's hand, kissed Émile on both cheeks, and sat down, more or less as if he were in his own house, although his heart was full. Mademoiselle Donet seemed to him a little thinner and paler. She must have grieved sorely. She now wore an air of constraint in his presence, as if she understood what she had not felt the week before under the first blow of her misfortune, and she exhibited an excessive deference toward him, a mournful humility, and made touching efforts to please him, as if to repay by her attentions the kindness he had manifested toward her. They were a long time at luncheon, talking over the business which had brought him there. She did not want so much money. It was too much. She earned enough to live on herself, but she only wished that Émile might find a few sous awaiting him when he grew up. César was firm, however, and even added a gift of a thousand francs for herself, for the expenses of mourning.

When he had taken his coffee, she asked:

"Do you smoke?"

"Yes—I have my pipe."

He felt in his pocket. Good heavens! He had forgotten it! He was becoming quite distressed about it when she offered him a pipe of his father's that had been put away in a closet. He took it up in his hand, recognized it, smelled it, spoke of its quality in a tone of emotion, filled it with tobacco, and lighted it. Then, he set Émile astride his knee, and gave him a ride, while she removed the tablecloth, and piled the soiled dishes under the sideboard, intending to wash them as soon as he was gone.

About three o'clock he rose regretfully, quite annoyed at the thought of having to go.

"Well! Mademoiselle Donet," he said, "I wish you good evening, and am delighted to have found you like this."

She remained standing before him, blushing, much

affected, and gazed at him while she thought of the father.

"Shall we not see one another again?" she said.

He replied simply:

"Why, yes, mademoiselle, if it gives you pleasure."

"Certainly, Monsieur César. Will next Thursday suit you?"

"Yes, Mademoiselle Donet."

"You will come to luncheon, of course?"

"Well—if you are so kind as to invite me, I can't refuse."

"It is understood, then, Monsieur César—next Thursday, at twelve, the same as to-day."

"Thursday at twelve, Mademoiselle Donet!"

Joseph Conrad

(1857–1924)

That he spoke English with a thick foreign accent and was twenty-one before he learned any English at all is perhaps the most astonishing aspect of the career of Joseph Conrad, one of the major English stylists. But it does not exhaust his unusual characteristics. Born Jozef Teodor Konrad Nalecz Korzeniowski in Russian-ruled Poland, he was the son of a Polish patriot who was exiled in Russia for his nationalist activities and died in 1869, leaving Conrad to be brought up by his maternal uncle and leaving him also with strong anti-Russian feelings which were to find expression in his powerful novel about a double agent, Under Western Eyes *(1910).*

In 1874 Conrad decided that he wanted to put to sea and made his first voyage on a French merchant ship. By 1878 he had signed on as an ordinary seaman on a small English coastal ship and begun to learn English. In 1886 he acquired both British citizenship and his master's certificate. In 1888 he received his first command and in 1890 took a steamboat up the Congo River, a voyage which not only made him severely ill but which haunted his imagination until he created out of it one of the most memorable short novels in the English language, Heart of Darkness. *He left the sea in 1895 when his first novel,* Almayer's Folly, *was published and settled down to a career as a writer. The following year he married an English girl and made his living as a writer until his death in 1924.*

As a novelist, Conrad proved himself both a master of English prose and of human psychology. Though for years he was considered a writer of adventure stories about the sea or the exotic places he had visited, his reputation today rests on his deep and subtle exploration of the moral and psychological ambiguities of existence. In Heart of Darkness *Kurtz is seen through the eyes of the narrator Marlowe (the intermediate narrator was one of Conrad's favorite devices) as an exemplar of the possibilities of human heroism and endurance despite the fact that he is also corrupted beyond redemption.* The Secret Sharer *(1912) depicts a young sea captain whose ship is becalmed in the Gulf of Siam apparently communicating with his double. But the captain is actually communicating with his own isolation and singularity. Conrad catches his characters in moments of great personal stress and tension, when they are faced with succumbing to the terror, loneliness, need for approval that exists within every man. Human sympathy in his novels and stories is aroused through the communion of those who have been challenged and who have come through the challenge with integrity.*

In such later novels as Nostromo *(1904),* Under Western Eyes, *and* The Secret Agent *(1906), Conrad turned his essentially pessimistic vision on politics and intrigue. His pessimism took a markedly aristocratic turn.*

Conrad's tremendous power and subtlety are to be found in his incessant attempt to find his secret self in his encounters with the sea. If he scorned the possibility of political solutions to human problems, this was in large part traceable to his need for total self-realization. He had served, as had his father before him, as an exile. But where his father's exile was distinctly political, Conrad's was more attuned to the inevitable exile of the artist.

Conrad's short stories are similar to his novels in that they focus almost exclusively on character development. Men are thrust into a crisis or a situation in which, in order to survive, they must rally the best within them. In the two white men we meet in "An Outpost of Progress," we witness a total moral disintegration. Both Kayerts and Carlier are "two perfectly insignificant and incapable individuals, whose existence is only rendered possible through the high organization of civilized crowds." Their ghastly end is seen as the jungle's implacable response to what they brought to it. "An Outpost of Progress" is vintage Conrad—a great story by a great writer.

An Outpost of Progress

There were two white men in charge of the trading station. Kayerts, the chief, was short and fat; Carlier, the assistant, was tall, with a large head and a very broad trunk perched upon a long pair of thin legs. The third man on the staff was a Sierra Leone nigger, who maintained that his name was Henry Price. However, for some reason or other, the

natives down the river had given him the name of Makola,
and it stuck to him through all his wanderings about the
country. He spoke English and French with a warbling
accent, wrote a beautiful hand, understood bookkeeping,
and cherished in his innermost heart the worship of evil
spirits. His wife was a negress from Loanda, very large
and very noisy. Three children rolled about in sunshine
before the door of his low, shed-like dwelling. Makola,
taciturn and impenetrable, despised the two white men.
He had charge of a small clay storehouse with a dried-
grass roof, and pretended to keep a correct account of
beads, cotton cloth, red kerchiefs, brass wire, and other
trade goods it contained. Besides the storehouse and
Makola's hut, there was only one large building in the
cleared ground of the station. It was built neatly of reeds,
with a veranda on all the four sides. There were three
rooms in it. The one in the middle was the living room,
and had two rough tables and a few stools in it. The other
two were the bedrooms for the white men. Each had a
bedstead and a mosquito net for all furniture. The plank
floor was littered with the belongings of the white men;
open half-empty boxes, torn wearing apparel, old boots;
all the things dirty, and all the things broken, that accumulate mysteriously round untidy men. There was also
another dwelling place some distance away from the
buildings. In it, under a tall cross much out of the perpen-
dicular, slept the man who had seen the beginning of all
this; who had planned and had watched the construction
of this outpost of progress. He had been, at home, an
unsuccessful painter who, weary of pursuing fame on an
empty stomach, had gone out there through high protec-
tions. He had been the first chief of that station. Makola
had watched the energetic artist die of fever in the just-
finished house with his usual kind of "I told you so" indifference. Then, for a time, he dwelt alone with his family, his account books, and the Evil Spirit that rules the
lands under the equator. He got on very well with his god.
Perhaps he had propitiated him by a promise of more
white men to play with, by and by. At any rate the director
of the Great Trading Company, coming up in a steamer
that resembled an enormous sardine box with a flat-roofed
shed erected on it, found the station in good order, and
Makola as usual quietly diligent. The director had the
cross put up over the first agent's grave, and appointed
Kayerts to the post. Carlier was told off as second in
charge. The director was a man ruthless and efficient, who

at times, but very imperceptibly, indulged in grim humor. He made a speech to Kayerts and Carlier, pointing out to them the promising aspect of their station. The nearest trading post was about three hundred miles away. It was an exceptional opportunity for them to distinguish themselves and to earn percentages on the trade. This appointment was a favor done to beginners. Kayerts was moved almost to tears by his director's kindness. He would, he said, by doing his best, try to justify the flattering confidence, etc., etc. Kayerts had been in the Administration of the Telegraphs, and knew how to express himself correctly. Carlier, an ex-noncommissioned officer of cavalry in an army guaranteed from harm by several European powers, was less impressed. If there were commissions to get, so much the better; and, trailing a sulky glance over the river, the forests, the impenetrable bush that seemed to cut off the station from the rest of the world, he muttered between his teeth, "We shall see, very soon."

Next day, some bales of cotton goods and a few cases of provisions having been thrown on shore, the sardine-box steamer went off, not to return for another six months. On the deck the director touched his cap to the two agents, who stood on the bank waving their hats, and turning to an old servant of the Company on his passage to headquarters, said, "Look at those two imbeciles. They must be mad at home to send me such specimens. I told those fellows to plant a vegetable garden, build new storehouses and fences, and construct a landing stage. I bet nothing will be done! They won't know how to begin. I always thought the station on this river useless, and they just fit the station!"

"They will form themselves there," said the old stager with a quiet smile.

"At any rate, I am rid of them for six months," retorted the director.

The two men watched the steamer round the bend, then, ascending arm in arm the slope of the bank, returned to the station. They had been in this vast and dark country only a very short time, and as yet always in the midst of other white men, under the eye and guidance of their superiors. And now, dull as they were to the subtle influences of surroundings, they felt themselves very much alone, when suddenly left unassisted to face the wilderness; a wilderness rendered more strange, more incomprehensible by the mysterious glimpses of the vigorous life it contained. They were two perfectly insignificant and incapable individuals, whose existence is only rendered possible through the high organization of civilized crowds. Few men realize that their life, the very essence of their character, their capabilities and their audacities, are only the expression of their belief in the safety of their surroundings. The courage, the composure, the confidence; the emotions and principles; every great and every insignificant thought belongs not to the individual but to the crowd: to the crowd that believes blindly in the irresistible force of its institutions and of its morals, in the power of its police and of its opinion. But the contact with pure unmitigated savagery, with primitive nature and primitive man, brings sudden and profound trouble into the heart. To the sentiment of being alone of one's kind, to the clear perception of the loneliness of one's thoughts, of one's sensations—to the negation of the habitual, which is safe, there is added the affirmation of the unusual, which is dangerous; a suggestion of things vague, uncontrollable, and repulsive, whose discomposing intrusion excites the imagination and tries the civilized nerves of the foolish and the wise alike.

Kayerts and Carlier walked arm in arm, drawing close to one another as children do in the dark, and they had the same, not altogether unpleasant, sense of danger which one half suspects to be imaginary. They chatted persistently in familiar tones. "Our station is prettily situated," said one. The other assented with enthusiasm, enlarging volubly on the beauties of the situation. Then they passed near the grave. "Poor devil!" said Kayerts. "He died of fever, didn't he?" muttered Carlier, stopping short. "Why," retorted Kayerts, with indignation, "I've been told that the fellow exposed himself recklessly to the sun. The climate here, everybody says, is not at all worse than at home, as long as you keep out of the sun. Do you hear that, Carlier? I am chief here, and my orders are that you should not expose yourself to the sun!" He assumed his superiority jocularly, but his meaning was serious. The idea that he would, perhaps, have to bury Carlier and remain alone, gave him an inward shiver. He felt suddenly that this Carlier was more precious to him here, in the center of Africa, than a brother could be anywhere else. Carlier, entering into the spirit of the thing, made a military salute and answered in a brisk tone, "Your orders shall be attended to, chief!" Then he burst out laughing, slapped Kayerts on the back and shouted, "We shall let life run easily here! Just sit still and gather in the ivory those savages will bring. This country has its good points, after all!" They both laughed loudly while Carlier thought: "That poor Kayerts; he is so fat and unhealthy. It would be awful if I had to bury him here. He is a man I respect." . . . Before they reached the veranda of their house they called one another "my dear fellow."

The first day they were very active, pottering about with hammers and nails and red calico, to put up curtains, make their house habitable and pretty; resolved to settle down comfortably to their new life. For them an impossible task. To grapple effectually with even purely material problems requires more serenity of mind and more lofty courage than people generally imagine. No two beings could have been more unfitted for such a struggle. Society, not from any tenderness, but because of its strange needs, had taken care of those two men, forbidding them all independent thought, all initiative, all departure from routine; and forbidding it under pain of death. They could only live on condition of being machines. And now, released from the fostering care of men with pens behind the ears, or of men with gold lace on the sleeves, they were like those life-long prisoners who, liberated after many years, do not know what use to make of their freedom. They did not know what use to make of their faculties, being both, through want of practice, incapable of independent thought.

At the end of two months Kayerts often would say, "If it was not for my Melie, you wouldn't catch me here." Melie was his daughter. He had thrown up his post in the Administration of the Telegraphs, though he had been for seventeen years perfectly happy there, to earn a dowry for his girl. His wife was dead, and the child was being brought up by his sisters. He regretted the streets, the pavements, the cafés, his friends of many years; all the things he used to see, day after day; all the thoughts suggested by familiar things—the thoughts effortless, monotonous, and soothing of a Government clerk; he regretted all the gossip, the small enmities, the mild venom, and the little jokes of Government offices. "If I had had a decent brother-in-law," Carlier would remark, "a fellow with a heart, I would not be here." He had left the army and had made himself so obnoxious to his family by his laziness and impudence, that an exasperated brother-in-law had made superhuman efforts to procure him an appointment in the Company as a second-class agent. Having not a penny in the world he was compelled to accept this means

of livelihood as soon as it became quite clear to him that
there was nothing more to squeeze out of his relations. He,
like Kayerts, regretted his old life. He regretted the clink
of saber and spurs on a fine afternoon, the barrack-room
witticisms, the girls of garrison towns; but, besides, he had
also a sense of grievance. He was evidently a much ill-used
man. This made him moody, at times. But the two men got
on well together in the fellowship of their stupidity and
laziness. Together they did nothing, absolutely nothing,
and enjoyed the sense of the idleness for which they were
paid. And in time they came to feel something resembling
affection for one another.

They lived like blind men in a large room, aware only
of what came in contact with them (and of that only im-
perfectly), but unable to see the general aspect of things.
The river, the forest, all the great land throbbing with
life, were like a great emptiness. Even the brilliant sunshine disclosed nothing intelligible. Things appeared and
disappeared before their eyes in an unconnected and aimless kind of way. The river seemed to come from nowhere
and flow nowhither. It flowed through a void. Out of that
void, at times, came canoes, and men with spears in their
hands would suddenly crowd the yard of the station. They
were naked, glossy black, ornamented with snowy shells
and glistening brass wire, perfect of limb. They made an
uncouth babbling noise when they spoke, moved in a
stately manner, and sent quick, wild glances out of their
startled, never-resting eyes. Those warriors would squat
in long rows, four or more deep, before the veranda, while
their chiefs bargained for hours with Makola over an ele-
phant tusk. Kayerts sat on his chair and looked down on
the proceedings, understanding nothing. He stared at them
with his round blue eyes, called out to Carlier, "Here,
look! look at that fellow there—and that other one, to the
left. Did you ever see such a face? Oh, the funny brute!"

Carlier, smoking native tobacco in a short wooden pipe,
would swagger up twirling his mustaches, and surveying
the warriors with haughty indulgence, would say:

"Fine animals. Brought any bone? Yes? It's not any too
soon. Look at the muscles of that fellow—third from the
end. I wouldn't care to get a punch on the nose from him.
Fine arms, but legs no good below the knee. Couldn't
make cavalry men of them." And after glancing down
complacently at his own shanks, he always concluded,
"Pah! Don't they stink! You, Makola! Take that herd

over to the fetish" (the storehouse was in every station called the fetish, perhaps because of the spirit of civilization it contained) "and give them up some of the rubbish you keep there. I'd rather see it full of bone than full of rags."

Kayerts approved.

"Yes, yes! Go and finish that palaver over there, Mr. Makola. I will come round when you are ready, to weigh the tusk. We must be careful." Then turning to his companion: "This is the tribe that lives down the river; they are rather aromatic. I remember, they had been once before here. D'ye hear that row? What a fellow has got to put up with in this dog of a country! My head is split."

Such profitable visits were rare. For days the two pioneers of trade and progress would look on their empty courtyard in the vibrating brilliance of vertical sunshine. Below the high bank, the silent river flowed on glittering and steady. On the sands in the middle of the stream, hippos and alligators sunned themselves side by side. And stretching away in all directions, surrounding the insignificant cleared spot of the trading post, immense forests, hiding fateful complications of fantastic life, lay in the eloquent silence of mute greatness. The two men understood nothing, cared for nothing but for the passage of days that separated them from the steamer's return. Their predecessor had left some torn books. They took up these wrecks of novels, and, as they had never read anything of the kind before, they were surprised and amused. Then during long days there were interminable and silly discussions about plots and personages. In the center of Africa they made acquaintance of Richelieu and of d'Artagnan, of Hawk's Eye and of Father Goriot, and of many other people. All these imaginary personages became subjects for gossip as if they had been living friends. They discounted their virtues, suspected their motives, decried their successes; were scandalized at their duplicity or were doubtful about their courage. The accounts of crimes filled them with indignation, while tender or pathetic passages moved them deeply. Carlier cleared his throat and said in a soldierly voice, "What nonsense!" Kayerts, his round eyes suffused with tears, his fat cheeks quivering, rubbed his bald head, and declared, "This is a splendid book. I had no idea there were such clever fellows in the world." They also found some old copies of a home paper. That print discussed what it was pleased to call "Our Colonial Expansion" in high-flown language. It spoke much of the

rights and duties of civilization, of the sacredness of the
civilizing work, and extolled the merits of those who went
about bringing light, and faith, and commerce to the dark
places of the earth. Carlier and Kayerts read, wondered,
and began to think better of themselves. Carlier said one
evening, waving his hand about, "In a hundred years,
there will be perhaps a town here. Quays, and warehouses,
and barracks, and—and—billiard rooms. Civilization, my
boy, and virtue—and all. And then, chaps will read that
two good fellows, Kayerts and Carlier, were the first
civilized men to live in this very spot!" Kayerts nodded,
"Yes, it is a consolation to think of that." They seemed
to forget their dead predecessor; but, early one day,
Carlier went out and replanted the cross firmly. "It used
to make me squint whenever I walked that way," he
explained to Kayerts over the morning coffee. "It made
me squint, leaning over so much. So I just planted it upright. And solid, I promise you! I suspended myself with
both hands to the cross-piece. Not a move. Oh, I did that
properly."

At times Gobila came to see them. Gobila was the chief
of the neighboring villages. He was a gray-headed savage,
thin and black, with a white cloth round his loins and a
mangy panther skin hanging over his back. He came up
with long strides of his skeleton legs, swinging a staff as
tall as himself, and, entering the common room of the
station, would squat on his heels to the left of the door.
There he sat, watching Kayerts, and now and then making
a speech which the other did not understand. Kayerts,
without interrupting his occupation, would from time to
time say in a friendly manner: "How goes it, you old
image?" and they would smile at one another. The two
whites had a liking for that old and incomprehensible
creature, and called him Father Gobila. Gobila's manner
was paternal, and he seemed really to love all white men.
They all appeared to him very young, indistinguishably
alike (except for stature), and he knew that they were all
brothers, and also immortal. The death of the artist, who
was the first white man whom he knew intimately, did not
disturb this belief, because he was firmly convinced that
the white stranger had pretended to die and got himself
buried for some mysterious purpose of his own, into which
it was useless to inquire. Perhaps it was his way of going
home to his own country? At any rate, these were his
brothers, and he transferred his absurd affection to them.
They returned it in a way. Carlier slapped him on the

back, and recklessly struck off matches for his amusement. Kayerts was always ready to let him have a sniff at the ammonia bottle. In short, they behaved just like that other white creature that had hidden itself in a hole in the ground. Gobila considered them attentively. Perhaps they were the same being with the other—or one of them was. He couldn't decide—clear up that mystery; but he remained always very friendly. In consequence of that friendship the women of Gobila's village walked in single file through the reedy grass, bringing every morning to the station, fowls, and sweet potatoes, and palm wine, and sometimes a goat. The Company never provisions the stations fully, and the agents required those local supplies to live. They had them through the good will of Gobila, and lived well. Now and then one of them had a bout of fever, and the other nursed him with gentle devotion. They did not think much of it. It left them weaker, and their appearance changed for the worse. Carlier was hollow-eyed and irritable. Kayerts showed a drawn, flabby face above the rotundity of his stomach, which gave him a weird aspect. But being constantly together, they did not notice the change that took place gradually in their appearance, and also in their dispositions.

Five months passed in that way.

Then, one morning, as Kayerts and Carlier, lounging in their chairs under the veranda, talked about the approaching visit of the steamer, a knot of armed men came out of the forest and advanced towards the station. They were strangers to that part of the country. They were tall, slight, draped classically from neck to heel in blue fringed cloths, and carried percussion muskets over their bare right shoulders. Makola showed signs of excitement, and ran out of the storehouse (where he spent all his days) to meet these visitors. They came into the courtyard and looked about them with steady, scornful glances. Their leader, a powerful and determined-looking Negro with bloodshot eyes, stood in front of the veranda and made a long speech. He gesticulated much, and ceased very suddenly.

There was something in his intonation, in the sounds of the long sentences he used, that startled the two whites. It was like a reminiscence of something not exactly familiar, and yet resembling the speech of civilized men. It sounded like one of those impossible languages which sometimes we hear in our dreams.

"What lingo is that?" said the amazed Carlier. "In the

first moment I fancied the fellow was going to speak French. Anyway, it is a different kind of gibberish to what we ever heard."

"Yes," replied Kayerts. "Hey, Makola, what does he say? Where do they come from? Who are they?"

But Makola, who seemed to be standing on hot bricks, answered hurriedly, "I don't know. They come from very far. Perhaps Mrs. Price will understand. They are perhaps bad men."

The leader, after waiting for a while, said something sharply to Makola, who shook his head. Then the man, after looking round, noticed Makola's hut and walked over there. The next moment Mrs. Makola was heard speaking with great volubility. The other strangers—they were six in all—strolled about with an air of ease, put their heads through the door of the storeroom, congregated round the grave, pointed understandingly at the cross, and generally made themselves at home.

"I don't like those chaps—and, I say, Kayerts, they must be from the coast; they've got firearms," observed the sagacious Carlier.

Kayerts also did not like those chaps. They both, for the first time, became aware that they lived in conditions where the unusual may be dangerous, and that there was no power on earth outside of themselves to stand between them and the unusual. They became uneasy, went in and loaded their revolvers. Kayerts said, "We must order Makola to tell them to go away before dark."

The strangers left in the afternoon, after eating a meal prepared for them by Mrs. Makola. The immense woman was excited, and talked much with the visitors. She rattled away shrilly, pointing here and there at the forests and at the river. Makola sat apart and watched. At times he got up and whispered to his wife. He accompanied the strangers across the ravine at the back of the station-ground, and returned slowly looking very thoughtful. When questioned by the white men he was very strange, seemed not to understand, seemed to have forgotten French—seemed to have forgotten how to speak altogether. Kayerts and Carlier agreed that the nigger had had too much palm wine.

There was some talk about keeping a watch in turn, but in the evening everything seemed so quiet and peaceful that they retired as usual. All night they were disturbed by a lot of drumming in the villages. A deep, rapid roll nearby would be followed by another far off—then all ceased. Some short appeals would rattle out here and there, then all mingle together, increase, become vigorous and sustained, would spread out over the forest, roll through the night, unbroken and ceaseless, near and far, as if the whole land had been one immense drum booming out steadily an appeal to heaven. And through the deep and tremendous noise sudden yells that resembled snatches of songs from a madhouse darted shrill and high in discordant jets of sound which seemed to rush far above the earth and drive all peace from under the stars.

Carlier and Kayerts slept badly. They both thought they had heard shots fired during the night—but they could not agree as to the direction. In the morning Makola was gone somewhere. He returned about noon with one of yesterday's strangers, and eluded all Kayerts' attempts to close with him: had become deaf apparently. Kayerts wondered. Carlier, who had been fishing off the bank, came back and remarked while he showed his catch, "The niggers seem to be in a deuce of a stir; I wonder what's up. I saw about fifteen canoes cross the river during the two hours I was there fishing." Kayerts, worried, said, "Isn't this Makola very queer today?" Carlier advised, "Keep all our men together in case of some trouble."

II

There were ten station men who had been left by the Director. Those fellows, having engaged themselves to the Company for six months (without having any idea of a month in particular and only a very faint notion of time in general), had been serving the cause of progress for upwards of two years. Belonging to a tribe from a very distant part of the land of darkness and sorrow, they did not run away, naturally supposing that as wandering strangers they would be killed by the inhabitants of the country; in which they were right. They lived in straw huts on the slope of a ravine overgrown with reedy grass, just behind the station buildings. They were not happy, regretting the festive incantations, the sorceries, the human sacrifices of their own land; where they also had parents, brothers, sisters, admired chiefs, respected magicians, loved friends, and other ties supposed generally to be human. Besides, the rice rations served out by the Company did not agree with them, being a food unknown to their land, and to which they could not get used. Consequently they were unhealthy and miserable. Had they been of any other tribe they would have made up their minds to die—for nothing is easier to certain savages than suicide —and so have escaped from the puzzling difficulties of existence. But belonging, as they did, to a warlike tribe with filed teeth, they had more grit, and went on stupidly living through disease and sorrow. They did very little work, and had lost their splendid physique. Carlier and Kayerts doctored them assiduously without being able to bring them back into condition again. They were mustered every morning and told off to different tasks—grass-cutting, fence-building, tree-felling, etc., etc., which no power on earth could induce them to execute efficiently. The two whites had practically very little control over them.

In the afternoon Makola came over to the big house and found Kayerts watching three heavy columns of smoke rising above the forests. "What is that?" asked Kayerts. "Some villages burn," answered Makola, who seemed to have regained his wits. Then he said abruptly: "We have got very little ivory; bad six months' trading. Do you like get a little more ivory?"

"Yes," said Kayerts, eagerly. He thought of percentages which were low.

"Those men who came yesterday are traders from Loanda who have got more ivory than they can carry home. Shall I buy? I know their camp."

"Certainly," said Kayerts. "What are those traders?"

"Bad fellows," said Makola, indifferently. "They fight with people, and catch women and children. They are bad men, and got guns. There is a great disturbance in the country. Do you want ivory?"

"Yes," said Kayerts. Makola said nothing for a while. Then: "Those workmen of ours are no good at all," he muttered, looking round. "Station in very bad order, sir. Director will growl. Better get a fine lot of ivory, then he say nothing."

"I can't help it; the men won't work," said Kayerts. "When will you get that ivory?"

"Very soon," said Makola. "Perhaps tonight. You leave it to me, and keep indoors, sir. I think you had better give some palm wine to our men to make a dance this evening. Enjoy themselves. Work better tomorrow. There's plenty palm wine—gone a little sour."

Kayerts said "yes," and Makola, with his own hands, carried big calabashes to the door of his hut. They stood there till the evening, and Mrs. Makola looked into every one. The men got them at sunset. When Kayerts and Carlier retired, a big bonfire was flaring before the men's huts. They could hear their shouts and drumming. Some men from Gobila's village had joined the station hands, and the entertainment was a great success.

In the middle of the night, Carlier, waking suddenly, heard a man shout loudly; then a shot was fired. Only one. Carlier ran out and met Kayerts on the veranda. They were both startled. As they went across the yard to call Makola, they saw shadows moving in the night. One of them cried, "Don't shoot! It's me, Price." Then Makola appeared close to them. "Go back, go back, please," he urged, "you spoil all." "There are strange men about," said Carlier. "Never mind; I know," said Makola. Then he whispered, "All right. Bring ivory. Say nothing! I know my business." The two white men reluctantly went back to the house, but did not sleep. They heard footsteps, whispers, some groans. It seemed as if a lot of men came in, dumped heavy things on the ground, squabbled a long time, then went away. They lay on their hard beds and thought: "This Makola is invaluable." In the morning Carlier came out, very sleepy, and pulled at the cord of the big bell. The station hands mustered every morning to the sound of the bell. That morning nobody came. Kayerts turned out also, yawning. Across the yard they saw Makola come out of his hut, a tin basin of soapy water in his hand. Makola, a civilized nigger, was very neat in his person. He threw the soapsuds skillfully over a wretched little yellow cur he had, then turning his face to the agent's house, he shouted from the distance, "All the men gone last night!"

They heard him plainly, but in their surprise they both yelled out together: "What!" Then they stared at one another. "We are in a proper fix now," growled Carlier. "It's incredible!" muttered Kayerts. "I will go to the huts and see," said Carlier, striding off. Makola coming up found Kayerts standing alone.

"I can hardly believe it," said Kayerts tearfully. "We took care of them as if they had been our children."

"They went with the coast people," said Makola after a moment of hesitation.

"What do I care with whom they went—the ungrateful brutes!" exclaimed the other. Then with sudden suspicion, and looking hard at Makola, he added: "What do you know about it?"

Makola moved his shoulders, looking down on the ground. "What do I know? I think only. Will you come and look at the ivory I've got there? It is a fine lot. You never saw such."

He moved towards the store. Kayerts followed him mechanically, thinking about the incredible desertion of the men. On the ground before the door of the fetish lay six splendid tusks.

"What did you give for it?" asked Kayerts, after surveying the lot with satisfaction.

"No regular trade," said Makola. "They brought the ivory and gave it to me. I told them to take what they most wanted in the station. It is a beautiful lot. No station can show such tusks. Those traders wanted carriers badly, and our men were no good here. No trade, no entry in books; all correct."

Kayerts nearly burst with indignation. "Why!" he shouted, "I believe you have sold our men for these tusks!" Makola stood impassive and silent. "I—I—will—I," stuttered Kayerts. "You fiend!" he yelled out.

"I did the best for you and the Company," said Makola, imperturbably. "Why you shout so much? Look at this tusk."

"I dismiss you! I will report you—I won't look at the tusk. I forbid you to touch them. I order you to throw them into the river. You—you!"

"You very red, Mr. Kayerts. If you are so irritable in the sun, you will get fever and die—like the first chief!" pronounced Makola impressively.

They stood still, contemplating one another with intense eyes, as if they had been looking with effort across immense distances. Kayerts shivered. Makola had meant no more than he said, but his words seemed to Kayerts full of ominous menace! He turned sharply and went away to the house. Makola retired into the bosom of his family; and the tusks, left lying before the store, looked very large and valuable in the sunshine.

Carlier came back on the veranda. "They're all gone, hey?" asked Kayerts from the far end of the common room in a muffled voice. "You did not find anybody?"

"Oh, yes," said Carlier, "I found one of Gobila's people lying dead before the huts—shot through the body. We heard that shot last night."

Kayerts came out quickly. He found his companion

staring grimly over the yard at the tusks, away by the store. They both sat in silence for a while. Then Kayerts related his conversation with Makola. Carlier said nothing. At the midday meal they ate very little. They hardly exchanged a word that day. A great silence seemed to lie heavily over the station and press on their lips. Makola did not open the store; he spent the day playing with his children. He lay full-length on a mat outside his door, and the youngsters sat on his chest and clambered all over him. It was a touching picture. Mrs. Makola was busy cooking all day as usual. The white men made a somewhat better meal in the evening. Afterwards, Carlier smoking his pipe strolled over to the store; he stood for a long time over the tusks, touched one or two with his foot, even tried to lift the largest one by its small end. He came back to his chief, who had not stirred from the veranda, threw himself in the chair and said:

"I can see it! They were pounced upon while they slept heavily after drinking all that palm wine you've allowed Makola to give them. A put-up job! See? The worst is, some of Gobila's people were there, and got carried off too, no doubt. The least drunk woke up, and got shot for his sobriety. This is a funny country. What will you do now?"

"We can't touch it, of course," said Kayerts.

"Of course not," assented Carlier.

"Slavery is an awful thing," stammered out Kayerts in an unsteady voice.

"Frightful—the sufferings," grunted Carlier with conviction.

They believed their words. Everybody shows a respectful deference to certain sounds that he and his fellows can make. But about feelings people really know nothing. We talk with indignation or enthusiasm; we talk about oppression, cruelty, crime, devotion, self-sacrifice, virtue, and we know nothing real beyond the words. Nobody knows what suffering or sacrifice mean—except, perhaps, the victims of the mysterious purpose of these illusions.

Next morning they saw Makola very busy setting up in the yard the big scales used for weighing ivory. By and by Carlier said: "What's that filthy scoundrel up to?" and lounged out into the yard. Kayerts followed. They stood watching. Makola took no notice. When the balance was swung true, he tried to lift a tusk into the scale. It was too heavy. He looked up helplessly without a word, and for a minute they stood round that balance as mute and still as

three statues. Suddenly Carlier said: "Catch hold of the
other end, Makola—you beast!" and together they swung
the tusk up. Kayerts trembled in every limb. He muttered,
"I say! O! I say!" and putting his hand in his pocket found
there a dirty bit of paper and the stump of a pencil. He
turned his back on the others, as if about to do something
tricky, and noted stealthily the weights which Carlier
shouted out to him with unnecessary loudness. When all
was over Makola whispered to himself: "The sun's very
strong here for the tusks." Carlier said to Kayerts in a
careless tone: "I say, chief, I might just as well give him
a lift with this lot into the store."

As they were going back to the house Kayerts observed
with a sigh: "It had to be done." And Carlier said: "It's
deplorable, but, the men being Company's men the ivory
is Company's ivory. We must look after it." "I will report
to the Director, of course," said Kayerts. "Of course; let
him decide," approved Carlier.

At midday they made a hearty meal. Kayerts sighed
from time to time. Whenever they mentioned Makola's
name they always added to it an opprobrious epithet. It
eased their conscience. Makola gave himself a half-holiday,
and bathed his children in the river. No one from Gobila's
villages came near the station that day. No one came the
next day, and the next, nor for a whole week. Gobila's
people might have been dead and buried for any sign of
life they gave. But they were only mourning for those they
had lost by the witchcraft of white men, who had brought
wicked people into their country. The wicked people were
gone, but fear remained. Fear always remains. A man
may destroy everything within himself, love and hate and
belief, and even doubt; but as long as he clings to life he
cannot destroy fear: the fear, subtle, indestructible, and
terrible, that pervades his being; that tinges his thoughts;
that lurks in his heart; that watches on his lips the struggle
of his last breath. In his fear, the mild old Gobila offered
extra human sacrifices to all the Evil Spirits that had taken
possession of his white friends. His heart was heavy. Some
warriors spoke about burning and killing, but the cautious
old savage dissuaded them. Who could foresee the woe
those mysterious creatures, if irritated, might bring? They
should be left alone. Perhaps in time they would disappear
into the earth as the first one had disappeared. His people
must keep away from them, and hope for the best.

Kayerts and Carlier did not disappear, but remained
above on this earth, that, somehow, they fancied had be-

come bigger and very empty. It was not the absolute and dumb solitude of the post that impressed them so much as an inarticulate feeling that something from within them was gone, something that worked for their safety, and had kept the wilderness from interfering with their hearts. The images of home; the memory of people like them, of men that thought and felt as they used to think and feel, receded into distances made indistinct by the glare of unclouded sunshine. And out of the great silence of the surrounding wilderness, its very hopelessness and savagery seemed to approach them nearer, to draw them gently, to look upon them, to envelop them with a solicitude irresistible, familiar, and disgusting.

Days lengthened into weeks, then into months. Gobila's people drummed and yelled to every new moon, as of yore, but kept away from the station. Makola and Carlier tried once in a canoe to open communications, but were received with a shower of arrows, and had to fly back to the station for dear life. That attempt set the country up and down the river into an uproar that could be very distinctly heard for days. The steamer was late. At first they spoke of delay jauntily, then anxiously, then gloomily. The matter was becoming serious. Stores were running short. Carlier cast his lines off the bank, but the river was low, and the fish kept out in the stream. They dared not stroll far away from the station to shoot. Moreover, there was no game in the impenetrable forest. Once Carlier shot a hippo in the river. They had no boat to secure it, and it sank. When it floated up it drifted away, and Gobila's people secured the carcass. It was the occasion for a national holiday, but Carlier had a fit of rage over it and talked about the necessity of exterminating all the niggers before the country could be made habitable. Kayerts mooned about silently; spent hours looking at the portrait of his Melie. It represented a little girl with long bleached tresses and a rather sour face. His legs were much swollen, and he could hardly walk. Carlier, undermined by fever, could not swagger any more, but kept tottering about, still with a devil-may-care air, as became a man who remembered his crack regiment. He had become hoarse, sarcastic, and inclined to say unpleasant things. He called it "being frank with you." They had long ago reckoned their percentages on trade, including in them that last deal of "this infamous Makola." They had also concluded not to say anything about it. Kayerts hesitated at first—was afraid of the Director.

"He has seen worse things done on the quiet," maintained Carlier, with a hoarse laugh. "Trust him! He won't thank you if you blab. He is no better than you or me. Who will talk if we hold our tongues? There is nobody here."

That was the root of the trouble! There was nobody there; and being left there alone with their weakness, they became daily more like a pair of accomplices than like a couple of devoted friends. They had heard nothing from home for eight months. Every evening they said, "Tomorrow we shall see the steamer." But one of the Company's steamers had been wrecked, and the Director was busy with the other, relieving very distant and important stations on the main river. He thought that the useless station, and the useless men, could wait. Meantime Kayerts and Carlier lived on rice boiled without salt, and cursed the Company, all Africa, and the day they were born. One must have lived on such diet to discover what ghastly trouble the necessity of swallowing one's food may become. There was literally nothing else in the station but rice and coffee; they drank the coffee without sugar. The last fifteen lumps Kayerts had solemnly locked away in his box, together with a half-bottle of cognac, "in case of sickness," he explained. Carlier approved. "When one is sick," he said, "any little extra like that is cheering."

They waited. Rank grass began to sprout over the courtyard. The bell never rang now. Days passed, silent, exasperating, and slow. When the two men spoke, they snarled; and their silences were bitter, as if tinged by the bitterness of their thoughts.

One day after a lunch of boiled rice, Carlier put down his cup untasted, and said: "Hang it all! Let's have a decent cup of coffee for once. Bring out that sugar, Kayerts!"

"For the sick," muttered Kayerts, without looking up.

"For the sick," mocked Carlier. "Bosh! . . . Well! I am sick."

"You are no more sick than I am, and I go without," said Kayerts in a peaceful tone.

"Come! Out with that sugar, you stingy old slave dealer."

Kayerts looked up quickly. Carlier was smiling with marked insolence. And suddenly it seemed to Kayerts that he had never seen that man before. Who was he? He knew nothing about him. What was he capable of? There was a surprising flash of violent emotion within him, as if in the presence of something undreamt-of, dangerous, and final. But he managed to pronounce with composure:

"That joke is in very bad taste. Don't repeat it."

"Joke!" said Carlier, hitching himself forward on his seat. "I am hungry—I am sick—I don't joke! I hate hypocrites. You are a hypocrite. You are a slave dealer. I am a slave dealer. There's nothing but slave dealers in this cursed country. I mean to have sugar in my coffee today, anyhow!"

"I forbid you to speak to me in that way," said Kayerts with a fair show of resolution.

"You!—What?" shouted Carlier, jumping up.

Kayerts stood up also. "I am your chief," he began, trying to master the shakiness of his voice.

"What?" yelled the other. "Who's chief? There's no chief here. There's nothing here: there's nothing but you and I. Fetch the sugar—you pot-bellied ass."

"Hold your tongue. Go out of this room," screamed Kayerts. "I dismiss you—you scoundrel!"

Carlier swung a stool. All at once he looked dangerously in earnest. "You flabby, good-for-nothing civilian—take that!" he howled.

Kayerts dropped under the table, and the stool struck the grass inner wall of the room. Then, as Carlier was trying to upset the table, Kayerts in desperation made a blind rush, head low, like a cornered pig would do, and overturning his friend, bolted along the veranda, and into his room. He locked the door, snatched his revolver, and stood panting. In less than a minute Carlier was kicking at the door furiously, howling, "If you don't bring out that sugar, I will shoot you at sight, like a dog. Now then—one—two—three. You won't? I will show you who's the master."

Kayerts thought the door would fall in, and scrambled through the square hole that served for a window in his room. There was then the whole breadth of the house between them. But the other was apparently not strong enough to break in the door, and Kayerts heard him running round. Then he also began to run laboriously on his swollen legs. He ran as quickly as he could, grasping the revolver, and unable yet to understand what was happening to him. He saw in succession Makola's house, the store, the river, the ravine, and the low bushes; and he saw all those things again as he ran for the second time round the house. Then again they flashed past him. That morning he could not have walked a yard without a groan.

And now he ran. He ran fast enough to keep out of sight of the other man.

Then as, weak and desperate, he thought, "Before I finish the next round I shall die," he heard the other man stumble heavily, then stop. He stopped also. He had the back and Carlier the front of the house, as before. He heard him drop into a chair cursing, and suddenly his own legs gave way, and he slid down into a sitting posture with his back to the wall. His mouth was as dry as a cinder, and his face was wet with perspiration—and tears. What was it all about? He thought it must be a horrible illusion; he thought he was dreaming; he thought he was going mad! After a while he collected his senses. What did they quarrel about? That sugar! How absurd! He would give it to him—didn't want it himself. And he began scrambling to his feet with a sudden feeling of security. But before he had fairly stood upright, a common-sense reflection occurred to him and drove him back into despair. He thought: "If I give way now to that brute of a soldier, he will begin this horror again tomorrow—and the day after—every day —raise other pretensions, trample on me, torture me, make me his slave—and I will be lost! Lost! The steamer may not come for days—may never come." He shook so that he had to sit down on the floor again. He shivered forlornly. He felt he could not, would not move any more. He was completely distracted by the sudden perception that the position was without issue—that death and life had in a moment become equally difficult and terrible.

All at once he heard the other push his chair back; and he leaped to his feet with extreme facility. He listened and got confused. Must run again! Right or left? He heard footsteps. He darted to the left, grasping his revolver, and at the very same instant, as it seemed to him, they came into violent collision. Both shouted with surprise. A loud explosion took place between them; a roar of red fire, thick smoke; and Kayerts, deafened and blinded, rushed back thinking: "I am hit—it's all over." He expected the other to come round—to gloat over his agony. He caught hold of an upright of the roof—"All over!" Then he heard a crashing fall on the other side of the house, as if somebody had tumbled headlong over a chair—then silence. Nothing more happened. He did not die. Only his shoulder felt as if it had been badly wrenched, and he had lost his revolver. He was disarmed and helpless! He waited for his fate. The other man made no sound. It was a stratagem.

He was stalking him now! Along what side? Perhaps he was taking aim this very minute!

After a few moments of an agony frightful and absurd, he decided to go and meet his doom. He was prepared for every surrender. He turned the corner, steadying himself with one hand on the wall; made a few paces, and nearly swooned. He had seen on the floor, protruding past the other corner, a pair of turned-up feet. A pair of white naked feet in red slippers. He felt deadly sick, and stood for a time in profound darkness. Then Makola appeared before him, saying quietly: "Come along, Mr. Kayerts. He is dead." He burst into tears of gratitude; a loud, sobbing fit of crying. After a time he found himself sitting in a chair and looking at Carlier, who lay stretched on his back. Makola was kneeling over the body.

"Is this your revolver?" asked Makola, getting up.

"Yes," said Kayerts; then he added very quickly, "He ran after me to shoot me—you saw!"

"Yes, I saw," said Makola. "There is only one revolver; where's his?"

"Don't know," whispered Kayerts in a voice that had become suddenly very faint.

"I will go and look for it," said the other, gently. He made the round along the veranda, while Kayerts sat still and looked at the corpse. Makola came back empty-handed, stood in deep thought, then stepped quietly into the dead man's room, and came out directly with a revolver, which he held up before Kayerts. Kayerts shut his eyes. Everything was going round. He found life more terrible and difficult than death. He had shot an unarmed man.

After meditating for a while, Makola said softly, pointing at the dead man who lay there with his right eye blown out:

"He died of fever." Kayerts looked at him with a stony stare. "Yes," repeated Makola, thoughtfully, stepping over the corpse, "I think he died of fever. Bury him tomorrow."

And he went away slowly to his expectant wife, leaving the two white men alone on the veranda.

Night came, and Kayerts sat unmoving on his chair. He sat quiet as if he had taken a dose of opium. The violence of the emotions he had passed through produced a feeling of exhausted serenity. He had plumbed in one short afternoon the depths of horror and despair, and now found repose in the conviction that life had no more secrets for him: neither had death! He sat by the corpse thinking;

thinking very actively, thinking very new thoughts. He
seemed to have broken loose from himself altogether. His
old thoughts, convictions, likes and dislikes, things he respected and things he abhorred, appeared in their true
light at last! Appeared contemptible and childish, false
and ridiculous. He reveled in his new wisdom while he sat
by the man he had killed. He argued with himself about
all things under heaven with that kind of wrong-headed
lucidity which may be observed in some lunatics. Incidentally he reflected that the fellow dead there had been a
noxious beast anyway; that men died every day in thousands; perhaps in hundreds of thousands—who could tell?
—and that in the number, that one death could not possibly make any difference; couldn't have any importance, at
least to a thinking creature. He, Kayerts, was a thinking
creature. He had been all his life, till that moment, a believer in a lot of nonsense like the rest of mankind—who
are fools; but now he thought! He knew! He was at peace;
he was familiar with the highest wisdom! Then he tried to
imagine himself dead, and Carlier sitting in his chair
watching him; and his attempt met with such unexpected
success, that in a very few moments he became not at all
sure who was dead and who was alive. This extraordinary
achievement of his fancy startled him, however, and by a
clever and timely effort of mind he saved himself just in
time from becoming Carlier. His heart thumped, and he
felt hot all over at the thought of that danger. Carlier!
What a beastly thing! To compose his now disturbed nerves
—and no wonder!—he tried to whistle a little. Then, suddenly, he fell asleep, or thought he had slept; but at any
rate there was a fog, and somebody had whistled in the
fog.

He stood up. The day had come, and a heavy mist had
descended upon the land: the mist penetrating, enveloping, and silent; the morning mist of tropical lands; the
mist that clings and kills; the mist white and deadly, im-
maculate and poisonous. He stood up, saw the body, and
threw his arms above his head with a cry like that of a
man who, waking from a trance, finds himself immured
forever in a tomb. *"Help! . . . My God!"*

A shriek inhuman, vibrating, and sudden, pierced like a
sharp dart the white shroud of that land of sorrow. Three
short, impatient screeches followed, and then, for a time,
the fog-wreaths rolled on, undisturbed, through a formidable silence. Then many more shrieks, rapid and piercing,
like the yells of some exasperated and ruthless creature,

rent the air. Progress was calling to Kayerts from the river.
Progress and civilization and all the virtues. Society was
calling to its accomplished child to come, to be taken care
of, to be instructed, to be judged, to be condemned; it
called him to return to that rubbish heap from which he
had wandered away, so that justice could be done.

Kayerts heard and understood. He stumbled out of the
veranda, leaving the other man quite alone for the first
time since they had been thrown there together. He groped
his way through the fog, calling in his ignorance upon the
invisible heaven to undo its work. Makola flitted by in the
mist, shouting as he ran:

"Steamer! Steamer! They can't see. They whistle for the
station. I go ring the bell. Go down to the landing, sir. I
ring."

He disappeared, Kayerts stood still. He looked upwards;
the fog rolled low over his head. He looked round like a
man who has lost his way; and he saw a dark smudge, a
cross-shaped stain, upon the shifting purity of the mist.
As he began to stumble towards it, the station bell rang in
a tumultuous peal its answer to the impatient clamor of
the steamer.

The Managing Director of the Great Civilizing Company (since we know that civilization follows trade)
landed first, and incontinently lost sight of the steamer.
The fog down by the river was exceedingly dense; above,
at the station, the bell rang unceasing and brazen.

The Director shouted loudly to the steamer:

"There is nobody down to meet us; there may be something wrong, though they are ringing. You had better
come, too!"

And he began to toil up the steep bank. The captain
and the engine-driver of the boat followed behind. As they
scrambled up the fog thinned, and they could see their Director a good way ahead. Suddenly they saw him start
forward, calling to them over his shoulder: "Run! Run to
the house! I've found one of them. Run, look for the
other!"

He had found one of them! And even he, the man of
varied and startling experience, was somewhat discomposed by the manner of this finding. He stood and fumbled
in his pockets (for a knife) while he faced Kayerts, who
was hanging by a leather strap from the cross. He had evidently climbed the grave, which was high and narrow, and
after tying the end of the strap to the arm, had swung

himself off. His toes were only a couple of inches above the ground; his arms hung stiffly down; he seemed to be standing rigidly at attention, but with one purple cheek playfully posed on the shoulder. And, irreverently, he was putting out a swollen tongue at his Managing Director.

Anton Chekhov

(1860–1904)

Anton Chekhov was born in Taganrog near the Sea of Azov, the son of a small and fanatically religious grocer who moved to Moscow when Chekhov was sixteen in order to escape being sent to debtors' prison. Chekhov finished school and then rejoined his family in Moscow, where he studied medicine at the University. It was while he was a university student that he first discovered he had contracted the disease (tuberculosis) which was to cut his life short. This did not keep him from writing the sketches and stories, for the most part humorous, with which he hoped to help his impoverished family. In 1886 Motley Stories brought him to public attention. After he received his medical degree, Chekhov continued to write with even greater fervor than he pursued his career as a physician. "Medicine is my lawful wife and literature is my mistress," he said.

Chekhov's later years were marked by his work with the Moscow Art Theatre. Like his stories, his plays are neither pure comedy nor tragedy but a mixture of both. Plagued by tuberculosis, he doggedly continued to write. He courageously embraced the cause of Alfred Dreyfus in a country whose reactionary government and inherent anti-Semitism made such a stand particularly hazardous. Despite his depressed financial state, he offered his medical services free to the peasants and downtrodden. He moved from place to place in quest of a climate in which his tuberculosis could be controlled. In 1901 he married Olga Knipper, one of the leading actresses of the Moscow Art Theatre. Their brief life together seems to have been remarkably happy for him. He died in 1904, in Badenweiler, a German health resort where he had been sent by his doctor. The freight car which brought his body to Moscow, where a huge funeral was given him, carried the sign "For Carting Fresh Oysters" on it. It was an irony which Chekhov, that master of ironists, would undoubtedly have appreciated.

Chekhov's earlier stories, designed for a popular audience, were for the most part light and comic. His later style aimed at rendering an absolutely faithful version of life. In his own words, "the aim of fiction is absolute and honest truth." Like the plays which he began to write with Ivanov (1888), his stories are characterized by their remarkable simplicity. But they are deeply suffused with a strong social conscience and a pervasive humanitarianism. Chekhov's literary mode and point of view are subsumed under the term "Chekhovian," that unique, deceptive simplicity of style and tone which illuminates the similarities between all forms of human isolation and men's desperately inarticulate reaching out for ways to communicate with one another.

In the traditional sense, there are no heroes in Chekhov's work. In his stories, heroism is the common fate of humanity. They reflect his deep compassion for the poor, the trapped, the frustrated, the confused. Through medicine, Chekhov relieved man's pains and agonies. Through his stories and plays he portrayed the cruel dilemmas and inescapable oppressions of the human condition.

"The House with the Mansard" is representative of the best of Chekhov in its subtle blending of theme and background, its revelation of the mind of the artist, its "artistic distance" from the characters, and its completely intimate involvement in their lives, its perfect evocation of the Chekhovian mood.

Anton Chekhov is widely recognized as one of the true short story masters. His influence is even greater than de Maupassant's. His psychological probings into the nature of heroism are as subtle and profound as Conrad's. Chekhov's influence is writ large in such writers as Katherine Anne Porter, Katherine Mansfield, Babel, and Joyce. But it goes beyond these obvious examples. Hardly any writer of short stories since Chekhov has failed to be influenced by what he did.

But no writer survives by his influence alone. In his relatively short life, Chekhov wrote a vast number of extraordinary, unique stories. It was Gorky, his friend and disciple, who summed up the singular quality of Chekhov's stories when he wrote how, in each of them, one could "hear the quiet, deep sigh of a pure and human heart, the hopeless sigh of sympathy for men who do not know how to respect human dignity. . . ." What distinguishes Chekhov's stories is their interplay of objectivity and compassion. Few writers have been less given to judging the lives of their creations. Chekhov sympathized with all the downtrodden, the deprived, the enervated middle class, the decadent aristocracy. His Russia was monotonous and boring. But, paradoxically, Chekhov found through his insight and compassion, the life that lies within and beyond this universal ennui and futility.

The House with the Mansard

An Artist's Story

I

It happened six or seven years ago, when I was living in one of the districts of the province of T——, on the estate of a landowner called Byelokurov, a young man who got up very early, went about in a long sleeveless peasant coat, drank beer in the evenings, and was always complaining to me that he never met with sympathy from anyone, anywhere. He lived in a lodge in the garden, and I in the old manor house, in an enormous salon with columns, where the only furniture was a wide divan on which I slept, and a table at which I played patience. Here, even in calm weather, there was always a humming sound in the old Amos stoves, and during a thunderstorm the whole house shook as though it were about to crack into pieces; this was somewhat frightening, especially at night, when the ten great windows were suddenly lit up by a flash of lightning.

Condemned by fate to a life of perpetual idleness, I did absolutely nothing. For hours at a time I gazed out the window at the sky, the birds, the garden walks, read everything that was brought me by the post, and slept. Occasionally I left the house and wandered about till late in the evening.

One day as I was returning home I unexpectedly came upon an estate I had never seen before. The sun was already sinking, and evening shadows lay across the flowering rye. Two rows of towering old fir trees, so densely planted that they formed almost solid walls, enclosed an avenue of somber beauty. I climbed the fence with no difficulty, and proceeded along the avenue, slipping on the fir needles which lay almost two inches deep on the ground. It was still and dark but for a shimmer of golden light high in the treetops, which here and there cast rainbows

on the spider webs. The fragrance of fir needles was
almost suffocating. I soon turned into a long avenue of
lime trees. Here, too, everything was desolate and aged;
last year's leaves rustled mournfully underfoot, and shadows lurked among the trees. From an ancient orchard on
the right came the faint, reluctant note of an oriole—the
bird, too, was probably old. And then the lime trees came
to an end; I walked by a white house with a veranda and
a mansard roof, and there suddenly opened before me a
view of a courtyard, a wide pond with a bathhouse, a
clump of willows, and on the farther bank a village with
a tall, slender belfry on which a cross glowed in the last
rays of the setting sun. For a moment I was under the
spell of something familiar and very dear to me, as though
I had seen this very same landscape at some time in my
childhood.

At the white stone gateway that led from the courtyard
to the open fields—a solid, old-fashioned pair of gates
adorned with lions—stood two girls. One of them, the
elder, slender, pale, and very beautiful, with masses of
auburn hair and a stubborn little mouth, looked very
severe and scarcely took any notice of me; the other, however, still very young—not more than seventeen or eighteen—also slender and pale, but with a large mouth and
large eyes, gazed at me with astonishment as I walked by,
said something in English, then looked confused; and it
seemed to me that I had also known these two charming
faces at some remote time. I returned home feeling as if I
had had a dream.

Not long after this, one midday when Byelokurov and
I were taking a walk near the house, there was an unexpected rustling of grass and a carriage drove into the
yard; in it sat one of the girls I had seen—the elder. She
had come with a subscription list to ask help for the victims of a fire. Without looking at us she very seriously
and precisely told us how many houses in the village of
Siyanovo had burned down, the number of men, women,
and children left homeless, and what steps the relief com-
mittee, of which she was a member, proposed to take. She
gave us the list to sign, then put it away and immediately
said good-bye.

"You've quite forgotten us, Pyotr Petrovich," she said
to Byelokurov, as she gave him her hand. "Come and see
us, and if Monsieur N———— (she mentioned my name)
would care to see how the admirers of his talent live, and
will come with you, my mother and I would be delighted."

I bowed.

When she had gone Pyotr Petrovich began telling me about her. The girl, he said, was of a good family; her name was Lidia Volchaninova, and both the estate on which she lived with her mother and sister and the village on the other side of the pond were called Shelkovka. Her father had once held a prominent position in Moscow, and had died with the rank of privy councilor. Although they had ample means, the Volchaninovs lived in the country summer and winter, never leaving their estate; Lidia taught in the zemstvo school in Shelkovka, her own village, and received a salary of twenty-five rubles a month. She spent nothing on herself but what she earned, and was proud of being self-supporting.

"An interesting family," said Byelokurov. "Let us go and visit them one day. They will be delighted to see you."

One day after dinner—it was a holiday—we thought of the Volchaninovs and set out for Shelkovka to see them. We found the mother and both daughters at home. The mother, Yekaterina Pavlovna, who apparently had once been beautiful but now was stouter than her age warranted, suffered from asthma, and was melancholy and absent-minded. She undertook to entertain me with talk about painting. Having learned from her daughter that I might perhaps visit Shelkovka, she had hastily called to mind two or three of my landscapes that she had seen at exhibitions in Moscow, and now asked me what I had intended to express by them. Lidia, or, as she was called at home, Lida, talked more to Byelokurov than to me. Serious and unsmiling, she asked him why he did not work in the zemstvo, and why he had never attended any of its meetings.

"It's not right, Pyotr Petrovich," she said reproachfully. "It's not right. It's a shame!"

"True, Lida, true," her mother agreed. "It is not right."

"Our whole district is in the hands of Balagin," Lida continued, turning to me. "He's the chairman of the board, and he's distributed all the district offices among his nephews and sons-in-law, and he does whatever he likes. He ought to be opposed. We young people ought to form a strong party. But you see what our young men are like. It's a shame, Pyotr Petrovich!"

The younger sister, Zhenya, remained silent while they talked of the zemstvo. She took no part in serious conversation, being considered not quite grown up by her family; they still called her "Misuce," as though she were a little girl, because as a child that was her way of saying "Mrs." to her governess. She kept looking at me with curiosity, and when I examined the photograph album she explained it to me: "That's my uncle . . . that's my god-father . . ." and she drew her little finger across the portraits, childishly brushing against me with her shoulder, and I could see her delicate, undeveloped bosom, her thin shoulders, her plait, and her slender little body tightly drawn in by a sash.

We played croquet and lawn tennis, walked about in the garden, drank tea, and then sat a long time over supper. After the huge, empty salon with columns, I felt somehow at home in this small, cozy house in which there were no oleographs on the walls and the servants were addressed politely; it all seemed very young and pure, thanks to the presence of Lida and Misuce, and everything breathed integrity. At supper Lida again spoke to Byelokurov about the zemstvo, Balagin, and school libraries. She was a spirited, sincere girl with convictions, and it was interesting to listen to her, though she talked a great deal and in a loud voice—perhaps because she was accustomed to speaking in school. My friend Pyotr Petrovich, on the other hand, who from his student days had retained the habit of reducing every conversation to an argument, was tedious, vapid, and long-winded, and spoke with the obvious desire of appearing to be a clever man with progressive views. Gesticulating, he overturned the sauceboat with his cuff, making a large pool on the tablecloth, which apparently was noticed by no one but me.

The night was dark and still as we walked home.

"Good breeding does not consist in not upsetting the sauceboat, but in not noticing it if someone else does," said Byelokurov, with a sigh. "Yes, an admirable, intellectual family. I'm terribly out of touch with nice people, terribly! And all because of work, work, work!"

He talked of how hard one had to work if one wanted to be a model farmer. And I thought: what a muddled, slothful fellow he is! When he spoke of anything serious his exertion expressed itself in a prolonged series of "er-er-er's"; and he worked exactly as he spoke—slowly, always late, never getting anything done on time. I had no faith in his capacity for business, if only because the letters I gave him to post remained in his pocket for weeks.

"And the hardest thing of all," he muttered, as he walked along beside me, "the hardest thing of all is that you

work and work, and never get any sympathy from anyone.
No sympathy whatsoever!"

II

I began to frequent the Volchaninovs'. Generally I sat
on the lowest step of the veranda; oppressed by dissatisfaction with myself, and filled with regrets for my life,
which was passing so rapidly and uninterestingly, I was
forever thinking how good it would be to tear out of my
breast the heart that had grown so heavy. Meanwhile,
they talked on the veranda, and I could hear the rustling
of their dresses and of pages being turned. I soon grew
accustomed to the idea that during the day Lida received
the sick, distributed books, and frequently went to the
village carrying a parasol but without a hat, and in the
evening talked in a loud voice about the zemstvo and
schools. Whenever the conversation turned on practical
matters, this slender, beautiful, invariably austere girl with
the exquisitely chiseled little mouth would turn to me and
in a dry tone say, "This won't interest you. . . ."

She did not find me sympathetic. She disliked me for
being a landscape painter and not depicting the needs of
the people in my pictures, and also for being indifferent,
as she thought, to what she so strongly believed in. I remember once driving along the shore of Lake Baikal and
meeting a Buryat girl on horseback, dressed in a shirt and
trousers of blue Chinese cotton; I asked her if she would
sell me her pipe, and as we talked she stared contemptuously at my European features and my hat; in a moment
she grew bored talking to me, and with a wild shout galloped away. In exactly the same way Lida despised me
as an alien. She gave no outward sign of her dislike, but I
could feel it; and as I sat there on the lowest step of the
veranda I experienced a feeling of irritation, and remarked
that treating peasants when one was not a doctor was to
deceive them, and that it was easy to be philanthropic
when one had over five thousand acres of land.

Her sister, Misuce, had no such cares, and spent her life
in complete idleness, as I did. As soon as she got up in the
morning she would take up a book and start to read, sitting
on the veranda in a deep armchair, her feet scarcely touching the floor; or she would seclude herself in the avenue of

lime trees, or walk beyond the gates into a field. She spent
the entire day poring over a book, but only an occasional
tired, dazed look and the extreme pallor of her face revealed that this reading was a mental strain. When I arrived, as soon as she caught sight of me she would flush
slightly, drop her book, and, looking into my face with her
large eyes, would eagerly tell me whatever had happened—
that the chimney in the servants' quarters had been on fire,
or that one of the workmen had caught a big fish in the
pond. On ordinary days she usually wore a light blouse
and a dark blue skirt. We took walks together, picked
cherries for jam, went rowing in the boat; and when she
jumped up to reach a cherry or when she pulled the oars,
her thin, delicate arms could be seen through the wide,
transparent sleeves of her blouse. Sometimes I would sketch
while she stood by my side and watched me with delight.

One Sunday at the end of July I arrived at the Volchaninovs' about nine o'clock in the morning. I walked through
the park, keeping at a distance from the house, looking
for white mushrooms, which were plentiful that summer,
and marking the places where I found them so that later
I could come and gather them with Zhenya. A warm breeze
was blowing. I saw Zhenya and her mother, both in light
holiday dresses, walking home from church, Zhenya holding her hat against the wind. Afterwards I could hear them
having tea on the veranda.

For a carefree person like myself, ever seeking an excuse
for perpetual idleness, these festive summer mornings in
country houses have always held a singular charm. When
the garden, all green and sparkling with dew, lies radiant
and joyous in the sunshine, when there is a fragrance of
mignonette and oleander near the house, when young people, all charmingly dressed and gay, having just returned
from church, are drinking tea in the garden, and when
one knows that all these healthy, well-fed, handsome people
are going to do nothing the whole day long, then one
wishes that all of life could be like this. These are the
thoughts I had as I walked in the garden, and I was quite
prepared to stroll about, without occupation and without
aim, the whole day, the whole summer.

Zhenya came with a basket; her expression revealed that
she had known, or at any rate felt, that she would find me
in the garden. We gathered mushrooms and talked, and
when she asked me a quesiton she walked a little ahead in
order to see my face.

"Yesterday a miracle took place in the village," she said.

"Lame Pelageya has been ill a whole year, and no doctors or medicines did her any good, but yesterday an old woman whispered something over her, and she isn't ill any more!"

"That's of no importance," I said. "You don't have to seek miracles only among the sick and the old. Isn't health a miracle? And life itself? Anything that is beyond understanding is a miracle."

"But aren't you afraid of what you don't understand?"

"No, I approach phenomena that I do not understand boldly, and do not defer to them. I am above them. Man must recognize his superiority to lions, tigers, the stars, to everything in nature, even to what is beyond understanding and appears to be miraculous, otherwise he is not a man but a mouse, afraid of everything."

Zhenya thought that, being an artist, I knew a great deal and could accurately divine what I did not know. She longed for me to lead her into the domain of the eternal and the beautiful, to that higher realm where, in her opinion, I was quite at home, and she talked to me of God, eternal life, and the miraculous. And I, unwilling to admit that my self and my imagination would perish forever after death, replied, "Yes, man is immortal." And she listened, believed, and never demanded proof.

As we walked toward the house she suddenly stopped and said, "Our Lida is a remarkable person. Don't you think so? I love her with all my heart; I would readily sacrifice my life for her. But tell me"—Zhenya touched my sleeve with her finger—"tell me why you always argue with her. Why do you become so irritated?"

"Because she is wrong."

Zhenya shook her head in protest, and tears came into her eyes. "That is inconceivable!" she exclaimed.

At that moment Lida, having just returned from somewhere, was standing near the veranda with a riding whip in her hand, a graceful, beautiful figure in the bright sunlight, giving orders to one of the workmen. Bustling about and talking loudly, she took care of two or three sick people, then, with a preoccupied, businesslike expression, walked from room to room, opening one cupboard after another, finally going to the attic. It was a long time before they could find her to call her to dinner, and by the time she came we had already finished the soup.

For some reason I remember and love all these petty details and, although nothing special happened, I still have a vivid memory of that whole day. After dinner Zhenya read, lying in the deep armchair, and I sat on the lowest step of the veranda. We did not talk. The sky was overcast, and a thin, fine rain began to fall. It was hot; the wind had gone down, and it seemed as though the day would never end. Yekaterina Pavlovna, still heavy with sleep, came out onto the veranda carrying a fan.

"Oh, Mama," said Zhenya, kissing her hand, "it's not good for you to sleep during the day!"

They adored each other. When one of them went into the garden, the other stood on the veranda looking toward the trees and called, "Oo-hoo, Zhenya!" or "Mamochka, where are you?" They always said their prayers together, sharing an identical faith, and understood each other perfectly, even without words. And their attitude toward people was the same. Yekaterina Pavlovna also became accustomed to my presence, and soon grew attached to me; when I did not come for two or three days she sent to ask if I was well. She, too, gazed admiringly at my sketches, and with the same candor and talkativeness as Misuce, told me everything that happened, often confiding to me her domestic secrets.

She stood in awe of her elder daughter. Lida was never affectionate, and spoke only of serious matters; she lived a life apart, and to her mother and sister was the sacred, somewhat enigmatic figure that an admiral, sequestered in his cabin, is to his sailors. "Our Lida is a remarkable person," her mother would often say, "isn't she?"

And now, as the soft rain fell, we talked of Lida.

"She is a remarkable person," said her mother; then, with a cautious glance over her shoulder, she added in a conspiratorial undertone, "You'd have to search with a lantern by daylight to find another like her! But, you know, I'm beginning to be somewhat alarmed. The school, the dispensary, books—that's all very well, but why go to extremes? She's almost twenty-four, you know; it's time she thought seriously about herself. If you go on like that with books and dispensaries, you don't see that life is passing. . . . She ought to marry."

Zhenya, pale from reading, her hair in disorder, raised her head and spoke as if to herself, while looking at her mother. "Mamochka, it all rests with God's will." And again she was immersed in her book.

Byelokurov arrived wearing his peasant coat and an embroidered shirt. We played croquet and lawn tennis, when it grew dark sat a long time over supper, and Lida again talked about schools and Balagin, who had the whole district under his thumb.

As I left the Volchaninovs that evening, I carried away the impression of a long, long, idle day, and a melancholy awareness that everything in this world, however long it may last, comes to an end. Zhenya accompanied us to the gateway, and perhaps because I had spent the entire day from beginning to end with her, I began to feel that I should be lonely without her, that this whole charming family was very close to me; and for the first time all summer I had a desire to paint.

"Tell me, why do you lead such a dull, colorless life?" I asked Byelokurov as we walked home together. "My life is dull, difficult, monotonous, because I am a painter, an odd person; from my youth I have been torn by envy, dissatisfaction with myself, and misgivings about my work, and I have always been poor, a vagabond. But you—you're a healthy, normal man, a landowner and a gentleman—why do you live so uninterestingly? Why do you take so little from life? Why, for instance, haven't you fallen in love with Lida or Zhenya?"

"You forget that I love another woman," replied Byelokurov.

He was referring to his friend, Lyubov Ivanovna, who was living in the lodge with him. Every day I used to see this lady, plump, podgy, and pompous as a fattened goose, walking about the garden, always with a parasol, dressed in the Russian national costume and strings of beads. The servant was continually calling her either to a meal or to drink tea. Three years before, she had rented one of the lodges for the summer, and had stayed on, apparently forever. She was ten years older than he, and kept him well in hand, so much so that he even had to ask her permission to leave the house. She was given to sobbing in loud, masculine tones, and I used to send word to say that if she did not stop I would give up my room. She stopped.

When we reached home Byelokurov seated himself on the divan and, with a scowl, fell to pondering; I walked up and down the room, stirred by a sweet emotion, as if I were in love. I wanted to talk about the Volchaninovs.

"Lida could fall in love only with a member of the zemstvo, someone who is just as fascinated by hospitals and schools as she is," I said. "Oh, for the sake of such a girl, not only could one become a member of the zemstvo, but even, as in the fairy tale, wear out a pair of iron boots. And Misuce? How adorable that Misuce is!"

Byelokurov, with his drawling "er-er-er," held forth at length on the malady of the age—pessimism. He spoke emphatically, in a tone that suggested I was debating with him. Hundreds of versts of desolate, monotonous, sunparched steppe cannot bring on the depression that is induced by one man who sits and talks, and gives no sign of ever going.

"It's not a question of either pessimism or optimism," I said irritably. "It's simply that ninety-nine out of a hundred people have no brains."

Byelokurov took this as a reflection on himself, was offended, and went away.

III

"The prince is visiting in Maloziomovo, and sends you his greetings," said Lida, removing her gloves as she came in. "He had a great deal of interesting news. . . . And he promised to raise the question of a medical station at Maloziomovo again at the next meeting of the provincial assembly, but he says there's not much hope." Then, turning to me, she added, "Excuse me, I keep forgetting that this sort of thing can be of no interest to you."

I felt exasperated. "Why of no interest to me?" I asked, shrugging my shoulders. "You don't care to hear my opinions, but I assure you, the question is of the greatest interest to me."

"It is?"

"Yes, it is. In my opinion there is absolutely no need for a medical station at Maloziomovo."

My irritation communicated itself to her. "And what is there a need for—landscape paintings?"

"No, not for landscape paintings either. There is no need for anything there."

She finished taking off her gloves and opened a newspaper which had just come by post; a moment later, in a quiet voice, evidently trying to control herself, she said, "Last week Anna died in childbirth; if there had been a medical station in the neighborhood she would be alive now. It seems to me that even landscape painters ought to have some sort of convictions about this matter."

"I have very definite convictions about it, I assure you," I replied. But she hid behind the newspaper as if unwilling to hear me. "In my opinion, medical stations, schools, libraries, dispensaries, under existing conditions, serve only to enslave the people. They are fettered by a great chain,

and you do not sever the chain, you simply add new links
to it—those are my convictions."

She raised her eyes to my face and smiled derisively, but
I went on, trying to catch hold of my main idea.

"What matters is not that Anna died in childbirth, but
that all these Annas, Mavras, Pelageyas are oppressed by
work from morning till night, and are all ill from over-
work; their entire lives they're trembling for their sick and
hungry children and doctoring themselves in fear of sickness and death; they fade early, age early, and die in filth
and stench. Their children grow up and it's the same story,
and so it goes on for hundreds of years, millions of people
living worse than animals—in constant dread, and all for
a mere crust of bread. The whole horror of their situation
lies in the fact that they never have time to think of their
souls, never have time to recollect their own image and
likeness; hunger, cold, animal fear, massive work, like
an avalanche, block all roads to spiritual activity—to the
very thing that distinguishes a human being from an animal, to the only thing that makes life worth living. You
come to their aid with hospitals and schools, but this does
not free them from their shackles; on the contrary, it further enslaves them, since, by introducing new prejudices,
you increase the number of their wants; not to mention
the fact that they have to pay the zemstvo for their drugs
and books, which only increases their burden."

"I am not going to argue with you," said Lida, putting
down her newspaper. "I've heard all that before. I will
say only one thing: it is impossible just to sit with your
hands in your lap. True, we are not saving mankind, and
perhaps we do make mistakes; but we do what we can—
and in that we are right. The highest and most sacred task
of a civilized man is to serve his neighbor, and we are en-
deavoring to serve as best we can. You may not like it,
but then, one can't please everyone."

"True, Lida, true," said her mother.

She was always timid in Lida's presence, anxiously
glancing at her whenever she wanted to speak, fearful of
saying something superfluous or inappropriate, and she
never contradicted her, but always concurred: true, Lida,
true.

"Teaching the peasants to read and write, giving them
books of wretched little precepts and adages, and medical
stations, can no more lessen their ignorance or lower their
death rate than the light from your windows can illuminate
this huge garden," I said. "You're not giving them any-

thing; by meddling in the lives of these people you do nothing but create new needs, new obligations to work."

"Oh, my God! But we must do something!" exclaimed Lida irately. Her tone made it evident that she considered my arguments trifling and contemptible.

"The people must be freed from heavy physical labor," I said. "They must be relieved of their yoke, given a respite, so that they do not spend their whole lives at the stove, at the washtub, in the fields, but may also have time to think of their souls, of God, and to develop their spiritual faculties. This spiritual activity—the continual search for truth and the meaning of life—is the vocation of every human being. Make it unnecessary for them to work like beasts of burden, let them feel that they are free, and you will see what a mockery these books and dispensaries are. Once a man becomes conscious of his true vocation, he can be satisfied only by religion, science, art—not by these trifles."

"Free them from work!" Lida smiled. "Do you really think that is possible?"

"Yes. Take upon yourself a share of their labor. If all of us, city and country dwellers alike, everyone without exception, would agree to divide among ourselves the work that is expended in satisfying the physical needs of mankind, each of us would be required to work perhaps two or three hours a day, no more. Imagine if we all, rich and poor alike, worked only three hours a day, and were free the rest of the time! Imagine too, if in order to depend still less upon our bodies, and to work less, we were to invent machines to replace our work, and tried to reduce the quantity of our needs to the minimum! We would harden ourselves and our children, so that they should not fear hunger and cold, and we should not continually tremble for their health like Anna, Mavra, and Pelageya. Imagine if we no longer doctored ourselves, maintained dispensaries, tobacco factories, distilleries—what a lot of free time we should have as a result! All of us together would devote this leisure to science and the arts. Just as the peasants sometimes work as a community to repair the roads, so all of us, as a community, would search for truth and the meaning of life, and—I am convinced of this—the truth would very soon be discovered, mankind would be delivered from this perpetual, agonizing, oppressive fear of death, and even from death itself."

"But you are contradicting yourself," said Lida. "You keep talking about science, but you reject literacy."

"Literacy, when a man can use it only to read tavern signs, or an occasional book that he doesn't understand—that kind of literacy we have had since the time of Rurik; Gogol's Petrushka has long been able to read, and yet, as the village was in Rurik's day, so it has remained. It is not literacy that is needed, but the freedom for a wide development of our spiritual faculties. It is not schools that are needed, but universities!"

"And you reject medicine, too."

"Yes, it would be required only for the study of diseases as natural phenomena, and not for their cure. If anything is treated, let it be the cause of the disease rather than the disease itself. Remove the principal cause, physical labor, and there will be no disease. I do not acknowledge a science that cures," I continued, growing excited. "Science and art, when they are genuine, aspire not to temporary, not to partial goals, but to the eternal and the universal—they seek the truth and the meaning of life; they seek God, the soul, and when they are harnessed to the necessities and the evils of the day, to dispensaries, to libraries, they can only complicate and encumber life. We have plenty of doctors, chemists, lawyers, plenty of literate men; but we have no biologists, mathematicians, philosophers, poets. All of our intellectual and spiritual energies have gone into the satisfaction of temporary, passing needs. . . . Scientists, writers, and painters work hard; thanks to them, the comforts of life increase daily, the demands of the body are multiplied; meanwhile, truth is a long way off and man continues to be the most rapacious, the most unclean of animals, and everything tends to the degeneration of the majority of mankind, and the permanent loss of all the vital capacities. In such conditions, the life of the artist has no meaning, and the more talented he is the more bizarre and incomprehensible is his role, as, on examination, it appears that he is working for the amusement of a rapacious, filthy animal, and supporting the existing order. I don't care to work for this, and I will not. . . . Nothing is of any use; let the world sink to the depths of hell!"

"Misuce, leave the room!" said Lida, evidently considering my language pernicious to so young a girl.

Zhenya looked mournfully from her sister to her mother, and went out.

"Such charming things are generally said when people wish to justify their indifference," said Lida. "It is easier to denounce schools and hospitals than it is to teach or heal."

"True, Lida, true," her mother said.

"You threaten to give up working," Lida continued.
"You obviously have a high regard for your work. Let us
stop arguing; we shall never agree, since I value the most
imperfect of these libraries and dispensaries, of which
you have just spoken so contemptuously, more highly than
all the landscape paintings in the world." She abruptly
turned to her mother and began speaking in a quite different tone. "The prince is very much changed, and much
thinner than when he was last with us. They are sending
him to Vichy."

She went on talking to her mother about the prince in
order to avoid speaking to me. Her face was burning, and
to conceal her agitation she bent low over the table as if
she were shortsighted, and pretended to read the newspaper. My presence was disagreeable to her. I took my
leave and went home.

IV

Outside all was quiet; the village on the other side of the
pond was already asleep and not a light was to be seen but
for the pale reflections of the stars on the water. At the
gate with the lions Zhenya was standing motionless, waiting to walk a little way with me.

"Everyone is asleep in the village," I said, trying to discern her face in the darkness. I could see her sad, dark
eyes fixed upon me. "The innkeeper and the horse thieves
are sleeping peacefully, while we respectable people argue
and irritate each other."

It was a melancholy August night—melancholy because
already there was a scent of autumn in the air. The moon
was rising behind a purple cloud, barely lighting the road
and the dark fields of winter corn on either side of it. From
time to time a star fell. Zhenya walked along the road beside me, trying not to look at the sky, to avoid seeing the
shooting stars, which for some reason frightened her.

"I think that you are right," she said, shivering from the
damp night air. "If people, all together, could devote
themselves to spiritual activity, soon they would know
everything."

"Of course! We are higher beings, and if we actually
realized the full power of human genius, and lived only for
higher purposes, ultimately we should become like gods.

But that will never be—mankind will degenerate, and not a trace of genius will remain."

When the gates were out of sight, Zhenya stopped and hastily shook my hand.

"Good night," she said, shivering; her shoulders were covered with nothing about a thin blouse, and she was shrinking from the cold. "Come tomorrow."

The thought of being left alone in this irritated state of dissatisfaction both with myself and other people terrified me, and I, too, tried not to look at the falling stars.

"Stay with me a little longer," I said. "Please."

I was in love with Zhenya. I think I loved her because she always met me when I came, and walked with me when I went away; because her face, when she looked at me, was rapt and tender. How touchingly beautiful were her pale face, her slender neck and arms, her weakness, her idleness, her books! And her mind? I surmised that hers was a remarkable intellect; I was enchanted by the scope of her ideas, perhaps because she thought so differently from the austere and beautiful Lida, who did not like me. Zhenya loved me because I was an artist; I had conquered her heart with my talent, and I had a passionate desire to paint only for her; I dreamed of her as my little queen, who one day would hold sway with me over these trees, these fields, the mists, the dawn—all this miraculous, bewitching nature, in whose midst I had till now felt hopelessly alone and useless.

"Stay with me a moment longer," I pleaded. "I entreat you!"

I took off my coat and put it over her chilly shoulders; she laughed and flung it off, afraid of looking ugly or absurd in a man's coat, and at that instant I took her in my arms and covered her face, her shoulders, her hands, with kisses. . . .

"Till tomorrow," she whispered, and cautiously, as though fearing to violate the stillness of the night, embraced me. "We have no secrets from one another. I must tell my mother and sister at once. . . . It's frightening! Mama's all right, she likes you—but Lida!"

She ran back toward the gate.

"Good-bye!" she called.

For a moment I stood listening to the sound of her running footsteps. I had no desire to go home; there was no reason for me to go there. I stood lost in thought, then slowly made my way back, to look once more at the house in which she lived, the dear, simple old house, with the mansard windows that seemed to be peering down at me like eyes, understanding everything. I walked past the veranda and sat on a bench near the tennis court in the darkness under an ancient elm tree, from where I could look at the house. In the windows of the mansard, where Misuce had her room, there was bright light, then a soft green glow—someone had put a shade over the lamp. Shadows moved about. . . . I was filled with tenderness, serenity, and satisfaction with myself—satisfaction that I could let myself be carried away and fall in love; and at the same time I was made uneasy by the thought that at this very moment, only a few paces from me, in one of the rooms of that house, was Lida, who did not like me, perhaps even hated me. I sat there waiting to see if Zhenya would come out, and as I listened for her it seemed to me that I could hear the sound of voices in the mansard.

An hour passed. The green light was extinguished, and the shadows were seen no more. The moon stood high above the house, shedding its light upon the sleeping garden and its paths; dahlias and the roses in the flower bed at the front of the house were clearly visible, and everything seemed to be of one color. It began to grow cold. I left the garden, picked up my coat on the road, and slowly made my way home.

When I arrived at the Volchaninovs' the following day after dinner, the glass door into the garden stood wide open. I sat down on the veranda, expecting that at any moment Zhenya would appear from behind the flower bed on the lawn, in one of the avenues, or that I should hear her voice from within the house. I went into the drawing room, then into the dining room. There was not a soul to be seen. From the dining room I walked down a long corridor to the entrance hall and back again. There were several doors in this corridor and through one of them I heard Lida's voice.

"To the crow somewhere . . . God . . ." she was speaking in a loud, distinct voice, probably dictating. "God sent a piece of cheese . . . to the crow . . . somewhere. . . . Who's there?" she suddenly called, hearing my step.

"It is I."

"Oh! Excuse me, I can't come out to you just now; I'm giving Dasha her lesson."

"Is Yekaterina Pavlovna in the garden?"

"No, she and my sister left this morning for a visit to my aunt in the province of Penza. And in the winter they will probably go abroad," she added after a pause. "God

sent . . . the crow . . . a piece . . . of cheese. . . . Have you
written it?"

I went back by the same way I had come that first day,
but in reverse: from the courtyard to the garden, past the
house, then along the avenue of lime trees. . . . At this
point I was overtaken by a small boy who handed me a
note: "I told my sister everything, and she insists that we
part," I read. "I could not bring myself to hurt her by
disobeying. God will give you happiness. Forgive me. If
you only knew how bitterly Mama and I are weeping!"

Then came the dark avenue of fir trees, and the broken-
down fence. . . . In the field where then the rye had been
in flower and quails had called, now there were cattle grazing, and hobbled horses. Here and there the winter corn
was bright green on the hills. A sober, prosaic mood took
possession of me, and I felt ashamed of all I had said at
the Volchaninovs', and bored with life, as I had been
before. When I got home I packed my things, and that
evening went to Petersburg.

I never saw the Volchaninovs again. Not long ago, on
my way to the Crimea, I met Byelokurov in the train. He
still wore his peasant coat and an embroidered shirt, and
when I asked him how he was he replied, "Thanks to your
prayers." We began to talk and he told me he had sold
his estate and bought a smaller one, which he had put in
Lyubov Ivanovna's name. He could tell me little about
the Volchaninovs. Lida, he said, was still living in Shelkovka, and teaching in the school; gradually she had succeeded in gathering round her a circle of people who were
in sympathy with her ideas, and who formed a strong
party; at the last zemstvo elections they had ousted
Balagin, who until then had held the whole district under
his thumb. About Zhenya he could tell me only that she
no longer lived at home, and that he did not know where
she was.

I am beginning to forget the house with the mansard,
and only now and then, when I am painting or reading,
suddenly, for no apparent reason, I recall the green light
in the window, the sound of my footsteps echoing through
the field at night as I walked home, in love, and chafing
my cold hands. And even more rarely, when I am oppressed by loneliness and feeling sad, I dimly remember,
and little by little begin to feel that I too am being remembered and waited for, and that we shall meet. . . .

Misuce, where are you?

—1896

Rudyard Kipling

(1865–1936)

Born in Bombay, India, Kipling's point of view should logically have been that of the English sahib, especially since his father was curator of the Lahore Museum and a well-known illustrator. More often than not, however, he manages to transcend the limitations of his class and to see things through the eyes of the British Tommy doing his duty in a land he does not like and for a cause he cannot understand.

Like the narrator of "The Man Who Would Be King," Kipling worked in India as a journalist after having been sent to school in England. He returned to England in 1889, found his fame as a poet and short story writer growing, married an American in 1892, and lived in Vermont until 1897. After a violent quarrel with his brother-in-law, he once again returned to England where he spent the rest of his life.

"The Man Who Would Be King" is a first-rate, distinctively Kiplingesque adventure story. Peachy Carnahan and Daniel Dravot are commoners, but they are also (and for Kipling this was most important) Englishmen in a non-English land, come to seek their rightful position as conquerors. Kipling here depicts the code of honor, the loyalty that exists between these two men and the native, Billy Fish, their dignity, their great physical strength, and their final overthrow as a result of over-extended ambition. As in so much of Kipling's fiction, what finally destroys the relationship between the men is the desire for a woman. Steeped in a fundamentalist religiosity, "The Man Who Would Be King" portrays not so much the world of the nineteenth-century Englishman as his desires.

As a poet, Kipling's roots are in the strong communal rhythms of the Methodist hymns on which he was raised. But in his Barrack Room Ballads (1890) he infused these rhythms with a feeling for the life of the common British soldiers serving overseas. The Ballads met with instantaneous popularity.

In Kipling's fiction, as well as in his poetry, we discern a number of dominant themes: sympathy for the Tommy, a devotion to a code of schoolboy honor and

226

duty which Kipling took from his own life in an English public school, a somewhat simplified notion of Darwinian evolution which led to his acceptance of "the white man's burden," and a recognition that the moral and psychological problems presented by imperialism are a subtle and worthy subject for art.

For better or for worse, Kipling seems destined to occupy the position of court imperialist in the history of English literature, the poet who urged Englishmen to "take up the white man's burden" and who predicted that East and West would never meet. Despite the great fame he enjoyed during his lifetime, and despite his considerable power as a creative artist, Kipling's literary reputation has declined ever since he became the first Englishman to receive the Nobel Prize for Literature in 1907. Though an eloquent case for Kipling has been made out by critics as diverse as T. S. Eliot, George Orwell, and Edmund Wilson, literary historians have, by and large, brushed over Kipling. His considerable and varied achievements are rarely adequately represented in anthologies of English literature.

The Man Who Would Be King

"Brother to a Prince and fellow to a beggar if he be found worthy."

The Law, as quoted, lays down a fair conduct of life, and one not easy to follow. I have been fellow to a beggar again and again under circumstances which prevented either of us finding out whether the other was worthy. I have still to be brother to a Prince, though I once came near to kinship with what might have been a veritable King and was promised the reversion of a Kingdom— army, lawcourts, revenue and policy all complete. But, today, I greatly fear that my King is dead, and if I want a crown I must go and hunt it for myself.

The beginning of everything was in a railway train upon the road to Mhow from Ajmir. There had been a Deficit in the Budget, which necessitated traveling, not Second-class, which is only half as dear as First-class, but by Intermediate, which is very awful indeed. There are no cushions in the Intermediate class, and the population are either Intermediate, which is Eurasian, or native, which for a long night journey is nasty, or Loafer, which is amusing though intoxicated. Intermediates do not patronize refreshment-rooms. They carry their food in bundles and pots, and buy sweets from the native sweetmeat-sellers, and drink the roadside water. That is why in the hot weather Intermediates are taken out of the carriages dead, and in all weathers are most properly looked down upon.

My particular Intermediate happened to be empty till I reached Nasirabad, when a huge gentleman in shirt-sleeves entered, and, following the custom of Intermediates, passed the time of day. He was a wanderer and a vagabond like myself, but with an educated taste for whiskey. He told tales of things he had seen and done, of out-of-the-way corners of the Empire into which he had penetrated, and of adventures in which he risked his life for a few days' food. "If India was filled with men like you and me, not knowing more than the crows where they'd get their next day's rations, it isn't seventy millions of revenue the land would be paying—it's seven hundred millions," said he; and as I looked at his mouth and chin I was disposed to agree with him. We talked politics—the politics of Loaferdom that sees things from the underside where the lath and plaster is not smoothed off—and we talked postal arrangements because my friend wanted to send a telegram back from the next station to Ajmir, which is the turning-off place from the Bombay to the Mhow line as you travel westward. My friend had no money beyond eight annas which he wanted for dinner, and I had no money at all, owing to the hitch in the Budget before mentioned. Further, I was going into a wilderness where, though I should resume touch with the Treasury, there were no telegraph offices. I was, therefore, unable to help him in any way.

"We might threaten a Station-master, and make him send a wire on tick," said my friend, "but that'd mean inquiries for you and for me, and I've got my hands full these days. Did you say you are traveling back along this line within any days?"

"Within ten," I said.

"Can't you make it eight?" said he. "Mine is rather urgent business."

"I can send your telegram within ten days if that will serve you," I said.

"I couldn't trust the wire to fetch him now I think of it. It's this way. He leaves Delhi on the 23d for

Bombay. That means he'll be running through Ajmir about the night of the 23d."

"But I'm going into the Indian Desert," I explained.

"Well *and* good," said he. "You'll be changing at Marwar Junction to get into Jodhpore territory—you must do that—and he'll be coming through Marwar Junction in the early morning of the 24th by the Bombay Mail. Can you be at Marwar Junction on that time? 'Twon't be inconveniencing you because I know that there's precious few pickings to be got out of these Central India States—even though you pretend to be correspondent of the *Backwoodsman*."

"Have you ever tried that trick?" I asked.

"Again and again, but the Residents finds you out, and then you get escorted to the Border before you've time to get your knife into them. But about my friend here. I *must* give him a word o' mouth to tell him what's come to me or else he won't know where to go. I would take it more than kind of you if you was to come out of Central India in time to catch him at Marwar Junction, and say to him:—'He has gone South for the week.' He'll know what that means. He's a big man with a red beard, and a great swell he is. You'll find him sleeping like a gentleman with all his luggage round him in a Second-class compartment. But don't you be afraid. Slip down the window, and say:—'He has gone South for the week,' and he'll tumble. It's only cutting your time to stay in those parts by two days. I ask you as a stranger—going to the West," he said, with emphasis.

"Where have *you* come from?" said I.

"From the East," said he, "and I am hoping that you will give him the message on the Square—for the sake of my Mother as well as your own."

Englishmen are not usually softened by appeals to the memory of their mothers, but for certain reasons, which will be fully apparent, I saw fit to agree.

"It's more than a little matter," said he, "and that's why I ask you to do it—and now I know that I can depend on you doing it. A Second-class carriage at Marwar Junction, and a redhaired man asleep in it. You'll be sure to remember. I get out at the next station, and I must hold on there till he comes or sends me what I want."

"I'll give the message if I catch him," I said, "and for the sake of your Mother as well as mine I'll give you a word of advice. Don't try to run the Central India States just now as the correspondent of the *Backwoods-*

man. There's a real one knocking about here, and it might lead to trouble."

"Thank you," said he, simply, "and when will the swine be gone? I can't starve because he's ruining my work. I wanted to get hold of the Degumber Rajah down here about his father's widow, and give him a jump."

"What did he do to his father's widow, then?"

"Filled her up with red pepper and slippered her to death as she hung from a beam. I found that out myself and I'm the only man that would dare going into the State to get hush-money for it. They'll try to poison me, same as they did in Chortumna when I went on the loot there. But you'll give the man at Marwar Junction my message?"

He got out at a little roadside station, and I reflected. I had heard, more than once, of men personating correspondents of newspapers and bleeding small Native States with threats of exposure, but I had never met any of the caste before. They lead a hard life, and generally die with great suddenness. The Native States have a wholesome horror of English newspapers, which may throw light on their peculiar methods of government, and do their best to choke correspondents with champagne, or drive them out of their mind with four-in-hand barouches. They do not understand that nobody cares a straw for the internal administration of Native States so long as oppression and crime are kept within decent limits, and the ruler is not drugged, drunk, or diseased from one end of the year to the other. Native States were created by Providence in order to supply picturesque scenery, tigers, and tall-writing. They are the dark places of the earth, full of unimaginable cruelty, touching the Railway and the Telegraph on one side, and, on the other, the days of Harun-al-Raschid. When I left the train I did business with divers Kings, and in eight days passed through many changes of life. Sometimes I wore dress-clothes and consorted with Princes and Politicals, drinking from crystal and eating from silver. Sometimes I lay out upon the ground and devoured what I could get, from a plate made of a flapjack, and drank the running water, and slept under the same rug as my servant. It was all in the day's work.

Then I headed for the Great Indian Desert upon the proper date, as I had promised, and the night Mail set me down at Marwar Junction, where a funny little, happy-go-lucky, native-managed railway runs to Jodhpore. The

Bombay Mail from Delhi makes a short halt at Marwar.
She arrived as I got in, and I had just time to hurry to her
platform and go down the carriages. There was only one
Second-class on the train. I slipped the window and looked
down upon a flaming red beard, half covered by a railway
rug. That was my man, fast asleep, and I dug him gently in
the ribs. He woke with a grunt and I saw his face in the
light of the lamps. It was a great and shining face.

"Tickets again?" said he.

"No," said I. "I am to tell you that he is gone South
for the week. He is gone South for the week!"

The train had begun to move out. The red man rubbed
his eyes. "He has gone South for the week," he repeated.
"Now that's just like his impidence. Did he say that I was
to give you anything?—'Cause I won't."

"He didn't," I said, and dropped away, and watched
the red lights die out in the dark. It was horribly cold
because the wind was blowing off the sands. I climbed
into my own train—not an Intermediate Carriage this time
—and went to sleep.

If the man with the beard had given me a rupee I should
have kept it as a memento of a rather curious affair. But
the consciousness of having done my duty was my only reward.

Later on I reflected that two gentlemen like my friends
could not do any good if they foregathered and personated
correspondents of newspapers, and might, if they "stuck
up" one of the little rat-trap states of Central India or
Southern Rajputana, get themselves into serious difficulties.
I therefore took some trouble to describe them as accurately as I could remember to people who would be interested
in deporting them: and succeeded, so I was later informed, in having them headed back from the Degumber
borders.

Then I became respectable, and returned to an Office
where there were no Kings and no incidents except the
daily manufacture of a newspaper. A newspaper office
seems to attract every conceivable sort of person, to the
prejudice of discipline. Zenana-mission ladies arrive, and
beg that the Editor will instantly abandon all his duties
to describe a Christian prize-giving in a back-slum of a
perfectly inaccessible village; Colonels who have been
overpassed for commands sit down and sketch the outline
of a series of ten, twelve, or twenty-four leading articles
on Seniority *versus* Selection; missionaries wish to know
why they have not been permitted to escape from their

regular vehicles of abuse and swear at a brother-mission-ary under special patronage of the editorial We; stranded theatrical companies troop up to explain that they can-not pay for their advertisements, but on their return from New Zealand or Tahiti will do so with interest; inventors of patent punkah-pulling machines, carriage couplings and unbreakable swords and axle-trees call with specifications in their pockets and hours at their disposal; tea-com-panies enter and elaborate their prospectuses with the office pens; secretaries of ball-committees clamor to have the glories of their last dance more fully expounded; strange ladies rustle in and say:—"I want a hundred lady's cards printed *at once,* please," which is manifestly part of an Editor's duty; and every dissolute ruffian that ever tramped the Grand Trunk Road makes it his business to ask for employment as a proofreader. And, all the time, the telephone-bell is ringing madly, and Kings are being killed on the Continent, and Empires are saying—"You're another," and Mister Gladstone is calling down brimstone upon the British Dominions, and the little black copy-boys are whining, *"kaa-pi chay-ha-yeh"* (copy wanted) like tired bees, and most of the paper is as blank as Modred's shield.

But that is the amusing part of the year. There are other six months wherein none ever come to call, and the thermometer walks inch by inch up to the top of the glass, and the office is darkened to just above reading light, and the press machines are red-hot of touch, and nobody writes anything but accounts of amusements in the Hill-stations or obituary notices. Then the telephone becomes a tinkling terror, because it tells you of the sud-den deaths of men and women that you knew intimately, and the prickly-heat covers you as with a garment, and you sit down and write:—"A slight increase of sickness is reported from the Khuda Janta Khan District. The out-break is purely sporadic in its nature, and, thanks to the energetic efforts of the District authorities, is now almost at an end. It is, however, with deep regret we record the death, etc."

Then the sickness really breaks out, and the less re-cording and reporting the better for the peace of the subscribers. But the Empires and the Kings continue to divert themselves as selfishly as before, and the Foreman thinks that a daily paper really ought to come out once in twenty-four hours, and all the people at the Hill-stations in the middle of their amusements say:—"Good gracious!

Why can't the paper be sparkling? I'm sure there's plenty going on up here."

That is the dark half of the moon, and as the advertisements say, "must be experienced to be appreciated."

It was in that season, and a remarkably evil season, that the paper began running the last issue of the week on Saturday night, which is to say Sunday morning, after the custom of a London paper. This was a great convenience, for immediately after the paper was put to bed, the dawn would lower the thermometer from 96° to almost 84° for half an hour, and in that chill—you have no idea how cold is 84° on the grass until you begin to pray for it —a very tired man could set off to sleep ere the heat roused him.

One Saturday night it was my pleasant duty to put the paper to bed alone. A King or courtier or a courtesan or a community was going to die or get a new Constitution, or do something that was important on the other side of the world, and the paper was to be held open till the latest possible minute in order to catch the telegram. It was a pitchy black night, as stifling as a June night can be, and the *loo,* the red-hot wind from the westward, was booming among the tinder-dry trees and pretending that the rain was on its heels. Now and again a spot of almost boiling water would fall on the dust with the flop of a frog, but all our weary world knew that was only pretence. It was a shade cooler in the press-room than the office, so I sat there, while the type ticked and clicked, and the night-jars hooted at the windows, and the all but naked compositors wiped the sweat from their foreheads and called for water. The thing that was keeping us back, whatever it was, would not come off, though the *loo* dropped and the last type was set, and the whole round earth stood still in the choking heat, with its fingers on its lip, to wait the event. I drowsed, and wondered whether the telegraph was a blessing, and whether this dying man, or struggling people, was aware of the inconvenience the delay was causing. There was no special reason beyond the heat and worry to make tension, but, as the clock hands crept up to three o'clock and the machines spun their fly-wheels two and three times to see that all was in order, before I said the word that would set them off, I could have shrieked aloud.

Then the roar and rattle of the wheels shivered the quiet into little bits. I rose to go away, but two men in white clothes stood in front of me. The first one said:—

"It's him!" The second said:—"So it is!" And they both laughed almost as loudly as the machinery roared, and mopped their foreheads. "We see there was a light burning across the road and we were sleeping in that ditch there for coolness, and I said to my friend here, The office is open. Let's come along and speak to him as turned us back from the Degumber State," said the smaller of the two. He was the man I had met in the Mhow train, and his fellow was the red-bearded man of Marwar Junction. There was no mistaking the eyebrows of the one or the beard of the other.

I was not pleased, because I wished to go to sleep, not to squabble with loafers. "What do you want?" I asked.

"Half an hour's talk with you cool and comfortable, in the office," said the red-bearded man. "We'd *like* some drink—the Contrack doesn't begin yet, Peachey, so you needn't look—but what we really want is advice. We don't want money. We ask you as a favor, because you did us a bad turn about Degumber."

I led from the press-room to the stifling office with the maps on the walls, and the red-haired man rubbed his hands. "That's something like," said he. "This was the proper shop to come to. Now, Sir, let me introduce to you Brother Peachey Carnehan, that's him, and Brother Daniel Dravot, that is *me,* and the less said about our professions the better, for we have been most things in our time. Soldier, sailor, compositor, photographer, proof-reader, street-preacher, and correspondents of the *Back-woodsman* when we thought the paper wanted one. Carnehan is sober, and so am I. Look at us first and see that's sure. It will save you cutting into my talk. We'll take one of your cigars apiece, and you shall see us light."

I watched the test. The men were absolutely sober, so I gave them each a tepid peg.

"Well *and* good," said Carnehan of the eyebrows, wiping the froth from his moustache. "Let me talk now, Dan. We have been all over India, mostly on foot. We have been boiler-fitters, engine-drivers, petty contractors, and all that, and we have decided that India isn't big enough for such as us."

They certainly were too big for the office. Dravot's beard seemed to fill half the room and Carnehan's shoulders the other half, as they sat on the big table. Carnehan continued:—"The country isn't half worked out because they that governs it won't let you touch it. They spend all their blessed time in governing it, and you can't lift a spade, nor chip a rock, nor look for oil, nor anything like that without all the Government saying—'Leave it alone and let us govern.' Therefore, such as it is, we will let it alone, and go away to some other place where a man isn't crowded and can come to his own. We are not little men, and there is nothing that we are afraid of except Drink, and we have signed a Contrack on that. *Therefore,* we are going away to be Kings."

"Kings in our own right," muttered Dravot.

"Yes, of course," I said. "You've been tramping in the sun, and it's a very warm night, and hadn't you better sleep over the notion? Come to-morrow."

"Neither drunk nor sunstruck," said Dravot. "We have slept over the notion half a year, and require to see Books and Atlases, and we have decided that there is only one place now in the world that two strong men can Sar-a-*whack*. They call it Kafiristan. By my reckoning it's the top right-hand corner of Afghanistan, not more than three hundred miles from Peshawur. They have two-and-thirty heathen idols there, and we'll be the thirty-third. It's a mountainous country, and the women of those parts are very beautiful."

"But that is provided against in the Contrack," said Carnehan. "Neither Women nor Liqu-or, Daniel."

"And that's all we know, except that no one has gone there, and they fight, and in any place where they fight, a man who knows how to drill men can always be a King. We shall go to those parts and say to any King we find—'D' you want to vanquish your foes?' and we will show him how to drill men; for that we know better than anything else. Then we will subvert that King and seize his Throne and establish a Dynasty."

"You'll be cut to pieces before you're fifty miles across the Border," I said. "You have to travel through Afghanistan to get to that country. It's one mass of mountains and peaks and glaciers, and no Englishman has been through it. The people are utter brutes, and even if you reached them you couldn't do anything."

"That's more like," said Carnehan. "If you could think us a little more mad we would be more pleased. We have come to you to know about this country, to read a book about it, and to be shown maps. We want you to tell us that we are fools and to show us your books." He turned to the bookcases.

"Are you at all in earnest?" I said.

"A little," said Dravot, sweetly. "As big a map as you

have got, even if it's all blank where Kafiristan is, and any
books you've got. We can read, though we aren't very educated."

I uncased the big thirty-two-miles-to-the-inch map of
India, and two smaller Frontier maps, hauled down
volume INF-KAN of the *Encyclopædia Britannica,* and
the men consulted them.

"See here!" said Dravot, his thumb on the map. "Up to
Jagdallak, Peachey and me know the road. We was there
with Roberts's Army. We'll have to turn off to the right at
Jagdallak through Laghmann territory. Then we get among
the hills—fourteen thousand feet—fifteen thousand—it
will be cold work there, but it don't look very far on the
map."

I handed him Wood on the *Sources of the Oxus.* Carnehan was deep in the *Encyclopædia.*

"They're a mixed lot," said Dravot, reflectively; "and
it won't help us to know the names of their tribes. The more
tribes the more they'll fight, and the better for us. From
Jagdallak to Ashan. H'mm!"

"But all the information about the country is as sketchy
and inaccurate as can be," I protested. "No one knows
anything about it really. Here's the file of the *United
Services' Institute.* Read what Bellew says."

"Blow Bellew!" said Carnehan. "Dan, they're an all-
fired lot of heathens, but this book here says they think
they're related to us English."

I smoked while the men pored over *Raverty, Wood,*
the maps and the *Encyclopædia.*

"There is no use your waiting," said Dravot, politely.
"It's about four o'clock now. We'll go before six o'clock
if you want to sleep, and we won't steal any of the papers.
Don't you sit up. We're two harmless lunatics, and if you
come, to-morrow evening, down to the Serai we'll say good-
bye to you."

"You *are* two fools," I answered. "You'll be turned
back at the Frontier or cut up the minute you set foot
in Afghanistan. Do you want any money or a recommenda-
tion down-country? I can help you to the chance of work
next week."

"Next week we shall be hard at work ourselves, thank
you," said Dravot. "It isn't so easy being a King as it
looks. When we've got our Kingdom in going order we'll
let you know, and you can come up and help us to govern
it."

"Would two lunatics make a Contrack like that?" said

Carnehan, with subdued pride, showing me a greasy half-sheet of note-paper on which was written the following. I copied it then and there, as a curiosity:

> This Contract between me and you persuing witnesseth in the name of God—Amen and so forth.
>
> (One)   That me and you will settle this matter together: i.e., to be Kings of Kafiristan.
>
> (Two)   That you and me will not, while this matter is being settled, look at any Liquor, nor any woman, black, white or brown, so as to get mixed up with one or the other harmful.
>
> (Three) That we conduct ourselves with dignity and discretion, and if one of us gets into trouble the other will stay by him.
>
> Signed by you and me this day.
> Peachey Taliaferro Carnehan.
> Daniel Dravot.
> Both Gentlemen at Large.

"There was no need for the last article," said Carnehan, blushing modestly; "but it looks regular. Now you know the sort of men that loafers are—we loafers, Dan, until we get out of India—and *do* yo   hat we would sign a Contrack like that unless we   arnest? We have kept away from the two thin   ake life worth having."

"You won't enjoy your lives much   you are going to try this idiotic adventure. D   office on fire," I said, "and go away before nin

I left them still poring over th   making notes on the back of the "Contra   to come down to the Serai to-morrow," wer   g words.

The Kumharsen Serai is the   quare sink of humanity where the strings o   horses from the North load and unload. A   ties of Central Asia may be found there   f the folk of India proper. Balkh and Bok   eet Bengal and Bombay, and try to draw ey   can buy ponies, turquoises, Persian pussy-ca   s, fat-tailed sheep and musk in the Kumharsen   get many strange things for nothing. In the aft   went down there to see whether my friends intende   keep their word or were lying about drunk.

A priest attired in fragments of ribbons and rags stalked up to me, gravely twisting a child's paper whirligig. Behind

him was his servant bending under the load of a crate of
mud toys. The two were loading up two camels, and the
inhabitants of the Serai watched them with shrieks of
laughter.

"The priest is mad," said a horse-dealer to me. "He is
going up to Kabul to sell toys to the Amir. He will either
be raised to honor or have his head cut off. He came in
here this morning and has been behaving madly ever
since."

"The witless are under the protection of God," stammered a flat-cheeked Usbeg in broken Hindi. "They foretell
future events."

"Would they could have foretold that my caravan would
have been cut up by the Shinwaris almost within shadow
of the Pass!" grunted the Eusufzai agent of a Rajputana
trading-house whose goods had been feloniously diverted
into the hands of other robbers just across the Border,
and whose misfortunes were the laughing-stock of the
bazaar. "Ohé, priest, whence come you and whither do you
go?"

"From Roum have I come," shouted the priest, waving
his whirligig; "from Roum, blown by the breath of a
hundred devils across the sea! O thieves, robbers, liars,
blessing of Pir Khan on pigs, dogs, and perjurers! Who
will take the Protected of God to the North to sell charms
that are never still to the Amir? The camels shall not gall,
the sons shall not fall sick, and the wives shall remain faithful while they are away, of the men who give me place
in their caravan. Who will assist me to slipper the King of
the Ross with a golden slipper with a silver heel? The
protection of Pir Khan be upon his labors!" He spread out
the skirts of his gaberdine and pirouetted between the lines
of tethered horses.

"There starts a caravan from Peshawur to Kabul in
twenty days, *Huzrut*," said the Eusufzai trader. "My camels
go therewith. Do thou also go and bring us good-luck."

"I will go even now!" shouted the priest. "I will depart
upon my winged camels, and be at Peshawur in a day!
Ho! Hazar Mir Khan," he yelled to his servant, "drive out
the camels, but let me first mount my own."

He leaped on the back of his beast as it knelt, and,
turning round to me, cried:—"Come thou also, Sahib,
a little along the road, and I will sell thee a charm—an
amulet that shall make thee King of Kafiristan."

Then the light broke upon me, and I followed the two

camels out of the Serai till we reached open road and the priest halted.

"What d' you think o' that?" said he in English. "Carnehan can't talk their patter, so I've made him my servant. He makes a handsome servant. 'Tisn't for nothing that I've been knocking about the country for fourteen years. Didn't I do that talk neat? We'll hitch on to a caravan at Peshawur till we get to Jagdallak, and then we'll see if we can get donkeys for our camels, and strike into Kafiristan. Whirligigs for the Amir, O Lord! Put your hand under the camel-bags and tell me what you feel."

I felt the butt of a Martini, and another and another.

"Twenty of 'em," said Dravot, placidly. "Twenty of 'em, and ammunition to correspond, under the whirligigs and the mud dolls."

"Heaven help you if you are caught with those things!" I said. "A Martini is worth her weight in silver among the Pathans."

"Fifteen hundred rupees of capital—every rupee we could beg, borrow, or steal—are invested on these two camels," said Dravot. "We won't get caught. We're going through the Khaiber with a regular caravan. Who'd touch a poor mad priest?"

"Have you got everything you want?" I asked, overcome with astonishment.

"Not yet, but we shall soon. Give us a memento of your kindness, *Brother*. You did me a service yesterday, and that time in Marwar. Half my Kingdom shall you have, as the saying is." I slipped a small charm compass from my watch-chain and handed it up to the priest.

"Good-bye," said Dravot, giving me hand cautiously. "It's the last time we'll shake hands with an Englishman these many days. Shake hands with him, Carnehan," he cried, as the second camel passed me.

Carnehan leaned down and shook hands. Then the camels passed away along the dusty road, and I was left alone to wonder. My eye could detect no failure in the disguises. The scene in Serai attested that they were complete to the native mind. There was just the chance, therefore, that Carnehan and Dravot would be able to wander through Afghanistan without detection. But, beyond, they would find death, certain and awful death.

Ten days later a native friend of mine, giving me the news of the day from Peshawur, wound up his letter with:—"There has been much laughter here on account of a certain mad priest who is going in his estimation to sell petty gauds and insignificant trinkets which he ascribes as great charms to H. H. the Amir of Bokhara. He passed through Peshawur and associated himself to the Second Summer caravan that goes to Kabul. The merchants are pleased because through superstition they imagine that such mad fellows bring good-fortune."

The two, then, were beyond the Border. I would have prayed for them, but, that night, a real King died in Europe, and demanded an obituary notice.

The wheel of the world swings through the same phases again and again. Summer passed and winter thereafter, and came and passed again. The daily paper continued and I with it, and upon the third summer there fell a hot night, a night-issue, and a strained waiting for something to be telegraphed from the other side of the world, exactly as had happened before. A few great men had died in the past two years, the machines worked with more clatter, and some of the trees in the Office garden were a few feet taller. But that was all the difference.

I passed over to the press-room, and went through just a scene as I have already described. The nervous tension was stronger than it had been two years before, and I felt the heat more acutely. At three o'clock I cried, "Print off," and turned to go, when there crept to my chair what was left of a man. He was bent into a circle, his head was sunk between his shoulders, and he moved his feet one over the other like a bear. I could hardly see whether he walked or crawled—this rag-wrapped, whining cripple who addressed me by name, crying that he was come back. "Can you give me a drink?" he whimpered. "For the Lord's sake, give me a drink!"

I went back to the office, the man following with groans of pain, and I turned up the lamp.

"Don't you know me?" he gasped, dropping into a chair, and he turned his drawn face, surmounted by a shock of grey hair, to the light.

I looked at him intently. Once before had I seen eyebrows that met over the nose in an inch-broad black band, but for the life of me I could not tell where.

"I don't know you," I said, handing him the whiskey. "What can I do for you?"

He took a gulp of the spirit raw, and shivered in spite of the suffocating heat.

"I've come back," he repeated; "and I was the King of Kafiristan—me and Dravot—crowned Kings we was!

In this office we settled it—you setting there and giving
us the books. I am Peachey—Peacey Taliaferro Carnehan,
and you've been setting here ever since—O Lord!"

I was more than a little astonished, and expressed my
feelings accordingly.

"It's true," said Carnehan, with a dry cackle, nursing his feet, which were wrapped in rags. "True as gospel.
Kings we were, with crowns upon our heads—me and
Dravot—poor Dan—oh, poor, poor Dan, that would
never take advice, not though I begged of him!"

"Take the whiskey," I said, "and take your own time.
Tell me all you can recollect of everything from beginning to end. You got across the border on your camels,
Dravot dressed as a mad priest and you his servant. Do
you remember that?"

"I ain't mad—yet, but I shall be that way soon. Of
course I remember. Keep looking at me, or maybe my
words will go all to pieces. Keep looking at me in my eyes
and don't say anything."

I leaned forward and looked into his face as steadily
as I could. He dropped one hand upon the table and I
grasped it by the wrist. It was twisted like a bird's claw,
and upon the back was a ragged, red, diamond-shaped
scar.

"No, don't look there. Look at *me*," said Carnehan.

"That comes afterward, but for the Lord's sake don't
distrack me. We left with the caravan, me and Dravot
playing all sorts of antics to amuse the people we were with.
Dravot used to make us laugh in the evenings when all
the people was cooking their dinners—cooking their dinners, and . . . what did they do then? They lit little fires
with sparks that went into Dravot's beard, and we all
laughed—fit to die. Little red fires they was, going into
Dravot's big red beard—so funny." His eyes left mine and
he smiled foolishly.

"You went as far as Jagdallak with that caravan," I said,
at a venture, "after you had lit those fires. To Jagdallak,
where you turned off to try to get into Kafiristan."

"No, we didn't neither. What are you talking about? We
turned off before Jagdallak, because we heard the roads
was good. But they wasn't good enough for our two camels
—mine and Dravot's. When we left the caravan, Dravot
took off all his clothes and mine too, and said we would
be heathen, because the Kafirs didn't allow Mohammedans
to talk to them. So we dressed betwixt and between, and
such a sight as Daniel Dravot I never saw yet nor expect

to see again. He burned half his beard, and slung a sheep-skin over his shoulder, and shaved his head into patterns. He shaved mine, too, and made me wear outrageous things to look like a heathen. That was in a most mountainous country, and our camels couldn't go along any more because of the mountains. They were tall and black, and coming home I saw them fight like wild goats—there are lots of goats in Kafiristan. And these mountains, they never keep still, no more than the goats. Always fighting they are, and don't let you sleep at night."

"Take some more whiskey," I said, very slowly "What did you and Daniel Dravot do when the camels could go no further because of the rough roads that led into Kafiristan?"

"What did which do? There was a party called Peachey Taliaferro Carnehan that was with Dravot. Shall I tell you about him? He died out there in the cold. Slap from the bridge fell old Peachey, turning and twisting in the air like a penny whirligig that you can sell to the Amir.—No; they was two for three ha' pence, those whirligigs, or I am much mistaken and woful sore. And then these camels were no use, and Peachey said to Dravot—'For the Lord's sake, let's get out of this before our heads are chopped off,' and with that they killed the camels all among the mountains, not having anything in particular to eat, but first they took off the boxes with the guns and the ammunition, till two men came along driving four mules. Dravot up and dances in front of them, singing,—'Sell me four mules.' Says the first man,—'If you are rich enough to buy, you are rich enough to rob'; but before ever he could put his hand to his knife, Dravot breaks his neck over his knee, and the other party runs away. So Carnehan loaded the mules with the rifles that was taken off the camels, and together we starts forward into those bitter cold mountaineous parts, and never a road broader than the back of your hand."

He paused for a moment, while I asked him if he could remember the nature of the country through which he had journeyed.

"I am telling you as straight as I can, but my head isn't as good as it might be. They drove nails through it to make me hear better how Dravot died. The country was mountaineous and the mules were most contrary, and the inhabitants was dispersed and solitary. They went up and up, and down and down, and that other party, Carnehan, was imploring of Dravot not to sing and whistle so loud, for fear of bringing down the tremenjus avalanches. But Dravot says that if a King couldn't sing it wasn't worth being King, and whacked the mules over the rump, and never took no heed for ten cold days. We came to a big level valley all among the mountains, and the mules were near dead, so we killed them, not having anything in special for them or us to eat. We sat upon the boxes, and played odd and even with the cartridges that was jolted out.

"Then ten men with bows and arrows ran down that valley, chasing twenty men with bows and arrows, and the row was tremenjus. They was fair men—fairer than you or me—with yellow hair and remarkable well built. Says Dravot, unpacking the guns—'This is the beginning of the business. We'll fight for the ten men,' and with that he fires two rifles at the twenty men, and drops one of them at two hundred yards from the rock where we was sitting. The other men began to run, but Carnehan and Dravot sits on the boxes picking them off at all ranges, up and down the valley. Then we goes up to the ten men that had run across the snow too, and they fires a footy little arrow at us. Dravot he shoots above their heads and they all falls down flat. Then he walks over them and kicks them, and then he lifts them up and shakes hands all round to make them friendly like. He calls them and gives them the boxes to carry, and waves his hand for all the world as though he was King already. They takes the boxes and him across the valley and up the hill into pine wood on the top, where there was half a dozen big stone idols. Dravot he goes to the biggest—a fellow they call Imbra—and lays a rifle and a cartridge at his feet, rubbing his nose respectful with his own nose, patting him on the head, and saluting in front of it. He turns round to the men and nods his head, and says,—'That's all right. I'm in the know too, and all these old jim-jams are my friends.' Then he opens his mouth and points down it, and when the first man brings him food, he says—'No'; and when the second man brings him food, he says—'No'; but when one of the old priests and the boss of the village brings him food, he says —'Yes'; very haughty, and eats it slow. That was how we came to our first village, without any trouble, just as though we had tumbled from the skies. But we tumbled from one of those damned rope-bridges, you see, and you couldn't expect a man to laugh much after that."

"Take some more whiskey and go on," I said. "That was the first village you came into. How did you get to be King?"

"I wasn't King," said Carnehan. "Dravot he was the King, and a handsome man he looked with the gold crown on his head and all. Him and the other party stayed in that village, and every morning Dravot sat by the side of old Imbra, and the people came and worshipped. That was Dravot's order. Then a lot of men came into the valley, and Carnehan and Dravot picks them off with the rifles before they knew where they was, and runs down into the valley and up again the other side, and finds another village, same as the first one, and the people all falls down flat on their faces, and Dravot says,—'Now what is the trouble between you two villages?' and the people points to a woman, as fair as you or me, that was carried off, and Dravot takes her back to the first village and counts up the dead—eight there was. For each dead man Dravot pours a little milk on the ground and waves his arms like a whirligig and 'That's all right,' says he. Then he and Carnehan takes the big boss of each village by the arm and walks them down the valley, and shows them how to scratch a line with a spear right down the valley, and gives each a sod of turf from both sides o' the line. Then all the people comes down and shouts like the devil and all, and Dravot says,—'Go and dig the land, and be fruitful and multiply,' which they did, though they didn't understand. Then we asks the names of things in their lingo—bread and water and fire and idols and such, and Dravot leads the priest of each village up to the idol, and says he must sit there and judge the people, and if anything goes wrong he is to be shot.

"Next week they was all turning up the land in the valley as quiet as bees and much prettier, and the priests heard all the complaints and told Dravot in dumb show what it was about. 'That's just the beginning,' says Dravot. 'They think we're Gods.' He and Carnehan picks out twenty good men and shows them how to click off a rifle, and form fours, and advance in line, and they was very pleased to do so, and clever to see the hang of it. Then he takes out his pipe and his baccy-pouch and leaves one at one village and one at the other, and off we two goes to see what was to be done in the next valley. That was all rock, and there was a little village there, and Carnehan says,—'Send 'em to the old valley to plant,' and takes 'em there and gives 'em some land that wasn't took before. They were a poor lot, and we blooded 'em with a kid before letting 'em into the new Kingdom. That was to impress the people, and then they settled down quiet, and Carne-

han went back to Dravot who had got into another valley,
all snow and ice and most mountaineous. There was no
people there and the Army got afraid, so Dravot shoots
one of them, and goes on till he finds some people in a
village, and the Army explains that unless the people wants
to be killed they had better not shoot their little matchlock;
for they had matchlocks. We makes friends with the priest
and I stays there alone with two of the Army, teaching the
men how to drill, and a thundering big Chief comes across
the snow with kettle-drums and horns twanging, because
he heard there was a new God kicking about. Carnehan
sights for the brown of the men half a mile across the
snow and wings one of them. Then he sends a message to
the Chief that, unless he wished to be killed, he must come
and shake hands with me and leave his arms behind. The
Chief comes alone first, and Carnehan shakes hands with
him and whirls his arms about, same as Dravot used, and
very much surprised that Chief was, and strokes my eyebrows. Then Carnehan goes alone to the Chief, and asks
him in dumb show if he had an enemy he hated. 'I have,'
says the Chief. So Carnehan weeds out the pick of his men,
and sets the two of the Army to show them drill and at
the end of two weeks the men can manœuvre about as well
as Volunteers. So he marches with the Chief to a great
big plain on the top of a mountain, and the Chief's men
rushes into a village and takes it; we three Martinis firing
into the brown of the enemy. So we took that village too,
and I gives the Chief a rag from my coat and says, 'Occupy
till I come'; which was scriptural. By way of a reminder,
when me and the Army was eighteen hundred yards away,
I drops a bullet near him standing on the snow, and all
the people falls flat on their faces. Then I sends a letter
to Dravot, wherever he be by land or by sea."

At the risk of throwing the creature out of train I interrupted—"How could you write a letter up yonder?"

"The letter?—Oh!—The Letter! Keep looking at me between the eyes, please. It was a string-talk letter, that
we'd learned the way of it from a blind beggar in the
Punjab."

I remember that there had once come to the office a
blind man with a knotted twig and a piece of string
which he wound round the twig according to some cypher
of his own. He could, after the lapse of days or hours,
repeat the sentence which he had reeled up. He had reduced the alphabet to eleven primitive sounds; and tried
to teach me his method, but failed.

"I sent that letter to Dravot," said Carnehan; "and told him to come back because this Kingdom was growing too big for me to handle, and then I struck for the first valley, to see how the priests were working. They called the village we took along with the Chief, Bashkai, and the first village we took, Er-Heb. The priests at Er-Heb was doing all right, but they had a lot of pending cases about land to show me, and some men from another village had been firing arrows at night. I went out and looked for that village and fired four rounds at it from a thousand yards. That used all the cartridges I cared to spend, and I waited for Dravot, who had been away two or three months, and I kept my people quiet.

"One morning I heard the devil's own noise of drums and horns, and Dan Dravot marches down the hill with his Army and a tail of hundreds of men, and, which was the most amazing—a great gold crown on his head. 'My Gord, Carnehan,' says Daniel, 'this is a tremenjus business, and we've got the whole country as far as it's worth having. I am the son of Alexander by Queen Semiramis, and you're my younger brother and a God too! It's the biggest thing we've ever seen. I've been marching and fighting for six weeks with the Army, and every footy little village for fifty miles has come in rejoiceful; and more than that, I've got the key of the whole show, as you'll see, and I've got a crown for you! I told 'em to make two of 'em at a place called Shu, where the gold lies in the rock like suet in mutton. Gold I've seen, and turquoise I've kicked out of the cliffs, and there's garnets in the sands of the river, and here's a chunk of amber that a man brought me. Call up all the priests and, here, take your crown.'

"One of the men opens a black hair bag and I slips the crown on. It was too small and too heavy, but I wore it for the glory. Hammered gold it was—five pound weight, like a hoop of a barrel.

"'Peachey,' says Dravot, 'we don't want to fight no more. The Craft's the trick so help me!' and he brings forward that same Chief that I left at Bashkai—Billy Fish we called him afterward, because he was so like Billy Fish that drove the big tank-engine at Mach on the Bolan in the old days. 'Shake hands with him,' says Dravot, and I shook hands and nearly dropped, for Billy Fish gave me the Grip. I said nothing, but tried him with the Fellow Craft Grip. He answers, all right, and I tried the Master's Grip, but that was a slip. 'A Fellow Craft he is!' I says to Dan. 'Does he know the word?' 'He does,' says Dan, 'and all the priests know. It's a miracle! The Chiefs and the priests can work a Fellow Craft Lodge in a way that's very like ours, and they've cut the marks on the rocks, but they don't know the Third Degree, and they've come to find out. It's Gord's Truth. I've known these long years that the Afghans knew up to the Fellow Craft Degree, but this is a miracle. A God and a Grand-Master of the Craft am I, and a Lodge in the Third Degree I will open, and we'll raise the head priests and the Chiefs of the villages.'

" 'It's against all the law,' I says, 'holding a Lodge without warrant from any one; and we never held office in any Lodge.'

" 'It's a master-stroke of policy,' says Dravot. 'It means running the country as easy as a four-wheeled bogy on a down grade. We can't stop to inquire now, or they'll turn against us. I've forty Chiefs at my heel, and passed and raised according to their merit they shall be. Billet these men on the villages and see that we run up a Lodge of some kind. The temple of Imbra will do for the Lodge-room. The women must make aprons as you show them. I'll hold a levee of Chiefs to-night and Lodge to-morrow.'

"I was fair run off my legs, but I wasn't such a fool as not to see what a pull this Craft business gave us. I showed the priests' families how to make aprons of the degrees, but for Dravot's apron the blue border and marks was made of turquoise lumps on white hide, not cloth. We took a great square stone in the temple for the Master's chair, and little stones for the officers' chairs, and painted the black pavement with white squares, and did what we could to make things regular.

"At the levee which was held that night on the hillside with big bonfires, Dravot gives out that him and me were Gods and sons of Alexander, and Past Grand-Masters in the Craft, and was come to make Kafiristan a country where every man should eat in peace and drink in quiet, and specially obey us. Then the Chiefs come round to shake hands, and they was so hairy and white and fair it was just shaking hands with old friends. We gave them names according as they was like men we had known in India—Billy Fish, Holly Dilworth, Pikky Kergan that was Bazaar-master when I was at Mhow, and so on and so on.

"*The* most amazing miracle was at Lodge next night. One of the old priests was watching us continuous, and I felt uneasy, for I knew we'd have to fudge the Ritual, and I didn't know what the men knew. The old priest was a stranger come in from beyond the village of Bashkai.

The minute Dravot puts on the Master's apron that the girls had made for him, the priest fetches a whoop and a howl, and tries to overturn the stone that Dravot was sitting on. 'It's all up now,' I says. 'That comes of meddling with the Craft without warrant!' Dravot never winked an eye, not when ten priests took and tilted over the Grand-Master's chair—which was to say the stone of Imbra. The priest begins rubbing the bottom end of it to clear away the black dirt, and presently he shows all the other priests the Master's Mark, same as was on Dravot's apron, cut into the stone. Not even the priests of the temple of Imbra knew it was there. The old chap falls flat on his face at Dravot's feet and kisses 'em. 'Luck again,' says Dravot, across the Lodge to me, 'they say it's the missing Mark that no one could understand the why of. We're more than safe now.' Then he bangs the butt of his gun for a gavel and says:—'By virtue of the authority vested in me by my own right hand and the help of Peachey, I declare myself Grand-Master of all Freemasonry in Kafiristan in this the Mother Lodge o' the country, and King of Kafiristan equally with Peachey!' At that he puts on his crown and I puts on mine—I was doing Senior Warden—and we opens the Lodge in most ample form. It was a amazing miracle! The priests moved in Lodge through the first two degrees almost without telling, as if the memory was coming back to them. After that, Peachey and Dravot raised such as was worthy—high priests and Chiefs of far-off villages. Billy Fish was the first, and I can tell you we scared the soul out of him. It was not in any way according to Ritual, but it served our turn. We didn't raise more than ten of the biggest men because we didn't want to make the Degree common. And they was clamoring to be raised.

" 'In another six months,' says Dravot, 'we'll hold another Communication and see how you are working.' Then he asks them about their villages, and learns that they was fighting one against the other and were fair sick and tired of it. And when they wasn't doing that they was fighting with the Mohammedans. 'You can fight those when they come into our country,' says Dravot. 'Tell off every tenth man of your tribes for a Frontier guard, and send two hundred at a time to this valley to be drilled. Nobody is going to be shot or speared any more so long as he does well, and I know that you won't cheat me because you're white people—sons of Alexander—and not like common, black Mohammedans. You are *my* people

and by God,' says he, running off into English at the end
—'I'll make a damned fine Nation of you, or I'll die in the
making!'

"I can't tell all we did for the next six months because
Dravot did a lot I couldn't see the hang of, and he learned
their lingo in a way I never could. My work was to help
the people plough, and now and again go out with some
of the Army and see what the other villages were doing,
and make 'em throw rope-bridges across the ravines which
cut up the country horrid. Dravot was very kind to me,
but when he walked up and down in the pine wood pulling
that bloody red beard of his with both fists I knew he was
thinking plans I could not advise him about, and I just
waited for orders.

"But Dravot never showed me disrespect before the
people. They were afraid of me and the Army, but they
loved Dan. He was the best of friends with the priests and
the Chiefs; but any one could come across the hills with
a complaint and Dravot would hear him out fair, and call
four priests together and say what was to be done. He
used to call in Billy Fish from Bashkai, and Pikky Kergan
from Shu, and an old Chief we called Kafuzelum—it was
like enough to his real name—and hold councils with 'em
when there was any fighting to be done in small villages.
That was his Council of War, and the four priests of
Bashkai, Shu, Khawak, and Madora was his Privy Council.
Between the lot of 'em they sent me, with forty men and
twenty rifles, and sixty men carrying turquoises, into the
Ghorband country to buy those hand-made Martini rifles
that come out of the Amir's workshops at Kabul, from
one of the Amir's Herati regiments that would have sold
the very teeth out of their mouths for turquoises.

"I stayed in Ghorband a month, and gave the Governor
there the pick of my baskets for hush-money, and bribed
the Colonel of the regiment some more, and, between the
two and the tribes-people, we got more than a hundred
hand-made Martinis, a hundred good Kohat Jezails that'll
throw to six hundred yards, and forty man-loads of very
bad ammunition for the rifles. I came back with what I
had, and distributed 'em among the men that the Chiefs
sent to me to drill. Dravot was too busy to attend to those
things, but the old Army that we first made helped me, and
we turned out five hundred men that could drill, and two
hundred that knew how to hold arms pretty straight. Even
those cork-screwed, hand-made guns was a miracle to
them. Dravot talked big about powder-shops and factories,

walking up and down in the pine wood when the winter
was coming on.

"'I won't make a Nation,' says he. 'I'll make an Empire! These men aren't niggers; they're English! Look at
their eyes—look at their mouths. Look at the way they
stand up. They sit on chairs in their own houses. They're
the Lost Tribes, or something like it, and they've grown
to be English. I'll take a census in the spring if the priests
don't get frightened. There must be a fair two million of
'em in these hills. The villages are full o' little children.
Two million people—two hundred and fifty thousand
fighting men—and all English! They only want the rifles
and a little drilling. Two hundred and fifty thousand men,
ready to cut in on Russia's right flank when she tries for
India! Peachey, man,' he says, chewing his beard in great
hunks, 'we shall be Emperors—Emperors of the Earth!
Rajah Brooke will be a suckling to us. I'll treat with the
Viceroy on equal terms. I'll ask him to send me twelve
picked English—twelve that I know of—to help us govern
a bit. There's Mackray, Sergeant-pensioner at Segowli—
many's the good dinner he's given me, and his wife a pair
of trousers. There's Donkin, the Warder of Tounghoo
Jail; there's hundreds that I could lay my hand on if I
was in India. The Viceroy shall do it for me. I'll send a
man through in the spring for those men, and I'll write for
a dispensation from the Grand Lodge for what I've done
as Grand-Master. That—and all the Sniders that'll be
thrown out when the native troops in India take up the
Martini. They'll be worn smooth, but they'll do for fighting in these hills. Twelve English, a hundred thousand
Sniders run through the Amir's country in driblets—I'd be
content with twenty thousand in one year—and we'd be
an Empire. When everything was shipshape, I'd hand over
the crown—this crown I'm wearing now—to Queen
Victoria on my knees, and she'd say: "Rise up, Sir Daniel
Dravot." Oh, it's big! It's big, I tell you! But there's so
much to be done in every place—Bashkai, Khawak, Shu,
and everywhere else.'

"'What is it?' I says. 'There are no more men coming in to be drilled this autumn. Look at those fat, black
clouds. They're bringing the snow.'

"'It isn't that,' says Daniel, putting his hand very hard
on my shoulder; 'and I don't wish to say anything that's
against you, for no other living man would have followed
me and made me what I am as you have done. You're a
first-class Commander-in-Chief, and the people know you;

but—it's a big country, and somehow you can't help me, Peachey, in the way I want to be helped.'

" 'Go to your blasted priests, then!' I said, and I was sorry when I made that remark, but it did hurt me sore to find Daniel talking so superior when I'd drilled all the men, and done all he told me.

" 'Don't let's quarrel, Peachey,' says Daniel, without cursing. 'You're a King too, and the half of this Kingdom is yours; but can't you see, Peachey, we want cleverer men than us now—three or four of 'em, that we can scatter about for our Deputies. It's a hugeous great State, and I can't always tell the right thing to do, and I haven't time for all I want to do, and here's the winter coming on and all.' He put half his beard into his mouth, and it was as red as the gold of his crown.

" 'I'm sorry, Daniel,' says I. 'I've done all I could. I've drilled the men and shown the people how to stack their oats better; and I've brought in those tinware rifles from Ghorband—but I know what you're driving at. I take it Kings always feel oppressed that way.'

" 'There's another thing, too,' says Dravot, walking up and down. 'The winter's coming and these people won't be giving much trouble, and if they do we can't move about. I want a wife.'

" 'For Gord's sake leave the women alone!' I says. 'We've both got all the work we can, though I am a fool. Remember the Contrack, and keep clear o' women.'

" 'The Contrack only lasted till such time as we was Kings; and Kings we have been these months past,' says Dravot, weighing his crown in his hand. 'You go get a wife too, Peachey—a nice, strappin', plump girl that'll keep you warm in the winter. They're prettier than English girls, and we can take the pick of 'em. Boil 'em once or twice in hot water, and they'll come as fair as chicken and ham.'

" 'Don't tempt me!' I says. 'I will not have any dealings with a woman, not till we are a dam' side more settled than we are now. I've been doing the work o' two men, and you've been doing the work o' three. Let's lie off a bit, and see if we can get some better tobacco from Afghan country and run in some good liquor; but no women.'

" 'Who's talking o' women?' says Dravot. 'I said wife —a Queen to breed a King's son for the King. A Queen out of the strongest tribe, that'll make them your blood-brothers, and that'll lie by your side and tell you all the people thinks about you and their own affairs. That's what I want.'

" 'Do you remember that Bengali woman I kept at Mogul Serai when I was a plate-layer?' says I. 'A fat lot o' good she was to me. She taught me the lingo and one or two other things; but what happened? She ran away with the Station Master's servant and half my month's pay. Then she turned up at Dadur Junction in tow of a half-caste, and had the impidence to say I was her husband —all among the drivers in the running-shed!'

" 'We've done with that,' says Dravot. 'These women are whiter than you or me, and a Queen I will have for the winter months.'

" 'For the last time o' asking, Dan, do *not*,' I says. 'It'll only bring us harm. The Bible says that Kings ain't to waste their strength on women, 'specially when they've got a new raw Kingdom to work over.'

" 'For the last time of answering I will,' said Dravot, and he went away through the pine-trees looking like a big red devil. The low sun hit his crown and beard on one side and the two blazed like hot coals.

"But getting a wife was not as easy as Dan thought. He put it before the Council, and there was no answer till Billy Fish said that he'd better ask the girls. Dravot damned them all round. 'What's wrong with me?' he shouts, standing by the idol Imbra. 'Am I a dog or am I not enough of a man for your wenches? Haven't I put the shadow of my hand over this country? Who stopped the last Afghan raid?' It was me really, but Dravot was too angry to remember. 'Who brought your guns? Who repaired the bridges? Who's the Grand-Master of the sign cut in the stone?' and he thumped his hand on the block that he used to sit on in Lodge, and at Council, which opened like Lodge always. Billy Fish said nothing and no more did the others. 'Keep your hair on, Dan,' said I; 'and ask the girls. That's how it's done at Home, and these people are quite English.'

" 'The marriage of the King is a matter of State,' says Dan, in a white-hot rage, for he could feel, I hope, that he was going against his better mind. He walked out of the Council-room, and the others sat still, looking at the ground.

" 'Billy Fish,' says I to the Chief of Bashkai, 'what's the difficulty here? A straight answer to a true friend.' 'You know,' says Billy Fish. 'How should a man tell you who know everything? How can daughters of men marry Gods or Devils? It's not proper.'

"I remembered something like that in the Bible; but if, after seeing us as long as they had, they still believed we were Gods, it wasn't for me to undeceive them.

" 'A God can do anything,' says I. 'If the King is fond of a girl he'll not let her die.' 'She'll have to,' said Billy Fish. 'There are all sorts of Gods and Devils in these mountains, and now and again a girl marries one of them and isn't seen any more. Besides, you two know the Mark cut in the stone. Only the Gods know that. We thought you were men till you showed the sign of the Master.'

"I wished then that we had explained about the loss of the genuine secrets of a Master-Mason at the first go-off; but I said nothing. All that night there was a blowing of horns in a little dark temple half-way down the hill, and I heard a girl crying fit to die. One of the priests told us that she was being prepared to marry the King.

" 'I'll have no nonsense of that kind,' says Dan. 'I don't want to interfere with your customs, but I'll take my own wife.' 'The girl's a little bit afraid,' says the priest. 'She thinks she's going to die, and they are a-heartening of her up down in the temple.'

" 'Hearten her very tender, then,' says Dravot, 'or I'll hearten you with the butt of a gun so that you'll never want to be heartened again.' He licked his lips, did Dan, and stayed up walking about more than half the night, thinking of the wife that he was going to get in the morning. I wasn't any means comfortable, for I knew that dealings with a woman in foreign parts, though you was a crowned King twenty times over, could not but be risky. I got up very early in the morning while Dravot was asleep, and I saw the priests talking together in whispers, and the Chiefs talking together too, and they looked at me out of the corners of their eyes.

" 'What is up, Fish?' I says to the Bashkai man, who was wrapped up in his furs and looking splendid to behold.

" 'I can't rightly say,' says he; 'but if you can induce the King to drop all this nonsense about marriage, you'll be doing him and me and yourself a great service.'

" 'That I do believe,' says I. 'But sure, you know, Billy, as well as me, having fought against and for us, that the King and me are nothing more than two of the finest men that God Almighty ever made. Nothing more, I do assure you.'

" 'That may be,' says Billy Fish, 'and yet I should be sorry if it was.' He sinks his head upon his great fur cloak for a minute and thinks. 'King,' says he, 'be you man or God or Devil, I'll stick by you to-day. I have twenty of my men with me, and they will follow me. We'll go to Bashkai until the storm blows over.'

"A little snow had fallen in the night, and everything was white except the greasy fat clouds that blew down and down from the north. Dravot came out with his crown on his head, swinging his arms and stamping his feet, and looking more pleased than Punch.

" 'For the last time, drop it, Dan,' says I, in a whisper. 'Billy Fish here says that there will be a row.'

" 'A row among my people!' says Dravot. 'Not much. Peachey, you're a fool not to get a wife too. Where's the girl?' says he, with a voice as loud as the braying of a jackass. 'Call up all the Chiefs and priests, and let the Emperor see if his wife suits him.'

"There was no need to call any one. They were all there leaning on their guns and spears round the clearing in the centre of the pine wood. A deputation of priests went down to the little temple to bring up the girl, and the horns blew up fit to wake the dead. Billy Fish saunters round and gets as close to Daniel as he could, and behind him stood his twenty men with matchlocks. Not a man of them under six feet. I was next to Dravot, and behind me was twenty men of the regular Army. Up comes the girl, and a strapping wench she was, covered with silver and turquoises but white as death, and looking back every minute at the priests.

" 'She'll do,' said Dan, looking her over. 'What's to be afraid of, lass? Come and kiss me.' He puts his arm round her. She shuts her eyes, gives a bit of a squeak, and down goes her face in the side of Dan's flaming red beard.

" 'The slut's bitten me!' says he, clapping his hand to his neck, and, sure enough, his hand was red with blood. Billy Fish and two of his matchlock-men catches hold of Dan by the shoulders and drags him into the Bashkai lot, while the priests howl in their lingo,—'Neither God nor Devil but a man!' I was all taken aback, for a priest cut at me in front, and the Army behind began firing into the Bashkai men.

" 'God A-mighty!' says Dan. 'What is the meaning o' this?'

" 'Come back! Come away!' says Billy Fish. 'Ruin and Mutiny is the matter. We'll break for Bashkai if we can.'

"I tried to give some sort of orders to my men—the men o' the regular Army—but it was no use, so I fired into the brown of 'em with an English Martini and drilled three beggars in a line. The valley was full of shouting, howling creatures, and every soul was shrieking, 'Not a God nor a Devil but only a man!' The Bashkai troops stuck to Billy Fish all they were worth, but their matchlocks wasn't half as good as the Kabul breech-loaders, and four of them dropped. Dan was bellowing like a bull, for he was very wrathy; and Billy Fish had a hard job to prevent him running out at the crowd.

" 'We can't stand,' says Billy Fish. 'Make a run for it down the valley! The whole place is against us.' The matchlock-men ran, and we went down the valley in spite of Dravot's protestations. He was swearing horribly and crying out that he was a King. The priests rolled great stones on us, and the regular Army fired hard, and there wasn't more than six men, not counting Dan, Billy Fish, and Me, that came down to the bottom of the valley alive.

"Then they stopped firing and the horns in the temple blew again. 'Come away—for Gord's sake come away!' says Billy Fish. 'They'll send runners out to all the villages before ever we get to Bashkai. I can protect you there, but I can't do anything now.'

"My own notion is that Dan began to go mad in his head from that hour. He stared up and down like a stuck pig. Then he was all for walking back alone and killing the priests with his bare hands; which he could have done. 'An Emperor am I,' says Daniel, 'and next year I shall be a Knight of the Queen.'

" 'All right, Dan,' says I; 'but come along now while there's time.'

" 'It's your fault,' says he, 'for not looking after your Army better. There was mutiny in the midst, and you didn't know—you damned engine-driving, plate-laying, missionary's-pass-hunting hound!' He sat upon a rock and called me every foul name he could lay tongue to. I was too heart-sick to care, though it was all his foolishness that brought the smash.

" 'I'm sorry, Dan,' says I, 'but there's no accounting for natives. This business is our Fifty-Seven. Maybe we'll make something out of it yet, when we've got to Bashkai.'

" 'Let's get to Bashkai,' says Dan, 'and, by God, when I come back here again I'll sweep the valley so there isn't a bug in a blanket left!'

"We walked all that day, and all that night Dan was stumping up and down on the snow, chewing his beard and muttering to himself.

" 'There's no hope o' getting clear,' said Billy Fish. 'The priests will have sent runners to the villages to say that you are only men. Why didn't you stick on as Gods till things was more settled? I'm a dead man,' says Billy Fish, and he throws himself down on the snow and begins to pray to his Gods.

"Next morning we was in a cruel bad country—all up and down, no level ground at all, and no food either. The six Bashkai men looked at Billy Fish hungry-wise as if they wanted to ask something, but they said never a word. At noon we came to the top of a flat mountain all covered with snow, and when we climbed up into it, behold, there was an Army in position waiting in the middle!

" 'The runners have been very quick,' says Billy Fish, with a little bit of a laugh. 'They are waiting for us.'

"Three or four men began to fire from the enemy's side, and a chance shot took Daniel in the calf of the leg. That brought him to his senses. He looks across the snow at the Army, and sees the rifles that we had brought into the country.

" 'We're done for,' says he. 'They are Englishmen, these people,—and it's my blasted nonsense that has brought you to this. Get back, Billy Fish, and take your men away; you've done what you could, and now cut for it. Carnehan,' says he, 'shake hands with me and go along with Billy. Maybe they won't kill you. I'll go and meet 'em alone. It's me that did it. Me, the King!'

" 'Go!' says I. 'Go to Hell, Dan. I'm with you here. Billy Fish, you clear out, and we two will meet those folk.'

" 'I'm a Chief,' says Billy Fish, quite quiet. 'I stay with you. My men can go.'

"The Bashkai fellows didn't wait for a second word but ran off, and Dan and Me and Billy Fish walked across to where the drums were drumming and the horns were horning. It was cold—awful cold. I've got that cold in the back of my head now. There's a lump of it there."

The punkah-coolies had gone to sleep. Two kerosene lamps were blazing in the office, and the perspiration poured down my face and splashed on the blotter as I leaned forward. Carnehan was shivering, and I feared that his mind might go. I wiped my face, took a fresh grip of the piteously mangled hands, and said:—"What happened after that?"

The momentary shift of my eyes had broken the clear current.

"What was you pleased to say?" whined Carnehan. "They took them without any sound. Not a little whisper all along the snow, not though the King knocked down the first man that set hand on him—not though old Peachey fired his last cartridge into the brown of 'em. Not a single solitary sound did those swines make. They just closed up tight, and I tell you their furs stunk. There was a man called Billy Fish, a good friend of us all, and they cut his throat, Sir, then and there, like a pig; and the King kicks up the bloody snow and says:—'We've had a dashed fine run for our money. What's coming next?' But Peachey, Peachey Taliaferro, I tell you, Sir, in confidence as betwixt two friends, he lost his head, Sir. No, he didn't neither. The King lost his head, so he did, all along o' one of those cunning rope-bridges. Kindly let me have the paper-cutter, Sir. It tilted this way. They marched him a mile across that snow to a rope-bridge over a ravine with a river at the bottom. You may have seen such. They prodded him behind like an ox. 'Damn your eyes!' says the King. 'D'you suppose I can't die like a gentleman?' He turns to Peachey—Peachey that was crying like a child. 'I've brought you to this, Peachey,' says he. 'Brought you out of your happy life to be killed in Kafiristan, where you was late Commander-in-Chief of the Emperor's forces. Say you forgive me, Peachey.' 'I do,' says Peachey. 'Fully and freely do I forgive you, Dan.' 'Shake hands, Peachey,' says he. 'I'm going now.' Out he goes, looking neither right nor left, and when he was plumb in the middle of those dizzy dancing ropes, 'Cut, you beggars,' he shouts; and they cut, and old Dan fell, turning round and round and round twenty thousand miles, for he took half an hour to fall till he struck the water, and I could see his body caught on a rock with the gold crown close beside.

"But do you know what they did to Peachey between two pine trees? They crucified him, Sir, as Peachey's hand will show. They used wooden pegs for his hands and his feet; and he didn't die. He hung there and screamed, and they took him down next day, and said it was a miracle that he wasn't dead. They took him

down—poor old Peachey that hadn't done them any harm
—that hadn't done them any . . ."

He rocked to and fro and wept bitterly, wiping his eyes
with the back of his scarred hands and moaning like a
child for some ten minutes.

"They was cruel enough to feed him up in the temple,
because they said he was more of a God than old Daniel
that was a man. Then they turned him out on the snow,
and told him to go home, and Peachey came home in about
a year, begging along the roads quite safe; for Daniel
Dravot he walked before and said:—'Come along,
Peachey. It's a big thing we're doing.' The mountains they
danced at night, and the mountains they tried to fall on
Peachey's head, but Dan he held up his hand, and
Peachey came along bent double. He never let go of Dan's
hand, and he never let go of Dan's head. They gave it to
him as a present in the temple, to remind him not to
come again, and though the crown was pure gold, and
Peachey was starving, never would Peachey sell the same.
You knew Dravot, Sir! You knew Right Worshipful
Brother Dravot! Look at him now!"

He fumbled in the mass of rags round his bent waist;
brought out a black horsehair bag embroidered with silver
thread; and shook therefrom on to my table—the dried,
withered head of Daniel Dravot! The morning sun that
had long been paling the lamps struck the red beard and
blind sunken eyes; struck, too, a heavy circlet of gold
studded with raw turquoises, that Carnehan placed tenderly on the battered temples.

"You behold now," said Carnehan, "the Emperor in
his habit as he lived—the King of Kafiristan with his
crown upon his head. Poor old Daniel that was a monarch
once!"

I shuddered, for, in spite of defacements manifold, I
recognized the head of the man of Marwar Junction.
Carnehan rose to go. I attempted to stop him. He was
not fit to walk abroad. "Let me take away the whiskey,
and give me a little money," he gasped. "I was a King
once. I'll go to the Deputy Commissioner and ask to set
in the Poorhouse till I get my health. No, thank you, I
can't wait till you get a carriage for me. I've urgent private
affairs—in the south—at Marwar."

He shambled out of the office and departed in the
direction of the Deputy Commissioner's house. That day
at noon I had occasion to go down the blinding hot Mall,
and I saw a crooked man crawling along the white dust

of the roadside, his hat in his hand, quavering dolorously
after the fashion of street-singers at Home. There was not
a soul in sight, and he was out of all possible earshot of
the houses. And he sang through his nose, turning his head
from right to left:

> The Son of Man goes forth to war,
>   A golden crown to gain;
> His blood-red banner streams afar—
>   Who follows in his train?

I waited to hear no more, but put the poor wretch into
my carriage and drove him off to the nearest missionary
for eventual transfer to the Asylum. He repeated the hymn
twice while he was with me whom he did not in the least
recognize, and I left him singing it to the missionary.

Two days later I inquired after his welfare of the
Superintendent of the Asylum.

"He was admitted suffering from sunstroke. He died
early yesterday morning," said the Superintendent. "Is it
true that he was half an hour bareheaded in the sun at
midday?"

"Yes," said I, "but do you happen to know if he had
anything upon him by any chance when he died?"

"Not to my knowledge," said the Superintendent.

And there the matter rests.

José Vasconcelos
(1882–1959)

Very little of José Vasconcelos' work has been translated into English, and his reputation in both the United States and England is still to be made. "The Boar Hunt" is one of the few stories available in English at the present time. But in his native Mexico, Vasconcelos is considered a master of fictional technique.

Like other famous Latin-American writers, Vasconcelos has served his country not merely as a writer but as an educator and statesman. From 1920 to 1924, he was head of the National University of Mexico and he served as minister of education under the regime of Álvaro Obregón. In 1929 he was a candidate for the Mexican presidency, but was unsuccessful.

"The Boar Hunt" creates the kind of tension characteristic of suspense stories. But Vasconcelos takes us beyond the incident itself into a penetrating look at the nature of killing. The story has obvious political and moral overtones.

The Boar Hunt

We were four companions, and we went by the names of our respective nationalities: the Colombian, the Peruvian, the Mexican; the fourth, a native of Ecuador, was called Quito for short. Unforeseen chance had joined us together a few years ago on a large sugar plantation on the Peruvian coast. We worked at different occupations during the day and met during the evening in our off time. Not being Englishmen, we did not play cards. Instead, our constant discussions led to disputes. These didn't stop us from wanting to see each other the next night, however, to continue the interrupted debates and support them with new arguments. Nor did the rough sentences of the preceding wrangles indicate a lessening of our affection, of which we assured ourselves reciprocally with the clasping of hands and a look. On Sundays we used to go on hunting parties. We roamed the fertile glens, stalking, generally with poor results, the game of the warm region around the coast, or we entertained ourselves killing birds that flew in the sunlight during the siesta hour.

We came to be tireless wanderers and excellent marksmen. Whenever we climbed a hill and gazed at the imposing range of mountains in the interior, its attractiveness stirred us and we wanted to climb it. What attracted us more was the trans-Andean region: fertile plateaus extending on the other side of the range in the direction of the Atlantic toward the immense land of Brazil. It was as if primitive nature called us to her breast. The vigor of the fertile, untouched jungles promised to rejuvenate our minds, the same vigor which rejuvenates the strength and the thickness of the trees each year. At times we devised crazy plans. As with all things that are given a lot of thought, these schemes generally materialized. Ultimately nature and events are largely what our imaginations make them out to be. And so we went ahead planning and acting. At the end of the year, with arranged vacations, accumulated money, good rifles, abundant munitions, stone- and mudproof boots, four hammocks, and a half dozen faithful Indians, our caravan descended the Andean slopes, leading to the endless green ocean.

At last we came upon a village at the edge of the Marañón River. Here we changed our safari. The region we were going to penetrate had no roads. It was unexplored underbrush into which we could enter only by going down the river in a canoe. In time we came to the area where we proposed to carry out the purpose of our journey, the hunting of wild boars.

We had been informed that boars travel in herds of several thousands, occupying a region, eating grass and staying together, exploiting the grazing areas, organized just like an army. They are very easy to kill if one attacks them when they are scattered out satisfying their appetites —an army given over to the delights of victory. When they march about hungry, on the other hand, they are usually vicious. In our search we glided down river between imposing jungles with our provisions and the company of three faithful Indian oarsmen.

One morning we stopped at some huts near the river. Thanks to the information gathered there, we decided to disembark a little farther on in order to spend the night on land and continue the hunt for the boars in the thicket the following day.

Sheltered in a backwater, we came ashore, and after a short exploration found a clearing in which to make camp. We unloaded the provisions and the rifles, tied the boat securely, then with the help of the Indians set up our camp one half kilometer from the river bank. In marking the path to the landing, we were careful not to lose ourselves in the thicket. The Indians withdrew toward their huts, promising to return two days later. At dawn we would set out in search of the prey.

Though night had scarcely come and the heat was great, we gathered at the fire to see each other's faces, to look instinctively for protection. We talked a little, smoked, confessed to being tired, and decided to go to bed. Each hammock had been tied by one end to a single tree, firm though not very thick in the trunk. Stretching out from this axis in different directions, the hammocks were supported by the other end on other trunks. Each of us carried his rifle, cartridges, and some provisions which couldn't remain exposed on the ground. The sight of the weapons made us consider the place where we were, surrounded by the unknown. A slight feeling of terror made us laugh, cough, and talk. But fatigue overcame us, that heavy fatigue which compels the soldier to scorn danger, to put down his rifle, and to fall asleep though the most persistent enemy pursues him. We scarcely noticed the supreme grandeur of that remote tropical night.

I don't know whether it was the light of the magnificent dawn or the strange noises which awakened me and made me sit up in my hammock and look carefully at my surroundings. I saw nothing but the awakening of that life which at night falls into the lethargy of the jungle. I called my sleeping companions and, alert and seated in our hanging beds, we dressed ourselves. We were preparing to jump to the ground when we clearly heard a somewhat distant, sudden sound of rustling branches. Since it did not continue, however, we descended confidently, washed our faces with water from our canteens, and slowly prepared and enjoyed breakfast. By about 11:00 in the morning we were armed and bold and preparing to make our way through the jungle.

But then the sound again. Its persistence and proximity in the thicket made us change our minds. An instinct made us take refuge in our hammocks. We cautiously moved our cartridges and rifles into them again, and without consulting each other we agreed on the idea of putting our provisions safely away. We passed them up into the hammocks, and we ourselves finally climbed in. Stretched out face down, comfortably suspended with rifles in hand, we did not have to wait long. Black, agile boars quickly appeared from all directions. We welcomed them with shouts of joy and well-aimed shots. Some fell immediately, giving comical snorts, but many more came out of the jungle. We shot again, spending all the cartridges in the magazine. Then we stopped to reload. Finding ourselves safe in the height of our hammocks, we continued after a pause.

We counted dozens of them. At a glance we made rapid calculations of the magnitude of the destruction, while the boars continued to come out of the jungle in uncountable numbers. Instead of going on their way or fleeing, they seemed confused. All of them emerged from the jungle where it was easy for us to shoot them. Occasionally we had to stop firing because the frequent shooting heated the barrels of our rifles. While they were cooling we smoked and were able to joke, celebrating our good fortune. The impotent anger of the boars amazed us. They raised their tusks in our direction, uselessly threatening us. We laughed at their snorts, quietly aimed at those who were near, and Bang! a dead boar. We carefully studied the angle of the shoulder blade so that the bullet would cross the heart. The slaughter lasted for hours.

At 4:00 P.M. we noticed an alarming shortage of our ammunition. We had been well supplied and had shot at will. Though the slaughter was gratifying, the boars must have numbered, as we had been informed previously, several thousands, because their hordes didn't diminish. On the contrary, they gathered directly beneath our hammocks in increasing groups. They slashed furiously at the trunk of the tree which held the four points of the hammocks. The marks of the tusks remained on the hard bark. Not without a certain fear we watched them gather compactly, tenaciously, in tight masses against the resisting trunk. We wondered what would happen to a man who fell within their reach. Our shots were now sporadic, well aimed, carefully husbanded. They did not drive away the aggressive beasts, but only redoubled their fury. One of us ironically noted that from being the attackers we had gone on the defensive. We did not laugh very long at the joke.

Now we hardly shot at all. We needed to save our
cartridges.

The afternoon waned and evening came upon us. After
consulting each other, we decided to eat in our hammocks.
We applauded ourselves for taking the food up—meat,
bread, and bottles of water. Stretching ourselves on our
hammocks, we passed things to each other, sharing what
we needed. The boars deafened us with their angry snorts.

After eating, we began to feel calm. We lit cigars. Surely
the boars would go. Their numbers were great, but they
would finally leave peacefully. As we said so, however, we
looked with greedy eyes at the few unused cartridges that
remained. Our enemies, like enormous angry ants, stirred
beneath us, encouraged by the ceasing of our fire. From
time to time we carefully aimed and killed one or two of
them, driving off the huge group of uselessly enraged boars
at the base of the trunk which served as a prop for our
hammocks.

Night enveloped us almost without our noticing the
change from twilight. Anxiety also overtook us. When
would the cursed boars leave? Already there were enough
dead to serve as trophies to several dozen hunters. Our
feat would be talked about; we had to show ourselves
worthy of such fame. Since there was nothing else to do,
it was necessary to sleep. Even if we had had enough
bullets it would have been impossible to continue the fight
in the darkness. It occurred to us to start a fire to drive
the herd off with flames, but apart from the fact that we
couldn't leave the place in which we were suspended, there
were no dry branches in the lush forest. Finally, we slept.

We woke up a little after midnight. The darkness was
profound, but the well-known noise made us aware that
our enemies were still there. We imagined they must be
the last ones which were leaving, however. If a good army
needs several hours to break camp and march off, what
can be expected of a vile army of boars but disorder and
delay? The following morning we would fire upon the
stragglers, but this painful thought bothered us: they were
in large and apparently active numbers. What were they
up to? Why didn't they leave? We thus spent long hours
of worry. Dawn finally came, splendid in the sky but noisy
in the jungle still enveloped inwardly in shadows. We
eagerly waited for the sun to penetrate the foliage in order
to survey the appearance of the field of battle of the day
before.

What we finally saw made us gasp. It terrified us. The

boars were painstakingly continuing the work which they had engaged in throughout the entire night. Guided by some extraordinary instinct, with their tusks they were digging out the ground underneath the tree from which our hammocks hung; they gnawed the roots and continued to undermine them like large, industrious rats. Presently the tree was bound to fall and we with it, among the beasts. From that moment we neither thought nor talked. In desperation we used up our last shots, killing more ferocious beasts. Still the rest renewed their activity. They seemed to be endowed with intelligence. However much we concentrated our fire against them, they did not stop their attack against the tree.

Soon our shots stopped. We emptied our pistols, and then silently listened to the tusks gnawing beneath the soft, wet, pleasant-smelling earth. From time to time the boars pressed against the tree, pushing it and making it creak, eager to smash it quickly. We looked on hypnotized by their devilish activity. It was impossible to flee because the black monsters covered every inch in sight. It seemed to us that, by a sudden inspiration, they were preparing to take revenge on us for the ruthless nature of man, the unpunished destroyer of animals since the beginning of time. Our imagination, distorted by fear, showed us our fate as an atonement for the unpardonable crimes implicit in the struggle of biological selection. Before my eyes passed the vision of sacred India, where the believer refuses to eat meat in order to prevent the methodical killing of beasts and in order to atone for man's evil, bloody, treacherous slaughter, such as ours, for mere vicious pleasure. I felt that the multitude of boars was raising its accusing voice against me. I now understood the infamy of the hunter, but what was repentance worth if I was going to die with my companions, hopelessly devoured by that horde of brutes with demonlike eyes?

Stirred by terror and without realizing what I was doing, I hung from the upper end of my hammock, I balanced myself in the air, I swung in a long leap, I grasped a branch of a tree facing the one on which the boars were digging. From there I leaped to other branches and to others, reviving in myself habits which the species had forgotten.

The next moment a terrifying sound and unforgettable cries told me of the fall of the tree and the end of my companions. I clung to a trunk, trembling and listening to the chattering of my jaws. Later, the desire to flee gave

me back my strength. Leaning out over the foliage, I
looked for a path, and I saw the boars in the distance,
marching in compressed ranks and holding their insolent
snouts in the air. I knew that they were now withdrawing,
and I got down from the tree. Horror overwhelmed me as
I approached the site of our encampment, but some idea
of duty made me return there. Perhaps one of my friends
had managed to save himself. I approached hesitantly.
Each dead boar made me tremble with fear.

But what I saw next was so frightful that I could not fix
it clearly in my mind: remains of clothing—and footwear.
There was no doubt; the boars had devoured them. Then
I ran toward the river, following the tracks we had made
two days before. I fled with great haste, limbs stiff from
panic.

Running with long strides, I came upon a boat. With
great effort, I managed to row to the huts. There I went
to bed with a high fever which lasted many days.

I will participate in no more hunts. I will contribute, if
I have to, to the extermination of harmful beasts. But I
will not kill for pleasure. I will not amuse myself with the
ignoble pleasure of the hunt.

Sherwood Anderson

(1876–1941)

The confusion between fact and fiction in the life of Sherwood Anderson stems from his effort to attribute his strange breakdown in 1912 to his deliberate decision to abandon a thriving business in order to begin a new life as a writer. Until that episode, however, his life epitomized the American success story. Born into a poor family in Camden, Ohio, he grew up in another small Ohio town, Clyde. At fourteen he quit school, worked at a number of jobs, joined the National Guard, and did patrol duty in Cuba after the Spanish-American War. Mustered out of the Guard, he returned to Ohio and enrolled in high school at the age of twenty-three. After later success as a writer of advertising copy, he soon found himself at the head of his own paint factory, the Anderson Manufacturing Company. According to his autobiography, he walked out of his successful business one day while dictating a letter to his secretary. But the truth seems far less romantic or dramatic. Apparently harassed by family and business problems, as well as four novels which he had started without being able to bring any of them to a successful completion, he seems to have suffered a nervous breakdown. Four days after his departure from the Anderson Manufacturing Company, he was found wandering in Cleveland, an apparent victim of exhaustion and amnesia. The importance of Anderson's flight is the great symbolic significance it took on for younger American writers who saw in it an action as momentous as Nora's walking out the door at the conclusion of Ibsen's A Doll's House.

Anderson next went to Chicago where he was accepted into the circle of writers who made up the Chicago Renaissance—Floyd Dell, Ben Hecht, Edgar Lee Masters, and Theodore Dreiser. Chicago was to prove far more hospitable to him than the cities in which he was to continue his restless wandering—New York, Paris, New Orleans.

There remains something essentially midwestern in Anderson's work. The influence he was to have on Hemingway, on Faulkner, on Thomas Wolfe is the influence of a man gripped by the struggles and confusions of Middle America. The powerful voice he gave to Middle America still sets his fiction apart from his many imitators. The flatness of the plains, the small dusty towns, the passing of life amidst loneliness and despair and the desire for something larger, some cosmic hunger of the sensitive individual—all stem from Anderson's own boyhood in Ohio and all are at the root of the brief revelations which make his best fiction so distinctive. The stories in his most memorable book, Winesburg, Ohio *(1919), are filled with the same haunting desperation that one finds in Edgar Lee Masters'* Spoon River Anthology *and the poetry of Edwin Arlington Robinson. This is the quality which the novelist Herbert Gold had in mind when he described Anderson as "one of the purest, most intense, poets of loneliness."*

Anderson's novels fall far short of his three excellent collections of stories, Winesburg, Ohio; The Triumph of the Egg *(1921); and* Horses and Men *(1923). His forays into novel writing, like his ostensibly autobiographical narratives (in which he seems to have changed fact at will and to have tried to portray himself as a far more rebellious figure than he actually was), simply do not achieve the power of his short stories. The sense of place that seized Anderson's own imagination is graphically transmitted to the reader in a story such as "Sophistication." Today, even more than when Anderson wrote it in 1919, it reads like a farewell to small-town America, somewhat more nostalgic in tone than Anderson intended it to be. For even the America to which he defiantly addressed himself has disappeared.*

Sophistication

It was early evening of a day in the late fall and the Winesburg County Fair had brought crowds of country people into town. The day had been clear and the night came on warm and pleasant. On the Trunion Pike, where the road after it left town stretched away between berry fields now covered with dry brown leaves, the dust from passing wagons arose in clouds. Children, curled into little balls, slept on the straw scattered on wagon beds. Their hair was full of dust and their fingers black and sticky. The dust rolled away over the fields and the departing sun set it ablaze with colors.

In the main street of Winesburg crowds filled the stores

and the sidewalks. Night came on, horses whinnied, the
clerks in the stores ran madly about, children became lost
and cried lustily, an American town worked terribly at the
task of amusing itself.

Pushing his way through the crowds in Main Street,
young George Willard concealed himself in the stairway
leading to Doctor Reefy's office and looked at the people.
With feverish eyes he watched the faces drifting past under
the store lights. Thoughts kept coming into his head and
he did not want to think. He stamped impatiently on the
wooden steps and looked sharply about. "Well, is she going
to stay with him all day? Have I done all this waiting for
nothing?" he muttered.

George Willard, the Ohio village boy, was fast growing
into manhood and new thoughts had been coming into his
mind. All that day, amid the jam of people at the Fair, he
had gone about feeling lonely. He was about to leave
Winesburg to go away to some city where he hoped to get
work on a city newspaper and he felt grown up. The mood
that had taken possession of him was a thing known to
men and unknown to boys. He felt old and a little tired.
Memories awoke in him. To his mind his new sense of
maturity set him apart, made of him a half-tragic figure.
He wanted someone to understand the feeling that had
taken possession of him after his mother's death.

There is a time in the life of every boy when he for the
first time takes the backward view of life. Perhaps that is
the moment when he crosses the line into manhood. The
boy is walking through the street of his town. He is thinking of the future and of the figure he will cut in the world.
Ambitions and regrets awake within him. Suddenly something happens; he stops under a tree and waits as for a
voice calling his name. Ghosts of old things creep into his
consciousness; the voices outside of himself whisper a
message concerning the limitations of life. From being
quite sure of himself and his future he becomes not at all
sure. If he be an imaginative boy a door is torn open and
for the first time he looks out upon the world, seeing, as
though they marched in procession before him, the countless figures of men who before his time have come out of
nothingness into the world, lived their lives and again disappeared into nothingness. The sadness of sophistication
has come to the boy. With a little gasp he sees himself as
merely a leaf blown by the wind through the streets of his
village. He knows that in spite of all the stout talk of his
fellows he must live and die in uncertainty, a thing blown

by the winds, a thing destined like corn to wilt in the sun.
He shivers and looks eagerly about. The eighteen years he
has lived seem but a moment, a breathing space in the
long march of humanity. Already he hears death calling.
With all his heart he wants to come close to some other
human, touch someone with his hands, be touched by the
hand of another. If he prefers that the other be a woman,
that is because he believes that a woman will be gentle,
that she will understand. He wants, most of all, understanding.

When the moment of sophistication came to George
Willard his mind turned to Helen White, the Winesburg
banker's daughter. Always he had been conscious of the
girl growing into womanhood as he grew into manhood.
Once on a summer night when he was eighteen, he had
walked with her on a country road and in her presence
had given way to an impulse to boast, to make himself
appear big and significant in her eyes. Now he wanted to
see her for another purpose. He wanted to tell her of the
new impulses that had come to him. He had tried to make
her think of him as a man when he knew nothing of manhood and now he wanted to be with her and to try to
make her feel the change he believed had taken place in
his nature.

As for Helen White, she also had come to a period of
change. What George felt, she in her young woman's way
felt also. She was no longer a girl and hungered to reach
into the grace and beauty of womanhood. She had come
home from Cleveland, where she was attending college, to
spend a day at the Fair. She also had begun to have memories. During the day she sat in the grand-stand with a
young man, one of the instructors from the college, who
was a guest of her mother's. The young man was of a
pedantic turn of mind and she felt at once he would not
do for her purpose. At the Fair she was glad to be seen in
his company as he was well dressed and a stranger. She
knew that the fact of his presence would create an impression. During the day she was happy, but when night came
on she began to grow restless. She wanted to drive the
instructor away, to get out of his presence. While they sat
together in the grand-stand and while the eyes of former
schoolmates were upon them, she paid so much attention
to her escort that he grew interested. "A scholar needs
money. I should marry a woman with money," he mused.

Helen White was thinking of George Willard even as he
wandered gloomily through the crowds thinking of her.

She remembered the summer evening when they had walked together and wanted to walk with him again. She thought that the months she had spent in the city, the going to theatres and the seeing of great crowds wandering in lighted thoroughfares, had changed her profoundly. She wanted him to feel and be conscious of the change in her nature.

The summer evening together that had left its mark on the memory of both the young man and woman had, when looked at quite sensibly, been rather stupidly spent. They had walked out of town along a country road. Then they had stopped by a fence near a field of young corn and George had taken off his coat and let it hang on his arm. "Well. I've stayed here in Winesburg—yes—I've not yet gone away but I'm growing up," he had said. "I've been reading books and I've been thinking. I'm going to try to amount to something in life.

"Well," he explained, "that isn't the point. Perhaps I'd better quit talking."

The confused boy put his hand on the girl's arm. His voice trembled. The two started to walk back along the road toward town. In his desperation George boasted, "I'm going to be a big man, the biggest that ever lived here in Winesburg," he declared. "I want you to do something, I don't know what. Perhaps it is none of my business. I want you to try to be different from other women. You see the point. It's none of my business I tell you. I want you to be a beautiful woman. You see what I want."

The boy's voice failed and in silence the two came back into town and went along the street to Helen White's house. At the gate he tried to say something impressive. Speeches he had thought out came into his head, but they seemed utterly pointless. "I thought—I used to think—I had it in my mind you would marry Seth Richmond. Now I know you won't," was all he could find to say as she went through the gate and toward the door of her house.

On the warm fall evening as he stood in the stairway and looked at the crowd drifting through Main Street, George thought of the talk beside the field of young corn and was ashamed of the figure he had made of himself. In the street the people surged up and down like cattle confined in a pen. Buggies and wagons almost filled the narrow thoroughfare. A band played and small boys raced along the sidewalk, diving between the legs of men. Young men with shining red faces walked awkwardly about with girls on their arms. In a room above one of the stores, where a dance was to be held, the fiddlers tuned their instruments. The broken sounds floated down through an open window and out across the murmur of voices and the loud blare of the horns of the band. The medley of sounds got on young Willard's nerves. Everywhere, on all sides, the sense of crowding, moving life closed in about him. He wanted to run away by himself and think. "If she wants to stay with that fellow she may. Why should I care? What difference does it make to me?" he growled and went along Main Street and through Hern's grocery into a side street.

George felt so utterly lonely and dejected that he wanted to weep but pride made him walk rapidly along, swinging his arms. He came to Westley Moyer's livery barn and stopped in the shadows to listen to a group of men who talked of a race Westley's stallion, Tony Tip, had won at the Fair during the afternoon. A crowd had gathered in front of the barn and before the crowd walked Westley, prancing up and down and boasting. He held a whip in his hand and kept tapping the ground. Little puffs of dust arose in the lamplight. "Hell, quit your talking," Westley exclaimed. "I wasn't afraid, I knew I had 'em beat all the time. I wasn't afraid."

Ordinarily George Willard would have been intensely interested in the boasting of Moyer, the horseman. Now it made him angry. He turned and hurried away along the street. "Old windbag," he sputtered. "Why does he want to be bragging? Why don't he shut up?"

George went into a vacant lot and as he hurried along, fell over a pile of rubbish. A nail protruding from an empty barrel tore his trousers. He sat down on the ground and swore. With a pin he mended the torn place and then arose and went on. "I'll go to Helen White's house, that's what I'll do. I'll walk right in. I'll say that I want to see her. I'll walk right in and sit down, that's what I'll do," he declared, climbing over a fence and beginning to run.

On the veranda of Banker White's house Helen was restless and distraught. The instructor sat between the mother and daughter. His talk wearied the girl. Although he had also been raised in an Ohio town, the instructor began to put on the airs of the city. He wanted to appear cosmopolitan. "I like the chance you have given me to study the background out of which most of our girls come," he declared. "It was good of you, Mrs. White, to have me down for the day." He turned to Helen and laughed. "Your life is still bound up with the life of this town?" he asked. "There are people here in whom you are interested?" To the girl his voice sounded pompous and heavy.

Helen arose and went into the house. At the door leading to a garden at the back she stopped and stood listening. Her mother began to talk. "There is no one here fit to associate with a girl of Helen's breeding," she said.

Helen ran down a flight of stairs at the back of the house and into the garden. In the darkness she stopped and stood trembling. It seemed to her that the world was full of meaningless people saying words. Afire with eagerness she ran through a garden gate and turning a corner by the banker's barn, went into a little side street. "George! Where are you, George?" she cried, filled with nervous excitement. She stopped running, and leaned against a tree to laugh hysterically. Along the dark little street came George Willard, still saying words. "I'm going to walk right into her house. I'll go right in and sit down," he declared as he came up to her. He stopped and stared stupidly. "Come on," he said and took hold of her hand. With hanging heads they walked away along the street under the trees. Dry leaves rustled under foot. Now that he had found her George wondered what he had better do and say.

At the upper end of the fair ground, in Winesburg, there is a half-decayed old grand-stand. It has never been painted and the boards are all warped out of shape. The fair ground stands on top of a low hill rising out of the valley of Wine Creek and from the grand-stand one can see at night, over a cornfield, the lights of the town reflected against the sky.

George and Helen climbed the hill to the fair ground, coming by the path past Waterworks Pond. The feeling of loneliness and isolation that had come to the young man in the crowded streets of his town was both broken and intensified by the presence of Helen. What he felt was reflected in her.

In youth there are always two forces fighting in people. The warm unthinking little animal struggles against the thing that reflects and remembers, and the older, the more sophisticated thing had possession of George Willard. Sensing his mood, Helen walked beside him filled with respect. When they got to the grand-stand they climbed up under the roof and sat down on one of the long bench-like seats.

There is something memorable in the experience to be

had by going into a fair ground that stands at the edge of
a Middle Western town on a night after the annual fair has
been held. The sensation is one never to be forgotten. On
all sides are ghosts, not of the dead, but of living people.
Here, during the day just passed, have come the people
pouring in from the town and the country around. Farmers
with their wives and children and all the people from the
hundreds of little frame houses have gathered within these
board walls. Young girls have laughed and men with beards
have talked of the affairs of their lives. The place has been
filled to overflowing with life. It has itched and squirmed
with life and now it is night and the life has all gone away.
The silence is almost terrifying. One conceals oneself
standing silently beside the trunk of a tree and what there
is of a reflectve tendency in his nature is intensified. One
shudders at the thought of the meainglessness of life while
at the same instant, and if the people of the town are his
people, one loves life so intensely that tears come into
the eyes.

In the darkness under the roof of the grand-stand,
George Willard sat beside Helen White and felt very keenly
his own insignificance in the scheme of existence. Now
that he had come out of town where the presence of the
people stirring about, busy with a multitude of affairs,
had been so irritating the irritation was all gone. The presence of Helen renewed and refreshed him. It was as though
her woman's hand was assisting him to make some minute
readjustment of the machinery of his life. He began to
think of the people in the town where he had always lived
with something like reverence. He had reverence for Helen.
He wanted to love and to be loved by her, but he did not
want at the moment to be confused by her womanhood.
In the darkness he took hold of her hand and when she
crept close put a hand on her shoulder. A wind began to
blow and he shivered. With all his strength he tried to
hold and to understand the mood that had come upon him.
In that high place in the darkness the two oddly sensitive
human atoms held each other tightly and waited. In the
mind of each was the same thought. "I have come to this
lonely place and here is this other," was the substance of
the thing felt.

In Winesburg the crowded day had run itself out into
the long night of the late fall. Farm horses jogged away
along lonely country roads pulling their portion of weary
people. Clerks began to bring samples of goods in off the
sidewalks and lock the doors of stores. In the Opera House

a crowd had gathered to see a show and further down
Main Street the fiddlers, their instruments tuned, sweated
and worked to keep the feet of youth flying over a dance
floor.

In the darkness in the grand-stand Helen White and
George Willard remained silent. Now and then the spell
that held them was broken and they turned and tried in
the dim light to see into each others eyes. They kissed but
that impulse did not last. At the upper end of the fair
ground a half dozen men worked over horses that had
raced during the afternoon. The men had built a fire and
were heating kettles of water. Only their legs could be seen
as they passed back and forth in the light. When the wind
blew the little flames of the fire danced crazily about.

George and Helen arose and walked away into the
darkness. They went along a path past a field of corn that
had not yet been cut. The wind whispered among the dry
corn blades. For a moment during the walk back into
town the spell that held them was broken. When they had
come to the crest of Waterworks Hill they stopped by a
tree and George again put his hands on the girl's shoulders.
She embraced him eagerly and then again they drew
quickly back from that impulse. They stopped kissing and
stood a little apart. Mutual respect grew big in them. They
were both embarrassed and to relieve their embarrassment
dropped into the animalism of youth. They laughed and
began to pull and haul at each other. In some way chas-
tened and purified by the mood they had been in they
became, not man and woman, not boy and girl, but excited
little animals.

It was so they went down the hill. In the darkness they
played like two splendid young things in a young world.
Once, running swiftly forward, Helen tripped George and
he fell. He squirmed and shouted. Shaking with laughter,
he rolled down the hill. Helen ran after him. For just a
moment she stopped in the darkness. There is no way of
knowing what woman's thoughts went through her mind
but, when the bottom of the hill was reached and she
came up to the boy, she took his arm and walked beside
him in dignified silence. For some reason they could not
have explained they had both got from their silent evening
together the thing needed. Man or boy, woman or girl,
they had for a moment taken hold of the thing that makes
the mature life of men and women in the modern world
possible.

James Joyce

(1882–1941)

Born and raised in Dublin, Joyce had to exile himself from Ireland in order to create from the turmoil of the life he lived and observed there what a substantial number of readers and critics believe is the outstanding achievement of modern English fiction. The son of a talented but dissolute father—the very antithesis of Franz Kafka's authoritarian father—and the eldest of ten children, Joyce saw his family drift into genteel poverty, moving from house to house, each of them one step down on the social scale. If Dublin was the matrix out of which Joyce created his fiction, then the Jesuit education he received between the ages of six and sixteen, first at Clongowes Woods College and then at Belvedere College, was the crucible in which his antecedents as a writer were formed and his lifelong argument with Catholicism, a vital source of his fiction, began to take shape. The Jesuits left an indelible mark upon Joyce. Few writers have been so steeped in the classics and the study of languages as he was.

After taking his B.A. at University College in Dublin, Joyce left for Paris, returned to Dublin for his mother's final illness, then permanently exiled himself with Nora Barnacle, a vivacious but uneducated Galway girl, at first in Trieste, then in Zurich, and from 1920 to 1940 in Paris, where he lived and was lionized by other writers as one of the great prose experimentalists of modern times. The war forced him to flee the Nazis and to take refuge in Zurich where he died in 1941.

Joyce's fame rests on four books. Dubliners *(1915) is a group of related stories which shed a remarkable light on all aspects of Dublin life. The city becomes a microcosm of all western cities and the men and women who populate Joyce's pages are embodiments of man's fate. Joyce left Dublin in order to re-create it, a task which he began with* Dubliners, *continued with the autobiographical* A Portrait of the Artist as a Young Man *(1916), with* Ulysses *(1922), and culminated in* Finnegans Wake *(1939) in which Joyce's penchant for puns and word play explodes in a vast symbolic dream that has kept legions of critics and explicators busy trying to* put it all together in the thirty-one years since its publication. That they have succeeded only in approaching its almost impenetrable mysteries can be taken as evidence that Joyce's final novel was intended to destroy the novel as an art form or that the casual reader has no place in so densely rich and complex a dream universe. Some critics have unkindly suggested that Joyce would want no place there either.

Dubliners is the simplest and most immediate of Joyce's books. What binds the stories together is not merely Joyce's technique, his creation of the famed short story epiphanies, nor even the geographic explorations of Dublin life. Rather, it is the haunting texture of these stories. Joyce's Dublin stands as a fictional summation of modern experience. The only other contemporary writer to approach this achievement is William Faulkner, who created a similar microcosm out of his Yoknapatawpha County.

No story in Dubliners exhibits the quality of "summation" better than "The Dead," which Joyce's biographer, Richard Ellman, described as his "first song of exile." The writing brilliantly and sensitively captures the accents and the psychological interiors of the Irish middle class. For here we see not only Gabriel Conroy and his wife as victims of the dead, of the memories which spring to life at a particular moment and so embrace our future with our pasts, but we see all of Dublin as a world haunted by its past. The carefully arranged symbols, the glimpses of Dublin monuments, the party at Gabriel's aunts' home, all are deeply evocative of that moment when the artist fuses past and present. Few contemporary stories are as richly textured, as lyrical, and as compassionate and sensitively told as "The Dead."

The Dead

Lily, the caretaker's daughter, was literally run off her feet. Hardly had she brought one gentleman into the little pantry behind the office on the ground floor and helped him off with his overcoat than the wheezy hall-door bell clanged again and she had to scamper along the bare hallway to let in another guest. It was well for her she had not to attend to the ladies also. But Miss Kate and Miss Julia had thought of that and had converted the bathroom upstairs into a ladies' dressing-room. Miss Kate and Miss Julia were there, gossiping and laughing and fussing, walking after each other to the head of the stairs, peering down over the banisters and calling down to Lily to ask her who had come.

It was always a great affair, the Misses Morkan's annual dance. Everybody who knew them came to it, members of the family, old friends of the family, the members of Julia's choir, any of Kate's pupils that were grown up enough and even some of Mary Jane's pupils too. Never once had it fallen flat. For years and years it had gone off in splendid style as long as anyone could remember; ever since Kate and Julia, after the death of their brother Pat, had left the house in Stoney Batter and taken Mary Jane, their only niece, to live with them in the dark gaunt house on Usher's Island, the upper part of which they had rented from Mr Fulham, the corn-factor on the ground floor. That was a good thirty years ago if it was a day. Mary Jane, who was then a little girl in short clothes, was now the main prop of the household for she had the organ in Haddington Road. She had been through the Academy and gave a pupils' concert every year in the upper room of the Antient Concert Rooms. Many of her pupils belonged to better-class families on the Kingstown and Dalkey line. Old as they were, her aunts also did their share. Julia, though she was quite grey, was still the leading soprano in Adam and Eve's, and Kate, being too feeble to go about much, gave music lessons to beginners on the old square piano in the back room. Lily, the caretaker's daughter, did housemaid's work for them. Though their life was modest they believed in eating well; the best of everything: diamond-bone sirloins, three-shilling tea and the best bottled stout. But Lily seldom made a mistake in the orders so that she got on well with her three mistresses. They were fussy, that was all. But the only thing they would not stand was back answers.

Of course they had good reason to be fussy on such a night. And then it was long after ten o'clock and yet there was no sign of Gabriel and his wife. Besides they were dreadfully afraid that Freddy Malins might turn up screwed. They would not wish for worlds that any of Mary Jane's pupils should see him under the influence; and when he was like that it was sometimes very hard to manage him. Freddy Malins always came late but they wondered what could be keeping Gabriel: and that was

what brought them every two minutes to the banisters to
ask Lily had Gabriel or Freddy come.

—O, Mr Conroy, said Lily to Gabriel when she opened
the door for him, Miss Kate and Miss Julia thought you
were never coming. Good-night, Mrs Conroy.

—I'll engage they did, said Gabriel, but they forget that
my wife here takes three mortal hours to dress herself.

He stood on the mat, scraping the snow from his
goloshes, while Lily led his wife to the foot of the stairs
and called out:

—Miss Kate, here's Mrs Conroy.

Kate and Julia came toddling down the dark stairs at
once. Both of them kissed Gabriel's wife, said she must be
perished alive and asked was Gabriel with her.

—Here I am as right as the mail, Aunt Kate! Go on up.
I'll follow, called out Gabriel from the dark.

He continued scraping his feet vigorously while the three
women went upstairs, laughing, to the ladies' dressing-
room. A light fringe of snow lay like a cape on the
shoulders of his overcoat and like toecaps on the toes of
his goloshes; and, as the buttons of his overcoat slipped
with a squeaking noise through the snow-stiffened frieze,
a cold fragrant air from out-of-doors escaped from crevices
and folds.

—Is it snowing again, Mr Conroy? asked Lily.

She had preceded him into the pantry to help him off
with his overcoat. Gabriel smiled at the three syllables she
had given his surname and glanced at her. She was a slim,
growing girl, pale in complexion and with hay-coloured
hair. The gas in the pantry made her look still paler.
Gabriel had known her when she was a child and used to
sit on the lowest step nursing a rag doll.

—Yes, Lily, he answered, and I think we're in for a
night of it.

He looked up at the pantry ceiling, which was shaking
with the stamping and shuffling of feet on the floor above,
listened for a moment to the piano and then glanced at
the girl, who was folding his overcoat carefully at the end
of a shelf.

—Tell me, Lily, he said in a friendly tone, do you still
go to school?

—O no, sir, she answered. I'm done schooling this year
and more.

—O, then, said Gabriel gaily, I suppose we'll be going to
your wedding one of these fine days with your young man,
eh?

The girl glanced back at him over her shoulder and said with great bitterness:

—The men that is now is only all palaver and what they can get out of you.

Gabriel coloured as if he felt he had made a mistake and, without looking at her, kicked off his goloshes and flicked actively with his muffler at his patent-leather shoes.

He was a stout tallish young man. The high colour of his cheeks pushed upwards even to his forehead where it scattered itself in a few formless patches of pale red; and on his hairless face there scintillated restlessly the polished lenses and the bright gilt rims of the glasses which screened his delicate and restless eyes. His glossy black hair was parted in the middle and brushed in a long curve behind his ears where it curled slightly beneath the groove left by his hat.

When he had flicked lustre into his shoes he stood up and pulled his waistcoat down more tightly on his plump body. Then he took a coin rapidly from his pocket.

—O Lily, he said, thrusting it into her hands, it's Christmas-time, isn't it? Just . . . here's a little. . . .

He walked rapidly towards the door.

—O no, sir! cried the girl, following him. Really, sir, I wouldn't take it.

—Christmas-time! Christmas-time! said Gabriel, almost trotting to the stairs and waving his hand to her in deprecation.

The girl, seeing that he had gained the stairs, called out after him:

—Well, thank you, sir.

He waited outside the drawing-room door until the waltz should finish, listening to the skirts that swept against it and to the shuffling of feet. He was still discomposed by the girl's bitter and sudden retort. It had cast a gloom over him which he tried to dispel by arranging his cuffs and the bows of his tie. Then he took from his waistcoat pocket a little paper and glanced at the headings he had made for his speech. He was undecided about the lines from Robert Browning for he feared they would be above the heads of his hearers. Some quotation that they could recognise from Shakespeare or from the Melodies would be better. The indelicate clacking of the men's heels and the shuffling of their soles reminded him that their grade of culture differed from his. He would only make himself ridiculous by quoting poetry to them which they could not understand. They would think that he was airing his superior education. He would fail with them just as he had failed with the girl in the pantry. He had taken up a wrong tone. His whole speech was a mistake from first to last, an utter failure.

Just then his aunts and his wife came out of the ladies' dressing-room. His aunts were two small plainly dressed old women. Aunt Julia was an inch or so the taller. Her hair, drawn low over the tops of her ears, was grey; and grey also, with darker shadows, was her large flaccid face. Though she was stout in build and stood erect her slow eyes and parted lips gave her the appearance of a woman who did not know where she was or where she was going. Aunt Kate was more vivacious. Her face, healthier than her sister's, was all puckers and creases, like a shrivelled red apple, and her hair, braided in the same old-fashioned way, had not lost its ripe nut colour.

They both kissed Gabriel frankly. He was their favourite nephew, the son of their dead elder sister, Ellen, who had married T. J. Conroy of the Port and Docks.

—Gretta tells me you're not going to take a cab back to Monkstown to-night, Gabriel, said Aunt Kate.

—No, said Gabriel, turning to his wife, we had quite enough of that last year, hadn't we. Don't you remember, Aunt Kate, what a cold Gretta got out of it? Cab windows rattling all the way, and the east wind blowing in after we passed Merrion. Very jolly it was. Gretta caught a dreadful cold.

Aunt Kate frowned severely and nodded her head at every word.

—Quite right, Gabriel, quite right, she said. You can't be too careful.

—But as for Gretta there, said Gabriel, she'd walk home in the snow if she were let.

Mrs Conroy laughed.

—Don't mind him, Aunt Kate, she said. He's really an awful bother, what with green shades for Tom's eyes at night and making him do the dumb-bells, and forcing Eva to eat the stirabout. The poor child! And she simply hates the sight of it! . . . O, but you'll never guess what he makes me wear now!

She broke out into a peal of laughter and glanced at her husband, whose admiring and happy eyes had been wandering from her dress to her face and hair. The two aunts laughed heartily too, for Gabriel's solicitude was a standing joke with them.

—Goloshes! said Mrs Conroy. That's the latest. Whenever it's wet underfoot I must put on my goloshes. To-night even he wanted me to put them on, but I wouldn't. The next thing he'll buy me will be a diving suit.

Gabriel laughed nervously and patted his tie reassuringly while Aunt Kate nearly doubled herself, so heartily did she enjoy the joke. The smile soon faded from Aunt Julia's face and her mirthless eyes were directed towards her nephew's face. After a pause she asked:

—And what are goloshes, Gabriel?

—Goloshes, Julia! exclaimed her sister. Goodness me, don't you know what goloshes are? You wear them over your . . . over your boots, Gretta, isn't it?

—Yes, said Mrs Conroy. Guttapercha things. We both have a pair now. Gabriel says everyone wears them on the continent.

—O, on the continent, murmured Aunt Julia, nodding her head slowly.

Gabriel knitted his brows and said, as if he were slightly angered:

—It's nothing very wonderful but Gretta thinks it very funny because she says the word reminds her of Christy Minstrels.

—But tell me, Gabriel, said Aunt Kate, with brisk tact. Of course, you've seen about the room. Gretta was saying . . .

—O, the room is all right, replied Gabriel. I've taken one in the Gresham.

—To be sure, said Aunt Kate, by far the best thing to do. And the children, Gretta, you're not anxious about them?

—O, for one night, said Mrs Conroy. Besides, Bessie will look after them.

—To be sure, said Aunt Kate again. What a comfort it is to have a girl like that, one you can depend on! There's that Lily, I'm sure I don't know what has come over her lately. She's not the girl she was at all.

Gabriel was about to ask his aunt some questions on this point but she broke off suddenly to gaze after her sister who had wandered down the stairs and was craning her neck over the banisters.

—Now, I ask you, she said, almost testily, where is Julia going? Julia! Julia! Where are you going?

Julia, who had gone halfway down one flight, came back and announced blandly:

—Here's Freddy.

At the same moment a clapping of hands and a final

flourish of the pianist told that the waltz had ended. The drawing-room door was opened from within and some couples came out. Aunt Kate drew Gabriel aside hurriedly and whispered into his ear:

—Slip down, Gabriel, like a good fellow and see if he's all right, and don't let him up if he's screwed. I'm sure he's screwed. I'm sure he is.

Gabriel went to the stairs and listened over the banisters. He could hear two persons talking in the pantry. Then he recognised Freddy Malins' laugh. He went down the stairs noisily.

—It's such a relief, said Aunt Kate to Mrs Conroy, that Gabriel is here. I always feel easier in my mind when he's here. . . . Julia, there's Miss Daly and Miss Power will take some refreshment. Thanks for your beautiful waltz, Miss Daly. It made lovely time.

A tall wizen-faced man, with a stiff grizzled moustache and swarthy skin, who was passing out with his partner, said:

—And may we have some refreshment, too, Miss Morkan?

—Julia, said Aunt Kate summarily, and here's Mr Browne and Miss Furlong. Take them in, Julia, with Miss Daly and Miss Power.

—I'm the man for the ladies, said Mr Browne, pursing his lips until his moustache bristled and smiling in all his wrinkles. You know, Miss Morkan, the reason they are so fond of me is—

He did not finish his sentence, but, seeing that Aunt Kate was out of earshot, at once led the three young ladies into the back room. The middle of the room was occupied by two square tables placed end to end, and on these Aunt Julia and the caretaker were straightening and smoothing a large cloth. On the sideboard were arrayed dishes and plates, and glasses and bundles of knives and forks and spoons. The top of the closed square piano served also as a sideboard for viands and sweets. At a smaller sideboard in one corner two young men were standing, drinking hop-bitters.

Mr Browne led his charges thither and invited them all, in jest, to some ladies' punch, hot, strong and sweet. As they said they never took anything strong he opened three bottles of lemonade for them. Then he asked one of the young men to move aside, and, taking hold of the decanter, filled out for himself a goodly measure of whisky. The young men eyed him respectfully while he took a trial sip.

—God help me, he said, smiling, it's the doctor's orders.

His wizened face broke into a broader smile, and the three young ladies laughed in musical echo to his pleasantry, swaying their bodies to and fro, with nervous jerks of their shoulders. The boldest said:

—O, now, Mr Browne, I'm sure the doctor never ordered anything of the kind.

Mr Browne took another sip of his whisky and said, with sidling mimicry:

—Well, you see, I'm like the famous Mrs Cassidy, who is reported to have said: *Now, Mary Grimes, if I don't take it, make me take it, for I feel I want it.*

His hot face had leaned forward a little too confidentially and he had assumed a very low Dublin accent so that the young ladies, with one instinct, received his speech in silence. Miss Furlong, who was one of Mary Jane's pupils, asked Miss Daly what was the name of the pretty waltz she had played; and Mr Browne, seeing that he was ignored, turned promptly to the two young men who were more appreciative.

A red-faced young woman, dressed in pansy, came into the room, excitedly clapping her hands and crying:

—Quadrilles! Quadrilles!

Close on her heels came Aunt Kate, crying:

—Two gentlemen and three ladies, Mary Jane!

—O, here's Mr Bergin and Mr Kerrigan, said Mary Jane. Mr Kerrigan, will you take Miss Power? Miss Furlong, may I get you a partner? Mr Bergin. O, that'll just do now.

—Three ladies, Mary Jane, said Aunt Kate.

The two young gentlemen asked the ladies if they might have the pleasure, and Mary Jane turned to Miss Daly.

—O, Miss Daly, you're really awfully good, after playing for the last two dances, but really we're so short of ladies to-night.

—I don't mind in the least, Miss Morkan.

—But I've a nice partner for you, Mr Bartell D'Arcy, the tenor. I'll get him to sing later on. All Dublin is raving about him.

—Lovely voice, lovely voice! said Aunt Kate.

As the piano had twice begun the prelude to the first figure Mary Jane led her recruits quickly from the room. They had hardly gone when Aunt Julia wandered slowly into the room, looking behind her at something.

—What is the matter, Julia? asked Aunt Kate anxiously. Who is it?

Julia, who was carrying in a column of table-napkins, turned to her sister and said, simply, as if the question had surprised her:

—It's only Freddy, Kate, and Gabriel with him.

In fact right behind her Gabriel could be seen piloting Freddy Malins across the landing. The latter, a young man of about forty, was of Gabriel's size and build, with very round shoulders. His face was fleshy and pallid, touched with colour only at the thick hanging lobes of his ears and at the wide wings of his nose. He had coarse features, a blunt nose, a convex and receding brow, tumid and protruded lips. His heavy-lidded eyes and the disorder of his scanty hair made him look sleepy. He was laughing heartily in a high key at a story which he had been telling Gabriel on the stairs and at the same time rubbing the knuckles of his left fist backwards and forwards into his left eye.

—Good-evening, Freddy, said Aunt Julia.

Freddy Malins bade the Misses Morkan good-evening in what seemed an offhand fashion by reason of the habitual catch in his voice and then, seeing that Mr Browne was grinning at him from the sideboard, crossed the room on rather shaky legs and began to repeat in an undertone the story he had just told to Gabriel.

—He's not so bad, is he? said Aunt Kate to Gabriel.

Gabriel's brows were dark but he raised them quickly and answered:

—O no, hardly noticeable.

—Now, isn't he a terrible fellow! she said. And his poor mother made him take the pledge on New Year's Eve. But come on, Gabriel, into the drawing-room.

Before leaving the room with Gabriel she signalled to Mr Browne by frowning and shaking her forefinger in warning to and fro. Mr Browne nodded in answer and, when she had gone, said to Freddy Malins:

—Now, then, Teddy, I'm going to fill you out a good glass of lemonade just to buck you up.

Freddy Malins, who was nearing the climax of his story, waved the offer aside impatiently but Mr Browne, having first called Freddy Malins' attention to a disarray in his dress, filled out and handed him a full glass of lemonade. Freddy Malins' left hand accepted the glass mechanically, his right hand being engaged in the mechanical readjustment of his dress. Mr Browne, whose face was once more wrinkling with mirth, poured out for himself a glass of whisky while Freddy Malins exploded, before he had well reached the climax of his story, in a kink of high-

pitched bronchitic laughter and, setting down his untasted and overflowing glass, began to rub the knuckles of
his left fist backwards and forwards into his left eye, repeating words of his last phrase as well as his fit of
laughter would allow him.

Gabriel could not listen while Mary Jane was playing
her Academy piece, full of runs and difficult passages,
to the hushed drawing-room. He liked music but the piece
she was playing had no melody for him and he doubted
whether it had any melody for the other listeners, though
they had begged Mary Jane to play something. Four
young men, who had come from the refreshment-room to
stand in the doorway at the sound of the piano, had gone
away quietly in couples after a few minutes. The only
persons who seemed to follow the music were Mary Jane
herself, her hands racing along the key-board or lifted
from it at the pauses like those of a priestess in momentary
imprecation, and Aunt Kate standing at her elbow to turn
the page.

Gabriel's eyes, irritated by the floor, which glittered with
beeswax under the heavy chandelier, wandered to the wall
above the piano. A picture of the balcony scene in *Romeo
and Juliet* hung there and beside it was a picture of the
two murdered princes in the Tower which Aunt Julia had
worked in red, blue and brown wools when she was a girl.
Probably in the school they had gone to as girls that kind
of work had been taught, for one year his mother had
worked for him as a birthday present a waistcoat of purple
tabinet, with little foxes' heads upon it, lined with brown
satin and having round mulberry buttons. It was strange
that his mother had had no musical talent though Aunt
Kate used to call her the brains carrier of the Morkan
family. Both she and Julia had always seemed a little
proud of their serious and matronly sister. Her photograph
stood before the pierglass. She held an open book on her
knees and was pointing out something in it to Constantine
who, dressed in a man-o'-war suit, lay at her feet. It was
she who had chosen the names for her sons for she was
very sensible of the dignity of family life. Thanks to her,
Constantine was now senior curate in Balbriggan and,
thanks to her, Gabriel himself had taken his degree in the
Royal University. A shadow passed over his face as he
remembered her sullen opposition to his marriage. Some
slighting phrases she had used still rankled in his memory;
she had once spoken of Gretta as being country cute and

that was not true of Gretta at all. It was Gretta who had
nursed her during all her last long illness in their house at
Monkstown.

He knew that Mary Jane must be near the end of her
piece for she was playing again the opening melody with
runs of scales after every bar and while he waited for the
end the resentment died down in his heart. The piece
ended with a trill of octaves in the treble and a final deep
octave in the bass. Great applause greeted Mary Jane as,
blushing and rolling up her music nervously, she escaped
from the room. The most vigorous clapping came from
the four young men in the doorway who had gone away to
the refreshment-room at the beginning of the piece but
had come back when the piano had stopped.

Lancers were arranged. Gabriel found himself partnered
with Miss Ivors. She was a frank-mannered talkative young
lady, with a freckled face and prominent brown eyes. She
did not wear a low-cut bodice and the large brooch which
was fixed in the front of her collar bore on it an Irish
device.

When they had taken their places she said abruptly:

—I have a crow to pluck with you.

—With me? said Gabriel.

She nodded her head gravely.

—What is it? asked Gabriel, smiling at her solemn
manner.

—Who is G. C.? answered Miss Ivors, turning her eyes
upon him.

Gabriel coloured and was about to knit his brows, as if
he did not understand, when she said bluntly:

—O, innocent Amy! I have found out that you write
for *The Daily Express*. Now, aren't you ashamed of yourself?

—Why should I be ashamed of myself? asked Gabriel,
blinking his eyes and trying to smile.

—Well, I'm ashamed of you, said Miss Ivors frankly. To
say you'd write for a rag like that. I didn't think you were
a West Briton.

A look of perplexity appeared on Gabriel's face. It was
true that he wrote a literary column every Wednesday in
The Daily Express, for which he was paid fifteen shillings.
But that did not make him a West Briton surely. The books
he received for review were almost more welcome than the
paltry cheque. He loved to feel the covers and turn over
the pages of newly printed books. Nearly every day when
his teaching in the college was ended he used to wander

down the quays to the second-hand booksellers, to Hickey's on Bachelor's Walk, to Webb's or Massey's on Aston's Quay, or to O'Clohissey's in the by-street. He did not know how to meet her charge. He wanted to say that literature was above politics. But they were friends of many years' standing and their careers had been parallel, first at the University and then as teachers: he could not risk a grandiose phrase with her. He continued blinking his eyes and trying to smile and murmured lamely that he saw nothing political in writing reviews of books.

When their turn to cross had come he was still perplexed and inattentive. Miss Ivors promptly took his hand in a warm grasp and said in a soft friendly tone:

—Of course, I was only joking. Come, we cross now.

When they were together again she spoke of the University question and Gabriel felt more at ease. A friend of hers had shown her his review of Browning's poems. That was how she had found out the secret: but she liked the review immensely. Then she said suddenly:

—O, Mr Conroy, will you come for an excursion to the Aran Isles this summer? We're going to stay there a whole month. It will be splendid out in the Atlantic. You ought to come. Mr Clancy is coming, and Mr Kilkelly and Kathleen Kearney. It would be splendid for Gretta too if she'd come. She's from Connacht, isn't she?

—Her people are, said Gabriel shortly.

—But you will come, won't you? said Miss Ivors, laying her warm hand eagerly on his arm.

—The fact is, said Gabriel, I have already arranged to go—

—Go where? asked Miss Ivors.

—Well, you know, every year I go for a cycling tour with some fellows and so—

—But where? asked Miss Ivors.

—Well, we usually go to France or Belgium or perhaps Germany, said Gabriel awkwardly.

—And why do you go to France and Belgium, said Miss Ivors, instead of visiting your own land?

—Well, said Gabriel, it's partly to keep in touch with the languages and partly for a change.

—And haven't you your own language to keep in touch with—Irish? asked Miss Ivors.

—Well, said Gabriel, if it comes to that, you know, Irish is not my language.

Their neighbours had turned to listen to the cross-examination. Gabriel glanced right and left nervously and tried to keep his good humour under the ordeal which was making a blush invade his forehead.

—And haven't you your own land to visit, continued Miss Ivors, that you know nothing of, your own people, and your own country?

—O, to tell you the truth, retorted Gabriel suddenly, I'm sick of my own country, sick of it!

—Why? asked Miss Ivors.

Gabriel did not answer for his retort had heated him.

—Why? repeated Miss Ivors.

They had to go visiting together and, as he had not answered her, Miss Ivors said warmly:

—Of course, you've no answer.

Gabriel tried to cover his agitation by taking part in the dance with great energy. He avoided her eyes for he had seen a sour expression on her face. But when they met in the long chain he was surprised to feel his hand firmly pressed. She looked at him from under her brows for a moment quizzically until he smiled. Then, just as the chain was about to start again, she stood on tiptoe and whispered into his ear:

—West Briton!

When the lancers were over Gabriel went away to a remote corner of the room where Freddy Malins' mother was sitting. She was a stout feeble old woman with white hair. Her voice had a catch in it like her son's and she stuttered slightly. She had been told that Freddy had come and that he was nearly all right. Gabriel asked her whether she had had a good crossing. She lived with her married daughter in Glasgow and came to Dublin on a visit once a year. She answered placidly that she had had a beautiful crossing and that the captain had been most attentive to her. She spoke also of the beautiful house her daughter kept in Glasgow, and of all the nice friends they had there. While her tongue rambled on Gabriel tried to banish from his mind all memory of the unpleasant incident with Miss Ivors. Of course the girl or woman, or whatever she was, was an enthusiast but there was a time for all things. Perhaps he ought not to have answered her like that. But she had no right to call him a West Briton before people, even in joke. She had tried to make him ridiculous before people, heckling him and staring at him with her rabbit's eyes.

He saw his wife making her way towards him through the waltzing couples. When she reached him she said into his ear:

—Gabriel, Aunt Kate wants to know won't you carve the goose as usual. Miss Daly will carve the ham and I'll do the pudding.

—All right, said Gabriel.

—She's sending in the younger ones first as soon as this waltz is over so that we'll have the table to ourselves.

—Were you dancing? asked Gabriel.

—Of course I was. Didn't you see me? What words had you with Molly Ivors?

—No words. Why? Did she say so?

—Something like that. I'm trying to get that Mr D'Arcy to sing. He's full of conceit, I think.

—There were no words, said Gabriel moodily, only she wanted me to go for a trip to the west of Ireland and I said I wouldn't.

His wife clasped her hands excitedly and gave a little jump.

—O, do go, Gabriel, she cried. I'd love to see Galway again.

—You can go if you like, said Gabriel coldly.

She looked at him for a moment, then turned to Mrs Malins and said:

—There's a nice husband for you, Mrs Malins.

While she was threading her way back across the room Mrs Malins, without adverting to the interruption, went on to tell Gabriel what beautiful places there were in Scotland and beautiful scenery. Her son-in-law brought them every year to the lakes and they used to go fishing. Her son-in-law was a splendid fisher. One day he caught a fish, a beautiful big big fish, and the man in the hotel boiled it for their dinner.

Gabriel hardly heard what she said. Now that supper was coming near he began to think again about his speech and about the quotation. When he saw Freddy Malins coming across the room to visit his mother Gabriel left the chair free for him and retired into the embrasure of the window. The room had already cleared and from the back room came the clatter of plates and knives. Those who still remained in the drawing-room seemed tired of dancing and were conversing quietly in little groups. Gabriel's warm trembling fingers tapped the cold pane of the window. How cool it must be outside! How pleasant it would be to walk out alone, first along by the river and then through the park! The snow would be lying on the branches of the trees and forming a bright cap on the

top of the Wellington Monument. How much more pleasant it would be there than at the supper-table!

He ran over the headings of his speech: Irish hospitality,
sad memories, the Three Graces, Paris, the quotation from
Browning. He repeated to himself a phrase he had written
in his review: *One feels that one is listening to a thought-
tormented music.* Miss Ivors had praised the review. Was
she sincere? Had she really any life of her own behind
all her propagandism? There had never been any ill-feeling
between them until that night. It unnerved him to think
that she would be at the supper-table, looking up at him
while he spoke with her critical quizzing eyes. Perhaps she
would not be sorry to see him fail in his speech. An idea
came into his mind and gave him courage. He would say,
alluding to Aunt Kate and Aunt Julia: *Ladies and Gentlemen, the generation which is now on the wane among us
may have had its faults but for my part I think it had
certain qualities of hospitality, of humour, of humanity,
which the new and very serious and hypereducated generation that is growing up around us seems to me to lack.*
Very good: that was one for Miss Ivors. What did he care
that his aunts were only two ignorant old women?

A murmur in the room attracted his attention. Mr
Browne was advancing from the door, gallantly escorting
Aunt Julia, who leaned upon his arm, smiling and hanging
her head. An irregular musketry of applause escorted her
also as far as the piano and then, as Mary Jane seated herself on the stool, and Aunt Julia, no longer smiling, half
turned so as to pitch her voice fairly into the room,
gradually ceased. Gabriel recognised the prelude. It was
that of an old song of Aunt Julia's—*Arrayed for the Bridal.*
Her voice, strong and clear in tone, attacked with great
spirit the runs which embellish the air and though she
sang very rapidly she did not miss even the smallest of
the grace notes. To follow the voice, without looking at the
singer's face, was to feel and share the excitement of swift
and secure flight. Gabriel applauded loudly with all the
others at the close of the song and loud applause was
borne in from the invisible supper-table. It sounded so
genuine that a little colour struggled into Aunt Julia's face
as she bent to replace in the music-stand the old leather-
bound song-book that had her initials on the cover.
Freddy Malins, who had listened with his head perched
sideways to hear her better, was still applauding when
everyone else had ceased and talking animatedly to his
mother who nodded her head gravely and slowly in

acquiescence. At last, when he could clap no more, he stood up suddenly and hurried across the room to Aunt Julia whose hand he seized and held in both his hands, shaking it when words failed him or the catch in his voice proved too much for him.

—I was just telling my mother, he said, I never heard you sing so well, never. No, I never heard your voice so good as it is to-night. Now! Would you believe that now? That's the truth. Upon my word and honour that's the truth. I never heard your voice sound so fresh and so . . . so clear and fresh, never.

Aunt Julia smiled broadly and murmured something about compliments as she released her hand from his grasp. Mr Browne extended his open hand towards her and said to those who were near him in the manner of a showman introducing a prodigy to an audience:

—Miss Julia Morkan, my latest discovery!

He was laughing very heartily at this himself when Freddy Malins turned to him and said:

—Well, Browne, if you're serious you might make a worse discovery. All I can say is I never heard her sing half so well as long as I am coming here. And that's the honest truth.

—Neither did I, said Mr Browne. I think her voice has greatly improved.

Aunt Julia shrugged her shoulders and said with meek pride:

—Thirty years ago I hadn't a bad voice as voices go.

—I often told Julia, said Aunt Kate emphatically, that she was simply thrown away in that choir. But she never would be said by me.

She turned as if to appeal to the good sense of the others against a refractory child while Aunt Julia gazed in front of her, a vague smile of reminiscence playing on her face.

—No, continued Aunt Kate, she wouldn't be said or led by anyone, slaving there in that choir night and day, night and day. Six o'clock on Christmas morning! And all for what?

—Well, isn't it for the honour of God, Aunt Kate? asked Mary Jane, twisting round on the piano-stool and smiling.

Aunt Kate turned fiercely on her niece and said:

—I know all about the honour of God, Mary Jane, but I think it's not at all honourable for the pope to turn out the women out of the choirs that have slaved there all their lives and put little whipper-snappers of boys over their heads. I suppose it is for the good of the Church if the pope does it. But it's not just, Mary Jane, and it's not right.

She had worked herself into a passion and would have continued in defence of her sister for it was a sore subject with her but Mary Jane, seeing that all the dancers had come back, intervened pacifically:

—Now, Aunt Kate, you're giving scandal to Mr Browne who is of the other persuasion.

Aunt Kate turned to Mr Browne, who was grinning at this allusion to his religion, and said hastily:

—O, I don't question the pope's being right. I'm only a stupid old woman and I wouldn't presume to do such a thing. But there's such a thing as common everyday politeness and gratitude. And if I were in Julia's place I'd tell that Father Healy straight up to his face . . .

—And besides, Aunt Kate, said Mary Jane, we really are all hungry and when we are hungry we are all very quarrelsome.

—And when we are thirsty we are also quarrelsome, added Mr Browne.

—So that we had better go to supper, said Mary Jane, and finish the discussion afterwards.

On the landing outside the drawing-room Gabriel found his wife and Mary Jane trying to persuade Miss Ivors to stay for supper. But Miss Ivors, who had put on her hat and was buttoning her cloak, would not stay. She did not feel in the least hungry and she had already overstayed her time.

—But only for ten minutes, Molly, said Mrs Conroy. That won't delay you.

—To take a pick itself, said Mary Jane, after all your dancing.

—I really couldn't, said Miss Ivors.

—I am afraid you didn't enjoy yourself at all, said Mary Jane hopelessly.

—Ever so much, I assure you, said Miss Ivors, but you really must let me run off now.

—But how can you get home? asked Mrs Conroy.

—O, it's only two steps up the quay.

Gabriel hesitated a moment and said:

—If you will allow me, Miss Ivors, I'll see you home if you really are obliged to go.

But Miss Ivors broke away from them.

—I won't hear of it, she cried. For goodness sake go

in to your suppers and don't mind me. I'm quite well able to take care of myself.

—Well, you're the comical girl, Molly, said Mrs Conroy frankly.

—*Beannacht libh,* cried Miss Ivors, with a laugh, as she ran down the staircase.

Mary Jane gazed after her, a moody puzzled expression on her face, while Mrs Conroy leaned over the banisters to listen for the hall-door. Gabriel asked himself was he the cause of her abrupt departure. But she did not seem to be in ill humour: she had gone away laughing. He stared blankly down the staircase.

At that moment Aunt Kate came toddling out of the supper-room, almost wringing her hands in despair.

—Where is Gabriel? she cried. Where on earth is Gabriel? There's everyone waiting in there, stage to let, and nobody to carve the goose!

—Here I am, Aunt Kate! cried Gabriel, with sudden animation, ready to carve a flock of geese, if necessary.

A fat brown goose lay at one end of the table and at the other end, on a bed of creased paper strewn with sprigs of parsley, lay a great ham, stripped of its outer skin and peppered over with crust crumbs, a neat paper frill round its shin, and beside this was a round of spiced beef. Between these rival ends ran parallel lines of side-dishes: two little minsters of jelly, red and yellow; a shallow dish full of blocks of blancmange and red jam, a large green leaf-shaped dish with a stalk-shaped handle, on which lay bunches of purple raisins and peeled almonds, a companion dish on which lay a solid rectangle of Smyrna figs, a dish of custard topped with grated nutmeg, a small bowl full of chocolates and sweets wrapped in gold and silver papers and a glass vase in which stood some tall celery stalks. In the centre of the table there stood, as sentries to a fruit-stand which upheld a pyramid of oranges and American apples, two squat old-fashioned decanters of cut glass, one containing port and the other dark sherry. On the closed square piano a pudding in a huge yellow dish lay in waiting and behind it were three squads of bottles of stout and ale and minerals, drawn up according to the colours of their uniforms, the first two black, with brown and red labels, the third and smallest squad white, with transverse green sashes.

Gabriel took his seat boldly at the head of the table and, having looked to the edge of the carver, plunged his fork firmly into the goose. He felt quite at ease now for he was an expert carver and liked nothing better than to find himself at the head of a well-laden table.

—Miss Furlong, what shall I send you? he asked. A wing or a slice of the breast?

—Just a small slice of the breast.

—Miss Higgins, what for you?

—O, anything at all, Mr Conroy.

While Gabriel and Miss Daly exchanged plates of goose and plates of ham and spiced beef Lily went from guest to guest with a dish of hot floury potatoes wrapped in a white napkin. This was Mary Jane's idea and she had also suggested apple sauce for the goose but Aunt Kate had said that plain roast goose without apple sauce had always been good enough for her and she hoped she might never eat worse. Mary Jane waited on her pupils and saw that they got the best slices and Aunt Kate and Aunt Julia opened and carried across from the piano bottles of stout and ale for the gentlemen and bottles of minerals for the ladies. There was a great deal of confusion and laughter and noise, the noise of orders and counter-orders, of knives and forks, of corks and glass-stoppers. Gabriel began to carve second helpings as soon as he had finished the first round without serving himself. Everyone protested loudly so that he compromised by taking a long draught of stout for he had found the carving hot work. Mary Jane settled down quietly to her supper but Aunt Kate and Aunt Julia were still toddling round the table, walking on each other's heels, getting in each other's way and giving each other unheeded orders. Mr Browne begged of them to sit down and eat their suppers and so did Gabriel but they said there was time enough so that, at last, Freddy Malins stood up and, capturing Aunt Kate, plumped her down on her chair amid general laughter.

When everyone had been well served Gabriel said, smiling:

—Now, if anyone wants a little more of what vulgar people call stuffing let him or her speak.

A chorus of voices invited him to begin his own supper and Lily came forward with three potatoes which she had reserved for him.

—Very well, said Gabriel amiably, as he took another preparatory draught, kindly forget my existence, ladies and gentlemen, for a few minutes.

He set to his supper and took no part in the conversation with which the table covered Lily's removal of the plates. The subject of talk was the opera company which was then at the Theatre Royal. Mr Bartell D'Arcy, the tenor, a dark-complexioned young man with a smart moustache, praised very highly the leading contralto of the company but Miss Furlong thought she had a rather vulgar style of production. Freddy Malins said there was a negro chieftain singing in the second part of the Gaiety panto-mime who had one of the finest tenor voices he had ever heard.

—Have you heard him? he asked Mr Bartell D'Arcy across the table.

—No, answered Mr Bartell D'Arcy carelessly.

—Because, Freddy Malins explained, now I'd be curious to hear your opinion of him. I think he has a grand voice.

—It takes Teddy to find out the really good things, said Mr Browne familiarly to the table.

—And why couldn't he have a voice too? asked Freddy Malins sharply. Is it because he's only a black?

Nobody answered this question and Mary Jane led the table back to the legitimate opera. One of her pupils had given her a pass for *Mignon.* Of course it was very fine, she said, but it made her think of poor Georgina Burns. Mr Browne could go back farther still, to the old Italian com-panies that used to come to Dublin—Tietjens, Ilma de Murzka, Campanini, the great Trebelli, Giuglini, Ravelli, Aramburo. Those were the days, he said, when there was something like singing to be heard in Dublin. He told too of how the top gallery of the old Royal used to be packed night after night, of how one night an Italian tenor had sung five encores to *Let Me Like a Soldier Fall,* introduc-ing a high C every time, and of how the gallery boys would sometimes in their enthusiasm unyoke the horses from the carriage of some great *prima donna* and pull her them-selves through the streets to her hotel. Why did they never play the grand old operas now, he asked, *Dinorah, Lu-crezia Borgia?* Because they could not get the voices to sing them: that was why.

—O, well, said Mr Bartell D'Arcy, I presume there are as good singers to-day as there were then.

—Where are they? asked Mr Browne defiantly.

—In London, Paris, Milan, said Mr Bartell D'Arcy warmly. I suppose Caruso, for example, is quite as good, if not better than any of the men you have mentioned.

—Maybe so, said Mr Browne. But I may tell you I doubt it strongly.

—O, I'd give anything to hear Caruso sing, said Mary Jane.

—For me, said Aunt Kate, who had been picking a bone, there was only one tenor. To please me, I mean. But I suppose none of you ever heard of him.

—Who was he, Miss Morkan? asked Mr Bartell D'Arcy politely.

—His name, said Aunt Kate, was Parkinson. I heard him when he was in his prime and I think he had then the purest tenor voice that was ever put into a man's throat.

—Strange, said Mr Bartell D'Arcy. I never even heard of him.

—Yes, yes, Miss Morkan is right, said Mr Browne. I remember hearing of old Parkinson but he's too far back for me.

—A beautiful pure sweet mellow English tenor, said Aunt Kate with enthusiasm.

Gabriel having finished, the huge pudding was transferred to the table. The clatter of forks and spoons began again. Gabriel's wife served out spoonfuls of the pudding and passed the plates down the table. Midway down they were held up by Mary Jane, who replenished them with raspberry or orange jelly or with blancmange and jam. The pudding was of Aunt Julia's making and she received praises for it from all quarters. She herself said that it was not quite brown enough.

—Well, I hope, Miss Morkan, said Mr Browne, that I'm brown enough for you because, you know, I'm all brown.

All the gentlemen, except Gabriel, ate some of the pudding out of compliment to Aunt Julia. As Gabriel never ate sweets the celery had been left for him. Freddy Malins also took a stalk of celery and ate it with his pudding. He had been told that celery was a capital thing for the blood and he was just then under doctor's care. Mrs Malins, who had been silent all through the supper, said that her son was going down to Mount Melleray in a week or so. The table then spoke of Mount Melleray, how bracing the air was down there, how hospitable the monks were and how they never asked for a penny-piece from their guests.

—And do you mean to say, asked Mr Browne incredulously, that a chap can go down there and put up there as if it were a hotel and live on the fat of the land and then come away without paying a farthing?

—O, most people give some donation to the monastery when they leave, said Mary Jane.

—I wish we had an institution like that in our Church, said Mr Browne candidly.

He was astonished to hear that the monks never spoke, got up at two in the morning and slept in their coffins. He asked what they did it for.

—That's the rule of the order, said Aunt Kate firmly.

—Yes, but why? asked Mr Browne.

Aunt Kate repeated that it was the rule, that was all. Mr Browne still seemed not to understand. Freddy Malins explained to him, as best he could, that the monks were trying to make up for the sins committed by all the sinners in the outside world. The explanation was not very clear for Mr Browne grinned and said:

—I like that idea very much but wouldn't a comfortable spring bed do them as well as a coffin?

—The coffin, said Mary Jane, is to remind them of their last end.

As the subject had grown lugubrious it was buried in a silence of the table during which Mrs Malins could be heard saying to her neighbour in an indistinct undertone:

—They are very good men, the monks, very pious men.

The raisins and almonds and figs and apples and oranges and chocolates and sweets were now passed about the table and Aunt Julia invited all the guests to have either port or sherry. At first Mr Bartell D'Arcy refused to take either but one of his neighbours nudged him and whispered something to him upon which he allowed his glass to be filled. Gradually as the last glasses were being filled the conversation ceased. A pause followed, broken only by the noise of the wine and by unsettlings of chairs. The Misses Morkan, all three, looked down at the tablecloth. Someone coughed once or twice and then a few gentlemen patted the table gently as a signal for silence. The silence came and Gabriel pushed back his chair and stood up.

The patting at once grew louder in encouragement and then ceased altogether. Gabriel leaned his ten trembling fingers on the tablecloth and smiled nervously at the company. Meeting a row of upturned faces he raised his eyes to the chandelier. The piano was playing a waltz tune and he could hear the skirts sweeping against the drawing-room door. People, perhaps, were standing in the snow on the quay outside, gazing up at the lighted windows and listening to the waltz music. The air was pure there. In the distance lay the park where the trees were weighted with snow. The Wellington Monument wore a gleaming cap of

snow that flashed westward over the white field of Fifteen
Acres.

He began:

—Ladies and Gentlemen.

—It has fallen to my lot this evening, as in years past,
to perform a very pleasing task but a task for which I
am afraid my poor powers as a speaker are all too inadequate.

—No, no! said Mr Browne.

—But, however that may be, I can only ask you to-
night to take the will for the deed and to lend me your
attention for a few moments while I endeavour to express
to you in words what my feelings are on this occasion.

—Ladies and Gentlemen. It is not the first time that we
have gathered together under this hospitable roof, around
this hospitable board. It is not the first time that we have
been the recipients—or perhaps, I had better say, the
victims—of the hospitality of certain good ladies.

He made a circle in the air with his arm and paused.
Everyone laughed or smiled at Aunt Kate and Aunt Julia
and Mary Jane who all turned crimson with pleasure.
Gabriel went on more boldly:

—I feel more strongly with every recurring year that
our country has no tradition which does it so much honour
and which it should guard so jealously as that of its
hospitality. It is a tradition that is unique as far as my
experience goes (and I have visited not a few places
abroad) among the modern nations. Some would say,
perhaps, that with us it is rather a failing than anything to
be boasted of. But granted even that, it is, to my mind, a
princely failing, and one that I trust will long be cultivated
among us. Of one thing, at least, I am sure. As long as
this one roof shelters the good ladies aforesaid—and I
wish from my heart it may do so for many and many a
long year to come—the tradition of genuine warm-hearted
courteous Irish hospitality, which our forefathers have
handed down to us and which we in turn must hand down
to our descendants, is still alive among us.

A hearty murmur of assent ran round the table. It shot
through Gabriel's mind that Miss Ivors was not there and
that she had gone away discourteously: and he said with
confidence in himself:

—Ladies and Gentlemen.

—A new generation is growing up in our midst, a generation actuated by new ideas and new principles. It is
serious and enthusiastic for these new ideas and its enthu-

siasm, even when it is misdirected, is, I believe, in the
main sincere. But we are living in a sceptical age, and, if I may
use the phrase, a thought-tormented age: and sometimes
I fear that this new generation, educated or hypereducated
as it is, will lack those qualities of humanity, of hospitality,
of kindly humour which belonged to an older day. Listening to-night to the names of all those great singers of the
past it seemed to me, I must confess, that we were living
in a less spacious age. Those days might, without exag-
geration, be called spacious days: and if they are gone beyond recall let us hope, at least, that in gatherings such
as this we shall still speak of them with pride and affection,
still cherish in our hearts the memory of those dead and
gone great ones whose fame the world will not willingly
let die.

—Hear, hear! said Mr Browne loudly.

—But yet, continued Gabriel, his voice falling into a
softer inflection, there are always in gatherings such as
this sadder thoughts that will recur to our minds: thoughts
of the past, of youth, of changes, of absent faces that we
miss here to-night. Our path through life is strewn with
many such sad memories: and were we to brood upon
them always we could not find the heart to go on bravely
with our work among the living. We have all of us living
duties and living affections which claim, and rightly claim,
our strenuous endeavours.

—Therefore, I will not linger on the past. I will not let
any gloomy moralising intrude upon us here to-night. Here
we are gathered together for a brief moment from the
bustle and rush of our everyday routine. We are met here
as friends, in the spirit of good-fellowship, as colleagues,
also to a certain extent, in the true spirit of *camaraderie*,
and as the guests of—what shall I call them?—the Three
Graces of the Dublin musical world.

The table burst into applause and laughter at this sally.
Aunt Julia vainly asked each of her neighbours in turn
to tell her what Gabriel had said.

—He says we are the Three Graces, Aunt Julia, said
Mary Jane.

Aunt Julia did not understand but she looked up, smiling, at Gabriel, who continued in the same vein:

—Ladies and Gentlemen.

—I will not attempt to play to-night the part that Paris
played on another occasion. I will not attempt to choose
between them. The task would be an invidious one and
one beyond my poor powers. For when I view them in

turn, whether it be our chief hostess herself, whose good
heart, whose too good heart, has become a byword with
all who know her, or her sister, who seems to be gifted
with perennial youth and whose singing must have been a
surprise and a revelation to us all to-night, or, last but not
least, when I consider our youngest hostess, talented, cheerful, hard-working and the best of nieces, I confess, Ladies
and Gentlemen, that I do not know to which of them I
should award the prize.

Gabriel glanced down at his aunts and, seeing the large
smile on Aunt Julia's face and the tears which had risen to
Aunt Kate's eyes, hastened to his close. He raised his glass
of port gallantly, while every member of the company
fingered a glass expectantly, and said loudly:

—Let us toast them all three together. Let us drink to
their health, wealth, long life, happiness and prosperity
and may they long continue to hold the proud and self-
won position which they hold in their profession and the
position of honour and affection which they hold in our
hearts.

All the guests stood up, glass in hand, and, turning
towards the three seated ladies, sang in unison, with Mr
Browne as leader:

> *For they are jolly gay fellows,*
> *For they are jolly gay fellows,*
> *For they are jolly gay fellows,*
> *Which nobody can deny.*

Aunt Kate was making frank use of her handkerchief
and even Aunt Julia seemed moved. Freddy Malins beat
time with his pudding-fork and the singers turned towards
one another, as if in melodious conference, while they
sang, with emphasis:

> *Unless he tells a lie,*
> *Unless he tells a lie.*

Then, turning once more towards their hostesses, they
sang:

> *For they are jolly gay fellows,*
> *For they are jolly gay fellows,*
> *For they are jolly gay fellows,*
> *Which nobody can deny.*

The acclamation which followed was taken up beyond the door of the supper-room by many of the other guests and renewed time after time, Freddy Malins acting as officer with his fork on high.

The piercing morning air came into the hall where they were standing so that Aunt Kate said:

—Close the door, somebody. Mrs Malins will get her death of cold.

—Browne is out there, Aunt Kate, said Mary Jane.

—Browne is everywhere, said Aunt Kate, lowering her voice.

Mary Jane laughed at her tone.

—Really, she said archly, he is very attentive.

—He has been laid on here like the gas, said Aunt Kate in the same tone, all during the Christmas.

She laughed herself this time good-humouredly and then added quickly:

—But tell him to come in, Mary Jane, and close the door. I hope to goodness he didn't hear me.

At that moment the hall-door was opened and Mr Browne came in from the doorstep, laughing as if his heart would break. He was dressed in a long green overcoat with mock astrakhan cuffs and collar and wore on his head an oval fur cap. He pointed down the snow-covered quay from where the sound of shrill prolonged whistling was borne in.

—Teddy will have all the cabs in Dublin out, he said.

Gabriel advanced from the little pantry behind the office, struggling into his overcoat and, looking round the hall, said:

—Gretta not down yet?

—She's getting on her things, Gabriel, said Aunt Kate.

—Who's playing up there? asked Gabriel.

—Nobody. They're all gone.

—O no, Aunt Kate, said Mary Jane. Bartell D'Arcy and Miss O'Callaghan aren't gone yet.

—Someone is strumming at the piano, anyhow, said Gabriel.

Mary Jane glanced at Gabriel and Mr Browne and said with a shiver:

—It makes me feel cold to look at you two gentlemen muffled up like that. I wouldn't like to face your journey home at this hour.

—I'd like nothing better this minute, said Mr Browne

stoutly, than a rattling fine walk in the country or a fast drive with a good spanking goer between the shafts.

—We used to have a very good horse and trap at home, said Aunt Julia sadly.

—The never-to-be-forgotten Johnny, said Mary Jane, laughing.

Aunt Kate and Gabriel laughed too.

—Why, what was wonderful about Johnny? asked Mr Browne.

—The late lamented Patrick Morkan, our grandfather, that is, explained Gabriel, commonly known in his later years as the old gentleman, was a glue-boiler.

—O, now, Gabriel, said Aunt Kate, laughing, he had a starch mill.

—Well, glue or starch, said Gabriel, the old gentleman had a horse by the name of Johnny. And Johnny used to work in the old gentleman's mill, walking round and round in order to drive the mill. That was all very well; but now comes the tragic part about Johnny. One fine day the old gentleman thought he'd like to drive out with the quality to a military review in the park.

—The Lord have mercy on his soul, said Aunt Kate compassionately.

—Amen, said Gabriel. So the old gentleman, as I said, harnessed Johnny and put on his very best tall hat and his very best stock collar and drove out in grand style from his ancestral mansion somewhere near Back Lane, I think.

Everyone laughed, even Mrs Malins, at Gabriel's manner and Aunt Kate said:

—O now, Gabriel, he didn't live in Back Lane, really. Only the mill was there.

—Out from the mansion of his forefathers, continued Gabriel, he drove with Johnny. And everything went on beautifully until Johnny came in sight of King Billy's statue: and whether he fell in love with the horse King Billy sits on or whether he thought he was back again in the mill, anyhow he began to walk round the statue.

Gabriel paced in a circle round the hall in his goloshes amid the laughter of the others.

—Round and round he went, said Gabriel, and the old gentleman, who was a very pompous old gentleman, was highly indignant. *Go on, sir! What do you mean, sir? Johnny! Johnny! Most extraordinary conduct! Can't understand the horse!*

The peals of laughter which followed Gabriel's imitation of the incident were interrupted by a resounding knock at

the hall-door. Mary Jane ran to open it and let in Freddy
Malins. Freddy Malins, with his hat well back on his head
and his shoulders humped with cold, was puffing and
steaming after his exertions.

—I could only get one cab, he said.

—O, we'll find another along the quay, said Gabriel.

—Yes, said Aunt Kate. Better not keep Mrs Malins
standing in the draught.

Mrs Malins was helped down the front steps by her son
and Mr Browne and, after many manœuvres, hoisted into
the cab. Freddy Malins clambered in after her and spent
a long time settling her on the seat, Mr Browne helping
him with advice. At last she was settled comfortably and
Freddy Malins invited Mr Browne into the cab. There
was a good deal of confused talk, and then Mr Browne
got into the cab. The cabman settled his rug over his
knees, and bent down for the address. The confusion
grew greater and the cabman was directed differently by
Freddy Malins and Mr Browne, each of whom had his
head out through a window of the cab. The difficulty was to
know where to drop Mr Browne along the route and
Aunt Kate, Aunt Julia and Mary Jane helped the discussion from the doorstep with cross-directions and con-
tradictions and abundance of laughter. As for Freddy
Malins he was speechless with laughter. He popped his
head in and out of the window every moment, to the great
danger of his hat, and told his mother how the discussion
was progressing till at last Mr Browne shouted to the bewildered cabman above the din of everybody's laughter:

—Do you know Trinity College?

—Yes, sir, said the cabman.

—Well, drive bang up against Trinity College gates, said
Mr Browne, and then we'll tell you where to go. You
understand now?

—Yes, sir, said the cabman.

—Make like a bird for Trinity College.

—Right, sir, cried the cabman.

The horse was whipped up and the cab rattled off along
the quay amid a chorus of laughter and adieus.

Gabriel had not gone to the door with the others. He
was in a dark part of the hall gazing up the staircase. A
woman was standing near the top of the first flight, in the
shadow also. He could not see her face but he could see the
terracotta and salmonpink panels of her skirt which the
shadow made appear black and white. It was his wife.
She was leaning on the banisters, listening to something.

Gabriel was surprised at her stillness and strained his ear
to listen also. But he could hear little save the noise of
laughter and dispute on the front steps, a few chords struck
on the piano and a few notes of a man's voice singing.

He stood still in the gloom of the hall, trying to catch
the air that the voice was singing and gazing up at his
wife. There was grace and mystery in her attitude as if
she were a symbol of something. He asked himself what
is a woman standing on the stairs in the shadow, listening to
distant music, a symbol of. If he were a painter he would
paint her in that attitude. Her blue felt hat would show off
the bronze of her hair against the darkness and the dark
panels of her skirt would show off the light ones. *Distant
Music* he would call the picture if he were a painter.

The hall-door was closed; and Aunt Kate, Aunt Julia
and Mary Jane came down the hall, still laughing.

—Well, isn't Freddy terrible? said Mary Jane. He's
really terrible.

Gabriel said nothing but pointed up the stairs towards
where his wife was standing. Now that the hall-door was
closed the voice and the piano could be heard more clearly. Gabriel held up his hand for them to be silent. The
song seemed to be in the old Irish tonality and the singer
seemed uncertain both of his words and of his voice. The
voice, made plaintive by distance and by the singer's
hoarseness, faintly illuminated the cadence of the air with
words expressing grief:

> *O, the rain falls on my heavy locks*
> *And the dew wets my skin,*
> *My babe lies cold . . .*

—O, exclaimed Mary Jane. It's Bartell D'Arcy singing
and he wouldn't sing all the night. O, I'll get him to sing a
song before he goes.

—O do, Mary Jane, said Aunt Kate.

Mary Jane brushed past the others and ran to the staircase but before she reached it the singing stopped and the
piano was closed abruptly.

—O, what a pity! she cried. Is he coming down, Gretta?

Gabriel heard his wife answer yes and saw her come
down towards them. A few steps behind her were Mr
Bartell D'Arcy and Miss O'Callaghan.

—O, Mr D'Arcy, cried Mary Jane, it's downright mean
of you to break off like that when we were all in raptures
listening to you.

—I have been at him all the evening, said Miss O'Callaghan, and Mrs Conroy too and he told us he had a dreadful cold and couldn't sing.

—O, Mr D'Arcy, said Aunt Kate, now that was a great fib to tell.

—Can't you see that I'm as hoarse as a crow? said Mr D'Arcy roughly.

He went into the pantry hastily and put on his overcoat. The others, taken aback by his rude speech, could find nothing to say. Aunt Kate wrinkled her brows and made signs to the others to drop the subject. Mr D'Arcy stood swathing his neck carefully and frowning.

—It's the weather, said Aunt Julia, after a pause.

—Yes, everybody has colds, said Aunt Kate readily, everybody.

—They say, said Mary Jane, we haven't had snow like it for thirty years; and I read this morning in the newspapers that the snow is general all over Ireland.

—I love the look of snow, said Aunt Julia sadly.

—So do I, said Miss O'Callaghan. I think Christmas is never really Christmas unless we have the snow on the ground.

—But poor Mr D'Arcy doesn't like the snow, said Aunt Kate, smiling.

Mr D'Arcy came from the pantry, fully swathed and buttoned, and in a repentant tone told them the history of his cold. Everyone gave him advice and said it was a great pity and urged him to be very careful of his throat in the night air. Gabriel watched his wife who did not join in the conversation. She was standing right under the dusty fanlight and the flame of the gas lit up the rich bronze of her hair which he had seen her drying at the fire a few days before. She was in the same attitude and seemed unaware of the talk about her. At last she turned towards them and Gabriel saw that there was colour on her cheeks and that her eyes were shining. A sudden tide of joy went leaping out of his heart.

—Mr D'Arcy, she said, what is the name of that song you were singing?

—It's called *The Lass of Aughrim*, said Mr D'Arcy, but I couldn't remember it properly. Why? Do you know it?

—*The Lass of Aughrim*, she repeated. I couldn't think of the name.

—It's a very nice air, said Mary Jane. I'm sorry you were not in voice tonight.

—Now, Mary Jane, said Aunt Kate, don't annoy Mr D'Arcy. I won't have him annoyed.

Seeing that all were ready to start she shepherded them to the door where good-night was said:

—Well, good-night, Aunt Kate, and thanks for the pleasant evening.

—Good-night, Gabriel. Good-night, Gretta!

—Good-night, Aunt Kate, and thanks ever so much. Good-night, Aunt Julia.

—O, good-night, Gretta, I didn't see you.

—Good-night, Mr D'Arcy. Good-night, Miss O'Callaghan.

—Good-night, Miss Morkan.

—Good-night, again.

—Good-night, all. Safe home.

—Good-night. Good-night.

The morning was still dark. A dull yellow light brooded over the houses and the river; and the sky seemed to be descending. It was slushy underfoot; and only streaks and patches of snow lay on the roofs, on the parapets of the quay and on the area railings. The lamps were still burning redly in the murky air and, across the river, the palace of the Four Courts stood out menacingly against the heavy sky.

She was walking on before him with Mr Bartell D'Arcy, her shoes in a brown parcel tucked under one arm and her hands holding her skirt up from the slush. She had no longer any grace of attitude but Gabriel's eyes were still bright with happiness. The blood went bounding along his veins; and the thoughts went rioting through his brain, proud, joyful, tender, valorous.

She was walking on before him so lightly and so erect that he longed to run after her noiselessly, catch her by the shoulders and say something foolish and affectionate into her ear. She seemed to him so frail that he longed to defend her against something and then to be alone with her. Moments of their secret life together burst like stars upon his memory. A heliotrope envelope was lying beside his breakfast-cup and he was caressing it with his hand. Birds were twittering in the ivy and the sunny web of the curtain was shimmering along the floor: he could not eat for happiness. They were standing on the crowded platform and he was placing a ticket inside the warm palm of her glove. He was standing with her in the cold, looking in through a grated window at a man making bottles in a roaring furnace. It was very cold. Her face, fragrant in the

cold air, was quite close to his; and suddenly she called
out to the man at the furnace:

—Is the fire hot, sir?

But the man could not hear her with the noise of the
furnace. It was just as well. He might have answered rude-
ly.

A wave of yet more tender joy escaped from his heart
and went coursing in warm flood along his arteries. Like the
tender fires of stars moments of their life together, that no
one knew of or would ever know of, broke upon and illu-
mined his memory. He longed to recall to her those moments, to make her forget the years of their dull existence
together and remember only their moments of ecstasy. For
the years, he felt, had not quenched his soul or hers. Their
children, his writing, her household cares had not quenched
all their souls' tender fire. In one letter that he had written
to her then he had said: *Why is it that words like these
seem to me so dull and cold? Is it because there is no word
tender enough to be your name?*

Like distant music these words that he had written years
before were borne towards him from the past. He longed
to be alone with her. When the others had gone away, when
he and she were in their room in the hotel, then they
would be alone together. He would call her softly:

—Gretta!

Perhaps she would not hear at once: she would be undressing. Then something in his voice would strike her. She
would turn and look at him. . . .

At the corner of Winetavern Street they met a cab. He
was glad of its rattling noise as it saved him from conversation. She was looking out of the window and seemed
tired. The others spoke only a few words, pointing out
some building or street. The horse galloped along wearily
under the murky morning sky, dragging his old rattling
box after his heels, and Gabriel was again in a cab with
her, galloping to catch the boat, galloping to their honey-
moon.

As the cab drove across O'Connell Bridge Miss O'Callaghan said:

—They say you never cross O'Connell Bridge without
seeing a white horse.

—I see a white man this time, said Gabriel.

—Where? asked Mr Bartell D'Arcy.

Gabriel pointed to the statue, on which lay patches of
snow. Then he nodded familiarly to it and waved his
hand.

—Good-night, Dan, he said gaily.

When the cab drew up before the hotel Gabriel jumped out and, in spite of Mr Bartell D'Arcy's protest, paid the driver. He gave the man a shilling over his fare. The man saluted and said:

—A prosperous New Year to you, sir.

—The same to you, said Gabriel cordially.

She leaned for a moment on his arm in getting out of the cab and while standing at the curbstone, bidding the others good-night. She leaned lightly on his arm, as lightly as when she had danced with him a few hours before. He had felt proud and happy then, happy that she was his, proud of her grace and wifely carriage. But now, after the kindling again of so many memories, the first touch of her body, musical and strange and perfumed, sent through him a keen pang of lust. Under cover of her silence he pressed her arm closely to his side; and, as they stood at the hotel door, he felt that they had escaped from their lives and duties, escaped from home and friends and run away together with wild and radiant hearts to a new adventure.

An old man was dozing in a great hooded chair in the hall. He lit a candle in the office and went before them to the stairs. They followed him in silence, their feet falling in soft thuds on the thickly carpeted stairs. She mounted the stairs behind the porter, her head bowed in the ascent, her frail shoulders curved as with a burden, her skirt girt tightly about her. He could have flung his arms about her hips and held her still for his arms were trembling with desire to seize her and only the stress of his nails against the palms of his hands held the wild impulse of his body in check. The porter halted on the stairs to settle his guttering candle. They halted too on the steps below him. In the silence Gabriel could hear the falling of the molten wax into the tray and the thumping of his own heart against his ribs.

The porter led them along a corridor and opened a door. Then he set his unstable candle down on a toilet-table and asked at what hour they were to be called in the morning.

—Eight, said Gabriel.

The porter pointed to the tap of the electric-light and began a muttered apology but Gabriel cut him short.

—We don't want any light. We have light enough from the street. And I say, he added, pointing to the candle, you might remove that handsome article, like a good man.

The porter took up his candle again, but slowly for he

was surprised by such a novel idea. Then he mumbled good-
night and went out. Gabriel shot the lock to.

A ghostly light from the street lamp lay in a long shaft
from one window to the door. Gabriel threw his overcoat
and hat on a couch and crossed the room towards the
window. He looked down into the street in order that his
emotion might calm a little. Then he turned and leaned
against a chest of drawers with his back to the light.
She had taken off her hat and cloak and was standing before a large swinging mirror, unhooking her waist. Gabriel
paused for a few moments, watching her, and then said:

—Gretta!

She turned away from the mirror slowly and walked
along the shaft of light towards him. Her face looked so
serious and weary that the words would not pass Gabriel's
lips. No it was not the moment yet.

—You looked tired, he said.

—I am a little, she answered.

—You don't feel ill or weak?

—No, tired: that's all.

She went on to the window and stood there, looking out.
Gabriel waited again and then, fearing that diffidence was
about to conquer him, he said abruptly:

—By the way, Gretta!

—What is it?

—You know that poor fellow Malins? he said quickly.

—Yes. What about him?

—Well, poor fellow, he's a decent sort of chap after all,
continued Gabriel in a false voice. He gave me back that
sovereign I lent him and I didn't expect it really. It's a
pity he wouldn't keep away from that Browne, because he's
not a bad fellow at heart.

He was trembling now with annoyance. Why did she
seem so abstracted? He did not know how he could begin.
Was she annoyed, too, about something? If she would only
turn to him or come to him of her own accord! To take
her as she was would be brutal. No, he must see some
ardour in her eyes first. He longed to be master of her
strange mood.

—When did you lend him the pound? she asked, after
a pause.

Gabriel strove to restrain himself from breaking out
into brutal language about the sottish Malins and his
pound. He longed to cry to her from his soul, to crush her
body against his, to overmaster her. But he said:

—O, at Christmas, when he opened that little Christmas-card shop in Henry Street.

He was in such a fever of rage and desire that he did not hear her come from the window. She stood before him for an instant, looking at him strangely. Then, suddenly raising herself on tiptoe and resting her hands lightly on his shoulders, she kissed him.

—You are a very generous person, Gabriel, she said.

Gabriel, trembling with delight at her sudden kiss and at the quaintness of her phrase, put his hands on her hair and began smoothing it back, scarcely touching it with his fingers. The washing had made it fine and brilliant. His heart was brimming over with happiness. Just when he was wishing for it she had come to him of her own accord. Perhaps her thoughts had been running with his. Perhaps she had felt the impetuous desire that was in him and then the yielding mood had come upon her. Now that she had fallen to him so easily he wondered why he had been so diffident.

He stood, holding her head between his hands. Then, slipping one arm swiftly about her body and drawing her towards him, he said softly:

—Gretta dear, what are you thinking about?

She did not answer nor yield wholly to his arm. He said again, softly:

—Tell me what it is, Gretta. I think I know what is the matter. Do I know?

She did not answer at once. Then she said in an outburst of tears:

—O, I am thinking about that song, *The Lass of Aughrim*.

She broke loose from him and ran to the bed and, throwing her arms across the bed-rail, hid her face. Gabriel stood stock-still for a moment in astonishment and then followed her. As he passed in the way of the cheval-glass he caught sight of himself in full length, his broad, well-filled shirt-front, the face whose expression always puzzled him when he saw it in a mirror and his glimmering gilt-rimmed eyeglasses. He halted a few paces from her and said:

—What about the song? Why does that make you cry?

She raised her head from her arms and dried her eyes with the back of her hand like a child. A kinder note than he had intended went into his voice.

—Why, Gretta? he asked.

—I am thinking about a person long ago who used to sing that song.

—And who was the person long ago? asked Gabriel, smiling.

—It was a person I used to know in Galway when I was living with my grandmother, she said.

The smile passed away from Gabriel's face. A dull anger began to gather again at the back of his mind and the dull fires of his lust began to glow angrily in his veins.

—Someone you were in love with? he asked ironically.

—It was a young boy I used to know, she answered, named Michael Furey. He used to sing that song, *The Lass of Aughrim.* He was very delicate.

Gabriel was silent. He did not wish her to think that he was interested in this delicate boy.

—I can see him so plainly, she said after a moment. Such eyes as he had: big dark eyes! And such an expression in them—an expression!

—O then, you were in love with him? said Gabriel.

—I used to go out walking with him, she said, when I was in Galway.

A thought flew across Gabriel's mind.

—Perhaps that was why you wanted to go to Galway with that Ivors girl? he said coldly.

She looked at him and asked in surprise:

—What for?

Her eyes made Gabriel feel awkward. He shrugged his shoulders and said:

—How do I know? To see him perhaps.

She looked away from him along the shaft of light towards the window in silence.

—He is dead, she said at length. He died when he was only seventeen. Isn't it a terrible thing to die so young as that?

—What was he? asked Gabriel, still ironically.

—He was in the gasworks, she said.

Gabriel felt humiliated by the failure of his irony and by the evocation of this figure from the dead, a boy in the gasworks. While he had been full of memories of their secret life together, full of tenderness and joy and desire, she had been comparing him in her mind with another. A shameful consciousness of his own person assailed him. He saw himself as a ludicrous figure, acting as a pennyboy for his aunts, a nervous well-meaning sentimentalist, orating to vulgarians and idealising his own clownish lusts, the pitiable fatuous fellow he had caught a glimpse of in the mirror. Instinctively he turned his back more to the light lest she might see the shame that burned upon his forehead.

He tried to keep up his tone of cold interrogation but his voice when he spoke was humble and indifferent.

—I suppose you were in love with this Michael Furey, Gretta, he said.

—I was great with him at that time, she said.

Her voice was veiled and sad. Gabriel, feeling now how vain it would be to try to lead her whither he had purposed, caressed one of her hands and said, also sadly:

—And what did he die of so young, Gretta? Consumption, was it?

—I think he died for me, she answered.

A vague terror seized Gabriel at this answer as if, at that hour when he had hoped to triumph, some impalpable and vindictive being was coming against him, gathering forces against him in its vague world. But he shook himself free of it with an effort of reason and continued to caress her hand. He did not question her again for he felt that she would tell him of herself. Her hand was warm and moist: it did not respond to his touch but he continued to caress it just as he had caressed her first letter to him that spring morning.

—It was in the winter, she said, about the beginning of the winter when I was going to leave my grandmother's and come up here to the convent. And he was ill at the time in his lodgings in Galway and wouldn't be let out and his people in Oughterard were written to. He was in decline, they said, or something like that. I never knew rightly.

She paused for a moment and sighed.

—Poor fellow, she said. He was very fond of me and he was such a gentle boy. We used to go out together, walking, you know, Gabriel, like the way they do in the country. He was going to study singing only for his health. He had a very good voice, poor Michael Furey.

—Well; and then? asked Gabriel.

—And then when it came to the time for me to leave Galway and come up to the convent he was much worse and I wouldn't be let see him so I wrote a letter saying I was going up to Dublin and would be back in the summer and hoping he would be better then.

She paused for a moment to get her voice under control and then went on:

—Then the night before I left I was in my grandmother's house in Nuns' Island, packing up, and I heard gravel thrown up against the window. The window was so wet I couldn't see so I ran downstairs as I was and slipped out the back into the garden and there was the poor fellow at the end of the garden, shivering.

—And did you not tell him to go back? asked Gabriel.

—I implored of him to go home at once and told him he would get his death in the rain. But he said he d: i not want to live. I can see his eyes as well as well! !ie was standing at the end of the wall where there was a tree.

—And did he go home? asked Gabriel.

—Yes, he went home. And when I was only a week in the convent he died and he was buried in Oughterard where his people came from. O, the day I heard that, that he was dead!

She stopped, choking with sobs, and, overcome by emotion, flung herself face downward on the bed, sobbing in the quilt. Gabriel held her hand for a moment longer, irresolutely, and then, shy of intruding on her grief, let it fall gently and walked quietly to the window.

She was fast asleep.

Gabriel, leaning on his elbow, looked for a few moments unresentfully on her tangled hair and half-open mouth, listening to her deep-drawn breath. So she had had that romance in her life: a man had died for her sake. It hardly pained him now to think how poor a part he, her husband, had played in her life. He watched her while she slept as though he and she had never lived together as man and wife. His curious eyes rested long upon her face and on her hair: and, as he thought of what she must have been then, in that time of her first girlish beauty, a strange friendly pity for her entered his soul. He did not like to say even to himself that her face was no longer beautiful but he knew that it was no longer the face for which Michael Furey had braved death.

Perhaps she had not told him all the story. His eyes moved to the chair over which she had thrown some of her clothes. A petticoat string dangled to the floor. One boot stood upright, its limp upper fallen down: the fellow of it lay upon its side. He wondered at his riot of emotions of an hour before. From what had it proceeded? From his aunt's supper, from his own foolish speech, from the wine and the dancing, the merry-making when saying good-night in the hall, the pleasure of the walk along the river in the snow. Poor Aunt Julia! She, too, would soon be a shade with the shade of Patrick Morkan and his horse. He had caught that haggard look upon her face for a moment when she was singing *Arrayed for the Bridal*. Soon, perhaps, he would be sitting in that same drawing-room, dressed in black, his silk hat on his knees. The blinds would be drawn down and Aunt Kate would be sitting beside him, crying and blowing her nose and telling him how Julia had died. He would cast about in his mind for some words that might console her, and would find only lame and useless ones. Yes, yes: that would happen very soon.

The air of the room chilled his shoulders. He stretched himself cautiously along under the sheets and lay down beside his wife. One by one they were all becoming shades. Better pass boldly into that other world, in the full glory of some passion, than fade and wither dismally with age. He thought of how she who lay beside him had locked in her heart for so many years that image of her lover's eyes when he had told her that he did not wish to live.

Generous tears filled Gabriel's eyes. He had never felt like that himself towards any woman but he knew that such a feeling must be love. The tears gathered more thickly in his eyes and in the partial darkness he imagined he saw the form of a young man standing under a dripping tree. Other forms were near. His soul had approached that region where dwell the vast hosts of the dead. He was conscious of, but could not apprehend, their wayward and flickering existence. His own identity was fading out into a grey impalpable world: the solid world itself which these dead had one time reared and lived in was dissolving and dwindling.

A few light taps upon the pane made him turn to the window. It had begun to snow again. He watched sleepily the flakes, silver and dark, falling obliquely against the lamplight. The time had come for him to set out on his journey westward. Yes, the newspapers were right: snow was general all over Ireland. It was falling on every part of the dark central plain, on the treeless hills, falling softly upon the Bog of Allen and, farther westward, softly falling into the dark mutinous Shannon waves. It was falling, too, upon every part of the lonely churchyard on the hill where Michael Furey lay buried. It lay thickly drifted on the crooked crosses and headstones, on the spears of the little gate, on the barren thorns. His soul swooned slowly as he heard the snow falling faintly through the universe and faintly falling, like the descent of their last end, upon all the living and the dead.

Franz Kafka

(1883–1924)

Franz Kafka was possessed of a vision steeped in meta-physical irony and pessimism. Perhaps the crowning irony enveloping him was his emergence as one of the major figures of twentieth-century literature. Not only was little of his work published during his lifetime, but he left in-structions for his literary executor, Max Brod, to burn all of his manuscripts. Fortunately, Brod chose to ignore his instructions. The posthumous publication of The Trial *(1925) and* The Castle *(1926) permanently estab-lished Kafka as one of the most influential writers of the twentieth century. Like that of de Sade, Kafka's name has become an integral part of our language. Even the casual reader immediately identifies an actual or fictional situation as "Kafkaesque."*

Kafka's life, like his fiction, is a study of the contrast between the surface appearance of things and the fre-quently terrifying realities which lie beneath that surface. Born in Prague to middle-class Czech-Jewish parents, Kafka became a lawyer and worked for the Austrian government in the Workman's Compensation Bureau. He wrote only in his spare time at home. The world he created in his fiction is a mirror image of the turmoil of his own personal life. Probably the strongest influence on both his life and work was his father's authoritarian per-sonality, which dominated Kafka until his death. Out of this relationship, Kafka created a logical terror. Like Poe, he saw terror as man's natural state. And he mixed fanta-sy and reality by presenting the most nightmarish situa-tions in a matter-of-fact style. His stylistic technique and his surrealistic vision have exercised a profound and per-vasive influence on the development of modern literature as well as the film and drama. Kafka's influence is clearly apparent not only in the writing of such major con-temporaries as Borges and Camus but also in the films of Ingmar Bergman.

"The Hunger Artist" is an excellent example of Kafka's extraordinary control of tone. Its opening is a simple statement of fact, the full significance of which only grad-ually dawns on the reader. The bizarre events which culminate in the dead hunger artist's replacement in the cage by the powerful young panther are presented in a

strikingly precise manner. Kafka probably intended this story as an allegory of the artist's position in society, but it can be interpreted in political or social terms as well. The hunger artist is a victim of changes in fashion. He is expected to appeal to a fickle and sensation-seeking audience at the very time that he begins to recognize that he cannot help but fast. Had he found the food he liked, he, too, would have eaten. His profession no longer provides him with pride in his accomplishments. The panther who takes his place is "wild," but the panther "seemed not even to miss his freedom." The panther is actually far tamer than the hunger artist, but the crowds see only his image. Having long since deserted the hunger artist, they flock to see the "wild" creature.

A Hunger Artist

During these last decades the interest in professional fasting has markedly diminished. It used to pay very well to stage such great performances under one's own management, but today that is quite impossible. We live in a different world now. At one time the whole town took a lively interest in the hunger artist; from day to day of his fast the excitement mounted; everybody wanted to see him at least once a day; there were people who bought season tickets for the last few days and sat from morning till night in front of his small barred cage; even in the nighttime there were visiting hours, when the whole effect was heightened by torch flares; on fine days the cage was set out in the open air, and then it was the children's special treat to see the hunger artist; for their elders he was often just a joke that happened to be in fashion, but the children stood open-mouthed, holding each other's hands for greater security, marveling at him as he sat there pallid in black tights, with his ribs sticking out so prominently, not even on a seat but down among straw on the ground, sometimes giving a courteous nod, answering questions with a constrained smile, or perhaps stretching an arm through the bars so that one might feel how thin it was, and then again withdrawing deep into himself, paying no attention to anyone or anything, not even to the all-important striking of the clock that was the only piece of furniture in his cage,

but merely staring into vacancy with half-shut eyes, now
and then taking a sip from a tiny glass of water to moisten
his lips.

Besides casual onlookers there were also relays of permanent watchers selected by the public, usually butchers,
strangely enough, and it was their task to watch the hunger
artist day and night, three of them at a time, in case he
should have some secret recourse to nourishment. This was
nothing but a formality, instituted to reassure the masses,
for the initiates knew well enough that during his fast the
artist would never in any circumstances, not even under
forcible compulsion, swallow the smallest morsel of food;
the honor of his profession forbade it. Not every watcher,
of course, was capable of understanding this, there were
often groups of night watchers who were very lax in carrying out their duties and deliberately huddled together in a
retired corner to play cards with great absorption, obviously
intending to give the hunger artist the chance of a little
refreshment, which they supposed he could draw from some
private hoard. Nothing annoyed the artist more than such
watchers; they made him miserable; they made his fast
seem unendurable; sometimes he mastered his feebleness
sufficiently to sing during their watch for as long as he
could keep going, to show them how unjust their suspicions
were. But that was of little use; they only wondered at his
cleverness in being able to fill his mouth even while singing. Much more to his taste were the watchers who sat
close up to the bars, who were not content with the dim
night lighting of the hall but focused him in the full glare of
the electric pocket torch given them by the impresario. The
harsh light did not trouble him at all; in any case he could
never sleep properly, and he could always drowse a little,
whatever the light, at any hour, even when the hall was
thronged with noisy onlookers. He was quite happy at the
prospect of spending a sleepless night with such watchers;
he was ready to exchange jokes with them, to tell them
stories out of his nomadic life, anything at all to keep them
awake and demonstrate to them again that he had no
eatables in his cage and that he was fasting as not one of
them could fast. But his happiest moment was when the
morning came and an enormous breakfast was brought
them, at his expense, on which they flung themselves with
the keen appetite of healthy men after a weary night of
wakefulness. Of course there were people who argued that
this breakfast was an unfair attempt to bribe the watchers,
but that was going rather too far, and when they were in-

vited to take on a night's vigil without a breakfast, merely
for the sake of the cause, they made themselves scarce, although they stuck stubbornly to their suspicions.

Such suspicions, anyhow, were a necessary accompaniment to the profession of fasting. No one could possibly
watch the hunger artist continuously, day and night, and
so no one could produce first hand evidence that the fast
had really been rigorous and continuous; only the artist
himself could know that, he was therefore bound to be the
sole completely satisfied spectator of his won fast. Yet for
other reasons he was never satisfied; it was not perhaps
mere fasting that had brought him to such skeleton thin-
ness that many people had regretfully to keep away from
his exhibitions, because the sight of him was too much for
them, perhaps it was dissatisfaction with himself that had
worn him down. For he alone knew, what no other initiate
knew, how easy it was to fast. It was the easiest thing in
the world. He made no secret of this, yet people did not
believe him; at the best they set him down as modest. Most
of them, however, thought he was out for publicity or else
was some kind of cheat who found it easy to fast because
he had discovered a way of making it easy, and then had
the impudence to admit the fact, more or less. He had to
put up with all that, and in the course of time had got used
to it, but his inner dissatisfaction always rankled, and never
yet, after any term of fasting—this must be granted to his
credit—had he left the cage of his own free will. The
longest period of fasting was fixed by his impresario at
forty days, beyond that term he was not allowed to go, not
even in great cities, and there was good reason for it, too.
Experience had proved that for about forty days the interest
of the public could be stimulated by a steadily increasing
pressure of advertisement, but after that the town began to
lose interest, sympathetic support began notably to fall off;
there were of course local variations as between one town
and another or one country and another, but as a general
rule forty days marked the limit. So on the fortieth day the
flower-bedecked cage was opened, enthusiastic spectators
filled the hall, a military band played, two doctors entered
the cage to measure the results of the fast, which were announced through a megaphone, and finally two young
ladies appeared, blissful at having been selected for the
honor, to help the hunger artist down the few steps leading to a small table on which was spread a carefully chosen
invalid repast. And at this very moment the artist always

turned stubborn. True, he would entrust his bony arms to the outstretched helping hands of the ladies bending over him, but stand up he would not. Why stop fasting at this particular moment, after forty days of it? He had held out for a long time, an illimitably long time; why stop now, when he was in his best fasting form, or rather, not yet quite in his best fasting form? Why should he be cheated of the fame he would get for fasting longer, for being not only the record hunger artist of all time, which presumably he was already, but for beating his own record by a performance beyond human imagination, since he felt that there were no limits to his capacity for fasting? His public pretended to admire him so much, why should it have so little patience with him; if he could endure fasting longer, why shouldn't the public endure it? Besides, he was tired, he was comfortable sitting in the straw, and now he was supposed to lift himself to his full height and go down to a meal the very thought of which gave him a nausea that only the presence of the ladies kept him from betraying, and even that with an effort. And he looked up into the eyes of the ladies who were apparently so friendly and in reality so cruel, and shook his head, which felt too heavy on its strengthless neck. But then there happened yet again what always happened. The impresario came forward, without a word—for the band made speech impossible—lifted his arms in the air above the artist, as if inviting Heaven to look down upon its creature here in the straw, this suffering martyr, which indeed he was, although in quite another sense; grasped him round the emaciated waist, with exaggerated caution, so that the frail condition he was in might be appreciated; and committed him to the care of the blenching ladies, not without secretly giving him a shaking so that his legs and body tottered and swayed. The artist now submitted completely; his head lolled on his breast as if it had landed there by chance; his body was hollowed out; his legs in a spasm of self-preservation clung close to each other at the knees, yet scraped on the ground as if it were not really solid ground; as if they were only trying to find solid ground; the whole weight of his body, a featherweight after all, relapsed onto one of the ladies, who, looking round for help and panting a little—this post of honor was not at all what she had expected it to be—first stretched her neck as far as she could to keep her face at least free from contact with the artist, then finding this impossible, and her more fortunate companion not coming to her aid but merely holding extended on her own trembling hand the

little bunch of knucklebones that was the artist's, to the
great delight of the spectators burst into tears and had to be
replaced by an attendant who had long been stationed in
readiness. Then came the food, a little of which the impresario managed to get between the artist's lips, while he
sat in a kind of half-fainting trance, to the accompaniment
of cheerful patter designed to distract the public's attention
from the artist's condition; after that, a toast was drunk
to the public, supposedly prompted by a whisper from the
artist in the impresario's ear; the band confirmed it with a
mighty flourish, the spectators melted away, and no one had
any cause to be dissatisfied with the proceedings, no one
except the hunger artist himself, he only, as always.

So he lived for many years, with small regular intervals
of recuperation, in visible glory, honored by the world, yet
in spite of that troubled in spirit, and all the more troubled
because no one would take his trouble seriously. What
comfort could he possibly need? What more could he
possibly wish for? And if some good-natured person, feeling sorry for him, tried to console him by pointing out that
his melancholy was probably caused by fasting, it could
happen, especially when he had been fasting for some time,
that he reacted with an outburst of fury and to the general
alarm began to shake the bars of his cage like a wild
animal. Yet the impresario had a way of punishing these
outbreaks which he rather enjoyed putting into operation.
He would apologize publicly for the artist's behavior, which
was only to be excused, he admitted, because of the irrita-
bility caused by fasting; a condition hardly to be understood by well-fed people; then by natural transition he went
on to mention the artist's equally incomprehensible boast
that he could fast for much longer than he was doing; he
praised the high ambition, the good will, the great self-
denial undoubtedly implicit in such a statement; and then
quite simply countered it by bringing out photographs,
which were also on sale to the public, showing the artist
on the fortieth day of a fast lying in bed almost dead from
exhaustion. This perversion of the truth, familiar to the
artist though it was, always unnerved him afresh and
proved too much for him. What was a consequence of the
premature ending of his fast was here presented as the
cause of it! To fight against this lack of understanding,
against a whole world of non-understanding, was impossible. Time and again in good faith he stood by the bars
listening to the impresario, but as soon as the photographs
appeared he always let go and sank with a groan back on

to his straw, and the reassured public could once more come close and gaze at him.

A few years later when the witnesses of such scenes called them to mind, they often failed to understand themselves at all. For meanwhile the aforementioned change in public interest had set in; it seemed to happen almost overnight; there may have been profound causes for it, but who was going to bother about that; at any rate the pampered hunger artist suddenly found himself deserted one fine day by the amusement seekers, who went streaming past him to other more favored attractions. For the last time the impresario hurried him over half Europe to discover whether the old interest might still survive here and there; all in vain; everywhere, as if by secret agreement, a positive revulsion from professional fasting was in evidence. Of course it could not really have sprung up so suddenly as all that, and many premonitory symptoms which had not been sufficiently remarked or suppressed during the rush and glitter of success now came retrospectively to mind, but it was now too late to take any countermeasures. Fasting would surely come into fashion again at some future date, yet that was no comfort for those living in the present. What, then, was the hunger artist to do? He had been applauded by thousands in his time and could hardly come down to showing himself in a street booth at village fairs, and as for adopting another profession, he was not only too old for that but too fanatically devoted to fasting. So he took leave of the impresario, his partner in an unparalleled career, and hired himself to a large circus; in order to spare his own feelings he avoided reading the conditions of his contract.

A large circus with its enormous traffic in replacing and recruiting men, animals, and apparatus can always find a use for people at any time, even for a hunger artist, provided of course that he does not ask too much, and in this particular case anyhow it was not only the artist who was taken on but his famous and long-known name as well. Indeed, considering the peculiar nature of his performance, which was not impaired by advancing age, it could not be objected that here was an artist past his prime, no longer at the height of his professional skill, seeking a refuge in some quiet corner of a circus; on the contrary, the hunger artist averred that he could fast as well as ever, which was entirely credible. He even alleged that if he were allowed to fast as he liked, and this was at once promised him without more ado, he could astound the world by establishing a record never yet achieved, a statement which certainly pro-

voked a smile among the other professionals, since it left
out of account the change in public opinion, which the
hunger artist in his zeal conveniently forgot.

He had not, however, actually lost his sense of the real
situation and took it as a matter of course that he and his
cage should be stationed, not in the middle of the ring as a
main attraction, but outside, near the animal cages, on a
site that was after all easily accessible. Large and gaily
painted placards made a frame for the cage and announced
what was to be seen inside it. When the public came throng-
ing out in the intervals to see the animals, they could
hardly avoid passing the hunger artist's cage and stopping
there for a moment. Perhaps they might even have stayed
longer had not those pressing behind them in the narrow
gangway, who did not understand why they should be held
up on their way towards the excitements of the menagerie,
made it impossible for anyone to stand gazing quietly for
any length of time. And that was the reason why the
hunger artist, who had of course been looking forward to
these visiting hours as the main achievement of his life,
began instead to shrink from them. At first he could hardly
wait for the intervals; it was exhilarating to watch the
crowds come streaming his way, until only too soon—not
even the most obstinate self-deception, clung to almost
consciously, could hold out against the fact—the conviction was borne in upon him that these people, most of
them, to judge from their actions, again and again, without
exception, were all on their way to the menagerie. And
the first sight of them from the distance remained the best.
For when they reached his cage he was at once deafened
by the storm of shouting and abuse that arose from the
two contending factions, which renewed themselves continuously, of those who wanted to stop and stare at him—
he soon began to dislike them more than the others—not
out of real interest but only out of obstinate self-assertive-
ness, and those who wanted to go straight on to the animals.
When the first great rush was past, the stragglers came
along, and these, whom nothing could have prevented from
stopping to look at him as long as they had breath, raced
past with long strides, hardly even glancing at him, in their
haste to get to the menagerie in time. And all too rarely
did it happen that he had a stroke of luck, when some
father of a family fetched up before him with his children,
pointed a finger at the hunger artist and explained at length
what the phenomenon meant, telling stories of earlier years

when he himself had watched similar but much more thrilling performances, and the children, still rather uncomprehending, since neither inside nor outside school had they been sufficiently prepared for this lesson—what did they care about fasting—yet showed by the brightness of their intent eyes that new and better times might be coming. Perhaps, said the hunger artist to himself many a time, things would be a little better if his cage were set not quite so near the menagerie. That made it too easy for people to make their choice, to say nothing of what he suffered from the stench of the menagerie, the animals' restlessness by night, the carrying past of raw lumps of flesh for the beasts of prey, the roaring at feeding times, which depressed him continually. But he did not dare to lodge a complaint with the management; after all, he had the animals to thank for the troops of people who passed his cage, among whom there might always be one here and there to take an interest in him, and who could tell where they might seclude him if he called attention to his existence and thereby to the fact that, strictly speaking, he was only an impediment on the way to the menagerie.

A small impediment, to be sure; one that grew steadily less. People grew familiar with the strange idea that they could be expected, in times like these, to take an interest in a hunger artist, and with this familiarity the verdict went out against him. He might fast as much as he could, and he did so; but nothing could save him now, people passed him by. Just try to explain to anyone the art of fasting! Anyone who has no feeling for it cannot be made to understand it. The fine placards grew dirty and illegible, they were torn down; the little notice board telling the number of fast days achieved, which at first was changed carefully every day, had long stayed at the same figure, for after the first few weeks even this small task seemed pointless to the staff; and so the artist simply fasted on and on, as he had once dreamed of doing, and it was no trouble to him, just as he had always foretold, but no one counted the days, no one, not even the artist himself, knew what records he was already breaking, and his heart grew heavy. And when once in a time some leisurely passer-by stopped, made merry over the old figure on the board and spoke of swindling, that was in its way the stupidest lie ever invented by indifference and inborn malice, since it was not the hunger artist who was cheating, he was working honestly, but the world was cheating him of his reward.

Many more days went by, however, and that too came to an end. An overseer's eye fell on the cage one day and he asked the attendants why this perfectly good cage should be left standing there unused with dirty straw inside it; nobody knew, until one man, helped out by the notice board, remembered about the hunger artist. They poked into the straw with sticks and found him in it. "Are you still fasting?" asked the overseer, "when on earth do you mean to stop?" "Forgive me, everybody," whispered the hunger artist; only the overseer, who had his ear to the bars, understood him. "Of course," said the overseer, and tapped his forehead with a finger to let the attendants know what state the man was in, "we forgive you." "I always wanted you to admire my fasting," said the hunger artist. "We do admire it," said the overseer, affably. "But you shouldn't admire it," said the hunger artist. "Well then we don't admire it," said the overseer, "but why shouldn't we admire it?" "Because I have to fast, I can't help it," said the hunger artist. "What a fellow you are," said the overseer, "and why can't you help it?" "Because," said the hunger artist, lifting his head a little and speaking, with his lips pursed, as if for a kiss, right into the overseer's ear, so that no syllable might be lost, "because I couldn't find the food I liked. If I had found it, believe me, I should have made no fuss and stuffed myself like you or anyone else." These were his last words, but in his dimming eyes remained the firm, though no longer proud, persuasion that he was still continuing to fast.

"Well, clear this out now!" said the overseer, and they buried the hunger artist, straw and all. Into the cage they put a young panther. Even the most insensitive felt it refreshing to see this wild creature leaping around the cage that had so long been dreary. The panther was all right. The food he liked was brought him without hesitation by the attendants; he seemed not even to miss his freedom; his noble body, furnished almost to the bursting point with all that it needed, seemed to carry freedom around with it too; somewhere in his jaws it seemed to lurk; and the joy of life streamed with such ardent passion from his throat that for the onlookers it was not easy to stand the shock of it. But they braced themselves, crowded round the cage, and did not want ever to move away.

David Henry Lawrence

(1885–1930)

D. H. Lawrence's life was framed between the polarities created by his mother and father, the one a strong-willed former schoolteacher plagued by a marriage which she considered beneath her, the other a jovial, barely literate coal miner. Lawrence was conquered by the ambitions of his mother, but it was an ambiguous victory. Throughout his life, he both sought mystical communion in love and conceived of the will as the power which allowed for the ultimate differentiation among men. No writer has more honestly and profoundly probed the relations between the sexes. Few writers have so successfully and sympathetically depicted the mean and grinding lives of working-class men and women.

Under his mother's prodding, Lawrence attended Nottingham High School, studied at Nottingham University for a short period of time, then taught biology. At the age of twenty-six, he published his first novel, The White Peacock. From that point on, he devoted himself to writing. His mother had died a year before the novel was published. Lawrence ultimately eloped with a married German mother of three children, Frieda von Richthoven. They wandered through the world together, living at various times in Italy, Mexico, Ceylon, Australia, and New Mexico, in each place seeking to throw off the strictures of a civilization which Lawrence believed had divided man's body and soul and had separated man from nature.

Lawrence was only forty-five when he succumbed to tuberculosis. Throughout his life he struggled with frailty and illness. Yet in spite of his handicaps, his literary output was prodigious. He wrote with intense dedication. The range of his work is not limited to novels such as Sons and Lovers (1913), Women in Love (1920), Lady Chatterley's Lover (1928). It encompasses distinguished travel books, essays, short stories. In fact, Lawrence's three volumes of short stories constitute what is probably the most memorable body of short fiction written in our century by an English writer. In these stories we find passionate expressions of Lawrence's deeply held convic-

tion that rapacious materialism and social rigidities lie at the root of modern man's sickness and alienation.

"The Prussian Officer" illustrates the way in which Lawrence shapes his characters to point up and criticize the struggles and dilemmas of civilized man. The officer represents man civilized beyond the point which his consciousness can endure. The soldier, on the other hand, moves in harmony with the dictates of his body and his environment. The conflict between the two leads to their deaths. Neither the soldier's naturalness nor the officer's rigidity is triumphant. The dissociation from nature, the fear of spontaneity, the relationship of past and present— these are given memorable form in one of the finest stories in the English language.

No writer of our century, not even Joyce, has been the subject of more attention by critics and literary historians than Lawrence. One of the greatest of English novelists, he is also among the most fascinating of literary men. Since his death other writers have found in Lawrence a steady source of inspiration testifying to his profound and pervasive influence both in the work they have produced and in the philosophies they have adopted.

The Prussian Officer

I

They had marched more than thirty kilometers since dawn, along the white, hot road where occasional thickets of trees threw a moment of shade, then out into the glare again. On either hand, the valley, wide and shallow, glittered with heat; dark green patches of rye, pale young corn, fallow and meadow and black pine woods spread in a dull, hot diagram under a glistening sky. But right in front the mountains ranged across, pale blue and very still, snow gleaming gently out of the deep atmosphere. And towards the mountains, on and on, the regiment marched between the rye fields and the meadows, between the scraggy fruit trees set regularly on either side the high road. The burnished, dark green rye threw off a suffocating heat, the mountains drew gradually nearer and more distinct. While the feet of the soldiers grew hotter, sweat ran through their hair under their helmets, and their knap-

sacks could burn no more in contact with their shoulders,
but seemed instead to give off a cold, prickly sensation.

He walked on and on in silence, staring at the mountains ahead, that rose sheer out of the land, and stood
fold behind fold, half earth, half heaven, the heaven, the
barrier with slits of soft snow, in the pale, bluish peaks.

He could now walk almost without pain. At the start,
he had determined not to limp. It had made him sick
to take the first steps, and during the first mile or so,
he had compressed his breath, and the cold drops of
sweat had stood on his forehead. But he had walked it
off. What were they after all but bruises! He had looked
at them, as he was getting up: deep bruises on the backs
of his thighs. And since he had made his first step in the
morning, he had been conscious of them, till now he had
a tight, hot place in his chest, with suppressing the pain,
and holding himself in. There seemed no air when he
breathed. But he walked almost lightly.

The Captain's hand had trembled at taking his coffee
at dawn: his orderly saw it again. And he saw the fine
figure of the Captain wheeling on horseback at the farmhouse ahead, a handsome figure in pale blue uniform with
facings of scarlet, and the metal gleaming on the black
helmet and the sword-scabbard, and dark streaks of sweat
coming on the silky bay horse. The orderly felt he was
connected with that figure moving so suddenly on horseback: he followed it like a shadow, mute and inevitable
and damned by it. And the officer was always aware of
the tramp of the company behind, the march of his
orderly among the men.

The Captain was a tall man of about forty, gray at the
temples. He had a handsome, finely knit figure, and
was one of the best horsemen in the West. His orderly,
having to rub him down, admired the amazing riding
muscles of his loins.

For the rest, the orderly scarcely noticed the officer
any more than he noticed himself. It was rarely he saw
his master's face: he did not look at it. The Captain had
reddish-brown, stiff hair, that he wore short upon his
skull. His mustache was also cut short and bristly over
a full, brutal mouth. His face was rather rugged, the
cheeks thin. Perhaps the man was the more handsome for
the deep lines in his face, the irritable tension of his brow,
which gave him the look of a man who fights with life.
His fair eyebrows stood bushy over light blue eyes that
were always flashing with cold fire.

He was a Prussian aristocrat, haughty and overbearing. But his mother had been a Polish Countess. Having made too many gambling debts when he was young, he had ruined his prospects in the Army, and remained an infantry captain. He had never married: his position did not allow of it, and no woman had ever moved him to it. His time he spent riding—occasionally he rode one of his own horses at the races—and at the officers' club. Now and then he took himself a mistress. But after such an event, he returned to duty with his brow still more tense, his eyes still more hostile and irritable. With the men, however, he was merely impersonal, though a devil when roused; so that, on the whole, they feared him, but had no great aversion from him. They accepted him as the inevitable.

To his orderly he was at first cold and just and indifferent: he did not fuss over trifles. So that his servant knew practically nothing about him, except just what orders he would give, and how he wanted them obeyed. That was quite simple. Then the change gradually came.

The orderly was a youth of about twenty-two, of medium height, and well built. He had strong, heavy limbs, was swarthy, with a soft, black, young mustache. There was something altogether warm and young about him. He had firmly marked eyebrows over dark, expressionless eyes, that seemed never to have thought, only to have received life direct through his senses, and acted straight from instinct.

Gradually the officer had become aware of his servant's young, vigorous, unconscious presence about him. He could not get away from the sense of the youth's person, while he was in attendance. It was like a warm flame upon the older man's tense, rigid body, that had become almost unliving, fixed. There was something so free and self-contained about him, and something in the young fellow's movement, that made the officer aware of him. And this irritated the Prussian. He did not choose to be touched into life by his servant. He might easily have changed his man, but he did not. He now very rarely looked direct at his orderly, but kept his face averted, as if to avoid seeing him. And yet as the young soldier moved unthinking about the apartment, the elder watched him, and would notice the movement of his strong young shoulders under the blue cloth, the bend of his neck. And it irritated him. To see the soldier's young, brown, shapely peasant's hand grasp the loaf or the wine-bottle sent a flash of hate or of anger through the elder man's blood. It was not that the youth was clumsy: it was rather the blind, instinctive sureness of movement of an unhampered young animal that irritated the officer to such a degree.

Once, when a bottle of wine had gone over, and the red gushed out on to the tablecloth, the officer had started up with an oath, and his eyes, bluey like fire, had held those of the confused youth for a moment. It was a shock for the young soldier. He felt something sink deeper, deeper into his soul, where nothing had ever gone before. It left him rather blank and wondering. Some of his natural completeness in himself was gone, a little uneasiness took its place. And from that time an undiscovered feeling had held between the two men.

Henceforward the orderly was afraid of really meeting his master. His subconsciousness remembered those steely blue eyes and the harsh brows, and did not intend to meet them again. So he always stared past his master, and avoided him. Also, in a little anxiety, he waited for the three months to have gone, when his time would be up. He began to feel a constraint in the Captain's presence, and the soldier even more than the officer wanted to be left alone, in his neutrality as servant.

He had served the Captain for more than a year, and knew his duty. This he performed easily, as if it were natural to him. The officer and his commands he took for granted, as he took the sun and the rain, and he served as a matter of course. It did not implicate him personally.

But now if he were going to be forced into a personal interchange with his master he would be like a wild thing caught; he felt he must get away.

But the influence of the young soldier's being had penetrated through the officer's stiffened discipline, and perturbed the man in him. He, however, was a gentleman, with long, fine hands and cultivated movements, and was not going to allow such a thing as the stirring of his innate self. He was a man of passionate temper, who had always kept himself suppressed. Occasionally there had been a duel, an outburst before the soldiers. He knew himself to be always on the point of breaking out. But he kept himself hard to the idea of the Service. Whereas the young soldier seemed to live out his warm, full nature, to give it off in his very movements, which had a certain zest, such as wild animals have in free movement. And this irritated the officer more and more.

In spite of himself, the Captain could not regain his

neutrality of feeling towards his orderly. Nor could he leave the man alone. In spite of himself, he watched him, gave him sharp orders, tried to take up as much of his time as possible. Sometimes he flew into a rage with the young soldier, and bullied him. Then the orderly shut himself off, as it were out of earshot, and waited, with sullen, flushed face, for the end of the noise. The words never pierced to his intelligence. He made himself, protectively, impervious to the feelings of his master.

He had a scar on his left thumb, a deep seam going across the knuckle. The officer had long suffered from it, and wanted to do something to it. Still it was there, ugly and brutal on the young, brown hand. At last the Captain's reserve gave way. One day, as the orderly was smoothing out the tablecloth, the officer pinned down his thumb with a pencil, asking:

"How did you come by that?"

The young man winced and drew back at attention.

"A wood ax, Herr Hauptmann," he answered.

The officer waited for further explanation. None came. The orderly went about his duties. The elder man was sullenly angry. His servant avoided him. And the next day he had to use all his will power to avoid seeing the scarred thumb. He wanted to get hold of it and— A hot flame ran in his blood.

He knew his servant would soon be free, and would be glad. As yet, the soldier had held himself off from the elder man. The Captain grew madly irritable. He could not rest when the soldier was away, and when he was present, he glared at him with tormented eyes. He hated those fine, black brows over the unmeaning, dark eyes, he was infuriated by the free movement of the handsome limbs, which no military discipline could make stiff. And he became harsh and cruelly bullying, using contempt and satire. The young soldier only grew more mute and expressionless.

"What cattle were you bred by, that you can't keep straight eyes? Look me in the eyes when I speak to you."

And the soldier turned his dark eyes to the other's face, but there was no sight in them: he stared with the slightest possible cast, holding back his sight, perceiving the blue of his master's eyes, but receiving no look from them. And the elder man went pale, and his reddish eyebrows twitched. He gave his order, barrenly.

Once he flung a heavy military glove into the young soldier's face. Then he had the satisfaction of seeing the black eyes flare up into his own, like a blaze when straw is thrown on a fire. And he had laughed with a little tremor and a sneer.

But there were only two months more. The youth instinctively tried to keep himself intact: he tried to serve the officer as if the latter were an abstract authority and not a man. All his instinct was to avoid personal contact, even definite hate. But in spite of himself the hate grew, responsive to the officer's passion. However, he put it in the background. When he had left the Army he could dare acknowledge it. By nature he was active, and had many friends. He thought what amazing good fellows they were. But, without knowing it, he was alone. Now this solitariness was intensified. It would carry him through his term. But the officer seemed to be going irritably insane, and the youth was deeply frightened.

The soldier had a sweetheart, a girl from the mountains, independent and primitive. The two walked together, rather silently. He went with her, not to talk, but to have his arm round her, and for the physical contact. This eased him, made it easier for him to ignore the Captain; for he could rest with her held fast against his chest. And she, in some unspoken fashion, was there for him. They loved each other.

The Captain perceived it, and was mad with irritation. He kept the young man engaged all the evenings long, and took pleasure in the dark look that came on his face. Occasionally, the eyes of the two men met, those of the younger sullen and dark, doggedly unalterable, those of the elder sneering with restless contempt.

The officer tried hard not to admit the passion that had got hold of him. He would not know that his feeling for his orderly was anything but that of a man incensed by his stupid, perverse servant. So, keeping quite justified and conventional in his consciousness, he let the other thing run on. His nerves, however, were suffering. At last he slung the end of a belt in his servant's face. When he saw the youth start back, the pain-tears in his eyes and the blood on his mouth, he had felt at once a thrill of deep pleasure and of shame.

But this, he acknowledged to himself, was a thing he had never done before. The fellow was too exasperating. His own nerves must be going to pieces. He went away for some days with a woman.

It was a mockery of pleasure. He simply did not want the woman. But he stayed on for his time. At the end of it, he came back in an agony of irritation, torment, and misery. He rode all the evening, then came straight in to supper. His orderly was out. The officer sat with his long, fine hands lying on the table, perfectly still, and all his blood seemed to be corroding.

At last his servant entered. He watched the strong, easy young figure, the fine eyebrows, the thick black hair. In a week's time the youth had got back his old well-being. The hands of the officer twitched and seemed to be full of mad flame. The young man stood at attention, unmoving, shut off.

The meal went in silence. But the orderly seemed eager. He made a clatter with the dishes.

"Are you in a hurry?" asked the officer, watching the intent, warm face of his servant. The other did not reply.

"Will you answer my question?" said the Captain.

"Yes, sir," replied the orderly, standing with his pile of deep Army plates. The Captain waited, looked at him, then asked again:

"Are you in a hurry?"

"Yes, sir," came the answer, that sent a flash through the listener.

"For what?"

"I was going out, sir."

"I want you this evening."

There was a moment's hesitation. The officer had a curious stiffness of countenance.

"Yes, sir," replied the servant, in his throat.

"I want you to-morrow evening also—in fact, you may consider your evenings occupied, unless I give you leave."

The mouth with the young mustache set close.

"Yes, sir," answered the orderly, loosening his lips for a moment.

He again turned to the door.

"And why have you a piece of pencil in your ear?"

The orderly hesitated, then continued on his way without answering. He set the plates in a pile outside the door, took the stump of pencil from his ear, and put it in his pocket. He had been copying a verse for his sweetheart's birthday card. He returned to finish clearing the table. The officer's eyes were dancing, he had a little, eager smile.

"Why have you a piece of pencil in your ear?" he asked.

The orderly took his hands full of dishes. His master was standing near the great green stove, a little smile on his face, his chin thrust forward. When the young soldier saw him his heart suddenly ran hot. He felt blind. Instead of answering, he turned dazedly to the door. As he was crouching to set down the dishes, he was pitched forward by a kick from behind. The pots went in a stream down the stairs, he clung to the pillar of the banisters. And as he was rising he was kicked heavily again, and again, so that he clung sickly to the post for some moments. His master had gone swiftly into the room and closed the door. The maid-servant downstairs looked up the staircase and made a mocking face at the crockery disaster.

The officer's heart was plunging. He poured himself a glass of wine, part of which he spilled on the floor, and gulped the remainder, leaning against the cool, green stove. He heard his man collecting the dishes from the stairs. Pale, as if intoxicated, he waited. The servant entered again. The Captain's heart gave a pang, as of pleasure, seeing the young fellow bewildered and uncertain on his feet, with pain.

"Schöner!" he said.

The soldier was a little slower in coming to attention.

"Yes, sir!"

The youth stood before him, with pathetic young mustache, and fine eyebrows very distinct on his forehead of dark marble.

"I asked you a question."

"Yes, sir."

The officer's tone bit like acid.

"Why had you a pencil in your ear?"

Again the servant's heart ran hot, and he could not breathe. With dark, strained eyes, he looked at the officer, as if fascinated. And he stood there sturdily planted, unconscious. The withering smile came into the Captain's eyes, and he lifted his foot.

"I—I forgot it—sir," panted the soldier, his dark eyes fixed on the other man's dancing blue ones.

"What was it doing there?"

He saw the young man's breast heaving as he made an effort for words.

"I had been writing."

"Writing what?"

Again the soldier looked him up and down. The officer could hear him panting. The smile came into the blue eyes. The soldier worked his dry throat, but could not speak. Suddenly the smile lit like a flame on the officer's

face, and a kick came heavily against the orderly's thigh.
The youth moved a pace sideways. His face went dead,
with two black, staring eyes.

"Well?" said the officer.

The orderly's mouth had gone dry, and his tongue
rubbed in it as on dry brown-paper. He worked his throat.
The officer raised his foot. The servant went stiff.

"Some poetry, sir," came the crackling, unrecognizable
sound of his voice.

"Poetry, what poetry?" asked the Captain with a sickly
smile.

Again there was the working in the throat. The Captain's heart had suddenly gone down heavily, and he stood
sick and tired.

"For my girl, sir," he heard the dry, inhuman sound.

"Oh!" he said, turning away. "Clear the table."

"Click!" went the soldier's throat; then again, "click!"
and then the half-articulate:

"Yes, sir."

The young soldier was gone, looking old, and walking
heavily.

The officer, left alone, held himself rigid, to prevent
himself from thinking. His instinct warned him that he
must not think. Deep inside him was the intense gratification of his passion, still working powerfully. Then there
was a counter-action, a horrible breaking down of something inside him, a whole agony of reaction. He stood
there for an hour motionless, a chaos of sensations, but
rigid with a will to keep blank his consciousness, to prevent his mind grasping. And he held himself so until the
worst of the stress had passed, when he began to drink,
drank himself to an intoxication, till he slept obliterated.
When he woke in the morning he was shaken to the base
of his nature. But he had fought off the realization of
what he had done. He had prevented his mind from taking it in, had suppressed it along with his instincts, and
the conscious man had nothing to do with it. He felt
only as after a bout of intoxication, weak, but the affair
itself all dim and not to be recovered. Of the drunken-
ness of his passion he successfully refused remembrance.
And when his orderly appeared with coffee, the officer
assumed the same self he had had the morning before.
He refused the event of the past night—denied it had
ever been—and was successful in his denial. He had not
done any such thing—not he himself. Whatever there
might be lay at the door of a stupid, insubordinate servant.

The orderly had gone about in a stupor all the evening. He drank some beer because he was parched, but not much, the alcohol made his feeling come back, and he could not bear it. He was dulled, as if nine-tenths of the ordinary man in him were inert. He crawled about disfigured. Still, when he thought of the kicks, he went sick, and when he thought of the threat of more kicking, in the room afterwards, his heart went hot and faint, and he panted, remembered the one that had come. He had been forced to say, "For my girl." He was much too done even to want to cry. His mouth hung slightly open, like an idiot's. He felt vacant, and wasted. So, he wandered at his work, painfully, and very slowly and clumsily, fumbling blindly with the brushes, and finding it difficult, when he sat down, to summon the energy to move again. His limbs, his jaw, were slack and nerveless. But he was very tired. He got to bed at last, and slept inert, relaxed, in a sleep that was rather stupor than slumber, a dead night of stupefaction shot through with gleams of anguish.

In the morning were the maneuvers. But he woke even before the bugle sounded. The painful ache in his chest, the dryness of his throat, the awful steady feeling of misery made his eyes come awake and dreary at once. He knew, without thinking, what had happened. And he knew that the day had come again, when he must go on with his round. The last bit of darkness was being pushed out of the room. He would have to move his inert body and go on. He was so young, and had known so little trouble, that he was bewildered. He only wished it would stay night, so that he could lie still, covered up by the darkness. And yet nothing would prevent the day from coming, nothing would save him from having to get up and saddle the Captain's horse, and make the Captain's coffee. It was there, inevitable. And then, he thought, it was impossible. Yet they would not leave him free. He must go and take the coffee to the Captain. He was too stunned to understand it. He only knew it was inevitable—inevitable, however long he lay inert.

At last, after heaving at himself, for he seemed to be a mass of inertia, he got up. But he had to force every one of his movements from behind, with his will. He felt lost, and dazed, and helpless. Then he clutched hold of the bed, the pain was so keen. And looking at his thighs, he saw the darker bruises on his swarthy flesh and he knew that, if he pressed one of his fingers on one of the bruises, he should faint. But he did not want to

faint—he did not want anybody to know. No one should
ever know. It was between him and the Captain. There
were only the two people in the world now—himself and
the Captain.

Slowly, economically, he got dressed and forced himself
to walk. Everything was obscure, except just what he
had his hands on. But he managed to get through his
work. The very pain revived his dull senses. The worst
remained yet. He took the tray and went up to the Captain's room. The officer, pale and heavy, sat at the table.
The orderly, as he saluted, felt himself put out of existence. He stood still for a moment submitting to his
own nullification—then he gathered himself, seemed to
regain himself, and then the Captain began to grow
vague, unreal, and the younger soldier's heart beat up.
He clung to this situation—that the Captain did not exist
—so that he himself might live. But when he saw his
officer's hand tremble as he took the coffee, he felt everything falling shattered. And he went away, feeling as if
he himself were coming to pieces, disintegrated. And when
the Captain was there on horseback, giving orders, while
he himself stood, with rifle and knapsack, sick with pain,
he felt as if he must shut his eyes—as if he must shut
his eyes on everything. It was only the long agony of
marching with a parched throat that filled him with one
single, sleep-heavy intention: to save himself.

II

He was getting used even to his parched throat. That
the snowy peaks were radiant among the sky, that the
whity-green glacier-river twisted through its pale shoals,
in the valley below, seemed almost supernatural. But he
was going mad with fever and thirst. He plodded on un-
complaining. He did not want to speak, not to anybody.
There were two gulls, like flakes of water and snow, over
the river. The scent of green rye soaked in sunshine
came like a sickness. And the march continued, monot-
onously, almost like a bad sleep.

At the next farmhouse, which stood low and broad
near the high road, tubs of water had been put out. The
soldiers clustered round to drink. They took off their

helmets, and the steam mounted from their wet hair. The Captain sat on horseback, watching. He needed to see his orderly. His helmet threw a dark shadow over his light, fierce eyes, but his mustache and mouth and chin were distinct in the sunshine. The orderly must move under the presence of the figure of the horseman. It was not that he was afraid, or cowed. It was as if he were disemboweled, made empty, like an empty shell. He felt himself as nothing, a shadow creeping under the sunshine. And, thirsty as he was, he could scarcely drink, feeling the Captain near him. He would not take off his helmet to wipe his wet hair. He wanted to stay in shadow, not to be forced into consciousness. Starting, he saw the light heel of the officer prick the belly of the horse; the Captain cantered away, and he himself could relapse into vacancy.

Nothing, however, could give him back his living place in the hot, bright morning. He felt like a gap among it all. Whereas the Captain was prouder, overriding. A hot flash went through the young servant's body. The Captain was firmer and prouder with life, he himself was empty as a shadow. Again the flash went through him, dazing him out. But his heart ran a little firmer.

The company turned up the hill, to make a loop for the return. Below, from among the trees, the farm-bell clanged. He saw the laborers, mowing barefoot at the thick grass, leave off their work and go downhill, their scythes hanging over their shoulders, like long, bright claws curving down behind them. They seemed like dream-people, as if they had no relation to himself. He felt as in a blackish dream: as if all the other things were there and had form, but he himself was only a consciousness, a gap that could think and perceive.

The soldiers were tramping silently up the glaring hillside. Gradually his head began to revolve, slowly, rhythmically. Sometimes it was dark before his eyes, as if he saw this world through a smoked glass, frail shadows and unreal. It gave him a pain in his head to walk.

The air was too scented, it gave no breath. All the lush green-stuff seemed to be issuing its sap, till the air was deathly, sickly with the smell of greenness. There was the perfume of clover, like pure honey and bees. Then there grew a faint acrid tang—they were near the beeches; and then a queer clattering noise, and a suffocating, hideous smell; they were passing a flock of sheep, a shepherd in a black smock, holding his crook. Why should

the sheep huddle together under this fierce sun? He felt
that the shepherd would not see him, though he could see
the shepherd.

At last there was the halt. They stacked rifles in a
conical stack, put down their kit in a scattered circle
around it, and dispersed a little, sitting on a small knoll
high on the hillside. The clatter began. The soldiers were
steaming with heat, but were lively. He sat still, seeing
the blue mountains rising upon the land, twenty kilometers away. There was a blue fold in the ranges, then
out of that, at the foot, the broad, pale bed of the river,
stretches of whity-green water between pinkish-gray shoals
among the dark pine woods. There it was, spread out a
long way off. And it seemed to come downhill, the river.
There was a raft being steered, a mile away. It was a
strange country. Nearer, a red-roofed, broad farm with
white base and square dots of windows crouched beside
the wall of beech foliage on the wood's edge. There were
long strips of rye and clover and pale green corn. And
just at his feet, below the knoll, was a darkish bog, where
globe flowers stood breathless, still on their slim stalks.
And some of the pale gold bubbles were burst, and a
broken fragment hung in the air. He thought he was
going to sleep.

Suddenly something moved into this colored mirage
before his eyes. The Captain, a small, light-blue and scarlet
figure, was trotting evenly between the strips of corn,
along the level brow of the hill. And the man making
flag-signals was coming on. Proud and sure moved the
horseman's figure, the quick, bright thing, in which was
concentrated all the light of this morning, which for the
rest lay a fragile, shining shadow. Submissive, apathetic,
the young soldier sat and stared. But as the horse slowed
to a walk, coming up the last steep path, the great flash
flared over the body and soul of the orderly. He sat waiting. The back of his head felt as if it were weighted with
a heavy piece of fire. He did not want to eat. His hands
trembled slightly as he moved them. Meanwhile the officer
on horseback was approaching slowly and proudly. The
tension grew in the orderly's soul. Then again, seeing the
Captain ease himself on the saddle, the flash blazed through
him.

The Captain looked at the patch of light blue and scarlet,
and dark heads, scattered closely on the hillside. It pleased
him. The command pleased him. And he was feeling
proud. His orderly was among them in common subjection.

The officer rose a little on his stirrups to look. The young soldier sat with averted, dumb face. The Captain relaxed on his seat. His slim-legged, beautiful horse, brown as a beech nut, walked proudly uphill. The Captain passed into the zone of the company's atmosphere: a hot smell of men, of sweat, of leather. He knew it very well. After a word with the lieutenant, he went a few paces higher, and sat there, a dominant figure, his sweat-marked horse swishing its tail, while he looked down on his men, on his orderly, a nonentity among the crowd.

The young soldier's heart was like fire in his chest, and he breathed with difficulty. The officer, looking downhill, saw three of the young soldiers, two pails of water between them, staggering across a sunny green field. A table had been set up under a tree, and there the slim lieutenant stood, importantly busy. Then the Captain summoned himself to an act of courage. He called his orderly.

The flame leapt into the young soldier's throat as he heard the command, and he rose blindly, stifled. He saluted, standing below the officer. He did not look up. But there was the flicker in the Captain's voice.

"Go to the inn and fetch me . . ." the officer gave his commands. "Quick!" he added.

At the last word, the heart of the servant leapt with a flash, and he felt the strength come over his body. But he turned in mechanical obedience, and set off at a heavy run downhill, looking almost like a bear, his trousers bagging over his military boots. And the officer watched this blind, plunging run all the way.

But it was only the outside of the orderly's body that was obeying so humbly and mechanically. Inside had gradually accumulated a core into which all the energy of that young life was compact and concentrated. He executed his commission, and plodded quickly back uphill. There was a pain in his head, as he walked, that made him twist his features unknowingly. But hard there in the center of his chest was himself, himself, firm, and not to be plucked to pieces.

The Captain had gone up into the wood. The orderly plodded through the hot, powerfully smelling zone of the company's atmosphere. He had a curious mass of energy inside him now. The Captain was less real than himself. He approached the green entrance to the wood. There, in the half-shade, he saw the horse standing, the sunshine and the flickering shadow of leaves dancing over his brown body. There was a clearing where timber had lately been felled. Here, in the gold-green shade beside the brilliant cup of sunshine, stood two figures, blue and pink, the bits of pink showing out plainly. The Captain was talking to his lieutenant.

The orderly stood on the edge of the bright clearing, where great trunks of trees, stripped and glistening, lay stretched like naked, brown-skinned bodies. Chips of wood littered the trampled floor, like splashed light, and the bases of the felled trees stood here and there, with their raw, level tops. Beyond was the brilliant, sunlit green of a beech.

"Then I will ride forward," the orderly heard his Captain say. The lieutenant saluted and strode away. He himself went forward. A hot flash passed through his belly, as he tramped towards his officer.

The Captain watched the rather heavy figure of the young soldier stumble forward, and his veins, too, ran hot. This was to be man to man between them. He yielded before the solid, stumbling figure with bent head. The orderly stooped and put the food on a level-sawn tree-base. The Captain watched the glistening, sun-inflamed, naked hands. He wanted to speak to the young soldier, but could not. The servant propped a bottle against his thigh, pressed open the cork, and poured out the beer into the mug. He kept his head bent. The Captain accepted the mug.

"Hot!" he said, as if amiably.

The flame sprang out of the orderly's heart, nearly suffocating him.

"Yes, sir," he replied, between shut teeth.

And he heard the sound of the Captain's drinking, and he clenched his fists, such a strong torment came into his wrists. Then came the faint clang of the closing of the pot-lid. He looked up. The Captain was watching him. He glanced swiftly away. Then he saw the officer stoop and take a piece of bread from the tree-base. Again the flash of flame went through the young soldier, seeing the stiff body stoop beneath him, and his hands jerked. He looked away. He could feel the officer was nervous. The bread fell as it was being broken. The officer ate the other piece. The two men stood tense and still, the master laboriously chewing his bread, the servant staring with averted face, his fist clenched.

Then the young soldier started. The officer had pressed open the lid of the mug again. The orderly watched the lid of the mug, and the white hand that clenched the handle, as if he were fascinated. It was raised. The youth followed it with his eyes. And then he saw the thin, strong throat of the elder man moving up and down as he drank, the strong jaw working. And the instinct which had been jerking at the young man's wrist suddenly jerked free. He jumped, feeling as if it were rent in two by a strong flame.

The spur of the officer caught in a tree-root, he went down backwards with a crash, the middle of his back thudding sickeningly against a sharp-edged tree-base, the pot flying away. And in a second the orderly, with serious, earnest young face, and underlip between his teeth, had got his knee in the officer's chest and was pressing the chin backward over the farther edge of the tree-stump, pressing, with all his heart, behind in a passion of relief, the tension of his wrists exquisite with relief. And with the base of his palms he shoved at the chin, with all his might. And it was pleasant, too, to have that chin, that hard jaw already slightly rough with beard, in his hands. He did not relax one hair's breadth, but, all the force of all his blood exulting in his thrust, he shoved back the head of the other man, till there was a little "cluck" and a crunching sensation. Then he felt as if his head went to vapor. Heavy convulsions shook the body of the officer, frightening and horrifying the young soldier. Yet it pleased him, too, to repress them. It pleased him to keep his hands pressing back the chin, to feel the chest of the other man yield in expiration to the weight of his strong, young knees, to feel the hard twitchings of the prostrate body jerking his own whole frame, which was pressed down on it.

But it went still. He could look into the nostrils of the other man, the eyes he could scarcely see. How curiously the mouth was pushed out, exaggerating the full lips, and the mustache bristling up from them. Then, with a start, he noticed the nostrils gradually filled with blood. The red brimmed, hesitated, ran over, and went in a thin trickle down the face to the eyes.

It shocked and distressed him. Slowly, he got up. The body twitched and sprawled there, inert. He stood and looked at it in silence. It was a pity *it* was broken. It represented more than the thing which had kicked and bullied him. He was afraid to look at the eyes. They were hideous now, only the whites showing, and the blood running to them. The face of the orderly was drawn with horror at the sight. Well, it was so. In his heart he was satisfied. He had hated the face of the Captain. It was extinguished now. There was a heavy relief in the orderly's soul. That was as it should be. But he could not bear to see the long, military body lying broken over the tree-base, the fine fingers crisped. He wanted to hide it away.

Quickly, busily, he gathered it up and pushed it under the felled tree-trunks, which rested their beautiful, smooth length either end on logs. The face was horrible with blood. He covered it with the helmet. Then he pushed the limbs straight and decent, and brushed the dead leaves off the fine cloth of the uniform. So, it lay quite still in the shadow under there. A little strip of sunshine ran along the breast, from a chink between the logs. The orderly sat by it for a few moments. Here his own life also ended.

Then, through his daze, he heard the lieutenant, in a loud voice, explaining to the men outside the wood, that they were to suppose the bridge on the river below was held by the enemy. Now they were to march to the attack in such and such a manner. The lieutenant had no gift of expression. The orderly, listening from habit, got muddled. And when the lieutenant began it all again he ceased to hear.

He knew he must go. He stood up. It surprised him that the leaves were glittering in the sun, and the chips of wood reflecting white from the ground. For him a change had come over the world. But for the rest it had not—all seemed the same. Only he had left it. And he could not go back. It was his duty to return with the beer-pot and the bottle. He could not. He had left all that. The lieutenant was still hoarsely explaining. He must go, or they would overtake him. And he could not bear contact with any one now.

He drew his fingers over his eyes, trying to find out where he was. Then he turned away. He saw the horse standing in the path. He went up to it and mounted. It hurt him to sit in the saddle. The pain of keeping his seat occupied him as they cantered through the wood. He would not have minded anything, but he could not get away from the sense of being divided from the others. The path led out of the trees. On the edge of the wood he pulled up and stood watching. There in the spacious sunshine of the valley soldiers were moving in a little swarm. Every now and then, a man harrowing on a strip of fallow shouted to his oxen, at the turn. The village and the white-towered church were small in the sunshine. And he no longer belonged to it—he sat there, beyond, like a man outside in the dark. He had gone out from everyday life into the unknown, and he could not, he even did not want to go back.

Turning from the sun-blazing valley, he rode deep into the wood. Tree-trunks, like people standing gray and still, took no notice as he went. A doe, herself a moving bit of sunshine and shadow, went running through the flecked shade. There were bright green rents in the foliage. Then it was all pine wood, dark and cool. And he was sick with pain, he had an intolerable great pulse in his head, and he was sick. He had never been ill in his life. He felt lost, quite dazed with all this.

Trying to get down from the horse, he fell, astonished at the pain and his lack of balance. The horse shifted uneasily. He jerked its bridle and sent it cantering jerkily away. It was his last connection with the rest of things.

But he only wanted to lie down and not be disturbed. Stumbling through the trees, he came on a quiet place where beeches and pine trees grew on a slope. Immediately he had lain down and closed his eyes, his consciousness went racing on without him. A big pulse of sickness beat in him as if it throbbed through the whole earth. He was burning with dry heat. But he was too busy, too tearingly active in the incoherent race of delirium to observe.

III

He came to with a start. His mouth was dry and hard, his heart beat heavily, but he had not the energy to get up. His heart beat heavily. Where was he?—the barracks— at home? There was something knocking. And, making an effort, he looked round—trees, and litter of greenery, and reddish, bright, still pieces of sunshine on the floor. He did not believe he was himself, he did not believe what he saw. Something was knocking. He made a struggle towards consciousness, but relapsed. Then he struggled again. And gradually his surroundings fell into relationship with himself. He knew, and a great pang of fear went through his heart. Somebody was knocking. He could see the heavy, black rags of a fir tree overhead. Then everything went black. Yet he did not believe he had closed his eyes. He had not. Out of the blackness sight slowly emerged again. And some one was knocking. Quickly, he saw the blood-disfigured face of his Captain which he hated. And he held himself still with horror. Yet, deep inside him, he knew that it was so, the Captain should be

dead. But the physical delirium got hold of him. Some one
was knocking. He lay perfectly still, as if dead, with fear.
And he went unconscious.

When he opened his eyes again, he started, seeing something creeping swiftly up a tree-trunk. It was a little bird.
And the bird was whistling overhead. Tap-tap-tap—it was
the small, quick bird rapping the tree-trunk with its beak,
as if its head were a little round hammer. He watched it
curiously. It shifted sharply, in its creeping fashion. Then,
like a mouse, it slid down the bare trunk. Its swift creeping
sent a flash of revulsion through him. He raised his head.
It felt a great weight. Then, the little bird ran out of the
shadow across a still patch of sunshine, its little head bob-
bing swiftly, its white legs twinkling brightly for a moment.
How neat it was in its build, so compact, with pieces of
white on its wings. There were several of them. They were
so pretty—but they crept like swift, erratic mice, running
here and there among the beech-mast.

He lay down again exhausted, and his consciousness
lapsed. He had a horror of the little creeping birds. All
his blood seemed to be darting and creeping in his head.
And yet he could not move.

He came to with a further ache of exhaustion. There
was the pain in his head, and the horrible sickness, and
his inability to move. He had never been ill in his life.
He did not know where he was or what he was. Probably
he had got sunstroke. Or what else?—he had silenced the
Captain forever—some time ago—oh, a long time ago.
There had been blood on his face, and his eyes had turned
upwards. It was all right, somehow. It was peace. But now
he had got beyond himself. He had never been here before.
Was it life, or not life? He was by himself. They were
in a big, bright place, those others, and he was outside.
The town, all the country, a big bright place of light: and
he was outside, here, in the darkened open beyond, where
each thing existed alone. But they would all have to come
out there sometime, those others. Little, and left behind
him, they all were. There had been father and mother and
sweetheart. What did they all matter? This was the open
land.

He sat up. Something scuffled. It was a little brown
squirrel running in lovely, undulating bounds over the
floor, its red tail completing the undulation of its body—
and then, as it sat up, furling and unfurling. He watched
it, pleased. It ran on again, friskily, enjoying itself. It flew
wildly at another squirrel, and they were chasing each

other, and making little scolding, chattering noises. The
soldier wanted to speak to them. But only a hoarse sound
came out of his throat. The squirrels burst away—they
flew up the trees. And then he saw the one peeping round
at him, halfway up a tree-trunk. A start of fear went
through him, though, in so far as he was conscious, he
was amused. It still stayed, its little, keen face staring at
him halfway up the tree-trunk, its little ears pricked up,
its clawy little hands clinging to the bark, its white breast
reared. He started from it in panic.

Struggling to his feet, he lurched away. He went on
walking, walking, looking for something—for a drink. His
brain felt hot and inflamed for want of water. He stumbled
on. Then he did not know anything. He went unconscious
as he walked. Yet he stumbled on, his mouth open.

When, to his dumb wonder, he opened his eyes on the
world again, he no longer tried to remember what it was.
There was thick, golden light behind golden-green glitter-
ings, and tall gray-purple shafts, and darknesses further
off, surrounding him, growing deeper. He was conscious
of a sense of arrival. He was amid the reality, on the real,
dark bottom. But there was the thirst burning in his brain.
He felt lighter, not so heavy. He supposed it was newness.
The air was muttering with thunder. He thought he was
walking wonderfully swiftly and was coming straight to
relief—or was it to water?

Suddenly he stood still with fear. There was a tremendous flare of gold, immense—just a few dark trunks like
bars between him and it. All the young level wheat was
burnished gold glaring on its silky green. A woman, full-
skirted, a black cloth on her head for head-dress, was
passing like a block of shadow through the glistening,
green corn, into the full glare. There was a farm, too, pale
blue in shadow, and the timber black. And there was a
church spire, nearly fused away in the gold. The woman
moved on, away from him. He had no language with
which to speak to her. She was the bright, solid unreality.
She would make a noise of words that would confuse him,
and her eyes would look at him without seeing him. She
was crossing there to the other side. He stood against a
tree.

When at last he turned, looking down the long, bare
grove whose flat bed was already filling dark, he saw the
mountains in a wonder-light, not far away, and radiant.
Behind the soft, gray ridge of the nearest range the further
mountains stood golden and pale gray, the snow all radiant

like pure, soft gold. So still, gleaming in the sky, fashioned pure out of the ore of the sky, they shone in their silence. He stood and looked at them, his face illuminated. And like the golden, lustrous gleaming of the snow he felt his own thirst bright in him. He stood and gazed, leaning against a tree. And then everything slid away into space.

During the night the lightning fluttered perpetually, making the whole sky white. He must have walked again. The world hung livid round him for moments, fields a level sheen of gray-green light, trees in dark bulk, and the range of clouds black across a white sky. Then the darkness fell like a shutter, and the night was whole. A faint flutter of a half-revealed world, that could not quite leap out of the darkness!—Then there again stood a sweep of pallor for the land; dark shapes looming, a range of clouds hanging overhead. The world was a ghostly shadow, thrown for a moment upon the pure darkness, which returned ever whole and complete.

And the mere delirium of sickness and fever went on inside him—his brain opening and shutting like the night—then sometimes convulsions of terror from something with great eyes that stared round a tree—then the long agony of the march, and the sun decomposing his blood—then the pang of hate for the Captain, followed by a pang of tenderness and ease. But everything was distorted, born of an ache and resolving into an ache.

In the morning he came definitely awake. Then his brain flamed with the sole horror of thirstiness! The sun was on his face, the dew was steaming from his hot clothes. Like one possessed, he got up. There, straight in front of him, blue and cool and tender, the mountains ranged across the pale edge of the morning sky. He wanted them —he wanted them alone—he wanted to leave himself and be identified with them. They did not move, they were still and soft, with white, gentle markings of snow. He stood still, mad with suffering, his hands crisping and clutching. Then he was twisting in a paroxysm on the grass.

He lay still, in a kind of dream of anguish. His thirst seemed to have separated itself from him, and to stand apart, a single demand. Then the pain he felt was another single self. Then there was the clog of his body, another separate thing. He was divided among all kinds of separate beings. There was some strange, agonized connection between them, but they were drawing further apart. Then they would all split. The sun, drilling down on him, was drilling through the bond. Then they would all fall, fall

through the everlasting lapse of space. Then again, his
consciousness reasserted itself. He roused on to his elbow
and stared at the gleaming mountains. There they ranked,
all still and wonderful between earth and heaven. He
stared till his eyes went black, and the mountains, as they
stood in their beauty, so clean and cool, seemed to have
it, that which was lost in him.

IV

When the soldiers found him, three hours later, he was
lying with his face over his arm, his black hair giving off
heat under the sun. But he was still alive. Seeing the open,
black mouth the young soldiers dropped him in horror.

He died in the hospital at night, without having seen
again.

The doctors saw the bruises on his legs, behind, and
were silent.

The bodies of the two men lay together, side by side,
in the mortuary, the one white and slender, but laid rigidly
at rest, the other looking as if every moment it must rouse
into life again, so young and unused, from a slumber.

Katherine Mansfield

(1888–1923)

Katherine Mansfield was born in New Zealand, the daughter of a highly successful businessman, Harold Beauchamp, who was later knighted. She was schooled in New Zealand, an open and pioneering society, and completed her education at Queens College in London. She returned to New Zealand in 1908, found herself extremely dissatisfied with its provincialism, went back to London in 1908, made an unfortunate marriage, left her husband, and had to flee to Germany to have a baby which she had conceived by another man. The baby was lost by a miscarriage. Her German retreat formed the basis for the bitter sketches she published as In a German Pension (1911). She returned to London where, unable to get a divorce, she formed a liaison with the critic John Middleton Murry whom she did not marry until her husband divorced her in 1918. In 1917 she discovered she had developed tuberculosis, and journeyed to France and Switzerland in a vain attempt to recapture her health. By 1922 Miss Mansfield was so ill that she was forced to give up writing. She died the following year.

In 1920 Miss Mansfield published her first collection of short stories, Bliss. Two other collections followed: The Garden Party (1922) and The Dove's Nest.

Modeling herself on Chekhov, whom she greatly admired, Katherine Mansfield made the modern short story a highly subtle and suggestive instrument. She is a writer who avoids the crude and obvious confrontation with her subjects. Her skillful manipulation of symbols and objects reveals life as a not-too-obvious amalgam of the comic and the tragic. Her fiction is essentially an expression of her yearning for freedom. But she is nonetheless capable of looking coolly and incisively at and through the shams and cruelties of English life and society. Miss Mansfield was not a prolific writer. The total body of her work is small. But her meticulous technique, her exquisitely sensitive and precise rendering of the nuances in people's speech and action, and her carefully crafted narrative technique have exerted a marked influence on the short story writers of our time.

*"Bliss" is a simple, subtle story that builds to a shat-
tering climax when the young wife realizes that her husband is having an affair with a woman she admires.
"Bliss" is Miss Mansfield at her characteristic best, full of
telling details, intensely critical and probing in its revelations and insights.*

Bliss

Although Bertha Young was thirty she still had moments
like this when she wanted to run instead of walk, to take
dancing steps on and off the pavement, to bowl a hoop, to
throw something up in the air and catch it again, or to
stand still and laugh at—nothing—at nothing, simply.

What can you do if you are thirty and, turning the
corner of your own street, you are overcome, suddenly,
by a feeling of bliss—absolute bliss!—as though you'd
suddenly swallowed a bright piece of that late afternoon
sun and it burned in your bosom, sending out a little
shower of sparks into every particle, into every finger and
toe? . . .

Oh, is there no way you can express it without being
"drunk and disorderly"? How idiotic civilization is! Why
be given a body if you have to keep it shut up in a case
like a rare, rare fiddle?

"No, that about the fiddle is not quite what I mean," she
thought, running up the steps and feeling in her bag for the
key—she'd forgotten it, as usual—and rattling the letter-
box. "It's not what I mean, because—Thank you, Mary"—
she went into the hall. "Is Nurse back?"

"Yes, M'm."

"And has the fruit come?"

"Yes, M'm. Everything's come."

"Bring the fruit up to the dining-room, will you? I'll
arrange it before I go upstairs."

It was dusky in the dining-room and quite chilly. But all
the same Bertha threw off her coat; she could not bear the
tight clasp of it another moment, and the cold air fell on
her arms.

But in her bosom there was still that bright glowing
place—that shower of little sparks coming from it. It was

almost unbearable. She hardly dared to breathe for fear of fanning it higher, and yet she breathed deeply, deeply. She hardly dared to look into the cold mirror—but she did look, and it gave her back a woman, radiant, with smiling, trembling lips, with big, dark eyes and an air of listening, waiting for something . . . divine to happen . . . that she knew must happen . . . infallibly.

Mary brought in the fruit on a tray and with it a glass bowl, and a blue dish, very lovely, with a strange sheen on it as though it had been dipped in milk.

"Shall I turn on the light, M'm?"

"No, thank you. I can see quite well."

There were tangerines and apples stained with strawberry pink. Some yellow pears, smooth as silk, some white grapes covered with a silver bloom and a big cluster of purple ones. These last she had bought to tone in with the new dining-room carpet. Yes, that did sound rather farfetched and absurd, but it was really why she had bought them. She had thought in the shop: "I must have some purple ones to bring the carpet up to the table." And it had seemed quite sensible at the time.

When she had finished with them and had made two pyramids of these bright round shapes, she stood away from the table to get the effect—and it really was most curious. For the dark table seemed to melt into the dusky light and the glass dish and the blue bowl to float in the air. This, of course in her present mood, was so incredibly beautiful. . . . She began to laugh.

"No, no. I'm getting hysterical." And she seized her bag and coat and ran upstairs to the nursery.

Nurse sat at a low table giving Little B her supper after her bath. The baby had on a white flannel gown and a blue woollen jacket, and her dark, fine hair was brushed up into a funny little peak. She looked up when she saw her mother and began to jump.

"Now, my lovey, eat it up like a good girl," said Nurse, setting her lips in a way that Bertha knew, and that meant she had come into the nursery at another wrong moment.

"Has she been good, Nanny?"

"She's been a little sweet all the afternoon," whispered Nanny. "We went to the park and I sat down on a chair and took her out of the pram and a big dog came along and put its head on my knee and she clutched its ear, tugged it. Oh, you should have seen her."

Bertha wanted to ask if it wasn't rather dangerous to let her clutch at a strange dog's ear. But she did not dare to.

She stood watching them, her hands by her sides, like the poor little girl in front of the rich little girl with the doll.

The baby looked up at her again, stared, and then smiled so charmingly that Bertha couldn't help crying:

"Oh, Nanny, do let me finish giving her her supper while you put the bath things away."

"Well, M'm, she oughtn't to be changed hands while she's eating," said Nanny, still whispering. "It unsettles her; it's very likely to upset her."

How absurd it was. Why have a baby if it has to be kept —not in a case like a rare, rare fiddle—but in another woman's arms? "Oh, I must!" she said.

Very offended, Nanny handed her over.

"Now, don't excite her after her supper. You know you do, M'm. And I have such a time with her after!"

Thank heaven! Nanny went out of the room with the bath towels.

"Now I've got you to myself, my little precious," said Bertha, as the baby leaned against her.

She ate delightfully, holding up her lips for the spoon and then waving her hands. Sometimes she wouldn't let the spoon go; and sometimes, just as Bertha had filled it, she waved it away to the four winds.

When the soup was finished Bertha turned round to the fire.

"You're nice—you're very nice!" said she, kissing her warm baby. "I'm fond of you. I like you."

And, indeed, she loved Little B so much—her neck as she bent forward, her exquisite toes as they shone transparent in the firelight—that all her feeling of bliss came back again, and again she didn't know how to express it— what to do with it.

"You're wanted on the telephone," said Nanny, coming back in triumph and seizing *her* Little B.

Down she flew. It was Harry.

"Oh, is that you, Ber? Look here. I'll be late. I'll take a taxi and come along as quickly as I can, but get dinner put back ten minutes—will you? All right?"

"Yes, perfectly. Oh, Harry!"

"Yes?"

What had she to say? She'd nothing to say. She only wanted to get in touch with him for a moment. She couldn't absurdly cry: "Hasn't it been a divine day!"

"What is it?" rapped out the little voice.

"Nothing. *Entendu*," said Bertha, and hung up the receiver, thinking how more than idiotic civilization was.

They had people coming to dinner. The Norman Knights—a very sound couple—he was about to start a theatre, and she was awfully keen on interior decoration, a young man, Eddie Warren, who had just published a little book of poems and whom everybody was asking to dine, and a "find" of Bertha's called Pearl Fulton. What Miss Fulton did, Bertha didn't know. They had met at the club and Bertha had fallen in love with her, as she always did fall in love with beautiful women who had something strange about them.

The provoking thing was that, though they had been about together and met a number of times and really talked, Bertha couldn't yet make her out. Up to a certain point Miss Fulton was rarely, wonderfully frank, but the certain point was there, and beyond that she would not go.

Was there anything beyond it? Harry said, "No." Voted her dullish, and "cold like all blond women, with a touch, perhaps, of anæmia of the brain." But Bertha wouldn't agree with him; not yet, at any rate.

"No, the way she has of sitting with her head a little on one side, and smiling, has something behind it, Harry, and I must find out what that something is."

"Most likely it's a good stomach," answered Harry.

He made a point of catching Bertha's heels with replies of that kind . . . "liver frozen, my dear girl," or "pure flatulence," or "kidney disease," . . . and so on. For some strange reason Bertha liked this, and almost admired it in him very much.

She went into the drawing-room and lighted the fire; then, picking up the cushions, one by one, that Mary had disposed so carefully, she threw them back on to the chairs and the couches. That made all the difference; the room came alive at once. As she was about to throw the last one she surprised herself by suddenly hugging it to her, passionately, passionately. But it did not put out the fire in her bosom. Oh, on the contrary!

The windows of the drawing-room opened on to a balcony overlooking the garden. At the far end, against the wall, there was a tall, slender pear tree in fullest, richest bloom; it stood perfect, as though becalmed against the jade-green sky. Bertha couldn't help feeling, even from this distance, that it had not a single bud or a faded petal. Down below, in the garden beds, the red and yellow tulips, heavy with flowers, seemed to lean upon the dusk. A grey cat, dragging its belly, crept across the lawn, and a black one, its shadow, trailed after. The sight of them, so intent and so quick, gave Bertha a curious shiver.

"What creepy things cats are!" she stammered, and she turned away from the window and began walking up and down. . . .

How strong the jonquils smelled in the warm room. Too strong? Oh, no. And yet, as though overcome, she flung down on a couch and pressed her hands to her eyes.

"I'm too happy—too happy!" she murmured.

And she seemed to see on her eyelids the lovely pear tree with its wide open blossoms as a symbol of her own life.

Really—really—she had everything. She was young. Harry and she were as much in love as ever, and they got on together splendidly and were really good pals. She had an adorable baby. They didn't have to worry about money. They had this absolutely satisfactory house and garden. And friends—modern, thrilling friends, writers and painters and poets or people keen on social questions—just the kind of friends they wanted. And then there were books, and there was music, and she had found a wonderful little dressmaker, and they were going abroad in the summer, and their new cook made the most superb omelettes. . . .

"I'm absurd. Absurd!" She sat up; but she felt quite dizzy, quite drunk. It must have been the spring.

Yes, it was the spring. Now she was so tired she could not drag herself upstairs to dress.

A white dress, a string of jade beads, green shoes and stockings. It wasn't intentional. She had thought of this scheme hours before she stood at the drawing-room window.

Her petals rustled softly into the hall, and she kissed Mrs. Norman Knight, who was taking off the most amusing orange coat with a procession of black monkeys round the hem and up the fronts.

". . . Why! Why! Why is the middle-class so stodgy—so utterly without a sense of humour! My dear, it's only by a fluke that I am here at all—Norman being the protective fluke. For my darling monkeys so upset the train that it rose to a man and simply ate me with its eyes. Didn't laugh—wasn't amused—that I should have loved. No, just stared—and bored me through and through."

"But the cream of it was," said Norman, pressing a large tortoise-shell-rimmed monocle into his eye, "you don't mind me telling this, Face, do you?" (In their home and

among their friends they called each other Face and Mug.)
"The cream of it was when she, being full fed, turned to
the woman beside her and said: 'Haven't you ever seen
a monkey before?'"

"Oh, yes!" Mrs. Norman Knight joined in the laughter.
"Wasn't that too absolutely creamy?"

And a funnier thing still was that now her coat was off
she did look like a very intelligent monkey—who had even
made that yellow silk dress out of scraped banana skins.
And her amber ear-rings; they were like little dangling
nuts.

"This is a sad, sad fall!" said Mug, pausing in front of
Little B's perambulator. "When the perambulator comes
into the hall—" and he waved the rest of the quotation
away.

The bell rang. It was lean, pale Eddie Warren (as usual)
in a state of acute distress.

"It *is* the right house, *isn't* it?" he pleaded.

"Oh, I think so—I hope so," said Bertha brightly.

"I have had such a *dreadful* experience with a taxi-man;
he was *most* sinister. I couldn't get him to stop. The *more*
I knocked and called the *faster* he went. And *in* the moonlight this *bizarre* figure with the *flattened* head *crouching*
over the *lit-tle* wheel . . ."

He shuddered, taking off an immense white silk scarf.
Bertha noticed that his socks were white, too—most
charming.

"But how dreadful!" she cried.

"Yes, it really was," said Eddie, following her into the
drawing-room. "I saw myself *driving* through Eternity in
a *timeless* taxi."

He knew the Norman Knights. In fact, he was going to
write a play for N.K. when the theatre scheme came off.

"Well, Warren, how's the play?" said Norman Knight,
dropping his monocle and giving his eye a moment in
which to rise to the surface before it was screwed down
again.

And Mrs. Norman Knight: "Oh, Mr. Warren, what
happy socks!"

"*I am* so glad you like them," said he, staring at his feet.
"They seem to have got so *much* whiter since the moon
rose." And he turned his lean sorrowful young face to
Bertha. "There *is* a moon, you know."

She wanted to cry: "I am sure there is—often—often!"

He really was a most attractive person. But so was Face,
crouched before the fire in her banana skins, and so was

Mug, smoking a cigarette and saying as he flicked the ash: "Why doth the bridegroom tarry?"

"There he is, now."

Bang went the front door open and shut. Harry shouted: "Hullo, you people. Down in five minutes." And they heard him swarm up the stairs. Bertha couldn't help smiling; she knew how he loved doing things at high pressure. What, after all, did an extra five minutes matter? But he would pretend to himself that they mattered beyond measure. And then he would make a great point of coming into the drawing-room, extravagantly cool and collected.

Harry had such a zest for life. Oh, how she appreciated it in him. And his passion for fighting—for seeking in everything that came up against him another test of his power and of his courage—that, too, she understood. Even when it made him just occasionally to other people, who didn't know him well, a little ridiculous perhaps. . . . For there were moments when he rushed into battle where no battle was. . . . She talked and laughed and positively forgot until he had come in (just as she had imagined) that Pearl Fulton had not turned up.

"I wonder if Miss Fulton has forgotten?"

"I expect so," said Harry. "Is she on the 'phone?"

"Ah! There's a taxi, now." And Bertha smiled with that little air of proprietorship that she always assumed while her women finds were new and mysterious. "She lives in taxis."

"She'll run to fat if she does," said Harry coolly, ringing the bell for dinner. "Frightful danger for blond women."

"Harry—don't," warned Bertha, laughing up at him.

Came another tiny moment, while they waited, laughing and talking, just a trifle too much at their ease, a trifle too unaware. And then Miss Fulton, all in silver, with a silver fillet binding her pale blond hair, came in smiling, her head a little on one side. "Am I late?"

"No, not at all," said Bertha. "Come along." And she took her arm and they moved into the dining-room.

What was there in the touch of that cool arm that could fan—fan—start blazing—blazing—the fire of bliss that Bertha did not know what to do with?

Miss Fulton did not look at her; but then she seldom did look at people directly. Her heavy eyelids lay upon her eyes and the strange half smile came and went upon her lips as though she lived by listening rather than seeing. But Bertha knew, suddenly, as if the longest, most intimate look had passed between them—as if they had said to each other: "You, too?"—that Pearl Fulton, stirring the beautiful red soup in the grey plate, was feeling just what she was feeling.

And the others? Face and Mug, Eddie and Harry, their spoons rising and falling—dabbing their lips with their napkins, crumbling bread, fiddling with the forks and glasses and talking.

"I met her at the Alpha show—the weirdest little person. She'd not only cut off her hair, but she seemed to have taken a dreadfully good snip off her legs and arms and her neck and her poor little nose as well."

"Isn't she very *liée* with Michael Oat?"

"The man who wrote *Love in False Teeth?*"

"He wants to write a play for me. One act. One man. Decides to commit suicide. Gives all the reasons why he should and why he shouldn't. And just as he has made up his mind either to do it or not to do it—curtain. Not half a bad idea."

"What's he going to call it—'Stomach Trouble'?"

"I *think* I've come across the *same* idea in a lit-tle French review, *quite* unknown in England."

No, they didn't share it. They were dears—dears—and she loved having them there, at her table, and giving them delicious food and wine. In fact, she longed to tell them how delightful they were, and what a decorative group they made, how they seemed to set one another off and how they reminded her of a play by Chekhov!

Harry was enjoying his dinner. It was part of his—well, not his nature, exactly, and certainly not his pose—his—something or other—to talk about food and to glory in his "shameless passion for the white flesh of the lobster" and "the green of pistachio ices—green and cold like the eyelids of Egyptian dancers."

When he looked up at her and said: "Bertha, this is a very admirable *soufflé!*" she almost could have wept with childlike pleasure.

Oh, why did she feel so tender towards the whole world tonight? Everything was good—was right. All that happened seemed to fill again her brimming cup of bliss.

And still, in the back of her mind, there was the pear tree. It would be silver now, in the light of poor dear Eddie's moon, silver as Miss Fulton, who sat there turning a tangerine in her slender fingers that were so pale a light seemed to come from them.

What she simply couldn't make out—what was miraculous—was how she should have guessed Miss Fulton's

mood so exactly and so instantly. For she never doubted
for a moment that she was right, and yet what had she to
go on? Less than nothing. "I believe this does happen very,
very rarely between women. Never between men," thought
Bertha. "But while I am making the coffee in the drawing-
room perhaps she will 'give a sign.' "

What she meant by that she did not know, and what
would happen after that she could not imagine.

While she thought like this she saw herself talking and
laughing. She had to talk because of her desire to laugh.

"I must laugh or die."

But when she noticed Face's funny little habit of tucking
something down the front of her bodice—as if she kept a
tiny, secret hoard of nuts there, too—Bertha had to dig
her nails into her hands—so as not to laugh too much.

It was over at last. And: "Come and see my new coffee
machine," said Bertha.

"We only have a new coffee machine once a fortnight,"
said Harry. Face took her arm this time; Miss Fulton bent
her head and followed after.

The fire had died down in the drawing-room to a red,
flickering "nest of baby phœnixes," said Face.

"Don't turn up the light for a moment. It is so lovely."
And down she crouched by the fire again. She was always
cold . . . "without her little red flannel jacket, of course,"
thought Bertha.

At that moment Miss Fulton "gave the sign."

"Have you a garden?" said the cool, sleepy voice.

This was so exquisite on her part that all Bertha could
do was to obey. She crossed the room, pulled the curtains
apart, and opened those long windows. "There!" she
breathed.

And the two women stood side by side looking at the
slender, flowering tree. Although it was so still it seemed,
like the flame of a candle, to stretch up, to point, to quiver
in the bright air, to grow taller and taller as they gazed—
almost to touch the rim of the round, silver moon.

How long did they stand there? Both, as it were, caught
in that circle of unearthly light, understanding each other
perfectly, creatures of another world, and wondering what
they were to do in this one with all this blissful treasure
that burned in their bosoms and dropped, in silver flowers,
from their hair and hands?

For ever—for a moment? And did Miss Fulton murmur,
"Yes. Just *that*." Or did Bertha dream it?

Then the light was snapped on and Face made the coffee

and Harry said: "My dear Mrs. Knight, don't ask me about my baby. I never see her. I shan't feel the slightest interest in her until she has a lover," and Mug took his eye out of the conservatory for a moment and then put it under glass again and Eddie Warren drank his coffee and set down the cup with a face of anguish as though he had drunk and seen the spider.

"What I want to do is to give the young men a show. I believe London is simply teeming with first-chop, unwritten plays. What I want to say to 'em is: 'Here's the theatre. Fire ahead.' "

"You know, my dear, I am going to decorate a room for the Jacob Nathans. Oh, I am so tempted to do a fried-fish scheme, with the backs of the chairs shaped like frying pans and lovely chip potatoes embroidered all over the curtains."

"The trouble with our young writing men is that they are still too romantic. You can't put out to sea without being seasick and wanting a basin. Well, why won't they have the courage of those basins?"

"A *dreadful* poem about a *girl* who was *violated* by a beggar *without* a nose in a lit-tle wood. . . ."

Miss Fulton sank into the lowest, deepest chair and Harry handed round the cigarettes.

From the way he stood in front of her shaking the silver box and saying abruptly: "Egyptian? Turkish? Virginian? They're all mixed up," Bertha realized that she not only bored him; he really disliked her. And she decided from the way Miss Fulton said: "No, thank you, I won't smoke," that she felt it, too, and was hurt.

"Oh, Harry, don't dislike her. You are quite wrong about her. She's wonderful, wonderful. And, besides, how can you feel so differently about someone who means so much to me. I shall try to tell you when we are in bed to-night what has been happening. What she and I have shared."

At those last words something strange and almost terrifying darted into Bertha's mind. And this something blind and smiling whispered to her: "Soon these people will go. The house will be quiet—quiet. The lights will be out. And you and he will be alone together in the dark room—the warm bed. . . ."

She jumped up from her chair and ran over to the piano.

"What a pity someone does not play!" she cried. "What a pity somebody does not play."

For the first time in her life Bertha Young desired her husband.

Oh, she loved him—she'd been in love with him, of course, in every other way, but just not in that way. And, equally, of course, she'd understood that he was different. They'd discussed it so often. It had worried her dreadfully at first to find that she was so cold, but after a time it had not seemed to matter. They were so frank with each other —such good pals. That was the best of being modern.

But now—ardently! ardently! The word ached in her ardent body! Was this what that feeling of bliss had been leading up to? But then—

"My dear," said Mrs. Norman Knight, "you know our shame. We are the victims of time and train. We live in Hampstead. It's been so nice."

"I'll come with you into the hall," said Bertha. "I loved having you. But you must not miss the last train. That's so awful, isn't it?"

"Have a whisky, Knight, before you go?" called Harry.

"No, thanks, old chap."

Bertha squeezed his hand for that as she shook it.

"Good night, good-bye," she cried from the top step, feeling that this self of hers was taking leave of them for ever.

When she got back into the drawing-room the others were on the move.

". . . Then you can come part of the way in my taxi."

"I shall be *so* thankful *not* to have to face *another* drive *alone* after my *dreadful* experience."

"You can get a taxi at the rank just at the end of the street. You won't have to walk more than a few yards."

"That's a comfort. I'll go and put on my coat."

Miss Fulton moved towards the hall and Bertha was following when Harry almost pushed past.

"Let me help you."

Bertha knew that he was repenting his rudeness—she let him go. What a boy he was in some ways—so impulsive— so—simple. And Eddie and she were left by the fire.

"I *wonder* if you have seen Bilks' *new* poem called *Table d'Hôte*," said Eddie softly. "It's *so* wonderful. In the last Anthology. Have you got a copy? I'd *so* like to *show* it to you. It begins with an *incredibly* beautiful line: 'Why Must it Always be Tomato Soup?'"

"Yes," said Bertha. And she moved noiselessly to a table opposite the drawing-room door and Eddie glided noiselessly after her. She picked up the little book and gave it to him; they had not made a sound.

While he looked it up she turned her head towards the hall. And she saw . . . Harry with Miss Fulton's coat in his arms and Miss Fulton with her back turned to him and her head bent. He tossed the coat away, put his hands on her shoulders and turned her violently to him. His lips said: "I adore you," and Miss Fulton laid her moonbeam fingers on his cheeks and smiled her sleepy smile. Harry's nostrils quivered; his lips curled back in a hideous grin while he whispered: "To-morrow," and with her eyelids Miss Fulton said: "Yes."

"Here it is," said Eddie. " 'Why Must it Always be Tomato Soup?' It's so *deeply* true, don't you feel? Tomato soup is so *dreadfully* eternal."

"If you prefer," said Harry's voice, very loud, from the hall, "I can 'phone you a cab to come to the door."

"Oh, no. It's not necessary," said Miss Fulton, and she came up to Bertha and gave her the slender fingers to hold.

"Good-bye. Thank you so much."

"Good-bye," said Bertha.

Miss Fulton held her hand a moment longer.

"Your lovely pear tree!" she murmured.

And then she was gone, with Eddie following, like the black cat following the grey cat.

"I'll shut up shop," said Harry, extravagantly cool and collected.

"Your lovely pear tree—pear tree—pear tree!"

Bertha simply ran over to the long windows.

"Oh, what is going to happen now?" she cried.

But the pear tree was as lovely as ever and as full of flower and as still.

Isaac Babel

(1894–1940?)

Isaac Babel was the most consummate prose writer to emerge from the Russian Revolution, and it was very possibly this, as much as his inability to play the fawning sycophant, that eventually led to his arrest and murder by the Soviet police. Babel's ability to absorb and reflect the chaos of revolutionary Russia in his short stories sets him apart from all of his contemporaries. His stories seem the work of a man who stripped himself of ego and self-righteousness. They are as elemental as the weather, and they seem, at moments, to have written themselves.

Babel was the son of a salesman for agricultural machines who opened his own business in Odessa (which was to remain Babel's Paris and which was to serve as the setting for many of his best stories). He attended the Nicholas 1 Commercial School and began to write short stories in French before he met Gorky, who apparently encouraged him to address himself in Russian to the world of Odessan Jews—those shopkeepers, clerks, thieves, pimps, and lovers who spring to such memorable life in his short stories. In Babel's time Odessa had a rich and still-flourishing Jewish cultural life, and the influence of its culture can easily be seen in Babel's first book, Odessa Stories *(1923). This was followed by* Red Cavalry *(1926), a volume of stories which grew out of his service as a war correspondent in Budenny's cavalry, perhaps the finest portrait that we have in fiction of the early years of the Russian Revolution. After the emergence of Stalin and the crackdown on intellectuals and artists that accelerated in the 1930s, Babel found himself under increasing pressure to publish fiction that was merely propaganda. He seems to have expected his arrest in May 1939 for many of his associates had been arrested and/or murdered in the terror of 1936–1938. The exact date of his death is not known nor has it ever been officially released, despite the fact that he was exonerated of all charges by the Soviet judiciary after the thaw.*

Babel's Collected Stories *were published in English in 1955 and his* Collected Works *appeared in the Soviet Union in 1957; they were sold out within two days and have never been reprinted. But Babel is cherished by younger Russians as well as by those who look forward to the emergence of an honest art in the Soviet Union for his immense talent and his deep compassion for people, a compassion that one discovers even in the midst of the violence that so many of his stories depict.*

In 1969 a new collection of Babel's stories never before published in English (some of them never published in the Soviet Union) was issued under the title You Must Know Everything. *Like the two other collections of Babel's stories, this one derives from his peculiar position in Russia. His is a world in which swift and senseless violence appears again and again; the physical and the intellectual are played off against one another; the world of nature and the world of books and education seem at odds. In the story reprinted here, one can easily see how Babel's parents filled him with that messianic passion for education so characteristic of Jews emerging from Russian ghettoes. Babel's world is full of promise and dread, and in capturing it he also captured the sense of expectation that the Revolution brought in its wake.*

You Must Know Everything

On Saturdays I always came home late, after my six lessons at school. Walking home through the streets never seemed to me a waste of time. It was very good for daydreaming, and everything looked so nice and familiar. I knew all the signs, the stonework of the houses, the storefronts. I knew them in some special way all my own, and I was quite convinced that I saw in them what really mattered, the mysterious something that we adults call the "essence of things." It was all very firmly fixed in my mind. If anybody happened to mention one of the stores, I could immediately picture its sign, with the gilt letters and the scratch in the left-hand corner, the girl cashier with her high hairdo, and the aura clinging to the place, which was unlike the aura of any other store. And it was from such stores, people, auras, and theater posters that I pieced together my native city of Odessa. I remember, feel, and love it to this very day. I know it as one knows the fragrance of one's mother's skin—the flavor of love, words, smiles. I love it because I grew up in it, was happy, sad, and dreamed my dreams—fervent dreams that will never return.

I always walked along the main street, which was the most crowded. The Saturday I am going to write about was at the beginning of spring. At that time of year we didn't have that mild and soft air which, in Central Russia, is so exquisite over some quiet river or gentle valley. We had a slight glinting chill in the air, a hint of passion with a cold edge to it. I was just a kid at the time and knew nothing about anything, but, blossoming and rosy-cheeked, I was affected by the spring just the same. I always took my time on the way home from school. I scrutinized every jewel in the jeweler's shop and read the theater posters from beginning to end. Once I was studying the pale-pink corsets with crinkly garters at Madame Rosalie's and was just about to move on when I bumped into a tall student with a large black mustache. He was grinning all over his face and he said, "Having a good look, eh?" I blushed. He gave me a knowing pat on the back and said condescendingly, "Keep it up, old fellow. Good for you! All the best!" He guffawed, turned on his heel, and walked away. I was very embarrassed, went straight home, and never again stopped to gaze into Madame Rosalie's shopwindow.

I was supposed to spend this particular Saturday at home with my grandmother. She had her own room at the far end of the apartment, behind the kitchen. In the corner of her room there was a stove; Grandmother always felt cold. It was always hot and stuffy in her room, and this made me miserable and I wanted to escape. On this day I took all my paraphernalia—books, music stand, and violin—into Grandmother's room. The table was already laid for me. Grandmother sat in her corner while I ate. Neither of us said a word. The door was shut and we were alone. For dinner I had cold gefilte fish with horseradish —a dish for the sake of which it would pay one to convert to Judaism—a thick, tasty soup, roast meat and onions, lettuce, fruit salad, coffee, pie, and apples. I ate it all. I may have been a daydreamer, but I also had an appetite. Grandmother cleared the table, and the room became neat and clean. There were some sickly-looking flowers on the windowsill. The only living things that Grandmother loved were her son, her grandson, her dog Mimi, and flowers. Mimi also came in, curled up on the sofa, and immediately fell asleep. She was a terrible sleepyhead but a wonderful dog—kind, sensible, small, and goodlooking. She was a pug, with a light-colored coat. She had not grown fat and flabby in her old age but had kept herself in good trim. She lived out the whole of her life of fifteen years with us, from birth to death, and, naturally enough, she loved us all, particularly Grandmother, who was so hard and merciless. Some other time I will tell the story of their silent and furtive friendship. It is a good, moving, and tender story.

Anyway, there we were, all three of us—Grandmother, Mimi, and I. Mimi was sleeping; Grandmother, in a good humor, sat in the corner in her silk Sabbath dress; and I was supposed to do my lessons. It was a difficult day for me. I had already had six lessons at school, and now my music teacher, Mr. Sorokin, was supposed to come, and so was Mr. L., my Hebrew teacher, to give a lesson we had missed. Peysson, the French teacher, might also come, and I had to prepare a lesson for him. There would be no trouble with L.—we were old friends—but music and those scales were sheer misery!

I spread out my exercise books and began to do my lessons. Grandmother did not interrupt me—God forbid! Her face was drawn and blank because of her reverence for my work. She fastened her round, bright yellow eyes on me. Whenever I turned over a page, they followed the movement of my hand. Anybody else would have been made very ill at ease by this fixed and ever-watchful gaze, but I had grown used to it. Later she would listen to me rehearse my lessons. She was at home only in Yiddish, and her Russian was very bad—she garbled it in her own peculiar way, using a lot of Polish and Yiddish words. Of course, she couldn't read or write in Russian, and she would hold a Russian book upside down. But this didn't prevent her from going through my lessons with me from beginning to end. She couldn't understand a word, but she listened intently, and the music of the words was sweet to her ears. She was full of reverence for learning, had great faith in me, and wanted me to become a rich man.

When I had finished with the lessons, I did some reading. At that time I was reading Turgenev's "First Love." I liked everything about it—the vivid words, descriptions, and conversations—but that afternoon I was particularly thrilled by the scene in which Vladimir's father strikes Zinaida on the cheek with his riding crop. I could hear the swish of the whip and feel the momentary keen and painful sting of its supple thong. This upset me in some unaccountable way, and at this point I had to stop reading and walk up and down the room. But Grandmother just sat there without moving a muscle, and even the hot, stifling air was quite motionless, as though it knew that I was busy and must not be disturbed. The room was getting hotter all the time. Mimi began to snore slightly. It was quiet—eerily quiet, with not a sound from the outside world. Everything seemed weird to me at that moment, and I wanted to run away from it all, but also to stay there forever. The darkening room, Grandmother's yellow eyes, her tiny figure wrapped in a shawl, hunched up and silent in the corner, the heat, the closed door, the crack of the whip, its loud swish—only now do I understand how bizarre all this was, and how much it affected me.

I was startled out of my troubled state by the ringing of the doorbell. It was Mr. Sorokin. I hated him at that moment. I hated his wretched scales, all this meaningless, futile, squawking music. It must be said that Sorokin was a splendid fellow. He had close-cut hair, fine large hands, and magnificent full lips. Today, under Grandmother's eye, he had to teach me for a whole hour—even a little over —and really give value for money. He got no credit for his pains. The old woman's eyes followed his every movement coldly and intently, and were quite indifferent and aloof to him. Grandmother had no time for strangers. She expected them to do their duty by us, and that was all. We began our lesson. I was not afraid of Grandmother, but for a whole hour I had to bear the brunt of poor Sorokin's unusual devotion to duty. He felt very out of place in this remote room, in the presence of the peacefully sleeping dog and the frosty old woman sitting in the corner. At last he took his leave. Grandmother coldly gave him her large leathery and wrinkled hand, but she made not the slightest movement with it. As he left, he bumped into a chair.

I endured the following hour as well—Mr. L.'s Hebrew lesson—and the moment came when the door closed behind him, too. By now it was nightfall. Faraway specks of gold lit up in the sky. The deep shaft of our courtyard was flooded with moonlight. In the neighbors' apartment, a woman's voice began to sing, "Why do I love you so madly?" The rest of my family had gone to the theater. I felt depressed and tired. I had read so much and done such a lot of work. The servant girl brought in the samovar. Grandmother lit a lamp. This immediately mellowed the room; the dark, massive furniture was bathed in soft light. Mimi woke up, took a walk through the other rooms, and then came back to us to wait for supper. Grandmother was a great tea drinker. She had kept a gingerbread for me. We both drank a lot of tea. The sweat began to glisten in the deeply etched seams of her face. "Do you want to go to bed?" she asked. "No," I replied. We began to talk, and once again I listened to Grandmother's stories. Long, long ago, there was a Jew who kept an inn. He was poor, married, and weighed down by a large family, and he sold vodka without a license. A government inspector came to see him and started making trouble for him. He went to a rabbi and said, "Rebbe, a government inspector is plaguing the life out of me. Ask God to help me." "Go in peace," the rabbi said to him. "The government inspector will quiet down." The Jew went home. He found the inspector on the doorstep of his inn. He was lying there dead, with his belly all purple and swollen up.

Grandmother fell silent. The samovar hummed away. The neighbor was still singing. Everything was covered with blinding moonlight. Mimi began to wag her tail—she was hungry.

"In the old days, people had faith," Grandmother said. "Life was simpler. When I was a little girl, the Poles rebelled. We lived next to the estate of a Polish count. The Czar himself used to come and visit him. They used to make merry for seven days at a stretch. I would run up to the hall after dark and look in through the lighted windows. The count had a daughter, and she had the finest pearls in all the world. Then there was this rebellion. Some soldiers came and dragged the old count out onto the square. We all stood around and cried. The soldiers dug a hole in the ground. They wanted to blindfold the old man, but he said he didn't want it. He stood in front of them and gave them the order to shoot. He was a big man with gray hair. The peasants liked him. Just as they were burying him, a courier came racing up. He had a pardon from the Czar."

The samovar was slowly going out. Grandmother drank her last glass of tea, which had gone cold by now, and sucked a piece of sugar in her toothless mouth. "Your grandfather," she said, "was a great one for telling stories. He didn't believe in anything, but he trusted people. He gave away all his money to his friends, but when he came to them for help they threw him downstairs, and that made him a little queer in the head." And she went on to tell me about my grandfather. He was a big man with a sharp tongue, passionate and overbearing. He played the violin, wrote essays at night, and knew all languages. He was ruled by an insatiable thirst for knowledge and life. A general's daughter had fallen in love with their elder son, and this had been the son's undoing. He became a wanderer and a gambler, and he died in Canada at the age of thirty-seven. All Grandmother had left was my father and me. Everything else was gone. For her, day was turning into night and death was coming slowly. She fell silent again, then lowered her head and began to cry. "Study!" she suddenly said with great vehemence. "Study and you will have everything—wealth and fame! You must know *everything*. The whole world will fall at your feet and grovel before you. Everybody must envy you. Do not trust people. Do not have friends. Do not lend them money. Do not give them your heart!"

She said no more. There was silence in the room. She was thinking about years gone by and all her troubles. She was thinking about my future, and her stern commandments pressed down heavily—and forever—on my weak, untried shoulders. In the dark corner the iron stove glowed red hot and gave off a fierce heat. I was hot and stifled, and I wanted to run outside into the fresh air and escape, but I hadn't even the strength to raise my head. There was a crash of crockery in the kitchen. Grandmother went in there. It was suppertime. The next moment, I heard her harsh and angry voice. She was shouting at the servant girl. I felt awkward and upset. She had just been full of such peace and sadness. The servant was answering back. "Get out, you little slut!" I heard my grandmother shout with uncontrollable rage in an unbearably loud and shrill voice. "I am the one who gives orders here! You are breaking my things. Get out!" I could not stand the raucous, metallic sound of her voice. I could see her through the half-opened door. Her face was taut, her lower lip was trembling with fury, her throat was all swollen. The servant was trying to reply. "Get out!" Grandmother said. Now everything was quiet. The servant, with hunched shoulders and on tiptoe, as though she was afraid to hurt the silence, crept out of the kitchen. We had supper without exchanging a single word. We ate well and plentifully, and took our time over it. Grandmother's translucent eyes were motionless, and I did not know what they were looking at.

Katherine Anne Porter

(1894–   )

Katherine Anne Porter was born in Indian Creek, Texas, was educated in southern schools for girls, and began her writing career as a journalist. She traveled extensively in the United States, Europe, and Mexico during the 1920s. It was then that her stories, published in a number of little magazines, began to attract attention. Her first book was a collection of short stories, Flowering Judas *(1930), which immediately established her as one of the major contemporary short story writers. In the years that followed, three additional collections of her short stories appeared,* Hacienda *(1934),* Pale Horse, Pale Rider *(1939), and* The Leaning Tower *(1944). At the age of sixty-eight, Miss Porter published her first novel,* Ship of Fools *(1962).*

Katherine Anne Porter is one of America's most accomplished stylists and short story writers. She has published relatively little in her long and distinguished career, but each of her stories has a uniquely recognizable quality. They are modern in tone and style, painstakingly shaped and reshaped to an exquisite perfection.

Miss Porter's sensitive prose style clearly suggests that she might, had she chosen, been an equally accomplished poet. Her uncanny feel and incessant search for the exact word for the exact emotion, her meticulously wrought characters and scenes place her in the ranks of such masters of the short story as Flaubert and James.

"He," which first appeared in Flowering Judas, *is less cosmopolitan than many of Miss Porter's other stories, but it shares with them a compassion for the common lot of mankind, especially for the rural poor. Despite their technical sophistication, Miss Porter's stories are, at least in part, a product of American populism. The opening sentence of "He"—"Life was very hard for the Whipples."—sets forth in Miss Porter's characteristically understated fashion the ineluctably short and simple annals of a family helplessly and hopelessly trapped. While she manages to keep her artistic distance from the Whipples, they do not become for her objects of scorn or ridicule. Their lives move like the seasons,*

deeper and deeper into relentless poverty. Their simple-minded mute son is one more burden which they accept as they accept drought or floods because they simply have no choice.

He

Life was very hard for the Whipples. It was hard to feed all the hungry mouths, it was hard to keep the children in flannels during the winter, short as it was: "God knows what would become of us if we lived North," they would say: keeping them decently clean was hard. "It looks like our luck won't never let up on us," said Mr. Whipple, but Mrs. Whipple was all for taking what was sent and calling it good, anyhow when the neighbors were in earshot. "Don't ever let a soul hear us complain," she kept saying to her husband. She couldn't stand to be pitied. "No, not if it comes to it that we have to live in a wagon and pick cotton around the country," she said, "nobody's going to get a chance to look down on us."

Mrs. Whipple loved her second son, the simple-minded one, better than she loved the other two children put together. She was forever saying so, and when she talked with certain of her neighbors she would even throw in her husband and her mother for good measure.

"You needn't keep on saying it around," said Mr. Whipple; "you'll make people think nobody else has any feeling about Him but you."

"It's natural for a mother," Mrs. Whipple would remind him. "You know yourself it's more natural for a mother to be that way. People don't expect so much of fathers, some way."

This didn't keep the neighbors from talking plainly among themselves. "A Lord's pure mercy if He should die," they said. "It's the sins of the fathers," they agreed among themselves. "There's bad blood and bad doings somewhere, you can bet on that." This behind the Whipples' backs. To their faces everybody said, "He's not so bad off. He'll be all right yet. Look how He grows!"

Mrs. Whipple hated to talk about it, she tried to keep her mind off it, but every time anybody set foot in the house, the subject always came up, and she had to talk about Him first, before she could get on to anything else. It seemed to ease her mind. "I wouldn't have anything happen to Him for all the world, but it just looks like I can't keep Him out of mischief. He's so strong and active, He's always into everything; He was like that since He could walk. It's actually funny sometimes, the way He can do anything; it's laughable to see Him up to His tricks. Emly has more accidents; I'm forever tying up her bruises, and Adna can't fall a foot without cracking a bone. But He can do anything and not get a scratch. The preacher said such a nice thing once when he was here. He said, and I'll remember it to my dying day, 'The innocent walk with God—that's why He don't get hurt.'" Whenever Mrs. Whipple repeated these words, she always felt a warm pool spread in her breast, and the tears would fill her eyes, and then she could talk about something else.

He did grow and He never got hurt. A plank blew off the chicken house and struck Him on the head and He never seemed to know it. He had learned a few words, and after this He forgot them. He didn't whine for food as the other children did, but waited until it was given Him; He ate squatting in the corner, smacking and mumbling. Rolls of fat covered Him like an overcoat, and He could carry twice as much wood and water as Adna. Emly had a cold in the head most of the time—"She takes after me," said Mrs. Whipple—so in bad weather they gave her the extra blanket off His cot. He never seemed to mind the cold.

Just the same, Mrs. Whipple's life was a torment for fear something might happen to Him. He climbed the peach trees much better than Adna and went skittering along the branches like a monkey, just a regular monkey. "Oh, Mrs. Whipple, you hadn't ought to let Him do that. He'll lose His balance sometime. He can't rightly know what He's doing."

Mrs. Whipple almost screamed out at the neighbor. "He *does* know what He's doing! He's as able as any other child! Come down out of there, you!" When He finally reached the ground she could hardly keep her hands off Him for acting like that before people, a grin all over His face and her worried sick about Him all the time.

"It's the neighbors," said Mrs. Whipple to her husband. "Oh, I do mortally wish they would keep out of

our business. I can't afford to let Him do anything for
fear they'll come nosing around about it. Look at the
bees, now. Adna can't handle them, they sting him up
so; I haven't got time to do everything, and now I don't
dare let Him. But if He gets a sting He don't really mind."

"It's just because He ain't got sense enough to be
scared of anything," said Mr. Whipple.

"You ought to be ashamed of yourself," said Mrs.
Whipple, "talking that way about your own child. Who's
to take up for Him if we don't, I'd like to know? He sees
a lot that goes on, He listens to things all the time. And
anything I tell Him to do He does it. Don't never let
anybody hear you say such things. They'd think you
favored the other children over Him."

"Well, now, I don't, and you know it, and what's the
use of getting all worked up about it? You always think
the worst of everything. Just let Him alone, He'll get
along somehow. He gets plenty to eat and wear, don't
He?" Mr. Whipple suddenly felt tired out. "Anyhow,
it can't be helped now."

Mrs. Whipple felt tired too, she complained in a tired
voice. "What's done can't never be undone, I know that
good as anybody; but He's my child, and I'm not going to
have people say anything. I'm sick of people coming around
saying things all the time."

In the early fall Mrs. Whipple got a letter from her
brother saying he and his wife and two children were
coming over for a little visit next Sunday week. "Put
the big pot in the little one," he wrote at the end. Mrs.
Whipple read this part out loud twice, she was so pleased.
Her brother was a great one for saying funny things.
"We'll just show him that's no joke," she said; "we'll just
butcher one of the suckling pigs."

"It's a waste, and I don't hold with waste the way we
are now," said Mr. Whipple. "That pig'll be worth money
by Christmas."

"It's a shame and a pity we can't have a decent meal's
vittles once in a while when my own family comes to see
us," said Mrs. Whipple. "I'd hate for his wife to go back
and say there wasn't a thing in the house to eat. My God,
it's better than buying up a great chance of meat in town.
There's where you'd spend the money!"

"All right, do it yourself then," said Mr. Whipple.
"Christamighty, no wonder we can't get ahead!"

The question was how to get the little pig away from
his ma, a great fighter, worse than a Jersey cow. Adna

wouldn't try it; "That sow'd rip my insides out all over the pen." "All right, old fraidy," said Mrs. Whipple, "*He's* not scared. Watch *Him* do it." And she laughed as though it was all a good joke and gave Him a little push towards the pen. He sneaked up and snatched the pig right away from the teat and galloped back and was over the fence with the sow raging at His heels. The little black squirming thing was screeching like a baby in a tantrum, stiffening its back and stretching its mouth to the ears. Mrs. Whipple took the pig with her face stiff and sliced its throat with one stroke. When He saw the blood He gave a great jolting breath and ran away. "But He'll forget and eat plenty, just the same," thought Mrs. Whipple. Whenever she was thinking, her lips moved making words. "He'd eat it all if I didn't stop Him. He'd eat up every mouthful from the other two if I'd let Him."

She felt badly about it. He was ten years old now and a third again as large as Adna, who was going on fourteen. "It's a shame, a shame," she kept saying under her breath, "and Adna with so much brains!"

She kept on feeling badly about all sorts of things. In the first place it was the man's work to butcher; the sight of the pig scraped pink and naked made her sick. He was too fat and soft and pitiful-looking. It was simply a shame the way things had to happen. By the time she had finished it up, she almost wished her brother would stay at home.

Early Sunday morning Mrs. Whipple dropped everything to get Him all cleaned up. In an hour He was dirty again, with crawling under fences after a possum, and straddling along the rafters of the barn looking for eggs in the hayloft. "My Lord, look at you now after all my trying! And here's Adna and Emly staying so quiet. I get tired trying to keep you decent. Get off that shirt and put on another, people will say I don't half dress you!" And she boxed Him on the ears, hard. He blinked and blinked and rubbed His head, and His face hurt Mrs. Whipple's feelings. Her knees began to tremble, she had to sit down while she buttoned His shirt. "I'm just all gone before the day starts."

The brother came with his plump healthy wife and two great roaring hungry boys. They had a grand dinner, with the pig roasted to a crackling in the middle of the table, full of dressing, a pickled peach in his mouth and plenty of gravy for the sweet potatoes.

"This looks like prosperity all right," said the brother; "you're going to have to roll me home like I was a barrel when I'm done."

Everybody laughed out loud; it was fine to hear them laughing all at once around the table. Mrs. Whipple felt warm and good about it. "Oh, we've got six more of these; I say it's as little as we can do when you come to see us so seldom."

He wouldn't come into the dining room, and Mrs. Whipple passed it off very well. "He's timider than my other two," she said, "He'll just have to get used to you. There isn't everybody He'll make up with; you know how it is with some children, even cousins." Nobody said anything out of the way.

"Just like my Alfy here," said the brother's wife. "I sometimes got to lick him to make him shake hands with his own grandmammy."

So that was over, and Mrs. Whipple loaded up a big plate for Him first, before everybody. "I always say He ain't to be slighted, no matter who else goes without," she said, and carried it to Him herself.

"He can chin Himself on the top of the door," said Emly, helping along.

"That's fine, He's getting along fine," said the brother.

They went away after supper. Mrs. Whipple rounded up the dishes, and sent the children to bed and sat down and unlaced her shoes. "You see?" she said to Mr. Whipple. "That's the way my whole family is. Nice and considerate about everything. No out-of-the-way remarks—they *have* got refinement. I get awfully sick of people's remarks. Wasn't that pig good?"

Mr. Whipple said, "Yes, we're out three hundred pounds of pork, that's all. It's easy to be polite when you come to eat. Who knows what they had in their minds all along?"

"Yes, that's like you," said Mrs. Whipple. "I don't expect anything else from you. You'll be telling me next that my own brother will be saying around that we made Him eat in the kitchen! Oh, my God!" she rocked her head in her hands, a hard pain started in the very middle of her forehead. "Now it's all spoiled, and everything was so nice and easy. All right, you don't like them and you never did—all right, they'll not come here again soon, never you mind! But they *can't* say He wasn't dressed every lick as good as Adna—oh, honest, sometimes I wish I was dead!"

"I wish you'd let up," said Mr. Whipple. "It's bad enough as it is."

It was a hard winter. It seemed to Mrs. Whipple that they hadn't ever known anything but hard times, and now to cap it all a winter like this. The crops were about half of what they had a right to expect; after the cotton was in it didn't do much more than cover the grocery bill. They swapped off one of the plow horses, and got cheated, for the new one died of the heaves. Mrs. Whipple kept thinking all the time it was terrible to have a man you couldn't depend on not to get cheated. They cut down on everything, but Mrs. Whipple kept saying there are things you can't cut down on, and they cost money. It took a lot of warm clothes for Adna and Emly, who walked four miles to school during the three-months session. "He sets around the fire a lot, He won't need so much," said Mr. Whipple. "That's so," said Mrs. Whipple, "and when He does the outdoor chores He can wear your tarpaullion coat. I can't do no better, that's all."

In February He was taken sick, and lay curled up under His blanket looking very blue in the face and acting as if He would choke. Mr. and Mrs. Whipple did everything they could for Him for two days, and then they were scared and sent for the doctor. The doctor told them they must keep Him warm and give Him plenty of milk and eggs. "He isn't as stout as He looks, I'm afraid," said the doctor. "You've got to watch them when they're like that. You must put more cover onto Him, too."

"I just took off His big blanket to wash," said Mrs. Whipple, ashamed. "I can't stand dirt."

"Well, you'd better put it back on the minute it's dry," said the doctor, "or He'll have pneumonia."

Mr. and Mrs. Whipple took a blanket off their own bed and put His cot in by the fire. "They can't say we didn't do everything for Him," she said, "even to sleeping cold ourselves on His account."

When the winter broke He seemed to be well again, but He walked as if His feet hurt Him. He was able to run a cotton planter during the season.

"I got it all fixed up with Jim Ferguson about breeding the cow next time," said Mr. Whipple. "I'll pasture the bull this summer and give Jim some fodder in the fall. That's better than paying out money when you haven't got it."

"I hope you didn't say such a thing before Jim Ferguson," said Mrs. Whipple. "You oughtn't to let him know we're so down as all that."

"Godamighty, that ain't saying we're down. A man is

got to look ahead sometimes. *He* can lead the bull over today. I need Adna on the place."

At first Mrs. Whipple felt easy in her mind about sending Him for the bull. Adna was too jumpy and couldn't be trusted. You've got to be steady around animals. After He was gone she started thinking, and after a while she could hardly bear it any longer. She stood in the lane and watched for Him. It was nearly three miles to go and a hot day, but He oughtn't to be so long about it. She shaded her eyes and stared until colored bubbles floated in her eyeballs. It was just like everything else in life, she must always worry and never know a moment's peace about anything. After a long time she saw Him turn into the side lane, limping. He came on very slowly, leading the big hulk of an animal by a ring in the nose, twirling a little stick in His hand, never looking back or sideways, but coming on like a sleepwalker with His eyes half shut.

Mrs. Whipple was scared sick of bulls; she had heard awful stories about how they followed on quietly enough, and then suddenly pitched on with a bellow and pawed and gored a body to pieces. Any second now that black monster would come down on Him; my God, He'd never have sense enough to run.

She mustn't make a sound nor a move; she mustn't get the bull started. The bull heaved his head aside and horned the air at a fly. Her voice burst out of her in a shriek, and she screamed at Him to come on, for God's sake. He didn't seem to hear her clamor, but kept on twirling His switch and limping on, and the bull lumbered along behind him as gently as a calf. Mrs. Whipple stopped calling and ran towards the house, praying under her breath: "Lord, don't let anything happen to Him. Lord, you *know* people will say we oughtn't to have sent Him. You *know* they'll say we didn't take care of Him. Oh, get Him home, safe home, safe home, and I'll look out for Him better! Amen."

She watched from the window while He led the beast in, and tied him up in the barn. It was no use trying to keep up, Mrs. Whipple couldn't bear another thing. She sat down and rocked and cried with her apron over her head.

From year to year the Whipples were growing poorer. The place just seemed to run down of itself, no matter how hard they worked. "We're losing our hold," said Mrs. Whipple. "Why can't we do like other people and watch for our best chances? They'll be calling us poor white trash next."

"When I get to be sixteen I'm going to leave," said Adna. "I'm going to get a job in Powell's grocery store. There's money in that. No more farm for me."

"I'm going to be a school-teacher," said Emly. "But I've got to finish the eighth grade, anyhow. Then I can live in town. I don't see any chances here."

"Emly takes after my family," said Mrs. Whipple. "Ambitious every last one of them, and they don't take second place for anybody."

When fall came Emly got a chance to wait on table in the railroad eating-house in the town near-by, and it seemed such a shame not to take it when the wages were good and she could get her food too, that Mrs. Whipple decided to let her take it, and not bother with school until the next session. "You've got plenty of time," she said. "You're young and smart as a whip."

With Adna gone too, Mr. Whipple tried to run the farm with just Him to help. He seemed to get along fine, doing His work and part of Adna's without noticing it. They did well enough until Christmas time, when one morning He slipped on the ice coming up from the barn. Instead of getting up He thrashed round and round, and when Mr. Whipple got to Him, He was having some sort of fit.

They brought Him inside and tried to make Him sit up, but He blubbered and rolled, so they put Him to bed and Mr. Whipple rode to town for the doctor. All the way there and back he worried about where the money was to come from: it sure did look like he had about all the troubles he could carry.

From then on He stayed in bed. His legs swelled up double their size, and the fits kept coming back. After four months, the doctor said, "It's no use, I think you'd better put Him in the County Home for treatment right away. I'll see about it for you. He'll have good care there and be off your hands."

"We don't begrudge Him any care, and I won't let Him out of my sight," said Mrs. Whipple. "I won't have it said I sent my sick child off among strangers."

"I know how you feel," said the doctor. "You can't tell me anything about that, Mrs. Whipple. I've got a boy of my own. But you'd better listen to me. I can't do anything more for Him, that's the truth."

Mr. and Mrs. Whipple talked it over a long time that

night after they went to bed. "It's just charity," said Mrs. Whipple, "that's what we've come to, charity! I certainly never looked for this."

"We pay taxes to help support the place just like everybody else," said Mr. Whipple, "and I don't call that taking charity. I think it would be fine to have Him where He'd get the best of everything . . . and besides, I can't keep up with these doctor bills any longer."

"Maybe that's why the doctor wants us to send Him —he's scared he won't get his money," said Mrs. Whipple.

"Don't talk like that," said Mr. Whipple, feeling pretty sick, "or we won't be able to send Him."

"Oh, but we won't keep Him there long," said Mrs. Whipple. "Soon's He's better, we'll bring Him right back home."

"The doctor has told you and told you time and again He can't ever get better, and you might as well stop talking," said Mr. Whipple.

"Doctors don't know everything," said Mrs. Whipple, feeling almost happy. "But anyhow, in the summer Emly can come home for a vacation and Adna can get down for Sundays: we'll all work together and get on our feet again, and the children will feel they've got a place to come to."

All at once she saw it full summer again, with the garden going fine, and new white roller shades up all over the house, and Adna and Emly home, so full of life, all of them happy together. Oh, it could happen, things would ease up on them.

They didn't talk before Him much, but they never knew just how much He understood. Finally the doctor set the day, and a neighbor who owned a double-seated carryall offered to drive them over. The hospital would have sent an ambulance, but Mrs. Whipple couldn't stand to see Him going away looking so sick as all that. They wrapped Him in blankets, and the neighbor and Mr. Whipple lifted Him into the back seat of the carryall beside Mrs. Whipple, who had on her black shirtwaist. She couldn't stand to go looking like charity.

"You'll be all right, I guess I'll stay behind," said Mr. Whipple. "It don't look like everybody ought to leave the place at once."

"Besides, it ain't as if He was going to stay forever," said Mrs. Whipple to the neighbor. "This is only for a little while."

They started away, Mrs. Whipple holding to the edges

of the blankets to keep Him from sagging sideways. He sat there blinking and blinking. He worked His hands out and began rubbing His nose with His knuckles, and then with the end of the blanket. Mrs. Whipple couldn't believe what she saw; He was scrubbing away big tears that rolled out of the corners of His eyes. He sniveled and made a gulping noise. Mrs. Whipple kept saying, "Oh, honey, you don't feel so bad, do you? You don't feel so bad, do you?" for He seemed to be accusing her of something. Maybe He remembered that time she boxed His ears, maybe He had been scared that day with the bull, maybe He had slept cold and couldn't tell her about it; maybe He knew they were sending Him away for good and all because they were too poor to keep Him. Whatever it was, Mrs. Whipple couldn't bear to think of it. She began to cry, frightfully, and wrapped her arms tight around Him. His head rolled on her shoulder: she had loved Him as much as she possibly could, there were Adna and Emly who had to be thought of too, there was nothing she could do to make up to Him for His life. Oh, what a mortal pity He was ever born.

They came in sight of the hospital, with the neighbor driving very fast, not daring to look behind him.

Jorge Luis Borges

(1899–   )

Born in Buenos Aires, Jorge Luis Borges was educated abroad in Spain and Switzerland. His work has been affected by such writers as Poe, Baudelaire, and Kafka. A short story writer of increasing stature, he has also written essays, detective stories, novels, poems, and movie scripts. Until a few years ago Borges was largely unknown in the English-speaking world. But as more and more translations of his work have become available, he has emerged as one of the most prominent of Latin-American writers and one of the modern writers who, like Beckett and Nabokov, has exerted a substantial influence on his younger contemporaries.

With the publication of Labyrinths, Selected Stories and Other Writing *(1962) in English, Borges became one of the favorites of the American literary avant-garde.*

"The Secret Miracle" is characteristic of Borges' brilliance as a writer. Set in Nazi-occupied Prague, the story is actually a passionate yet Kafkaesque defense of the immortality bestowed by art, an immortality which is the gift not of an individual but of a culture. Despite its official tone, the last sentence of "The Secret Miracle" is haunted by the threat of a civilization bent on destroying itself through its own inhumanity.

The Secret Miracle

And God had him die for a hundred years and then revived him and said:
   "How long have you been here?"
   "A day or a part of a day," he answered.

Koran, II, 261

The night of March 14, 1943, in an apartment in the Zeltnergasse of Prague, Jaromir Hladik, the author of the unfinished drama entitled *The Enemies,* of *Vindication of Eternity* and of a study of the indirect Jewish sources of Jakob Böhme, had a dream of a long game of chess. The players were not two persons, but two illustrious families; the game had been going on for centuries. Nobody could remember what the stakes were, but it was rumored that they were enormous, perhaps infinite; the chessmen and the board were in a secret tower. Jaromir (in his dream) was the first-born of one of the contending families. The clock struck the hour for the game, which could not be postponed. The dreamer raced over the sands of a rainy desert, and was unable to recall either the pieces or the rules of chess. At that moment he awoke. The clangor of the rain and of the terrible clocks ceased. A rhythmic, unanimous noise, punctuated by shouts of command, arose from the Zeltnergasse. It was dawn, and the armored vanguard of the Third Reich was entering Prague.

On the nineteenth the authorities received a denunciation; that same nineteenth, toward evening, Jaromir Hladik was arrested. He was taken to an aseptic, white barracks on the opposite bank of the Moldau. He was unable to refute a single one of the Gestapo's charges; his mother's family name was Jaroslavski, he was of Jewish blood, his study on Böhme had a marked Jewish emphasis, his signature had been one more on the protest against the *Anschluss.* In 1928 he had translated the *Sepher Yezirah* for the publishing house of Hermann Barsdorf. The fulsome catalogue of the firm had exaggerated, for publicity purposes, the translator's reputation, and the catalogue had been examined by Julius Rothe, one of the officials who held Hladik's fate in his hands. There is not a person who, except in the field of his own specialization, is not credulous; two or three adjectives in Gothic type were enough to persuade Julius Rothe of Hladik's importance, and he ordered him sentenced to death *pour encourager les autres.* The execution was set for March 29th, at 9:00 A.M. This delay (whose importance the reader will grasp later) was owing to the desire on the authorities' part to proceed impersonally and slowly, after the manner of vegetables and plants.

Hladik's first reaction was mere terror. He felt he would not have shrunk from the gallows, the block, or the knife, but that death by a firing squad was unbearable. In vain he tried to convince himself that the plain, unvarnished fact of dying was the fearsome thing, not the attendant

circumstances. He never wearied of conjuring up these
circumstances, senselessly trying to exhaust all their possible variations. He infinitely anticipated the process of his
dying, from the sleepless dawn to the mysterious volley.
Before the day set by Julius Rothe he died hundreds of
deaths in courtyards whose forms and angles strained geo-
metrical probabilities, machine-gunned by variable soldiers
in changing numbers, who at times killed him from a distance, at others from close by. He faced these imaginary
executions with real terror (perhaps with real bravery);
each simulacrum lasted a few seconds. When the circle
was closed, Jaromir returned once more and interminably
to the tremulous vespers of his death. Then he reflected that
reality does not usually coincide with our anticipation of
it; with a logic of his own he inferred that to foresee a cir-
cumstantial detail is to prevent its happening. Trusting in
this weak magic, he invented, *so that they would not happen,* the most gruesome details. Finally, as was natural, he
came to fear that they were prophetic. Miserable in the
night, he endeavored to find some way to hold fast to the
fleeting substance of time. He knew that it was rushing
headlong toward the dawn of the twenty-ninth. He rea-
soned aloud: "I am now in the night of the twenty-second;
while this night lasts (and for six nights more), I am in-
vulnerable, immortal." The nights of sleep seemed to him
deep, dark pools in which he could submerge himself.
There were moments when he longed impatiently for the
final burst of fire that would free him, for better or for
worse, from the vain compulsion of his imaginings. On the
twenty-eighth, as the last sunset was reverberating from
the high barred windows, the thought of his drama, *The
Enemies,* deflected him from these abject considerations.

Hladik had rounded forty. Aside from a few friendships
and many habits, the problematic exercise of literature
constituted his life. Like all writers, he measured the
achievements of others by what they had accomplished,
asking of them that they measure him by what he envisaged or planned. All the books he had published had
left him with a complex feeling of repentance. His studies
of the work of Böhme, of Ibn Ezra, and of Fludd had been
characterized essentially by mere application; his translation of the *Sepher Yezirah,* by carelessness, fatigue, and
conjecture. *Vindication of Eternity* perhaps had fewer
shortcomings. The first volume gave a history of man's
various concepts of eternity, from the immutable Being
of Parmenides to the modifiable Past of Hinton. The second

denied (with Francis Bradley) that all the events of the
universe make up a temporal series, arguing that the number of man's possible experiences is not infinite, and that
a single "repetition" suffices to prove that time is a fallacy
. . . Unfortunately, the arguments that demonstrate this
fallacy are equally fallacious. Hladik was in the habit of
going over them with a kind of contemptuous perplexity.
He had also composed a series of Expressionist poems; to
the poet's chagrin they had been included in an anthology
published in 1924, and no subsequent anthology but in-
herited them. From all this equivocal, uninspired past
Hladik had hoped to redeem himself with his drama in
verse, *The Enemies*. (Hladik felt the verse form to be
essential because it makes it impossible for the spectators
to lose sight of irreality, one of art's requisites.)

The drama observed the unities of time, place, and action. The scene was laid in Hradčany, in the library of
Baron von Roemerstadt, on one of the last afternoons of
the nineteenth century. In the first scene of the first act
a strange man visits Roemerstadt. (A clock was striking
seven, the vehemence of the setting sun's rays glorified the
windows, a passionate, familiar Hungarian music floated in
the air.) This visit is followed by others; Roemerstadt does
not know the people who are importuning him, but he
has the uncomfortable feeling that he has seen them
somewhere, perhaps in a dream. They all fawn upon him,
but it is apparent—first to the audience and then to the
Baron—that they are secret enemies, in league to ruin him.
Roemerstadt succeeds in checking or evading their involved schemings. In the dialogue mention is made of his
sweetheart, Julia von Weidenau, and a certain Jaroslav
Kubin, who at one time pressed his attentions on her.
Kubin has now lost his mind, and believes himself to be
Roemerstadt. The dangers increase; Roemerstadt, at the
end of the second act, is forced to kill one of the conspira-
tors. The third and final act opens. The incoherencies
gradually increase; actors who had seemed out of the play
reappear; the man Roemerstadt killed returns for a moment.
Someone points out that evening has not fallen; the clock
strikes seven, the high windows reverberate in the western
sun, the air carries an impassioned Hungarian melody.
The first actor comes on and repeats the lines he had
spoken in the first scene of the first act. Roemerstadt speaks
to him without surprise; the audience understands that
Roemerstadt is the miserable Jaroslav Kubin. The drama

has never taken place; it is the circular delirium that Kubin lives and relives endlessly.

Hladik had never asked himself whether this tragicomedy of errors was preposterous or admirable, well thought out or slipshod. He felt that the plot I have just sketched was best contrived to cover up his defects and point up his abilities and held the possibility of allowing him to redeem (symbolically) the meaning of his life. He had finished the first act and one or two scenes of the third; the metrical nature of the work made it possible for him to keep working it over, changing the hexameters, without the manuscript in front of him. He thought how he still had two acts to do, and that he was going to die very soon. He spoke with God in the darkness: "If in some fashion I exist, if I am not one of Your repetitions and mistakes, I exist as the author of *The Enemies*. To finish this drama, which can justify me and justify You, I need another year. Grant me these days, You to whom the centuries and time belong." This was the last night, the most dreadful of all, but ten minutes later sleep flooded over him like a dark water.

Toward dawn he dreamed that he had concealed himself in one of the naves of the Clementine Library. A librarian wearing dark glasses asked him: "What are you looking for?" Hladik answered: "I am looking for God." The librarian said to him: "God is in one of the letters on one of the pages of one of the four hundred thousand volumes of the Clementine. My fathers and the fathers of my fathers have searched for this letter; I have grown blind seeking it." He removed his glasses, and Hladik saw his eyes, which were dead. A reader came in to return an atlas. "This atlas is worthless," he said, and handed it to Hladik, who opened it at random. He saw a map of India as in a daze. Suddenly sure of himself, he touched one of the tiniest letters. A ubiquitous voice said to him: "The time of your labor has been granted." At this point Hladik awoke.

He remembered that men's dreams belong to God, and that Maimonides had written that the words heard in a dream are divine when they are distinct and clear and the person uttering them cannot be seen. He dressed: two soldiers came into the cell and ordered him to follow them.

From behind the door, Hladik had envisaged a labyrinth of passageways, stairs, and separate buildings. The reality was less spectacular: they descended to an inner court by a narrow iron stairway. Several soldiers—some with uniform unbuttoned—were examining a motorcycle and discussing it. The sergeant looked at the clock; it was 8:44. They had to wait until it struck nine. Hladik, more insignificant than pitiable, sat down on a pile of wood. He noticed that the soldiers' eyes avoided his. To ease his wait, the sergeant handed him a cigarette. Hladik did not smoke; he accepted it out of politeness or humility. As he lighted it, he noticed that his hands were shaking. The day was clouding over; the soldiers spoke in low voices as though he were already dead. Vainly he tried to recall the woman of whom Julia von Weidenau was the symbol.

The squad formed and stood at attention. Hladik, standing against the barracks wall, waited for the volley. Someone pointed out that the wall was going to be stained with blood; the victim was ordered to step forward a few paces. Incongruously, this reminded Hladik of the fumbling preparations of photographers. A big drop of rain struck one of Hladik's temples and rolled slowly down his cheek; the sergeant shouted the final order.

The physical universe came to a halt.

The guns converged on Hladik, but the men who were to kill him stood motionless. The sergeant's arm eternized an unfinished gesture. On a paving stone of the courtyard a bee cast an unchanging shadow. The wind had ceased, as in a picture. Hladik attempted a cry, a word, a movement of the hand. He realized that he was paralyzed. Not a sound reached him from the halted world. He thought: "I am in hell, I am dead." He thought: "I am mad." He thought: "Time has stopped." Then he reflected that if that was the case, his mind would have stopped too. He wanted to test this; he repeated (without moving his lips) Vergil's mysterious fourth Eclogue. He imagined that the now remote soldiers must be sharing his anxiety; he longed to be able to communicate with them. It astonished him not to feel the least fatigue, not even the numbness of his protracted immobility. After an indeterminate time he fell asleep. When he awoke the world continued motionless and mute. The drop of water still clung to his cheek, the shadow of the bee to the stone. The smoke from the cigarette he had thrown away had not dispersed. Another "day" went by before Hladik understood.

He had asked God for a whole year to finish his work; His omnipotence had granted it. God had worked a secret miracle for him; German lead would kill him at the set hour, but in his mind a year would go by between the order and its execution. From perplexity he passed to stupor, from stupor to resignation, from resignation to sudden gratitude.

He had no document but his memory; the training he had acquired with each added hexameter gave him a discipline unsuspected by those who set down and forget temporary, incomplete paragraphs. He was not working for posterity or even for God, whose literary tastes were unknown to him. Meticulously, motionlessly, secretly, he wrought in time his lofty, invisible labyrinth. He worked the third act over twice. He eliminated certain symbols as over-obvious, such as the repeated striking of the clock, the music. Nothing hurried him. He omitted, he condensed, he amplified. In certain instances he came back to the original version. He came to feel an affection for the courtyard, the barracks; one of the faces before him modified his conception of Roemerstadt's character. He discovered that the wearying cacophonies that bothered Flaubert so much are mere visual superstitions, weakness and limitation of the written word, not the spoken . . . He concluded his drama. He had only the problem of a single phrase. He found it. The drop of water slid down his cheek. He opened his mouth in a maddened cry, moved his face, dropped under the quadruple blast.

Jaromir Hladik died on March 29, at 9:02 A.M.

William Faulkner

(1897–1962)

*Perhaps no other American writer of this century has
set himself so gigantic a creative task as Faulkner undertook in his extended saga of Yoknapatawpha County,
Mississippi. Universally acknowledged as one of the
masters of twentieth-century fiction, Faulkner is, in certain respects, an archaism. Employing a unique style,
replete with rather complex rhetorical strategies, he depicted a world that always led back to the nineteenth
century and to American Negro slavery. The scope of
his fiction is remarkable: his subject matter ranges from
slapstick comedy to almost Grecian tragedy, while his
technique moves from interpolated passages, broken time
sequences, and stream-of-consciousness to the straight
traditional narrative.*

*When Faulkner received the Nobel Prize for Literature
in 1949, he said, in his now famous acceptance speech,
that the purpose behind his writing had been the need
to depict "the human heart in conflict with itself," an
unusual statement, on the face of it, for a man whose
novels are filled with rape, pillage, and, above all, the
incredible degradations of American Negro slavery. And
yet, Faulkner can be said to have remained consistently
true to his purpose. His prose frequently has the ring
of the Old Testament moralist, and he reminds us, even
as he describes the violence, of the individual's potential
for goodness and courage. In his novels and stories about
Yoknapatawpha County, he sought to create an American
fictional equivalent to Balzac's Paris. In his rural landscapes his characters have depth and solidity; they
seem, as Faulkner himself seemed, rooted in the earth.*

*William Faulkner was born in New Albany, Mississip-
pi, of an old southern family that had fallen on hard
times after the Civil War. His grandfather had been a
colonel in the Confederate Army, had returned to the
defeated South to build a railroad, fight a duel, and write
a popular novel,* The White Rose of Memphis. *One of
Faulkner's brothers was also to become a novelist. The
family moved to the university town of Oxford, where
Faulkner spent most of his life. He attended Oxford
public schools, enlisted in the Royal Canadian Air*

*Force during World War I (an experience he drew upon
when he wrote his novel about stunt-flying, Pylon), and
then returned to Oxford where he enrolled at the University
of Mississippi as a special student and worked
in the post office. He then went to New Orleans, where
he became friendly with Sherwood Anderson who helped
him find a publisher for his first novel. He spent three
months in New York, toured Europe on foot, and returned
to Oxford to settle down as a writer.*

*Faulkner's early novels brought him critical recognition,
especially* Sartoris *(1929),* The Sound and the
Fury *(1929), and* As I Lay Dying *(1930). Many critics
still consider* The Sound and the Fury *Faulkner's finest
novel. It remains among the best adaptations of Joyce's
stream-of-consciousness technique.* Sanctuary *(1931),
which he claims to have written as a potboiler, brought
him popular success. His other important novels are*
Absalom, Absalom! *(1936),* Light in August *(1932), and
the three novels which comprise the Snopes trilogy,
one of the truly comic masterpieces of American literature,*
The Hamlet *(1940),* The Town *(1957), and* The
Mansion *(1959).*

*Faulkner's three volumes of stories were brought together
in 1950 as* The Collected Stories of William Faulkner.
*They reveal him to be almost as remarkable a short
story writer as he is a novelist. His only American peer
is Ernest Hemingway. In some of his stories, he seems to
find it difficult to stay within the boundaries of the traditional
short story form. But in such stories as "A Rose
for Emily," "Pantaloon in Black," "Shingles for the
Lord," "Was," and "Barn Burning," he created some of
his more memorable fiction. But of all his stories, "Red
Leaves" remains the most haunting. Like so much of his
work, it is saturated with the myths and legends of the
nineteenth-century South, a section of America which
passed into history before it found its greatest storyteller,
William Faulkner.*

Red Leaves

I

The two Indians crossed the plantation toward the slave
quarters. Neat with whitewash, of baked soft brick, the

two rows of houses in which lived the slaves belonging to the clan, faced one another across the mild shade of the lane marked and scored with naked feet and with a few home-made toys mute in the dust. There was no sign of life.

"I know what we will find," the first Indian said.

"What we will not find," the second said. Although it was noon, the lane was vacant, the doors of the cabins empty and quiet; no cooking smoke rose from any of the chinked and plastered chimneys.

"Yes. It happened like this when the father of him who is now the Man, died."

"You mean, of him who was the Man."

"Yao."

The first Indian's name was Three Basket. He was perhaps sixty. They were both squat men, a little solid, burgher-like; paunchy, with big heads, big, broad, dust-colored faces of a certain blurred serenity like carved heads on a ruined wall in Siam or Sumatra, looming out of a mist. The sun had done it, the violent sun, the violent shade. Their hair looked like sedge grass on burnt-over land. Clamped through one ear Three Basket wore an enameled snuffbox.

"I have said all the time that this is not the good way. In the old days there were no quarters, no Negroes. A man's time was his own then. He had time. Now he must spend most of it finding work for them who prefer sweating to do."

"They are like horses and dogs."

"They are like nothing in this sensible world. Nothing contents them save sweat. They are worse than the white people."

"It is not as though the Man himself had to find work for them to do."

"You said it. I do not like slavery. It is not the good way. In the old days, there was the good way. But not now."

"You do not remember the old way either."

"I have listened to them who do. And I have tried this way. Man was not made to sweat."

"That's so. See what it has done to their flesh."

"Yes. Black. It has a bitter taste, too."

"You have eaten of it?"

"Once. I was young then, and more hardy in the appetite than now. Now it is different with me."

"Yes. They are too valuable to eat now."

"There is a bitter taste to the flesh which I do not like."

"They are too valuable to eat, anyway, when the white men will give horses for them."

They entered the lane. The mute, meager toys—the fetish-shaped objects made of wood and rags and feathers —lay in the dust about the patinaed doorsteps, among bones and broken gourd dishes. But there was no sound from any cabin, no face in any door; had not been since yesterday, when Issetibbeha died. But they already knew what they would find.

It was in the central cabin, a house a little larger than the others, where at certain phases of the moon the Negroes would gather to begin their ceremonies before removing after nightfall to the creek bottom, where they kept the drums. In this room they kept the minor accessories, the cryptic ornaments, the ceremonial records which consisted of sticks daubed with red clay in symbols. It had a hearth in the center of the floor, beneath a hole in the roof, with a few cold wood ashes and a suspended iron pot. The window shutters were closed; when the two Indians entered, after the abashless sunlight they could distinguish nothing with the eyes save a movement, shadow, out of which eyeballs rolled, so that the place appeared to be full of Negroes. The two Indians stood in the doorway.

"Yao," Basket said. "I said this is not the good way."

"I don't think I want to be here," the second said.

"That is black man's fear which you smell. It does not smell as ours does."

"I don't think I want to be here."

"Your fear has an odor too."

"Maybe it is Issetibbeha which we smell."

"Yao. He knows. He knows what we will find here. He knew when he died what we should find here today." Out of the rank twilight of the room the eyes, the smell, of Negroes rolled about them. "I am Three Basket, whom you know," Basket said into the room. "We are come from the Man. He whom we seek is gone?" The Negroes said nothing. The smell of them, of their bodies, seemed to ebb and flux in the still hot air. They seemed to be musing as one upon something remote, inscrutable. They were like a single octopus. They were like the roots of a huge tree uncovered, the earth broken momentarily upon the writhen, thick, fetid tangle of its lightless and outraged life. "Come," Basket said. "You know our errand. Is he whom we seek gone?"

"They are thinking something," the second said. "I do not want to be here."

"They are knowing something," Basket said.

"They are hiding him, you think?"

"No. He is gone. He has been gone since last night. It happened like this before, when the grandfather of him who is now the Man died. It took us three days to catch him. For three days Doom lay above the ground, saying 'I see my horse and my dog. But I do not see my slave. What have you done with him that you will not permit me to lie quiet?'"

"They do not like to die."

"Yao. They cling. It makes trouble for us, always. A people without honor and without decorum. Always a trouble."

"I do not like it here."

"Nor do I. But then, they are savages; they cannot be expected to regard usage. That is why I say that this way is a bad way."

"Yao. They cling. They would even rather work in the sun than to enter the earth with a chief. But he is gone."

The Negroes had said nothing, made no sound. The white eyeballs rolled, wild, subdued; the smell was rank, violent. "Yes, they fear," the second said. "What shall we do now?"

"Let us go and talk with the Man."

"Will Moketubbe listen?"

"What can he do? He will not like to. But he is the Man now."

"Yao. He is the Man. He can wear the shoes with the red heels all the time now." They turned and went out. There was no door in the door frame. There were no doors in any of the cabins.

"He did that anyway," Basket said.

"Behind Issetibbeha's back. But now they are his shoes since he is the Man."

"Yao. Issetibbeha did not like it. I have heard. I know that he said to Moketubbe: 'When you are the Man, the shoes will be yours. But until then, they are my shoes.' But now Moketubbe is the Man; he can wear them."

"Yao," the second said. "He is the Man now. He used to wear the shoes behind Issetibbeha's back, and it was not known if Issetibbeha knew this or not. And then Issetibbeha became dead, who was not old, and the shoes are Moketubbe's, since he is the Man now. What do you think of that?"

"I don't think about it," Basket said. "Do you?"

"No," the second said.

"Good," Basket said. "You are wise."

II

The house sat on a knoll, surrounded by oak trees. The
front of it was one story in height, composed of the deck
house of a steamboat which had gone ashore and which
Doom, Issetibbeha's father, had dismantled with his slaves
and hauled on cypress rollers twelve miles home overland.
It took them five months. His house consisted at the time
of one brick wall. He set the steamboat broadside on to
the wall, where now the chipped and flaked gilding of the
rococo cornices arched in faint splendor above the gilt
lettering of the stateroom names above the jalousied doors.

Doom had been born merely a subchief, a Mingo, one
of three children on the mother's side of the family. He
made a journey—he was a young man then and New Orleans was a European city—from north Mississippi to
New Orleans by keel boat, where he met the Chevalier
Sœur Blonde de Vitry, a man whose social position, on its
face, was as equivocal as Doom's own. In New Orleans,
among the gamblers and cutthroats of the river front,
Doom, under the tutelage of his patron, passed as the chief,
the Man, the hereditary owner of that land which belonged
to the male side of the family; it was the Chevalier de
Vitry who called him *du homme,* and hence Doom.

They were seen everywhere together—the Indian, the
squat man with a bold, inscrutable, underbred face, and the
Parisian, the expatriate, the friend, it was said, of Caron-
delet and the intimate of General Wilkinson. Then they
disappeared, the two of them, vanishing from their old
equivocal haunts and leaving behind them the legend of
the sums which Doom was believed to have won, and some
tale about a young woman, daughter of a fairly well-to-
do West Indian family, the son and brother of whom
sought Doom with a pistol about his old haunts for some
time after his disappearance.

Six months later the young woman herself disappeared,
boarding the St. Louis packet, which put in one night at
a wood landing on the north Mississippi side, where the
woman, accompanied by a Negro maid, got off. Four Indians met her with a horse and wagon, and they traveled

for three days, slowly, since she was already big with child, to the plantation, where she found that Doom was now chief. He never told her how he accomplished it, save that his uncle and his cousin had died suddenly. At that time the house consisted of a brick wall built by shiftless slaves, against which was propped a thatched lean-to divided into rooms and littered with bones and refuse, set in the center of ten thousand acres of matchless parklike forest where deer grazed like domestic cattle. Doom and the woman were married there a short time before Issetibbeha was born, by a combination itinerant minister and slave trader who arrived on a mule, to the saddle of which was lashed a cotton umbrella and a three-gallon demijohn of whisky. After that, Doom began to acquire more slaves and to cultivate some of his land, as the white people did. But he never had enough for them to do. In utter idleness the majority of them led lives transplanted whole out of African jungles, save on the occasions when, entertaining guests, Doom coursed them with dogs.

When Doom died, Issetibbeha, his son, was nineteen. He became proprietor of the land and of the quintupled herd of blacks for which he had no use at all. Though the title of Man rested with him, there was a hierarchy of cousins and uncles who ruled the clan and who finally gathered in squatting conclave over the Negro question, squatting profoundly beneath the golden names above the doors of the steamboat.

"We cannot eat them," one said.

"Why not?"

"There are too many of them."

"That's true," a third said. "Once we started, we should have to eat them all. And that much flesh diet is not good for man."

"Perhaps they will be like deer flesh. That cannot hurt you."

"We might kill a few of them and not eat them," Issetibbeha said.

They looked at him for a while. "What for?" one said.

"That is true," a second said. "We cannot do that. They are too valuable; remember all the bother they have caused us, finding things for them to do. We must do as the white men do."

"How is that?" Issetibbeha said.

"Raise more Negroes by clearing more land to make corn to feed them, then sell them. We will clear the land

and plant it with food and raise Negroes and sell them to the white men for money."

"But what will we do with this money?" a third said.

They thought for a while.

"We will see," the first said. They squatted, profound, grave.

"It means work," the third said.

"Let the Negroes do it," the first said.

".Yao. Let them. To sweat is bad. It is damp. It opens the pores."

"And then the night air enters."

"Yao. Let the Negroes do it. They appear to like sweating."

So they cleared the land with the Negroes and planted it in grain. Up to that time the slaves had lived in a huge pen with a lean-to roof over one corner, like a pen for pigs. But now they began to build quarters, cabins, putting the young Negroes in the cabins in pairs to mate; five years later Issetibbeha sold forty head to a Memphis trader, and he took the money and went abroad upon it, his maternal uncle from New Orleans conducting the trip. At that time the Chevalier Sœur Blonde de Vitry was an old man in Paris, in a toupee and a corset, with a careful toothless old face fixed in a grimace quizzical and profoundly tragic. He borrowed three hundred dollars from Issetibbeha and in return he introduced him into certain circles; a year later Issetibbeha returned home with a gilt bed, a pair of girandoles by whose light it was said that Pompadour arranged her hair while Louis smirked at his mirrored face across her powdered shoulder, and a pair of slippers with red heels. They were too small for him, since he had not worn shoes at all until he reached New Orleans on his way abroad.

He brought the slippers home in tissue paper and kept them in the remaining pocket of a pair of saddlebags filled with cedar shavings, save when he took them out on occasion for his son, Moketubbe, to play with. At three years of age Moketubbe had a broad, flat, Mongolian face that appeared to exist in a complete and unfathomable lethargy, until confronted by the slippers.

Moketubbe's mother was a comely girl whom Issetibbeha had seen one day working in her shift in a melon patch. He stopped and watched her for a while—the broad, solid thighs, the sound back, the serene face. He was on his way to the creek to fish that day, but he didn't go any farther; perhaps while he stood there watching the unaware girl he may have remembered his own mother, the city woman, the fugitive with her fans and laces and her Negro blood, and all the tawdry shabbiness of that sorry affair. Within the year Moketubbe was born; even at three he could not get his feet into the slippers. Watching him in the still, hot afternoons as he struggled with the slippers with a certain monstrous repudiation of fact, Issetibbeha laughed quietly to himself. He laughed at Moketubbe and the shoes for several years, because Moketubbe did not give up trying to put them on until he was sixteen. Then he quit. Or Issetibbeha thought he had. But he had merely quit trying in Issetibbeha's presence. Issetibbeha's newest wife told him that Moketubbe had stolen and hidden the shoes. Issetibbeha quit laughing then, and he sent the woman away, so that he was alone. "Yao," he said. "I too like being alive, it seems." He sent for Moketubbe. "I give them to you," he said.

Moketubbe was twenty-five then, unmarried. Issetibbeha was not tall, but he was taller by six inches than his son and almost a hundred pounds lighter. Moketubbe was already diseased with flesh, with a pale, broad, inert face and dropsical hands and feet. "They are yours now," Issetibbeha said, watching him. Moketubbe had looked at him once when he entered, a glance brief, discreet, veiled.

"Thanks," he said.

Issetibbeha looked at him. He could never tell if Moketubbe saw anything, looked at anything. "Why will it not be the same if I give the slippers to you?"

"Thanks," Moketubbe said. Issetibbeha was using snuff at the time; a white man had shown him how to put the powder into his lip and scour it against his teeth with a twig of gum or of alphea.

"Well," he said, "a man cannot live forever." He looked at his son, then his gaze went blank in turn, unseeing, and he mused for an instant. You could not tell what he was thinking, save that he said half aloud: "Yao. But Doom's uncle had no shoes with red heels." He looked at his son again, fat, inert. "Beneath all that, a man might think of doing anything and it not be known until too late." He sat in a splint chair hammocked with deer thongs. "He cannot even get them on; he and I are both frustrated by the same gross meat which he wears. He cannot even get them on. But is that my fault?"

He lived for five years longer, then he died. He was sick

one night, and though the doctor came in a skunk-skin
vest and burned sticks, he died before noon.

That was yesterday; the grave was dug, and for twelve
hours now the People had been coming in wagons and carriages and on horseback and afoot, to eat the baked dog
and the succotash and the yams cooked in ashes and to
attend the funeral.

III

"It will be three days," Basket said, as he and the other
Indian returned to the house. "It will be three days and the
food will not be enough; I have seen it before."

The second Indian's name was Louis Berry. "He will
smell too, in this weather."

"Yao. They are nothing but a trouble and a care."

"Maybe it will not take three days."

"They run far. Yao. We will smell this Man before he
enters the earth. You watch and see if I am not right."

They approached the house.

"He can wear the shoes now," Berry said. "He can wear
them now in man's sight."

"He cannot wear them for a while yet," Basket said.
Berry looked at him. "He will lead the hunt."

"Moketubbe?" Berry said. "Do you think he will? A man
to whom even talking is travail?"

"What else can he do? It is his own father who will soon
begin to smell."

"That is true," Berry said. "There is even yet a price he
must pay for the shoes. Yao. He has truly bought them.
What do you think?"

"What do you think?"

"What do you think?"

"I think nothing."

"Nor do I. Issetibbeha will not need the shoes now. Let
Moketubbe have them; Issetibbeha will not care."

"Yao. Man must die."

"Yao. Let him; there is still the Man."

The bark roof of the porch was supported by peeled
cypress poles, high above the texas of the steamboat, shad-
ing an unfloored banquette where on the trodden earth
mules and horses were tethered in bad weather. On the
forward end of the steamboat's deck sat an old man and

two women. One of the women was dressing a fowl, the
other was shelling corn. The old man was talking. He was
barefoot, in a long linen frock coat and a beaver hat.

"This world is going to the dogs," he said. "It is being
ruined by white men. We got along fine for years and
years, before the white men foisted their Negroes upon
us. In the old days the old men sat in the shade and ate
stewed deer's flesh and corn and smoked tobacco and
talked of honor and grave affairs; now what do we do?
Even the old wear themselves into the grave taking care
of them that like sweating." When Basket and Berry
crossed the deck he ceased and looked up at them. His
eyes were querulous, bleared; his face was myriad with tiny
wrinkles. "He is fled also," he said.

"Yes," Berry said, "he is gone."

"I knew it. I told them so. It will take three weeks, like
when Doom died. You watch and see."

"It was three days, not three weeks," Berry said.

"Were you there?"

"No," Berry said. "But I have heard."

"Well, I was there," the old man said. "For three whole
weeks, through the swamps and the briers—" They went
on and left him talking.

What had been the saloon of the steamboat was now a
shell, rotting slowly; the polished mahogany, the carving
glinting momentarily and fading through the mold in
figures cabalistic and profound; the gutted windows were
like cataracted eyes. It contained a few sacks of seed or
grain, and the fore part of the running gear of a barouche,
to the axle of which two C-springs rusted in graceful
curves, supporting nothing. In one corner a fox cub ran
steadily and soundlessly up and down a willow cage; three
scrawny gamecocks moved in the dust, and the place was
pocked and marked with their dried droppings.

They passed through the brick wall and entered a big
room of chinked logs. It contained the hinder part of the
barouche, and the dismantled body lying on its side, the
window slatted over with willow withes, through which
protruded the heads, the still, beady, outraged eyes and
frayed combs of still more game chickens. It was floored
with packed clay; in one corner leaned a crude plow and
two hand-hewn boat paddles. From the ceiling, suspended
by four deer thongs, hung the gilt bed which Issetibbeha
had fetched from Paris. It had neither mattress nor springs,
the frame crisscrossed now by a neat hammocking of
thongs.

Issetibbeha had tried to have his newest wife, the young one, sleep in the bed. He was congenitally short of breath himself, and he passed the nights half reclining in his splint chair. He would see her to bed and, later, wakeful, sleeping as he did but three or four hours a night, he would sit in the darkness and simulate slumber and listen to her sneak infinitesimally from the gilt and ribboned bed, to lie on a quilt pallet on the floor until just before daylight. Then she would enter the bed quietly again and in turn simulate slumber, while in the darkness beside her Issetibbeha quietly laughed and laughed.

The girandoles were lashed by thongs to two sticks propped in a corner where a ten-gallon whisky keg lay also. There was a clay hearth; facing it, in the splint chair, Moketubbe sat. He was maybe an inch better than five feet tall, and he weighed two hundred and fifty pounds. He wore a broadcloth coat and no shirt, his round, smooth copper balloon of belly swelling above the bottom piece of a suit of linen underwear. On his feet were the slippers with the red heels. Behind his chair stood a stripling with a punkah-like fan made of fringed paper. Moketubbe sat motionless, with his broad, yellow face with its closed eyes and flat nostrils, his flipperlike arms extended. On his face was an expression profound, tragic, and inert. He did not open his eyes when Basket and Berry came in.

"He has worn them since daylight?" Basket said.

"Since daylight," the stripling said. The fan did not cease. "You can see."

"Yao," Basket said. "We can see." Moketubbe did not move. He looked like an effigy, like a Malay god in frock coat, drawers, naked chest, the trivial scarlet-heeled shoes.

"I wouldn't disturb him, if I were you," the stripling said.

"Not if I were you," Basket said. He and Berry squatted. The stripling moved the fan steadily. "O Man," Basket said, "listen." Moketubbe did not move. "He is gone," Basket said.

"I told you so," the stripling said. "I knew he would flee. I told you."

"Yao," Basket said. "You are not the first to tell us afterward what we should have known before. Why is it that some of you wise men took no steps yesterday to prevent this?"

"He does not wish to die," Berry said.

"Why should he not wish it?" Basket said.

"Because he must die some day is no reason," the

stripling said. "That would not convince me either, old man."

"Hold your tongue," Berry said.

"For twenty years," Basket said, "while others of his race sweat in the fields, he served the Man in the shade. Why should he not wish to die, since he did not wish to sweat?"

"And it will be quick," Berry said. "It will not take long."

"Catch him and tell him that," the stripling said.

"Hush," Berry said. They squatted, watching Moketubbe's face. He might have been dead himself. It was as though he were cased so in flesh that even breathing took place too deep within him to show.

"Listen, O Man," Basket said. "Issetibbeha is dead. He waits. His dog and his horse we have. But his slave has fled. The one who held the pot for him, who ate of his food, from his dish, is fled. Issetibbeha waits."

"Yao," Berry said.

"This is not the first time," Basket said. "This happened when Doom, thy grandfather, lay waiting at the door of the earth. He lay waiting three days, saying, 'Where is my Negro?' And Issetibbeha, thy father, answered, 'I will find him. Rest; I will bring him to you so that you may begin the journey.' "

"Yao," Berry said.

Moketubbe had not moved, had not opened his eyes.

"For three days Issetibbeha hunted in the bottom," Basket said. "He did not even return home for food, until the Negro was with him; then he said to Doom, his father, 'Here is thy dog, thy horse, thy Negro; rest.' Issetibbeha, who is dead since yesterday, said it. And now Issetibbeha's Negro is fled. His horse and his dog wait with him, but his Negro is fled."

"Yao," Berry said.

Moketubbe had not moved. His eyes were closed; upon his supine monstrous shape there was a colossal inertia, something profoundly immobile, beyond and impervious to flesh. They watched his face, squatting.

"When thy father was newly the Man, this happened," Basket said. "And it was Issetibbeha who brought back the slave to where his father waited to enter the earth." Moketubbe's face had not moved, his eyes had not moved. After a while Basket said, "Remove the shoes."

The stripling removed the shoes. Moketubbe began to pant, his bare chest moving deep, as though he were rising from beyond his unfathomed flesh back into life, like up from the water, the sea. But his eyes had not opened yet.

Berry said, "He will lead the hunt."

"Yao," Basket said. "He is the Man. He will lead the hunt."

IV

All that day the Negro, Issetibbeha's body servant, hidden in the barn, watched Issetibbeha's dying. He was forty, a Guinea man. He had a flat nose, a close, small head; the inside corners of his eyes showed red a little, and his prominent gums were a pale bluish red above his square, broad teeth. He had been taken at fourteen by a trader off Kamerun, before his teeth had been filed. He had been Issetibbeha's body servant for twenty-three years.

On the day before, the day on which Issetibbeha lay sick, he returned to the quarters at dusk. In that unhurried hour the smoke of the cooking fires blew slowly across the street from door to door, carrying into the opposite one the smell of the identical meat and bread. The women tended them; the men were gathered at the head of the lane, watching him as he came down the slope from the house, putting his naked feet down carefully in a strange dusk. To the waiting men his eyeballs were a little luminous.

"Issetibbeha is not dead yet," the headman said.

"Not dead," the body servant said. "Who not dead?"

In the dusk they had faces like his, the different ages, the thoughts sealed inscrutable behind faces like the death masks of apes. The smell of the fires, the cooking, blew sharp and slow across the strange dusk, as from another world, above the lane and the pickaninnies naked in the dust.

"If he lives past sundown, he will live until daybreak," one said.

"Who says?"

"Talk says."

"Yao. Talk says. We know but one thing." They looked at the body servant as he stood among them, his eyeballs a little luminous. He was breathing slow and deep. His chest was bare; he was sweating a little. "He knows. He knows it."

"Let us let the drums talk."

"Yao. Let the drums tell it."

The drums began after dark. They kept them hidden in the creek bottom. They were made of hollowed cypress trees, and the Negroes kept them hidden; why, none knew. They were buried in the mud on the bank of a slough; a lad of fourteen guarded them. He was undersized, and a mute; he squatted in the mud there all day, clouded over with mosquitoes, naked save for the mud with which he coated himself against the mosquitoes, and about his neck a fiber bag containing a pig's rib to which black shreds of flesh still adhered, and two scaly barks on a wire. He slobbered onto his clutched knees, drooling; now and then Indians came noiselessly out of the bushes behind him and stood there and contemplated him for a while and went away, and he never knew it.

From the loft of the stable where he lay hidden until dark and after, the Negro could hear the drums. They were three miles away, but he could hear them as though they were in the barn itself below him, thudding and thudding. It was as though he could see the fire too, and the black limbs turning into and out of the flames in copper gleams. Only there would be no fire. There would be no more light there than where he lay in the dusty loft, with the whispering arpeggios of rat feet along the warm and immemorial ax-squared rafters. The only fire there would be the smudge against mosquitoes where the women with nursing children crouched, their heavy sluggish breasts nippled full and smooth into the mouths of men children; contemplative, oblivious of the drumming, since a fire would signify life.

There was a fire in the steamboat, where Issetibbeha lay dying among his wives, beneath the lashed girandoles and the suspended bed. He could see the smoke, and just before sunset he saw the doctor come out, in a waistcoat made of skunk skins, and set fire to two clay-daubed sticks at the bows of the boat deck. "So he is not dead yet," the Negro said into the whispering gloom of the loft, answering himself; he could hear the two voices, himself and himself:

"Who not dead?"

"You are dead."

"Yao, I am dead," he said quietly. He wished to be where the drums were. He imagined himself springing out of the bushes, leaping among the drums on his bare, lean, greasy, invisible limbs. But he could not do that, because man leaped past life, into where death was; he dashed into death and did not die, because when death took a man, it took him just this side of the end of living. It was when death overran him from behind, still in life. The thin whisper of rat feet died in fainting gusts along the rafters. Once he had eaten rat. He was a boy then, but just come to America. They had lived ninety days in a three-foot-high 'tween-deck in tropic latitudes, hearing from topside the drunken New England captain intoning aloud from a book which he did not recognize for ten years afterward to be the Bible. Squatting in the stable so, he had watched the rat, civilized, by association with man reft of its inherent cunning of limb and eye; he had caught it without difficulty, with scarce a movement of his hand, and he ate it slowly, wondering how any of the rats had escaped so long. At that time he was still wearing the single white garment which the trader, a deacon in the Unitarian church, had given him, and he spoke then only his native tongue.

He was naked now, save for a pair of dungaree pants bought by Indians from white men, and an amulet slung on a thong about his hips. The amulet consisted of one half of a mother-of-pearl lorgnon which Issetibbeha had brought back from Paris, and the skull of a cottonmouth moccasin. He had killed the snake himself and eaten it, save the poison head. He lay in the loft, watching the house, the steamboat, listening to the drums, thinking of himself among the drums.

He lay there all night. The next morning he saw the doctor come out, in his skunk vest, and get on his mule and ride away, and he became quite still and watched the final dust from beneath the mule's delicate feet die away, and then he found that he was still breathing and it seemed strange to him that he still breathed air, still needed air. Then he lay and watched quietly, waiting to move, his eyeballs a little luminous, but with a quiet light, and his breathing light and regular, and saw Louis Berry come out and look at the sky. It was good light then, and already five Indians squatted in their Sunday clothes along the steamboat deck; by noon there were twenty-five there. That afternoon they dug the trench in which the meat would be baked, and the yams; by that time there were almost a hundred guests—decorous, quiet, patient in their stiff European finery—and he watched Berry lead Issetibbeha's mare from the stable and tie her to a tree, and then he watched Berry emerge from the house with the old hound which lay beside Issetibbeha's chair. He tied the hound to the tree too, and it sat there, looking gravely about at the faces. Then it began to howl. It was still howling at sundown, when the Negro climbed down the back wall of the barn and entered the spring branch, where it was already dusk. He began to run then. He could hear the hound howling behind him, and near the spring, already running, he passed another Negro. The two men, the one motionless and the other running, looked for an instant at each other as though across an actual boundary between two different worlds. He ran on into full darkness, mouth closed, fists doubled, his broad nostrils bellowing steadily.

He ran on in the darkness. He knew the country well, because he had hunted it often with Issetibbeha, following on his mule the course of the fox or the cat beside Issetibbeha's mare; he knew it as well as did the men who would pursue him. He saw them for the first time shortly before sunset of the second day. He had run thirty miles then, up the creek bottom, before doubling back; lying in a pawpaw thicket he saw the pursuit for the first time. There were two of them, in shirts and straw hats, carrying their neatly rolled trousers under their arms, and they had no weapons. They were middle-aged, paunchy, and they could not have moved very fast anyway; it would be twelve hours before they could return to where he lay watching them. "So I will have until midnight to rest," he said. He was near enough to the plantation to smell the cooking fires, and he thought how he ought to be hungry, since he had not eaten in thirty hours. "But it is more important to rest," he told himself. He continued to tell himself that, lying in the pawpaw thicket, because the effort of resting, the need and the haste to rest, made his heart thud the same as the running had done. It was as though he had forgot how to rest, as though the six hours were not long enough to do it in, to remember again how to do it.

As soon as dark came he moved again. He had thought to keep going steadily and quietly through the night, since there was nowhere for him to go, but as soon as he moved he began to run at top speed, breasting his panting chest, his broad-flaring nostrils through the choked and whipping darkness. He ran for an hour, lost by then, without direction, when suddenly he stopped, and after a time his thudding heart unraveled from the sound of the drums. By the sound they were not two miles away; he followed the sound until he could smell the smudge fire and taste the acrid smoke. When he stood among them the drums did not cease; only the headman came to him where he

stood in the drifting smudge, panting, his nostrils flaring
and pulsing, the hushed glare of his ceaseless eyeballs in
his mud-daubed face as though they were worked from
lungs.

"We have expected thee," the headman said. "Go, now."

"Go?"

"Eat, and go. The dead may not consort with the living;
thou knowest that."

"Yao. I know that." They did not look at one another.
The drums had not ceased.

"Wilt thou eat?" the headman said.

"I am not hungry. I caught a rabbit this afternoon, and
ate while I lay hidden."

"Take some cooked meat with thee, then."

He accepted the cooked meat, wrapped in leaves, and
entered the creek bottom again; after a while the sound of
the drums ceased. He walked steadily until daybreak. "I
have twelve hours," he said. "Maybe more, since the trail
was followed by night." He squatted and ate the meat and
wiped his hands on his thighs. Then he rose and removed
the dungaree pants and squatted again beside a slough and
coated himself with mud—face, arms, body and legs—and
squatted again, clasping his knees, his head bowed. When
it was light enough to see, he moved back into the swamp
and squatted again and went to sleep so. He did not dream
at all. It was well that he moved, for, waking suddenly in
broad daylight and the high sun, he saw the two Indians.
They still carried their neatly rolled trousers; they stood
opposite the place where he lay hidden, paunchy, thick,
soft-looking, a little ludicrous in their straw hats and shirt
tails.

"This is wearying work," one said.

"I'd rather be at home in the shade myself," the other
said. "But there is the Man waiting at the door to the
earth."

"Yao." They looked quietly about; stooping, one of them
removed from his shirt tail a clot of cockleburs. "Damn
that Negro," he said.

"Yao. When have they ever been anything but a trial
and a care to us?"

In the early afternoon, from the top of a tree, the Negro
looked down into the plantation. He could see Issetibbeha's
body in a hammock between the two trees where the horse
and the dog were tethered, and the concourse about the
steamboat was filled with wagons and horses and mules,
with carts and saddle-horses, while in bright clumps the

women and the smaller children and the old men squatted about the long trench where the smoke from the barbecuing meat blew slow and thick. The men and the big boys would all be down there in the creek bottom behind him, on the trail, their Sunday clothes rolled carefully up and wedged into tree crotches. There was a clump of men near the door to the house, to the saloon of the steamboat, though, and he watched them, and after a while he saw them bring Moketubbe out in a litter made of buckskin and persimmon poles; high hidden in his leafed nook the Negro, the quarry, looked quietly down upon his irrevocable doom with an expression as profound as Moketubbe's own. "Yao," he said quietly. "He will go then. That man whose body has been dead for fifteen years, he will go also."

In the middle of the afternoon he came face to face with an Indian. They were both on a footlog across a slough—the Negro gaunt, lean, hard, tireless and desperate; the Indian thick, soft-looking, the apparent embodiment of the ultimate and the supreme reluctance and inertia. The Indian made no move, no sound; he stood on the log and watched the Negro plunge into the slough and swim ashore and crash away into the undergrowth.

Just before sunset he lay behind a down log. Up the log in slow procession moved a line of ants. He caught them and ate them slowly, with a kind of detachment, like that of a dinner guest eating salted nuts from a dish. They too had a salt taste, engendering a salivary reaction out of all proportion. He ate them slowly, watching the unbroken line move up the log and into oblivious doom with a steady and terrific undeviation. He had eaten nothing else all day; in his caked mud mask his eyes rolled in reddened rims. At sunset, creeping along the creek bank toward where he had spotted a frog, a cottonmouth moccasin slashed him suddenly across the forearm with a thick, sluggish blow. It struck clumsily, leaving two long slashes across his arm like two razor slashes, and half sprawled with its own momentum and rage, it appeared for the moment utterly helpless with its own awkwardness and choleric anger. "Olé, grandfather," the Negro said. He touched its head and watched it slash him again across his arm, and again, with thick, raking, awkward blows. "It's that I do not wish to die," he said. Then he said it again—"It's that I do not wish to die"—in a quiet tone, of slow and low amaze, as though it were something that, until the words had said themselves, he found that he had not known, or had not known the depth and extent of his desire.

V

Moketubbe took the slippers with him. He could not wear them very long while in motion, not even in the litter where he was slung reclining, so they rested upon a square of fawnskin upon his lap—the cracked, frail slippers a little shapeless now, with their scaled patent-leather surfaces and buckleless tongues and scarlet heels, lying upon the supine obese shape just barely alive, carried through swamp and brier by swinging relays of men who bore steadily all day long the crime and its object, on the business of the slain. To Moketubbe it must have been as though, himself immortal, he were being carried rapidly through hell by doomed spirits which, alive, had contemplated his disaster, and, dead, were oblivious partners to his damnation.

After resting for a while, the litter propped in the center of the squatting circle and Moketubbe motionless in it, with closed eyes and his face at once peaceful for the instant and filled with inescapable foreknowledge, he could wear the slippers for a while. The stripling put them on him, forcing his big, tender, dropsical feet into them; whereupon into his face came again that expression tragic, passive and profoundly attentive, which dyspeptics wear. Then they went on. He made no move, no sound, inert in the rhythmic litter out of some reserve of inertia, or maybe of some kingly virtue such as courage or fortitude. After a time they set the litter down and looked at him, at the yellow face like that of an idol, beaded over with sweat. Then Three Basket or Had-Two-Fathers would say: "Take them off. Honor has been served." They would remove the shoes. Moketubbe's face would not alter, but only then would his breathing become perceptible, going in and out of his pale lips with a faint ah-ah-ah sound, and they would squat again while the couriers and the runners came up.

"Not yet?"

"Not yet. He is going east. By sunset he will reach Mouth of Tippah. Then he will turn back. We may take him tomorrow."

"Let us hope so. It will not be too soon."

"Yao. It has been three days now."

"When Doom died, it took only three days."

"But that was an old man. This one is young."

"Yao. A good race. If he is taken tomorrow, I will win a horse."

"May you win it."

"Yao. This work is not pleasant."

That was the day on which the food gave out at the plantation. The guests returned home and came back the next day with more food, enough for a week longer. On that day Issetibbeha began to smell; they could smell him for a long way up and down the bottom when it got hot toward noon and the wind blew. But they didn't capture the Negro on that day, nor on the next. It was about dusk on the sixth day when the couriers came up to the litter; they had found blood. "He has injured himself."

"Not bad, I hope," Basket said. "We cannot send with Issetibbeha one who will be of no service to him."

"Nor whom Issetibbeha himself will have to nurse and care for," Berry said.

"We do not know," the courier said. "He had hidden himself. He has crept back into the swamp. We have left pickets."

They trotted with the litter now. The place where the Negro had crept into the swamp was an hour away. In the hurry and excitement they had forgotten that Moketubbe still wore the slippers; when they reached the place Moketubbe had fainted. They removed the slippers and brought him to.

With dark, they formed a circle about the swamp. They squatted, clouded over with gnats and mosquitoes; the evening star burned low and close down the west, and the constellations began to wheel overhead. "We will give him time," they said. "Tomorrow is just another name for today."

"Yao. Let him have time." Then they ceased, and gazed as one into the darkness where the swamp lay. After a while the noise ceased, and soon the courier came out of the darkness.

"He tried to break out."

"But you turned him back?"

"He turned back. We feared for a moment, the three of us. We could smell him creeping in the darkness, and we could smell something else, which we did not know. That was why we feared, until he told us. He said to slay him there, since it would be dark and he would not have to see

the face when it came. But it was not that which we
smelled; he told us what it was. A snake had struck him.
That was two days ago. The arm swelled, and it smelled
bad. But it was not that which we smelled then, because
the swelling had gone down and his arm was no larger
than that of a child. He showed us. We felt the arm, all of
us did; it was no larger than that of a child. He said to
give him a hatchet so he could chop the arm off. But
tomorrow is today also."

"Yao. Tomorrow is today."

"We feared for a while. Then he went back into the
swamp."

"That is good."

"Yao. We feared. Shall I tell the Man?"

"I will see," Basket said. He went away. The courier
squatted, telling again about the Negro. Basket returned.
"The Man says that it is good. Return to your post."

The courier crept away. They squatted about the litter;
now and then they slept. Sometime after midnight the
Negro waked them. He began to shout and talk to himself,
his voice coming sharp and sudden out of the darkness,
then he fell silent. Dawn came; a white crane flapped
slowly across the jonquil sky. Basket was awake. "Let us
go now," he said. "It is today."

Two Indians entered the swamp, their movements noisy.
Before they reached the Negro they stopped, because he
began to sing. They could see him, naked and mud-caked,
sitting on a log, singing. They squatted silently a short distance away, until he finished. He was chanting something
in his own language, his face lifted to the rising sun. His
voice was clear, full, with a quality wild and sad. "Let him
have time," the Indians said, squatting, patient, waiting. He
ceased and they approached. He looked back and up at
them through the cracked mud mask. His eyes were bloodshot, his lips cracked upon his square short teeth. The mask
of mud appeared to be loose on his face, as if he might
have lost flesh since he put it there; he held his left arm
close to his breast. From the elbow down it was caked and
shapeless with black mud. They could smell him, a rank
smell. He watched them quietly until one touched him on
the arm. "Come," the Indian said. "You ran well. Do not
be ashamed."

VI

As they neared the plantation in the tainted bright morning, the Negro's eyes began to roll a little, like those of a horse. The smoke from the cooking pit blew low along the earth and upon the squatting and waiting guests about the yard and upon the steamboat deck, in their bright, stiff, harsh finery; the women, the children, the old men. They had sent couriers along the bottom, and another on ahead, and Issetibbeha's body had already been removed to where the grave waited, along with the horse and the dog, though they could still smell him in death about the house where he had lived in life. The guests were beginning to move toward the grave when the bearers of Moketubbe's litter mounted the slope.

The Negro was the tallest there, his high, close, mud-caked head looming above them all. He was breathing hard, as though the desperate effort of the six suspended and desperate days had catapulted upon him at once; although they walked slowly, his naked scarred chest rose and fell above the close-clutched left arm. He looked this way and that continuously, as if he were not seeing, as though sight never quite caught up with the looking. His mouth was open a little upon his big white teeth; he began to pant. The already moving guests halted, pausing, looking back, some with pieces of meat in their hands, as the Negro looked about at their faces with his wild, restrained, unceasing eyes.

"Will you eat first?" Basket said. He had to say it twice.

"Yes," the Negro said. "That's it. I want to eat."

The throng had begun to press back toward the center; the word passed to the outermost: "He will eat first."

They reached the steamboat. "Sit down," Basket said. The Negro sat on the edge of the deck. He was still panting, his chest rising and falling, his head ceaseless with its white eyeballs, turning from side to side. It was as if the inability to see came from within, from hopelessness, not from absence of vision. They brought food and watched quietly as he tried to eat it. He put the food into his mouth and chewed it, but chewing, the half-masticated matter began to emerge from the corners of his mouth and to drool down his chin, onto his chest, and after a while he stopped chewing and sat there, naked, covered with dried mud, the plate on his knees, and his mouth filled with a mass of chewed food, open, his eyes wide and unceasing, panting and panting. They watched him, patient, implacable, waiting.

"Come," Basket said at last.

"It's water I want," the Negro said. "I want water."

The well was a little way down the slope toward the quarters. The slope lay dappled with the shadows of noon, of that peaceful hour when, Issetibbeha napping in his chair and waiting for the noon meal and the long afternoon to sleep in, the Negro, the body servant, would be free. He would sit in the kitchen door then, talking with the women who prepared the food. Beyond the kitchen the lane between the quarters would be quiet, peaceful, with the women talking to one another across the lane and the smoke of the dinner fires blowing upon the pickaninnies like ebony toys in the dust.

"Come," Basket said.

The Negro walked among them, taller than any. The guests were moving on toward where Issetibbeha and the horse and the dog waited. The Negro walked with his high ceaseless head, his panting chest. "Come," Basket said. "You wanted water."

"Yes," the Negro said. "Yes." He looked back at the house, then down to the quarters, where today no fire burned, no face showed in any door, no pickaninny in the dust, panting. "It struck me here, raking me across this arm; once, twice, three times. I said, 'Olé, Grandfather.' "

"Come now," Basket said. The Negro was still going through the motion of walking, his knee action high, his head high, as though he were on a treadmill. His eyeballs had a wild, restrained glare, like those of a horse. "You wanted water," Basket said. "Here it is."

There was a gourd in the well. They dipped it full and gave it to the Negro, and they watched him try to drink. His eyes had not ceased as he tilted the gourd slowly against his caked face. They could watch his throat working and the bright water cascading from either side of the gourd, down his chin and breast. Then the water stopped. "Come," Basket said.

"Wait," the Negro said. He dipped the gourd again and tilted it against his face, beneath his ceaseless eyes. Again they watched his throat working and the unswallowed water sheathing broken and myriad down his chin, channeling his caked chest. They waited, patient, grave, decorous, implacable; clansman and guest and kin. Then the water ceased, though still the empty gourd tilted higher and higher, and still his black throat aped the vain motion of his frustrated swallowing. A piece of water-loosened mud carried away from his chest and broke at his muddy feet, and in the empty gourd they could hear his breath: ah-ah-ah.

"Come," Basket said, taking the gourd from the Negro and hanging it back in the well.

Bernard Malamud

(1914–   )

The emergence of a number of Jewish-American writers of significant talent since World War II is among the most notable trends in modern American fiction. The majority of these writers are simply Americans who happen to have been born Jews, but a few, most notably Saul Bellow and Bernard Malamud, have consciously sought in the Jewish experience a metaphor for the contemporary human condition. Bellow has probed that experience in such novels as The Victim *and* Herzog, *but Malamud has been even more consistent. In* The Fixer *(1966) and* The Assistant *(1957), he has chosen the Jewish condition as the vehicle for what he considers the writer's function: "To tell the truth about life." What Malamud means by truth is not strictly literary realism, a form which he has dismissed as "dead," but rather a combination of reality and fantasy designed to force the reader to perceive new combinations of circumstances which lead him through the daily heroism of existence into the very mystery of life. More perhaps than any of his contemporaries, Malamud has found his fictional heroes in average men and women struggling to discover an identity in the drab, confused circumstances of their lives. In an age steeped in self-conscious pessimism, Malamud has demonstrated his faith in man's ability to endure.*

Bernard Malamud was born in Brooklyn and educated in the New York City schools. He began to write while a student at Erasmus Hall High School in Brooklyn and continued at the City College of New York, where he received his B.A. in 1936. In 1942, he was awarded an M.A. from Columbia University. He held a number of jobs, ranging from a clerk in the Census Bureau to high school English teacher. In 1949 he left New York for a job teaching composition and literature at Oregon State College, an experience which bore fruit in what some critics consider his finest novel, A New Life *(1961). Since 1961 he has been writer-in-residence at Bennington College in Vermont.*

In The Magic Barrel *(1958) and* Idiots First *(1963), Malamud created stories which are different from any other contemporary American short stories. From the*

Jewish experience, Malamud seems to have gravitated toward a kind of spiritual mysticism; his world is filled, as is that of Isaac Bashevis Singer, with angels and spirits, apparitions that are half real, half fantasized. Malamud's mysticism, however, finds its expression in graphic, almost naturalistic, detail. In "The Magic Barrel," the colorless everyday world in which Salzman eats his fish and Leo searches his books is juxtaposed against the romantic world of promised love and sensuality, in which "violins and candles revolved in the sky." The story's conclusion is forcefully ambiguous, arousing in the reader the tantalizing suspicion that—just possibly— Salzman is a god-like schlemiel who has planned events in just this way.

"The Magic Barrel" is Malamud at the peak of his narrative powers. It is technically a brilliant achievement, vibrant with Malamud's characteristic warmth and compassion.

The Magic Barrel

Not long ago there lived in uptown New York, in a small, almost meager room, though crowded with books, Leo Finkle, a rabbinical student in the Yeshivah University. Finkle, after six years of study, was to be ordained in June and had been advised by an acquaintance that he might find it easier to win himself a congregation if he were married. Since he had no present prospects of marriage, after two tormented days of turning it over in his mind, he called in Pinye Salzman, a marriage broker whose two-line advertisement he had read in the *Forward*.

The matchmaker appeared one night out of the dark fourth-floor hallway of the graystone rooming house where Finkle lived, grasping a black, strapped portfolio that had been worn thin with use. Salzman, who had been long in the business, was of slight but dignified build, wearing an old hat, and an overcoat too short and tight for him. He smelled frankly of fish, which he loved to eat, and although he was missing a few teeth, his presence was not displeasing, because of an amiable manner curiously contrasted with mournful eyes. His voice, his lips, his wisp of beard, his bony fingers were animated, but give him a moment of repose and his mild blue eyes revealed a depth of sadness, a characteristic that put Leo a little at ease although the situation, for him, was inherently tense.

He at once informed Salzman why he had asked him to come, explaining that his home was in Cleveland, and that but for his parents, who had married comparatively late in life, he was alone in the world. He had for six years devoted himself almost entirely to his studies, as a result of which, understandably, he had found himself without time for a social life and the company of young women. Therefore he thought it the better part of trial and error—of embarrassing fumbling—to call in an experienced person to advise him on these matters. He remarked in passing that the function of the marriage broker was ancient and honorable, highly approved in the Jewish community, because it made practical the necessary without hindering joy. Moreover, his own parents had been brought together by a matchmaker. They had made, if not a financially profitable marriage—since neither had possessed any worldly goods to speak of—at least a successful one in the sense of their everlasting devotion to each other. Salzman listened in embarrassed surprise, sensing a sort of apology. Later, however, he experienced a glow of pride in his work, an emotion that had left him years ago, and he heartily approved of Finkle.

The two went to their business. Leo had led Salzman to the only clear place in the room, a table near a window that overlooked the lamp-lit city. He seated himself at the matchmaker's side but facing him, attempting by an act of will to suppress the unpleasant tickle in his throat. Salzman eagerly unstrapped his portfolio and removed a loose rubber band from a thin packet of much-handled cards. As he flipped through them, a gesture and sound that physically hurt Leo, the student pretended not to see and gazed steadfastly out the window. Although it was still February, winter was on its last legs, signs of which he had for the first time in years begun to notice. He now observed the round white moon, moving high in the sky through a cloud menagerie, and watched with half-open mouth as it penetrated a huge hen, and dropped out of her like an egg laying itself. Salzman, though pretending through eyeglasses he had just slipped on, to be engaged in scanning the writing on the cards, stole occasional glances at the young man's distinguished face, noting with pleasure the long, severe scholar's nose, brown eyes heavy with learning, sensitive yet ascetic lips, and a certain, almost hollow quality of the dark cheeks. He gazed around at shelves upon shelves of books and let out a soft, contented sigh.

When Leo's eyes fell upon the cards, he counted six spread out in Salzman's hand.

"So few?" he asked in disappointment.

"You wouldn't believe me how much cards I got in my office," Salzman replied. "The drawers are already filled to the top, so I keep them now in a barrel, but is every girl good for a new rabbi?"

Leo blushed at this, regretting all he had revealed of himself in a curriculum vitae he had sent to Salzman. He had thought it best to acquaint him with his strict standards and specifications, but in having done so, felt he had told the marriage broker more than was absolutely necessary.

He hesitantly inquired, "Do you keep photographs of your clients on file?"

"First comes family, amount of dowry, also what kind promises," Salzman replied, unbuttoning his tight coat and settling himself in the chair. "After comes pictures, rabbi."

"Call me Mr. Finkle. I'm not yet a rabbi."

Salzman said he would, but instead called him doctor, which he changed to rabbi when Leo was not listening too attentively.

Salzman adjusted his horn-rimmed spectacles, gently cleared his throat and read in an eager voice the contents of the top card:

"Sophie P. Twenty-four years. Widow one year. No children. Educated high school and two years college. Father promises eight thousand dollars. Has wonderful wholesale business. Also real estate. On the mother's side comes teachers, also one actor. Well known on Second Avenue."

Leo gazed up in surprise. "Did you say a widow?"

"A widow don't mean spoiled, rabbi. She lived with her husband maybe four months. He was a sick boy she made a mistake to marry him."

"Marrying a widow has never entered my mind."

"This is because you have no experience. A widow, especially if she is young and healthy like this girl, is a wonderful person to marry. She will be thankful to you the rest of her life. Believe me, if I was looking now for a bride, I would marry a widow."

Leo reflected, then shook his head.

Salzman hunched his shoulders in an almost imperceptible gesture of disappointment. He placed the card down on the wooden table and began to read another:

"Lily H. High school teacher. Regular. Not a substitute. Has savings and new Dodge car. Lived in Paris one year. Father is successful dentist thirty-five years. Interested in professional man. Well Americanized family. Wonderful opportunity.

"I knew her personally," said Salzman. "I wish you could see this girl. She is a doll. Also very intelligent. All day you could talk to her about books and theyater and what not. She also knows current events."

"I don't believe you mentioned her age?"

"Her age?" Salzman said, raising his brows. "Her age is thirty-two years."

Leo said after a while, "I'm afraid that seems a little too old."

Salzman let out a laugh. "So how old are you, rabbi?"

"Twenty-seven."

"So what is the difference, tell me, between twenty-seven and thirty-two? My own wife is seven years older than me. So what did I suffer?—Nothing. If Rothschild's a daughter wants to marry you, would you say on account her age, no?"

"Yes," Leo said dryly.

Salzman shook off the no in the yes. "Five years don't mean a thing. I give you my word that when you will live with her for one week you will forget her age. What does it mean five years—that she lived more and knows more than somebody who is younger? On this girl, God bless her, years are not wasted. Each one that it comes makes better the bargain."

"What subject does she teach in high school?"

"Languages. If you heard the way she speaks French, you will think it is music. I am in the business twenty-five years, and I recommend her with my whole heart. Believe me, I know what I'm talking, rabbi."

"What's on the next card?" Leo said abruptly.

Salzman reluctantly turned up the third card:

"Ruth K. Nineteen years. Honor student. Father offers thirteen thousand cash to the right bridegroom. He is a medical doctor. Stomach specialist with marvelous practice. Brother-in-law owns own garment business. Particular people."

Salzman looked as if he had read his trump card.

"Did you say nineteen?" Leo asked with interest.

"On the dot."

"Is she attractive?" He blushed. "Pretty?"

Salzman kissed his finger tips. "A little doll. On this I give you my word. Let me call the father tonight and you will see what means pretty."

But Leo was troubled. "You're sure she's that young?"

"This I am positive. The father will show you the birth certificate."

"Are you positive there isn't something wrong with her?" Leo insisted.

"Who says there is wrong?"

"I don't understand why an American girl her age should go to a marriage broker."

A smile spread over Salzman's face.

"So for the same reason you went, she comes."

Leo flushed. "I am pressed for time."

Salzman, realizing he had been tactless, quickly explained. "The father came, not her. He wants she should have the best, so he looks around himself. When we will locate the right boy he will introduce him and encourage. This makes a better marriage than if a young girl without experience takes for herself. I don't have to tell you this."

"But don't you think this young girl believes in love?" Leo spoke uneasily.

Salzman was about to guffaw but caught himself and said soberly, "Love comes with the right person, not before."

Leo parted dry lips but did not speak. Noticing that Salzman had snatched a glance at the next card, he cleverly asked, "How is her health?"

"Perfect," Salzman said, breathing with difficulty. "Of course, she is a little lame on her right foot from an auto accident that it happened to her when she was twelve years, but nobody notices on account she is so brilliant and also beautiful."

Leo got up heavily and went to the window. He felt curiously bitter and upbraided himself for having called in the marriage broker. Finally, he shook his head.

"Why not?" Salzman persisted, the pitch of his voice rising.

"Because I detest stomach specialists."

"So what do you care what is his business? After you marry her do you need him? Who says he must come every Friday night in your house?"

Ashamed of the way the talk was going, Leo dismissed Salzman, who went home with heavy, melancholy eyes.

Though he had felt only relief at the marriage broker's

418   *Bernard Malamud*

departure, Leo was in low spirits the next day. He explained it as arising from Salzman's failure to produce a suitable bride for him. He did not care for his type of clientele. But when Leo found himself hesitating whether to seek out another matchmaker, one more polished than Pinye, he wondered if it could be—his protestations to the contrary, and although he honored his father and mother—that he did not, in essence, care for the matchmaking institution? This thought he quickly put out of mind yet found himself still upset. All day he ran around in the woods—missed an important appointment, forgot to give out his laundry, walked out of a Broadway cafeteria without paying and had to run back with the ticket in his hand; had even not recognized his landlady in the street when she passed with a friend and courteously called out, "A good evening to you, Doctor Finkle." By nightfall, however, he had regained sufficient calm to sink his nose into a book and there found peace from his thoughts.

Almost at once there came a knock on the door. Before Leo could say enter, Salzman, commercial cupid, was standing in the room. His face was gray and meager, his expression hungry, and he looked as if he would expire on his feet. Yet the marriage broker managed, by some trick of the muscles, to display a broad smile.

"So good evening. I am invited?"

Leo nodded, disturbed to see him again, yet unwilling to ask the man to leave.

Beaming still, Salzman laid his portfolio on the table. "Rabbi, I got for you tonight good news."

"I've asked you not to call me rabbi. I'm still a student."

"Your worries are finished. I have for you a first-class bride."

"Leave me in peace concerning this subject." Leo pretended lack of interest.

"The world will dance at your wedding."

"Please, Mr. Salzman, no more."

"But first must come back my strength," Salzman said weakly. He fumbled with the portfolio straps and took out of the leather case an oily paper bag, from which he extracted a hard, seeded roll and a small, smoked whitefish. With a quick motion of his hand he stripped the fish out of its skin and began ravenously to chew. "All day in a rush," he muttered.

Leo watched him eat.

"A sliced tomato you have maybe?" Salzman hesitantly inquired.

"No."

The marriage broker shut his eyes and ate. When he had finished he carefully cleaned up the crumbs and rolled up the remains of the fish, in the paper bag. His spectacled eyes roamed the room until he discovered, amid some piles of books, a one-burner gas stove. Lifting his hat he humbly asked, "A glass tea you got, rabbi?"

Conscience-stricken, Leo rose and brewed the tea. He served it with a chunk of lemon and two cubes of lump sugar, delighting Salzman.

After he had drunk his tea, Salzman's strength and good spirits were restored.

"So tell me, rabbi," he said amiably, "you considered some more the three clients I mentioned yesterday?"

"There was no need to consider."

"Why not?"

"None of them suits me."

"What then suits you?"

Leo let it pass because he could give only a confused answer.

Without waiting for a reply, Salzman asked, "You remember this girl I talked to you—the high school teacher?"

"Age thirty-two?"

But, surprisingly, Salzman's face lit in a smile. "Age twenty-nine."

Leo shot him a look. "Reduced from thirty-two?"

"A mistake," Salzman avowed. "I talked today with the dentist. He took me to his safety deposit box and showed me the birth certificate. She was twenty-nine years last August. They made her a party in the mountains where she went for her vacation. When her father spoke to me the first time I forgot to write the age and I told you thirty-two, but now I remember this was a different client, a widow."

"The same one you told me about? I thought she was twenty-four?"

"A different. Am I responsible that the world is filled with widows?"

"No, but I'm not interested in them, nor for that matter, in school teachers."

Salzman pulled his clasped hands to his breast. Looking at the ceiling he devoutly exclaimed, "Yiddishe kinder, what can I say to somebody that he is not interested in high school teachers? So what then you are interested?"

Leo flushed but controlled himself.

"In what else will you be interested," Salzman went on,

"if you not interested in this fine girl that she speaks four languages and has personally in the bank ten thousand dollars? Also her father guarantees further twelve thousand. Also she has a new car, wonderful clothes, talks on all subjects, and she will give you a first-class home and children. How near do we come in our life to paradise?"

"If she's so wonderful, why wasn't she married ten years ago?"

"Why?" said Salzman with a heavy laugh. "—Why? Because she is *partikiler*. This is why. She wants the *best*."

Leo was silent, amused at how he had entangled himself. But Salzman had aroused his interest in Lily H., and he began seriously to consider calling on her. When the marriage broker observed how intently Leo's mind was at work on the facts he had supplied, he felt certain they would soon come to an agreement.

Late Saturday afternoon, conscious of Salzman, Leo Finkle walked with Lily Hirschorn along Riverside Drive. He walked briskly and erectly, wearing with distinction the black fedora he had that morning taken with trepidation out of the dusty hat box on his closet shelf, and the heavy black Saturday coat he had thoroughly whisked clean. Leo also owned a walking stick, a present from a distant relative, but quickly put temptation aside and did not use it. Lily, petite and not unpretty, had on something signifying the approach of spring. She was au courant, animatedly, with all sorts of subjects, and he weighed her words and found her surprisingly sound—score another for Salzman, whom he uneasily sensed to be somewhere around, hiding perhaps high in a tree along the street, flashing the lady signals with a pocket mirror; or perhaps a cloven-hoofed Pan, piping nuptial ditties as he danced his invisible way before them, strewing wild buds on the walk and purple grapes in their path, symbolizing fruit of a union, though there was of course still none.

Lily startled Leo by remarking, "I was thinking of Mr. Salzman, a curious figure, wouldn't you say?"

Not certain what to answer, he nodded.

She bravely went on, blushing, "I for one am grateful for his introducing us. Aren't you?"

He courteously replied, "I am."

"I mean," she said with a little laugh—and it was all in good taste, or at least gave the effect of being not in bad—"do you mind that we came together so?"

He was not displeased with her honesty, recognizing that

she meant to set the relationship aright, and understanding that it took a certain amount of experience in life, and courage, to want to do it quite that way. One had to have some sort of past to make that kind of beginning.

He said that he did not mind. Salzman's function was traditional and honorable—valuable for what it might achieve, which, he pointed out, was frequently nothing.

Lily agreed with a sigh. They walked on for a while and she said after a long silence, again with a nervous laugh, "Would you mind if I asked you something a little bit personal? Frankly, I find the subject fascinating." Although Leo shrugged, she went on half embarrassedly, "How was it that you came to your calling? I mean was it a sudden passionate inspiration?"

Leo, after a time, slowly replied, "I was always interested in the Law."

"You saw revealed in it the presence of the Highest?"

He nodded and changed the subject. "I understand that you spent a little time in Paris, Miss Hirschorn?"

"Oh, did Mr. Salzman tell you, Rabbi Finkle?" Leo winced but she went on, "It was ages ago and almost forgotten. I remember I had to return for my sister's wedding."

And Lily would not be put off. "When," she asked in a trembly voice, "did you become enamored of God?"

He stared at her. Then it came to him that she was talking not about Leo Finkle, but of a total stranger, some mystical figure, perhaps even passionate prophet that Salzman had dreamed up for her—no relation to the living or dead. Leo trembled with rage and weakness. The trickster had obviously sold her a bill of goods, just as he had him, who'd expected to become acquainted with a young lady of twenty-nine, only to behold, the moment he laid eyes upon her strained and anxious face, a woman past thirty-five and aging rapidly. Only his self-control had kept him this long in her presence.

"I am not," he said gravely, "a talented religious person," and in seeking words to go on, found himself possessed by shame and fear. "I think," he said in a strained manner, "that I came to God not because I loved Him, but because I did not."

This confession he spoke harshly because its unexpectedness shook him.

Lily wilted. Leo saw a profusion of loaves of bread go flying like ducks high over his head, not unlike the winged loaves by which he had counted himself to sleep last night.

Mercifully, then, it snowed, which he would not put past Salzman's machinations.

He was infuriated with the marriage broker and swore he would throw him out of the room the minute he reappeared. But Salzman did not come that night, and when Leo's anger had subsided, an unaccountable despair grew in its place. At first he thought this was caused by his disappointment in Lily, but before long it became evident that he had involved himself with Salzman without a true knowledge of his own intent. He gradually realized—with an emptiness that seized him with six hands—that he had called in the broker to find him a bride because he was incapable of doing it himself. This terrifying insight he had derived as a result of his meeting and conversation with Lily Hirschorn. Her probing questions had somehow irritated him into revealing—to himself more than her—the true nature of his relationship to God, and from that it had come upon him, with shocking force, that apart from his parents, he had never loved anyone. Or perhaps it went the other way, that he did not love God so well as he might, because he had not loved man. It seemed to Leo that his whole life stood starkly revealed and he saw himself for the first time as he truly was—unloved and loveless. This bitter but somehow not fully unexpected revelation brought him to a point of panic, controlled only by extraordinary effort. He covered his face with his hands and cried.

The week that followed was the worst of his life. He did not eat and lost weight. His beard darkened and grew ragged. He stopped attending seminars and almost never opened a book. He seriously considered leaving the Yeshivah, although he was deeply troubled at the thought of the loss of all his years of study—saw them like pages torn from a book, strewn over the city—and at the devastating effect of this decision upon his parents. But he had lived without knowledge of himself, and never in the Five Books and all the Commentaries—mea culpa—had the truth been revealed to him. He did not know where to turn, and in all this desolating loneliness there was no *to whom,* although he often thought of Lily but not once could bring himself to go downstairs and make the call. He became touchy and irritable, especially with his landlady, who asked him all manner of personal questions; on the other hand, sensing his own disagreeableness, he waylaid her on the stairs and apologized abjectly, until mortified, she ran from him. Out of this, however, he drew the consolation that he was a Jew and that a Jew suffered. But gradually, as the long and terrible week drew to a close, he regained his composure and some idea of purpose in life: to go on as planned. Although he was imperfect, the ideal was not. As for his quest of a bride, the thought of continuing afflicted him with anxiety and heartburn, yet perhaps with this new knowledge of himself he would be more successful than in the past. Perhaps love would now come to him and a bride to that love. And for this sanctified seeking who needed a Salzman?

The marriage broker, a skeleton with haunted eyes, returned that very night. He looked, withal, the picture of frustrated expectancy—as if he had steadfastly waited the week at Miss Lily Hirschorn's side for a telephone call that never came.

Casually coughing, Salzman came immediately to the point: "So how did you like her?"

Leo's anger rose and he could not refrain from chiding the matchmaker: "Why did you lie to me, Salzman?"

Salzman's pale face went dead white, the world had snowed on him.

"Did you not state that she was twenty-nine?" Leo insisted.

"I give you my word—"

"She was thirty-five, if a day. *At least* thirty-five."

"Of this don't be too sure. Her father told me—"

"Never mind. The worst of it was that you lied to her."

"How did I lie to her, tell me?"

"You told her things about me that weren't true. You made me out to be more, consequently less than I am. She had in mind a totally different person, a sort of semi-mystical Wonder Rabbi."

"All I said, you was a religious man."

"I can imagine."

Salzman sighed. "This is my weakness that I have," he confessed. "My wife says to me I shouldn't be a salesman, but when I have two fine people that they would be wonderful to be married, I am so happy that I talk too much." He smiled wanly. "This is why Salzman is a poor man."

Leo's anger left him. "Well, Salzman, I'm afraid that's all."

The marriage broker fastened hungry eyes on him.

"You don't want any more a bride?"

"I do," said Leo, "but I have decided to seek her in a

different way. I am no longer interested in an arranged marriage. To be frank, I now admit the necessity of pre-marital love. That is, I want to be in love with the one I marry."

"Love?" said Salzman, astounded. After a moment he remarked, "For us, our love is our life, not for the ladies. In the ghetto they—"

"I know, I know," said Leo. "I've thought of it often. Love, I have said to myself, should be a by-product of living and worship rather than its own end. Yet for my-self I find it necessary to establish the level of my need and fulfill it."

Salzman shrugged but answered, "Listen, rabbi, if you want love, this I can find for you also. I have such beauti-ful clients that you will love them the minute your eyes will see them."

Leo smiled unhappily. "I'm afraid you don't under-stand."

But Salzman hastily unstrapped his portfolio and with-drew a manila packet from it.

"Pictures," he said, quickly laying the envelope on the table.

Leo called after him to take the pictures away, but as if on the wings of the wind, Salzman had disappeared.

March came. Leo had returned to his regular routine. Although he felt not quite himself yet—lacked energy—he was making plans for a more active social life. Of course it would cost something, but he was an expert in cutting corners; and when there were no corners left he would make circles rounder. All the while Salzman's pic-tures had lain on the table, gathering dust. Occasionally as Leo sat studying, or enjoying a cup of tea, his eyes fell on the manila envelope, but he never opened it.

The days went by and no social life to speak of de-veloped with a member of the opposite sex—it was difficult, given the circumstances of his situation. One morning Leo toiled up the stairs to his room and stared out the window at the city. Although the day was bright his view of it was dark. For some time he watched the people in the street below hurrying along and then turned with a heavy heart to his little room. On the table was the packet. With a sudden relentless gesture he tore it open. For a half-hour he stood by the table in a state of excitement, examining the photographs of the ladies Salzman had included. Finally, with a deep sigh he put them down. There were six, of varying degrees of attractiveness, but look at them long enough and they all became Lily Hirschorn: all past their prime, all starved behind bright smiles, not a true personality in the lot. Life, despite their frantic yoohoo-ings, had passed them by; they were pictures in a brief case that stank of fish. After a while, however, as Leo attempted to return the photographs into the envelope, he found in it another, a snapshot of the type taken by a machine for a quarter. He gazed at it a moment and let out a cry.

Her face deeply moved him. Why, he could at first not say. It gave him the impression of youth—spring flowers, yet age—a sense of having been used to the bone, wasted; this came from the eyes, which were hauntingly familiar, yet absolutely strange. He had a vivid impression that he had met her before, but try as he might he could not place her although he could almost recall her name, as if he had read it in her own handwriting. No, this couldn't be; he would have remembered her. It was not, he affirmed, that she had an extraordinary beauty—no, though her face was attractive enough; it was that *something* about her moved him. Feature for feature, even some of the ladies of the photographs could do better; but she leaped forth to his heart—had *lived,* or wanted to—more than just wanted, perhaps regretted how she had lived—had some-how deeply suffered: it could be seen in the depths of those reluctant eyes, and from the way the light enclosed and shone from her, and within her, opening realms of possibility: this was her own. Her he desired. His head ached and eyes narrowed with the intensity of his gazing, then as if an obscure fog had blown up in the mind, he experienced fear of her and was aware that he had re-ceived an impression, somehow, of evil. He shuddered, saying softly, it is thus with us all. Leo brewed some tea in a small pot and sat sipping it without sugar, to calm himself. But before he had finished drinking, again with excitement he examined the face and found it good: good for Leo Finkle. Only such a one could understand him and help him seek whatever he was seeking. She might, perhaps, love him. How she had happened to be among the discards in Salzman's barrel he could never guess, but he knew he must urgently go find her.

Leo rushed downstairs, grabbed up the Bronx telephone book and searched for Salzman's home address. He was not listed, nor was his office. Neither was he in the Man-hattan book. But Leo remembered having written down the address on a slip of paper after he had read Salzman's

advertisement in the "personals" column of the *Forward*.
He ran up to his room and tore through his papers, without luck. It was exasperating. Just when he needed the
matchmaker he was nowhere to be found. Fortunately Leo
remembered to look in his wallet. There on a card he
found his name written and a Bronx address. No phone
number was listed, the reason—Leo now recalled—he had
originally communicated with Salzman by letter. He got
on his coat, put a hat on over his skull cap and hurried to
the subway station. All the way to the far end of the
Bronx he sat on the edge of his seat. He was more than
once tempted to take out the picture and see if the girl's
face was as he remembered it, but he refrained, allowing
the snapshot to remain in his inside coat pocket, content
to have her so close. When the train pulled into the station he was waiting at the door and bolted out. He quickly
located the street Salzman had advertised.

The building he sought was less than a block from the
subway, but it was not an office building, nor even a loft,
nor a store in which one could rent office space. It was a
very old tenement house. Leo found Salzman's name in
pencil on a soiled tag under the bell and climbed three
dark flights to his apartment. When he knocked, the door
was opened by a thin, asthmatic, gray-haired woman, in
felt slippers.

"Yes?" she said, expecting nothing. She listened without listening. He could have sworn he had seen her, too,
before but knew it was an illusion.

"Salzman—does he live here? Pinye Salzman," he said,
"the matchmaker?"

She stared at him a long minute. "Of course."

He felt embarrassed. "Is he in?"

"No." Her mouth, though left open, offered nothing
more.

"The matter is urgent. Can you tell me where his office
is?"

"In the air." She pointed upward.

"You mean he has no office?" Leo asked.

"In his socks."

He peered into the apartment. It was sunless and dingy,
one large room divided by a half-open curtain, beyond
which he could see a sagging metal bed. The near side of
the room was crowded with rickety chairs, old bureaus, a
three-legged table, racks of cooking utensils, and all the
apparatus of a kitchen. But there was no sign of Salzman

or his magic barrel, probably also a figment of the imagination. An odor of frying fish made Leo weak to the knees.

"Where is he?" he insisted. "I've got to see your husband."

At length she answered, "So who knows where he is? Every time he thinks a new thought he runs to a different place. Go home, he will find you."

"Tell him Leo Finkle."

She gave no sign she had heard.

He walked downstairs, depressed.

But Salzman, breathless, stood waiting at his door.

Leo was astounded and overjoyed. "How did you get here before me?"

"I rushed."

"Come inside."

They entered. Leo fixed tea, and a sardine sandwich for Salzman. As they were drinking he reached behind him for the packet of pictures and handed them to the marriage broker.

Salzman put down his glass and said expectantly, "You found somebody you like?"

"Not among these."

The marriage broker turned away.

"Here is the one I want." Leo held forth the snapshot.

Salzman slipped on his glasses and took the picture into his trembling hand. He turned ghastly and let out a groan.

"What's the matter?" cried Leo.

"Excuse me. Was an accident this picture. She isn't for you."

Salzman frantically shoved the manila packet into his portfolio. He thrust the snapshot into his pocket and fled down the stairs.

Leo, after momentary paralysis, gave chase and cornered the marriage broker in the vestibule. The landlady made hysterical outcries but neither of them listened.

"Give me back the picture, Salzman."

"No." The pain in his eyes was terrible.

"Tell me who she is then."

"This I can't tell you. Excuse me."

He made to depart, but Leo, forgetting himself, seized the matchmaker by his tight coat and shook him frenziedly.

"Please," sighed Salzman. *"Please."*

Leo ashamedly let him go. "Tell me who she is," he begged. "It's very important for me to know."

"She is not for you. She is a wild one—wild, without shame. This is not a bride for a rabbi."

"What do you mean wild?"

"Like an animal. Like a dog. For her to be poor was a sin. This is why to me she is dead now."

"In God's name, what do you mean?"

"Her I can't introduce to you," Salzman cried.

"Why are you so excited?"

"Why, he asks," Salzman said, bursting into tears. "This is my baby, my Stella, she should burn in hell."

Leo hurried up to bed and hid under the covers. Under the covers he thought his life through. Although he soon fell asleep he could not sleep her out of his mind. He woke, beating his breast. Though he prayed to be rid of her, his prayers went unanswered. Through days of torment he endlessly struggled not to love her; fearing success, he escaped it. He then concluded to convert her to goodness, himself to God. The idea alternately nauseated and exalted him.

He perhaps did not know that he had come to a final decision until he encountered Salzman in a Broadway cafeteria. He was sitting alone at a rear table, sucking the bony remains of a fish. The marriage broker appeared haggard, and transparent to the point of vanishing.

Salzman looked up at first without recognizing him. Leo had grown a pointed beard and his eyes were weighted with wisdom.

"Salzman," he said, "love has at last come to my heart."

"Who can love from a picture?" mocked the marriage broker.

"It is not impossible."

"If you can love her, then you can love anybody. Let me show you some new clients that they just sent me their photographs. One is a little doll."

"Just her I want," Leo murmured.

"Don't be a fool, doctor. Don't bother with her."

"Put me in touch with her, Salzman," Leo said humbly. "Perhaps I can be of service."

Salzman had stopped eating and Leo understood with emotion that it was now arranged.

Leaving the cafeteria, he was, however, afflicted by a tormenting suspicion that Salzman had planned it all to happen this way.

Leo was informed by letter that she would meet him on a certain corner, and she was there one spring night, waiting under a street lamp. He appeared, carrying a small bouquet of violets and rosebuds. Stella stood by the lamp post, smoking. She wore white with red shoes, which fitted his expectations, although in a troubled moment he had imagined the dress red, and only the shoes white. She waited uneasily and shyly. From afar he saw that her eyes—clearly her father's—were filled with desperate innocence. He pictured, in her, his own redemption. Violins and lit candles revolved in the sky. Leo ran forward with flowers outthrust.

Around the corner, Salzman, leaning against a wall, chanted prayers for the dead.

Isaac Bashevis Singer

(1904–   )

*Son and grandson of rabbis and brother of the great
Yiddish realistic novelist, I. J. Singer, Isaac Bashevis
Singer was born in Poland and lived there until 1935,
when his first novel, Satan in Goray, was published and
when he himself emigrated to the United States. Singer
began his writing career as a journalist for the Yiddish
press, with which he is still actively involved. A prominent translator, he has translated Thomas Mann's The
Magic Mountain into Yiddish. Singer has supervised the
translation of his own work into English by working
very closely with his translators. He is the one contemporary Yiddish writer who has had considerable influence on American writers.*

*Singer's appeal as a writer can be attributed, in large
measure, to his uniquely imaginative blend of Jewish
folklore and mysticism with modern psychological skepticism. One of the major Yiddish stylists, he seems as
much at home in the world of Hassidic mysticism as in
Freudian psychology. Few other contemporary writers
have been more successful in evoking the mood and
atmosphere of the supernatural. His creation of a miniature of contemporary life out of the world of the Eastern
European Jew explains why his work became so popular
during America's troubled 1960s.*

*"Gimpel the Fool," Singer's best-known story, is char-
acteristic of much of his work. Mixing rich folk comedy
with vivid insights into the tragic nature of existence, it
continues to exert a powerful hold over its readers. The
sainted fool is among the favorite themes of folklore
and literature, but here, in Gimpel, Singer transcends the
usual limitations of folklore to fashion a story in which
the individual's right to his illusions is viewed in terms
of society's inability to see itself as it really is. From
his inner world, Gimpel emerges with far greater dignity than any of his tormentors. In his ability to love and
his capacity to forgive those who have betrayed him
he achieves a near sublimity. His comic acceptance of
his fate makes him irresistibly, unforgettably human.*

430

Gimpel the Fool

I

I am Gimpel the fool. I don't think myself a fool. On the contrary. But that's what folks call me. They gave me the name while I was still in school. I had seven names in all: imbecile, donkey, flax-head, dope, glump, ninny, and fool. The last name stuck. What did my foolishness consist of? I was easy to take in. They said, "Gimpel, you know the rabbi's wife has been brought to childbed?" So I skipped school. Well, it turned out to be a lie. How was I supposed to know? She hadn't had a big belly. But I never looked at her belly. Was that really so foolish? The gang laughed and hee-hawed, stomped and danced and chanted a good-night prayer. And instead of the raisins they give when a woman's lying in, they stuffed my hand full of goat turds. I was no weakling. If I slapped someone he'd see all the way to Cracow. But I'm really not a slugger by nature. I think to myself: Let it pass. So they take advantage of me.

I was coming home from school and heard a dog barking. I'm not afraid of dogs, but of course I never want to start up with them. One of them may be mad, and if he bites there's not a Tartar in the world who can help you. So I made tracks. Then I looked around and saw the whole market place wild with laughter. It was no dog at all but Wolf-Lieb the Thief. How was I supposed to know it was he? It sounded like a howling bitch.

When the pranksters and leg-pullers found that I was easy to fool, every one of them tried his luck with me. "Gimpel, the Czar is coming to Frampol; Gimpel, the moon fell down in Turbeen; Gimpel, little Hodel Furpiece found a treasure behind the bathhouse." And I like a golem believed everyone. In the first place, everything is possible, as it is written in the Wisdom of the Fathers, I've forgotten just how. Second, I had to believe when the whole town came down on me! If I ever dared to say, "Ah, you're kidding!" there was trouble. People got an-

gry. "What do you mean! You want to call everyone a
liar?" What was I to do? I believed them, and I hope at
least that did them some good.

I was an orphan. My grandfather who brought me up
was already bent toward the grave. So they turned me
over to a baker, and what a time they gave me there!
Every woman or girl who came to bake a batch of noo-
dles had to fool me at least once. "Gimpel, there's a fair
in heaven; Gimpel, the rabbi gave birth to a calf in the
seventh month; Gimpel, a cow flew over the roof and
laid brass eggs." A student from the yeshiva came once
to buy a roll, and he said, "You, Gimpel, while you stand
here scraping with your baker's shovel the Messiah has
come. The dead have arisen." "Want do you mean?" I
said. "I heard no one blowing the ram's horn!" He said,
"Are you deaf?" And all began to cry, "We heard it, we
heard!" Then in came Rietze the Candle-dipper and called
out in her hoarse voice, "Gimpel, your father and mother
have stood up from the grave. They're looking for you."

To tell the truth, I knew very well that nothing of the
sort had happened, but all the same, as folks were talking,
I threw on my wool vest and went out. Maybe something
had happened. What did I stand to lose by looking? Well,
what a cat music went up! And then I took a vow to
believe nothing more. But that was no go either. They
confused me so that I didn't know the big end from the
small.

I went to the rabbi to get some advice. He said, "It is
written, better to be a fool all your days than for one
hour to be evil. You are not a fool. They are the fools.
For he who causes his neighbor to feel shame loses Paradise himself." Nevertheless the rabbi's daughter took me
in. As I left the rabbinical court she said, "Have you
kissed the wall yet?" I said, "No; what for?" She answered, "It's the law; you've got to do it after every visit."
Well, there didn't seem to be any harm in it. And she
burst out laughing. It was a fine trick. She put one over
on me, all right.

I wanted to go off to another town, but then everyone
got busy matchmaking, and they were after me so they
nearly tore my coat tails off. They talked at me and
talked until I got water on the ear. She was no chaste
maiden, but they told me she was virgin pure. She had a
limp, and they said it was deliberate, from coyness. She
had a bastard, and they told me the child was her little
brother. I cried, "You're wasting your time. I'll never

marry that whore." But they said indignantly, "What a
way to talk! Aren't you ashamed of yourself? We can
take you to the rabbi and have you fined for giving her a
bad name." I saw then that I wouldn't escape them so
easily and I thought: They're set on making me their butt.
But when you're married the husband's the master, and
if that's all right with her it's agreeable to me too. Besides, you can't pass through life unscathed, nor expect
to.

I went to her clay house, which was built on the sand,
and the whole gang, hollering and chorusing, came after
me. They acted like bear-baiters. When we came to the
well they stopped all the same. They were afraid to start
anything with Elka. Her mouth would open as if it were
on a hinge, and she had a fierce tongue. I entered the
house. Lines were strung from wall to wall and clothes
were drying. Barefoot she stood by the tub, doing the
wash. She was dressed in a worn hand-me-down gown of
plush. She had her hair put up in braids and pinned across
her head. It took my breath away, almost, the reek of it
all.

Evidently she knew who I was. She took a look at me
and said, "Look who's here! He's come, the drip. Grab a
seat."

I told her all; I denied nothing. "Tell me the truth,"
I said, "are you really a virgin, and is that mischievous
Yechiel actually your little brother? Don't be deceitful
with me, for I'm an orphan."

"I'm an orphan myself," she answered, "and whoever
tries to twist you up, may the end of his nose take a twist.
But don't let them think they can take advantage of me.
I want a dowry of fifty guilders, and let them take up
a collection besides. Otherwise they can kiss my you-
know-what." She was very plainspoken. I said, "It's the
bride and not the groom who gives a dowry." Then she
said, "Don't bargain with me. Either a flat 'yes' or a flat
'no'—Go back where you came from."

I thought: No bread will ever be baked from *this*
dough. But ours is not a poor town. They consented to
everything and proceeded with the wedding. It so happened that there was a dysentery epidemic at the time.
The ceremony was held at the cemetery gates, near the
little corpse-washing hut. The fellows got drunk. While
the marriage contract was being drawn up I heard the
most pious high rabbi ask, "Is the bride a widow or a
divorced woman?" And the sexton's wife answered for

her, "Both a widow and divorced." It was a black moment for me. But what was I to do, run away from under the marriage canopy?

There was singing and dancing. An old granny danced opposite me, hugging a braided white *chalah*. The master of revels made a "God 'a mercy" in memory of the bride's parents. The schoolboys threw burrs, as on Tishe b'Av fast day. There were a lot of gifts after the sermon: a noodle board, a kneading trough, a bucket, brooms, ladles, household articles galore. Then I took a look and saw two strapping young men carrying a crib. "What do we need this for?" I asked. So they said, "Don't rack your brains about it. It's all right, it'll come in handy." I realized I was going to be rooked. Take it another way though, what did I stand to lose? I reflected: I'll see what comes of it. A whole town can't go altogether crazy.

II

At night I came where my wife lay, but she wouldn't let me in. "Say, look here, is this what they married us for?" I said. And she said, "My monthly has come." "But yesterday they took you to the ritual bath, and that's afterward, isn't it supposed to be?" "Today isn't yesterday," said she, "and yesterday's not today. You can beat it if you don't like it." In short, I waited.

Not four months later she was in childbed. The townsfolk hid their laughter with their knuckles. But what could I do? She suffered intolerable pains and clawed at the walls. "Gimpel," she cried, "I'm going. Forgive me!" The house filled with women. They were boiling pans of water. The screams rose to the welkin.

The thing to do was to go to the House of Prayer to repeat Psalms, and that was what I did.

The townsfolk liked that, all right. I stood in a corner saying Psalms and prayers, and they shook their heads at me. "Pray, pray!" they told me. "Prayer never made any woman pregnant." One of the congregation put a straw to my mouth and said, "Hay for the cows." There was something to that too, by God!

She gave birth to a boy. Friday at the synagogue the sexton stood up before the Ark, pounded on the reading table, and announced, "The wealthy Reb Gimpel invites

the congregation to a feast in honor of the birth of a
son." The whole House of Prayer rang with laughter. My
face was flaming. But there was nothing I could do. After all, I *was* the one responsible for the circumcision
honors and rituals.

Half the town came running. You couldn't wedge another soul in. Women brought peppered chick-peas, and
there was a keg of beer from the tavern. I ate and drank
as much as anyone, and they all congratulated me. Then
there was a circumcision, and I named the boy after my
father, may he rest in peace. When all were gone and
I was left with my wife alone, she thrust her head through
the bed-curtain and called me to her.

"Gimpel," said she, "why are you silent? Has your ship
gone and sunk?"

"What shall I say?" I answered. "A fine thing you've
done to me! If my mother had known of it she'd have
died a second time."

She said, "Are you crazy, or what?"

"How can you make such a fool," I said, "of one who
should be the lord and master?"

"What's the matter with you?" she said. "What have
you taken it into your head to imagine?"

I saw that I must speak bluntly and openly. "Do you
think this is the way to use an orphan?" I said. "You
have borne a bastard."

She answered, "Drive this foolishness out of your head.
The child is yours."

"How can he be mine?" I argued. "He was born seventeen weeks after the wedding."

She told me then that he was premature. I said, "Isn't
he a little too premature?" She said she had had a grandmother who carried just as short a time and she resembled
this grandmother of hers as one drop of water does another. She swore to it with such oaths that you would
have believed a peasant at the fair if he had used them.
To tell the plain truth, I didn't believe her; but when I
talked it over next day with the schoolmaster he told me
that the very same thing had happened to Adam and
Eve. Two they went up to bed, and four they descended.

"There isn't a woman in the world who is not the
granddaughter of Eve," he said.

That was how it was; they argued me dumb. But then,
who really knows how such things are?

I began to forget my sorrow. I loved the child madly,
and he loved me too. As soon as he saw me he'd wave

his little hands and want me to pick him up, and when
he was colicky I was the only one who could pacify him.
I bought him a little bone teething ring and a little gilded
cap. He was forever catching the evil eye from someone,
and then I had to run to get one of those abracadabras
for him that would get him out of it. I worked like an
ox. You know how expenses go up when there's an infant
in the house. I don't want to lie about it; I didn't dislike
Elka either, for that matter. She swore at me and cursed,
and I couldn't get enough of her. What strength she had!
One of her looks could rob you of the power of speech.
And her orations! Pitch and sulphur, that's what they
were full of, and yet somehow also full of charm. I adored
her every word. She gave me bloody wounds though.

In the evening I brought her a white loaf as well as
a dark one, and also poppyseed rolls I baked myself. I
thieved because of her and swiped everything I could
lay hands on: macaroons, raisins, almonds, cakes. I hope
I may be forgiven for stealing from the Saturday pots
the women left to warm in the baker's oven. I would
take out scraps of meat, a chunk of pudding, a chicken
leg or head, a piece of tripe, whatever I could nip quickly. She ate and became fat and handsome.

I had to sleep away from home all during the week,
at the bakery. On Friday nights when I got home she always made an excuse of some sort. Either she had heartburn, or a stitch in the side, or hiccups, or headaches.
You know what women's excuses are. I had a bitter time
of it. It was rough. To add to it, this little brother of
hers, the bastard, was growing bigger. He'd put lumps on
me, and when I wanted to hit back she'd open her mouth
and curse so powerfully I saw a green haze floating before my eyes. Ten times a day she threatened to divorce
me. Another man in my place would have taken French
leave and disappeared. But I'm the type that bears it and
says nothing. What's one to do? Shoulders are from God,
and burdens too.

One night there was a calamity in the bakery; the oven
burst, and we almost had a fire. There was nothing to
do but go home, so I went home. Let me, I thought,
also taste the joy of sleeping in bed in mid-week. I didn't
want to wake the sleeping mite and tiptoed into the
house. Coming in, it seemed to me that I heard not the
snoring of one but, as it were, a double snore, one a
thin enough snore and the other like the snoring of a
slaughtered ox. Oh, I didn't like that! I didn't like it at all.

I went up to the bed, and things suddenly turned black.
Next to Elka lay a man's form. Another in my place
would have made an uproar, and enough noise to rouse
the whole town, but the thought occurred to me that
I might wake the child. A little thing like that—why
frighten a little swallow, I thought. All right then, I went
back to the bakery and stretched out on a sack of flour
and till morning I never shut an eye. I shivered as if
I had had malaria. "Enough of being a donkey," I said
to myself. "Gimpel isn't going to be a sucker all his
life. There's a limit even to the foolishness of a fool like
Gimpel."

In the morning I went to the rabbi to get advice, and
it made a great commotion in the town. They sent the
beadle for Elka right away. She came, carrying the child.
And what do you think she did? She denied it, denied
everything, bone and stone! "He's out of his head," she
said. "I know nothing of dreams or divinations." They
yelled at her, warned her, hammered on the table, but
she stuck to her guns: it was a false accusation, she said.

The butchers and the horse-traders took her part. One
of the lads from the slaughterhouse came by and said to
me, "We've got our eye on you, you're a marked man."
Meanwhile the child started to bear down and soiled itself. In the rabbinical court there was an Ark of the
Covenant, and they couldn't allow that, so they sent Elka
away.

I said to the rabbi, "What shall I do?"

"You must divorce her at once," said he.

"And what if she refuses?" I asked.

He said, "You must serve the divorce. That's all you'll
have to do."

I said, "Well, all right, Rabbi. Let me think about it."

"There's nothing to think about," said he. "You mustn't
remain under the same roof with her."

"And if I want to see the child?" I asked.

"Let her go, the harlot," said he, "and her brood of
bastards with her."

The verdict he gave was that I mustn't even cross her
threshold—never again, as long as I should live.

During the day it didn't bother me so much. I
thought: It was bound to happen, the abscess had to
burst. But at night when I stretched out upon the sacks
I felt it all very bitterly. A longing took me, for her and
for the child. I wanted to be angry, but that's my misfortune exactly, I don't have it in me to be really angry.

In the first place—this was how my thoughts went—
there's bound to be a slip sometimes. You can't live without errors. Probably that lad who was with her led her
on and gave her presents and what not, and women are
often long on hair and short on sense, and so he got
around her. And then since she denies it so, maybe I
was only seeing things? Hallucinations do happen. You
see a figure or a mannikin or something, but when you
come up closer it's nothing, there's not a thing there. And
if that's so, I'm doing her an injustice. And when I got
so far in my thoughts I started to weep. I sobbed so that
I wet the flour where I lay. In the morning I went to
the rabbi and told him that I had made a mistake. The
rabbi wrote on with his quill, and he said that if that
were so he would have to reconsider the whole case. Until he had finished I wasn't to go near my wife, but I
might send her bread and money by messenger.

III

Nine months passed before all the rabbis could come to
an agreement. Letters went back and forth. I hadn't realized that there could be so much erudition about a matter
like this.

Meanwhile Elka gave birth to still another child, a girl
this time. On the Sabbath I went to the synagogue and
invoked a blessing on her. They called me up to the
Torah, and I named the child for my mother-in-law—
may she rest in peace. The louts and loudmouths of the
town who came into the bakery gave me a going over.
All Frampol refreshed its spirits because of my trouble
and grief. However, I resolved that I would always believe
what I was told. What's the good of *not* believing? Today
it's your wife you don't believe; tomorrow it's God Himself you won't take stock in.

By an apprentice who was her neighbor I sent her
daily a corn or a wheat loaf, or a piece of pastry, rolls
or bagels, or, when I got the chance, a slab of pudding,
a slice of honeycake, or wedding strudel—whatever came
my way. The apprentice was a goodhearted lad, and more
than once he added something of his own. He had formerly annoyed me a lot, plucking my nose and digging
me in the ribs, but when he started to be a visitor to

my house he became kind and friendly. "Hey, you, Gimpel," he said to me, "you have a very decent little wife and two fine kids. You don't deserve them."

"But the things people say about her," I said.

"Well, they have long tongues," he said, "and nothing to do with them but babble. Ignore it as you ignore the cold of last winter."

One day the rabbi sent for me and said, "Are you certain, Gimpel, that you were wrong about your wife?"

I said, "I'm certain."

"Why, but look here! You yourself saw it."

"It must have been a shadow," I said.

"The shadow of what?"

"Just of one of the beams, I think."

"You can go home then. You owe thanks to the Yanover rabbi. He found an obscure reference in Maimonides that favored you."

I seized the rabbi's hand and kissed it.

I wanted to run home immediately. It's no small thing to be separated for so long a time from wife and child. Then I reflected: I'd better go back to work now, and go home in the evening. I said nothing to anyone, although as far as my heart was concerned it was like one of the Holy Days. The women teased and twitted me as they did every day, but my thought was: Go on, with your loose talk. The truth is out, like the oil upon the water. Maimonides says it's right, and therefore it is right!

At night, when I had covered the dough to let it rise, I took my share of bread and a little sack of flour and started homeward. The moon was full and the stars were glistening, something to terrify the soul. I hurried onward, and before me darted a long shadow. It was winter, and fresh snow had fallen. I had a mind to sing, but it was growing late and I didn't want to wake the householders. Then I felt like whistling, but I remembered that you don't whistle at night because it brings the demons out. So I was silent and walked as fast as I could.

Dogs in the Christian yards barked at me when I passed, but I thought: Bark your teeth out! What are you but mere dogs? Whereas I am a man, the husband of a fine wife, the father of promising children.

As I approached the house my heart started to pound as though it were the heart of a criminal. I felt no fear, but my heart went thump! thump! Well, no drawing back. I quietly lifted the latch and went in. Elka was asleep.

I looked at the infant's cradle. The shutter was closed, but the moon forced its way through the cracks. I saw the newborn child's face and loved it as soon as I saw it —immediately—each tiny bone.

Then I came nearer to the bed. And what did I see but the apprentice lying there beside Elka. The moon went out all at once. It was utterly black, and I trembled. My teeth chattered. The bread fell from my hands, and my wife waked and said, "Who is that, ah?"

I muttered, "It's me."

"Gimpel?" she asked. "How come you're here? I thought it was forbidden."

"The rabbi said," I answered and shook as with a fever.

"Listen to me, Gimpel," she said, "go out to the shed and see if the goat's all right. It seems she's been sick." I have forgotten to say that we had a goat. When I heard she was unwell I went into the yard. The nannygoat was a good little creature. I had a nearly human feeling for her.

With hesitant steps I went up to the shed and opened the door. The goat stood there on her four feet. I felt her everywhere, drew her by the horns, examined her udders and found nothing wrong. She had probably eaten too much bark. "Good night, little goat," I said. "Keep well." And the little beast answered with a "Maa" as though to thank me for the good will.

I went back. The apprentice had vanished.

"Where," I asked, "is the lad?"

"What lad?" my wife answered.

"What do you mean?" I said. "The apprentice. You were sleeping with him."

"The things I have dreamed this night and the night before," she said, "may they come true and lay you low, body and soul! An evil spirit has taken root in you and dazzles your sight." She screamed out, "You hateful creature! You moon calf! You spook! You uncouth man! Get out, or I'll scream all Frampol out of bed!"

Before I could move, her brother sprang out from behind the oven and struck me a blow on the back of the head. I thought he had broken my neck. I felt that something about me was deeply wrong, and I said, "Don't make a scandal. All that's needed now is that people should accuse me of raising spooks and *dybbuks*." For that was what she had meant. "No one will touch bread of my baking."

In short, I somehow calmed her.

"Well," she said, "that's enough. Lie down, and be shattered by wheels."

Next morning I called the apprentice aside. "Listen here, brother!" I said. And so on and so forth. "What do you say?" He stared at me as though I had dropped from the roof or something.

"I swear," he said, "you'd better go to an herb doctor or some healer. I'm afraid you have a screw loose, but I'll hush it up for you." And that's how the thing stood.

To make a long story short, I lived twenty years with my wife. She bore me six children, four daughters and two sons. All kinds of things happened, but I neither saw nor heard. I believed, and that's all. The rabbi recently said to me, "Belief in itself is beneficial. It is written that a good man lives by his faith."

Suddenly my wife took sick. It began with a trifle, a little growth upon the breast. But she evidently was not destined to live long; she had no years. I spent a fortune on her. I have forgotten to say that by this time I had a bakery of my own and in Frampol was considered to be something of a rich man. Daily the healer came, and every witch doctor in the neighborhood was brought. They decided to use leeches, and after that to try cupping. They even called a doctor from Lublin, but it was too late. Before she died she called me to her bed and said, "Forgive me, Gimpel."

I said, "What is there to forgive? You have been a good and faithful wife."

"Woe, Gimpel!" she said. "It was ugly how I deceived you all these years. I want to go clean to my Maker, and so I have to tell you that the children are not yours."

If I had been clouted on the head with a piece of wood it couldn't have bewildered me more.

"Whose are they?" I asked.

"I don't know," she said. "There were a lot . . . but they're not yours." And as she spoke she tossed her head to the side, her eyes turned glassy, and it was all up with Elka. On her whitened lips there remained a smile.

I imagined that, dead as she was, she was saying, "I deceived Gimpel. That was the meaning of my brief life."

IV

One night, when the period of mourning was done, as I lay dreaming on the flour sacks, there came the Spirit of Evil himself and said to me, "Gimpel, why do you sleep?"

I said, "What should I be doing? Eating *kreplach?*"

"The whole world deceives you," he said, "and you ought to deceive the world in your turn."

"How can I deceive all the world?" I asked him.

He answered, "You might accumulate a bucket of urine every day and at night pour it into the dough. Let the sages of Frampol eat filth."

"What about the judgment in the world to come?" I said.

"There is no world to come," he said. "They've sold you a bill of goods and talked you into believing you carried a cat in your belly. What nonsense!"

"Well then," I said, "and is there a God?"

He answered, "There is no God either."

"What," I said, *"is* there, then?"

"A thick mire."

He stood before my eyes with a goatish beard and horn, long-toothed, and with a tail. Hearing such words, I wanted to snatch him by the tail, but I tumbled from the flour sacks and nearly broke a rib. Then it happened that I had to answer the call of nature, and, passing, I saw the risen dough, which seemed to say to me, "Do it!" In brief, I let myself be persuaded.

At dawn the apprentice came. We kneaded the bread, scattered caraway seeds on it, and set it to bake. Then the apprentice went away, and I was left sitting in the little trench by the oven, on a pile of rags. Well, Gimpel, I thought, you've revenged yourself on them for all the shame they've put on you. Outside the frost glittered, but it was warm beside the oven. The flames heated my face. I bent my head and fell into a doze.

I saw in a dream, at once, Elka in her shroud. She called to me, "What have you done, Gimpel?"

I said to her, "It's all your fault," and started to cry.

"You fool!" she said. "You fool! Because I was false is everything false too? I never deceived anyone but my-

self. I'm paying for it all, Gimpel. They spare you nothing
here."

I looked at her face. It was black; I was startled and
waked, and remained sitting dumb. I sensed that everything hung in the balance. A false step now and I'd lose
Eternal Life. But God gave me His help. I seized the
long shovel and took out the loaves, carried them into
the yard, and started to dig a hole in the frozen earth.

My apprentice came back as I was doing it. "What are
you doing, boss?" he said, and grew pale as a corpse.

"I know what I'm doing," I said, and I buried it all
before his very eyes.

Then I went home, took my hoard from its hiding
place, and divided it among the children. "I saw your
mother tonight," I said. "She's turning black, poor thing."

They were so astounded they couldn't speak a word.

"Be well," I said, "and forget that such a one as Gimpel
ever existed." I put on my short coat, a pair of boots,
took the bag that held my prayer shawl in one hand, my
stock in the other, and kissed the *mezzuzah*. When people saw me in the street they were greatly surprised.

"Where are you going?" they said.

I answered, "Into the world." And so I departed from
Frampol.

I wandered over the land, and good people did not
neglect me. After many years I became old and white;
I heard a great deal, many lies and falsehoods, but the
longer I lived the more I understood that there were really no lies. Whatever doesn't really happen is dreamed at
night. It happens to one if it doesn't happen to another,
tomorrow if not today, or a century hence if not next
year. What difference can it make? Often I heard tales
of which I said, "Now this is a thing that cannot happen."
But before a year had elapsed I heard that it actually
had come to pass somewhere.

Going from place to place, eating at strange tables,
it often happens that I spin yarns—improbable things that
could never have happened—about devils, magicians,
windmills, and the like. The children run after me, calling,
"Grandfather, tell us a story." Sometimes they ask for
particular stories, and I try to please them. A fat young
boy once said to me, "Grandfather, it's the same story
you told us before." The little rogue, he was right.

So it is with dreams too. It is many years since I left
Frampol, but as soon as I shut my eyes I am there again.
And whom do you think I see? Elka. She is standing by

the washtub, as at our first encounter, but her face is shining and her eyes are as radiant as the eyes of a saint, and she speaks outlandish words to me, strange things. When I wake I have forgotten it all. But while the dream lasts I am comforted. She answers all my queries, and what comes out is that all is right. I weep and implore, "Let me be with you." And she consoles me and tells me to be patient. The time is nearer than it is far. Sometimes she strokes and kisses me and weeps upon my face. When I awaken I feel her lips and taste the salt of her tears.

No doubt the world is entirely an imaginary world, but it is only once removed from the true world. At the door of the hovel where I lie, there stands the plank on which the dead are taken away. The gravedigger Jew has his spade ready. The grave waits and the worms are hungry; the shrouds are prepared—I carry them in my beggar's sack. Another *shnorrer* is waiting to inherit my bed of straw. When the time comes I will go joyfully. Whatever may be there, it will be real, without complication, without ridicule, without deception. God be praised: there even Gimpel cannot be deceived.

John Steinbeck

(1902–1969)

*John Steinbeck's desire to become a writer led him to
six years at Stanford University (which he left without
taking a degree) and then to a variety of jobs as laborer,
field hand, and so on. From the beginning, he seems to
have been intent on exploring America. The Great Depression which devastated America provided him with
the exact focus he needed for his work. Against the background of an America suffering on an unprecedented
scale, his empathy for individuals struggling to survive
with dignity emerged. Steinbeck's almost scientific interest in the way individuals react to the stresses and
strains of existence is balanced by his deep and sincere
love of people. If at times he can be justifiably accused
of sentimentalizing his characters, he nevertheless remains one of the few major American writers of this
century to answer the indictment of mass alienation by
portraying men and women living and working together
in the face of hardship. It is this struggle which he depicts so movingly and graphically in* Tortilla Flat *(1935),*
In Dubious Battle *(1936),* Of Mice and Men *(1937),
and the memorable novel which treats the flight of the
Okies to California's green but exploited fields,* The
Grapes of Wrath *(1939).*

*First published in Steinbeck's only book of short
stories,* The Long Valley *(1938), "Flight" is set in the
Salinas Valley, whose beautiful but rugged terrain provides both landscape and inspiration for so much of
Steinbeck's fiction. On the realistic level, the story deals
with the death of a* paisano, *the kind of individual whom
Steinbeck described far more humorously in* Tortilla
Flat. *On another level, it offers a parable of the way in
which man faces up to his inevitable destruction. Steinbeck is careful not to tell the reader who Pepé's pursuers
are; they seem, at times, to be natural forces rather than
people. And they are as relentless as the "dark watchers"
Pepé's mother speaks about. There is even a hint in the
story that they may be supernatural. The one gift Pepé's
dead father has left him, the knife, is his sole inheritance.
Pepé's world has always been a world in which one is
prepared to flee. When he flees his pursuers, he takes*

445

*with him the knife and a rifle, artifacts of civilization
designed to enable a man to resist a wild natural world.
But, ironically, it is precisely an impersonal nature
which triumphs over Pepé. Steinbeck's great gifts as a
storyteller find dramatic and compassionate expression
in "Flight."*

*John Steinbeck's literary reputation has been consider-
ably greater among European critics than among his
fellow countrymen, perhaps because Steinbeck is an
especially difficult writer to classify. Labeled a primitivist,
a naturalist, a philosophical novelist, a sentimentalist, he
is like most important writers in that he fits none of
these categories. He is, rather, simply in the American
grain. Few American writers have been more successful in exploring the complexities that go to make up
American life; fewer still have managed to combine a
more fervent sense of social responsibility with a more
passionate commitment to democratic individualism.*

Flight

About fifteen miles below Monterey, on the wild coast,
the Torres family had their farm, a few sloping acres above
a cliff that dropped to the brown reefs and to the hissing
white waters of the ocean. Behind the farm the stone
mountains stood up against the sky. The farm buildings
huddled like little clinging aphids on the mountain skirts,
crouched low to the ground as though the wind might
blow them into the sea. The little shack, the rattling,
rotting barn were gray-bitten with sea salt, beaten by the
damp wind until they had taken on the color of the granite
hills. Two horses, a red cow and a red calf, half a dozen
pigs and a flock of lean, multi-colored chickens stocked
the place. A little corn was raised on the sterile slope, and
it grew short and thick under the wind, and all the cobs
formed on the landward sides of the stalks.

Mama Torres, a lean, dry woman with ancient eyes,
had ruled the farm for ten years, ever since her husband
tripped over a stone in the field one day and fell full
length on a rattlesnake. When one is bitten on the chest
there is not much that can be done.

Mama Torres had three children, two undersized black

ones of twelve and fourteen, Emilio and Rosy, whom
Mama kept fishing on the rocks below the farm when the
sea was kind and when the truant officer was in some distant part of Monterey County. And there was Pepé, the
tall smiling son of nineteen, a gentle, affectionate boy, but
very lazy. Pepé had a tall head, pointed at the top, and
from its peak, coarse black hair grew down like a thatch
all around. Over his smiling little eyes Mama cut a straight
bang so he could see. Pepé had sharp Indian cheekbones
and an eagle nose, but his mouth was as sweet and shapely
as a girl's mouth, and his chin was fragile and chiseled.
He was loose and gangling, all legs and feet and wrists,
and he was very lazy. Mama thought him fine and brave,
but she never told him so. She said, "Some lazy cow must
have got into thy father's family, else how could I have a
son like thee." And she said, "When I carried thee, a
sneaking lazy coyote came out of the brush and looked at
me one day. That must have made thee so."

Pepé smiled sheepishly and stabbed at the ground with
his knife to keep the blade sharp and free from rust. It
was his inheritance, that knife, his father's knife. The long
heavy blade folded back into the black handle. There was
a button on the handle. When Pepé pressed the button,
the blade leaped out ready for use. The knife was with
Pepé always, for it had been his father's knife.

One sunny morning when the sea below the cliff was
glinting and blue and the white surf creamed on the reef,
when even the stone mountains looked kindly, Mama
Torres called out the door of the shack, "Pepé, I have a
labor for thee."

There was no answer. Mama listened. From behind the
barn she heard a burst of laughter. She lifted her full long
skirt and walked in the direction of the noise.

Pepé was sitting on the ground with his back against a
box. His white teeth glistened. On either side of him
stood the two black ones, tense and expectant. Fifteen feet
away a redwood post was set in the ground. Pepé's right
hand lay limply in his lap, and in the palm the big black
knife rested. The blade was closed back into the handle.
Pepé looked smiling at the sky.

Suddenly Emilio cried, "Ya!"

Pepé's wrist flicked like the head of a snake. The blade
seemed to fly open in mid-air, and with a thump the point
dug into the redwood post, and the black handle quivered.
The three burst into excited laughter. Rosy ran to the
post and pulled out the knife and brought it back to Pepé.

He closed the blade and settled the knife carefully in his listless palm again. He grinned self-consciously at the sky.

"Ya!"

The heavy knife lanced out and sunk into the post again. Mama moved forward like a ship and scattered the play.

"All day you do foolish things with the knife, like a toy-baby," she stormed. "Get up on thy huge feet that eat up shoes. Get up!" She took him by one loose shoulder and hoisted at him. Pepé grinned sheepishly and came half-heartedly to his feet. "Look!" Mama cried. "Big lazy, you must catch the horse and put on him thy father's saddle. You must ride to Monterey. The medicine bottle is empty. There is no salt. Go thou now, Peanut! Catch the horse."

A revolution took place in the relaxed figure of Pepé. "To Monterey, me? Alone? Sí, Mama."

She scowled at him. "Do not think, big sheep, that you will buy candy. No, I will give you only enough for the medicine and the salt."

Pepé smiled. "Mama, you will put the hatband on the hat?"

She relented then. "Yes, Pepé. You may wear the hatband."

His voice grew insinuating. "And the green handkerchief, Mama?"

"Yes, if you go quickly and return with no trouble, the silk green handkerchief will go. If you make sure to take off the handkerchief when you eat so no spot may fall on it. . . ."

"Sí, Mama. I will be careful. I am a man."

"Thou? A man? Thou art a peanut."

He went into the rickety barn and brought out a rope, and he walked agilely enough up the hill to catch the horse.

When he was ready and mounted before the door, mounted on his father's saddle that was so old that the oaken frame showed through torn leather in many places, then Mama brought out the round black hat with the tooled leather band, and she reached up and knotted the green silk handkerchief about his neck. Pepé's blue denim coat was much darker than his jeans, for it had been washed much less often.

Mama handed up the big medicine bottle and the silver coins. "That for the medicine," she said, "and that for the salt. That for a candle to burn for the papa. That for *dulces* for the little ones. Our friend Mrs. Rodriquez will give you dinner and maybe a bed for the night. When you go to the church say only ten Paternosters and only twenty-five Ave Marias. Oh! I know, big coyote. You would sit there flapping your mouth over Aves all day while you looked at the candles and the holy pictures. That is not good devotion to stare at the pretty things."

The black hat, covering the high pointed head and black thatched hair of Pepé, gave him dignity and age. He sat the rangy horse well. Mama thought how handsome he was, dark and lean and tall. "I would not send thee now alone, thou little one, except for the medicine," she said softly. "It is not good to have no medicine, for who knows when the toothache will come, or the sadness of the stomach. These things are."

"Adios, Mama," Pepé cried. "I will come back soon. You may send me often alone. I am a man."

"Thou art a foolish chicken."

He straightened his shoulders, flipped the reins against the horse's shoulder and rode away. He turned once and saw that they still watched him, Emilio and Rosy and Mama. Pepé grinned with pride and gladness and lifted the tough buckskin horse to a trot.

When he had dropped out of sight over a little dip in the road, Mama turned to the black ones, but she spoke to herself. "He is nearly a man now," she said. "It will be a nice thing to have a man in the house again." Her eyes sharpened on the children. "Go to the rocks now. The tide is going out. There will be abalones to be found." She put the iron hooks into their hands and saw them down the steep trail to the reefs. She brought the smooth stone *metate* to the doorway and sat grinding her corn to flour and looking occasionally at the road over which Pepé had gone. The noonday came and then the afternoon, when the little ones beat the abalones on a rock to make them tender and Mama patted the tortillas to make them thin. They ate their dinner as the red sun was plunging down toward the ocean. They sat on the doorsteps and watched the big white moon come over the mountain tops.

Mama said, "He is now at the house of our friend Mrs. Rodriquez. She will give him nice things to eat and maybe a present."

Emilio said, "Some day I too will ride to Monterey for medicine. Did Pepé come to be a man today?"

Mama said wisely, "A boy gets to be a man when a man

is needed. Remember this thing. I have known boys forty years old because there was no need for a man."

Soon afterwards they retired, Mama in her big oak bed on one side of the room, Emilio and Rosy in their boxes full of straw and sheepskins on the other side of the room.

The moon went over the sky and the surf roared on the rocks. The roosters crowed the first call. The surf subsided to a whispering surge against the reef. The moon dropped toward the sea. The roosters crowed again.

The moon was near down to the water when Pepé rode on a winded horse to his home flat. His dog bounced out and circled the horse yelping with pleasure. Pepé slid off the saddle to the ground. The weathered little shack was silver in the moonlight and the square shadow of it was black to the north and east. Against the east the piling mountains were misty with light; their tops melted into the sky.

Pepé walked wearily up the three steps and into the house. It was dark inside. There was a rustle in the corner.

Mama cried out from her bed. "Who comes? Pepé, is it thou?"

"*Sí*, Mama."

"Did you get the medicine?"

"*Sí*, Mama."

"Well, go to sleep, then. I thought you would be sleeping at the house of Mrs. Rodriquez." Pepé stood silently in the dark room. "Why do you stand there, Pepé? Did you drink wine?"

"*Sí*, Mama."

"Well, go to bed then and sleep out the wine."

His voice was tired and patient, but very firm. "Light the candle, Mama. I must go away into the mountains."

"What is this, Pepé? You are crazy." Mama struck a sulphur match and held the little blue burr until the flame spread up the stick. She set light to the candle on the floor beside her bed. "Now, Pepé, what is this you say?" She looked anxiously into his face.

He was changed. The fragile quality seemed to have gone from his chin. His mouth was less full than it had been, the lines of the lips were straighter, but in his eyes the greatest change had taken place. There was no laughter in them any more nor any bashfulness. They were sharp and bright and purposeful.

He told her in a tired monotone, told her everything just as it had happened. A few people came into the kitchen of Mrs. Rodriquez. There was wine to drink. Pepé drank wine. The little quarrel—the man started toward Pepé and then the knife—it went almost by itself. It flew, it darted before Pepé knew it. As he talked, Mama's face grew stern, and it seemed to grow more lean. Pepé finished. "I am a man now, Mama. The man said names to me I could not allow."

Mama nodded. "Yes, thou art a man, my poor little Pepé. Thou art a man. I have seen it coming on thee. I have watched you throwing the knife into the post, and I have been afraid." For a moment her face had softened, but now it grew stern again. "Come! We must get you ready. Go. Awaken Emilio and Rosy. Go quickly."

Pepé stepped over to the corner where his brother and sister slept among the sheepskins. He leaned down and shook them gently. "Come, Rosy! Come, Emilio! The mama says you must arise."

The little black ones sat up and rubbed their eyes in the candlelight. Mama was out of bed now, her long black skirt over her nightgown. "Emilio," she cried. "Go up and catch the other horse for Pepé. Quickly now! Quickly." Emilio put his legs in his overalls and stumbled sleepily out the door.

"You heard no one behind you on the road?" Mama demanded.

"No, Mama. I listened carefully. No one was on the road."

Mama darted like a bird about the room. From a nail on the wall she took a canvas water bag and threw it on the floor. She stripped a blanket from her bed and rolled it into a tight tube and tied the ends with string. From a box beside the stove she lifted a flour sack half full of black stringy jerky. "Your father's black coat, Pepé. Here, put it on."

Pepé stood in the middle of the floor watching her activity. She reached behind the door and brought out the rifle, a long 38-56, worn shiny the whole length of the barrel. Pepé took it from her and held it in the crook of his elbow. Mama brought a little leather bag and counted the cartridges into his hand. "Only ten left," she warned. "You must not waste them."

Emilio put his head in the door. *"'Qui 'st 'l caballo,* Mama."

"Put on the saddle from the other horse. Tie on the blanket. Here, tie the jerky to the saddle horn."

Still Pepé stood silently watching his mother's frantic

activity. His chin looked hard, and his sweet mouth was drawn and thin. His little eyes followed Mama about the room almost suspiciously.

Rosy asked softly, "Where goes Pepé?"

Mama's eyes were fierce. "Pepé goes on a journey. Pepé is a man now. He has a man's thing to do."

Pepé straightened his shoulders. His mouth changed until he looked very much like Mama.

At last the preparation was finished. The loaded horse stood outside the door. The water bag dripped a line of moisture down the bay shoulder.

The moonlight was being thinned by the dawn and the big white moon was near down to the sea. The family stood by the shack. Mama confronted Pepé. "Look, my son! Do not stop until it is dark again. Do not sleep even though you are tired. Take care of the horse in order that he may not stop of weariness. Remember to be careful with the bullets—there are only ten. Do not fill thy stomach with jerky or it will make thee sick. Eat a little jerky and fill thy stomach with grass. When thou comest to the high mountains, if thou seest any of the dark watching men, go not near to them nor try to speak to them. And forget not thy prayers." She put her lean hands on Pepé's shoulders, stood on her toes and kissed him formally on both cheeks, and Pepé kissed her on both cheeks. Then he went to Emilio and Rosy and kissed both of their cheeks.

Pepé turned back to Mama. He seemed to look for a little softness, a little weakness in her. His eyes were searching, but Mama's face remained fierce. "Go now," she said. "Do not wait to be caught like a chicken."

Pepé pulled himself into the saddle. "I am a man," he said.

It was the first dawn when he rode up the hill toward the little canyon which let a trail into the mountains. Moonlight and daylight fought with each other, and the two warring qualities made it difficult to see. Before Pepé had gone a hundred yards, the outlines of his figure were misty; and long before he entered the canyon, he had become a gray, indefinite shadow.

Mama stood stiffly in front of her doorstep, and on either side of her stood Emilio and Rosy. They cast furtive glances at Mama now and then.

When the gray shape of Pepé melted into the hillside and disappeared, Mama relaxed. She began the high, whining keen of the death wail. "Our beautiful—our brave," she cried. "Our protector, our son is gone." Emilio and Rosy moaned beside her. "Our beautiful——our brave, he is gone." It was the formal wail. It rose to a high piercing whine and subsided to a moan. Mama raised it three times and then she turned and went into the house and shut the door.

Emilio and Rosy stood wondering in the dawn. They heard Mama whimpering in the house. They went out to sit on the cliff above the ocean. They touched shoulders. "When did Pepé come to be a man?" Emilio asked.

"Last night," said Rosy. "Last night in Monterey." The ocean clouds turned red with the sun that was behind the mountains.

"We will have no breakfast," said Emilio. "Mama will not want to cook." Rosy did not answer him. "Where is Pepé gone?" he asked.

Rosy looked around at him. She drew her knowledge from the quiet air. "He has gone on a journey. He will never come back."

"Is he dead? Do you think he is dead?"

Rosy looked back at the ocean again. A little steamer, drawing a line of smoke, sat on the edge of the horizon. "He is not dead," Rosy explained. "Not yet."

Pepé rested the big rifle across the saddle in front of him. He let the horse walk up the hill and he didn't look back. The stony slope took on a coat of short brush so that Pepé found the entrance to a trail and entered it.

When he came to the canyon opening, he swung once in his saddle and looked back, but the houses were swallowed in the misty light. Pepé jerked forward again. The high shoulder of the canyon closed in on him. His horse stretched out its neck and sighed and settled to the trail.

It was a well-worn path, dark soft leaf-mold earth strewn with broken pieces of sandstone. The trail rounded the shoulder of the canyon and dropped steeply into the bed of the stream. In the shallows the water ran smoothly, glinting in the first morning sun. Small round stones on the bottom were as brown as rust with sun moss. In the sand along the edges of the stream the tall, rich wild mint grew, while in the water itself the cress, old and tough, had gone to heavy seed.

The path went into the stream and emerged on the other side. The horse sloshed into the water and stopped. Pepé dropped his bridle and let the beast drink of the running water.

Soon the canyon sides became steep and the first giant

sentinel redwoods guarded the trail, great round red
trunks bearing foliage as green and lacy as ferns. Once
Pepé was among the trees, the sun was lost. A perfumed
and purple light lay in the pale green of the underbrush.
Gooseberry bushes and blackberries and tall ferns lined
the stream, and overhead the branches of the redwoods
met and cut off the sky.

Pepé drank from the water bag, and he reached into
the flour sack and brought out a black string of jerky. His
white teeth gnawed at the string until the tough meat
parted. He chewed slowly and drank occasionally from
the water bag. His little eyes were slumberous and tired,
but the muscles of his face were hard set. The earth of the
trail was black now. It gave up a hollow sound under the
walking hoofbeats.

The stream fell more sharply. Little waterfalls splashed
on the stones. Five-fingered ferns hung over the water and
dripped spray from their fingertips. Pepé rode half over
in his saddle, dangling one leg loosely. He picked a bay
leaf from a tree beside the way and put it into his mouth
for a moment to flavor the dry jerky. He held the gun
loosely across the pommel.

Suddenly he squared in his saddle, swung the horse from
the trail and kicked it hurriedly up behind a big redwood
tree. He pulled up the reins tight against the bit to keep
the horse from whinnying. His face was intent and his
nostrils quivered a little.

A hollow pounding came down the trail, and a horseman rode by, a fat man with red cheeks and a white stubble
beard. His horse put down its head and blubbered at the
trail when it came to the place where Pepé had turned off.
"Hold up!" said the man and he pulled up his horse's
head.

When the last sound of the hoofs died away, Pepé came
back into the trail again. He did not relax in the saddle
any more. He lifted the big rifle and swung the lever to
throw a shell into the chamber, and then he let down the
hammer to half cock.

The trail grew very steep. Now the redwood trees were
smaller and their tops were dead, bitten dead where the
wind reached them. The horse plodded on; the sun went
slowly overhead and started down toward the afternoon.

Where the stream came out of a side canyon, the trail
left it. Pepé dismounted and watered his horse and filled
up his water bag. As soon as the trail had parted from the
stream, the trees were gone and only the thick brittle sage

and manzanita and chaparral edged the trail. And the soft black earth was gone, too, leaving only the light tan broken rock for the trail bed. Lizards scampered away into the brush as the horse rattled over the little stones.

Pepé turned in his saddle and looked back. He was in the open now: he could be seen from a distance. As he ascended the trail the country grew more rough and terrible and dry. The way wound about the bases of great square rocks. Little gray rabbits skittered in the brush. A bird made a monotonous high creaking. Eastward the bare rock mountaintops were pale and powder-dry under the dropping sun. The horse plodded up and up the trail toward a little V in the ridge which was the pass.

Pepé looked suspiciously back every minute or so, and his eyes sought the tops of the ridges ahead. Once, on a white barren spur, he saw a black figure for a moment, but he looked quickly away, for it was one of the dark watchers. No one knew who the watchers were, nor where they lived, but it was better to ignore them and never to show interest in them. They did not bother one who stayed on the trail and minded his own business.

The air was parched and full of light dust blown by the breeze from the eroding mountains. Pepé drank sparingly from his bag and corked it tightly and hung it on the horn again. The trail moved up the dry shale hillside, avoiding rocks, dropping under clefts, climbing in and out of old water scars. When he arrived at the little pass he stopped and looked back for a long time. No dark watchers were to be seen now. The trail behind was empty. Only the high tops of the redwoods indicated where the stream flowed.

Pepé rode on through the pass. His little eyes were nearly closed with weariness, but his face was stern, relentless and manly. The high mountain wind coasted sighing through the pass and whistled on the edges of the big blocks of broken granite. In the air, a red-tailed hawk sailed over close to the ridge and screamed angrily. Pepé went slowly through the broken jagged pass and looked down on the other side.

The trail dropped quickly, staggering among broken rock. At the bottom of the slope there was a dark crease, thick with brush, and on the other side of the crease a little flat, in which a grove of oak trees grew. A scar of green grass cut across the flat. And behind the flat another mountain rose, desolate with dead rocks and starving little black bushes. Pepé drank from the bag again for the air was so dry that it encrusted his nostrils and burned his lips. He

put the horse down the trail. The hooves slipped and
struggled on the steep way, starting little stones that rolled
off into the brush. The sun was gone behind the westward
mountain now, but still it glowed brilliantly on the oaks
and on the grassy flat. The rocks and the hillsides still sent
up waves of the heat they had gathered from the day's sun.

Pepé looked up to the top of the next dry withered
ridge. He saw a dark form against the sky, a man's figure
standing on top of a rock, and he glanced away quickly
not to appear curious. When a moment later he looked up
again, the figure was gone.

Downward the trail was quickly covered. Sometimes the
horse floundered for footing, sometimes set his feet and
slid a little way. They came at last to the bottom where
the dark chaparral was higher than Pepé's head. He held
up his rifle on one side and his arm on the other to shield
his face from the sharp brittle fingers of the brush.

Up and out of the crease he rode, and up a little cliff.
The grassy flat was before him, and the round comfortable
oaks. For a moment he studied the trail down which he
had come, but there was no movement and no sound from
it. Finally he rode out over the flat, to the green streak,
and at the upper end of the damp he found a little spring
welling out of the earth and dropping into a dug basin
before it seeped out over the flat.

Pepé filled his bag first, and then he let the thirsty horse
drink out of the pool. He led the horse to the clump of
oaks, and in the middle of the grove, fairly protected from
sight on all sides, he took off the saddle and the bridle and
laid them on the ground. The horse stretched his jaws
sideways and yawned. Pepé knotted the lead rope about
the horse's neck and tied him to a sapling among the oaks,
where he could graze in a fairly large circle.

When the horse was gnawing hungrily at the dry grass,
Pepé went to the saddle and took a black string of jerky
from the sack and strolled to an oak tree on the edge of
the grove, from under which he could watch the trail. He
sat down in the crisp dry oak leaves and automatically felt
for his big black knife to cut the jerky, but he had no knife.
He leaned back on his elbow and gnawed at the tough
strong meat. His face was blank, but it was a man's face.

The bright evening light washed the eastern ridge, but
the valley was darkening. Doves flew down from the hills
to the spring, and the quail came running out of the brush
and joined them, calling clearly to one another.

Out of the corner of his eye Pepé saw a shadow grow out

of the bushy crease. He turned his head slowly. A big spotted wildcat was creeping toward the spring, belly to the ground, moving like thought.

Pepé cocked his rifle and edged the muzzle slowly around. Then he looked apprehensively up the trail and dropped the hammer again. From the ground beside him he picked an oak twig and threw it toward the spring. The quail flew up with a roar and the doves whistled away. The big cat stood up: for a long moment he looked at Pepé with cold yellow eyes, and then fearlessly walked back into the gulch.

The dusk gathered quickly in the deep valley. Pepé muttered his prayers, put his head down on his arm and went instantly to sleep.

The moon came up and filled the valley with cold blue light, and the wind swept rustling down from the peaks. The owls worked up and down the slopes looking for rabbits. Down in the brush of the gulch a coyote gabbled. The oak trees whispered softly in the night breeze.

Pepé started up, listening. His horse had whinnied. The moon was just slipping behind the western ridge, leaving the valley in darkness behind it. Pepé sat tensely gripping his rifle. From far up the trail he heard an answering whinny and the crash of shod hooves on the broken rock. He jumped to his feet, ran to his horse and led it under the trees. He threw on the saddle and cinched it tight for the steep trail, caught the unwilling head and forced the bit into the mouth. He felt the saddle to make sure the water bag and the sack of jerky were there. Then he mounted and turned up the hill.

It was velvet dark. The horse found the entrance to the trail where it left the flat, and started up, stumbling and slipping on the rocks. Pepé's hand rose up to his head. His hat was gone. He had left it under the oak tree.

The horse had struggled far up the trail when the first change of dawn came into the air, a steel grayness as light mixed thoroughly with dark. Gradually the sharp snaggled edge of the ridge stood out above them, rotten granite tortured and eaten by the winds of time. Pepé had dropped his reins on the horn, leaving direction to the horse. The brush grabbed at his legs in the dark until one knee of his jeans was ripped.

Gradually the light flowed down over the ridge. The starved brush and rocks stood out in the half light, strange and lonely in high perspective. Then there came warmth into the light. Pepé drew up and looked back, but he could see nothing in the darker valley below. The sky turned blue over the coming sun. In the waste of the mountainside, the poor dry brush grew only three feet high. Here and there, big outcroppings of unrotted granite stood up like moldering houses. Pepé relaxed a little. He drank from his water bag and bit off a piece of jerky. A single eagle flew over, high in the light.

Without warning Pepé's horse screamed and fell on its side. He was almost down before the rifle crash echoed up from the valley. From a hole behind the struggling shoulder, a stream of bright crimson blood pumped and stopped and pumped and stopped. The hooves threshed on the ground. Pepé lay half stunned beside the horse. He looked slowly down the hill. A piece of sage clipped off beside his head and another crash echoed up from side to side of the canyon. Pepé flung himself frantically behind a bush.

He crawled up the hill on his knees and on one hand. His right hand held the rifle up off the ground and pushed it ahead of him. He moved with the instinctive care of an animal. Rapidly he wormed his way toward one of the big outcroppings of granite on the hill above him. Where the brush was high he doubled up and ran, but where the cover was slight he wriggled forward on his stomach, pushing the rifle ahead of him. In the last little distance there was no cover at all. Pepé poised and then he darted across the space and flashed around the corner of the rock.

He leaned panting against the stone. When his breath came easier he moved along behind the big rock until he came to a narrow slit that offered a thin section of vision down the hill. Pepé lay on his stomach and pushed the rifle barrel through the slit and waited.

The sun reddened the western ridges now. Already the buzzards were settling down toward the place where the horse lay. A small brown bird scratched in the dead sage leaves directly in front of the rifle muzzle. The coasting eagle flew back toward the rising sun.

Pepé saw a little movement in the brush far below. His grip tightened on the gun. A little brown doe stepped daintily out on the trail and crossed it and disappeared into the brush again. For a long time Pepé waited. Far below he could see the little flat and the oak trees and the slash of green. Suddenly his eyes flashed back at the trail again. A quarter of a mile down there had been a quick movement in the chaparral. The rifle swung over. The front sight nestled in the V of the rear sight. Pepé studied for a moment and then raised the rear sight a notch. The little movement in the brush came again. The sight settled on it. Pepé squeezed the trigger. The explosion crashed down the mountain and up the other side, and came rattling back. The whole side of the slope grew still. No more movement. And then a white streak cut into the granite of the slit and a bullet whined away and a crash sounded up from below. Pepé felt a sharp pain in his right hand. A sliver of granite was sticking out from between his first and second knuckles and the point protruded from his palm. Carefully he pulled out the sliver of stone. The wound bled evenly and gently. No vein nor artery was cut.

Pepé looked into a little dusty cave in the rock and gathered a handful of spider web, and he pressed the mass into the cut, plastering the soft web into the blood. The flow stopped almost at once.

The rifle was on the ground. Pepé picked it up, levered a new shell into the chamber. And then he slid into the brush on his stomach. Far to the right he crawled, and then up the hill, moving slowly and carefully, crawling to cover and resting and then crawling again.

In the mountains the sun is high in its arc before it penetrates the gorges. The hot face looked over the hill and brought instant heat with it. The white light beat on the rocks and reflected from them and rose up quivering from the earth again, and the rocks and bushes seemed to quiver behind the air.

Pepé crawled in the general direction of the ridge peak, zigzagging for cover. The deep cut between his knuckles began to throb. He crawled close to a rattlesnake before he saw it, and when it raised its dry head and made a soft beginning whirr, he backed up and took another way. The quick gray lizards flashed in front of him, raising a tiny line of dust. He found another mass of spider web and pressed it against his throbbing hand.

Pepé was pushing the rifle with his left hand now. Little drops of sweat ran to the ends of his coarse black hair and rolled down his cheeks. His lips and tongue were growing thick and heavy. His lips writhed to draw saliva into his mouth. His little dark eyes were uneasy and suspicious. Once when a gray lizard paused in front of him on the parched ground and turned its head sideways he crushed it flat with a stone.

When the sun slid past noon he had not gone a mile. He crawled exhaustedly a last hundred yards to a patch of high sharp manzanita, crawled desperately, and when the patch was reached he wriggled in among the tough gnarly trunks and dropped his head on his left arm. There was little shade in the meager brush, but there was cover and safety. Pepé went to sleep as he lay and the sun beat on his back. A few little birds hopped close to him and peered and hopped away. Pepé squirmed in his sleep and he raised and dropped his wounded hand again and again.

The sun went down behind the peaks and the cool evening came, and then the dark. A coyote yelled from the hillside. Pepé started awake and looked about with misty eyes. His hand was swollen and heavy; a little thread of pain ran up the inside of his arm and settled in a pocket in his armpit. He peered about and then stood up, for the mountains were black and the moon had not yet risen. Pepé stood up in the dark. The coat of his father pressed on his arm. His tongue was swollen until it nearly filled his mouth. He wriggled out of the coat and dropped it in the brush, and then he struggled up the hill, falling over rocks and tearing his way through the brush. The rifle knocked against stones as he went. Little dry avalanches of gravel and shattered stone went whispering down the hill behind him.

After a while the old moon came up and showed the jagged ridge top ahead of him. By moonlight Pepé traveled more easily. He bent forward so that his throbbing arm hung away from his body. The journey uphill was made in dashes and rests, a frantic rush up a few yards and then a rest. The wind coasted down the slope rattling the dry stems of the bushes.

The moon was at meridian when Pepé came at last to the sharp backbone of the ridge top. On the last hundred yards of the rise no soil had clung under the wearing winds. The way was on solid rock. He clambered to the top and looked down on the other side. There was a draw like the last below him, misty with moonlight, brushed with dry struggling sage and chaparral. On the other side the hill rose up sharply and at the top the jagged rotten teeth of the mountain showed against the sky. At the bottom of the cut the brush was thick and dark.

Pepé stumbled down the hill. His throat was almost closed with thirst. At first he tried to run, but immediately he fell and rolled. After that he went more carefully. The moon was just disappearing behind the mountains when he came to the bottom. He crawled into the heavy brush feeling with his fingers for water. There was no water in the bed of the stream, only damp earth. Pepé laid his gun

down and scooped up a handful of mud and put it in his
mouth, and then he spluttered and scraped the earth from
his tongue with his finger, for the mud drew at his mouth
like a poultice. He dug a hole in the stream bed with his
fingers, dug a little basin to catch water; but before it was
very deep his head fell forward on the damp ground and
he slept.

The dawn came and the heat of the day fell on the earth,
and still Pepé slept. Late in the afternoon his head jerked
up. He looked slowly around. His eyes were slits of wari-
ness. Twenty feet away in the heavy brush a big tawny
mountain lion stood looking at him. Its long thick tail
waved gracefully, its ears erect with interest, not laid back
dangerously. The lion squatted down on its stomach and
watched him.

Pepé looked at the hole he had dug in the earth. A half
inch of muddy water had collected in the bottom. He tore
the sleeve from his hurt arm, with his teeth ripped out a
little square, soaked it in the water and put it in his mouth.
Over and over he filled the cloth and sucked it.

Still the lion sat and watched him. The evening came
down but there was no movement on the hills. No birds
visited the dry bottom of the cut. Pepé looked occasionally
at the lion. The eyes of the yellow beast drooped as though
he were about to sleep. He yawned and his long thin red
tongue curled out. Suddenly his head jerked around and
his nostrils quivered. His big tail lashed. He stood up and
slunk like a tawny shadow into the thick brush.

A moment later Pepé heard the sound, the faint far crash
of horses' hooves on gravel. And he heard something else,
a high whining yelp of a dog.

Pepé took his rifle in his left hand and he glided into
the brush almost as quietly as the lion had. In the darkening evening he crouched up the hill toward the next ridge.
Only when the dark came did he stand up. His energy was
short. Once it was dark he fell over the rocks and slipped
to his knees on the steep slope, but he moved on and on
up the hill, climbing and scrabbling over the broken hillside.

When he was far up toward the top, he lay down and
slept for a little while. The withered moon, shining on
his face, awakened him. He stood up and moved up the
hill. Fifty yards away he stopped and turned back, for he
had forgotten his rifle. He walked heavily down and poked
about in the brush, but he could not find his gun. At last
he lay down to rest. The pocket of pain in his armpit had

grown more sharp. His arm seemed to swell out and fall with every heartbeat. There was no position lying down where the heavy arm did not press against his armpit.

With the effort of a hurt beast, Pepé got up and moved again toward the top of the ridge. He held his swollen arm away from his body with his left hand. Up the steep hill he dragged himself, a few steps and a rest, and a few more steps. At last he was nearing the top. The moon showed the uneven sharp back of it against the sky.

Pepé's brain spun in a big spiral up and away from him. He slumped to the ground and lay still. The rock ridge top was only a hundred feet above him.

The moon moved over the sky. Pepé half turned on his back. His tongue tried to make words, but only a thick hissing came from between his lips.

When the dawn came, Pepé pulled himself up. His eyes were sane again. He drew his great puffed arm in front of him and looked at the angry wound. The black line ran up from his wrist to his armpit. Automatically he reached in his pocket for the big black knife, but it was not there. His eyes searched the ground. He picked up a sharp blade of stone and scraped at the wound, sawed at the proud flesh and then squeezed the green juice out in big drops. Instantly he threw back his head and whined like a dog. His whole right side shuddered at the pain, but the pain cleared his head.

In the gray light he struggled up the last slope to the ridge and crawled over and lay down behind a line of rocks. Below him lay a deep canyon exactly like the last, waterless and desolate. There was no flat, no oak trees, not even heavy brush in the bottom of it. And on the other side a sharp ridge stood up, thinly brushed with starving sage, littered with broken granite. Strewn over the hill there were giant outcroppings, and on the top the granite teeth stood out against the sky.

The new day was light now. The flame of sun came over the ridge and fell on Pepé where he lay on the ground. His coarse black hair was littered with twigs and bits of spider web. His eyes had retreated back into his head. Between his lips the tip of his black tongue showed.

He sat up and dragged his great arm into his lap and nursed it, rocking his body and moaning in his throat. He threw back his head and looked up into the pale sky. A big black bird circled nearly out of sight, and far to the left another was sailing near.

He lifted his head to listen, for a familiar sound had

come to him from the valley he had climbed out of; it was the crying yelp of hounds, excited and feverish, on a trail.

Pepé bowed his head quickly. He tried to speak rapid words but only a thick hiss came from his lips. He drew a shaky cross on his breast with his left hand. It was a long struggle to get to his feet. He crawled slowly and mechanically to the top of a big rock on the ridge peak. Once there, he arose slowly, swaying to his feet, and stood erect. Far below he could see the dark brush where he had slept. He braced his feet and stood there, black against the morning sky.

There came a ripping sound at his feet. A piece of stone flew up and a bullet droned off into the next gorge. The hollow crash echoed up from below. Pepé looked down for a moment and then pulled himself straight again.

His body jarred back. His left hand fluttered helplessly toward his breast. The second crash sounded from below. Pepé swung forward and toppled from the rock. His body struck and rolled over and over, starting a little avalanche. And when at last he stopped against a bush, the avalanche slid slowly down and covered up his head.

Frank O'Connor

(1903–1966)

Born Michael O'Donovan in the city of Cork, Frank O'Connor described his early life with humor and vivacity in his volume of short stories, An Only Child *(1961). His mother worked as a domestic; his father was an alcoholic laborer. His elementary school education ended when he left school at the age of fourteen, fortunately having come into contact with a great teacher, Daniel Corkery. During the Irish Civil War, O'Connor joined the Republican forces against the Free State government and was captured. He continued his education, as other writers have done, in prison. He then returned to more formal education, was encouraged in his writing by AE and Yeats. He is now the acknowledged master of the Irish short story. His first book of short stories,* Guests of the Nation, *was originally published in 1931. It was followed by six more collections of short stories.*

The great advantage that the Irish short story writers seem to have over their English contemporaries is that they have maintained the oral tradition which formed the basis for the development of the short story in Ireland as well as in all other lands. Professor Vivien Mercier maintains that "the Irish short story has stayed closer to its folk roots than any other national or ethnic school of fiction except the Jewish." Irrefutable proof of this is available in recordings O'Connor has made of his stories and of the stories of other Irish writers. Here O'Connor's fine speaking voice endows the Irish short story with a uniquely poetic quality.

The irresistible appeal of "My Oedipus Complex" (the appeal of much of O'Connor's fiction) lies in the sense that the humor of the story has been lived. It does not seem contrived. O'Connor here subjects the Freudian Oedipus complex to the open-eyed realistic point of view and personality of the child. It is a delicious strategy, executed with deft and devastating effect. In the warm, no-nonsense world O'Connor portrays, Freud doesn't stand a chance.

My Oedipus Complex

Father was in the army all through the war—the first war, I mean—so, up to the age of five, I never saw much of him, and what I saw did not worry me. Sometimes I woke and there was a big figure in khaki peering down at me in the candlelight. Sometimes in the early morning I heard the slamming of the front door and the clatter of nailed boots down the cobbles of the lane. These were Father's entrances and exits. Like Santa Claus he came and went mysteriously.

In fact, I rather liked his visits, though it was an uncomfortable squeeze between Mother and him when I got into the big bed in the early morning. He smoked, which gave him a pleasant musty smell, and shaved, an operation of astounding interest. Each time he left a trail of souvenirs—model tanks and Gurkha knives with handles made of bullet cases, and German helmets and cap badges and button-sticks, and all sorts of military equipment—carefully stowed away in a long box on top of the wardrobe, in case they ever came in handy. There was a bit of the magpie about Father; he expected everything to come in handy. When his back was turned, Mother let me get a chair and rummage through his treasures. She didn't seem to think so highly of them as he did.

The war was the most peaceful period of my life. The window of my attic faced southeast. My mother had curtained it, but that had small effect. I always woke with the first light and, with all the responsibilities of the previous day melted, feeling myself rather like the sun, ready to illumine and rejoice. Life never seemed so simple and clear and full of possibilities as then. I put my feet out from under the clothes—I called them Mrs. Left and Mrs. Right—and invented dramatic situations for them in which they discussed the problems of the day. At least Mrs. Right did; she was very demonstrative, but I hadn't the same control of Mrs. Left, so she mostly contented herself with nodding agreement.

They discussed what Mother and I should do during

the day, what Santa Claus should give a fellow for Christmas, and what steps should be taken to brighten the home. There was that little matter of the baby, for instance. Mother and I could never agree about that. Ours was the only house in the terrace without a new baby, and Mother said we couldn't afford one till Father came back from the war because they cost seventeen and six. That showed how simple she was. The Geneys up the road had a baby, and everyone knew they couldn't afford seventeen and six. It was probably a cheap baby, and Mother wanted something really good, but I felt she was too exclusive. The Geneys' baby would have done us fine.

Having settled my plans for the day, I got up, put a chair under the attic window, and lifted the frame high enough to stick out my head. The window overlooked the front gardens of the terrace behind ours, and beyond these it looked over a deep valley to the tall, red-brick houses terraced up the opposite hillside, which were all still in shadow, while those at our side of the valley were all lit up, though with long strange shadows that made them seem unfamiliar; rigid and painted.

After that I went into Mother's room and climbed into the big bed. She woke and I began to tell her of my schemes. By this time, though I never seemed to have noticed it, I was petrified in my nightshirt, and I thawed as I talked until, the last frost melted, I fell asleep beside her and woke again only when I heard her below in the kitchen, making the breakfast.

After breakfast we went into town; heard Mass at St. Augustine's and said a prayer for Father; and did the shopping. If the afternoon was fine we either went for a walk in the country or a visit to Mother's great friend in the convent, Mother St. Dominic. Mother had them all praying for Father, and every night, going to bed, I asked God to send him back safe from the war to us. Little, indeed, did I know what I was praying for!

One morning, I got into the big bed, and there, sure enough, was Father in his usual Santa Claus manner, but later, instead of uniform, he put on his best blue suit, and Mother was as pleased as anything. I saw nothing to be pleased about, because, out of uniform, Father was altogether less interesting, but she only beamed, and explained that our prayers had been answered, and off we went to Mass to thank God for having brought Father safely home.

The irony of it! That very day when he came in to dinner he took off his boots and put on his slippers, donned the dirty old cap he wore about the house to save him from colds, crossed his legs, and began to talk gravely to Mother, who looked anxious. Naturally, I disliked her looking anxious, because it destroyed her good looks, so I interrupted him.

"Just a moment, Larry!" she said gently.

This was only what she said when we had boring visitors, so I attached no importance to it and went on talking.

"Do be quiet, Larry!" she said impatiently. "Don't you hear me talking to Daddy?"

This was the first time I had heard those ominous words, "talking to Daddy," and I couldn't help feeling that if this was how God answered prayers, he couldn't listen to them very attentively.

"Why are you talking to Daddy?" I asked with as great a show of indifference as I could muster.

"Because Daddy and I have business to discuss. Now, don't interrupt again!"

In the afternoon, at Mother's request, Father took me for a walk. This time we went into town instead of out in the country, and I thought at first, in my usual optimistic way, that it might be an improvement. It was nothing of the sort. Father and I had quite different notions of a walk in town. He had no proper interest in trams, ships, and horses, and the only thing that seemed to divert him was talking to fellows as old as himself. When I wanted to stop he simply went on, dragging me behind him by the hand; when he wanted to stop I had no alternative but to do the same. I noticed that it seemed to be a sign that he wanted to stop for a long time whenever he leaned against a wall. The second time I saw him do it I got wild. He seemed to be settling himself forever. I pulled him by the coat and trousers, but, unlike Mother who, if you were too persistent, got into a wax and said: "Larry, if you don't behave yourself, I'll give you a good slap," Father had an extraordinary capacity for amiable inattention. I sized him up and wondered would I cry, but he seemed to be too remote to be annoyed even by that. Really, it was like going for a walk with a mountain! He either ignored the wrenching and pummeling entirely, or else glanced down with a grin of amusement from his peak. I had never met anyone so absorbed in himself as he seemed.

At teatime, "talking to Daddy" began again, complicated this time by the fact that he had an evening paper, and every few minutes he put it down and told Mother

something new out of it. I felt this was foul play. Man
for man, I was prepared to compete with him any time
for Mother's attention, but when he had it all made up
for him by other people it left me no chance. Several times
I tried to change the subject without success.

"You must be quiet while Daddy is reading, Larry,"
Mother said impatiently.

It was clear that she either genuinely liked talking to
Father better than talking to me, or else that he had some
terrible hold on her which made her afraid to admit the
truth.

"Mummy," I said that night when she was tucking me
up, "do you think if I prayed hard God would send Daddy
back to the war?"

She seemed to think about that for a moment.

"No, dear," she said with a smile. "I don't think he
would."

"Why wouldn't he, Mummy?"

"Because there isn't a war any longer, dear."

"But, Mummy, couldn't God make another war, if He
liked?"

"He wouldn't like to, dear. It's not God who makes
wars, but bad people."

"Oh!" I said.

I was disappointed about that. I began to think that
God wasn't quite what he was cracked up to be.

Next morning I woke at my usual hour, feeling like a
bottle of champagne. I put out my feet and invented a
long conversation in which Mrs. Right talked of the trouble she had with her own father till she put him in the
Home. I didn't quite know what the Home was but it
sounded the right place for Father. Then I got my chair
and stuck my head out of the attic window. Dawn was just
breaking, with a guilty air that made me feel I had caught
it in the act. My head bursting with stories and schemes,
I stumbled in next door, and in the half-darkness scrambled into the big bed. There was no room at Mother's side
so I had to get between her and Father. For the time being I had forgotten about him, and for several minutes
I sat bolt upright, racking my brains to know what I
could do with him. He was taking up more than his fair
share of the bed, and I couldn't get comfortable, so I gave
him several kicks that made him grunt and stretch. He
made room all right, though. Mother waked and felt for
me. I settled back comfortably in the warmth of the bed
with my thumb in my mouth.

"Mummy!" I hummed, loudly and contentedly.

"Sssh! dear," she whispered. "Don't wake Daddy!"

This was a new development, which threatened to be even more serious than "talking to Daddy." Life without my early-morning conferences was unthinkable.

"Why?" I asked severely.

"Because poor Daddy is tired."

This seemed to me a quite inadequate reason, and I was sickened by the sentimentality of her "poor Daddy." I never liked that sort of gush; it always struck me as insincere.

"Oh!" I said lightly. Then in my most winning tone: "Do you know where I want to go with you today, Mummy?"

"No, dear," she sighed.

"I want to go down the Glen and fish for thornybacks with my new net, and then I want to go out to the Fox and Hounds, and——"

"Don't-wake-Daddy!" she hissed angrily, clapping her hand across my mouth.

But it was too late. He was awake, or nearly so. He grunted and reached for the matches. Then he stared incredulously at his watch.

"Like a cup of tea, dear?" asked Mother in a meek, hushed voice I had never heard her use before. It sounded almost as though she were afraid.

"Tea?" he exclaimed indignantly. "Do you know what the time is?"

"And after that I want to go up the Rathcooney Road," I said loudly, afraid I'd forget something in all those interruptions.

"Go to sleep at once, Larry!" she said sharply.

I began to snivel. I couldn't concentrate, the way that pair went on, and smothering my early-morning schemes was like burying a family from the cradle.

Father said nothing, but lit his pipe and sucked it, looking out into the shadows without minding Mother or me. I knew he was mad. Every time I made a remark Mother hushed me irritably. I was mortified. I felt it wasn't fair; there was even something sinister in it. Every time I had pointed out to her the waste of making two beds when we could both sleep in one, she had told me it was healthier like that, and now here was this man, this stranger, sleeping with her without the least regard for her health!

He got up early and made tea, but though he brought Mother a cup he brought none for me.

"Mummy," I shouted, "I want a cup of tea, too."

"Yes, dear," she said patiently. "You can drink from Mummy's saucer."

That settled it. Either Father or I would have to leave the house. I didn't want to drink from Mother's saucer; I wanted to be treated as an equal in my own home, so, just to spite her, I drank it all and left none for her. She took that quietly, too.

But that night when she was putting me to bed she said gently:

"Larry, I want you to promise me something."

"What is it?" I asked.

"Not to come in and disturb poor Daddy in the morning. Promise?"

"Poor Daddy" again! I was becoming suspicious of everything involving that quite impossible man.

"Why?" I asked.

"Because poor Daddy is worried and tired and he doesn't sleep well."

"Why doesn't he, Mummy?"

"Well, you know, don't you, that while he was at the war Mummy got the pennies from the Post Office?"

"From Miss MacCarthy?"

"That's right. But now, you see, Miss MacCarthy hasn't any more pennies, so Daddy must go out and find us some. You know what would happen if he couldn't?"

"No," I said, "tell us."

"Well, I think we might have to go out and beg for them like the poor old woman on Fridays. We wouldn't like that, would we?"

"No," I agreed. "We wouldn't."

"So you'll promise not to come in and wake him?"

"Promise."

Mind you, I meant that. I knew pennies were a serious matter, and I was all against having to go out and beg like the old woman on Fridays. Mother laid out all my toys in a complete ring round the bed so that, whatever way I got out, I was bound to fall over one of them.

When I woke I remembered my promise all right. I got up and sat on the floor and played—for hours, it seemed to me. Then I got my chair and looked out the attic window for more hours. I wished it was time for Father to wake; I wished someone would make me a cup of tea. I didn't feel in the least like the sun; instead, I was bored and so very, very cold! I simply longed for the warmth and depth of the big featherbed.

At last I could stand it no longer. I went into the next room. As there was still no room at Mother's side I climbed over her and she woke with a start.

"Larry," she whispered, gripping my arm very tightly, "what did you promise?"

"But I did, Mummy," I wailed, caught in the very act. "I was quiet for ever so long."

"Oh, dear, and you're perished!" she said sadly, feeling me all over. "Now, if I let you stay will you promise not to talk?"

"But I want to talk, Mummy," I wailed.

"That has nothing to do with it," she said with a firmness that was new to me. "Daddy wants to sleep. Now, do you understand that?"

I understood it only too well. I wanted to talk, he wanted to sleep—whose house was it, anyway?

"Mummy," I said with equal firmness, "I think it would be healthier for Daddy to sleep in his own bed."

That seemed to stagger her, because she said nothing for a while.

"Now, once for all," she went on, "you're to be perfectly quiet or go back to your own bed. Which is it to be?"

The injustice of it got me down. I had convicted her out of her own mouth of inconsistency and unreasonableness, and she hadn't even attempted to reply. Full of spite, I gave Father a kick, which she didn't notice but which made him grunt and open his eyes in alarm.

"What time is it?" he asked in a panic-stricken voice, not looking at Mother but at the door, as if he saw someone there.

"It's early yet," she replied soothingly. "It's only the child. Go to sleep again. . . . Now, Larry," she added, getting out of bed, "you've wakened Daddy and you must go back."

This time, for all her quiet air, I knew she meant it, and knew that my principal rights and privileges were as good as lost unless I asserted them at once. As she lifted me, I gave a screech, enough to wake the dead, not to mind Father. He groaned.

"That damn child! Doesn't he ever sleep?"

"It's only a habit, dear," she said quietly, though I could see she was vexed.

"Well, it's time he got out of it," shouted Father, beginning to heave in the bed. He suddenly gathered all the bedclothes about him, turned to the wall, and then looked back over his shoulder with nothing showing only two small, spiteful, dark eyes. The man looked very wicked.

To open the bedroom door, Mother had to let me down, and I broke free and dashed for the farthest corner, screeching. Father sat bolt upright in bed.

"Shut up, you little puppy!" he said in a choking voice.

I was so astonished that I stopped screeching. Never, never had anyone spoken to me in that tone before. I looked at him incredulously and saw his face convulsed with rage. It was only then that I fully realized how God had codded me, listening to my prayers for the safe return of this monster.

"Shut up, you!" I bawled, beside myself.

"What's that you said?" shouted Father, making a wild leap out of the bed.

"Mick, Mick!" cried Mother. "Don't you see the child isn't used to you?"

"I see he's better fed than taught," snarled Father, waving his arms wildly. "He wants his bottom smacked."

All his previous shouting was as nothing to these obscene words referring to my person. They really made my blood boil.

"Smack your own!" I screamed hysterically. "Smack your own! Shut up! Shut up!"

At this he lost his patience and let fly at me. He did it with the lack of conviction you'd expect of a man under Mother's horrified eyes, and it ended up as a mere tap, but the sheer indignity of being struck at all by a stranger, a total stranger who had cajoled his way back from the war into our big bed as a result of my innocent intercession, made me completely dotty. I shrieked and shrieked, and danced in my bare feet, and Father, looking awkward and hairy in nothing but a short grey army shirt, glared down at me like a mountain out for murder. I think it must have been then that I realized he was jealous too. And there stood Mother in her nightdress, looking as if her heart was broken between us. I hoped she felt as she looked. It seemed to me that she deserved it all.

From that morning out my life was a hell. Father and I were enemies, open and avowed. We conducted a series of skirmishes against one another, he trying to steal my time with Mother and I his. When she was sitting on my bed, telling me a story, he took to looking for some pair of old boots which he alleged he had left behind him at the beginning of the war. While he talked to Mother I played loudly with my toys to show my total lack of concern. He created a terrible scene one evening when he came in from work and found me at his box, playing with his regimental badges, Gurkha knives and button-sticks. Mother got up and took the box from me.

"You mustn't play with Daddy's toys unless he lets you, Larry," she said severely. "Daddy doesn't play with yours."

For some reason Father looked at her as if she had struck him and then turned away with a scowl.

"Those are not toys," he growled, taking down the box again to see had I lifted anything. "Some of those curios are very rare and valuable."

But as time went on I saw more and more how he managed to alienate Mother and me. What made it worse was that I couldn't grasp his method or see what attraction he had for Mother. In every possible way he was less winning than I. He had a common accent and made noises at his tea. I thought for a while that it might be the newspapers she was interested in, so I made up bits of news of my own to read to her. Then I thought it might be the smoking, which I personally thought attractive, and took his pipes and went round the house dribbling into them till he caught me. I even made noises at my tea, but Mother only told me I was disgusting. It all seemed to hinge round that unhealthy habit of sleeping together, so I made a point of dropping into their bedroom and nosing round, talking to myself, so that they wouldn't know I was watching them, but they were never up to anything that I could see. In the end it beat me. It seemed to depend on being grown-up and giving people rings, and I realized I'd have to wait.

But at the same time I wanted him to see that I was only waiting, not giving up the fight. One evening when he was being particularly obnoxious, chattering away well above my head, I let him have it.

"Mummy," I said, "do you know what I'm going to do when I grow up?"

"No, dear," she replied. "What?"

"I'm going to marry you," I said quietly.

Father gave a great guffaw out of him, but he didn't take me in. I knew it must only be pretence. And Mother, in spite of everything, was pleased. I felt she was probably relieved to know that one day Father's hold on her would be broken.

"Won't that be nice?" she said with a smile.

"It'll be very nice," I said confidently. "Because we're going to have lots and lots of babies."

"That's right, dear," she said placidly. "I think we'll

have one soon, and then you'll have plenty of company."

I was no end pleased about that because it showed that in spite of the way she gave in to Father she still considered my wishes. Besides, it would put the Geneys in their place.

It didn't turn out like that, though. To begin with, she was very preoccupied—I supposed about where she would get the seventeen and six—and though Father took to staying out late in the evenings it did me no particular good She stopped taking me for walks, became as touchy as blazes, and smacked me for nothing at all. Sometimes I wished I'd never mentioned the confounded baby—I seemed to have a genius for bringing calamity on myself.

And calamity it was! Sonny arrived in the most appalling hullabaloo—even that much he couldn't do without a fuss —and from the first moment I disliked him. He was a difficult child—so far as I was concerned he was always difficult —and demanded far too much attention. Mother was simply silly about him, and couldn't see when he was only showing off. As company he was worse than useless. He slept all day, and I had to go round the house on tiptoe to avoid waking him. It wasn't any longer a question of not waking Father. The slogan now was "Don't-wake-Sonny!" I couldn't understand why the child wouldn't sleep at the proper time, so whenever Mother's back was turned I woke him. Sometimes to keep him awake I pinched him as well. Mother caught me at it one day and gave me a most unmerciful flaking.

One evening, when Father was coming in from work, I was playing trains in the front garden. I let on not to notice him; instead, I pretended to be talking to myself, and said in a loud voice: "If another bloody baby comes into this house, I'm going out."

Father stopped dead and looked at me over his shoulder.

"What's that you said?" he asked sternly.

"I was only talking to myself," I replied, trying to conceal my panic. "It's private."

He turned and went in without a word. Mind you, I intended it as a solemn warning, but its effect was quite different. Father started being quite nice to me. I could understand that, of course. Mother was quite sickening about Sonny. Even at mealtimes she'd get up and gawk at him in the cradle with an idiotic smile, and tell Father to do the same. He was always polite about it, but he looked so puzzled you could see he didn't know what she was talking about. He complained of the way Sonny cried at night, but she only got cross and said that Sonny never cried except when there was something up with him—which was a flaming lie, because Sonny never had anything up with him, and only cried for attention. It was really painful to see how simple-minded she was. Father wasn't attractive, but he had a fine intelligence. He saw through Sonny, and now he knew that I saw through him as well.

One night I woke with a start. There was someone beside me in the bed. For one wild moment I felt sure it must be Mother, having come to her senses and left Father for good, but then I heard Sonny in convulsions in the next room, and Mother saying: "There! There! There!" and I knew it wasn't she. It was Father. He was lying beside me, wide awake, breathing hard and apparently as mad as hell.

After a while it came to me what he was mad about. It was his turn now. After turning me out of the big bed, he had been turned out himself. Mother had no consideration now for anyone but that poisonous pup, Sonny. I couldn't help feeling sorry for Father. I had been through it all myself, and even at that age I was magnanimous. I began to stroke him down and say: "There! There!" He wasn't exactly responsive.

"Aren't you asleep either?" he snarled.

"Ah, come on and put your arm around us, can't you?" I said, and he did, in a sort of way. Gingerly, I suppose, is how you'd describe it. He was very bony but better than nothing.

At Christmas he went out of his way to buy me a really nice model railway.

Albert Camus

(1913–1960)

*Albert Camus was so uniquely a product of the world
of twentieth-century European man that it is virtually
impossible to conceive of his work as having been written at any other period in history. It is not merely that
Camus saw the writer's function as serving as man's conscience and took it upon himself to speak for that function in each of his own writings; he himself, as well as
his writing, seems to be distinctively a part of our time.
He has been incorporated into the very intellectual and
spiritual legacy he helped to create. With Orwell, Silone,
and perhaps Malraux and Faulkner, he appears to the
contemporary reader to be inseparable from the world
he has created.*

*Camus' fiction does not so much illuminate as it states
the human condition under which men labor. Called
"the absurd," for want, one suspects, of a more detailed
term, it limits man at the very same moment that it
strives to set him free. The responsibility of man is to
freedom, and this responsibility cannot be escaped even
if man accepts his sojourn on this earth as the stay of an
exile. It was exactly such a situation that Camus depicted in his first and most famous novel,* The Stranger
(1942).

*Camus, who today seems the archetypal French
literary intellectual, was born not in Paris but in Mon-
dovi, Algeria, of poor working-class parents. He attended
the university in Algeria where he began his career as a
journalist and continued his work in theater. He studied
philosophy and literature, participated in sports, and
seems to have led a happy, active existence.*

*When he was twenty-four, Camus discovered that he
had tuberculosis. Along with the Nazi occupation of
France, where he had gone to live and write, this event
seems to have been crucial in his development of the
concept of the absurd. Quite suddenly, he was thrust into
a world in which only death seemed imminent and inevitable. Existence itself was accidental, and what one
discovers in his fiction, as well as in his essays, is the
desire to shore man up against the threat implicit in the
recognition of existence as an accident. Such novels as*

The Stranger *and* The Plague *(1947) can be explained in no other way.*

The Myth of Sisyphus (1942), which was also pub- lished during the Nazi occupation of France, is Camus' philosophical attempt to express exactly what he means by "the absurd." "In a universe suddenly deprived of light and illusions, man feels himself an outsider. This exile is irrevocable, since he has no memories of a lost homeland and no hope of a promised land." Man's obligations remain; he is, as Sartre wrote, "man con- fronting this world." With Camus, this produced social activism, an insistence that the artist must make his presence known in tangible ways. During the war, he wrote for the French resistance and served as the editor of the underground newspaper, Combat. *Like Sartre, he was to remain politically active after the war as well. When he was only forty-seven, he was killed in an automobile crash, three years after he had been awarded the Nobel Prize for Literature.*

Camus' style is, like Flaubert's, the style of a classi- cist. In his major fiction, he writes as if he had measured the effect of every word. He is among those modern writers who insist that his reader participate in the creative act. The reader must, in fact, accept his own moral obli- gations in reading Camus. He molds mood to source in a way that few writers have been able to do. In "The Adulterous Woman," one of the stories from Exile and the Kingdom *(1957), he creates the moment of crisis and self-discovery in which the human mind is stripped of all its protective illusions and the protagonist is left to face her inner self. It is this revelation which we see so sensitively developed in the portrait of Janine.*

The Adulterous Woman

A housefly had been circling for the last few minutes in the bus, though the windows were closed. An odd sight here, it had been silently flying back and forth on tired wings. Janine lost track of it, then saw it light on her husband's motionless hand. The weather was cold. The fly shuddered with each gust of sandy wind that scratched against the windows. In the meager light of the winter morning, with a great fracas of sheet metal and axles, the vehicle was rolling, pitching, and making hardly any

progress. Janine looked at her husband. With wisps of
graying hair growing low on a narrow forehead, a broad
nose, a flabby mouth, Marcel looked like a pouting faun.
At each hollow in the pavement she felt him jostle against
her. Then his heavy torso would slump back on his wide-
spread legs and he would become inert again and absent,
with vacant stare. Nothing about him seemed active but
his thick hairless hands, made even shorter by the flannel
underwear extending below his cuffs and covering his
wrists. His hands were holding so tight to a little canvas
suitcase set between his knees that they appeared not to
feel the fly's halting progress.

Suddenly the wind was distinctly heard to howl and
the gritty fog surrounding the bus became even thicker.
The sand now struck the windows in packets as if hurled
by invisible hands. The fly shook a chilled wing, flexed its
legs, and took flight. The bus slowed and seemed on the
point of stopping. But the wind apparently died down, the
fog lifted slightly, and the vehicle resumed speed. Gaps of
light opened up in the dust-drowned landscape. Two or
three frail, whitened palm trees which seemed cut out of
metal flashed into sight in the window only to disappear
the next moment.

"What a country!" Marcel said.

The bus was full of Arabs pretending to sleep, shrouded
in their burnooses. Some had folded their legs on the seat
and swayed more than the others in the car's motion. Their
silence and impassivity began to weigh upon Janine; it
seemed to her as if she had been traveling for days with
that mute escort. Yet the bus had left only at dawn from
the end of the rail line and for two hours in the cold
morning it had been advancing on a stony, desolate plateau
which, in the beginning at least, extended its straight
lines all the way to reddish horizons. But the wind had
risen and gradually swallowed up the vast expanse. From
that moment on, the passengers had seen nothing more;
one after another, they had ceased talking and were
silently progressing in a sort of sleepless night, occasionally
wiping their lips and eyes irritated by the sand that filtered
into the car.

"Janine!" She gave a start at her husband's call. Once
again she thought how ridiculous that name was for
someone tall and sturdy like her. Marcel wanted to know
where his sample case was. With her foot she explored
the empty space under the seat and encountered an object
which she decided must be it. She could not stoop over

without gasping somewhat. Yet in school she had won the first prize in gymnastics and hadn't known what it was to be winded. Was that so long ago? Twenty-five years. Twenty-five years were nothing, for it seemed to her only yesterday when she was hesitating between an independent life and marriage, just yesterday when she was thinking anxiously of the time she might be growing old alone. She was not alone and that law student who always wanted to be with her was now at her side. She had eventually accepted him although he was a little shorter than she and she didn't much like his eager, sharp laugh or his black, protruding eyes. But she liked his courage in facing up to life, which he shared with all the French of this country. She also liked his crestfallen look when events or men failed to live up to his expectations. Above all, she liked being loved, and he had showered her with attentions. By so often making her aware that she existed for him he made her exist in reality. No, she was not alone. . . .

The bus, with many loud honks, was plowing its way through invisible obstacles. Inside the car, however, no one stirred. Janine suddenly felt someone staring at her and turned toward the seat across the aisle. He was not an Arab, and she was surprised not to have noticed him from the beginning. He was wearing the uniform of the French regiments of the Sahara and an unbleached linen cap above his tanned face, long and pointed like a jackal's. His gray eyes were examining her with a sort of glum disapproval, in a fixed stare. She suddenly blushed and turned back to her husband, who was still looking straight ahead in the fog and wind. She snuggled down in her coat. But she could still see the French soldier, long and thin, so thin in his fitted tunic that he seemed constructed of a dry, friable material, a mixture of sand and bone. Then it was that she saw the thin hands and burned faces of the Arabs in front of her and noticed that they seemed to have plenty of room, despite their ample garments, on the seat where she and her husband felt wedged in. She pulled her coat around her knees. Yet she wasn't so fat—tall and well rounded rather, plump and still desirable, as she was well aware when men looked at her, with her rather childish face, her bright, naïve eyes contrasting with this big body she knew to be warm and inviting.

No, nothing had happened as she had expected. When Marcel had wanted to take her along on his trip she had protested. For some time he had been thinking of this trip —since the end of the war, to be precise, when business

had returned to normal. Before the war the small dry-
goods business he had taken over from his parents on
giving up his study of law had provided a fairly good
living. On the coast the years of youth can be happy ones.
But he didn't much like physical effort and very soon had
given up taking her to the beaches. The little car took
them out of town solely for the Sunday afternoon ride.
The rest of the time he preferred his shop full of multi-
colored piece-goods shaded by the arcades of this half-
native, half-European quarter. Above the shop they lived
in three rooms furnished with Arab hangings and furniture from the Galerie Barbès. They had not had children.
The years had passed in the semi-darkness behind the half-
closed shutters. Summer, the beaches, excursions, the mere
sight of the sky were things of the past. Nothing seemed
to interest Marcel but business. She felt she had discovered
his true passion to be money, and, without really knowing
why, she didn't like that. After all, it was to her advantage.
Far from being miserly, he was generous, especially where
she was concerned. "If something happened to me," he
used to say, "you'd be provided for." And, in fact, it is
essential to provide for one's needs. But for all the rest,
for what is not the most elementary need, how to provide?
This is what she felt vaguely, at infrequent intervals. Meanwhile she helped Marcel keep his books and occasionally
substituted for him in the shop. Summer was always the
hardest, when the heat stifled even the sweet sensation of
boredom.

Suddenly, in summer as it happened, the war, Marcel
called up then rejected on grounds of health, the scarcity
of piece-goods, business at a standstill, the streets empty
and hot. If something happened now, she would no longer
be provided for. This is why, as soon as piece-goods came
back on the market, Marcel had thought of covering the
villages of the Upper Plateaus and of the South himself in
order to do without a middleman and sell directly to the
Arab merchants. He had wanted to take her along. She
knew that travel was difficult, she had trouble breathing,
and she would have preferred staying at home. But he was
obstinate and she had accepted because it would have
taken too much energy to refuse. Here they were and,
truly, nothing was like what she had imagined. She had
feared the heat, the swarms of flies, the filthy hotels reeking
of aniseed. She had not thought of the cold, of the biting
wind, of these semi-polar plateaus cluttered with moraines.
She had dreamed too of palm trees and soft sand. Now

she saw that the desert was not that at all, but merely stone, stone everywhere, in the sky full of nothing but stone-dust, rasping and cold, as on the ground, where nothing grew among the stones except dry grasses.

The bus stopped abruptly. The driver shouted a few words in that language she had heard all her life without ever understanding it. "What's the matter?" Marcel asked. The driver, in French this time, said that the sand must have clogged the carburetor, and again Marcel cursed this country. The driver laughed hilariously and asserted that it was nothing, that he would clean the carburetor and they'd be off again. He opened the door and the cold wind blew into the bus, lashing their faces with a myriad grains of sand. All the Arabs silently plunged their noses into their burnooses and huddled up. "Shut the door," Marcel shouted. The driver laughed as he came back to the door. Without hurrying, he took some tools from under the dashboard, then, tiny in the fog, again disappeared ahead without closing the door. Marcel sighed. "You may be sure he's never seen a motor in his life." "Oh, be quiet!" said Janine. Suddenly she gave a start. On the shoulder of the road close to the bus, draped forms were standing still. Under the burnoose's hood and behind a rampart of veils, only their eyes were visible. Mute, come from nowhere, they were staring at the travelers. "Shepherds," Marcel said.

Inside the car there was total silence. All the passengers, heads lowered, seemed to be listening to the voice of the wind loosed across these endless plateaus. Janine was all of a sudden struck by the almost complete absence of luggage. At the end of the railroad line the driver had hoisted their trunk and a few bundles onto the roof. In the racks inside the bus could be seen nothing but gnarled sticks and shopping-baskets. All these people of the South apparently were traveling empty-handed.

But the driver was coming back, still brisk. His eyes alone were laughing above the veils with which he too had masked his face. He announced that they would soon be under way. He closed the door, the wind became silent, and the rain of sand on the windows could be heard better. The motor coughed and died. After having been urged at great length by the starter, it finally sparked and the driver raced it by pressing on the gas. With a big hiccough the bus started off. From the ragged clump of shepherds, still motionless, a hand rose and then faded into the fog behind them. Almost at once the vehicle began to bounce on the road, which had become worse. Shaken up, the Arabs constantly swayed. Nonetheless, Janine was feeling overcome with sleep when there suddenly appeared in front of her a little yellow box filled with lozenges. The jackalsoldier was smiling at her. She hesitated, took one, and thanked him. The jackal pocketed the box and simultaneously swallowed his smile. Now he was staring at the road, straight in front of him. Janine turned toward Marcel and saw only the solid back of his neck. Through the window he was watching the denser fog rising from the crumbly embankment.

They had been traveling for hours and fatigue had extinguished all life in the car when shouts burst forth outside. Children wearing burnooses, whirling like tops, leaping, clapping their hands, were running around the bus. It was now going down a long street lined with low houses; they were entering the oasis. The wind was still blowing, but the walls intercepted the grains of sand which had previously cut off the light. Yet the sky was still cloudy. Amidst shouts, in a great screeching of brakes, the bus stopped in front of the adobe arcades of a hotel with dirty windows. Janine got out and, once on the pavement, staggered. Above the houses she could see a slim yellow minaret. On her left rose the first palm trees of the oasis, and she would have liked to go toward them. But although it was close to noon, the cold was bitter; the wind made her shiver. She turned toward Marcel and saw the soldier coming toward her. She was expecting him to smile or salute. He passed without looking at her and disappeared. Marcel was busy getting down the trunk of piece-goods, a black foot-locker perched on the bus's roof. It would not be easy. The driver was the only one to take care of the luggage and he had already stopped, standing on the roof, to hold forth to the circle of burnooses gathered around the bus. Janine, surrounded with faces that seemed cut out of bone and leather, besieged by guttural shouts, suddenly became aware of her fatigue. "I'm going in," she said to Marcel, who was shouting impatiently at the driver.

She entered the hotel. The manager, a thin, laconic Frenchman, came to meet her. He led her to a second-floor balcony overlooking the street and into a room which seemed to have but an iron bed, a white-enameled chair, an uncurtained wardrobe, and, behind a rush screen, a washbasin covered with fine sand-dust. When the manager had closed the door, Janine felt the cold coming from the

bare, whitewashed walls. She didn't know where to put
her bag, where to put herself. She had either to lie down
or to remain standing, and to shiver in either case. She
remained standing, holding her bag and staring at a sort
of window-slit that opened onto the sky near the ceiling.
She was waiting, but she didn't know for what. She was
aware only of her solitude, and of the penetrating cold,
and of a greater weight in the region of her heart. She
was in fact dreaming, almost deaf to the sounds rising
from the street along with Marcel's vocal outbursts, more
aware on the other hand of that sound of a river coming
from the window-slit and caused by the wind in the palm
trees, so close now, it seemed to her. Then the wind seemed
to increase and the gentle ripple of waters became a hissing
of waves. She imagined, beyond the walls, a sea of erect,
flexible palm trees unfurling in the storm. Nothing was
like what she had expected, but those invisible waves
refreshed her tired eyes. She was standing, heavy, with
dangling arms, slightly stooped, as the cold climbed her
thick legs. She was dreaming of the erect and flexible palm
trees and of the girl she had once been.

After having washed, they went down to the dining-
room. On the bare walls had been painted camels and
palm trees drowned in a sticky background of pink and
lavender. The arcaded windows let in a meager light.
Marcel questioned the hotel manager about the merchants.
Then an elderly Arab wearing a military decoration on his
tunic served them. Marcel, preoccupied, tore his bread
into little pieces. He kept his wife from drinking water.
"It hasn't been boiled. Take wine." She didn't like that,
for wine made her sleepy. Besides, there was pork on the
menu. "They don't eat it because of the Koran. But the
Koran didn't know that well-done pork doesn't cause
illness. We French know how to cook. What are you
thinking about?" Janine was not thinking of anything, or
perhaps of that victory of the cooks over the prophets.
But she had to hurry. They were to leave the next morning for still farther south; that afternoon they had to see
all the important merchants. Marcel urged the elderly Arab
to hurry the coffee. He nodded without smiling and pat-
tered out. "Slowly in the morning, not too fast in the
afternoon," Marcel said, laughing. Yet eventually the coffee
came. They barely took time to swallow it and went out
into the dusty, cold street. Marcel called a young Arab to
help him carry the trunk, but as a matter of principle

quibbled about the payment. His opinion, which he once more expressed to Janine, was in fact based on the vague principle that they always asked for twice as much in the hope of settling for a quarter of the amount. Janine, ill at ease, followed the two trunk-bearers. She had put on a wool dress under her heavy coat and would have liked to take up less space. The pork, although well done, and the small quantity of wine she had drunk also bothered her somewhat.

They walked along a diminutive public garden planted with dusty trees. They encountered Arabs who stepped out of their way without seeming to see them, wrapping themselves in their burnooses. Even when they were wearing rags, she felt they had a look of dignity unknown to the Arabs of her town. Janine followed the trunk, which made a way for her through the crowd. They went through the gate in an earthen rampart and emerged on a little square planted with the same mineral trees and bordered on the far side, where it was widest, with arcades and shops. But they stopped on the square itself in front of a small construction shaped like an artillery shell and painted chalky blue. Inside, in the single room lighted solely by the entrance, an old Arab with white mustaches stood behind a shiny plank. He was serving tea, raising and lowering the teapot over three tiny multicolored glasses. Before they could make out anything else in the darkness, the cool scent of mint tea greeted Marcel and Janine at the door. Marcel had barely crossed the threshold and dodged the garlands of pewter teapots, cups and trays, and the postcard displays when he was up against the counter. Janine stayed at the door. She stepped a little aside so as not to cut off the light. At that moment she perceived in the darkness behind the old merchant two Arabs smiling at them, seated on the bulging sacks that filled the back of the shop. Red-and-black rugs and embroidered scarves hung on the walls; the floor was cluttered with sacks and little boxes filled with aromatic seeds. On the counter, beside a sparkling pair of brass scales and an old yardstick with figures effaced, stood a row of loaves of sugar. One of them had been unwrapped from its coarse blue paper and cut into on top. The smell of wool and spices in the room became apparent behind the scent of tea when the old merchant set down the teapot and said good-day.

Marcel talked rapidly in the low voice he assumed when talking business. Then he opened the trunk, exhibited the wools and silks, pushed back the scale and yardstick to

spread out his merchandise in front of the old merchant.
He got excited, raised his voice, laughed nervously, like a
woman who wants to make an impression and is not sure
of herself. Now, with hands spread wide, he was going
through the gestures of selling and buying. The old man
shook his head, passed the tea tray to the two Arabs behind
him, and said just a few words that seemed to discourage
Marcel. He picked up his goods, piled them back into the
trunk, then wiped an imaginary sweat from his forehead.
He called the little porter and they started off toward the
arcades. In the first shop, although the merchant began by
exhibiting the same Olympian manner, they were a little
luckier. "They think they're God almighty," Marcel said,
"but they're in business too! Life is hard for everyone."

Janine followed without answering. The wind had almost
ceased. The sky was clearing in spots, A cold, harsh light
came from the deep holes that opened up in the thickness
of the clouds. They had now left the square. They were
walking in narrow streets along earthen walls over which
hung rotted December roses or, from time to time, a
pomegranate, dried and wormy. An odor of dust and coffee,
the smoke of a wood fire, the smell of stone and of sheep
permeated this quarter. The shops, hollowed out of the
walls, were far from one another; Janine felt her feet
getting heavier. But her husband was gradually becoming
more cheerful. He was beginning to sell and was feeling
more kindly; he called Janine "Baby"; the trip would not
be wasted. "Of course," Janine said mechanically, "it's
better to deal directly with them."

They came back by another street, toward the center.
It was late in the afternoon; the sky was now almost completely clear. They stopped in the square. Marcel rubbed
his hands and looked affectionately at the trunk in front
of them. "Look," said Janine. From the other end of the
square was coming a tall Arab, thin, vigorous, wearing a
sky-blue burnoose, soft brown boots and gloves, and bearing his bronzed aquiline face loftily. Nothing but the
chèche that he was wearing swathed as a turban distinguished him from those French officers in charge of native
affairs whom Janine had occasionally admired. He was
advancing steadily toward them, but seemed to be looking
beyond their group as he slowly removed the glove from
one hand. "Well," said Marcel as he shrugged his shoulders, "there's one who thinks he's a general." Yes, all of
them here had that look of pride; but this one, really, was
going too far. Although they were surrounded by the

empty space of the square, he was walking straight toward the trunk without seeing it, without seeing them. Then the distance separating them decreased rapidly and the Arab was upon them when Marcel suddenly seized the handle of the foot-locker and pulled it out of the way. The Arab passed without seeming to notice anything and headed with the same regular step toward the ramparts. Janine looked at her husband; he had his crestfallen look. "They think they can get away with anything now," he said. Janine did not reply. She loathed that Arab's stupid arrogance and suddenly felt unhappy. She wanted to leave and thought of her little apartment. The idea of going back to the hotel, to that icy room, discouraged her. It suddenly occurred to her that the manager had advised her to climb up to the terrace around the fort to see the desert. She said this to Marcel and that he could leave the trunk at the hotel. But he was tired and wanted to sleep a little before dinner. "Please," said Janine. He looked at her, suddenly attentive. "Of course, my dear," he said.

She waited for him in the street in front of the hotel. The white-robed crowd was becoming larger and larger. Not a single woman could be seen, and it seemed to Janine that she had never seen so many men. Yet none of them looked at her. Some of them, without appearing to see her, slowly turned toward her that thin, tanned face that made them all look alike to her, the face of the French soldier in the bus and that of the gloved Arab, a face both shrewd and proud. They turned that face toward the foreign woman, they didn't see her, and then, light and silent, they walked around her as she stood there with swelling ankles. And her discomfort, her need of getting away increased. "Why did I come?" But already Marcel was coming back.

When they climbed the stairs to the fort, it was five o'clock. The wind had died down altogether. The sky, completely clear, was now periwinkle blue. The cold, now drier, made their cheeks smart. Halfway up the stairs an old Arab, stretched out against the wall, asked them if they wanted a guide, but didn't budge, as if he had been sure of their refusal in advance. The stairs were long and steep despite several landings of packed earth. As they climbed, the space widened and they rose into an ever broader light, cold and dry, in which every sound from the oasis reached them pure and distinct. The bright air seemed to vibrate around them with a vibration increasing in length as they advanced, as if their progress struck from the crystal of light a sound wave that kept spreading out. And as soon as they reached the terrace and their gaze was lost in the vast horizon beyond the palm grove, it seemed to Janine that the whole sky rang with a single short and piercing note, whose echoes gradually filled the space above her, then suddenly died and left her silently facing the limitless expanse.

From east to west, in fact, her gaze swept slowly, without encountering a single obstacle, along a perfect curve. Beneath her, the blue-and-white terraces of the Arab town overlapped one another, splattered with the dark-red spots of peppers drying in the sun. Not a soul could be seen, but from the inner courts, together with the aroma of roasting coffee, there rose laughing voices or incomprehensible stamping of feet. Farther off, the palm grove, divided into uneven squares by clay walls, rustled its upper foliage in a wind that could not be felt up on the terrace. Still farther off and all the way to the horizon extended the ocher-and-gray realm of stones, in which no life was visible. At some distance from the oasis, however, near the wadi that bordered the palm grove on the west could be seen broad black tents. All around them a flock of motionless dromedaries, tiny at that distance, formed against the gray ground the black signs of a strange handwriting, the meaning of which had to be deciphered. Above the desert, the silence was as vast as the space.

Janine, leaning her whole body against the parapet, was speechless, unable to tear herself away from the void opening before her. Beside her, Marcel was getting restless. He was cold; he wanted to go back down. What was there to see here, after all? But she could not take her gaze from the horizon. Over yonder, still farther south, at that point where sky and earth met in a pure line—over yonder it suddenly seemed there was awaiting her something of which, though it had always been lacking, she had never been aware until now. In the advancing afternoon the light relaxed and softened; it was passing from the crystalline to the liquid. Simultaneously, in the heart of a woman brought there by pure chance a knot tightened by the years, habit, and boredom was slowly loosening. She was looking at the nomads' encampment. She had not even seen the men living in it; nothing was stirring among the black tents, and yet she could think only of them whose existence she had barely known until this day. Homeless, cut off from the world, they were a handful wandering over the vast territory she could see, which however was but a paltry part of an even greater expanse whose dizzying course stopped only thousands of miles farther south, where the first river finally waters the forest. Since the beginning of time, on the dry earth of this limitless land scraped to the bone, a few men had been ceaselessly trudging, possessing nothing but serving no one, poverty-stricken but free lords of a strange kingdom. Janine did not know why this thought filled her with such a sweet, vast melancholy that it closed her eyes. She knew that this kingdom had been eternally promised her and yet that it would never be hers, never again, except in this fleeting moment perhaps when she opened her eyes again on the suddenly motionless sky and on its waves of steady light, while the voices rising from the Arab town suddenly fell silent. It seemed to her that the world's course had just stopped and that, from that moment on, no one would ever age any more or die. Everywhere, henceforth, life was suspended—except in her heart, where, at the same moment, someone was weeping with affliction and wonder.

But the light began to move; the sun, clear and devoid of warmth, went down toward the west, which became slightly pink, while a gray wave took shape in the east ready to roll slowly over the vast expanse. A first dog barked and its distant bark rose in the now even colder air. Janine noticed that her teeth were chattering. "We are catching our death of cold," Marcel said. "You're a fool. Let's go back." But he took her hand awkwardly. Docile now, she turned away from the parapet and followed him. Without moving, the old Arab on the stairs watched them go down toward the town. She walked along without seeing anyone, bent under a tremendous and sudden fatigue, dragging her body, whose weight now seemed to her unbearable. Her exaltation had left her. Now she felt too tall, too thick, too white too for this world she had just entered. A child, the girl, the dry man, the furtive jackal were the only creatures who could silently walk that earth. What would she do there henceforth except to drag herself toward sleep, toward death?

She dragged herself, in fact, toward the restaurant with a husband suddenly taciturn unless he was telling how tired he was, while she was struggling weakly against a cold, aware of a fever rising within her. Then she dragged herself toward her bed, where Marcel came to join her and put the light out at once without asking anything of her. The room was frigid. Janine felt the cold creeping up while the fever was increasing. She breathed with difficulty, her blood pumped without warming her; a sort of fear grew within her. She turned over and the old iron bedstead groaned under her weight. No, she didn't want to fall ill. Her husband was already asleep; she too had to sleep; it was essential. The muffled sounds of the town reached her through the window-slit. With a nasal twang old phonographs in the Moorish cafés ground out tunes she recognized vaguely; they reached her borne on the sound of a slow-moving crowd. She must sleep. But she was counting black tents; behind her eyelids motionless camels were grazing; immense solitudes were whirling within her. Yes, why had she come? She fell asleep on that question.

She awoke a little later. The silence around her was absolute. But, on the edges of town, hoarse dogs were howling in the soundless night. Janine shivered. She turned over, felt her husband's hard shoulder against hers, and suddenly, half asleep, huddled against him. She was drifting on the surface of sleep without sinking in and she clung to that shoulder with unconscious eagerness as her safest haven. She was talking, but no sound issued from her mouth. She was talking, but she herself hardly heard what she was saying. She could feel only Marcel's warmth. For more than twenty years every night thus, in his warmth, just the two of them, even when ill, even when traveling, as at present . . . Besides, what would she have done alone at home? No child! Wasn't that what she lacked? She didn't know. She simply followed Marcel, pleased to know that someone needed her. The only joy he gave her was the knowledge that she was necessary. Probably he didn't love her. Love, even when filled with hate, doesn't have that sullen face. But what is his face like? They made love in the dark by feel, without seeing each other. Is there another love than that of darkness, a love that would cry aloud in daylight? She didn't know, but she did know that Marcel needed her and that she needed that need, that she lived on it night and day, at night especially—every night, when he didn't want to be alone, or to age or die, with that set expression he assumed which she occasionally recognized on other men's faces, the only common expression of those madmen hiding under an appearance of wisdom until the madness seizes them and hurls them desperately toward a woman's body to bury in it, without desire, everything terrifying that solitude and night reveals to them.

Marcel stirred as if to move away from her. No, he didn't love her; he was merely afraid of what was not she, and she and he should long ago have separated and slept

alone until the end. But who can always sleep alone? Some
men do, cut off from others by a vocation or misfortune,
who go to bed every night in the same bed as death.
Marcel never could do so—he above all, a weak and disarmed child always frightened by suffering, her own child
indeed who needed her and who, just at that moment, let
out a sort of whimper. She cuddled a little closer and put
her hand on his chest. And to herself she called him with
the little love-name she had once given him, which they
still used from time to time without even thinking of what
they were saying.

She called him with all her heart. After all, she too
needed him, his strength, his little eccentricities, and she
too was afraid of death. "If I could overcome that fear,
I'd be happy. . . ." Immediately, a nameless anguish seized
her. She drew back from Marcel. No, she was overcoming
nothing, she was not happy, she was going to die, in truth,
without having been liberated. Her heart pained her; she
was stifling under a huge weight that she suddenly discovered she had been dragging around for twenty years.
Now she was struggling under it with all her strength. She
wanted to be liberated even if Marcel, even if the others,
never were! Fully awake, she sat up in bed and listened to
a call that seemed very close. But from the edges of night
the exhausted and yet indefatigable voices of the dogs of
the oasis were all that reached her ears. A slight wind had
risen and she heard its light waters flow in the palm grove.
It came from the south, where desert and night mingled
now under the again unchanging sky, where life stopped,
where no one would ever age or die any more. Then the
waters of the wind dried up and she was not even sure of
having heard anything except a mute call that she could,
after all, silence or notice. But never again would she know
its meaning unless she responded to it at once. At once—
yes, that much was certain at least!

She got up gently and stood motionless beside the bed,
listening to her husband's breathing. Marcel was asleep.
The next moment, the bed's warmth left her and the cold
gripped her. She dressed slowly, feeling for her clothes in
the faint light coming through the blinds from the street-
lamps. Her shoes in her hand, she reached the door. She
waited a moment more in the darkness, then gently opened
the door. The knob squeaked and she stood still. Her heart
was beating madly. She listened with her body tense and,
reassured by the silence, turned her hand a little more.
The knob's turning seemed to her interminable. At last

she opened the door, slipped outside, and closed the door with the same stealth. Then, with her cheek against the wood, she waited. After a moment she made out, in the distance, Marcel's breathing. She faced about, felt the icy night air against her cheek, and ran the length of the balcony. The outer door was closed. While she was slipping the bolt, the night watchman appeared at the top of the stairs, his face blurred with sleep, and spoke to her in Arabic. "I'll be back," said Janine as she stepped out into the night.

Garlands of stars hung down from the black sky over the palm trees and houses. She ran along the short avenue, now empty, that led to the fort. The cold, no longer having to struggle against the sun, had invaded the night; the icy air burned her lungs. But she ran, half blind, in the darkness. At the top of the avenue, however, lights appeared, then descended toward her zigzagging. She stopped, caught the whir of turning sprockets and, behind the enlarging lights, soon saw vast burnooses surmounting fragile bicycle wheels. The burnooses flapped against her; then three red lights sprang out of the black behind her and disappeared at once. She continued running toward the fort. Halfway up the stairs, the air burned her lungs with such cutting effect that she wanted to stop. A final burst of energy hurled her despite herself onto the terrace, against the parapet, which was now pressing her belly. She was panting and everything was hazy before her eyes. Her running had not warmed her and she was still trembling all over. But the cold air she was gulping down soon flowed evenly inside her and a spark of warmth began to glow amidst her shivers. Her eyes opened at last on the expanse of night.

Not a breath, not a sound—except at intervals the muffled crackling of stones that the cold was reducing to sand —disturbed the solitude and silence surrounding Janine. After a moment, however, it seemed to her that the sky above her was moving in a sort of slow gyration. In the vast reaches of the dry, cold night, thousands of stars were constantly appearing, and their sparkling icicles, loosened at once, began to slip gradually toward the horizon. Janine could not tear herself away from contemplating those drifting flares. She was turning with them, and the apparently stationary progress little by little identified her with the core of her being, where cold and desire were now vying with each other. Before her the stars were falling one by one and being snuffed out among the stones of the desert, and each time Janine opened a little more to the night. Breathing deeply, she forgot the cold, the dead weight of others, the craziness or stuffiness of life, the long anguish of living and dying. After so many years of mad, aimless fleeing from fear, she had come to a stop at last. At the same time, she seemed to recover her roots and the sap again rose in her body, which had ceased trembling. Her whole belly pressed against the parapet as she strained toward the moving sky; she was merely waiting for her fluttering heart to calm down and establish silence within her. The last stars of the constellations dropped their clusters a little lower on the desert horizon and became still. Then, with unbearable gentleness, the water of night began to fill Janine, drowned the cold, rose gradually from the hidden core of her being and overflowed in wave after wave, rising up even to her mouth full of moans. The next moment, the whole sky stretched out over her, fallen on her back on the cold earth.

When Janine returned to the room, with the same precautions, Marcel was not awake. But he whimpered as she got back in bed and a few seconds later sat up suddenly. He spoke and she didn't understand what he was saying. He got up, turned on the light, which blinded her. He staggered toward the washbasin and drank a long draught from the bottle of mineral water. He was about to slip between the sheets when, one knee on the bed, he looked at her without understanding. She was weeping copiously, unable to restrain herself. "It's nothing, dear," she said, "it's nothing."